Nobody Would Listen: The Collected Mystery Stories of Elisabeth Sanxay Holding

Introduction by Curtis Evans

Stark House Press • Eureka California

ACKNOWLEDGMENTS

Nobody Would Listen (*Mystery Magazine*, August 1935)
The Kiskadee Bird (*Cosmopolitan*, July 1944)
The Blue Envelope (*Collier's Weekly,* September 30,1944)
The Unbelievable Baroness (*The American Magazine*, May 1945)
Farewell to a Corpse (*Mystery Book Magazine*, October 1946)
Farewell, Big Sister (*Ellery Queen Mystery Magazine*, July 1952)
Glitter of Diamonds (*Ellery Queen Mystery Magazine*, March 1955)
Very, Very Dark Mink (*The Saint Detective Magazine*, December 1956)
Shadow of Wings (*Magazine of Fantasy and Science Fiction*, July 1954)
The Strange Children (*Magazine of Fantasy and Science Fiction*, August 1955)
The Legacy (*Liberty*, December 1950)
Friday, the Nineteenth (*Magazine of Fantasy and Science Fiction*, Summer 1950)
Mollie: The Ideal Nurse (*The Century Magazine*, January 1921)
I'm the Man You Killed (*Maclean's*, March 1, 1937)
Game for Four Players (*Alfred Hitchcock's Mystery Magazine*, June 1958)
People Do Fall Downstairs (*Ellery Queen's Mystery Magazine*, August 1947)
Most Audacious Crime (*Nero Wolfe Mystery Magazine*, January 1954)
The Daring Doctor (*Alfred Hitchcock's Mystery Magazine*, March 1957)
The Chain of Death (*Liberty*, May-June 1930)

NOBODY WOULD LISTEN: THE COLLECTED MYSTERY STORIES
OF ELISABETH SANXAY HOLDING

Published by Stark House Press
1315 H Street
Eureka, CA 95501, USA
griffinskye3@sbcglobal.net
www.starkhousepress.com

All rights reserved by the Estate of Elisabeth Sanxay Holding. Reprinted
by permission of the Estate of Elisabeth Sanxay Holding.

"Getting behind Closed Doors in Elisabeth Holding's Short Crime Fiction"
copyright © 2021 by Curtis Evans

ISBN: 979-8-88601-015-2

Book and cover design by Mark Shepard, shepgraphics.com
Proofreading by Bill Kelly

PUBLISHER'S NOTE
This is a work of fiction. Names, characters, places and incidents are
either the products of the author's imagination or used fictionally, and
any resemblance to actual persons, living or dead, events or locales, is
entirely coincidental.

Without limiting the rights under copyright reserved above, no part of
this publication may be reproduced, stored, or introduced into a retrieval
system or transmitted in any form or by any means (electronic,
mechanical, photocopying, recording or otherwise) without the prior
written permission of both the copyright owner and the above publisher
of the book.

First Stark House Press Edition: February 2023

NOBODY WOULD LISTEN: THE COLLECTED MYSTERY STORIES OF ELISABETH SANXAY HOLDING

The Blue Envelope: George Nevill, the deputy commissioner of San Fernago, is presented with an interesting case when Miss Sylvester accuses Dulac, Mrs. Jones' chauffeur, of being a German spy. As far as Nevill knows, Dulac is the loyal Frenchman he seems, but Miss Sylvester knows better and is willing to go to any lengths to prove it.

Friday, the Nineteenth: Boyce is sick of his wife and his boring life. He and his neighbor Molly have been flirting for a while, but the time has come for them to do something about it. They agree to meet the next day at a downtown hotel. But when he awakes the following morning Boyce discovers that it's still Friday. Every morning is Friday! Can he and Molly ever escape this endless day and find Saturday together?

The Chain of Death: Gilbert Emery has been shot during an apparent robbery, but his daughter Lois thinks there is more to it. She convinces her uncle, Barty Clement, to come back to the house with her to investigate. Clement is a reluctant sleuth, but even he can see that something is amiss here—everyone hates Emery, and no one is telling a straight story to him or the police.

Three clever mystery stories plus 16 more, some set in the Caribbean, many set during the second World War, all infused with Holding's psychological twists and turns and her cool depiction of the contrariness of human nature.

Table of Contents

Nobody Would Listen: Getting behind Closed Doors
in Elisabeth Holding's Short Crime Fiction 7
1. Nobody Would Listen 22
2. The Kiskadee Bird 42
3. The Blue Envelope 55
4. The Unbelievable Baroness 68
5. Farewell to a Corpse 79
6. Farewell, Big Sister 161
7. Glitter of Diamonds 170
8. Very, Very Dark Mink 181
9. Shadow of Wings 196
10. The Strange Children 216
11. The Legacy 227
12. Friday, the Nineteenth 242
13. Mollie: The Ideal Nurse 255
14. I'm the Man You Killed 269
15. Game for Four Players 283
16. People Do Fall Downstairs 293
17. Most Audacious Crime 310
18. The Daring Doctor 325
19. The Chain of Death 340
Bibliography 420

Nobody Would Listen

Getting behind Closed Doors in
Elisabeth Holding's Short Crime Fiction

by Curtis Evans

In 1916 the White Enamel Refrigerator Company published, doubtlessly with an eye toward promoting sales of its fabulous labor-saving devices, a book prosaically entitled *Housewives Favorite Recipes for Cold Dishes, Dainties, Chilled Drinks, etc.* "Most of the hardships of kitchen work come from the fact that it deprives many housewives of the pleasure of entertaining," the editors of the gastronomic tome warned forebodingly. "The thought of going into a hot kitchen, after an evening at the theatre, to prepare a luncheon destroys all the anticipated pleasure of such an event." Happily, however, with *Housewives Favorite Recipes* in her culinary arsenal any woman materially blessed with one of these enameled white wonders could "easily prepare in advance a tempting repast and place it in her refrigerator knowing it will be in perfect condition, whenever she is prepared to serve it." Among the housewives who contributed to this reassuring collection of recipes was a bride of just three years, a Mrs. George Edwyn Holding of 39 Washington Square, Greenwich Village, who offered up for beleaguered wifely readers a concoction of veal and ham artfully suspended in that savory jelly known as aspic. In fact, twenty-seven-year-old Mrs. George Edwyn Holding was none other than future crime writer Elisabeth Sanxay Holding (1889-1955).

In 1920, four years after the publication of *Housewives Favorite Recipes*, housewife Elisabeth Sanxay Holding began laying out a bountiful spread of enticing fiction. Twenty-five novels from Holding's hand, eighteen of which concerned criminal wrongdoing in one form or another, appeared between 1920 and 1953, but additionally the author published scores of short fiction tales, serialized in a myriad of periodicals such as *The Smart Set, Munsey's Magazine, The Century, The Dial, Woman's Home Companion, Ladies' Home Journal, The American Magazine, Liberty, Maclean's, McClure's,* Munsey's, *Collier's Weekly, Cosmopolitan, Redbook,* Mystery, *Street & Smith's Detective Story Magazine,* and, latterly in her career, the digests *Magazine of Fantasy and Science Fiction, The Saint Detective Magazine, Nero Wolfe Mystery Magazine, Alfred Hitchcock's Mystery Magazine* and *Ellery Queen's Mystery Magazine*, the pinnacle of mid-century short crime writing. By 1933 Holding estimated that she had already published over 250 magazine stories, this made possible through the maintenance of a strict regimen under which she wrote from 8:30 in the morning until 6:00 in the evening, entirely in longhand. Altogether this steady output of highly disciplined writing was more than enough to place the author among the twentieth century's most prolific purveyors of popular fiction.

Whatever had inspired Elisabeth Sanxay Holding, a seemingly comfortably circumstanced and complacent young New York matron with not only a refrigerator but a husband and two toddler daughters to care for, to turn on such a gushing spigot of words? Certainly writing was an activity which Elisabeth genuinely enjoyed, having precociously composed her first short story at the age of seven and first submitted a tale for publication as the age of sixteen. (It was rejected, the first such of many.) But the heavy spate of writing which Holding commenced in the 1920s was motivated by something else: her constant, consuming fear of loss of social caste and, worse yet, sheer economic deprivation.

Elisabeth's tall, slender, black-eyed husband, George Edwyn Holding, who was thirty-seven years old years old when he wed his twenty-three-year-old bride, at first blush would seem to have been a promising provider. A native of Greenwich, England, George—the son of wealthy steam forge manufacturer Joseph Holding and Sophia Charlotte Quin, a Yorkshire cousin in some degree—during the last quarter of the nineteenth century resided with his parents, three brothers and sister at "Gothic House" in the posh neighborhood of Maze Hill. Having as a young man been employed as a stockbroker's clerk in London, George after the death in 1898 of his father, who seems not to have left the sizeable estate one might have anticipated, migrated to Christiansted, Danish West Indies, where his mother's brother John Thomas Quin served as Inspector of Schools. At Christiansted George took a job teaching languages. By the time of his marriage to Elisabeth in 1913, he held a position with a New York insurance company as an adjuster of marine insurance.

By 1920 George and Elisabeth Holding and their two young daughters, Skeffington Quin and Antonia Sanxay, born in 1917 and 1919 respectively, had departed Manhattan for the borough of Staten Island, then populated by fewer than 120,000 inhabitants. Residing with them in a much less tony five-year-old suburban Dutch Colonial house on a narrow lot were three additional adults: Elisabeth's mother, Edith

Gertrude Oliver, a divorced magazine editor; her younger sister, Eleanor Eaton Sanxay, a commercial artist recently separated from her husband, whom she later divorced; and her still teenaged half-brother, Humphrey Marshall Oliver, who would move to Florida and eventually become a Miami yacht broker.

In 1922 Elisabeth with her husband and daughters departed New York for a balmier clime in the British overseas territory of Bermuda, where George, who had remained a citizen of the United Kingdom, presumably had obtained some sort of consular position. Upon her marriage to a British national, Elisabeth by the terms of the Expatriation Act of 1907 had immediately lost her American citizenship, although she would regain it when the Holdings returned to the United States in 1930, the Act having since been amended. A photograph of Elisabeth and her two girls taken around this time shows a somewhat exhausted-looking woman in a large, overhanging hat. Later photos of the ever-increasingly plump author have cemented in people's minds the image of a mirthful, matronly woman incongruously writing murder fiction, like Queen of Crime Agatha Christie, yet a previously unknown early photo of Holding, probably taken early in her marriage, reveals a decidedly more bohemian looking individual, smiling and wearing a long string of beads, her left thumb hooked in her belt while she holds a cigarette in her right hand.

While living in Bermuda the family appears to have resided in splendor at Cedarhurst, a magnificent neoclassical mansion that currently serves as the residence of the U.S. Consul General to the island. Yet after the Holdings returned to the United States in 1930, at the outset of the Great Depression, Elisabeth and George separated (according to her daughter Antonia's 2006 obituary), compelling Elisabeth to rely more than ever upon her earnings as a popular fiction writer to support her family, particularly the crime novels which increasingly came to the fore from 1934 onward.

By the end of the decade, Elisabeth, her mother having passed away in 1938, resided with her two daughters at the Gramercy Park Hotel in Manhattan, giving her occupation as writer. George, now sixty-three years old and less than three years away from death, resided at the Hotel as well, but he lived apart from his family in another suite and seems to have held no remunerative occupation at this time, despite Holding's boast in publicity material that she was the wife of a "distinguished English diplomat." The prevalence of discontented and querulous male alcoholics in Elisabeth's fiction suggests a source of discord between the man and wife.

In a 2012 piece written for a prior Stark House reprint of Elisabeth

Sanxay Holding fiction, Elisabeth's granddaughter Judith Rose Ardon describes her grandmother's life as a desperate, unceasing bid, beset by her constant bad health, to keep the financial wolves from her family's doors, with Ardon's Grandfather George conspicuous only by his utter absence from the heroic family narrative:

> [Writing] was no hobby—it was an all-consuming effort. [Elisabeth] could not find peace without knowing she could provide for her mother, herself and her girls' future. The family fortunes were unpredictable, plagued by insecurity and lurching from the sale of one story to another….
> It was a wearing way to live. Her health was not good. In 1923, at the age of thirty-four, she had pneumonia and was tormented by how she could continue to provide for her two little girls. By the age of thirty-nine she was experiencing extreme fatigue…. Fatigue and depression continued to plague her but she strove to overcome all this by sheer force of will and strength of spirit driven by her fierce loyalty to her daughters.

Ardron writes that the spiritually indefatigable Elisabeth Sanxay Holding "came from a dynasty of strong women who were independent spirits in a world that had rigid ideas of a woman's role and place in the economic order." Certainly Elisabeth's sister and her mother, Edith Gertrude Oliver, qualified as such. Edith Oliver was the youngest of four children of Frederick Hollick, a noted nineteenth-century sexologist, and his wife, Eleanor Eliza Bailey. Although on account of his pioneering lectures and writings in the United States, the native English Dr. Hollick, author of *The Marriage Guide*, *The Origin of Life*, *The Diseases of Women* and many other books on sex and the human body, was harassed and subjected to obscenity trials, his work proving, as is so often true in such cases, extremely lucrative. Residing with his family on Staten Island in 1860, Hollick that year valued his wealth in personal and real property at fifty thousand dollars (some 1.6 million dollars today), a tally which demonstrates—if there ever had been any room for doubt—that, even in the years before the likes of such popular twentieth-century gurus as Alfred Kinsey and "Dr. Ruth," sex talk sold.

Although Frederick Hollick's own actual medical credentials evidently were questionable, however popular he may have been with deeply intrigued laypeople, his daughter Edith's eldest brother became a doctor and her sister married a doctor, while her other brother, Charles Arthur Hollick, became a prominent American paleobotanist and the curator of fossil plants at Columbia University and the New York

Botanical Garden. The baby of the family, Edith was the only Hollick offspring to have no scientific affiliation in her own life, in 1888 wedding twenty-six years old Charles Skeffington Sanxay. Elisabeth Sanxay was born to the couple the next year, followed two years later by her sister Eleanore, after which there were no more children from the union. The family resided at Columbia Heights in Brooklyn in a nineteenth-century row house, outwardly the picture of upper-class perfection.

In 1903, however, Charles Sanxay suddenly passed away from heart disease at the untimely age of forty, leaving his entire estate, in the will he had made but five days before his death, to be divided between "my two daughters, Lizzie and Eleanore," who were then only thirteen and eleven respectively, and making no mention whatever of Edith, his wife of fifteen years. In lieu of Edith, Charles appointed a special guardian for their girls. Obviously something had set Charles bitterly against his spouse—but what?

Just eighteen days after Charles' death—barely allowing her time to don and doff widow's weeds—Edith Sanxay wed another man, five years younger than she, named John Nicholas Oliver, a salesman of building specialties from Washington, D.C. The new couple moved out of New York City with Elisabeth and Eleanor (the latter as an adult dropped the final "E" from her name) to a nondescript new house located at 60 Brookside Place, New Rochelle, where they were joined, less than six months after the marriage, by Master Humphrey Marshall Oliver, Edith's newborn son by her new husband John.

By 1910 Elisabeth—who was educated in various private establishments and had graduated, along with her sister Eleanor, from the Packer Collegiate Institute (originally the Brooklyn Female Academy)—had taken employment as a governess, further indicating that her late father's money had not been sufficient for her to maintain the idealized life of an American gentlewoman (although in 1915 she and her sister numbered among the inheritors of their deceased Grandmother Fickett's substantial estate, valued at $22,000—nearly $600,000 today). By 1920 Elisabeth's mother Edith had parted from her successor spouse, the reason due this time not to death but rather divorce, thereby for a second time depriving herself of a source of steady masculine income. Edith, who never remarried, retained her ex-husband's surname, editing and publishing fiction under the name Edith Hollick Oliver. Tellingly, it was the Sanxay surname which Edith expunged, although it survives to the present day as the middle name of her vastly better-known crime writer daughter.

The most interesting thing about Edith's second husband likely was that he was one of the children of John Nicholas Oliver, Sr., a prominent nineteenth-century D.C. attorney, who two decades earlier had represented Lillie Christiancy in the divorce suit brought against her, on grounds of multiple infidelities, by her husband, former United States Senator and then current Minister Plenipotentiary to Peru Isaac P. Christiancy. The couple, whose age disparity was over four decades (at the time of their marriage in 1876, Lillie was twenty-one and her husband was sixty-three), had wed just eighteen months after the death of Christiancy's first wife, much to the chagrin of the senator's adult children.

Admittedly the Christiancy divorce saga, which occupied page after page in American newspapers across the country between 1881 and 1883 (though it is oddly forgotten today), took place several years before Elisabeth Sanxay Holding was even born, and Lillie's attorney, John N. Oliver, Sr., died in 1894, when Elisabeth was just five. Yet Elisabeth resided with her stepfather, John N. Oliver, Jr. during the decade between 1903 and 1913, from her mother Edith's marriage to her own; and it seems not unlikely that the case might have been recalled in her presence, especially given the circumstances of her mother's own precipitous second marriage. Coupled with the progressive views about women's sexuality held by her maternal grandfather Frederick Hollick, who died in 1900 when Elisabeth was eleven, and her own apparent marital challenges with her own husband, George Holding, it should come as no surprise that marital misery, infidelity, illegitimacy, alcoholism, divorce and men and women in general straying beyond the stricter confines of moral and sexual convention are recurrent themes in Elisabeth's crime fiction, recalling the work of her older contemporary Edith Wharton. Over and over Elisabeth Holding, like Edith Wharton, presents to her readers sagas of dark emotional problems hidden behind closed doors which even the miracle of modern appliances cannot solve.

□ □ □

Nobody Would Listen: Collected Crime Fiction of Elizabeth Sanxay Holding, gathers nineteen works of short crime fiction by the author, from "Mollie: The Ideal Nurse," published at the outset of Holding's writing career in *The Century* in January 1921, when she was just thirty years old, to "Game for Four Players," which appeared nearly four decades later in *Alfred Hitchcock's Mystery Magazine* in June 1958, more than three years after the author's premature death at the age of sixty-five in 1955. The publication of so much of Holding's short crime fiction in one mammoth volume is a signal moment in crime fiction history, giving the author, long acknowledged as one of the twentieth century's finest crime novelists, her due also as an accomplished chronicler of crime in its shorter forms.

Presumably the first piece of crime fiction which Holding published, the masterful "Mollie: The Ideal Nurse," tells the tale of Rob and Mrs. Keating, a couple with two young children in the capable care of Mollie, their nigh-perfect nursemaid—barring Steve, the drunken lout of a husband with whom Mollie unhappily comes encumbered. How does one deal with a problem like Mollie's mister? This short story—which like Susan Glaspell's courtroom (and classroom) classic "A Jury of Her Peers" (1917), includes serious subtext about marital relationships between couples, both genteel and menial—is told with perceptive wit and irony. "Once again there descended upon them that old fear well known to all [upper middle class] parents, that fear of their children," observes the author at one point, when Mollie, seemingly reconciled with Steve, leaves the Keatings. How much of this story was drawn from real life?

The vast majority of Holding's true short crime fiction dates from the 1940s and 1950s, the decades when the author achieved her pinnacle as a crime writer. However, two exceptions, aside from "Mollie", are the long novella "The Chain of Death," published serially in *Liberty* over May-June 1930 and "Nobody Would Listen," published in August 1935 in *Mystery*, a short-lived slick mystery magazine aimed at women readers. Published around the same time as her early crime novels *Miasma* (1929) and *Dark Power* (1930), "Chain" is very much of its time, with a country house murder, a victim whom everyone conveniently hated, an ill-assorted house party of suspects and stiff characters who periodically ejaculate at each other epithets like "You hound!" and "You swine!" There is even a wealthy dilettante amateur sleuth of sorts, though things happen *to* him rather than the other way around. Classic detective fiction was not really Holding's forte, yet this period piece is not without period charm.

An altogether grimmer tale, effectively anticipating the brilliant succession of Holding's deadly serious novels of psychological, or domestic, suspense that darkly commenced with *The Death Wish* (1934), is "Nobody Would Listen." Events in the story are seen through the perceptions of focal character Mrs. Morrissey, who accepts—the depressed economy being what it is—a position as cook and maid of all work at the isolated, forest shrouded cottage of two middle-aged single women, Mrs. Torrance and her companion Miss Raleigh. After witnessing repeated recriminatory outbursts between the two genteel ladies, Mrs. Morrissey direfully warns of impending violence to a wealthy neighbor, the local clergyman and the local doctor, but no one pays her heed. Reflects Mrs. Morrissey of this complacency: "It's because they're ladies ... If they were just poor people, or if they were foreigners, people would believe it." As in "Mollie," there is much discerning social observation in "Listen," although this time it comes, more unusually for the period, from a working-class perspective.

We know that Holding lived for eight years in Bermuda, where her husband evidently held some sort of diplomatic position between 1922 and 1930, and that during this time she, then a British citizen under American law like her husband, frequently traveled to islands in the Caribbean, where her husband had once lived. Between 1944 and 1957, a half-dozen Holding crime stories with Caribbean settings were published, these being "The Kiskadee Bird" (*Cosmopolitan*, 1944), "The Blue Envelope" (*Collier's Weekly,* 1944), "The Unbelievable Baroness" (*The American Magazine*), "People Do Fall Downstairs" (*Ellery Queen's Mystery Magazine*, 1947), "Most Audacious Crime" (*Nero Wolfe Mystery Magazine*, 1954) and "The Daring Doctor" (*Alfred Hitchcock's Mystery Hitchcock*, 1957). All of the wartime tales in some way concern the plights of war refugees, to whom the author displays decided sympathy.

"The Kiskadee Bird" takes place on the island of Puerto Azul, where Johnny Pepper has recently been appointed Deputy Police Commissioner. Like Holding's husband, Johnny has a "natural gift for tongues" and additionally his father was in the Consular Service. With the onset of World War Two his job has been mostly dealing with "queer people coming into Puerto Azul these days": sorting them out, examining their papers and asking them questions. The latest of these "queer people" to arrive at Puerto Azul, imperious Julia Alderton, daughter of American steel magnate Cyrus Alderton and a survivor of a ship torpedoed offshore, presents Johnny with an unusual problem indeed, one perhaps romantic as well as criminal.

The protagonist of "The Blue Envelope" is another Caribbean deputy police commissioner, George Neva of the island of San Fernago. He must determine whether the mysterious Alphonse Dulac is in fact a German spy and prevent an impulsive French refugee from getting herself killed. "The Unbelievable Baroness," the best of this trio of wartime tales in my view, takes place on the island of Buenaventura and presents a vexing problem for Lieutenant Martin Hardy, Acting High Chief Commissioner of United States Police Forces for the territory. The problem concerns an outsize refugee German baroness, her young companion Elsa Taube and her "unspeakable little dog," Gustel, to whom the baroness evinces surpassing devotion. "My little dog has eleven years," she touchingly explains, "I have to him a duty."

The later trio of crime tales with Caribbean settings all have a series sleuth, Captain Martin Consadine, Commissioner of Police on the island of Puerto Azul, a locale familiar from "The Kiskadee Bird." (We are not informed what became of Johnny Pepper.) In "People Do Fall Downstairs"—Holding's first publication in *Ellery Queen's Mystery Magazine*, which had been founded six years earlier—the newly arrived Consadine ("He had been a policeman in Ceylon, in Demerara, in Trinidad, and elsewhere; he had almost forgotten Ireland, where he was born, London, where he had been trained.") and Constable Merribel ("Merribel was invaluable to him, a portly coloured man of calm and decorous demeanour, with a colossal knowledge of the island and its inhabitants") encounter the classic "Did he fall or was he pushed?" conundrum at the household of Captain William Jarvis of the Merchant Marine, which consists of, besides Jarvis himself, his alcoholic brother and his brother's wife; handsy handyman Louis Hazen; and pious Irish cook Mary Gogarty.

Possibly with "Downstairs" Holding had been encouraged to introduce a series sleuth by Frederic Dannay, editor of *Ellery Queen's Mystery Magazine*, who liked stories with recurring detectives. Whatever the case, however, Consadine did not appear again in another tale for seven years, when "Most Audacious Crime" was published in the January 1954 issue of *Nero Wolfe Mystery Magazine*, a lesser, short-lived rival of *EQMM*. (During the final full year of her life, Holding published no novel and only a pair of short stories, suggesting the ill health which led to her demise in February 1955.) In "Crime" Consadine investigates strange goings-on at the Joblyn household, consisting of Howard Joblyn, an American geologist "down here on some sort of survey," Joblyn's wallflower wife, Natalie, and Natalie's forbidding spinster aunt, Miss Fanning. Their domestic situation has the poisonous tang of a true crime account.

In the final Consadine tale, Holding seems to have forgotten several details about her sleuth, giving his name as Dennis rather than Martin, his rank as Lieutenant rather than Captain and his locale as "the Caribbean island of St. Jerome" rather than Puerto Azul, while his assistant is now one Sergeant Mayblossom, "a stout colored man, looking soft as a teddy bear in his very snug white uniform, but in reality hard and muscular and alert, knowing everything about the island." (Mayblossom sounds a lot like Constable Merribel.) The story being published posthumously in *Alfred Hitchcock's Mystery Magazine* in March 1957, more than two years after the author's death, surely explains the inconsistencies. In it Consadine is tasked with untangling the matter of the mysterious Doctor Thomas Pauli, whom cantankerous

Mrs. Cobby claims is impudently impersonating her American professor spouse, who brought them to St. Jerome to complete a book, with the assistance of his Danish secretary Karen. Explodes Mrs. Cobby of Doctor Pauli, in a fine display of Fifties American paranoia: "He's a Communist! ... Who else would go prancing around the streets in a red necktie? The whole thing's a Communist plot...." However, Mayblossom explains to his superior that while back during the war years cranky Mrs. Cobby had cried wolf on numerous occasions about German spies and such, every now and then she turned out to hit the nail on the head....

Holding's Caribbean mysteries are attractive miniatures (comparatively speaking), but "Farewell to a Corpse," a lengthy novella set in exurban New York that was originally published in *Mystery Book Magazine* in October 1946, is the most substantial piece of short crime fiction that the author published in the postwar era, using murder to explore deeper matters than a puzzle. The editor of *MBM* perceptively described "Corpse" as "essentially a [moral] problem novel but [one] which combines elements of crime, danger and suspense to make it an outstanding mystery tale as well."

The protagonist of "Corpse," the amiable if somewhat feckless Felix Tellier, finds himself embroiled in a murder case, along with his wealthy, shrewish, daddy's girl wife Ildina; his overbearing father-in-law Leroy Fuller, who will make you want never to hear the word "Nope" again; his doggedly devoted pal Augie West, whom Ildina dismisses contemptuously as a "vulgar little beast"; and his lovely old friend, Stephanie, or "Taffy" as he calls her, whom he first knew back when she was a mere schoolgirl. For this novella, Holding drew on themes that go back in her crime fiction a dozen years to *The Death Wish*. Like the protagonist in that novel, Felix is an easygoing fellow starting to feel a sense of dissatisfaction with his jealously possessive, insecure wife and his company job. (He is Personnel Manager in his father-in-law's leather factory.) Increasingly he feels trapped in his life and yearns to become free again, to join the Merchant Marine and roam the seas in "space and freedom" as he once had planned. "Settled in a job, in a home, in a community," he thinks discontentedly, "sometimes, in vivid flashes, this stability seemed...like a yawning trap." To local liberal District Attorney Francis Bushey, Ildina provokingly blames the murder of their neighbor Mimi DePew on a tramp, or perhaps, recalling Mrs. Cobby from "The Daring Doctor," "one of those Communists who hate everyone with any money"; yet Felix senses that the true culprit lies closer to home.

How much of a character like Felix Tellier owe inspiration to Holding's own life and her husband we cannot know, but it seems not improbable that George Edwyn Holding, who roamed the Caribbean in his twenties before finally marrying at the age of thirty-seven, when he was working an adjuster in a marine insurance company, had a similar dissatisfaction with life's—and marriage's—confinements. Of his two-year-old marriage Felix tells himself: "Stop thinking about it. It will get better in time. People get adjusted to each other as time goes on. As time goes on, you get used to things, to anything, to everything, and you don't mind anymore."

On the question of divorce, a not uncommon occurrence in the Holding ménage (Elisabeth's half-brother would divorce his spouse as well), Taffy, whose mother Denise is twice divorced and thrice married, unexpectedly urges on Felix her belief in the inviolability of the legal union between man and wife, in words that read like a criticism of the author's mother: "I've known people who wouldn't turn away an old servant, no matter how trying and disagreeable and useless she was. But they'd turn away the husband or wife they'd chosen." Was this Holding's own view of marriage and divorce? Does this explain why she stuck it out with George, whatever their problems, for three decades, until his death in 1943? Did she feel all her life a sense of opprobrium over her mother's marital misadventures? In "Corpse" the odious Leroy Fuller sneers at Felix advancing the notion that anyone with Taffy's sordid upbringing could have a working moral compass: "Her mother had three husbands, two divorces. What do you think marriage means to her daughter? Not a damn thing."

Holding's second "farewell" story, her hard-boiled mystery parody "Farewell, Big Sister," was the second of the three stories by her which *Ellery Queen's Mystery Magazine* published, in July 1952. Anyone familiar with Raymond Chandler's crime writing will surmise that it is his work that is the target of the parody. Interestingly, the notoriously grouchy and acerbic Chandler was a self-professed great admirer of Holding, effusively declaring of her in correspondence: "For my money she's the top suspense writer of them all." Chandler worked on a screenplay for Holding's 1946 novel *The Innocent Mrs. Duff*, before giving it up because, he later claimed, of studio interference. (The projected film was never produced.) It is doubtful that Holding was aware of Chandler's esteem for her own work, but her amusing parody of his, which includes some notably surreal touches, is a knowing one. What would the hyper-sensitive Chandler have made of PI Coney Bassard (i.e., corny bastard) and Police Captain Canoodler?

The last of the three Holding crime stories which appeared in *Ellery Queen's Mystery Magazine*, "Glitter of Diamonds," published in March 1955, a month after the author's death, also mines a humorous vein, bearing something of a resemblance to "The Snowball Burglary," a thirty-three-year-old Reggie Fortune detective story by English mystery writer H. C. Bailey. Indeed, Lady Beryl, the protagonist of the tale, is a very English aristocrat, summering in the Connecticut Berkshires at a house lent her by an American friend. Lady Beryl has had imposed upon her as a companion one Mademoiselle Gervaise d'Arville, a very earnest leftist young woman with whom she has nothing in common and for whom she has nothing actually to do. To deal with the problem of Gervaise, Lady Beryl turns to crime, getting some unwitting help in the process from her equally earnest insurance investigator nephew Phillip Phipps. One would never guess from this sparklingly amusing story that its author was nearing her death.

Somewhat reminiscent of "Glitter of Diamonds," albeit in a dark vein, is "The Legacy," which was published in *Liberty* in 1950. In it, Mrs. Lamb, like Lady Beryl in "Diamonds," has a companion temporarily foisted upon her, in this case by a wealthy cousin, Laurie Jacobs, while Laurie is away, ostensibly touring Mexico. Laurie warns Mrs. Lamb of her domestic: "She's really wonderful, only she's got to be kept busy, or she gets queer"—and never have truer words been spoken.

Another posthumously published crime story by Holding is "Very, Very Dark Mink," which first appeared in *The Saint Detective Magazine* in December 1956, nearly two years after the author's passing. In "Mink" Albert Pennington, an employee in a New York steamship company, is called upon by an old love—the boss' much younger wife no less—to help put a stop to a blackmailer who menaces them both. Things take a surprising turn from there.

Holding's final original published tale, "Game for Four Players," which was published in *Alfred Hitchcock's Mystery Magazine* in June 1958, more than three years after the author's death, is another ironic tale of sexual shenanigans. When the story opens, down on her luck Desiree walks through "the dismal and almost empty lobby of the third-rate little hotel" to commence a game—a badger game—with an unsuspecting male at the dowdy hotel's so-called Paris Grill—but little does she realize how complicated this particular game will get. Like "Mink," "Game" could have made an excellent episode of the contemporary television series *Alfred Hitchcock Presents*.

In addition to short crime fiction, Holding in the 1950s published in the *Magazine of Fantasy and Science Fiction* a trio of intriguing tales of the uncanny, which one might liken unto contemporary works by authors Daphne du Maurier and Shirley Jackson. (Indeed, Jackson's work appeared in *MFSF* as well.) These stories are "Friday, the Nineteenth," "Shadow of Wings" and "The Strange Children." "Friday, the Nineteenth," published in *MFSF* in the summer of 1950, is an unnerving time dislocation tale, like a nightmarish version of the 1993 Bill Murray film *Groundhog Day*. "Shadow of Wings," published in *MFSF* in July 1954, was the final Holding story published during the author's lifetime. Readers will be reminded of "The Birds," Daphne du Maurier's classic apocalyptic novella (and the inspiration for the classic Alfred Hitchcock film), which first appeared in the United States the previous year in du Maurier's short fiction collection *Kiss Me Again, Stranger*. However, Holding takes the theme of strange actions by massed flocks of birds in a different direction. One point which Holding repeatedly urges—that ostensible scientific "experts" are not necessarily to be trusted by the public—startlingly has particular currency today, in this era of impassioned COVID mask protests and raucous school board meetings:

> That's it, said Stan to himself. That's the matter with us today. We all believe there are experts around, to fix up anything and everything. Soil erosion, rivers deflected, droughts, forests destroyed, natural resources wasted away. Never mind. Scientists will make food, control soil, or water. Plagues? Let 'em come, polio, flu, anything. Scientists will cope with them. They'll also deal with crime, insanity, family rows.
> ….we're trained to look for an expert, in any sort of trouble. Don't try to do anything for yourself, ever…. Don't try to figure out what sort of education and training your own children need. You'll ruin their lives. Call in a psychiatrist.

The last in this trio of Holding's "tall" tales is the only overtly supernatural one in the bunch: "The Strange Children," published in August 1955, seven months after Holding's voice was silenced by the grave. In this tale young Marjorie Smith's night of babysitting for a pair of children whom she has never met before turns very strange and unnerving indeed, especially after she spies the children up and out of bed and talking to an unknown man…. One might initially be reminded of the 1979 film shocker *When a Stranger Calls*, but the story takes an appropriately fantastical turn, becoming a meditation on the state of life after death.

Hear me out: The wonderful variety and high quality of the tales collected in *Nobody Would Listen* confirms Elisabeth Sanxay Holding's stature as one of the twentieth century's most significant crime writers, not only as a bridge between the so-called "Had I But Known" mysteries of Mary Roberts Rinehart and her many followers and the postwar psychological suspense and noir of such noted crime writers as Margaret Millar, Celia Fremlin, Shelley Smith, Charlotte Armstrong and Patricia Highsmith, but as a serious and versatile mainstream author who shared affinities with such towering literary figures as Edith Wharton, Susan Glaspell and Shirley Jackson. Acknowledging Holding's sad untimely death in the *Magazine of Fantasy and Science Fiction* in 1955, Editor Anthony Boucher pronounced that the author's "series of psychological suspense stories of murder" were "so far ahead of their times in delicacy and depth that she may almost be said to have created the modern murder novel." Her short fiction is not chump change either, as readers now will be able to see for themselves in this fine volume.

—November 2022
Germantown, TN

Curtis Evans received a PhD in American history in 1998. He is the author of *Masters of the "Humdrum" Mystery: Cecil John Charles Street, Freeman Wills Crofts, Alfred Walter Stewart and British Detective Fiction, 1920-1961* (2012) and most recently the editor of the Edgar nominated *Murder in the Closet: Essays on Queer Clues in Crime Fiction Before Stonewall* (2017) and, with Douglas G. Greene, the Richard Webb and Hugh Wheeler short crime fiction collection, *The Cases of Lieutenant Timothy Trant* (2019). He blogs on vintage crime fiction at The Passing Tramp.

Nobody Would Listen:
The Collected
Mystery Stories of
Elisabeth Sanxay Holding

Nobody Would Listen

Mrs. Morrissey had never before taken a position as general houseworker. She was a cook, and a good one. But times were hard, and from what Mrs. Cornelius at the agency had said, this seemed like a nice place, two ladies, no washing; and in the mountains. Mrs. Morrissey accepted it, sent her trunk by express, and bag in hand, took a train early in the morning for Fayville.

She liked riding in the train; she sat by the window looking out at the countryside, a sturdy little woman with gray hair, and deep-set dark blue eyes, and a composed and serious air. Yet, sedate as she was, there was a spirit of adventure in her, she liked new scenes, she liked not to know where she was going. She thought about one thing and another until the train stopped at Fayville—then she descended, the only passenger on the little platform.

There was a coupe waiting, and out of it got a woman, tall and straight, and well built, with splendid red hair that glistened like copper in the sun.

"Are you from the agency?"

"Yes, ma'am. Mrs. Morrissey, ma'am."

"I'm Miss Raleigh," said the other, in her cool pleasant voice.

Mrs. Morrissey got into the car, and Miss Raleigh took the wheel. She talked from time to time in a good-humored, sensible way, and Mrs. Morrissey was favorably impressed. This, she thought, was the sort of lady she liked to work for—reasonable, one who knew her own mind. She only hoped the other lady would be as nice.

They went past fields, empty in the blazing noonday sun, past farmhouses; presently they turned off the main road, and followed shady little lanes. The way was uphill now, and there was nothing but trees, miles and miles of trees, a glade of white birches where the sun struck through, a dark unstirring regiment of oaks, with ferns growing at their feet, delicate larches, and black spruce. For a while Mrs. Morrissey looked with pleasure on the green world, and found it restful; but after a time she liked it less.

"I'll be glad when we get out of the woods," she thought.

They turned into a lane no more than a narrow track through a pine wood.

"There's the house," said Miss Raleigh.

Before them stood a little half-timbered cottage, with a lawn of coarse grass before it, and the dark pines springing close about it. It had a curiously unreal theatrical look, and a very lonely one.

"How would you go out, at all?" thought Mrs. Morrissey, "the way you'd be in a forest, as soon as you stepped out of the door."

Carrying her bag, she followed Miss Raleigh up the path, and into a dim little hall.

"Josie!" called Miss Raleigh. "Here we are."

"You needn't scream," said another voice so close at hand that Mrs. Morrissey started, and from a room at the right came a frail little lady with dark hair, and thin rouged cheeks, wearing a pince-nez. "What is your name? Mrs. Morrissey? Come in here, please. I want to speak to you."

"Gloomy," thought Mrs. Morrissey, glancing at the sitting room with its brown velvet rug, and a purple brocaded sofa, ecru curtains across its closed windows. The frail little lady sat down, and Mrs. Morrissey stood before her.

"I am Mrs. Torrance," she said. "I'm the one who is employing you. I don't know whether that's been made clear to you. This is my house and Miss Raleigh is my companion."

"Yes, ma'am," said Mrs. Morrissey.

"You'll have a good home here," Mrs. Torrance went on. "And the work's not at all hard. I always try to be considerate … Your room is upstairs at the end of the hall … We'll expect only a light lunch today … A little omelette …"

"Yes, ma'am," said Mrs. Morrissey.

Many times in her fifty years had she gone into a stranger's house to live for she didn't know how long, to earn her living in conditions unknown to her. She had learned to accept vicissitudes calmly; if things were too hard, she would leave. She mounted the stairway in a philosophic mood. Mrs. Torrance had said she'd have a good home here. Well, she hoped it would be so.

Her room was unexpectedly fine, right on the same floor with the ladies. Yet she did not like it at all. The pine trees stood too close to the windows; they made the room dark. The furniture too was dark and massive, a big double bed with a green moiré spread, a big clothes press, a walnut washstand with a green and white basin and jug.

"I'd never in the world feel at home here," she thought.

She changed into a clean cotton dress and went down to find the kitchen. This first meal was something of an ordeal; she didn't know where things were kept, she didn't know the ladies' tastes. She remembered her last place. A big house with a butler, and three maids, and a chauffeur.

"I've never worked alone before," she thought, and sighed.

She was very glad when Miss Raleigh came to help her; a very nice lady, pleasant and friendly, yet dignified. She showed Mrs. Morrissey where the supplies were kept, helped her to set the table in the little dining room. Mrs. Morrissey was a little nervous about waiting on the table, for she had had no experience in that; she moved about carefully, her lips compressed, and she watched her two ladies trying to understand them. They talked very little, and she wondered if they had had a disagreement, or if they were always so quiet.

While she was washing the dishes, Mrs. Torrance came into the kitchen and told Mrs. Morrissey what there was in the house for dinner; the butcher came three times a week and they would give him an order tomorrow.

"The last cook had to leave very suddenly," she said. "Someone in her family was ill. Of course it made it hard for Miss Raleigh. She had to do all the cooking and the house work then."

"Putting Miss Raleigh in her place like," thought Mrs. Morrissey. "Always harping on that, Mrs. Torrance is."

She wished Mrs. Torrance would go away, so that she could get on with the dishes, but Mrs. Torrance wished to talk, and Mrs. Morrissey had to stand there, grave and respectful.

"Remember, Mrs. Morrissey, if there are any little difficulties, come straight to me. I'm not in good health, but I do keep the reins in my own hands. Naturally," she gave a little laugh, "when I pay all the bills."

"Yes, ma'am," said Mrs. Morrissey.

Left alone at last, she went on with the dishes, and when that was done she stepped out of the back door for a breath of air. She found herself in a little space of grass surrounded by fir trees, all rustling softly. There was nothing else to be seen, no vista, only the blue sky overhead, no sound but the trees rustling.

"Just the three of us here," she thought; "I don't like a house with no man in it."

She returned to the house to clean all the shelves. She heard no footsteps overhead, no sound, she had never been in such a quiet house. "What are they all doing, the both of them?" she thought. "It's too quiet, entirely."

"It was nearly four o'clock when she heard a car coming, and she was glad enough to hear it. The doorbell rang and she hastened to open it for a dark, serious, handsome young clergyman.

"Will you please ask Mrs. Torrance if she can see Mr. Boles?" he said.

He entered the sitting room, and Mrs. Morrissey was going towards the stairs when she saw Mrs. Torrance descending in haste.

"Is it Mr. Boles? Always let me know *at once* when Mr. Boles comes."

"Yes, ma'am."

Returning to the kitchen, Mrs. Morrissey heard Mrs. Torrance's voice. Clear, eager, almost girlish.

"Mr. Boles, I'm so glad. It does seem so long …"

Mrs. Morrissey put on the kettle, thinking they might be wanting tea, and she was right; in a few minutes Mrs. Torrance rang for her. She was sitting on the purple brocade sofa, beside Mr. Boles, and either she had put on more rouge or her thin cheeks were flushed.

"Some tea!" she said imperiously.

When Mrs. Morrissey returned with the tray, Miss Raleigh was there, very pleasant and young-looking in a sleeveless white dress. They all seemed very cheerful together.

It was time to think about dinner, now; Mrs. Morrissey wanted to make a good impression this first night, but the supplies were meagre and uninspiring; a very small leg of lamb, some potatoes, a cabbage.

"I'll make them a nice apple pie," she thought, and was rolling out the dough, when Mrs. Torrance came into the kitchen. For a moment she stood in silence, her little fingers interlacing.

"It's more than I can bear!" she cried suddenly. "Cissy's been at you already. *She's* the kind, helpful one, and I'm the tyrant. She's the good-natured one who puts up with everything from me. And nobody knows— or cares—what I put up with from her."

She wept, with a little lace handkerchief to her eyes. "She's turned everyone against me! Everyone! My own doctor, my old friend Amy Winter … And now she'll do the same with you. Even now you're thinking that she's the kindest … I fixed up your room myself. I put that handsome moiré spread on the bed … I pay good wages, and I am reasonable and considerate as ever I can be. But she gets all the credit."

This scene was very distressing to Mrs. Morrissey. She was shocked by Mrs. Torrance's lack of restraint. But she was sorry for her.

"And maybe there's something in what she says," she thought, "Miss Raleigh is smart."

But what sympathy she had felt Mrs. Torrance was lost a few hours later. With her own ears she had heard how Mrs. Torrance talked to Miss Raleigh at the dinner table.

"Really, Cissy, you're too obvious … If you're so desperately anxious to see Mr. Boles alone, you might think up a better excuse than pretending you want to borrow his music.…"

"Mr. Boles suggested my driving over to the parsonage."

"After you had hinted, and hinted. Really, Cissy, you're not a young girl, you know."

Every time Mrs. Morrissey went into the dining room it was going on, Mrs. Torrance, so spiteful, and Miss Raleigh so patient.

"Wasn't it just a little officious, Cissy, to give the blackberry jam to Amy Winter? I know you made it, and I'd have given you full credit for that. But after all, Amy is *my* friend, and that jam is supposed to be part of the household supplies."

"I'm sorry," said Miss Raleigh, gently, "I'm sorry that I forgot, even for a moment, that everything here belongs to you."

After that, they finished the meal in silence. Then, when Mrs. Morrissey was washing the dishes, she heard the piano. She looked in and saw Miss Raleigh playing, and it seemed to her very wonderful. She propped open the door into the dining room, so that she could hear better. Noble, beautiful music, it was, that somehow eased her heart.... She thought of her husband, who had died long ago. They had loved each other dearly, and she liked to remember him.

"It's as good as anything I ever heard on the radio," she thought. The music ceased, and she rose with a sigh and glanced about her kitchen to be sure it was immaculate. "But you'd never be able to do much with this floor," she thought. "I wonder, would Mrs. Torrance get some nice linoleum … I might speak to her tomorrow about it—if I make up my mind to stay."

For she was not at all sure that she wanted to stay. The wages were good and the work not too hard, and jobs were not too plentiful just now, but she wasn't at all sure....

The two ladies came down to breakfast promptly at eight, and as she brought in the coffee, Mrs. Morrissey glanced at them uneasily. She hoped earnestly that yesterday had been unusual, and that today they would be pleasant and cheerful together. They sat at the table in silence.

"Well, there's many don't feel like talking till after breakfast," thought Mrs. Morrissey.

When the ladies were served, she went upstairs to do the bedrooms; the sun was up but the trees shut away the light; there wasn't, she thought, one cheerful room in the place. But after she had got the house all in order, she felt better. Always living in the houses of strangers, it was easy for her to feel at home; and after she had worked for the little house, she liked it. She was humming quietly in the kitchen while she got the lunch when Miss Raleigh came in and closed the door.

"Mrs. Morrissey," she said, not smiling now, but pale and subdued, "I'm going to ask you to do something for me, and I don't want Mrs. Torrance to know. After lunch, I want you to slip out and take this note to Mrs. Winter and wait for an answer. It's quite a long walk, and I can't drive you without Mrs. Torrance noticing. And I can't telephone...."

"Yes, ma'am," said Mrs. Morrissey.

"Go down the lane until you reach the main road, and then turn up the hill. Mrs. Winter's is the first place you will come to. It's really quite a walk, and I'm sorry to ask you, but—" she paused a moment—"I'm not timid or nervous," she went on, "but I'm a little afraid ..." she paused again, "Mrs. Torrance is not herself. She's turned against me ... After nearly twenty years ... Perhaps you noticed?"

Timid and respectful, Mrs. Morrissey stood before her, and said nothing. When Miss Raleigh had gone she went on with her work.

"I wouldn't know the rights and wrongs of it," she thought, "and me only here since yesterday. But I do not like it at all."

When lunch had been served, and the dishes washed, she put on her black suit and her black straw hat and her black gloves, and left the house by the kitchen door. It was hot in the sun, and she was not accustomed to walking; she sighed when she reached the main road and saw the steep hill before her. On one side of the road were those endless woods, on the other side, a white fence, and looking over it she saw the tops of trees, far below her, in a dark cool ravine.

As she toiled up the hill, her shoes began to hurt. It was so hot that she took off her jacket and folded it neatly over her arm. She did not meet a single car, a single living creature, she heard nothing but the rustle of the trees, and now and then the clear note of some unseen bird.

Then to her great relief, she came to a stone wall, and presently to the entrance of a driveway. Sturdy and straight, she walked along, and was rewarded by the sight of a fine stone house with a terrace before it, and striped awnings, the sort of house in which she was accustomed to working. With a great longing, she thought of the orderly routine in a place like that, the pleasant companionship.

"But you cannot expect to have everything you want, in this world," she said to herself.

She went to the side door and was admitted by a butler, a heavy middle-aged man with a calm face. She told him she had a message for Mrs. Winters from Miss Raleigh, and was to wait for an answer.

"Sit down," he said, not professional now, but friendly, "I'll tell the madame."

Mrs. Morrissey was glad enough to sit down in the pantry. This house was quiet, but not like the cottage. She heard someone singing in the kitchen, a light quick step overhead. It was alive.

"The madame will see you," said the butler reappearing. "Jacobs, my name is."

"I'm Mrs. Morrissey."

"Pleased, Mrs. Morrissey. You must find it rather lonely down at the cottage … Maybe, some evening when some of us are driving into the village to the pictures, you'd do us the favor of coming along?"

"I'd be pleased to come, Mr. Jacobs, I like the pictures once in a while." She was wonderfully fortified by this conversation. She followed Jacobs through a swing door, and along a hall to a big library, where, sitting in an armchair was an elderly lady, stout, florid, and handsome with a crown of white hair.

"Now, what's all this?" she demanded. "Sit down, Mrs. Morrissey. You look as if you had some common sense." She stared at Mrs. Morrissey with candid appraisal. "You don't look like the others they've had in the cottage. Where have you worked before?"

Mrs. Morrissey sat with her gloved hands in her lap, and never had she felt more at ease.

"I'm a cook, ma'am," she answered simply. "I've never done general housework before. Mrs. Dennison was my last lady. Then there was Mrs. Lewis Porter, Junior—six years I was with her—and before that Miss Mildred Atterbury."

"Ha!" said Mrs. Winter, "I didn't know Miss Milly personally, but I know plenty of people who did.…"

She fell silent, still staring at Mrs. Morrissey. And Mrs. Morrissey sat waiting patiently. A real lady, Mrs. Winter, the sort she understood and admired.

"I don't know …" Mrs. Winter resumed. "There was a lot of talk about contesting Miss Milly's will … Did you notice anything queer about her?"

"She had her own little ways, ma'am."

"You know how to hold your tongue," said Mrs. Winter. "That's an admirable thing. But now I wish you'd talk. I'm the oldest friend Josie Torrance has. Cissy Raleigh has more sense in her little finger, than Josie has in her whole body. But Josie's my friend … If there's anything in this farrago … I'm treating you with confidence … Have you noticed anything queer in Mrs. Torrance?"

"No, ma'am," said Mrs. Morrissey after a pause, "just nervous-like."

"Very well," said Mrs. Winter. "Tell Miss Raleigh I'll think over her note, and I'll come down in a day or two. Now Bates can drive you back."

What Miss Raleigh had written in her note seemed obvious to Mrs. Morrissey; she had said that Mrs. Torrance was "queer."

"And that's a serious thing," she thought. "Well do I remember how them relatives were trying to make out that Miss Atterbury was queer, too, that way they'd get their money. It's a treacherous thing for Miss Raleigh to do."

She got out of the car before they came in sight of the house, and entered it stealthily by the back door.

"Quiet as the grave," she thought, trying not to step upon the stair that creaked. But she did tread on it inadvertently, and Miss Raleigh called her in a queer whisper.

"Mrs. Morrissey!"

She went to Miss Raleigh's room and opened the door. And Miss Raleigh was lying in bed, white as paper, her hands pressed against her stomach.

"Whatever is the matter, ma'am?" cried Mrs. Morrissey.

"Nothing ...!" said Miss Raleigh, and was suddenly and horribly sick.

"I'll send for the doctor, ma'am—"

"No ..." said Miss Raleigh. "Get me the brandy from my cupboard." She lay back on the pillows, white and obviously in pain; she sipped a little brandy from the glass Mrs. Morrissey held for her.

"Are you still suffering, ma'am?"

"I can stand pain," said Miss Raleigh.

"If you'll let me send for the doctor, ma'am?"

"No!" said Miss Raleigh, her voice unexpectedly clear, "I've had an attack of acute indigestion ... but it won't happen again." She closed her eyes with a faint grimace of pain. "I don't want you to mention this— to *anyone*, Mrs. Morrissey ... I know how to take care of myself...."

She fainted then, and Mrs. Morrissey took away the pillows so that she could lie flat, and bathed her face with water until her eyes opened.

"Ma'am, you ought to have the doctor—"

"No!" said Miss Raleigh. "If you'll make me a cup of good strong coffee."

Mrs. Morrissey had never done anything so quickly in her life; she was out of breath when she reached the room with the coffee on a tray. But Miss Raleigh was undoubtedly better and it was not Mrs. Morrissey's place to insist upon a doctor. She tidied the room, and made Miss Raleigh as comfortable as she could, and then she returned to the kitchen. She sat down to peel potatoes for dinner.

"I don't know," she said to herself. "Miss Raleigh was terrible bad ... It was not anything she had for her lunch, at all ... But maybe she ate something else ... What else would it be but indigestion? Like she said...."

She thought and thought while she peeled the potatoes and dropped them into a yellow bowl of clear water. She had worked all her life for women, it had been necessary for her to study these women, upon whom her daily bread, and her peace of mind depended. She did this unconsciously, and unconsciously had formed her estimate of Miss

Raleigh and Mrs. Torrance.

"They hadn't ought to be shut up here together," she said to herself. "Not feeling like they do."

There was a crash outside that made her spring to her feet; running to the window, she saw a broken medicine bottle on the gravel walk, with a dark liquid flowing sluggishly over the fragments.

"Now!" cried Mrs. Torrance's voice from above. "Now, try to go spreading your crazy lies about my poisoning you, Cissy Raleigh! You *are* crazy! A crazy old maid!"

"If you don't stop—" said Miss Raleigh, in quite a new voice, low and fierce.

"I won't stop!" cried Mrs. Torrance, almost in a scream. "A crazy old maid, making a fool of yourself about Mr. Boles ... Cissy! Don't you dare come near me! *Help!*"

Mrs. Morrissey ran out into the hall. She saw Mrs. Torrance fly out of Miss Raleigh's room, she saw Miss Raleigh catch her, and bend the frail little woman backward over the bannisters....

"Stop!" cried Mrs. Morrissey.

The scene dissolved with the confusing speed of a nightmare. Miss Raleigh went into her room, Mrs. Torrance stepped into the bathroom; they were both gone, the cottage was perfectly quiet again. Mrs. Morrissey returned to the kitchen and sat down heavily in a chair. She felt weak.

"It is a terrible thing," she thought. "God have mercy on them ... And something will have to be done."

The woods were very strange in the night; the road was darker than any Mrs. Morrissey has ever travelled.

"Hate," she thought. "The two of them shut up there together, and hating each other to the point of death. And then to see them come down to their dinner—talking, and smiling, with that in their hearts.

The ravine looked black as the pit; the road on this moonless night was a faint white trail.

"I wonder are there bears or the like?" thought Mrs. Morrissey, toiling up the mountain side in her respectable black suit and hat, "or tramps? Well, there's no use to be thinking of them, I have to do this, that's all there is to it."

It was a comfort to see the lights of the fine big house before her; it was a comfort to see Jacob's face when he opened the door.

"I'll have to see Mrs. Winter," she said, and sank into a chair. "My feet are near killing me, the way I'm not used to walking much."

"The madame's gone to bed," said Jacobs. "But if it's urgent—"

He went away, and Mrs. Morrissey closed her eyes, lapped in the comfort of the house. Mrs. Winter would know what to do. She would lift this burden from her shoulders.

"The madame will see you," said Jacobs. "I hope there's nothing gone wrong down at the cottage."

She liked Jacobs, but she couldn't talk about that. It wouldn't be proper. She followed him up the stairs, and into a large bedroom lighted by a rose shaded lamp, where Mrs. Winter lay in bed, propped up with pillows, and wearing a white dotted Swiss dressing jacket.

"Close the door," she said. "Sit down, Mrs. Morrissey. You look very tired. Now then, what's the trouble?"

"It's very bad, ma'am. They didn't ought to be left there alone another hour."

"They quarreled, I suppose," said Mrs. Winter, "but they're really fond of each other in their own way."

"Excuse me, ma'am, but—" it was extremely hard to say in this tranquil room—"they tried to kill each other today."

"Nonsense!" cried Mrs. Winter. "Explain!"

Mrs. Morrissey did so.

"Well, *that's* clear enough," said Mrs. Winter. "Cissy ate something that disagreed with her. And she's got the idea so firmly in her head that Josie is queer … As for the rest of it—the scene you saw in the hall … It's disgraceful! Two middle-aged women behaving in that hysterical fashion … It won't do! I'm coming down to see Josie on Friday."

"It hadn't ought to be left till Friday, ma'am. They tried to kill each other this very day."

"No, they didn't," said Mrs. Winter. "It's just because you don't understand them as I do. I can't come before Friday, but you needn't worry, Mrs. Morrissey. Now, I'm going to send you home in the car, and before you go, Jacobs will give you a glass of port and a biscuit. It's very conscientious of you to come all this way."

"Ma'am, it's dangerous!" cried Mrs. Morrissey. "You're Mrs. Torrance's friend, and I do beg you to do something at once."

"I can't do anything in the middle of the night," said Mrs. Winter, half laughing. "Go home now and get a good night's sleep, Mrs. Morrissey. You've told me all about the situation, and I'll take the responsibility."

Mrs. Morrissey couldn't enjoy her glass of port in the servants' dining room, could not respond to Jacobs' friendly conversation. She couldn't enjoy the drive back home in the big black car. The chauffeur was a nice young fellow, but she didn't feel like talking to him. As before she got out of the car at the head of the lane.

"It's lonely here, all right," said Gates the chauffeur.

"Lonely?" thought Mrs. Morrissey. "I never knew what it was to feel real lonely before."

When she wakened in the morning, a soft steady rain was falling from a slate-colored sky. The kitchen was dreary. The rain whispered on the grass, on the leaves. There was a smell of mould in the cupboard. It was so quiet and so lonely, that she was glad to hear Mrs. Torrance's step on the stair, in spite of the dread she felt in seeing either of her ladies alone. Mrs. Torrance wore a brown and white silk dress, she looked dainty and fragile and somehow a little touching, with her soft brown hair, and rouge on her thin cheeks. And she didn't talk about anything embarrassing, only the list for the grocer.

Miss Raleigh came down, and they sat at breakfast together as pleasant as could be.

"It's hard to believe," thought Mrs. Morrissey.

But she did believe what she had seen and heard, and her heart was like lead.

While the ladies were finishing their breakfast, she went upstairs to make the beds; she was passing along the upper hall when she heard Miss Raleigh speaking.

"Hello! *Hello!* What on earth's the matter with this telephone?"

"Nothing," said Mrs. Torrance. "I rang up the company yesterday, and told them to disconnect it. A man will come today or tomorrow, to take it out."

"Why did you do that?" asked Miss Raleigh, her voice suddenly cold.

"Because I consider it an unnecessary expense," said Mrs. Torrance. "The butcher and the grocer call three times a week, and you've got the car. I can't see the need for ringing up Mr. Boles almost every day."

"You shouldn't have done that," said Miss Raleigh. "We might need the telephone—"

"Dr. Kynes will probably be stopping this afternoon," Mrs. Torrance interrupted. "You can tell him how worried you are. You must certainly tell him about your mysterious illness, Cissy."

"I scarcely think so," said Miss Raleigh with a little laugh. "I'm quite well again now. And the poor man is bothered enough by some people's imaginary ailments."

"But, after all," said Mrs. Torrance, "there are *some* ailments which are not imaginary. People do die, you know, Cissy. That's why I'm going to change my will when Mr. Harvey comes out on Saturday. So that if anything does happen to me...."

Mrs. Morrissey stood by the kitchen window looking out into the faint rain.

"The way they speak ... God help us ...! The hate they've got in their hearts...."

When lunch was finished, she sat in a straight chair, waiting.

"Maybe Mrs. Winter will come, after she's thought it over. Or maybe the doctor will come. If he does, I will tell him. I don't want to be here tonight, this way. I will tell him ... But the worst is the things you couldn't tell. It's the way they look at each other, and their voices. I wish I could get out of this, but I can't until there's somebody in charge of it. I cannot leave the two of them alone. It would be on my conscience till my dying day."

At four o'clock she made herself a cup of tea, wondering in dread about the ladies, so very quiet upstairs. She was just finishing a second cup when a car drove up, and she opened the door for a burly, gray-haired man with a pleasant face. Before there was a chance to say a word, Miss Raleigh came hurrying down the stairs.

"Mrs. Torrance is resting, Dr. Kynes," she said, "but I'd like to speak to you about her, I'm very uneasy...."

She took him into the drawing-room and closed the door, and Mrs. Morrissey was about to return to the kitchen when she heard a little sound that made her look up. Mrs. Torrance was in the upper hall, leaning on the stair rail.

"Did you hear that, Mrs. Morrissey?" she asked. "Cissy's been trying that for some time. Trying to make people believe I'm insane. So that if I make a new will it won't be valid. But she doesn't make much headway."

She gave a short little laugh, and withdrew, and Mrs. Morrissey went into the kitchen.

She heard the doctor go upstairs, and it seemed a long time before he descended again. She met him in the hall.

"Excuse me, sir," she said. "But if you wouldn't mind stepping into the kitchen—"

She closed the door.

"It's about the two ladies," she said. "Something ought to be done."

"Mean, they quarrel? I've advised Mrs. Torrance to go away for a little trip. But she won't do it. They've got on each other's nerves. It's unfortunate, but it's nothing to worry about. Nothing serious."

"Sir," said Mrs. Morrissey, a tremor in her voice, "it *is* serious. They hate each other."

"All on the surface. At heart, they're devoted to each other." He smiled good-humoredly at her. "The whole trouble is that they haven't got enough to do."

"They tried to kill each other yesterday, sir,"

He patted Mrs. Morrissey's shoulder, and looked down into her troubled face.

"Don't worry," he said. "When you know them better, you'll understand … Lot of talk, that's all." He glanced at his watch. "Don't worry!" he said again. "I've got to hurry along now. But I'll be back in a day or two and I expect to find you laughing at this. I'm glad they've got a good, sensible woman like you with them...."

"Sir, if you'd—"

"I've got to go," he said. "If you want me at any time, ring me up."

"The telephone is cut off, sir."

"It'll be repaired," he said, and off he went.

Mrs. Morrissey cooked the best dinner she could with the materials on hand, but the two ladies ate almost nothing; they did not speak a word, and directly after the meal was finished, they went into the sitting room. The wind had risen, the branches of the trees tossed restlessly with an unceasing whisper. Now and then there was a rattling gust of rain against the windows.

"I'm not much of a one to read," thought Mrs. Morrissey, "but tonight I'd be glad of a magazine, or the like. If I'd my cards with me I'd play solitaire."

She did not know what to do with herself, she was not sleepy, she had no wish to go to her room. And she did not want to sit in the kitchen, and just think. Think of the miles and miles of trees all around, and nothing else. The telephone was dead....

"Just the three of us here," she thought. "It's wrong."

The sound of a car startled her; she heard someone coming up the steps of the veranda, and she went out into the hall. But Mrs. Torrance was there before her, holding open the door.

"Mr. Boles! Imagine you coming out in this weather!"

"Mrs. Torrance," he said, "I'm overwhelmed. Your generosity … I got your check in this morning's mail."

Through the half-opened door of the kitchen, Mrs. Morrissey could see him standing there in the hall, very handsome, very earnest, in a glistening rubber coat, his hat in his hand. Mrs. Torrance was looking up into his face with so soft a smile.

"I don't think you quite realize how much I love our little church in the woods," she said, "or how much I appreciate the wonderful work you are doing in the parish."

"It's very kind of you."

"I only wish I could help more. I've shut myself up too much. If I could help you even a little, Mr. Boles, visiting people, perhaps?"

"I'm sure you could."

"And I want to ask you this, Mr. Boles. Do you know of some honest respectable woman who'd like the position of personal maid to me? Really something *more* than a maid, *almost* a companion. Miss Raleigh's leaving me."

"I'm sorry to hear that."

"Miss Raleigh doesn't agree with my point of view about religion. Her chief interest is in the music, the ritual. And mine is in the charitable work."

"That's because I'm dependent upon charity myself," said Miss Raleigh from within the sitting room, and Mrs. Morrissey gave a little gasp. It was dreadful that Miss Raleigh should have heard what Mrs. Torrance had just said. Calling her a 'maid', making her out to be heartless and mean … "Josie's kind enough to allow me a salary," Miss Raleigh went on. "But of course I don't really earn it. I'm simply a pauper dependent on Josie's beautiful charity.… It's her ruling passion—at the moment. We actually don't have enough to eat, so that she can make those lavish donations. It's admirable, no doubt, but it's worried me. Josie's not a rich woman; she'll leave herself destitute."

"Oh, stop! Stop!" cried Mrs. Morrissey to herself.

"That will do, Cissy," said Mrs. Torrance gently. "You needn't worry. I shall give you enough to keep you in comfort."

"According to my station," said Miss Raleigh, "I don't want anything from you."

"No doubt you've feathered your nest," said Mrs. Torrance, "and you've ingratiated yourself … You try to steal everyone from me, with your flattery, and your lies. You've made up to Amy Winter, flattering her, and belittling me—"

"Ladies," cried Mr. Boles, "Please—!"

"You can see for yourself," said Miss Raleigh, "what a condition Josie is in, she's not *responsible*."

"Ladies," he said again, "Ladies—" He paused; when he spoke again, his young voice had dignity and authority. "Let us pray for a time, in silence. Let us pray that all anger and uncharitableness be purged from our hearts. Let us admit, in all humility that we have offended one against the other, and entreat the God of mercy to forgive us as we forgive our fellow creatures. Let us pray."

There was a long silence.

"Amen," said Mr. Boles.

"You're so wonderful, Mr. Boles!" said Mrs. Torrance with a sob. "No one has ever done me so much good."

"If any help has come to you, Mrs. Torrance, the credit is not mine. Can I leave now," he asked, "with the assurance that this little storm has passed?"

"Yes, Father," said Miss Raleigh unsteadily.

"No!" cried Mrs. Morrissey, in her heart. "It is worse now than ever it was."

She heard Mr. Boles taking leave, and she hurried out of the back door and round to the drive where his car stood. He was startled when she spoke to him from the darkness.

"Please sir, if you would say something more to the two ladies. Things are bad between them, sir, very bad."

"It's always sad to see old friends fall out," he said kindly. "But one does see it very often. The best of it is that if they're left alone, they settle the little difference."

"It's not a little difference, sir, it's hatred they have for each other."

"You're wrong," he answered her, "there's an affection—"

"They tried to kill each other," said Mrs. Morrissey, said it almost mechanically. She knew he wouldn't believe her. And indeed he paid no attention to the strange statement.

"I am a student of human nature," he said. "My work demands that. I understand the situation perfectly. Here are two ladies, no longer young, and leading a too isolated life. It's almost inevitable—that they should magnify minor irritations."

"It's you is the cause of the trouble," thought Mrs. Morrissey. "And you've made it worse for all your meaning so well. The things they've said about each other with you listening, they'll never forgive nor forget.... And aloud, "If you'd go back, sir, and talk to them some more. The way you did before, only more, *you* could influence them more, sir."

"But I can't go back now," he said, his young voice troubled. "It would be very awkward...."

"It will be worse if you leave them alone," she cried. "Please go back."

"I can't," he said; "it would be a mistake … But I'll call again tomorrow or the next day. And I believe—I hope there is a better feeling between them now."

"There isn't sir!"

"I'll return very shortly," he said, with a slight trace of stiffness in his manner. "And you mustn't take their quarrel too seriously. Goodnight!"

She sat down in the kitchen. The rain was drumming on the roof, rattling on the windows; the trees, she thought, sounded like the sea....

And then she heard the piano. She settled back in her chair with a sigh of relief. It would be a fine thing, she thought, to hear more of that music. But it wasn't fine now, it was too loud. It was dreadful. Mrs. Morrissey put her hands over her ears, yet still she heard it. It was as if the whole world was filled with violence. She wanted to run upstairs, and get away from it.

"Is Mrs. Torrance sitting in there with *that* going on," thought Mrs. Morrissey, and felt obliged to go down the hall and see.

But Miss Raleigh was alone in there, and she was terrible. Her profile looked sharp and white, her coppery hair glinted in the lamplight, her strong hands pounced upon the keys. There was an ominous and furious energy about her.

"Oh …!" said Mrs. Morrissey to herself, pressing the knuckles of her hand against her mouth.

She had not the words to express what she felt. But she knew that no one could keep Miss Raleigh shut up in a little cottage, no one could belittle and wound her with impunity.

As she turned toward the stairs, the dreadful music stopped, and there was a ringing silence. It was good to hear the rain come back in a gust. Mrs. Morrissey felt a sudden impulse to run up the stairs to the safety of her room. She had a notion that Miss Raleigh had come out of the sitting room, and was coming stealthily along behind her, with her white face, and glittering hair, and her strong hands … But it wouldn't do to run. She mounted the stairs slowly. The faint light that was always left burning in the upper hall was out. Mrs. Torrance's door was open, but no light came from her room.

"I don't care at all if it's my place to do it or not," she said, "I want that light on, this night."

She turned the wall switch with a faint click, but no light came. And from the darkness came a titter.

She got into her own room with sort of a rush, turned on the light and locked the door. Her heart was beating wildly; nothing in her life had ever frightened her so much as that giggle in the dark.

"Sitting in there, laughing," she thought. "What is it she's laughing at? I cannot stay here."

Her knees felt weak. She sat down in a chair. "I've done what I could. If nobody will listen to me, I cannot help it."

The rain rattled against the window, there were all those miles and miles of lonely forest outside … Her room was bright, and the door was locked; she was safe enough. But she couldn't stay like that. In vain she told herself that she had done all she could, and that what happened now was not her responsibility.

"There is nobody but me," she thought. "I've just got to do the best I can."

That was her creed. She unlocked her door, and sat where she could watch the hall, and listen. Miss Raleigh came upstairs, and went into her room. Mrs. Torrance's door remained open. Mrs. Morrissey waited as best she could, but sometimes she dozed. For so many years she had gone to bed early and got up early.

The rain ceased in the night, but at five o'clock it was still overcast and dark. She made herself a cup of tea and left the house, taking an umbrella with her. It would take her at least an hour to walk to Mrs. Winter's house, and maybe there would be nobody up at this time. She was allowing a margin for that; so that if she had to wait there, and walk home again she could get her ladies' breakfast ready by eight o'clock.

The lane was muddy, it was dark under the trees, at every step, the wind brought down a shower of cold drops. She put up her umbrella to protect her hat, but she didn't need it when she got out on the main road. A desperate sense of haste possessed her, she walked as fast as she could; as she mounted the hill, perspiration was running down her face, her gray hair was damp on the temples. The loose stones bruised her feet through the soles of her shoes. She was tired, in a queer way, too; she wondered if some illness were coming on her.

"I'll have the strength to go," she told herself. "The strength will be given to me—to go on."

But when she reached the fence that marked the beginning of Mrs. Winter's garden, she had to sit down by the roadside. The trees rustled overhead, a faint breeze blew against her flushed face.

"I'm that tired," she thought. And suddenly she felt sure that her errand was in vain. Mrs. Winter would not believe her now, any more than she had before, and more than Dr. Kynes, or Mr. Boles believed her.

"It's no use!" she said to herself.

Mrs. Winter, like the others, would find her own explanation for the deeds, the words of her ladies.

They hadn't seen Miss Raleigh at the piano. They hadn't heard Mrs. Torrance laugh all by herself in the dark. Mr. Boles had heard the dreadful things they said to each other, and even he wouldn't believe in their hate.

"It's because they're ladies," thought Mrs. Morrissey. "If they were just poor people, or if they were foreigners, people would believe it. Everyone knows what women'll do when they're in love. But nobody'll believe that Mrs. Torrance and Miss Raleigh are in love with Mr. Boles...." She sat there quietly, to recover her strength.

"I'll go back," she thought. "I'll do the best that I can by myself, for there's no one will help me."

She sat, staring before her with deep-set, dark blue eyes, letting the breeze blow against her face. She sighed and rose. Her feet were bruised, she limped as she started down the hill.

"I'll just keep an eye on them every minute," she thought. "And I'll let them know it. I won't be impudent. I'll just tell them, as respectful as I can, that they've got to behave themselves, or I'll call in the police."

By the time she reached the lane again, she was hobbling, drenched with perspiration, worn out, a little dizzy.

"What time would it be?" she thought.

She went in at the back door, and found the kettle steaming away on the stove.

"One of 'em been down here," she thought.

She had forgotten to bring the alarm clock down with her, and she went into the hall to look at the grandfather's clock there. The hall was dim; she thought she saw a bundle lying at the foot of the stairs. She went closer and saw that it was Mrs. Torrance.

She thought she could not move. But she had to. She knelt down beside that very quiet figure and lifted the hand. It was warm.

"Praise be to God!" she cried, and raised the limp body in her strong arms. But Mrs. Torrance's head fell forward in a queer way ... Too far forward.

Mrs. Morrissey laid her down again very gently.

"Miss Raleigh!" she called.

She didn't think there would be any answer. She remembered how she had seen Miss Raleigh bending Mrs. Torrance back over the stair rail....

"Miss Raleigh is gone," she thought. "There's no one here but the two of us ... No telephone ... I'll have to go all the way back to Mrs. Winter's...."

It surprised her to find that she was crying. She dried her eyes, and tried to think.

"Will I wait until the butcher comes? I do not like to leave her alone ... It is a bad way to end ... I'm certain she brought it on herself the way she was always mocking and jeering at the other. But it is a bad way to end—all alone—in her own house—with her neck broken."

She could not stop crying.

"I'll cover her up decent," she thought ... "The sheets are all cotton ... I'll get a linen table cloth. She has a right to that."

Tears blinded her. She nearly stumbled over Miss Raleigh, lying on the dining room floor, with her knees drawn up, and her hands clenched, and an awful sort of smile drawing back her lips.

Judson Green deposed that he was seventeen years old, and employed by his father to deliver meat. On Thursday morning he had gone to Mrs. Torrance's house, and the cook let him in, and told him to get the police. James Bascom, constable, deposed that he had reached the cottage at ten twenty-seven, and had found the two bodies covered with table cloths. He had questioned Mrs. Morrissey, and she had said that when she returned from an early morning walk, she had found both the ladies dead. She had been unable to summon help because the telephone was disconnected, and she had not wanted to leave the ladies alone.

Dr. Kynes gave evidence. Mrs. Torrance died of a broken neck, caused by a fall. Miss Raleigh died of arsenic poisoning. Traces of arsenic had been found in the cup of tea which Miss Raleigh had evidently been drinking, mixed with a good deal of sugar. No, he could not give any definite opinion as to which of them had died first, but he was inclined to think that Mrs. Torrance had pre-deceased Miss Raleigh. Yes, as far as his personal observation went, the two ladies had been devoted to each other. Miss Raleigh had spoken to him only the day before, of her anxiety about Mrs. Torrance's nervous condition. A little quarrel, now and then, but nothing serious.

Mr. Boles gave evidence, as one of the last persons who had spoken to the ladies. He had called the evening before to thank Mrs. Torrance for a most generous check. He was obliged to admit that there was a certain acrimony between the ladies at first, but before he had left they were quite reconciled.

"What I should call a little hot weather quarrel," he said, with his shy pleasant smile.

Mr. Harvey, Mrs. Torrance's lawyer, took the stand. Mrs. Torrance had asked him to come out on Saturday. No, she had not said for what purpose, but she was in the habit of consulting him frequently, about her investments, and so on. Her will provided for certain legacies to the church, and to distant relations, the residue of the estate to Miss Cecilia Raleigh. He had every reason to believe that the two ladies were greatly attached to each other.

Mrs. Morrissey was asked a great many questions about the exact position of the bodies, about the foods in the house. The coroner then asked her what she could tell about the relations between the two ladies. Had she ever heard them quarrel? Yes, she had. What were the causes and nature of those quarrels? Mrs. Morrissey answered, after considerable reflection, that at one time it was about the telephone. The coroner suppressed a smile. Had Mrs. Morrissey ever seen any receptacle containing a poisonous spray for roses: She had not? Very well. Mrs. Morrissey could stand down.

The coroner addressed the jury. They had heard the evidence, and it was their duty to give an opinion as to how the two women had died. The medical evidence showed the probability or possibility that Mrs. Torrance had died first, and that Miss Raleigh, her devoted friend had died shortly afterwards from arsenic poisoning. The jury didn't take long. In their opinion, Mrs. Torrance had died from an accidental fall down the stairs, and Miss Raleigh had committed suicide, whilst of an unsound mind, distracted by shock and grief.

Mrs. Winter had attended the inquest, and when it was over, she approached Mrs. Morrissey.

"What are you going to do now?" she asked.

"I'll be going to my brother's, ma'am, till I find a new place."

"Would you like to come and work for me?"

"I would indeed, ma'am."

"Mrs. Morrissey …"

"Ma'am?"

"You remember coming to see me last week?"

"Yes, ma'am."

"You remember what you told me?"

"No, ma'am," said Mrs. Morrissey.

"Do you think you'll ever remember it, when you're talking to your family, or your friends?"

"I will not, ma'am?"

They looked at each other steadily.

"Thank you …" said Mrs. Winter. "I was fond of Josie … if I'd listened to you … You're a fine woman, Mrs. Morrissey, and you've got sense. You can stay with me as long as you please, and when you leave, or when I die, you'll be provided for. I'll see Matthew Harvey about that today, before he goes back to town."

"Thank you, ma'am," said Mrs. Morrissey.

Later in the afternoon, Mrs. Morrissey, leaning back in the big black car, drove through the gates of Mrs. Winter's place. She turned her head and looked back down the hill, and for an instant she had a vision of Mrs. Torrance bending over a tea cup, in the dining room … Of Miss Raleigh coming upon her upstairs—and afterwards—sitting down to drink her tea.... Then she turned back to look at the house before her. She liked Jacobs and the chauffeur, she would have people to talk to, the orderly pleasant routine to which her life was attuned.

"A good home …" she thought.

The Kiskadee Bird

Johnny Pepper had recently been appointed deputy police commissioner in Puerto Azul. It was a step up for the young man, but one that he appreciated very little. His first choice would have been the Army, but he had been told he would be more useful here, and it was not for him to argue about that.

There were a lot of queer people coming into Puerto Azul these days, and it was his job to sort them out, to examine their papers and to ask them questions.

During the commissioner's absence, Johnny Pepper occupied his bungalow, and there was a bird frequenting the garden that amused him. "That the kiskadee bird, sah," Laura, the commissioner's stern Negro cook told him. "Sound to me like he speak in some foreign tongue, all the time asking, 'What you say? What you say?'"

And sure enough, if you listened to that bird, you could imagine it was saying over and over and over—"*Qu'est-ce qu'on dit? Qu'est-ce qu'on dit?*" Like me, Johnny Pepper thought.

The queer people came from the South American mainland—from Venezuela, Columbia, Brazil; they came from the French islands, from God knew where; they came in unbelievable old steamers, they came in schooners, some of them came by plane. And some of them came the hard way: in lifeboats; on rafts from torpedoed ships. But no matter how they got there, Johnny Pepper had to ask them questions—if they were alive.

What is your name? Prove it. Where did you come from? Let me see your papers, please. Where do you hope you're going? Kindly state in your own words what right you have to be on earth. Johnny Pepper could do this in four languages—English, French, German and Spanish; he had a natural gift for tongues and—his father having been in the Consular Service—he had been to school in many countries.

Twenty-seven, Johnny was a slim, fair-haired fellow with a foppish elegance about him in his white uniform. He was popular with the old Spanish families on the island, because he spoke their language so well and because he had such beautiful manners. And he filled the queer people with wildly unreasonable hopes.

Not that he meant to do that. Most of these people were trying to get somewhere else, and they found encouragement in the trouble he took over their precious, their life-or-death papers, and the patience he had with their dialects, and even with their desperate lies. Plenty of them wanted to stay here; just sit down here in a place where there could be a policeman like Johnny. "What will you take?" they whispered. "Will this be enough?"

As a matter of fact, there was little or nothing he could do for anybody. They were all caught in a giant machine that went grinding on; some people were sifted out and could go Somewhere Else, and other people were not so lucky, and they had to wait and wait, or be sent back. Anyhow, he hated it, and the proffered bribes made him feel sick.

It was the hurricane season, and with the island so overcrowded and supplies so perilously short, a fine hurricane that would destroy the crops and provide more patients for the overworked doctors and nurses would have been the last straw. He tapped the barometer on the commissioner's gallery and it jumped down a little; he sighed and sat down at the table, and the stern Laura brought him his breakfast.

The commissioner's garden was in a bad way, a tangle of bush and parched grass, and in the center of it a plaster fountain cracked in two. It had been set there for birds, and one bird was there this morning. Kiskadee, kiskadee, kiskadee, it chirped. Yes, that's me, Johnny Pepper thought, sighing again, thinking of the papers and the questions ahead of him.

One of his Negro constables came riding up on a bicycle. "Sah," he said gravely, "I come to report two castaways on Shark Point, sah, and one of which is a lady."

"What did you do with them, Kelson?"

"I provide them with water, sah, and I leave them. I fear the man dying, sah."

"Get a doctor from the hospital, Kelson, and I'll meet him at Shark Point."

"Yes, sah. And I think, sah, maybe the lady like a coat, sah, before she pass through the town."

The only coat Johnny Pepper had or needed to have in Puerto Azul was a raincoat; he took that with him in his car, setting out as soon as he had swallowed one cup of coffee.

He drove down the dusty road past the Botanical Gardens, where their three Italian prisoners of war were working; then he turned into the shore road. The sea was calm as a lake, sapphire-blue and sparkling in the morning sun, but just outside the harbor was the rusty funnel of a little steamer that had been caught there by a U-boat. Not far off he knew there was another one, lying on the bottom where the little fish went by in shoals and the sharks and the barracuda hunted alone.

He was well away from the town now, among low hills covered with bush; he rounded a curve and before him stood two tall jagged black rocks like a gateway to a strip of white sand. A boat was beached there, and two people were leaning against it, one on each side.

One of them struggled to rise as the car approached; a girl, it was, and she so startled Johnny that he let the car swerve a little. For a long time he had been seeing the dazed, the sick, the bereaved, the hopeless; it was surprising to see anyone so proud and magnificent.

She stood straight as an arrow, now that she was up. She was barefoot, dressed in a bleached rag of a skirt and a blouse in tatters; her thick black hair was loose and tangled about her shoulders, her face was darkly burned, her lips were cracked, her cheekbones stood out above her hollow cheeks. But she was beautiful, just as she was.

"Are you in charge here?" she asked.

"Pepper, deputy police commissioner," he answered.

"My name is Julia Alderton," she said, and he saw that she expected the name to mean something to him. But it did not.

"Thank you," he said politely. "The doctor'll be here any moment."

"I don't need a doctor," she said. "But *he* does."

Johnny went round to the other side of the boat and looked at the man lying there with his eyes closed, a young fellow, thin, browned, unshaven, but good-looking. And dead-looking. He had a pulse, though, and he was breathing.

"If you can tell me anything about him, Miss Alderton?" Johnny asked.

"His name is Eric," she said. "We just happened to get into the same boat when the ship was torpedoed. He was wonderful to me."

"I see! And your nationality, Miss Alderton?"

"I'm an American," she said. "My father is Cyrus Alderton."

"I see!" said Johnny again, never having heard of Cyrus Alderton.

The ambulance came along then, and out got Dr. Ridgeway, followed by two orderlies. He looked at the girl with surprise and went to examine the man.

"Has he any chance, doctor?" she asked.

"Hard to say," he answered. "He's in pretty poor shape. There's a head injury."

"Yes. He had a fall," she said. "I'd like to take him to a hotel, please."

"The hospital's the place for him, Miss Alderton."

"I'd like to have him near me," she said. "I'll get a room for him, and private nurses, and I'll help look after him."

You couldn't call her rude. She spoke civilly; she listened civilly. But she was the most regal creature Johnny Pepper had ever encountered.

"Well," Dr. Ridgeway said, "I don't see any objection to that, Miss

Alderton. If you're willing to take the responsibility ..." Naturally he didn't object. The two hospitals on the island were fantastically overcrowded.

"Afraid the hotel people wouldn't care much for that," Johnny Pepper said. "They're not keen on taking in seriously ill people."

"My father will pay anything they ask," said the girl, like a young queen. "I'd like Eric near me, where I can look after him."

"We-ell," said Johnny Pepper, "I could ask Rocky."

"Take me to the hotel and let me ask, will you?" she said.

Johnny took her to the Grand Royal Hotel, a big, old-fashioned place on the shore outside the town. The owner and manager was Mr. Luigi Buenarocca, an Italian from the Argentine, known in the island as "Rocky"; a shrewd man of business, not sentimental. When Johnny Pepper brought a barefoot girl in a raincoat into his private office, he was not at all pleased; he very definitely objected to taking a dying man into his hotel. "Bad for business," he said.

"I'll see that you don't lose by it," Julia said, and it was notable that she did not try to appeal to his better nature. "I'll take the three best rooms you have—for him and the nurse and myself—and I'll pay whatever rate you think is fair."

It was interesting to Johnny Pepper to see how she impressed Rocky. "It would be expensive," he said warningly.

"I'll leave that to you," she said, and then, after he had consented: "My father is Cyrus Alderton. He'll guarantee the bills."

In his line of business, Rocky knew about Americans, and he knew about Cyrus Alderton, the steel magnate, rich, rich, rich, and important now in the government. But just the same, he had consented before he heard the magic name. Extraordinary girl, Johnny thought.

Eric was brought in on a stretcher, and the nurse found some sodden papers in an oilskin case fastened under his belt. She brought them to Johnny, and Johnny learned that the man was Eric Eitel Thaler, aged twenty-four, a rating in the German Navy, and serving in a U-boat. This was a complication, and a bad one.

Johnny telephoned to Julia's room. "I'd like to see you as soon as it's convenient."

"Come along in half an hour," she said, and he did.

There was very little merchandise left in Puerto Azul now, but Julia had in some way got a sleeveless white cotton dress and white sandals; her black hair was soft and shining; she even wore lipstick, and that gave her thin sun-browned face an almost barbaric vividness.

She was more beautiful than ever, and she had nice manners too. She had had a tray sent up, with gin and vermouth and bitters and limes and ice, and she mixed cocktails and gave him one.

"Miss Alderton," he said, "I'm sorry to bother you now, when you ought to be resting, but I'm afraid it can't be helped."

"I understand that," she said. "Ask me whatever you want to know."

"This man Eric," he said. "I understand he was from your ship."

"No," she said. "We picked him up out of the water."

"We?"

"There were three of us to start with," she said. "The third officer and a steward and myself. The steward had broken his leg, and the third officer had some sort of head wound. But they didn't seem to be seriously hurt. I didn't realize … We got Eric into the boat, and he took the oars. And they just died. The third officer died that night, and the steward twenty-four hours later."

She spoke evenly and soberly, simply telling what had happened. But her face was haunted.

"You were aware, Miss Alderton, that this man Eric came from the U-boat?"

"What could we do?" she asked. "He was drowning, and we picked him up."

"How did he behave?"

"It was—wonderful," she answered slowly. "I don't understand German, but he made it obvious—how he felt. How grateful; how—humble."

And that's what you like, isn't it? Johnny thought.

"You understand, don't you, Miss Alderton, that this man is now a prisoner of war?"

"Yes," she said.

"And that he's incommunicado?"

She glanced at him and said nothing.

Johnny sent one of his constables to the governor with a full report of all this, and a request for a military guard. In the meantime he put one of his own men—whom he could ill afford to spare—inside the sickroom, and then he closed his office and stopped at the Yacht Club for a nightcap.

Nobody knew better than he how everything got around in the island; he took it for granted everyone would know about the castaways. But the talk he heard at the club astonished him. Quite a tale, it was, about Eric's chivalrous devotion to the beautiful American heiress; he had saved her life, and now she was nursing him, day and night.

God knew the people of Puerto Azul had little enough reason to be sentimental about U-boat crews. They need only take a look over their own harbor. The Yacht Club members, too, were a hard-bitten lot; most of them veterans of the former war. Yet this romantic fantasy seemed to delight them.

Julia must have started this tale, a disturbing one and very bad for public morale. "Fellow saved his own skin, that's all," Johnny said. "And Miss Alderton is not nursing him." But he could see that nobody liked his version. They preferred Julia's.

The next morning Cyrus Alderton began to make himself felt across some twelve hundred miles of ocean. A cable came from the British Consulate, New York, to Deputy Police Commissioner John Franklin Pepper, requesting him to extend every courtesy to Miss Julia Alderton. A special plane would be sent to fetch her home, and thought Johnny, the sooner the better.

She called him up in his office. "Mr. Pepper," she said, "will you please tell your policeman to let me see Eric?"

Polite, she was, but quietly certain he would do what she asked.

"I'm sorry, Miss Alderton," he answered, "but I can't make any exceptions. The man's a prisoner of war."

"He's unconscious, Mr. Pepper. And even if he wasn't, I don't understand German and he can't speak English."

"I'm sorry, Miss Alderton."

There was a moment's silence.

"Will you come and have a cocktail with me this afternoon, Mr. Pepper?" she asked.

"Oh, thank you very much, Miss Alderton," he said.

She's going to try to vamp me, he thought, and the idea was not disagreeable to him. As an eligible bachelor, he had experienced this before, but in a rather naïve way. This, he thought, would be different.

Early in the afternoon the governor's aide-de-camp rang him up. "I say, Pepper," he began, "this isn't official, y'know—only it would be appreciated in certain quarters if you could stretch a point and let this Miss A. see the prisoner now and then. Mean to say, under any conditions *you* think fit. It seems the fellow saved her life."

"No," said Johnny. "Sorry, but it can't be done."

Then came a hint of the iron hand within the velvet glove. "Thing is," said the blithe young A.D.C., "there seems to be a spot of doubt as to whether the chap exactly belongs to you. Mean to say, military prisoner, wouldn't you say?"

"I should," said Johnny. "You people can have him whenever you like."

"Oh, thanks. By the way, seeing you're so short of men, Pepper, H. E. thought you might take your constable off duty. Doctor says the prisoner'll never get out of his bed again."

"Maybe," said Johnny Pepper. "There's the possibility, though, that someone might try to communicate with him."

"He's unconscious, isn't he?" asked the A.D.C., with an air of innocence.

Johnny Pepper was curiously unhappy about this. He no longer thought that Julia was going to vamp him. She didn't need to; she was simply putting him aside, walking over him. It was true that he was very short of men; he couldn't properly afford to keep a constable sitting night and day in that room, and it must now look, to the governor and to everyone else, as if he did it from sheer petty obstinacy.

He went to Dr. Ridgeway. "Like to move this fellow to the hospital," he said.

"I shouldn't like to take the responsibility for moving him," said the doctor. "We haven't any room for him, either, Pepper. Why not let well enough alone? It can't be more than a few days."

"Very good," said Johnny, after a moment.

He went later in the afternoon to visit Julia. He was in a grim mood, ready to find her triumphant and condescending.

But there was no trace of anything like that. She was polite and grave, and she showed a serious and half-puzzled interest in him. She asked him about his career, and he told her that as time went on he would become a full commissioner, either here or in some other island.

"But don't you want to get to Washington or New York or London?" she asked. "Don't you want to be *in* things?"

As he saw it, he *was* in things, very much so. He was an insider, welcome at Government House; he had good connections. But that had no meaning at all for her; as they sat there talking, he began to get an idea of the world in which she had always lived; like the cinema, it was a world of yachts, hotels, houses like palaces, amazing luxuries and still more amazing independence. She was only twenty-four, but she had been to Europe, to Paris, alone, before the war; she had gone to Rio to visit a friend, and had stayed too long. She had had friends all over—in England, France, Italy, South America, Bermuda.

You hear of people who think they own the earth. Well, Julia was like that. She honestly believed that she could go anywhere; that she could get a check cashed anywhere; that she could do anything she damn pleased.

They drank their cocktails in her sitting room, and they tried to understand each other, the neat, alert young man, bred in an old and rigid tradition, and the gaunt and beautiful Yankee princess who from her dazzling Park Avenue world had come to this dreadful adventure. He found her fascinating, but he understood her less than ever and he was not sure he liked her very much.

She did not mention Eric, not once, and it occurred to Johnny Pepper that perhaps her interest had been nothing more than a whim. "Girls like that," he said to himself, "take people up and then drop them."

When he left her, he went to the room across the hall, where he found the doctor. The young German, burning with fever, lay in a clean white bed, his bandaged head moving incessantly on the pillow, his blue eyes heavy and blank.

"Any chance of his talking?" Johnny asked.

"It's hard to say," the doctor answered. "He may go out like this, or he may have a lucid interval."

"I'd like to know if this lucid interval comes along," said Johnny.

"Can't even let anyone die in peace, you policemen?" asked the doctor.

"No, we can't," said Johnny Pepper, with a sigh.

But he withdrew his constable, and he spoke to Nurse Fraser. "You understand no visitors?" he said.

"Yes, Mr. Pepper."

The man was dying, and the princess would be going home, and everyone would forget the whole thing, thought Johnny. But he was still uneasy about the prisoner. He came early the next morning to have a look at him, and from the corridor he saw Julia in the sickroom.

The young German was muttering faintly, and she bent over him, listening, her face grave, intent, unbelievably beautiful. It's not a whim, he thought. She cares a lot about this fellow.

"Miss Alderton," he said, "will you step out here, please?" She came out and stood before him. "Who let you go in there?" he asked.

"No one," she answered. "I kept my door open, and when I saw the nurse go out, I went in."

"I'll have to ask you to give me your word you won't go in there again."

"No," she said. "I can't do that."

At this early hour she was fully dressed, in the same white sleeveless dress, or another one like it, and he saw with a twinge of pain that she was wearing a big necklace of white and yellow shells that looked like a garland of flowers. It was charming, and it was beyond measure touching that she should have decked herself in this way.

"Miss Alderton," he said, "you're an American. You wouldn't like people to say that you were—sentimental about an enemy of your country." He hoped the word "sentimental" would nettle her.

"Mr. Pepper, I don't care what people say."

"Y'know," said Johnny Pepper, "whenever I hear anyone say that, it makes me think of a courtroom. The man—or the woman—standing in the dock has nothing to depend on except what people say. His—or her—life can depend on what the witnesses say; and in the end, on what the jury says."

"I'm not in the dock, Mr. Pepper."

"Miss Alderton, you've heard, I suppose, that they've picked up two lifeboats from the *Princess Ann*—your ship. It's not likely there'll be any more now. That means that forty people, more or less, are lost."

That bleak and haunted look came over her face again. She lowered her lashes, black and long and thick.

"This man is one of the people who did that," he said.

"Very well," she said. "He's dying. Isn't that enough for you?"

"He's lucky," said Johnny. "He's dying in a nice clean bed, with a nurse to give him water. Other people have to die in burning oil, or be eaten by sharks, or drown all alone."

She looked up at him then, with her dark eyes brilliant. "That's—pretty beastly," she said.

"But you can take it," said Johnny.

"Yes!" she said. "I can."

"And you still feel like holding his hand?"

"I still think I'm the judge of my own actions," she said, and moved away, back to her own room.

You still think you can do whatever you damn please, he thought. There aren't any laws or any rules, for you. There isn't any war, for you. Your Eric was wonderful to you. Humble to you. The forty people who died don't count. Nobody counts to Julia, daughter of Cyrus Alderton.

And he was a policeman, sworn to uphold the law; to deal impartially with the rich and the poor, the powerful and the helpless. There was no possible meeting ground for him and this girl; they could not be anything but enemies.

He had trained himself long ago never to lose his temper; he was equable, always the same. But he was not equable now, as he drove back to his office; he felt something that was close to bitterness against that girl.

His exacting day began, and he had no time to think of her. He could not stop for lunch until after two, and then he went to the Victoria Hotel in the town, to sit alone in the big dim dining room, looking over a sheaf of papers while he ate. He lighted a cigarette with his coffee, and suddenly he thought of her. It was almost like a vision; he saw her in his mind as he had seen her that morning, standing by the bedside of the dying man with that grave, intent look on her wonderful face.

She's—merciful, he thought, and however wrong her object, that was a quality he could not condemn. I was hard on her, he thought. Too hard, perhaps. If this fellow saved her life, or she thinks he did … You can understand a thing like that, even if you've got to put a stop to it.

He was not likely to see her again. The plane would be coming to fetch her home; she would fly away, back to her own dazzling world, and he would stay where he was. He would never see her again, or anyone like her. So proud, so unconquerable, so beautiful.

When he got back to his office, she called him up. "Mr. Pepper?" she said, with a faint note of doubt in her voice, "How would you feel about coming for a cocktail today?"

"Oh, thank you very much," he said.

He could not get away till late; the swift tropical dusk had come when he reached the hotel. He was surprised that she had asked him; he thought it more than possible that she had some ulterior motive in doing so, but just the same, he was glad. Her big, high-ceilinged sitting room was dim, and in that light her sunburned face looked pale; her thick hair was tied back from her forehead with a blue ribbon, and she had a wide ribbon like it around her narrow waist.

"Hello," she said, with that same note of doubt.

"Hello!" he answered.

The room was full of flowers, and on the desk he saw a stack of cables and wireless messages. She was important, a princess; it must be a new thing to her, to be thwarted by anyone.

She was the polite hostess again, mixing the cocktails. They sat down facing each other, and she tried to talk. He tried too, but it was all wrong. The room grew dark, and she turned on a lamp; it should have been cozy and pleasant then. But it was not; it was somehow sad.

There was a knock at the half-open door, and the doctor entered. "Sorry to disturb you, Miss Alderton," he said, "but you wanted to know, Pepper. I think we can expect a change in the patient before morning."

Julia rose quickly. "Do you mean he's going to get well?"

"I'm sorry," the doctor answered gently. "No. I mean, it's possible he may have a lucid interval before—" He left the phrase unfinished.

Julia remained standing after he had gone. "Why did you want to know about that?" she asked. "You're not going to ask him questions—while he's dying?"

"Afraid that's my job," said Johnny.

"Is that all you care about?" she asked. "Your job?"

"Oh, I hope not," he answered, polite, but uncomfortable, unhappy.

"If I ask you," she said, "if I beg you—will you let him die in peace?"

It occurred to Johnny—and it surprised him—that here was one of those temptations you hear about. He wanted to say yes. "I'm sorry," he said, "but I can't."

"You mean you won't do that for me?"

"I mean I can't," he said. "The man is an enemy of my country. If I can get any information from him, I must do it."

"Oh, that?" she said, and went over to the window and stood there, turned away from him.

If she loves that fellow, he thought, how far would she go for him? All the way, to treason? He couldn't answer that; he could not even guess what she might be capable of, or what sort of code she had.

He went across the hall to the sickroom. "I'll sleep in the hotel tonight," he said to Nurse Fraser. "If the patient regains consciousness, let me know at once, will you?"

He went to his office then, to catch up with his work, and there were people waiting for him. What is your name? Where do you come from? Why should you be here, or anywhere else? *Qu'est-ce qu'on dit?* Kiskadee … So. Mr. Luis Gomez, with his liquid dark eyes, is a British national from London, and the redheaded Señor Tom Kelly is a Peruvian? All mixed up; all thrusting their papers at him; all crazy-mad to get on the next ship and go Somewhere Else.

He went back to the Grand Royal Hotel for a late and solitary dinner, and then Rocky led him upstairs to an empty room. He took off his tunic and his shoes and lay down on the bed in the dark; he could hear the surf thundering against the shore; there must be a great wind blowing somewhere. But it was very quiet here, and he fell asleep.

A knock on the door waked him, and he got up to open the door for Nurse Fraser. "The patient is conscious, Mr. Pepper," she said.

"Thanks," he said. "Sit down here."

"I can't leave my patient, Mr. Pepper."

"I'll take the responsibility," said Johnny. "You sit here by the window and rest for the space of one cigarette."

She was glad to rest for a moment; she sighed as she sat down in the armchair. Johnny buttoned his tunic and put on his shoes. It was nearly four o'clock, and the hotel had a queer air; it was quiet, but not tranquil. There were people here paid to be awake all night: elevator boy, night clerk, watchman; and there were other people shut into their rooms, some of Johnny's especial people, waiting for a decision about their papers, waiting and hoping for new papers, people who wouldn't be resting.

He did not trouble to ring for the lift; he ran up the stairs to the floor above and along the corridor into the sickroom. He heard the man's voice, hoarse and troubled *"Schwester!"* he called. *"Schwester!"* A queer thing for him, the enemy, to be calling the good British Nurse Fraser his sister. *"Hilfe!"* he cried, and then was silent.

The door was ajar; Johnny pushed it open, and Julia was in there, bending over the bed. She had not heard him enter; she was too intent upon the dying man. Trying to ease these last moments, Johnny thought. She was wearing the white dress and the blue ribbon in her black hair; perhaps she had been waiting all night long for this opportunity. And that was a gentle and merciful thing.

He moved forward, and he saw that she had her hand over the dying man's mouth, and he was trying to pull it away.

"Miss Alderton!" said Johnny.

She snatched her hand away and stood up straight, and her gaunt face had a look of bleak and dreadful despair. "He—don't let him talk," she said. "The nurse—the doctor said he—mustn't talk. It's not good for him."

"Herr Kapitan!" said the man, with an effort. "*Hilfe! Mörderin.*"

"What is he saying?" Julia asked.

"*Mörderin!*" said the man clearly.

What was he saying? He said, "Help." He said, "Murderess."

"*Bitte, Herr Kapitan,*" said the man, in his well-schooled North German, "don't leave me alone with her. She tried already to kill me. She hit me on the head with a big flashlight."

"I want to know what he's saying," said Julia.

"Oh, little things that happened when he was a child," said Johnny. And in German: "Why did she hit you?"

"*Ach!*" said Eric. "She is a devil, that one! *Herr Kapitan*, listen once to what she does. The other two die, and I put them overboard. Then we are alone, that she-devil and I. Very good. I am a man, and she is a girl; not bad-looking, either. It came into my head I wanted her. So I took her in my arms. She fought like a cat! But I am a man; I was stronger."

"I—want to know what he's saying," said Julia.

"About his school friends," said Johnny, not looking at her.

"*Herr Kapitan!*" said Eric. "What is *she*? Only another woman. Many girls have loved me, only that one ... That night, when I was sleeping, she hit me on the head with the big flashlight. She tried to kill me, *Herr Kapitan!* After that I was afraid to go to sleep anymore. There she sat, staring at me with her big eyes and holding that flashlight. Even yet my head hurts me, *Herr Kapitan*. She is a devil," said Eric, and that, quite simply, was the way he saw it. There was no compunction in him, and no understanding of his monstrous offense against her. She was another woman, that was all; she was nothing.

"*Herr Kapitan,* she tried to kill me, and only because—" He tried to raise his hand to his bandaged head. "*Herr Kapitan,*" he said, "but—what is this?"

That was the end of him. In a moment Johnny drew the sheet up over his face.

"Is he—dead?" Julia asked.

"Yes, he's dead."

She was leaning against the wall; she looked exhausted. "He talked to you. I'd—like to know—what he said."

"Well, nothing much," said Johnny. "Rambling a bit, about his childhood."

His face was blank, innocent. But she was not convinced, and she must be convinced. It was not mercy that had kept her here beside the dying man; it was fear that he would tell what he had told.

"Did you think he might have some information useful to your country?"

That convinced her. She shuddered and stood up straight. "Yes. That was it."

"Well, it's too late now. If he had anything to tell, we'll never know now."

She would not want to go on living, Johnny thought, unless he and everyone else believed that. Her pride was vital to her; she must, at any cost, stand before the world as that proud and untouchable princess. *At any cost.*

In the moment of silence between them he became aware of the twitter of birds.

"Johnny," she said, "I'm going home today. My father could pull some strings. Maybe you could come to Washington?"

Johnny had a vision of Cyrus Alderton pulling strings to make a puppet dance.

The elevator door at the end of the long corridor rattled open and deliberate footsteps were coming toward them. Outside the window a kiskadee bird began. Kiskadee? Kiskadee? *Kiskadee?*

"Johnny?" she said, gently and sweetly.

"I'm afraid I couldn't manage that," he said, and raised her hand to his lips. "Happy landings, princess."

The gesture pleased her; her eyes were soft. "You've been very nice," she said.

They were, he thought, two people who might have loved each other. But their love would have been a battle in which one of them would have to lose too much. Let her go back to her own world, and let her go in all her beauty and her pride. He would stay here, where he belonged.

He went to the door with her, and as she went out, the doctor and Nurse Fraser came up to them. Outside the kiskadee bird went on with its impudent and eternal question that nobody ever answered.

The Blue Envelope

Mrs. Percy Effingham came to see George Nevill, deputy police commissioner of the island of San Fernago. She entered George Nevill's office with dignity, a stout coffee-colored woman in a starched dress down to her ankles and a bandanna on her head, on top of which sat a Panama hat.

"Mahning, Mr. Commissioner," she said. "I wish to complain a mon, sah."

"Good morning," said George, slim and neat as a cat in his white uniform, with his fair hair and his little yellow mustache. He was pleased to see Mrs. Effingham; he looked forward to hearing her complaint. He had a nostalgia for the good old days before the war, the cases of robbery, assault ... anything but the refugee cases, the papers he had to examine, the questions he had to ask of them.

"What man is it, Mrs. Effingham?" he asked.

"Name Dulac, sah."

"Mean Mrs. Jones' chauffeur?"

"That the mon, sah."

"Where did this take place?" George asked.

"In the market square, sah. This Dulac, he address my friend, and she turn she back on me, and then he grow bitter."

If it had been somebody else, George Nevill would have been inclined to dismiss the matter then and there. But Mrs. Effingham was not a woman to come with a frivolous complaint.

"What friend were you with?" he asked.

"A lady friend, sah, name Mis' Sylvester. When this Dulac address my friend again, I make a reproach, and he push me and he knock me hat off and use bod language."

"Well," said George, "if you have witnesses, we can charge Dulac. But in times like these ... Suppose I give him a hint to mend his manners, instead of bringing the case into court?"

"Mr. Commissioner, sah," said Mrs. Effingham, "that mon a German spy."

"Oh, come now!" said George.

"I speak the truth, sah."

"In the first place, he's not a German. In the second place, he's been investigated and there's nothing against him. Have you any facts—any grounds for what you say?"

"Just feel it to be the truth, sah."

There was seldom a day when George did not hear something like this. The inhabitants of the island accused the refugees of being spies; the refugees accused one another. People reported mysterious lights flashing on the shore; they overheard conversations they declared were plots; they brought letters they insisted were in codes.

"Well?" said George. "Do you want Dulac charged?"

"No, sah," said Mrs. Effingham. "Only wish to warn you, Mr. Commissioner."

"Well, we'll keep an eye on him," said George.

He let her go. He felt quite sure that she had something more than a "feeling" beneath her warning, but he was also sure that she had said all she intended to say.

"Jolly," he said to his favorite constable, "you might see if you can find a woman called Sylvester. Friend of Mrs. Effingham's."

"Know that lady, sah."

"Very good, then. Ask her to come in and see me, will you? And get out her dossier, if she has any."

Several hours later Constable Jolly approached the deputy commissioner.

"Got Mis' Sylvester here, sah," he said. "Here she dossier."

"Bring her in in five minutes," said George, and sat down to look through the papers.

Her name, he saw, was not Sylvester, but Sylvestre, Elena, widow, white, a French national, born in Spain, aged twenty-three, occupation dressmaker. She had come to San Fernago from Martinique six weeks ago and she had a permit to remain for three months. There were no remarks from the Immigration Department. This didn't tell him much, but all he wanted to know was why she had turned her back upon Dulac.

Constable Jolly opened the door and she came in. And George Nevill was astounded; he had not expected Mrs. Effingham's lady friend to be anything like this. A slight girl, all in black, with a pale, clear face, black hair, magnificent black eyes, an air of austere, rigidly controlled pride.

"Sit down, Mrs. Sylvestre," he said, and she took the chair opposite his desk. She had a wonderful face, narrow and fine, a stern and beautiful mouth; she had beautiful hands.

"You are a dressmaker, madam?"

"I know I am breaking the law by working," she said. "They told me when I came here that I was not allowed to work. But I have to."

"You're working here as a dressmaker?"

"No, sir, I am not a dressmaker. It was only that I didn't know what else to put down. I know how to embroider very well, and I have found some work like that to do."

"You have six weeks more to remain in San Fernago, señora. Where do you intend to go, at the end of that time?"

"I was going to Quebec to join my husband," she said. "But while I was on my way, he was executed there."

"This is a subject very painful to you, señora—"

"No, señor. Nothing is painful to me any longer. My husband was executed as a spy."

"You were aware of his activities?"

"No, señor. But I should have been. I should have known." She paused to reflect on her past. "I was very young, when our war came in Spain. My father was a man who loved our republic; he was shot by the Falangistas. My brother and I got out of Spain. In the small town where we went, we met with nothing but kindness. The family who took us in treated us like their own children. My brother and I will never forget, as long as we live, how much we owe to that family. And to France.

"There was a son in the family, a young composer, very talented. He was away in Germany, studying music; I did not see him for two years after we came to France. He believed, very sincerely, in that New Order for Europe, for France. I hated his ideas, but I loved him very much. He was young. I thought he would change when he had been home a little longer.

"When the danger of war came to his own country, he said that he had changed, and I believed him. We were married before the mobilization, and we went to Martinique. He said that the government sent him; perhaps that was true. But after we had been there a time, there were things that worried me, that frightened me. Only he denied everything—and I wanted very much to believe him. Then, after the fall of France, he arranged in some way—I don't know how—to be sent to Quebec. And that was the end."

"Señora, you have suffered very much. But you are young. Your life lies before you."

"I have lost my own country, and my second country, France," she said. "My brother was killed, fighting for France. I have nowhere to go. There is nothing before me, señor."

She meant that. She was, quite simply and obviously, that sort of girl. He had encountered that type before this, in Europe. It was not only grief that she felt, but shame; she felt herself irretrievably dishonored by her husband's treachery.

"I'd be obliged if you would answer a few more questions, señora. You were with Mrs. Effingham in the market yesterday. You were addressed by a man named Dulac, and you turned your back on him. Will you tell me why, señora?"

"I do not wish to speak to Germans, señor."

"Dulac is a Frenchman, señora."

"I disagree, señor."

"Why do you think he is a German?"

"I am quite sure I have seen him before, señor. In Martinique. He came to see my husband, he and another man, on a rainy night. They spoke German then. They were Germans, señor."

"If you believed that you recognized this man as a German, señora, why did you not come to me at once?"

"I thought you would order me to stop working, señor. I thought it would be better to put the idea into the head of the Mrs. Effingham."

Very well; she had put an idea into George Nevill's nimble brain. He was not at all impressed with the spy angle; he had met Dulac several times, he knew quite a lot about him, and all of it was favorable. But this girl's cool, proud resignation was intolerable. She was young and she was lovely; she had no business to be living in Mrs. Effingham's boardinghouse.

"Señora," he said, "it is possible that you might be of great assistance to us. You might be able to serve my country—and France."

"Señor, de quo manera?"

"If we could arrange a way for you to observe this man carefully," he said, "so that you could be, not quite sure, but entirely sure about him?"

She was beautiful now, with her lips parted and her dark eyes brilliant.

Almost all the other Americans in San Fernago had been ordered home or had gladly gone home long ago, but Mrs. Jones was an exception. It was not only that she was an old resident, a property owner, a very wealthy woman. She was an exception to all rules because of her goodness.

It was a goodness that nobody could question. There were people who hated her, but they hated her because of that goodness. George Nevill was fonder of her than he wished to be. She often came to see him, meddling in matters that were none of her business, trying to do illegal, shocking things, trying to give people things they were not entitled to, trying to help people evade the proper consequences of having wrong papers. She would come lumbering into his office, stout and shapeless, in a flowered print dress, with a big hat on her untidy dark hair, and she would offer to post a bond for someone highly suspect, she would propose some outrageous way to let someone stay here who had no right to stay anywhere on earth.

Mrs. Jones lived in a sort of stone castle on a hilltop; very imposing, it was, with turrets and a long stone terrace and all the rooms opening upon a patio with a fountain. Inside, the furniture was a jumble of fine old mahogany and the modern items that had appealed to Mrs. Jones' taste. And the whole place was overrun with servants. She admitted that there were not only the servants she paid, but their friends and relations uncounted by her.

There was nothing to be done with that woman. She had certainly been beautiful once, and she had let that go; she had thrown that away. As she threw away her money and her illimitable love.

He drove up to the tawdry castle late that afternoon, and a saucy little colored parlor maid opened the door and led him into the patio where Mrs. Jones sat, with half a dozen friends, enjoying a special punch she liked to serve. It was, to George Nevill, a horrible drink, a tourist drink; but he accepted a glass to please her. And he got her apart from the others and told her the story of Elena Sylvestre, omitting the spy angle.

She listened, leaning back in a huge teakwood chair. She wore a blue and white flowered dress, with a green sash around such waist as she had, and her very shapelessness seemed somehow right and reassuring; she looked like some mother goddess, with her long, gentle dark eyes, her wide and candid brow.

"She must come here, George," she said. "I'll ask her to embroider things for me. I'll go tomorrow and see her."

"Could you spare Dulac to drive me home?" George asked. "I let Jolly take my car."

She was only too glad to do so, and in a few moments Dulac drove up in the car. He was a good-looking young fellow, broad-shouldered and muscular, with an olive skin and level black brows; you might have said he was a typical Latin, only George's years in Europe made him avoid such judgments. He had met Danes who looked like Frenchmen, and Frenchmen who looked like Tatars, and Germans who looked like Italians. Dulac spoke French like a Parisian, but speech was no infallible gauge.

Yes. He could look like a Frenchman and speak like one, and still be something else. But there was absolutely nothing against him. He had come here from Cuba some six months ago, with his papers all in order and a perfectly straightforward story. He had heard there was a dearth of good mechanics in San Fernago, and that was very true, and he was a very good mechanic. Mrs. Jones had snapped him up, but she lent him willingly; he had repaired the governor's launch, he had done jobs for the Department of Works.

He was curt and sullen and nobody liked him—except Mrs. Jones. But he was an excellent worker, he never drank even a glass of wine, he minded his own business. If he was a spy, he was a good one.

"I understand you had some trouble in the market square yesterday," said George.

"Oh, that?" said Dulac with a shrug. "I saw a girl, very pretty, and spoke to her. Why not? And that damned—" He used vivid words for Mrs. Effingham. "She interfered. She got in my way and I pushed her aside and went off. That's all."

"That's not the way one behaves here," said George. "We don't care for it, Dulac."

"*Alors* ..." said Dulac with another shrug. "What harm has been done?"

"Don't do it again," said George.

Mrs. Jones telephoned to George in his office.

"I know you're busy," she said, "but I just wanted to tell you that I've got Elena here staying with me. She's a lovely girl, George."

"Yes," he said. "I think so."

"But she's so sad, George! So aloof. I'm going to try to cheer her up. Rest and good food and friendliness, don't you think?"

He said yes, but he thought that "cheering up" Elena Sylvestre would take more, even, than Mrs. Jones' immeasurable kindness. He felt sure that Elena would make no least effort to be happy; she would think it shameless. She expected and wished to pay for her husband's crime. *El honor. La familia. La patria.*

A few days later the girl herself came to see him. She was as pale, as slight, as grave as before, but there was a change in her; the look of bleak resignation was gone; she was more alive; and more beautiful. For a moment he thought that perhaps Mrs. Jones had succeeded.

"Yesterday, when the ship came in with mail," she said, in English, "he got letters."

"Post office says no," said George, because that was something he had looked into.

"They could come addressed to somebody else," she said. "But he got letters, Señor Nevill. Two. He read them, and then he locked them in a drawer. I saw this. I came to ask you something, señor." She went on in Spanish. "Señor, the police have some little instrument for opening locks,

no? If you will give me one of these, I will get the letters for you."
He explained, with all politeness, that this was impossible.

"Then, señor," she said, "if I telephone and tell you when this man is away from the house, will you send some policeman to open the drawer?"

"I'm sorry, señora, but we have nothing definite against this man. I'd have to get a search warrant to do as you ask, and I have no grounds for applying for one."

She was silent for a moment; then she raised her brilliant eyes to his face.

"I will get those letters, señor," she said.

"Señora," said George, "according to the law, it would be robbery for you to break open a drawer and take those letters."

"I will accept that responsibility, señor."

"Señora," he said, "do you find yourself well with Mrs. Jones?"

"But yes, señor! She is a saint, this friend of yours."

"I believe I can get you permission to stay here, señora, and permission to work. You can help in the hospital, perhaps. They need people badly. There are other things, many other ways to help."

"I am glad to do them, señor."

George Nevill had lived much among Spanish-speaking people, and when he spoke their noble and beautiful language he was a little transformed from his debonair and British self.

"Señora," he said, "live your life. Be useful. Be tranquil. And forget Dulac."

"Señor, I know that I have seen this man before. I know he is a German spy."

"Then, without doubt, something will reveal it. Leave it to fate, señora, or to God."

She rose.

"Thousand thanks, señor, for receiving me," she said. "When I have information, I shall ask the favor of another interview."

Nothing could deflect her, nothing could swerve her from her sole idea of atonement and vengeance.

There was a garden party at the Cricket Club, for some wartime charity, and George Nevill stopped in there; it was expected of him. And there, sitting at a table in a marquee, was Mrs. Jones.

He sat down in a canvas chair beside her and took off his helmet. He was hot and tired, and in a somber mood. He resented his fate. Everyone else was in the war, and he was kept here, like a watchdog. He did not know whether the company of Mrs. Jones was an irritation or a solace. She was serene, she was happy; in this world of anguish, she never lost her shining hope; there was always something she could do, some help she could offer. She was impossible, but he loved her.

"Drink your tea, George," she said. "I've got a *very* interesting bit of news for you. About Elena."

"D'you like her?" George asked.

"Very much," said Mrs. Jones. "She's the soul of honor. Only until lately I've been worried about her, George. She's been brooding so."

"And now she isn't brooding?"

"She's fallen in love!" said Mrs. Jones.

"No!" said George. "Who's the man?"

"Dulac!" said Mrs. Jones.

"Is it mutual?" he asked, after a moment.

"Oh, yes! They can't take their eyes off each other," said Mrs. Jones happily. "Of course, he hasn't the education Elena has, or the little social graces. But he's such a fine, steady boy. He's so practical, and Elena's so idealistic. I wish you could see them, George."

"I'd like to," he said. "Could I come this evening?"

"I've got to stay till the end," she said. "But if you'll wait, I'll drive you back, George."

"*They can't take their eyes off each other.*" He could not get that phrase out of his mind. He had a vision of Elena, in Mrs. Jones' vast baronial hall, with her magnificent dark eyes fixed upon Dulac, and it was enough to give him the shivers.

That was just how it was. They sat at dinner, in the vast hall, at a long refectory table with a lace cloth and blue candles in massive silver holders. There were seven for dinner, and Dulac was acting as butler; he poured the wine, he stood at the massive sideboard and gave low-voiced orders to the two colored maids; he was cool, efficient, alert in his white jacket.

And again and again Elena's dark eyes turned to him in his shadowy corner. She was all in black, as he had always seen her, but this was an evening dress, elegant, fitting beautifully to her fine thin body. George had never before seen her without a hat, and he was entranced by her hair, so thick, so smooth on her proud little head. She was beautiful, and she was terrible.

Just once did he get a good look at Dulac, as he leaned over to fill her glass. The look on his face was unmistakable; the hunger, the jealousy, the fury that is so often called by the name of love. And Elena, on her part, would like nothing better than to see him hanged by his strong young neck until he was dead. A touching little romance …

They went into the patio for coffee; they sat there under a sky glittering with stars, talking in polite, contented voices. George Nevill went to Elena's side.

"What are you doing?" he asked her in Spanish, speaking very low.

"I am going to trap this man for you," she said. "I cannot get any help from you, so I shall do it alone."

"Señora," he said, "you have lost all sense of proportion, all sense of—" He paused.

"Decency?" she suggested. "Very well, señor. I don't care at all what I do, as long as I can trap this man. This spy."

"Have you found one fact, señora, one smallest thing to prove him a spy?"

"I know his heart," she said. "He is altogether vile; cruel and false."

"Even if that is so, señora—"

"You can believe me, señor," she said. "I have taken this man as my lover, so that I can know."

Such anger filled him that he couldn't speak; he lighted a cigarette, standing beside her in the starlit dark.

"When I have trapped this man," she said, "I shall have paid my debt to the country my husband betrayed."

"Señora," he said, "you are destroying yourself."

"Señor, I don't care—if I can destroy him, too."

He threw down the cigarette and put his foot on it. "Good night, señora," he said.

He went to take leave of Mrs. Jones, and his great anger extended even to her, a little, because her goodness and her charity were lost and futile among these swift currents of hate and evil.

He did not want to go home. He went to the Yacht Club and played snooker until he was tired of it; then he had a drink and went to sit on the screened veranda overlooking the harbor; clouds were streaming across the sky, hiding the stars, and it was black as the pit. It was very late, but still George Nevill did not want to go home.

The sleepy steward came out, through the blackout curtain.

"Mr. Nevill, sah, Mis' Jones wish to speak to you, sah, on the telephone."

The light inside the club dazzled George; he closed his eyes as he took up the instrument.

"George," she said, "please come—at once."

"What's wrong? What's the matter?"

"It's Elena. I'm afraid—it's very bad. Please come, George."

He got into his car and drove off along the dark and empty roads; when he reached the fantastic castle, there was another car standing in the drive. He mounted the steps, and Dulac opened the door. The vast hall was softly lighted by shaded lamps; at one end of it, Mrs. Jones and another couple, the Wynnes, sat close together near a table on which playing cards were scattered. They all rose as he entered.

"Doctor Farrell is with her, George," Mrs. Jones said.

"Wait, please," he said. "All of you. Dulac, too."

He ran up the stairs; on the floor above, light showed under a door, and he knocked there. "It's Nevill," he said, and Farrell's voice said, "Come in."

She was lying on a big bed, straight and quiet, in an elaborate blue silk dressing gown, her thick shining black hair was pushed back from her forehead and spread out on the pillow; her face was grave and beautiful and very young.

"It's nearly over," said Farrell.

"Nothing to be done?" George asked.

"Nothing. I've sent for the ambulance, but it's too late. Barbituric poisoning. Suicide, I suppose. I found these under her pillow."

He handed George a little packet of letters with an elastic band around them. "Souvenirs, I suppose," he said. "Poor girl …"

George sat down by the lamp and looked through the letters. They were all addressed to "*lieber* Alphonse," all of them in German. Elena would not have been able to read them. Illiterate letters, from a forlorn refugee girl working at the hospital until they could find some place to send her. Love letters and nothing else. "I am sorry I cannot write to you in French," she said, in almost every one. "Maybe you won't understand what I write, *lieber* Alphonse, because you don't know German so good."

He put the rubber band around them again; these letters for which she had paid so monstrous a price. If they served any purpose at all, it was to confirm that Dulac was a Frenchman. He rose.

"I'm going down," he said. "Coming?"

"I'll wait here for the end," said Farrell. "She won't regain consciousness."

George went down the stairs, and again the three sitting there rose. Dulac stood in a corner with his arms folded.

"George," Mrs. Jones asked, "is she—"

"No," he answered.

"Can I go up to her, George?"

"I'm sorry. No. Sit down, please. You understand that I've got to ask some questions. Who found Mrs. Sylvestre in this condition?"

"I did," Mrs. Jones answered. "We were playing bridge, and I was dummy. I just went up to see how she was. She'd gone to bed very early …"

"Who was playing bridge, Mrs. Jones?"

"We three. And Dulac. He often makes a fourth with us," she said. To her there was nothing surprising in Dulac's coming to play cards with the guests he had recently waited upon in the dining room. "She looked—strange, and I couldn't wake her. So I came down and told Caroline. She's taken first aid and a home-nursing course. I asked her to go up, while I telephoned to Doctor Farrell."

Mrs. Jones was dry-eyed, and for all her immeasurable compassion, George Nevill had never seen her otherwise than quiet and steadfast. But young Mrs. Wynne was crying.

"Mrs. Wynne," he said, "will you describe exactly what you found when you went upstairs?"

She was a good little thing; she looked up at him through wet lashes.

"I could see—it was very serious," she said. "I couldn't feel any pulse. There was an empty medicine bottle there, but it was a prescription, and I couldn't tell what she'd taken. I didn't know what ought to be done for her. I felt sure it was suicide."

"Why, Mrs. Wynne?"

"The way she was lying there—with a blue envelope in her hand."

"Did you take this blue envelope, Mrs. Wynne?"

"Oh, no!" she said. "I didn't touch it."

Doctor Farrell was coming down the stairs now, slowly and heavily, and George waited for him.

"Doctor Farrell," said George, with a certain formality. "Did you find a blue envelope in the deceased's hand?"

"I did not," said Farrell. "Mrs. Jones, did you give this medicine of yours to Mrs. Sylvestre?"

"No," Mrs. Jones answered. "It had been in my bathroom cabinet for a long time—years. I'd only had one dose of it."

"Did you see this blue envelope, Mrs. Jones?" George asked.

"Why, yes," she answered, slowly. "I did pick up a blue envelope from the floor. But it was empty, and I threw it away."

"Where did you throw it, Mrs. Jones?"

"Why, I think I crumpled it up and threw it out the window," she said.

Now he knew she was lying. And only one motive could make that candid woman lie. "There are screens in all the windows here, aren't there?" he asked, and when she did not answer: "Let me see your bag, please, Mrs. Jones."

She had an evening bag in her hand, a rather dreadful little article of scarlet silk ruffled to look like a rose. She drew it up defensively against the bosom of her white satin dress.

"Why, George ..." she said. "No, really."

But when he came toward her, she handed it to him. It was hard for him to take it. He pulled the silken cord, and a delicate perfume came out. The blue envelope was in there, folded over; the address was typewritten. Mr. Alphonse Dulac, Post Office, San Fernago, General Delivery. Inside there were two sheets in fine German script.

Saboteur and spy, Dulac was, but not a very successful one. According to the letter's contents his superiors were not very well pleased with him.

George put the letter back into the envelope and looked at Mrs. Jones.

"George," said Mrs. Jones, "there must be some mistake—"

George did not answer. He was watching Dulac now, Dulac who was staring at Mrs. Jones with a look of intense loathing. Suddenly the muscles around his mouth gave way to exasperated rage.

"*No!*" cried Dulac.

They all turned to look at him and he moved forward, into a circle of light.

"I don't allow this!" he said, in English. "It's—disgusting."

"How's that?" George asked.

For a moment, Dulac was silent, his jaw set, his eyes brilliant. He was breathing fast, and there was sweat on his forehead.

"I don't allow this woman to accept any consequences for *me*," he said. "It's disgusting. What's the *matter* with her? She must be crazy. To ruin herself—to go to jail, to shield me? I don't allow it!"

"Dulac …" Mrs. Jones said faintly.

"Be quiet!" he said. "No more from you! I have lived here three months—and I have never seen anything like it, never! You throw away your money—everything, for this riffraff—this black trash—these dirty refugees that *we* kicked out. You give them everything. You have no pride; you have no honor. I despise you." He turned to George. "Arrest me! I killed that girl!"

"Dulac—" George began.

"Not Dulac," he said. He drew himself up rigidly and brought his heels together. "Lieutenant Grauhelm, of the German army."

He waited scornfully.

"Well?" he demanded. "Why don't you arrest me? I killed that girl. She stole letters from my room. I saw her. I knew then that she had been trying to make a fool of me, and *that* I don't allow, from any woman. But I didn't let her know that. I went to her room, with a fine glass of wine, full of this drug I took long ago from the bathroom."

He smiled, but his hands, straight at his sides, were trembling.

"Now everything is finished," he said. "I've had enough." His voice rose.

"I've had enough of this island—and all you slovenly, stupid people. I despise all of you—everything! I despise this damned heat—day after day. Day after day ..."

He drew the back of his hand across his forehead, and now his mouth was twitching.

"I was sent here to get information," he said. "Be sure I should have done so, very soon. All I needed was more time to be of real service to the Fatherland. They did not understand my problem here. I—I ..." And he seemed to be searching for words to bolster his position in the eyes of the present gathering. "But now I refuse to go on! I refuse, absolutely, to owe my life—to this disgusting American woman. I prefer to die."

The sound of the ambulance siren came to them, and he started violently.

"This woman shall not shield me!" he shouted. "I will take nothing from her! Arrest me—and you shall see how a German officer can die!"

Young Mrs. Wynne sat on the sofa beside Mrs. Jones, holding her hand; Wynne stood beside her; Farrell leaned back in a chair; George Nevill sat on the edge of a table.

The ambulance had taken away the mortal remains of Elena Sylvestre. Sergeant Welby and a Negro constable had taken away Lieutenant Grauhelm. It was very quiet here now.

"Will you—shoot him, George?" asked Mrs. Jones.

"Not me," said George. "We'll turn him over to the military."

"I wasn't trying to shield him," she said. "I thought the poor child had tried to kill herself—and that's considered a crime, isn't it? I thought that if she got well, she'd be deported, or perhaps put in prison."

Mrs. Jones looked very tired; she looked sorrowful. But she had her own solace and her own unfailing hope.

"I never suspected Dulac," she said. "Never!"

But you did him in, thought George Nevill. The girl who hated him couldn't get anything against him, couldn't break him down. But you did ... with all your kindness and goodness.

The Unbelievable Baroness

The *Carribiana* came into the harbor of Buenaventura before sunrise and anchored there in the pearly grayness. The immigration people and the port doctor went out to her in a launch, and with them went Lieutenant Martin Hardy, of the island police.

The steady trade wind blew; it was cool at this hour, and it was melancholy. Hardy thought of the days before the war, when the *Carribiana* had used to come in triumph, tourists lined up along the rail, a fleet of rowboats going out to meet her, the boatmen yelling with excitement. Sometimes the three-piece orchestra would be playing. And now she lay here dark and silent. Every voyage was a desperate adventure now; her two sister ships were at the bottom of the sea, and she stopped only long enough to leave a cargo of vitally needed stores for the island.

And refugees; a special variety. She sailed out of New York, and the refugees that she brought were people who, by heaven only knew what expedients and through what pains, had got themselves to the United States, and been turned away again. Some of them were going to South America, where they might or might not be acceptable; some of them tried to stay in Buenaventura. They were all guilty people and they knew it; they were all aware of having Wrong Papers. Some of them had become dazed with fatigue and disappointment and answered questions very stupidly; others had a dreadful jauntiness and told absurd, transparent lies.

"Very short list this trip, thank God!" said Crane, of the Immigration Department. "Only six coming ashore, and all of 'em in transit. No work for you this time, Martin, my boy."

The chief officer was waiting for them at the head of the accommodation ladder as they mounted, Crane and his colleague, the doctor with his little bag, and Martin Hardy neat and slim in his white uniform, his young face looking a little hollow.

They all went, according to custom, down to the dining saloon for coffee, and there Murchison, the purser, joined them. He sat down beside Martin. "Only one casualty," he said. "The Baroness has lost her dog."

"And who's the Baroness?" asked Martin.

"Ah …!" said Murchison. "You may well ask. But you'll see for yourself. You'll hear plenty from her about this dog."

"How does it happen that she's traveling with a dog, in these days?"

"Because she can make anything happen," said Murchison, with a grim smile on his wooden, sun-browned face. "She's come all the way from Germany with that unspeakable little dog. How she ever got the little beast into New York is unknown. Probably the same way she got it on board here. One of the crew brought it on as his own pet. We allow that, you know. Supposed to be good for morale. Then, as soon as we'd sailed, she pretended to buy the dog from the fellow. Took it into her cabin. We told her that was not allowed. But the dog stayed in the cabin."

"And it's disappeared?"

"Just this morning. Personally, I think it's a case of murder," said Murchison. "And justifiable. I'm fond of dogs, but this was such a pampered little beast ..."

They talked for a while about affairs in Buenaventura; they were old friends and they had plenty to say. Then a steward crossed the saloon and opened the blacked-over portholes, and there was the sun, very spectacular, standing on the rim of the sea. They finished their coffee and went up to the smoke-room, where the passengers were assembled.

"Vell?" said a loud, clear voice. "Have you yet any news from my dog, gentlemen?"

"That's her," said Murchison, with a sort of pride.

She was a spare woman, straight as a ramrod, with gray hair done high on her head, with a curly fringe over her forehead and a toque of artificial violets placed squarely on top. She wore a long, black skirt and a silk blouse with a high collar. In one black-gloved hand she carried a big alligator purse and in the other a neatly rolled black umbrella.

"No news yet, Baroness," said Murchison. "Now, if you'll please take your place in the line ..."

She went, with soldierly obedience, to the end of the short line that faced the table where Crane and his colleague sat.

"Elsa!" she called, in that loud and very clear voice. "Come!"

A girl came hurrying in from the deck, a thin, blond girl, shabbily dressed in black. But she was very pretty, and she was gay; she was the only person in the room who looked happy.

"You look again for Gustel?" the Baroness asked her.

"I look everywhere, madame," she answered, "but I don't find him. Don't you think that maybe in mistake he falls into the sea?"

"Foolery!" said the Baroness. "Gustel is too little to come over the top of a rail anywhere; also, he is too fat to be squeezing through. No! Not so! He is on this ship—*and I shall find him.*"

The other people in the line were soon disposed of and passed. There was a Roman Catholic priest; there were two middle-aged American men, upon legitimate business; there was a polite Italian going back to his home in Brazil. Then came the Baroness.

"With me comes also my young companion," she said. "Elsa Taube. We wait in your island to fare onward by airplane."

"What is your ultimate destination, madam?" asked Crane.

"Please?" she said, frowning.

"What is the end of your journey?"

"That shall only God know," she answered with simplicity "We try now to go in Brazil. If they allow it not—" She shrugged her stiff shoulders. "Mexico, perhaps. I don't know."

"You applied for permission to remain in the United States, madam?"

"Not allowed," she answered. "I have a cousin who is high with the Nazis, and they believe I, too, must be one of those picks."

"Picks …?" Crane repeated.

"Pigs …" murmured Martin, and she gave him a bow of acknowledgment.

Crane asked her and the girl a few more questions, and then he told her she might go ashore.

"Thank you," said the Baroness, "but I shall find first my little dog."

"We've made a thorough search, madam," said Murchison. "It isn't on board."

"Excuse!" she said. "My little dog has no wings to fly off. I cannot go without him."

"Sorry, madam, but the launch is waiting," said Murchison.

"I will pay some other launch. After I have found my little dog."

"Afraid you'll have to go now, madam," said Crane.

"Excuse! That cannot be. My little dog has eleven years. I have to him a duty."

Martin Hardy stepped forward and addressed her in German. "Gnädige Frau," he said, "allow me to introduce myself. Lieutenant Martin Hardy, Acting High Chief Commissioner of United States Police Forces for this territory. At your service."

He had been to school in Germany, and he understood something of the German thought processes. He had hoped to impress her, and it was so; she bowed her head.

"It is The Rule that passengers shall go in this launch," he said.

"The police then should look for my little dog, Herr Hardy."

"They're taking off cargo here," said Martin. "After that's done, I'll send a couple of men to look for the aforementioned dog, gracious lady. It's possible that he got into one of the holds."

"I thank you, Herr Acting High Chief," she said, and rose to go.

When Hardy got back to his office, he remembered to detail two men to go on board the *Carribiana* to look for a little dog. Then he thought no more about the Baroness....

Russell, Chief Inspector of Customs, called up Martin. "There's something here that smells," he said. "Fellow by the name of—wait—Castelloverdi, off the *Carribiana*."

"Yes," said Martin. That was the polite Italian.

"He had six pieces of luggage on board, and only five came on shore."

"Take it up with the ship's people," said Martin. "Don't bother me."

"Wait!" said Russell. "I'll tell you how it happened. We'd examined this Castelloverdi fellow's luggage. Everything was okay, and we were passing him out, when up comes a steward, fellow by the name of Hawkey, and he pipes up: 'I couldn't find that brown bag of yours, sir, and I wondered if you'd brought it ashore yourself.' Castelloverdi said it must have been mislaid, left on board, probably. He took it easy, very, very easy. He said, 'Oh, never mind! Nothing of any value. Don't bother.' … Now do you see?"

"Mean you think he passed it on to someone else to smuggle ashore for him?"

"Bright boy!" said Russell.

"It's still your case," said Martin, "but I'll have a talk with him. To oblige you."

When he hung up the instrument, the porter was standing beside him. "Lady want to see you, sir."

"What does she want?" said Martin.

"She say she tell nobody but—" The porter's impassive face quivered a little. "Nobody but the Acting High Chief Commissioner of the United States Police Forces."

"Oh, I see!" said Martin, remembering the Baroness. "Bring her in."

In she came, with the pretty Elsa. Martin rose, and she bent her gray head.

"Herr Acting High Commissioner," she said, in her loud, clear voice, "the officials tell me that my plane leaves tomorrow morning, early. My little dog is not yet found. I beg to stay here only until the next plane."

"I'll speak to the Immigration Department," said Martin, "but I'm afraid they won't consent. The regulations are pretty stiffly enforced, in times like these."

"Times like these!" she repeated. "What madness! They drive me out of my own land, those savages. In my part of the country my family, also my husband's family, ruled for hundreds of years. They did that very well, very wisely. There are people who are born to rule, and people who are born to obey. Today, Herr Hardy, the people who rule in my land are vulgar boors, ignorant savages."

There she sat, quietly certain that she was one who had been born to rule, to be obeyed.

"You had difficulties, then, with the Nazis, gracious lady?" Martin asked.

"How should it be otherwise?" she asked. "How should we bow our heads to that trash? My husband was seventy years old. All his life he spoke the truth, and when the time came he spoke the truth about the Schicklgruber. And for that they killed him. They called him a traitor, and they cut off his head."

"Gracious lady, allow me to express my deepest sympathy."

"Thank you," she said, with stern graciousness. "From the beginning I find you very sympathetic, Herr Lieutenant. That is why I come to beg of you a favor. I want very little anymore. I want only to protect the young Elsa here. She is a good girl, Herr Lieutenant, very faithful to me. She was born on my land, like her father and his father, for many generations. We have always protected her people, and it must continue to be so. Herr Lieutenant, is it not possible for the young Elsa to remain here?"

"I'm afraid not," said Marlin.

"She is young and strong, Herr Lieutenant. She can cook and sew; she is willing and obedient. Also, in Germany she was just beginning as a schoolteacher. Her people, you understand, were peasants, but my husband and I wished to give her a superior education. She could be useful here."

Martin glanced at the girl, wondering how she liked this. Their eyes met, and she smiled, cheerful as ever. Probably used to this, he thought.

"Herr Lieutenant," the Baroness went on, "I had never traveled before out of my own land. I never wished to. But since those savages robbed me and drove me out, I have been in many places. Only never have I seen any place so beautiful as your island. I did not know there were such places, with such a blue sea and such lovely flowers, also the mountains. And the people here, Herr Lieutenant, are so polite, so mild. You would think yourself in Paradise. I understand that I cannot stay, because of my oldness. I should not be very useful. But Elsa?"

"I'll see what I can do," said Martin. "But I'm afraid, gracious lady …"

"And you will get me permission to remain here until the next plane, if my little Gustel is not found today?"

"I'll try," he said. "But it may be impossible. You understand, gnädige Frau, that many accidents could befall a little dog on a ship. I have sent two men to search again. But if they don't find him this afternoon—I regret to say this, but in that case it is necessary to accept the fact that he will not be found."

"I do not accept that, Herr Lieutenant. A little dog does not vanish into the air. He does not throw himself into the sea, like an unhappy man. If he had died, his body would be found. *No,* Herr Lieutenant, it is not an accident." She rose. "It is a crime," she said.

He rose, too.

"I thank you for this attention," she said. "I hope you will get permission for the young Elsa to remain here, in this heaven-beautiful island. And I am sure you will get for me permission to remain here, if for one week only, in order that I may find my little dog."

He opened the door for her, and she went out, followed by Elsa. And Martin telephoned to Crane, in the Immigration Department, to plead the Baroness's case.

"Sorry, Martin," said Crane, "but we can't make an exception. She might get ill here, and then she couldn't go. And, to tell you the truth, it doesn't seem to me very important. Highhanded, arrogant old lady wants to stay and look for a dog that's obviously dead. I can't see why you're bothering about it."

"I'm sorry for her," said Martin. "And I rather like the old girl."

"Well, I'm afraid you're alone in that," said Crane. "No. I'm sorry, but she'll have to take the plane tomorrow, the girl, too."

So Martin sent a note to the Baroness's hotel, the best sort of note he could devise, to tell her that he could not help her and that she must leave, early in the morning. With Elsa, and without the little Gustel …

Mr. Castelloverdi had been waiting a long time, but he showed not the least impatience or resentment. He was a handsome man, a little stout, but vigorous and buoyant, with curly black hair and a black mustache.

"I'm sorry my bag is causing so much trouble," he said. "For myself, I don't really care at all. Nothing of value in it. Some clothes, some shirts, all very easy to replace."

"What's your theory about the bag, Mr. Castelloverdi?" asked Martin.

Mr. Castelloverdi smiled widely and spread out his hands. "But, my dear sir …! I leave the bag in my cabin. The door is not locked. There are dozens of people running around. What is easier than for someone to pick up a little bag and walk ashore with it?"

"There were only five other passengers," Martin observed. "Which one do you suspect?"

"My dear sir, I don't suspect anyone! I only try to make some little suggestion. It might be that some porter or steward let the bag fall into the water and then was afraid to admit it. A hundred things could happen. Personally, I don't care. I should like to sit in my hotel and enjoy a long, cold drink and a good cigar." He smiled ruefully. "But it seems to be like a crime, to lose a bag, eh?"

"Sorry to cause you so much trouble," said Martin politely. "You're a Brazilian national, Mr. Castelloverdi? Born there?"

"Born in Italy, my dear sir, but living in Brazil for twelve years."

"You speak English very well, Mr. Castelloverdi."

"I lived for some years in Brooklyn, where I was an importer of olive oil."

"You're leaving here by the next ship?"

"No, no. I leave by the plane for Trinidad tomorrow morning. My luggage comes after me, by ship."

"If you wait over for the next plane," said Martin, "we may be able to find that bag."

"My dear, good sir, I have business in Brazil!" said Mr. Castelloverdi, in good-humored protest. "Please believe that I don't care about this bag. If it comes to light, very good. If not—" He shrugged his shoulders.

Martin Hardy was reluctant to let him go. He did not trust the smiling and affable Mr. Castelloverdi; he did not like this affair of the missing bag. But there was no adequate reason or excuse for holding the man.

"Good-by!" said Mr. Castelloverdi pleasantly....

The telephone rang, and Martin waked up. He reached for the instrument and brought it into the bed, under the mosquito net.

"Hardy?" said a man's voice. "This is Lomax, out at the airfield. We're just about ready to take off, and this Baroness woman hasn't shown up."

"Call her hotel."

"We have. Naturally. But she's not there. The girl—companion—maid—whatever she is—is here, but she can't tell us anything. Says she went to the old lady's room, and when she didn't find her there, she came on here."

"Can you hold the plane?"

"Half an hour. That's the absolute limit."

"Okay!" said Martin, and called up the sergeant on duty at the police station.

"Send a man at once, Wells, to the Palace Hotel to make inquiries about a woman who should have turned up at the airfield."

"It wouldn't be a Baroness, would it, sir?" asked Wells.

"Yes. Why?"

"I was just thinking I'd better call you up, sir. There's a man here with a very queer story about her. Boatman by the name of Samson. He says this Baroness stole his boat."

"Let's hear the whole thing."

"Well, sir, he says this Baroness came down to the water front last night and offered him a five-dollar bill to take her out to the *Carribiana*. She said she'd left something on board. He agreed to that, but when they got near the ship, she said she wanted to get on board without being noticed. Samson didn't like that so much; it kind of worried him. But the lady seems to have impressed him. Elderly and—"

"Oh, yes!" said Martin. "Go ahead."

"Yes, sir. He rowed her up to the landing stage; nobody around. The old lady told him to wait, and she nipped up the accommodation ladder, lively as anyone. Samson waited, feeling pretty nervous, and in fifteen minutes or so back she came, carrying a little dog."

"A dog?" cried Martin.

"Yes, sir, she was carrying a little dog, and a bag. Samson helped her down the ladder, and as soon as she'd got the dog and the bag stowed in the boat, she told Samson she'd forgotten something—left a purse full of money in her cabin and she wanted him to go and get it for her. He didn't want to do that, but she bribed him well.

"He found the cabin, all right, but he couldn't find any purse. He hunted high and low, getting more and more nervous, and at last he gave it up. He went back on deck, and when he got to the head of the ladder, he saw that his boat was gone. The moon was down then, but he says he caught a glimpse of her, rowing away.

"He went to the fo'castle then and looked up a pal of his. The captain had gone ashore and was due back any moment, and this friend of Samson's managed to smuggle him on board the launch for the trip back. It came off all right, and Samson's got his fifteen dollars, but he's mad, sir. Wants this Baroness arrested for stealing his boat."

"Keep him there," said Martin. "I'll be along presently."

He got up and dressed, with practiced speed. He got into his car and drove along the dark and deserted roads to the town.

"So she found her little dog," he thought. "But where in God's name has she gone with it? Why didn't she let Samson row her back? Does she think she can find some place where she can hide away, on this heaven-beautiful island?"

The sky was beginning to grow light by the time he reached Harbor Street.

Puzzled, troubled, he stopped the car, on the chance that he would see that incredible woman somewhere on the quiet water front. And suddenly he heard the sound of oars.

It didn't have to be the Baroness. But the Harbor Patrol discouraged any small craft from moving after dark.

He got out of the car and walked to the end of the jetty. And now, in the fast-coming tropical dawn, he could see a boat, still forty or fifty yards from the shore, but coming slowly and steadily on.

"Ahoy, there!" he called. "Who are you?"

"Gives it Herr Lieutenant Hardy?" called that loud, clear voice.

"Yes. Can you get in? Need any help?"

She stopped rowing. "I wish to tell you something," she said. "Most important."

He jumped down into a rowboat and cast loose and started out toward her.

"Herr Lieutenant!" she called. "Do not come near! I have here a bomb."

"What—!"

"It is in the bag of that Castelloverdi. I pull it in the water with a rope, but I do not know if water destroys such a bomb."

He rowed toward her, fast.

"Herr Lieutenant, you shall not allow yourself to be up-blown!" she said sternly. "If it happens, if we are both killed, then that Castelloverdi will never be caught. He will blow up more ships. Herr Lieutenant, you shall think first of your country. That is your duty."

"Let the bag go."

"But it is evidence!" she said. "You should see it first. You have a torch?"

A little dog began to bark, loud and shrill.

"Ach, Gustel!" she said, with infinite indulgence. "Here then, Herr Lieutenant."

He sent the beam of the torch across the water, and with a great effort she pulled a bag out of the water, a small, brown bag.

"Let it go now," he said. "The water's not too deep here. We'll dredge it up later."

She dropped it back into the water, with a splash.

"Come in to the shore now, gracious lady."

"I regret, Herr Lieutenant, that I can no more. It is my oldness."

He brought his boat alongside hers and climbed in, carefully. The little dog was barking frantically now, standing on her knees. The sun was sliding up over the horizon, and in the pale light he could see the creature, a nameless breed, black, with a sharp muzzle.

"Where did you find your dog, gracious lady?" he asked.

"He was cruelly used," she said. "I found him in a drawer, his mouth tied, his little feet tied. The drawer was almost tight closed. He would soon have died, from lack of air."

"What drawer, gracious lady? In what cabin?"

"A cabin near mine. Where I found the bag."

"Whose cabin was it?"

She sat erect, absently stroking the little dog.

"When we were all at the Customs inspection," she said, "I heard that Castelloverdi has lost a bag. I thought that was something queer. I did not trust that man."

"Why did you not, gracious lady?"

"Perhaps you will think it is foolishness," she said. "Although I have heard that the Americans also have some understanding of dogs. I did not trust the man because the little Gustel did not trust him. Did not like him at all. Every time he saw this Castelloverdi, he would run before him and look up into his face and bark; sometimes also he growled."

"Did you suspect what was in the bag?"

"Never!" she said. "I thought only that perhaps he had given this bag to another person, for what reason I didn't know. When I saw it in the cabin, I opened it, and I found in it a mechanism."

She described it, carefully and intelligently.

"At first I thought I would throw it into the sea," she went on. "But then I thought no. It was necessary for you to see this, in order that you should arrest the man who wished to blow up the ship. I did not wish the boatman to be in danger, so I left him behind."

"I'm sorry," he said, "but in whose cabin did you find your little dog, gracious lady? And the bag?"

The rising sun shone on her and she closed her eyes. "In Elsa's cabin," she said.

"I'm sorry to ask you, but do you think she had something to do with this thing?"

"She is not a wicked girl, Herr Lieutenant. Only frivolous. She talked and laughed too much on the ship with that Castelloverdi. I forebade it, but I know that it continued. Herr Lieutenant, I am absolutely sure she did not know what was in that bag. In the first place she would have been shocked, and she would have come running to me. In the second place, Herr Lieutenant, why should he tell her? There was no need for him to share this dangerous secret. No. He had only to ask her— 'Fräulein, permit me to leave in the wardrobe of your cabin a little bag I don't wish to take ashore.' He could give her some reason, or none. She would think little of it."

"And Gustel ...?"

"You are an officer of the law, Herr Lieutenant," she said. "It is right to tell you what I believe. But I am sorry to do so. The night before we arrived here, I was waked up by hearing the little Gustel barking and barking outside in the alleyway. I got up and went out to see what was wrong with him, but I couldn't find him. I knocked at Elsa's door and I asked her if she had seen him. She answered me, 'No.' But I think he was in there, even while she spoke. I think he was barking outside her cabin because—there was someone in there he did not like. I think Elsa opened the door and let him in and made him be quiet. Then later she was frightened. She did not know what to do with him. It was not in her heart to kill him, but she left him—as I found him …"

He made the boat fast to the jetty; he got into his car with the Baroness and drove to the police station, where he called the airport.

"Yes," he said. "Yes, I see. I'll attend to it." He turned to the Baroness. "I'm sending a message ahead to Trinidad," he told her. "They'll be stopped and sent back here."

"'They'?" she said. "Elsa has gone? But the officials obliged her to go, of course."

"No," said Martin. "You would always prefer to hear the truth, gracious lady? She was told that she might remain here while a search was made for you. But she—went."

She turned away toward the window that overlooked the harbor. "Look!" she said.

The *Carribiana* was moving off, gray and grim against the golden sun. She flew no flags, these days, but she was familiar to everyone in the islands, as she doggedly made her round from one island to another, bringing the desperately needed cargoes of medicines, food, shoes, machine parts, the precious mail.

"Also, there she goes," said the Baroness.

"Thanks to you," said Martin.

"I am glad that such a chance comes to me in my oldness," she said. "But now, Herr Lieutenant? The plane has gone. Gustel and I shall leave on the next one?"

"You shall remain in Buenaventura, as long as you please. If that's what you wish."

"If I wish …!" she said. She held the little dog up to the window that had no glass. "Look, you little Gustel! You are in Paradise!"

Farewell to a Corpse

CHAPTER I

Felix Tellier stood in a corner, with a glass of champagne in one hand and a lighted cigarette in the other. But he could manage this; he was deft in everything, slim and neat, fair-haired and sharp-featured and wonderfully amiable.

He was hemmed in by people, all strangers, all with their backs turned to him, but he was quite content to be let alone and to observe. The hot July sun came in through the window behind him, and the noises of the city street; the air was heavy with tobacco smoke; the pink roses that stood about in bowls and vases were falling fast and the petals lay thick on the gray carpet. Denise's second wedding had been celebrated on Long Island, a good deal grander it had been, but with pink roses like this, and with this same air of high drama, almost tragedy.

That had been nine years ago, and it was remarkable how little Denise had changed. She stood at the far end of the long room, beside her third bridegroom, and she was lovely, slender and delicate, in a dark linen suit and a little black hat that showed her shining chestnut hair. There was a look of desperate gallantry on her pale face.

A woman standing in front of Felix looked back and up into his face—a thin, dark, stylish little monkey of a woman.

"Did you know that Boris is really a *baron?*" she asked. "He doesn't use his title, but Denise is actually a baroness. The whole thing has been so romantic, hasn't it?"

"Oh, yes!" said Felix, knowing nothing about the whole thing.

"I do hope she'll find *some* happiness," said the little dark woman. "She deserves it, doesn't she, after all she's been through?"

"Oh, yes!" Felix said again.

He did not know this woman who spoke to him so confidentially and she, he thought, couldn't know who he was. He was an uninvited and unexpected guest. He had not seen anyone here whom he remembered from the other wedding. But he had long ago found out for himself that Denise changed her friends often.

"Where's Taffy?" someone called, and he glanced up quickly.

"Where's Taffy? We want Taffy!" somebody else said, and then they all took it up. "We want Taffy!"

She came in from the hall, a tall girl, very slight in her gray dress with a high collar, her soft light-brown hair loose about her gentle face. Denise took one arm, the bridegroom took the other and Taffy stood there between her mother and her mother's new husband. She was not shy, or in any way awkward, but she was curiously aloof.

It must be easier for her now, at twenty-four, he thought. At that other wedding she had been only fifteen, a tall kid in a white party dress too childish for her, her hair specially waved in a frizzy bush. Yet even then she had had this gentle grace; even at fifteen she had had this touching and unconscious dignity.

He had been twenty-three himself then and very happy. He had gone to that wedding because some fellow he knew had asked him to come along and it was his nature to accept invitations. It was natural, too, for him to be kind to the kid Taffy. He had thought she was sweet. He had stood beside her while she waved good-by to her mother and that other husband until their car was out of sight.

"Could you come out to dinner with me, do you think?" he had asked her.

He had taken her in a taxi to an inn he had heard praised for its shore dinners.

"This is the first time I've ever been out to dinner with a boy," she had told him. "I'll *never* forget it."

He had never quite forgotten it, either. He had gone to Mexico that autumn and he had sent a postcard to Taffy in boarding school. She had answered with a letter, casual, amusing, a little rambling, the sort of letter he liked.

After that they had always written to each other. All through the nine years they had kept in touch with each other, in the casual way he so cherished. Months could go by without a word, and it made no difference. They had met from time to time; they always had a good time together; they always said *au revoir* without any definite plan for meeting again. That was what made it so perfect; they demanded nothing of each other, expected nothing.

It was over a year since he had seen her, but she was just the same. Standing in his corner he watched her with a sort of delight to see her so unchanged. Nobody like her, he thought.

The bride and groom were leaving now, moving toward the hall, arm in arm, and the guests went after them. An excited woman in pince-nez took a handful of rice out of a paper bag and threw it at them. Some of the grains caught in Denise's shining hair and she turned, with a look of grave astonishment. That was a mistake, Felix thought. Denise takes her weddings very seriously.

He stood by the window and looked out into the quiet upper East Side street. Three little girls from a different world were waiting out there, fascinated. A cook across the street was looking out through a barred window in the basement.

A chauffeur was holding open the door of a car. Denise got in, followed by her bridegroom, the door closed and off they went. The guests came streaming into the house again, the caterer's men moved around with more champagne and sandwiches. The stylish little monkey of a woman, who seemed as friendless here as Felix himself, laid her hand on his arm.

"Sweet, wasn't it?" she said, almost crying. "Sweet."

"Very," Felix said earnestly. "Now, if you'll excuse me just a moment."

And he went off to look for Taffy. She was not in the drawing room, she was not in the dining room across the hall. There was a butler there, glassy-eyed and unsteady on his feet.

"Where's Miss Stephanie, d'you know?" Felix asked him.

"She's upstairs, sir," the butler answered, with a hiccup that made him wince.

"Go up and tell her, will you, that Mr. Tellier is here."

"Undoubtedly, sir," said the butler, leaning against the back of a chair.

Felix looked at him and shook his head. Then he went into the hall and stood there for a moment, a little at a loss. He had never been in this house before. He did not know his way around in it, or even what people might be living in it.

It was a queer little house, a maisonette, narrow and dark, yet with a certain Denise-like smartness.

At the top of the stairs there was a half-open door facing him, He approached this and saw inside a rack where women's coats were hanging and a maid, in cap and apron, sitting in an armchair with her legs stretched out and her pumps kicked off.

"Will you tell Miss Stephanie that Mr. Tellier would like to see her?" he said.

"Miss Stephanie's room is at the end of the hall, sir," said the maid, without moving.

A household altogether typical of Denise, this was, without discipline or order, with that curious end-of-the-world atmosphere she produced. You could almost believe that the house and everybody and everything in it would vanish when the sun rose again. He went to the end of the hall and knocked at the door there.

"Come in!" said Taffy's slow and gentle voice.

CHAPTER II

The room he entered was empty, a funny, touching little room. On the floor were two rugs, blue, with white polar bears on them; there were a birchbark rocking-chair and table, a small white desk with bright-colored circus animals painted on it. There was a low white bookcase and on top of it a lamp made like an owl with yellow eyes. A door, leading to an inner room, stood ajar, and he could hear someone moving in there.

"Taffy?" he said.

"*Felix!*" she cried, and came running in. "Oh, Felix!"

She held out both hands to him, looking at him with her gray eyes brilliant, her lips parted.

"You forgot to invite me," he said. "But I saw the note in this morning's paper and I came, anyhow."

"Like the other time."

"That was the idea," he said.

"Felix, sit down. Will you have a cigarette?"

"Am I bothering you, Taffy? Are you busy?"

"Oh, no!" she said. "I was just packing a bag."

"Going away?"

"I thought I would," she said. "For the weekend, or maybe longer."

"Where?"

"Well, I saw an inn on Long Island advertised in a magazine, and I thought I'd go there."

"Don't you know anything about it?"

"Well, if I don't like it when I get there," she said, "I won't stay. I've got the names of some other inns."

"Why don't you visit someone, Taffy?"

"I don't feel like visiting, Felix. I want to stay at an inn for a while by myself. I never have, you know. A nice inn, with a real roof, and pine trees all around."

"We've got one rather like that, out at Spruce Lake," he said. "Look here! Why don't you go there? I've got my car here. I can drive you."

"Well, shall I, Felix?" she said with a doubting frown.

"Why not? First we'll have a gala dinner in town."

"Then I'll have to change," she said. "I shan't be long, Felix. My bags are all packed. Sit down in the armchair."

She took up a cardboard box with a lid on which seashells were glued in a crowded, hit-or-miss way; it was filled with cigarettes.

"Please help yourself," she said.

She went off into the other room and he lighted a cigarette and moved about, looking at her things. These were things from her childhood, making a little world all her own, bright and innocent, with the nostalgic charm of a fairy tale. She herself was like a maiden in a fairy tale—gentle and friendly, yet always aloof, able to go through forests of dark enchantment unharmed.

There's nobody like her, he thought. I knew that, the first time I saw her, when she was only fifteen. I knew she was—what's the word?—valuable—precious. Darling. All these years, even when we haven't seen each other, or haven't even written, it's just the same. Whenever we meet, we go on just where we left off. We're always perfectly easy together; we're always happy.

I wish to God I'd been able to make Ildina happy, he thought. I meant to. I thought I could. Ildina thought so, too. I've never been happy in my life, Felix, she had told him. But it will be different now. I'll be different.

Only she wasn't different, and wasn't happy. And neither was he. He remembered their breakfast that morning, Ildina sitting across the table from him—pale, handsome, sullen, in that negligee of yellow chiffon trimmed with strips of panther that he secretly thought sensational and a little comic.

He had seen the notice of Denise's wedding in the newspaper and he had lied to Ildina, in the serious, businesslike way that was growing easy to him.

"I'll have to go in to New York on business today," he had said.

"And you're planning to go away tomorrow for two weeks," Ildina had said.

"My dear girl," he had said, "I've got to go out to the Coast. It's a business matter—"

"That's a lie," she had said.

It was only partly a lie. There was business out there he was going to attend to, but the truth was that Macklin could have done it just as well. Let it go. She didn't believe him when he told the truth, and now it didn't matter.

"I'll be back in time for Mimi's party," he had said.

"I'm not going to Mimi's party," she had said.

Let it go. No use asking her why. She would say she didn't like Mimi. She didn't like anyone.

"You go, if you're so anxious about it," she had said, looking at him with her eyes narrowed.

He didn't care about going. He liked Mimi, and she was a neighbor of theirs. It was going to look conspicuously rude if they stayed away. But he was not going to argue with Ildina, and anyhow his old zest for parties had left him. All he really wanted now was to get away.

Only for a little while, only now and then. Whenever he managed to get away, it did all the good in the world. He always came home feeling cheerful, and hopeful, and Ildina would have little things to tell him. It'll work out all right, in the course of time, he thought. I'll get away tomorrow, get a little change.

He sighed, passed his hand down the back of his neat fair head, and he stopped thinking about Ildina. He could do that, when he wanted; he could stop thinking of anything much and feel nothing but a serene and healthy good humor.

He was stooping to look at the books on the shelves when Taffy spoke.

"Felix?"

She was standing in the doorway, in a long white cotton dress with a round neck and puff sleeves and two little white coral flowers in her long hair. She looked so lovely and so happy.

"That's a pretty dress, Taffy," he said.

"Thank you, Felix. I got it for the dances we give for soldiers."

"Do *you* go to those?" he asked.

"Why not?"

"Do you talk to the soldiers?"

"Not very much," she said. "I'm not very good. I just sort of float around and smile."

During the war, Felix had tried to enlist in some branch of the U. S. Armed Services, but had been turned down because he'd had malaria two or three times. He had been in San Francisco at the time and was on the way home, when he had met Ildina, and his plan of joining the Merchant Marine had been postponed. Little by little, it had faded.

His father-in-law had given him a job in a new branch of his leather business. They were busy now with various contracts, for the first time in his cheerful, wandering life, he was a settled man. Settled in a job, in a home, in a community. And sometimes, in vivid flashes, this stability seemed to him like a yawning trap.

It did now, when he thought of the soldiers who had danced with Taffy. I'm thirty-one, he thought. Those days are over.

"I'll take my bag along, Felix," Taffy said. "And then I'll never have to come back."

"Never?"

"No. Mother's rented the house."

"But your things? The furniture?"

"Oh, that's going into storage until I get settled somewhere."

"And now you don't live anywhere," he said.

She put on a loose rough white coat. He took her bag and they went out of the room and down the stairs. The floor below was crowded with the wedding guests, but no one took any notice of Taffy.

"We'd better go out the basement door," she said and led the way through a lively group of people to a flight of dark stairs at the end of the hall.

Denise's parties were always like this, he thought. They went on by themselves. She paid caterers and servants to run a show and she came to it like another guest herself, not at all responsible for anything. Maybe Taffy had lived here like a guest in a hotel.

She opened the barred door to the area and they went out, into broad daylight. The westering sun shone in her face and she narrowed her eyes against it.

The three little girls were still there, watching the house.

"Oo-o, lookit!" one of them cried. "Here's *another* bride!"

Taffy smiled at the children, her hair like a nimbus about her gentle face.

CHAPTER III

He drove easily through the city streets, and they did not talk, or try to talk. It was always like this when they were together; they could he silent, or they could speak, and it made no difference. He drove across the Washington Bridge and the river was pearly under the sky that was sheer light without color. He turned into a side road, and it was suddenly dusk there beneath the trees.

"Now!" she said, contentedly.

"Now what?"

"Now there's the country smell," she said.

"I didn't know you were so fond of the country, Taffy."

"It's coming over me in my old age," she said. "You know, Felix, when I was little, Father had a playhouse built for me in the garden, a real little house, with a sitting room and a bedroom, and a kitchen with an electric stove. It had red and white striped awnings and a little porch. You can imagine! I never was allowed to stay there all night but sometimes, late in the afternoon, I used to lie on the bed, and a tree outside used to brush against the window screen with this sound."

"You loved your little house?"

"So much ... Too much. I didn't want anyone to come into it, except my nurse once in a while. She was all right, because she was businesslike; she swept and dusted, as if it was *real*. Father used to come sometimes and sit on the tiny porch and smoke a pipe, and Mother used to come and bring me presents. I never liked any of them.

"I remember once she brought a tea set; it was very pretty, but much, much too little. It was for dolls. I made tea and gave her a cup, about the size of a thimble, and she drank it, so politely and sweetly. I hated it."

"A nasty, ungrateful little girl."

"I was. Were you a nasty little boy?"

"I was crazy," said Felix. "A completely crazy little dynamo, always getting into trouble. My father was a country doctor, overworked, tired. He must have needed a little peace and quiet. But my mother died and left him with two small boys and he never could get a housekeeper to stay very long."

"Where's your brother now, Felix?"

"Still in the Navy."

"Is he like you?"

"Couldn't be more different. He's a steady, disciplined sort of fellow. He did the things I left undone. He looked after Father, that last year. I was in Mexico, selling typewriters."

"We never talked about our childhoods before, Felix."

"Well, no. I never think about mine."

"I do," she said. "When this reconversion period's over, I'd like to build a little house, tiny, like that playhouse, and find a cozy old lady to live in it with me."

No, he thought. It won't be like that for you. You'll fall in love and you'll marry. You'll live in a big house, a big complicated, social life. That's what you were born to, and trained for; that's your fate.

"What do you do with yourself, Taffy?" he asked.

"Oh, I'm working in a day nursery. I've got two weeks' holiday now."

"Do you like that?"

"No," she answered. "I'm not good at it. I haven't got the right way with children. I'm too—vague. I think they need someone very definite, who'll tell them what to do, someone who knows the answers."

"Will you go back to it?"

"Oh, yes," she said. "Maybe I'll improve. Felix, there's a lake!"

He stopped the car so that she could look at it, the pale quiet water ringed with trees. Her face in the dusk looked very grave. He wondered what she was thinking about. She turned her head and looked at him.

"Where are we going to eat?" she asked earnestly.

That made him laugh.

"I thought you were meditating," he said. "Where would you like to eat? A roadhouse?"

"Don't we know where we're going?" she said. "I like that. Let's just drive along until we see a place we like. Unless you have to be anywhere at any special time, Felix?"

"I may be a little late," he had told Ildina. "Better not wait dinner for me. I'll get a bite somewhere." But she was always waiting for him, and when he came she would not believe what he said, whether it was true or whether it was a lie. So that a truth and a lie were equal.

Stop thinking about it. It will get better in time. People get adjusted to each other as time goes on. As time goes on, you get used to things, to anything, to everything, and you don't mind anymore.

Insects were chirping by the roadside now, and the low hills ahead of them looked dark against the sky. The air that blew against his face was cool and sweet.

I wish it was true that we weren't going anywhere, he thought.

But behind those hills lay his home, and that was where he was going.

He came to the end of the lane and turned into the highway, and it was forlorn there. There was a filling station, closed, the circular drive before it littered with paper. There was a tavern built like a huge Noah's Ark, all the windows dark. The street lights were dim and only trucks were moving along the road.

"Let's eat in that diner there," Taffy said.

"If you like diners—" he said.

They sat side by side at the counter and ordered ham and eggs. In the harsh overhead light Taffy's hair looked smooth and pale. She leaned her elbows on the counter and hooked her heels over the rung of the stool and her white dress hung almost to the floor.

We've eaten in a lot of queer little places together, he thought. That Spanish place near Brooklyn Bridge—in Automats—down at Coney Island. And in some very grand places, too. That first place where we had dinner together ... Lord! Eight years ago. A long time in anyone's life.

And he thought, I've come a long way since then. A hell of a long way. I've learned to work now. I've learned some discipline. I've got some sense of responsibility. I've improved. Or haven't I?

He would have liked to ask Taffy about that, but whenever he glanced at her, he gave up the idea. She was his friend. He was certain of that, but she was aloof from him in her own world.

Someone came up the steps of the diner and stopped abruptly in the doorway.

As Felix turned his head, the newcomer was about to beat a hasty retreat.

"Hello, Augie," said Felix with a gentle smile.

It was Augie West, in a snug-fitting blue suit, a blue-gray felt hat shadowing his thin, sad, dark face with froglike eyes and doleful mouth.

"I'm just going …" he said anxiously. "I saw your car and I just stopped."

"Taffy," said Felix. "This is my friend, Augie West. Augie, Miss Marlowe."

Augie took off his hat. He bowed politely to her.

"Miss Marlowe," he murmured correctly, and Taffy smiled at him with vague gentleness.

CHAPTER IV

That Impossible Little Man, that was what they called him in Spruce Lake, when they didn't call him worse. He had come, from God knew where, and rented a vast and imposing house. Van loads of furniture had come—very magnificent—tapestries, paintings, two grand pianos. And Augie lived alone with two servants in this splendor.

It was a queer thing the way Augie had got in bad from the very start. He had wanted to contribute money to everything. During the war he had offered his two cars and his little yacht for every sort of purpose.

He had offered his grounds for a Boy Scout picnic. But everything he did was wrong. He used to be a bootlegger, Ildina had told Felix. That wasn't true and Felix had told her so. It was just one of those tales that got around.

Ildina couldn't stand him. The one time he had set foot in their house she had let him see how she felt.

"He's a vulgar little beast," she had said.

"No," Felix had said. "He's not vulgar. He's a damn fine little guy."

"You like him because he truckles to you," Ildina had said.

"All right," Felix had said. "We'll let it go at that.…"

"What are you doing here, Augie?" Felix asked.

"Why, to tell you the truth, Felix, my car broke down a little way from here and I walked to the filling station to get a tow."

"We'll give you a lift home," said Felix.

"Oh, no," said Augie. "I can get a taxi, Felix."

"Please come along with us," said Taffy. "We're ready, aren't we, Felix?"

Felix very much wanted her to talk to Augie. He wanted her to *get* Augie, to see in him that quality he himself saw.

They went out of the diner and into the roadster, with Taffy between the two men, but she did not talk. Augie talked too much. He talked about his car, his boat, his garden, the books he had read lately, in a quick nervous outflow.

"It's disgusting, the way he brags," Ildina had said.

"He doesn't brag," Felix had said. "He's just trying to tell you what sort of fellow he is."

And he was doing it now, to Taffy.

"I'm a great reader," he said. "Mostly non-fiction. But music is my hobby. Sometimes I just play the piano for three or four hours straight in the evenings."

"That must be fun," said Taffy. You couldn't tell from her voice whether or not she was liking Augie.

"I'll take a shortcut, past the Club," Felix said, turning the car uphill into a private road.

Augie had wanted to belong to the Country Club. And Felix, counting on his own popularity, had proposed him. But they wouldn't have Augie West at any price, and he had to know it. Not so easy for the poor little guy to go there now. It would help if Taffy talked to him.

"Just drop me here, Felix, at the foot of the hill."

"We'll run you home in style, Augie."

There were a lot of cars parked along the drive out at the Country Club, and the screened veranda at the side of the Clubhouse was brilliantly lit. It was like a scene in a play—a long table set out there, decorated with flowers, eighteen or twenty people sitting at it; and at the head was Mimi Depew, blond, very thin in her pale-blue dress, smiling her gay, sweet silly smile.

"I'd forgotten about her party," Felix said. "I shouldn't—"

All the lights went out.

"Oh, what's happened?" Taffy cried, her hand on Felix's wrist.

Then the people on the veranda began to sing, in the dark.

"Happy birthday to you! Happy birthday, clear Mimi ..." A circlet of little flames, all slanting in one direction, as if floating forward in the dark. "Happy *birthday*, dear Mimi ..."

The lights came on again and Mimi rose, smiling down at the pink frosted cake before her.

Someone moved, and Felix saw Ildina there, handsome and dark and sullen in a white satin dress, with her pearls around her throat, not singing with the others, not smiling.

Why had she come? Felix thought, surprised.

He drove on, through the woods, to Augie's fine house.

"Well, thank you, Felix," said Augie. "Very glad to have met you, Miss Marlowe. Thank you."

He got out of the car and Felix drove down the hill to the highway.

He remembered driving along here once, alone, at dawn. The sun had been coming up over the marshes and the reeds were flushed with a rosy light; there had been a wonderful feeling of space and freedom …

"Do you live near here, Felix?" Taffy asked.

"Oh, yes. Up the next road. Would you like to see the house?"

"Yes, I should."

No sense in this, he thought. But after all, why not? I'm going away tomorrow, and when I get back, Taffy'll be gone. This is only a moment.

He turned off the highway, up a hill. He knew this road in the day and in the dark, in winter and in summer. There was a sign nailed to a tree. *Private—Keep Out*. Ildina had had that put up.

"What's the idea?" he had asked. "We don't care if people drive up here now and then. It's a dead end. There'd never be many."

"Dad worked for the money to buy this place for me," she had said. "And it means something to me. Nothing means anything to you …"

Maybe that's true, he thought. He had never owned anything he valued much. He had come to Ildina empty-handed and it was not for him to belittle her gifts.

Private. Keep Out. They had a wine-cellar that was kept locked; they had a safe hidden in the wall; they had had a burglar alarm installed. Everybody had to keep out; Taffy, too.

It came into his head then that Taffy could never set foot in that house, and that if Ildina ever saw her, ever even heard of her, she would say the things she did say.

Driving up the dark private road he remembered the first time he had seen how it was with her. They had been married only a few months and they had come into New York for the weekend—he couldn't remember why. Only that it had been a gala time. They had taken a suite at a hotel, they had gone to a play and then to a night club.

She had grown silent, sat with her eyes lowered, her face blank. He had seen that something was wrong, and he had tried to get her talking; but she would answer only curtly. She refused to dance. "Shall we go home?" he had asked, and she much to had answered, "Yes."

It was late when they got back to the hotel, and he had begun to undress. But Ildina had sat in a chair, still with her eyes lowered and that heavy blank look on her face.

"What's the matter?" he had asked.

"Did you think I didn't notice?" she had asked.

"Notice what?"

"The way you looked at that girl," she had said. "That half-naked little bitch with the tambourine."

"But, good Lord!" he had cried. "Everybody was looking at her. That's what she's there for."

"I saw the look on your face," she had said. "It was—*horrible*."

He had been surprised and at heart a little repelled, but he had tried to be reasonable, tried to win her back to a good humor.

"You don't love me," she had said. "You never did."

He had tried, that time, to make her believe in his love. But not anymore. Now when she made her sudden furious accusations he was only patient, and all he wanted now was to get away from the sound of her voice and to stay away until her fury was spent.

"You never loved me!" she had said. "It was only my money."

The first time she had said that, he had turned his back and walked away, sick with anger and disgust. She had had to go after him that time. But she had said it again and again, and he no longer troubled to deny it.

On his way home from San Francisco, nearly two years ago, he had stopped over in San Antonio to see an old friend, and at the hotel there he had met Ildina. She had just returned from a tour in Mexico, all by herself. She was always alone. The other people in the hotel called her snobbish and arrogant.

But he had thought she was somehow touching, so young, so handsome and so ill-liked, and had gone out of his way to be friendly to her. She had been hostile and suspicious in the beginning. She had taken the Mexican trip to get over a broken engagement. She had been hurt and bitter, and he had made her happy. She had been lonely, and he had given her a gay comradeship that she had never known before. She had turned to him, in the end, and had clung to him in a sort of desperation.

We could have been happy, he thought. We were, for a while. But she won't let herself be happy. Well ... he sighed. As time goes on ... he thought. I don't know.

CHAPTER V

The lighted windows of the house shone through the trees.

"What a big house, Felix!" Taffy said.

"Very big."

"It's queer to think of you walking around in there."

"I don't walk around there much," he said. "People don't, you know."

"It would be even queerer to think of you sitting still," she said.

"Ildina isn't home," he said. As if that had any meaning.

"Isn't she?" said Taffy.

She accepted what he said, always, without any questions. He had written to tell her of his marriage and she had sent a present—to Mr. and Mrs. Felix Tellier—a silver lion, made in Denmark. He had never shown it to Ildina and Taffy had never mentioned it again. She had never suggested meeting Ildina, never had asked a question about her. He could drive her, his faithful friend, past the house where he lived, and not even stop the car, and she would accept that, too.

But it was unbearable.

"Would you like to sit on the terrace and smoke a cigarette, Taffy?" he asked.

"Love to, Felix."

Wonderful invitation, he thought. You can't go into the house, because the servants might see you and tell Ildina. But you can sit out here in the dark, and if anyone tells Ildina about that, you can deny it.

The chairs had been taken in. She sat on the broad stone balustrade and the light from the window shone on her gleaming dress.

"When will your mother be back?" he asked.

"In two weeks," she said. "She and Boris are going to live in an apartment hotel."

"And what about you?"

"They want to get a room in the hotel for me, and maybe I'll do that."

"What else could you do?"

"Well, practically anything," she said. "I could get a little apartment, or I could get a job in Detroit, helping in a day nursery. Or I could go somewhere else."

"People are supposed to live somewhere, my good girl. They're supposed to have addresses."

"Plenty of time for all that," she said amiably, and they were both silent for a time.

"That must be the library," Taffy said. "Where you can sit and read."

He hated that room, with the big red leather armchairs, the big mahogany desk, where no one ever worked, the shelves of books that no one ever read, the shaded lamps, the air of tranquil comfort—where there was no ease.

The telephone on the desk began to ring. Let it ring.

He sat still, and in a moment in came Carrie, pert and pretty in her black uniform and cap, to answer it.

"Mr. Tellier?" she said. "Just a moment, sir. I'll see …"

She put the telephone down and went out into the hall; Felix met her as she was opening the front door.

"I thought I heard your car, sir," she said. "There's someone on the telephone for you, sir."

"Who is it?"

"I didn't get the name, sir," she answered, looking up into his face.

It was bad luck that she had heard the car, and that she knew someone was out there on the terrace, but it couldn't be helped now. He went into the library and took up the telephone.

"This is Tellier," he said.

"Mr. Tellier," said a man's voice, "this is F. T. Bushey speaking, District Attorney for Spruce Lake. Is Mrs. Tellier at home now?"

"Mrs. Tellier?" Felix repeated, frowning. "I—"

"I'm here," said Ildina, from the doorway. "Who is it, Felix?"

"Says his name is Bushey."

"I'll speak to him," she said, and came across the room, tall and sullen and unhurrying in her white dress. She sat down on the edge of the desk and took up the telephone.

"This is Mrs. Tellier," she said. "Yes, I've been home about half an hour … But why? An accident? What sort of accident? Oh, I see … Yes, certainly."

She hung up the instrument.

"There's been an accident at the Club," she said. "Mimi Depew's been shot."

"Shot? What do you mean? By mistake?"

"How do I know? This Bushey'll be here presently. He wants to ask me questions. You had better say I came home with you."

"Did he say whether Mimi's badly hurt?"

"Oh, yes," said Ildina. "She's dead."

"Dead?" he said. "Mimi's *dead!*"

"So that Bushey said. Someone shot Mimi through the window."

"How can you take it like that?" he demanded. "As if you didn't give a damn?"

"I'm not going to pretend to be crazy about Mimi Depew!"

"You were sitting at the table with her an hour ago. At her birthday party."

"How did you know I was there?"

"I saw you. I drove Augie home."

"And you didn't stop in to take me home?"

Taffy! he thought in a panic.

Never mind what Ildina thought or said, he had to get Taffy safely away. He put his hand into his pocket and drew it out empty.

"I left my cigarettes in the car," he said. "I'll be right back."

He went out on the terrace but he did not see her there. He went down the steps and opened the door of the car. She was not there. The bag was gone. He dared not call her here. He started along the drive, dismay and fear rising and rising. When he had gone far enough he called her name.

"Taffy?"

The trees rustled overhead. He heard the quiet rush of a car along the highway and nothing else.

Mimi was shot, he thought. A tramp? A madman?

He went all the way to the main road. He called her name once more, and then he turned back. He went up the hill in a hurry, his heart beating fast in familiar alarm.

Where did she go? he thought. Where could she go all by herself, with that bag?

As he reached the steps of the terrace, a car was coming up the drive. He got into the house and closed the door before the occupants of the car had picked him out.

"Where have you been?" Ildina asked.

The bell rang and Felix opened the door. Two men stood there, one of them a policeman in uniform.

"Mr. Tellier?" said the man not in uniform. "I'd like a few words with Mrs. Tellier, please. Kennedy, you can wait here."

He followed Felix into the library where Ildina sat at the edge of the desk, smoking.

"Mrs. Tellier?" he said. "I am Francis Bushey, District Attorney for Spruce Lake County."

CHAPTER VI

He was a stout, deep-chested, young man, with shoulders too broad for his height, pale and thin-lipped, with fiery dark eyes. He wore his dark hair somewhat long behind the ears, and brushed back from his forehead. He looks like a ham actor, Felix thought.

"Sit down, won't you?" said Ildina casually.

"Thank you. I should like to ask you a few questions, Mrs. Tellier, in connection with the shocking occurrence at the Country Club."

"I can't tell you anything."

"Mrs. Depew was shot," Bushey stated, looking sternly at her, "while she sat at the table among her friends."

"Yes. You told me on the telephone."

"I wondered if you were not at the table when the shooting occurred?"

"No, I went home early."

"You heard the shot?"

"No."

"What did you do, Mrs. Tellier, when you left the clubhouse?"

"I went down the hill to the highway. I was going towards home, but

I hoped to find my husband driving by in the car and I got in with him and came home."

It's a mistake to lie to him, Felix thought. I don't know why she's doing it.

"When you left the table, Mrs. Tellier," Bushey went on, "you stopped in the powder room to get your wrap?"

"No. I didn't bother with it."

"You simply rose from the table and walked out of the clubhouse, Mrs. Tellier?"

There was a note in Bushey's voice that disturbed Felix, a note of shocked reproach.

"Yes," Ildina answered.

"You said good-by to Mrs. Depew?"

"No."

"Did you say good-by to anyone? Did you tell anyone that you were leaving?"

That must sound damn queer to Bushey, Felix thought, but as a matter of fact, it's typical of Ildina. I've seen her do that before—simply walk out in the middle of a cocktail party. She's done that without telling even me. Sometimes I'd hurry after her and then after a lot of trouble, I'd find out that somebody had said something or done something which offended her.

"Mrs. Tellier doesn't care much for parties, you know," he said to Bushey.

"No?" said Bushey. "Mrs. Tellier, when you left the clubhouse, did you see anyone in the garden?"

"No."

"There is a clump of pine trees at the side of the veranda. Would it have been possible for anyone to stand there without being seen by you?"

"She couldn't," Felix began, but Bushey turned on him sharply.

"Kindly let Mrs. Tellier answer for herself," he said. "Mrs. Tellier, could it have been possible for anyone to stand there?"

"I don't know," she answered scornfully. "I didn't look at this clump of trees."

My God! thought Felix. Was that a trap? To find out if she'd been at the side of the clubhouse? Where the man must have stood to shoot Mimi? No, that's nonsense. He couldn't think Ildina knew anything....

"Was Mrs. Depew a close friend of yours, Mrs. Tellier?"

"No."

"Were you on good terms with Mrs. Depew?"

"I suppose so. She asked me to her party."

"Mrs. Tellier, did Mrs. Depew ever speak to you of any threats made against her?"

"No. I never talked to her alone."

"Did you ever hear Mrs. Depew mention an enemy?"

"No," Ildina answered with a sigh, and lighted another cigarette.

"No doubt this is very tedious to you," said Bushey, affronted. "But it happens to be necessary."

"All right," said Ildina. "Let's get it over with."

"Mr. Tellier."

"Oh, me?" said Felix.

"From what direction did you appear at the Club?"

"Oh! From the south. I was driving back from New York."

"Did you see anyone in the vicinity of the Club who seemed to be acting in any way unusual? Any car?"

"No. I can't think of anything."

"Were you alone in your car?"

"Yes," said Felix.

"Had you made any arrangement for meeting Mrs. Tellier outside the Club?"

"No. No, I hadn't. It was just chance."

"You're well acquainted with Mrs. Depew's social circle, Mr. Tellier?"

"Fairly well, yes."

"Did you ever hear anyone in that circle express animosity toward Mrs. Depew?"

"No," Felix answered. "Everybody liked her."

"Why does it have to be someone like us?" Ildina demanded. "Why couldn't it be a tramp? Or one of those Communists who hate everyone with any money?"

Ildina on the subject of Communists was something wonderful. I'd better stop her, Felix thought.

"I don't consider that probable, Mrs. Tellier," said Bushey. "In the first place, the fact that this crime was committed on Mrs. Depew's birthday gives it, in my opinion, the appearance of a premeditated crime of personal vengeance. There were six other women present, all of the same social standing as Mrs. Depew. But she was singled out."

He's very much concerned about social standing, Felix thought. So is Ildina.

"There are plenty of people around who'd be delighted to shoot any of us," said Ildina. "And the police do nothing about them."

"I think the police in this vicinity are more than reasonably efficient Mrs. Tellier."

"Do you?" she countered sharply.

"I intend to pursue this investigation to the end," he said. "Without fear or favor. I don't make any distinction between people of a certain social circle, and any other citizens."

"You can't treat people of any standing like riff-raff," said Ildina.

"I make *no* distinction."

"Ildina, you're tired and upset," said Felix. He turned to Bushey. "The thing's been a great shock to my wife. Couldn't we call it a day?"

"Very well," said Bushey stiffly. "But I consider it grossly improper that your District Attorney should be swayed by any consideration of wealth and social standing."

"Who pays the taxes for—" Ildina began, but Felix interrupted her.

"Never mind," he said. "We're both ready to help, Mr. Bushey."

"I'm glad to hear that, Mr. Tellier," said Bushey. "It will probably be necessary to question you both again. You understand, of course, that you mustn't leave the district without communicating with me. Good night."

CHAPTER VII

Felix was silent until he heard the door close.

"Ildina," he said, "There's no use in antagonizing the man."

"I know that's your theory," she said. "To get on with everybody. But I don't mind antagonizing people."

No, he thought, glaring at her, you enjoy it. She looked very handsome, still sitting on the edge of the desk. She looked proud and vivid and alive now.

"I made that Bushey pretty uncomfortable," she said.

Felix moved about the room.

"Ildina," he said presently. "Why did you tell him that tale about meeting me and driving home with me?"

"I don't want him or anyone else to know that I had to come home alone."

"Well, you didn't have to, Ildina. You could have waited."

"I'd had enough of that party. I only went because I thought I'd find you there."

"Look here, Ildina, we talked it over and you said you didn't want to go. I told you I wasn't going without you."

"Then it looks as if I didn't believe what you told me, doesn't it?"

He felt suddenly sick of all this. He was so worried about Taffy, he was so very sorry about poor, gay Mimi, and that was enough without the misery of a scene with Ildina.

"You're tired," he said. "I'll get you a drink."

He mixed highballs for both of them and he thought of how often he had done this, persuaded her to take a drink or two with him, so that the sharp, cruel shape of the barrier between them softened and they could talk with friendliness. Sometimes he could even make her laugh.

That was what he so badly wanted now, not to explain and argue, to defend himself, but an interlude without hostility.

"Here's to us," he said, raising his glass.

She was always pleased by that toast.

"Here's to us!" she repeated.

To us. Just us two, alone here together, away from the rest of the world. And against the rest of the world.

Felix was by habit an early riser and he had learned many little techniques for not disturbing Ildina.

"You've got to promise never to leave the house without saying goodby to me," she had said long ago. "It's *horrible* to think of you creeping out and leaving me asleep."

So he had promised, and he now left without waking her. But whenever he could manage to eat breakfast alone, he liked that.

This morning he was almost desperately anxious to be alone. If I could call up the Inn, I'd find out if Taffy's there, but not from the house. Carrie might hear him and he was quite certain that she told Ildina everything. He dressed in the bathroom quickly and neatly as he did all things. He went down the stairs, leaden-hearted about Taffy.

He thought of Mimi Depew, too, but briefly. He was aware that he had not yet begun to feel what he surely must feel later on, the shock, the regret. All that was put aside, overshadowed by his anxiety for Taffy.

"Good morning, Mr. Tellier," said Carrie, as he entered the dining room.

"Good morning," he answered, in the special tone he had for Carrie, very businesslike, almost curt.

He was a little afraid of Carrie. She was a pretty girl, with dead-black hair in a curly fringe across her forehead, dark, blue eyes, an upturned nose. If he had come across her somewhere else, in other circumstances, he might have thought her an amusing, saucy little thing. But not here, in Ildina's house. She was far too much alive, too much aware of Mimi!

"Carrie's a very well-behaved, respectable girl," Ildina often said, and Felix never contradicted it, "Carrie's absolutely devoted to me," Ildina would say, and that, too, he never denied. But he thought Ildina was mistaken on both counts.

"Wasn't that the dreadfullest thing that happened up to the Club last night, Mr. Tellier?" she said.

"Yes," said Felix.

"It's in the papers," said Carrie.

"Yes," said Felix. "Sure to be."

"I guess it was one of those maniacs," said Carrie, setting a half-grapefruit before him.

The doorbell rang and she went to answer it.

"It's Mr. West," she said, coming back. "He's waiting out on the terrace."

"Bring him—no, I'll go out," said Felix, rising.

Augie had been in this house once. "Stop in and have a drink," Felix had said and he should have known better. Ildina had received him with cold amazement and Augie had been at his worst with her. He had talked and talked, in his almost frantic anxiety to interest her, to show her what manner of man he was.

Horrible, vulgar little man, Ildina said later to Felix.

He was waiting on the terrace, in gray slacks and a snug brown jacket, his black hair sleek, his frog-eyes brilliant.

"Felix, I was afraid you would be worrying about Miss Marlowe," he said quickly.

"My God, I was," said Felix. "Do you know where she is?"

"She's at the Inn, Felix. She called me up last night."

"Called you?"

"Yes. You see, Felix, when you got that telephone call she thought that maybe you—well—you'd be busy, so she went away."

When she saw Ildina there, she went away.

"Where did she go?"

"She walked down to the highway and she stopped in at a filling station and looked up my number in the book and she called me up. You see, Felix, she did not know the name of the Inn she was going to and she thought I'd probably know. So I got out my car and I drove down after her and I took her to The Inn."

"Good! Did she ask you to come and let me know, Augie?"

"Why, no. No, she didn't, Felix. When I said I thought you'd be worrying, she seemed surprised. She's—" He paused. "Of course, I don't know her, but I got the impression that she's not used to having anyone worry about her."

"You're right," said Felix briefly.

"She doesn't think enough of herself," said Augie. "She doesn't know what she's like."

No, Felix thought. She doesn't ask for anything, doesn't expect anything.

Augie ran his finger round the inside of his collar. He was embarrassed by something he was going to say, but he kept his anxious gaze upon Felix's face.

"What I thought was this, Felix," he said. "Miss Marlowe agreed. I mean, if you haven't mentioned it yet, why, maybe it's just as well not to say anything about anyone being with you, don't you think?"

"Yes," said Felix, almost curtly. "I told Bushey I was alone."

It was hard for him to face the fact that he had come close to involving Taffy in a very unsavory scandal. It was hard, very hard for him to admit that he had no right to see Taffy, ever. It could bring her nothing but harm.

"Thanks for telling me, Augie," he said. "Will you—do you want to sit down and have a smoke?"

It was hard to admit, in so many words, that he could not ask this man, for whom he had a genuine regard and liking, to set foot in this house. Ildina might come down and, if she saw Augie, she would make him miserable.

"Well, no, thanks, Felix," Augie said. "I'll be getting along."

"I'd like to drop in and see you some day," said Felix.

"Do that!" cried Augie fervently. "Do that, Felix."

CHAPTER VIII

Augie went down the steps and got into his purple roadster. During the war Felix had heard people say that people like Augie were sure to have plenty of gas, shortage or no shortage. Felix had taken pains to explain, whenever he could, that Augie was even over-scrupulous about any sort of rationing—that his conspicuous, deluxe car was six years old.

It was no use. Augie was just in bad. When he had a Boy Scout troop out from New York for a picnic on his grounds, he was accused of showing off. He could do nothing right.

I can't help him, Felix thought. I can't help Taffy, either. I can't make her happy, can't do anything for her.

He went back to his breakfast, in a mood he had never known before, troubled, puzzled, very ill-pleased with himself.

I want to call up Taffy, he thought. It seems only natural, only friendly, to do that. But maybe I shouldn't.

He was sure she would understand if he did not call her up. If years went by without a word from him. He was sure she would not blame him and would not forget him. She asked nothing, expected nothing of him.

He went up the stairs to wake Ildina, and it came into his mind that she expected the impossible from him. She was lying on her side, her rich dark hair loose on the pillow. Her pale face had a look of sullen unhappiness, even in sleep.

"I'm off," he said, kissing her cheek.

"Oh!" she said, sitting up and putting her arm around his neck. "Felix, you won't be taking the trip to the Coast today. That Bushey man said we mustn't leave Spruce Lake."

She looked triumphant. This, he thought, was all that Mimi's death meant to her. It had stopped Felix from getting away.

"No," he said. "I'll postpone it."

"You'll be home to lunch, Felix?"

"Yes," he said.

He got the car out of the garage, the car that Ildina had given him. He drove down the private road that everyone else must keep out of, and along the highway.

I've got to call up Taffy, he thought. It's too damned indifferent and offhand to let her go without a word.

He stopped at a drugstore where there was a booth. He got the Inn and asked for Miss Marlowe.

"Hello?" said her light sweet voice.

"It's me, Taffy. I just—"

"Oh," she said. "Can't you possibly call a little later? Mr. Bushey's here now."

He hung up the telephone without another word and went back to the car.

Bushey's there! he thought, overwhelmed. There with Taffy! But why? What does it mean?

There was nothing he could do.

He got back into the car, haunted by the echo of her gentle voice, by the vision of her, last night, in her white dress. He was utterly cut off from her now. If Ildina ever finds out about her, he thought. *How* could I have taken such a chance?

The factory was a cheerful place, red brick, with wide windows. On either side of the drive, lined with double rows of cars, were flowerbeds—his idea. His idea—to open a canteen where the workers could get tea and coffee and eat their lunches in comfort.

"You're good at personnel," Leroy Fuller, his father-in-law, had said, and that was a lot, coming from him, for he had no very high opinion of Felix. He had made him Personnel Manager, with a good salary, and he accepted almost all of Felix's proposals.

It was a good job, far better than anything Felix had ever had, or even expected. He had never been ambitious. He had always been able to earn enough money to live in the way he liked, and that had been just enough.

A job here, a deal there, buying, selling, on commission, in the West

Indies, Central America, Mexico. He had never been really hard up, never had been without decent clothes. He had been, always, the sort of young fellow who is asked to join the board of your Club or Tennis Club.

But he had never before been what he was now—settled, established, with many obligations. And with no freedom. This job he could not leave, or this town. Here was his life, lying straight and flat before him, the road he had chosen.

He had been learning to accept it. The job itself was interesting to him. He liked the neighbors. And if he and Ildina didn't get on very well, that would change and improve, as time went on. Whenever he was out of the house, away from her, he could forget all about it and be happy and careless.

But this morning a sort of desperation filled him. That straight, flat road before him, now seemed lined with high walls, over which he must never climb, never even look. Taffy was on the other side of the wall, free as air, wandering, tall, slight and lovely, wherever she pleased.

I can't see Taffy again, he thought. Maybe never again.

He went into the building and up to his office where his secretary, Miss Larsen, was waiting for him, the mail opened and sorted. When he had first come here, Frieda Larsen had been one of the typists, all sitting together in the big office.

She had never had a secretarial job. Felix had picked her out. She was far from being a glamorous girl, tall, bony and pale, with a big nose and long light hair, austerely dressed. She had had little hope of a position like this, and she knew it. She knew what Felix had done for her. And to repay him, she was the best secretary in the world, utterly devoted and loyal.

"I'll have to cancel my reservation," Felix told her.

"Oh, I'm sorry, Mr. Tellier!" she said. "A little change would have been good for you."

"By the way, what are you doing about your vacation?" he asked.

"Oh, we'll see how things work out," she answered. "Maybe you'll be going away later...."

All her plans depended upon him, and he wished it were not so.

He sat down and began to look over his mail, then studied the appointments she had written down for him. Before this, even when there had been a bad time with Ildina, he had slipped easily into the current of the business day, had been able to forget any exasperation, and could go back to her refreshed, in good humor, ready and willing to take a lot of trouble to make Ildina happy again.

But this morning he felt no interest in his work. He lighted one cigarette after the other, taking up the letters again and again, and looking at them with a frown, as if making some important decision.

He had an appointment at ten with a foreman in whose shop an unusual amount of friction had suddenly developed. With an effort he pulled himself together. He was able to talk to the man in the right way.

"Well, it could be I got mad too easy," said the foreman, a Swede, with a long, sober face. "You see, Mr. Tellier, I got trouble at home." It came out, in a slow, steady sing-song. "My wife, she wants to spend, spend, spend. You make good money, what you so stingy for? Don't you want me to have nothing nice?"

"Do you give her an allowance?" he asked.

"To run the house, yes. To buy all the monkey business she wants, no. I tell that woman, good times don't last forever. I don't get no younger. In the good times I save for the bad times. But no, every morning she's at me. She sees a fur coat. She wants to put down money, pay installments for it. I never buy installments. What we buy, we pay for cash."

"No children, have you, Jensen?"

"No," said Jensen. "No. When we had, it would be difference."

"That's hard on Mrs. Jensen."

"It's hard," Jensen admitted.

"If you told her you'd give her a little extra every week," Felix suggested.

"Already she gets too much. Spends, spends, spends. All kinds of monkey business."

"If you gave her a little more, if you told her she could get the fur coat when she'd saved enough cash, I bet you'd see a big change," said Felix. "She'd be more careful, if she had something to save for. And she'd be happy."

"She's got a good home. A good, steady man. What she has to have a fur coat for?"

"It'll make her proud of you. She'll tell the other women! 'See how much my husband thinks of me.'"

That appealed to Jensen. He was stubborn and yielded slowly, but the picture of himself as an outstandingly generous husband, envied by other women, took hold of his imagination.

"Well, we see," he said, rising. "Women make plenty trouble, Mr. Tellier."

CHAPTER IX

Domestic troubles and drink, Felix thought. Same old story, over and over. When a man's unhappy at home he starts to slip on his job.

"Mr. Bushey to see you, Mr. Tellier," said Miss Larsen.

"Oh," said Felix. "Bring him in, please."

It was necessary to placate Bushey. He rose and stood waiting for him, with a smile. But Bushey did not smile.

"Good morning," Bushey said.

"Morning. Sit down, won't you? Cigarette?"

"I don't smoke, thank you," said Bushey, and sat down opposite the desk, pale, severe, noble. "Captain Wicks is conducting the police investigation very ably, but I, personally, am questioning the people involved in this case."

"I see," said Felix.

"And I'm not at all satisfied," said Bushey, looking straight at Felix. He was obviously in a very ill-humor, and that could be dangerous.

"I'm getting no cooperation," he said, raising his voice a little. "A woman has been murdered, and the members of her social circle show no willingness whatever to cooperate with me in my investigation. On the contrary, information is being deliberately withheld."

"By whom, for instance?" Felix asked, very uneasy.

"By your wife, for one," said Bushey. "I've just seen Mrs. Tellier again and she was—I can't call it anything but hostile. Openly hostile. She even goes so far as to impugn my motives."

"She doesn't mean that," said Felix. "It's simply—"

"Mrs. Tellier suggests that I am determined to find someone in her social circle guilty. She went so far as to use the word 'persecution.'"

Oh, God! thought Felix. Why does she get her back up this way? It's bad. It's dangerous.

"She's naturally very much upset," he explained, feebly enough.

"I don't find her so," said Bushey. "I don't find Mrs. Tellier unduly disturbed by the murder of the woman who had been her hostess that evening. I'll admit, Mr. Tellier, that if it had not been for the clear and convincing evidence of Miss Jenkins—"

"Who's Miss Jenkins?"

"You don't know the name?" said Bushey, still more affronted. "This young woman has been employed by you for a year, and you don't know her name? Very well, let us call her Carrie."

"What evidence did she give?" Felix asked.

"She was able to testify definitely that Mrs. Tellier came home with you in your car at a time which establishes the fact that she could not have been near the Club when the shot was fired. She told me that you and Mrs. Tellier were sitting on the terrace of your house when I telephoned."

It was Taffy she saw, thought Felix. It's got to stay like that.

"*Otherwise*, I should find Mrs. Tellier's account of her activities last night extremely—" said Bushey, he paused—"suspicious."

"Oh, but, see here!" said Felix. "My wife scarcely knew Mimi—Mrs. Depew."

"Mrs. Tellier suddenly rose from the table and left the party. She made no excuses. She did not take leave of her hostess, or of anyone else. According to her own story, she simply walked out of the clubhouse, in formal evening dress. She did not send for a taxi. She set off on foot. She went down the drive to the highway and there, at precisely that moment, you came by in your car. That's a remarkable coincidence, Mr. Tellier."

"Yes," Felix admitted. "But those things do happen."

"A very remarkable coincidence," said Bushey.

Felix lighted a cigarette.

If you knew Ildina, he thought, it's not so damn surprising to hear that she walked out on a party. But if you didn't know her, and if she were arrogant and hostile about it, it would look queer. She'd have to be more civil to Bushey.

"There are several remarkable features in this case," Bushey went on. "The other guests at the birthday party all take the same attitude as Mrs. Tellier. They all talk about 'a tramp.' Even the deceased man's husband."

"But that's natural enough. Who else could have done it?"

"I don't find it natural. Every indication points to a premeditated crime. Yet every member of her social circle shows the same desire to hush the thing up. It won't work, Mr. Tellier."

"I don't think anyone wants to hush it up," said Felix. "It's simply that nobody knows anything."

"I'm by no means convinced of that, Mr. Tellier. By no means!" He rose and pushed back the thick dark hair behind one ear, in a gesture of stern impatience. "I am convinced that a majority of the members of Mrs. Depew's social circle whom I have interviewed, have deliberately withheld information."

"You don't mean you think one of her friends had anything to do with it?" Felix asked, astounded.

"I said 'information,' Mr. Tellier. I believe that many of the dead woman's friends could give me important information as to the motives behind this crime. I came here this morning in the hope that you can volunteer something."

"But I don't know anything."

"I suggest that you know the undercurrent in that circle, Mr. Tellier. You know the jealousies, the quarrels, the rivalries beneath the surface."

"I don't. I give you my word I don't know of anyone who ever had a grudge against poor Mimi."

"I understand that the late Mrs. Depew was in the habit of drinking in bars, in the company of men other than her husband."

"You couldn't call it a 'habit.' Sometimes she'd take a drink with someone she knew, at the Club, at a hotel."

"Did Mrs. Depew frequently drink with you?"

"No. Not frequently."

"Mr. Tellier. What is your impression of the relations between the late Mrs. Depew and her husband?"

"Oh, very harmonious," said Felix.

Well, harmonious enough. Edgar Depew was a good twenty-five years older than his wife, a stiff and formal man, wonderfully boring. Mimi had laughed at him a little. She had laughed at everything, but she had, Felix thought, a genuine appreciation of the man's integrity and decency and his great generosity to her.

"Mr. Tellier, I suggest that you are not fully cooperating with me in this investigation," said Bushey.

"I give you my word I don't know anything whatever that could help you."

"And you're not particularly interested, are you, Mr. Tellier, in discovering and punishing the murderer of this woman who was, you admit, a friend of yours."

As a matter of fact, I'm not, Felix thought, surprised. He had not given a moment's thought to Mimi's possible killer. His first anxiety had been to keep Taffy out of this. He was concerned now with protecting Ildina from the consequences of her own arrogance.

"I intend to solve this case," said Bushey. "I intend to find the *motive* behind this wanton killing, and the motive will lead me straight to the murderer. I shall succeed, Mr. Tellier. Make no mistake about it."

Felix believed that. It was all very well for Ildina to fight the man's obsession with "social circles" and be so offensive and ridiculous, all very well to be amused by his theatrical looks, his grandiloquent speech, but was it wise? There was a fiery, almost furious energy in him, a formidable doggedness.

"I wish you luck," said Felix.

CHAPTER X

At noon Felix left his office and went out of the building. The workers were streaming out from the side entrances, and he stopped at the head of the steps, waiting until the drive was clear.

There were men stopping to light pipes, men and women lighting cigarettes. There were pretty girls in slacks with bright bandannas on their heads.

In this weather, few people used the cafeteria. Some of them went across the road to the diner that stood there. Some of the men beyond sat on the grassy bank to open their lunch boxes.

He watched them with a pang of envy. Even the middle-aged men with lined faces were having this hour of freedom. They could relax, they could talk to each other. They belonged to a brotherhood from which he was shut out now.

He lighted a cigarette himself and got into his car. And he hated the car. He was one of the big shots now, and he hated that. Beyond anything he would have liked to go into the diner, sit on a stool, and talk to anyone, say anything he pleased, with no thought of tact or expediency.

He wanted and tried, to think about Mimi, but he could not. He thought of Ildina. I'll have to warn her about Bushey, he thought. Bushey could make a lot of trouble for her if he felt like it. If she keeps on needling him, he'll concentrate on her. He'll question her until she loses her temper and gives herself away.

Of course, Bushey doesn't seriously suspect her of strolling out of the club and shooting Mimi through the window, Felix told himself. But if he finds out that I didn't pick her up in the car, he could use that as an excuse to make things damned unpleasant for her.

He turned into that private road and up to the house. He got out, reluctant and heavy-hearted and went into the hall. The sound of a voice from the library stopped him.

"Oh, Lord!" he said to himself. "That's too much."

It was Leroy Fuller's voice. He and his father-in-law had never had any sort of quarrel, no significant, open disagreement. Yet there was not one subject upon which they did not at heart disagree.

Moving forward a few steps, Felix could see Fuller in there, standing with his back to a window, a tall, lean man, all brown, a weather-beaten face with high cheekbones, a sardonic mouth, light brown hair, alert brown eyes. Ildina was leaning back in her chair, looking up at him—

the one person in the world, Felix thought, whom she wholly trusted.

He sighed and went into the room.

"Hello!" he said, holding out his hand. "It's a surprise to have you here."

And, as always when his father-in-law came here, Felix was acutely aware that this was Ildina's house, not his. He was not a host welcoming a guest.

"I read in the morning's paper about this shooting at your clubhouse," Fuller said. "Saw Ildina's name so I came out."

"What did it say about Ildina?" Felix asked.

"Here—" said Fuller, taking up a newspaper and stabbing at a paragraph with his forefinger.

"Among the guests questioned by District Attorney Francis Bushey," Fuller read aloud, "was Mrs. Ildina Tellier, daughter of Leroy Fuller, well-known leather manufacturer …"

Mrs. "Ildina"—daughter of Leroy Fuller—wife of nobody in particular. Felix unfolded the paper and saw a picture of Mimi, thin and laughing. SLAIN SOCIETY MATRON. Seeing it here before him in print, he realized for the first time the sheer drama of the thing. That gay pretty young woman, shot dead at her birthday party, among her friends, her husband at her side!

"It's incredible!" Felix said "Who'd do such a thing?"

"You don't know much about her, do you?" Fuller asked. "Only since you've come here?"

"Not much," said Felix. "But there was nothing very subtle about Mimi. Easy to see what type she was."

"There aren't any 'types,'" said Fuller.

"She was a bitch," said Ildina.

"Ildina!" Felix protested.

"Lunch is served, madam," said Carrie, from the doorway, and Ildina rose and led the way to the dining room.

"What do you think of *this*, Felix?" she asked.

"Of what, Ildina?"

"This!" she said, leaning forward and touching the fluted silver in the center of the table.

"Oh—very nice," said Felix.

"I had it made," she said. "I ordered it eight months ago, to surprise you and it just came this morning."

"Very nice," Felix said again.

The blank, sullen look so familiar to him, came over her face. He had disappointed her and he knew it. She wanted and expected him to notice and praise all the things that she bought, and as a rule, he tried, just to make her happy. But not today. What she had said about Mimi, her whole attitude toward this tragedy, sickened and angered him.

"What I'm going to do is to look into the woman's past history," said Fuller. "I've got a man on the job already."

"The police will, probably."

"I've got my own man," said Fuller. "He's a fellow I've used before." He began to eat the jellied madrilène before him. "Ildina tells me this fellow Bushey has got it in for her."

"He needs careful handling," said Felix briefly.

"Maybe," said Fuller. "And maybe he needs to have the fear of God put into him."

Fear of Leroy Fuller is what you mean, thought Felix. He's to tremble before Leroy Fuller and his money. Well, he won't.

For the first time in his life, Felix, himself, felt sullen. He made no more effort to lighten the meal than did Ildina herself. So that's going to be the line, he thought.

In order to keep Bushey from "annoying" Ildina, they're going to try to dig up something to discredit Mimi. Anything will do. They'll find something, something foolish. Mimi wasn't any too discreet. They'll distort it into something shameful. But there's one thing they won't be able to do. They won't buy Bushey. And they won't frighten him.

The soup was removed and Carrie brought in crab meat in ramekins.

"This is good," said Fuller.

There was no more conversation. It's a funny thing, Felix thought, but there's nothing much worse than a meal in silence. It gets you down.

"No coffee, thanks," he said. "I'll have to be getting back."

"I want a word with you first," said Fuller.

"You'll be here when I get back, won't you?" said Felix. "I have an appointment."

"This won't keep," said Fuller. "You'll excuse us, Ildina."

"Go in the library," she said. "I'll stay here and drink my coffee."

All their words were like commands, they were together, side by side, and he was an outsider.

In the library he lighted a cigarette and remained standing, and Fuller, too.

"There's this," said Fuller. "Ildina told me about leaving the party and walking home alone through the woods. No reason why she shouldn't. She made a mistake, telling Bushey you picked her up."

"I agree with you," said Felix. "I don't think he believed it."

"He believes it, all right," said Fuller. "On account of this girl, Carrie." He took a leather cigarette case out of his pocket. "I had a talk with Carrie this morning," he said. "Mina's very pleased with the girl. Thinks she told Bushey that tale about seeing Ildina on the terrace simply out of loyalty."

Felix started, and turned his head away a little.

"Ildina's wrong," said Leroy Fuller. "I talked to Carrie, went over her story carefully. She didn't see or hear Ildina come in the side door. She believes she did see her with you on the terrace. All right. Who was it she saw out there?"

It seemed to Felix that every nerve and muscle in his body tautened, to meet this danger. This was something to fight.

"Nobody," said Felix. "It's her imagination."

"There was someone there all right," said Leroy Fuller. "Some woman you brought here. You might as well tell me."

"There was nobody," said Felix. He didn't much care whether Fuller believed him or not. This was a thing to fight and he would fight it.

"Very well," said Fuller, "I'll find out."

CHAPTER XI

On the way back to the factory, Felix stopped again at the drugstore and telephoned to Miss Marlowe at the Inn. Miss Marlowe's room did not answer.

"Any message, sir?" asked the operator.

"Nothing, thanks," said Felix.

No message. He could not speak to Taffy, could not see her. He was utterly cut off from her. But he had to warn her. He must tell her to leave here at once. Still shut in the booth, he lighted a cigarette and tried to think of a way. Again he thought, and called Augie's number.

"This is Mr. West's residence," said a deep grave voice.

"Mr. Tellier would like to speak to him," said Felix and in a few moments Augie's eager voice sounded in his ear.

"Felix?"

"Augie, look here. I won't go into details now, but I want Miss Marlowe to get out of this place at once. This afternoon. Can you give her that message?"

"But Felix, there are some complications."

"What? What complications?"

"Felix, could you stop around here? Then I could explain things. Stop in for a drink after you leave the office?"

"Yes," said Felix promptly.

"Around five-thirty, say?"

"Yes," Felix said, again. "No! Wait … Four-thirty, if it suits you, Augie."

Because if he was not home by six, Ildina would telephone to the office.

"Any time suits me, Felix," said Augie. "Any time at all."

What did he mean by *complications?* Felix asked himself. There's nothing to stop her from leaving here, and she's got to go. Before Fuller finds out anything more. She's *got* to go.

He left his office at a quarter to four—so tense, so anxious that he believed himself to be angry. Angry at Augie, for speaking of complications. Angry at Denise for abandoning her daughter; angry even at Taffy because she had not already left here. She ought to care more about herself, he thought. A girl like her can't go wandering about like that. She ought to get an apartment with another girl. She ought to visit an aunt or someone.

He had never been inside Augie's house but he had sat on the veranda two or three times. He was accustomed to the exterior, an old house finely proportioned, with tall white pillars up the front, set among noble old trees.

"Too big," the real estate agent had explained once to Felix. "White elephant, a place like that. People are kicking because I sold the place to this funny little guy. They say it's spoiled the neighborhood. But hell, Felix! That place had been on the market for God knows how many years, and then along comes this little guy, checkbook in hand …"

Felix mounted the steps and crossed the wide veranda. He rang the bell and the door was opened promptly by Augie's butler, a genuine import from England, and faultless except that he was a very old man.

"Good afternoon, sir," he said. "Mr. West is expecting you, sir." He took Felix's hat, and led him down the hall, past a handsome and somewhat florid drawing room on one side, a somewhat somber dining room opposite it to a room in the back of the house. Like the others, this room was large and lofty, but it was simple, with a bare, polished floor and white curtains at the windows, and bare pearl-gray walls.

Against the inner wall stood two grand pianos side by side and across from this a little oasis of coziness, a Chinese rug before the fireplace, a long gleaming table with blue and yellow china inkstand and candlesticks to match, two blue armchairs, each with a small table beside it.

On the white mantelpiece was a plaster bust, one of these musical johnnies, Felix thought, looking at the thin, sorrowful face, the hair brushed back from the forehead with a vertical furrow above the nose.

"That's my brother," said Augie's voice behind him.

"I didn't know you had a brother," Felix said.

"He's gone now," said Augie. "He's dead. But you'd be surprised if you heard his name. He was world-famous."

In ordinary circumstances, Felix would have asked questions, encouraged Augie to talk about his brother. But not now.

"Miss Marlowe ought to go home," he said. "What did you mean by 'complications,' Augie?"

"Sit down, Felix. Will you have tea? Or Mason can make a mean mint julep."

"That would be fine. Now let's hear."

Augie rang a bell set in the wall, and gave his order to Mason, then he sat down in the second armchair.

"Well, you see, Felix, the police started to check on any strangers that were in this neighborhood last night, and that led them to Taffy." A dark flush rose in his face. "She asked me to call her that. She told me to call her that."

"All right. Go ahead."

"Well, Bushey went to see her, and he seemed to think the whole thing was pretty phony. I mean, a girl like that, a society girl, coming to the Inn after two o'clock and without a reservation."

"Yes. He would think that."

"He wanted to know why she'd come here, and she said she'd heard about the place from me. She told him it was such a nice night, she started to walk. She said she asked someone for directions and when she found it was a couple of miles, she stopped at the filling station and called me up, and I came and drove her to the Inn. That was quick thinking, Felix."

"Did it satisfy Bushey?"

"Well, more or less. But he told her to stick around for a while."

"I don't believe he has any right to do that, if she wants to go home."

"It's better not to start anything, Felix."

"Why? She's got nothing to do with his damned investigation. I want her to get away from here, at once. I've got good reasons."

"Well, she'll be over in a few moments, Felix."

"Here?"

"Yes. She wants me to take her out to dinner. She had me over to the Inn for lunch today. You see, Felix, it's her idea we ought to be seen around together. I mean, to make it look natural."

"Yes," said Felix.

It was probably a good idea. The best in the circumstances, but he didn't like it. He did not want her here, within striking distance of Leroy Fuller.

"As soon as Bushey left here, she called me up and told me what she'd said to him, so that when he got here, I was ready for him," Augie went on. "We're saying that we used to go around together in New York. Everything looks good, Felix. We've even got it fixed about that diner.

If the fellow there comes forward, we're saying I left her there while I went on an errand, and you happened along, on your way home and then I came back for her."

"That doesn't fit in with her starting to walk. The fellow in the diner probably saw us all get into my car."

"Our story is, we get out at the station. I have to go home for a phone call and she says she'll take the first taxi that turns up, see? Then she gets tired of waiting and she starts to walk to the Inn."

"It's phony, all right," said Felix.

"It's phony," Augie agreed. "But I guess we'll get by with it."

And the thing that lay behind all these "complications," the reason for this, had not been mentioned. All this elaborate network of lies had been constructed only to hide one fact, that Taffy had sat for ten minutes on the terrace of his house. No, *Ildina's* house. And that fact had to be concealed at any cost, as carefully as if it were an actual crime.

"I wish I'd never brought her out here!" Felix cried. "I ought to have known better."

"She's not blaming you, Felix."

"She never blames anybody."

"She was telling me how you first met, and all that," Augie went on. "She said it seemed like every time she was feeling low about things, you'd come along and make it all right. And that goes for me, too, Felix."

"How do you mean?" Felix asked, with a quick frown.

"There have been times, Felix," said Augie earnestly, "when I've been just about what you'd say at the end of my tether. Then you'd come along. You'd say come and have a drink, something like that. Out of this world you are."

"Me?"

"A prince," said Augie. "That's what the bartender in the Tavern said the other day, Felix. 'Mr. Tellier's a prince,' he said. You make people happy, somehow. Maybe because the things that bother other people don't bother you."

CHAPTER XII

Mason came in then with two frosted glasses on a tray. Felix took a sip, vaguely troubled by Augie's words. But he dismissed that.

"There's this," he began, when the doorbell rang.

"Here she is," said Augie, springing to his feet.

He went out of the room, and came back in a moment with Taffy.

But had she always been like this? he thought. Had she changed, or was it that he had never seen before what she was? She was wearing a sheer, pale-blue blouse with long sleeves, and a black skirt, and two little blue flowers at her temples. She stood beside Augie, a little taller than he, straight and easy and gentle. And she was not that sweet, dreamy child, wandering through a fairy tale, whom he could make happy with a present, a treat.

He noticed the faint hollow beneath her cheekbones, the patient set of her mouth. All these nine years she had been living her own life, not an easy one, not a happy one, and he had never thought of that.

Time after time he had come back to her, like someone eagerly opening a closed door to take out a treasured object, to look at it, admire it, rejoice in it. And look it up again.

He had never wondered what she did or what she thought. She was simply *there*, part of his life. He could not imagine life without her. Wherever he had gone he had found things to send to Taffy, things to please her, or make her laugh. Whenever he had turned homeward it was Taffy he was going back to, certain that she was waiting.

She had waited, and he had deserted her. She was the best and dearest thing he had ever had, and he had let her go. He stood before her now, empty-handed. There was nothing he could bring her now but pain and trouble.

"Taffy, I'm sorry," he said.

Her fingers tightened over his for a moment, then she drew away her hand.

"Well, don't be, Felix," she said.

"When did Bushey say you could leave?"

"Oh. A couple of days, he said. But I don't mind a bit. I like the Inn, and Augie's taking me around and giving me a good time."

"I'll see about some more drinks," said Augie, and went out of the room.

Taffy sat down in one of the blue armchairs, and Felix sat on the edge of the long table, beside her.

"I'm afraid there's going to be trouble," he said.

"I don't think so, Felix."

It was almost impossible to say what he had to say.

"You see, Taffy ... Ildina's father knows there was someone on the terrace with me."

"But, after all, Felix, that's nothing so awful," she said.

"He could make it pretty bad."

"Felix, I've seen for myself how much gossip people can live through, and be none the worse for it."

She means her mother, he thought. But that's altogether different. Denise loves the limelight; she makes a drama out of everything. And she's the sort of woman who can get away with anything. But not Taffy.

He heard the doorbell ring, and it made him uneasy. Everything could do that now. He felt like a criminal—guilty, fearful, ready to start at a shadow. And now he heard the voice least welcome to him of any in the world.

"I want to see Mr. Tellier."

"Yes, sir," said the butler. "I'll see if he's here, sir."

"He's here," snapped Leroy Fuller. "Take this and pay off my taxi. No tip for that highway robber."

"Excuse me, sir. If you'll be kind enough to wait here, sir."

But Leroy Fuller did not wait. He came on down the hall and stopped in the doorway of the music room. Felix rose, cold with dismay. It seemed to him the greatest possible misfortune that Fuller should ever set eyes on Taffy.

"Saw your car outside," said Fuller. "So I thought you'd give me a lift home."

Augie came in then, with three frosted glasses on a tray. He stopped, looking up at the newcomer,

"You West?" asked Fuller.

"Yes. Yes, I am."

"I stopped in to see you," said Fuller. "But it'll keep. Some other time, when you're alone."

He looked now at Taffy, sitting in the blue armchair, and she looked up at him, steadily.

"How about an introduction?" said Fuller.

"But—I don't know your name," said Augie.

"Felix does," said Fuller.

Felix was silent. He knew well enough how futile this was, but he would not, he could not, speak her name to Leroy Fuller.

"Well?" said Fuller.

"My name is Stephanie Marlowe," she said.

"I've been hearing about you," said Fuller. "You're the mysterious stranger who arrived at the Inn last night. You're in the evening paper. Ready, Felix?"

"Yes," Felix said. "Good night," he said to Taffy, and "Good night" to Augie, standing there with the tray.

They went out, and got into the roadster. Fuller brought out a newspaper stuffed behind the seat, and read aloud.

"'Society Girl Quizzed in Club Slaying.' I was going to get around to her, but I had West first on my list."

"What 'list'?" Felix asked.

"West's home is right in line with the Club. Must be able to see the

Club from his windows."

"Are you going to suggest that Augie West walked out of his house and shot a woman he'd never spoken to?"

"You'd be surprised at all I'm going to suggest," said Leroy Fuller, with a sort of grim joyousness. "I didn't know I'd have the luck to kill two birds with one stone."

"Who are your birds?"

"I'm going to get Bushey off Ildina's neck. He's making her nervous. And I'm going to get you out of the picture, I hope."

"Just how?"

"I never wanted Ildina to marry you," said Leroy Fuller. "You knew that. I tried to make her see what you are. A lightweight. A damn playboy. Condescending."

"'Condescending?'"

"That's the word," said Fuller. "You were going to make the poor little rich girl happy. Show her how to live and all that. Well, you haven't done it. She's not happy."

This open hostility surprised and disconcerted Felix. He had known from the beginning that his father-in-law had no high opinion of him, but this direct attack was completely unexpected.

"Suppose you let Ildina and me manage our own affairs," he said.

"Nope," said Fuller with the same air of cool satisfaction. "I'm going to tell her."

"Tell her what?"

"That you brought a woman here," said Fuller. "Now I know who the woman was."

"If you do—" Felix began and stopped.

"If I do, then what?" Fuller demanded.

Then what?

CHAPTER XIII

Leroy Fuller got out and went into the house, and Felix drove the car into the garage.

I've got to get hold of myself, he thought. Let him tell Ildina. There's nothing to tell. This isn't serious.

But when he lighted a cigarette, his hand was unsteady. I'd better deny everything, he thought. Better say I don't know Taffy, never saw her before today. She's someone that Augie knows. That's all. I'll keep her out of this, no matter what I have to say or do.

He walked slowly to the house, making an almost desperate effort at nonchalance.

I've got to remember that I'm not guilty, he thought. I must not feel guilty. I've done nothing to offend or injure Ildina.

He felt that if he kept that in mind, he could deal better with whatever was coming. He was going to lie, but it was a harmless lie. There was nothing wrong to conceal. Nothing.

He opened the door with his latch key and entered the house.

"Felix?" Ildina called from the library, and as he entered, Leroy Fuller rose and strolled off to the dining room, at home here. Ildina was leaning back in an armchair, her long legs straight out, ankles crossed. She was smoking a cigarette in a cardboard holder.

"Who is this Marlowe woman?" she asked evenly.

He could not go on with this.

"Ildina," he said, standing before her. "Whatever your father has told you, I give you my word there's nothing in it."

"I don't believe your word," she said. "You told me you saw me at the Club. You thought I was safely out of the way, and you brought this woman here, to *my* house."

"It's—not like that," he said.

"Then what is it like?" she asked. "Who is she? You left your office early. You went to your common little Augie's house to meet her."

"Ildina," he said. "Don't go on. It's—"

"It's *what?*"

"I can't explain to you," he said "You wouldn't believe anything I said."

"Don't bother," she said. "Dad's got a man investigating that woman. He'll find out about her. Everything about her."

"There's nothing to find out. She's a well-bred, well-behaved girl."

"Oh! You admit that you know her!"

"I've known her since she was a kid," he said.

"And you've never even mentioned her name to me."

"Why the devil should I? You'd only have twisted the whole thing into something cheap and ugly. As you always do. You wouldn't believe I had any decency. You won't believe I've been faithful to you."

"You haven't!" she said, rising. "Never! You've cheated me from the very beginning. I was miserable and you thought it would be fun to make me happy. But it wasn't fun, was it? I just didn't turn into someone like you. Someone absolutely shallow and heartless.

"When I married you it was because I didn't want anyone else. But right from the beginning you liked other people just as much as me. And now you like other people more, much, much more. This Marlowe woman—"

"Leave her out of this, please," said Felix curtly.

"I won't! I'll drag her into it. I'll make her wish she'd never heard of you."

"If you annoy her—"

"*I* 'annoy' *her?* This woman you brought into my house? She ran away fast enough that time. But the next time she won't get away. I'm going there."

"If you do that," said Felix, "I'm finished."

"I'm going to do it. I'm going to see her."

"Good-by," he said, and turned away.

He went out of the house and along the drive, and there was nothing in his heart but a hot anger that filled him with a driving energy. He didn't care where he went, what he did. I'll never go back, he thought. I can't stop her from going to see Taffy, making a scene, a scandal. But I'll never see her again. I'm finished.

He walked along the boulevard, keeping to the grass at one side. A stream of long-haul trucks was coming out from the city, and on the inside track of the broad road, private cars went by with a rush.

I have no car now, he thought, with a sudden curious pleasure, as if a burden had been lifted. No job either, he thought. Well, that's no headache. I've never had any trouble finding jobs, and I shan't now. I'll sign on with the Merchant Marine, go to sea again.

He thought of Taffy. No, he thought. I won't go away until there's no chance of any trouble for her. No, I'll get a job in a big automobile plant, working at a machine. Tomorrow. Maybe at noon, tomorrow, he would be sitting on a stool in a diner, a man among other men, saying what he pleased, able to get on with his fellows, and able to hold his own.

Through all his anger, his dread and anxiety about Taffy, the hopeful careless happiness native to him was rising again. It was a sweet, fresh hour. The sun was low in the clear lemon-colored sky and an inland breeze was blowing. He could forget his anger now, and begin again to feel at peace.

For he was profoundly, fundamentally good-tempered. There was no envy in him; he never wanted to take anything away from anyone. He had never in his life wanted to dominate anyone. He was ready enough to fight for his own when it was necessary, but he was never irritable or suspicious or uneasy. He could and he did let other people alone, and—more than anything else in the world—he wanted to be let alone himself.

He was alone now, with the fresh wind blowing on his face, and a healthy hope beginning to stir. I'll stay at the Washington tonight, he thought. Then tomorrow I'll look around.

The Washington was a square red-brick building, flush with the street, facing the railroad station. He had been at the bar here before, and it was his wish to go there now, for a cocktail before dinner.

But as he stood at the desk, waiting for the clerk's attention, he dismissed the idea. He was too likely to find someone who knew him, who would ask him what he was doing there. For Ildina's sake, he didn't want that. Let her give any version she liked of his absence and he would back it up.

"Baggage, sir?" the clerk asked.

"Not tonight," Felix said. He paid for the room in advance and the clerk pushed forward the register.

For a moment he thought of using another name. Tellier might well be familiar to the clerk. But there were too many complications. He signed and took the key and went to the newsstand. He bought a paper book and three or four magazines and went upstairs in the elevator to his room. His beautiful room, bleak, neat, the walls sickly, a fuzzy green bedspread, a green runner on the chest of drawers.

Standing by the window, he looked down at the familiar street. He saw faces that were familiar to him. But he was alone here, and he was free.

I'll go out presently and get a toothbrush and razor, he thought. And to be without any possessions at all was like beginning life all over again.

Now he could telephone to Taffy without haste, without a sense of guilt and apprehension.

CHAPTER XIV

Felix did not intend to warn Taffy of Ildina's threat to visit her. He would have done anything in the world to prevent that, but he was helpless. The only solace he had was in his feeling that Taffy could endure a thing like that better than other people. He would hate it, but, he thought, she would soon be away from here and she would forget it.

I just want to speak to her, he thought. Just to let her know I'm here. Standing by. He called the Inn, and she was at home.

"Oh, Felix?" she said.

"I'm here at the Hotel Washington," he said.

"Oh, are you?" she said.

He knew it was not her way to ask questions, yet her polite acceptance of his news gave him an odd feeling of disappointment. He did not want to tell her, flatly, that he had left Ildina, but it must be obvious to her.

"Felix," she said. "Could we stop in and see you?"

"Here?"

"Yes. Augie's coming any moment to take me out to dinner somewhere. Could we stop and have a cocktail with you?"

He thought about that for a moment. But even if Ildina finds out about it, he thought, as long as she comes with Augie, it can't make things any worse. Only not in the lounge downstairs, not in public. That would be too much like an insult to Ildina. A cheerful little party as soon as he had left her.

"Better come straight up here," he said. "Room six-twelve."

"Six-twelve," she repeated. "In about half an hour, Felix."

He telephoned to the bar for a shaker of Martinis, and three glasses.

He washed, smoothed his short, neat hair with his hands, straightened his tie. He remembered that year he had had a bungalow in Trinidad, and used to ask people in for cocktails. His houseboy had made very good canapes. He would arrange flowers in the long sitting room, these added a nice air of festivity. He wanted that again. He wanted to see people in uncritical, unthinking friendliness.

He called the bar again.

"Look here!" he said, "can you send up some little things, sandwiches, something like that?"

"We got pretzels, sir," answered a hopeless voice. "And peanuts. That's all."

Felix glanced at his watch and went downstairs, to the drugstore next to the hotel. He bought cigarettes and then wandered around, looking in the showcase.

"Can I help you?" said the girl behind the counter.

"Just looking," said Felix. "I thought there might be something for a little party?"

The girl was interested at once.

"Well ..." she said, musing. "I don't know ... Well, listen! We've got these, left over from Easter."

From under the counter she brought out a cardboard box, and in it were little crepe paper baskets, pink, green and yellow.

"What are they?" Felix asked.

"You put candy in them," she explained. "You put them around at everybody's place."

"Have you got any candy?"

"Oh, yes! These fruit drops would look cute."

He bought three baskets, and, on the girl's recommendation, a package of paper napkins with a floral design. When he got back to his room, the cocktails were there, and the waiter.

"Thank you, sir," said the waiter and departed.

Felix spread three napkins on the table, and set the baskets, a little crumpled, a little dusty, on them. He was, as always, completely without self-consciousness. He was never bothered by the fear that he might be ridiculous. Simply, he had wanted a touch of something festive and this was the best he could do. He was entertaining guests in his own home and he was pleased about it.

There was a knock at the door. He opened it and Taffy was there, tall, very slight in a black dress, with a little black hat on the back of her head.

"Hello, Felix."

"Hello, Taffy. Where's Augie?"

"He's coming later."

I'll leave the door open till he comes, Felix thought. Better that way.

"Sit here, Taffy," he said. "By the window. There! Shall we wait for Augie, or will you have a drink now?"

"Oh, let's wait!" she said, drawing off her black gloves. "Augie's having a very bad time now."

"How? What's wrong?"

"He didn't want to tell you, but I thought you'd rather hear now."

"Yes. Certainly."

"Mr. Fuller's found out a lot of things, in just this little while." she said. "He's—" She paused.

"Yes!" said Felix. "He's a go-getter and a human dynamo, and all that. What's he found out?"

"Well … when Mrs. Depew was shot, there was a man standing beside her. MacLoughlin is his name."

"Oh, yes! I know him."

"Mr. Fuller says the shot was meant for MacLoughlin. He says Augie hates him."

"Well, he doesn't," said Felix. "But if he did, he'd be justified. MacLoughlin's a damn snob and a stuffed shirt. He's done every mean, petty thing you could imagine, to get Augie out of here. But is Fuller suggesting that Augie took a gun and tried to kill him?"

"Yes."

"That's damn nonsense! Even the people who can't stand Augie wouldn't believe that."

"You see," said Taffy. "He's been arrested for murder before."

"What!"

"He was accused of murdering his brother five years ago."

"Taffy, I don't believe it!"

"He told me about it himself. He lived with his brother in some very deluxe Park Avenue apartment. It was summer and they'd given the servants a holiday. But one of the maids came back unexpectedly to get something, and she found Louis, the brother, with his throat cut. Augie was sleeping so soundly they couldn't wake him. They took him to a hospital. They said he'd killed his brother and then tried to kill himself with sleeping pills."

"My God!" said Felix, his face turning white.

"His brother had left him a great deal of money. One of the elevator boys had overheard them quarreling earlier that evening. Augie says it's true. They did quarrel. Louis was getting involved with a woman Augie thought was ruining him, spoiling his work, and his whole life. He'd been so upset by the quarrel that he took sleeping medicine. He thinks that maybe, without meaning to, he repeated the dose and it proved fatal."

Taffy took a deep breath. "Anyhow he was arrested and sent to prison without bail," she went on. "But before the trial, the woman he didn't like, came forward with a letter Louis had written her just before he died. He'd told her he was going to cut his throat. So they let Augie go. He changed his name and he tried to start over again. Only he loved his brother so …"

"They can't have any case against Augie for this thing."

"He had a license for a gun," said Taffy. "He says he can't find the gun."

"Even that's nothing."

Taffy shook her head, her expression troubled and uneasy.

"He's got what the police think is a motive," said Taffy. "He had the opportunity, too. He could have got out of his house by a side door without any of the servants noticing, and he could have got back the same way. It's only a few moments' walk to the Club right across the hilltop."

"Taffy! How is he taking it?"

"He's—crushed," she said. "That's the only word for it. He's so kindly, so desperately anxious to be friendly to everybody. He can't understand how he could even be suspected of such a horrible thing."

CHAPTER XV

Felix was silent, standing beside her chair, his fair head bent. He was startled to realize how easily he had forgotten about Mimi and her cruel death. He was surprised to realize how little concerned he was with justice, how little he felt even of curiosity.

His paramount care had been to keep Taffy out of this.

"Taffy," he said. "When is Bushey going to let you go?"

"He'd let me go now," she said. "He doesn't approve of me. He thinks I'm a frivolous 'society girl,' but he's not interested in me as a suspect. It's the police now. Captain Wicks and Mr. Fuller."

"Fuller has no authority to keep you here."

"He puts ideas into Captain Wicks' head. He's found out things about us, too, Felix. That we've known each other a long time. That you came to Mother's reception. He's found people who saw us leave the house together in your car."

That was a hard thing, a hard thing to hear.

"But, after all," Felix said. "Nobody can make anything much out of that."

"I didn't know—" she said.

"Didn't know what, Taffy?"

"I didn't know that you—weren't happy," she said. "If I had known, I wouldn't have come with you."

"I'm afraid I don't quite understand, Taffy."

"Ever since we first met I've thought of you as being happy," she said. "It was a wonderful thing to think. It was a comfort. Sometimes, when the whole world looked so mixed up and miserable, I'd think, well, there's Felix. He's one person who isn't mixed up and miserable. I thought your marriage was like that. Just happy and clear."

"No," he said briefly. "It was a mistake."

"If I'd known that, I'd never have seen you."

"But, Taffy, I don't see—"

"I wouldn't want you to be happy with me."

"Taffy, you're not responsible. It wouldn't have lasted anyhow. It was a mistake, altogether. From the beginning. My mistake. My fault. But now it's over."

"You're not going back?"

"No," he said.

She turned away her head. She moved so that he could see her face.

There were tears caught in her lashes. And he'd never seen her in tears before.

"Taffy, dear, what's wrong?" he cried and when she did not answer, he took her hand. "Taffy, dear!"

"I'm so sorry," she said. "So sorry!"

"Well, don't be. It's not a tragedy, dear. Ildina's young and very good-looking. She'll get over this. She'll marry someone else."

"Don't!" she said. "Please don't. I've heard that so many times, from so many other people. I *don't believe* it, Felix. It can't be true."

"Don't believe what, dear? That a marriage can be simply a mistake? And that people have a right to another chance?"

"About 'getting over it,'" she said. "I've seen so many divorced couples being so friendly together. And of all the couples I know, there's one who hasn't got over it."

"Well, that's hard luck," said Felix. "But, after all, if one of them is damn wretched in the marriage—"

She tried to draw away her hand, but he held it tight. She looked up at him then, her gray eyes brilliant with tears.

"When you get married, it's like opening a door into your life," she said. "You ask, you beg somebody there to come in. You ask the person to live there, and be at home, and share everything with you. Then you get bored, or irritated. You ask the person you invited to come in to go out. You want to be alone, or you want someone else. The one who's sent away *doesn't* 'get over it.'"

He was impressed and dismayed by her fervor.

"But, Taffy," he said. "Do you mean you think people ought to stay together even if one of them is a drunkard, or a brute, or utterly unfaithful, for instance?"

"Those are big things," she said. "I've known so many people who got divorces, but never for one of the big things. Always from boredom and irritation, or just wanting a change."

"Don't you think there's any case for happiness, Taffy?"

"Being happy can't be a *reason* for anything. And if you have to be cruel to snake yourself happy ... I've known people who wouldn't turn away an old servant, no matter how trying and disagreeable and useless she was. But they'd turn away the husband or wife they'd chosen."

"Taffy, we can all make mistakes," he said.

"Then we can pay for them," she said.

Her hand moved in his but he could not bear to let her go.

"Taffy," he said. "Maybe you don't quite understand, dear."

"Oh, I do!" she said. "Father got tired of Mother. That's what it really was. He thought he'd like someone else for a change. I was only a little girl but I used to listen to Mother talking to her friends. She was horribly hurt and humiliated, but she was wonderful about it. She had the same idea that *you* have. She thought Father had a right to be free if he felt like it.

"She gave him a divorce as quickly as she could. She was lonely and unhappy, and she married again. And when she got tired of poor old Jeff, she asked him for a divorce. He cried. I saw him. I was terribly fond of Jeff. I was only thirteen but he talked to me. He said, 'I haven't any right to try to keep Denise ...'"

"Taffy," he said, and released he hand.

"Yes, Felix?"

But he did not know anything more to say. She thought the less of him for his wretched marriage. She wanted him to go back to it.

And I can't, he thought. I've got away now. I'm not going back.

The elevator door rattled open and someone was coming along the corridor.

In a moment Augie stood in the doorway, smiling anxiously, his hands twitching with nervousness.

"Sorry I'm late, Felix," he said. "Do you mind if I forego the drink? Taffy and I—we'd better be leaving. You know you have to get to places early these days, even with a reservation."

"That's right," Felix said.

He didn't want to keep them here. He watched them covertly, and it seemed to him that Taffy's manner with Augie was just what it had been with himself, just the same polite and gentle gaiety, the same friendly ease. That hurt.

So I'm not anyone special, he thought. Maybe she's the same to everyone. How do I know?

"You like one person as much as another," Ildina had once said to him.

And now he knew what she meant. He went out to the elevator with them, and Taffy held out her hand to him. She squeezed his fingers hard, looking straight into his eyes. She smiled and he smiled at her, and maybe it didn't mean anything.

Then they were gone, the tall, fair girl and the luckless Augie. I hope to heaven he won't have any serious trouble with the police, Felix thought. He's such a damn *good* little guy, so generous and so straight. Hard to see how anyone, even a policeman, could believe *he'd* shoot anyone dead.

CHAPTER XVI

It was seven o'clock now and Felix was hungry. It wouldn't do, he thought, to go down to the restaurant. Anyone who saw him there, eating alone, a few miles from his house, would deduce some grave domestic trouble. He called room service and ordered a meal, and while he waited, he put the paper baskets and the napkins on the tray with the cocktail glasses.

Not much of a party, he thought. I'm sorry. I'm sorry Taffy thinks I ought to go back to Ildina. Only, she doesn't know what the setup was. It couldn't have lasted much longer, in any case. We've been coming closer and closer to the breaking point. Just about anything would have caused it. Ildina hasn't been any happier than I.

No. It was a mistake. My fault. My mistake. But the only thing to do now, is to cancel it. We're both young. We can both make a fresh start.

His heart began to lighten a little, thinking of a fresh start, a new road. When his dinner came, he sat by the open window to eat it, by the last of the daylight. Taffy might disapprove of his new freedom, but it would not make much difference.

She didn't turn her back on people for doing things she did not admire. She was still here, in his life—he had not lost her. And as time goes on ... he thought.

He went down to the drugstore again, bought a razor, a tooth brush, a pocket comb, and a few other things he needed, only a small package. He had a couple of thousand dollars in the bank. Money he had saved before his marriage. Money he'd earned since. And he could make more.

He strolled along the street in the dusk.

Some of the little shops were open, bright and cozy. A harsh white light burned in the jeweler's empty room, a red sign flashed on and off outside Barney's Bar and Grill.

It was quiet here, yet it seemed to him that there was a tense excitement in the air, like a scene on a stage, when something is going to happen. It had been a long time since he had walked along a street in this way, not knowing or caring about time, not knowing or caring where he went.

I'd like to go back to Mexico, he thought. Back to Trinidad. To Bahia. Taffy would like those places. Santos in the rain. She'd like those little ships going from one island to another. When I lost my bags off Mayeguez, I went ashore with nothing and it felt like this.

He met a cat taking a walk, proud and leisurely, but with twitching, tensely alert ears. Funny little animals, he thought. They live in deadly danger all the time, but they don't seem to have any complexes.

He went back to the hotel, and the lobby had, for him, the same quality he had felt in the streets. The men who sat there smoking and reading under the glittering chandeliers seemed to be waiting for a cue. He glanced at the bar where a radio was turned on. A line of men sat at the bar, listening to a frantic voice describing a baseball game.

His room was better than ever. Someone had come in and turned down the bed. A cool breeze blew in. It was magically tranquil. He sat down under a lamp and picked up a magazine.

The telephone rang.

"There's a young lady to see you, sir," said the clerk.

"Oh," said Felix. "I'll be right down."

It's Taffy, he thought, without any reason. But then suppose it's

Ildina?

Very well. He had no thought of avoiding Ildina. He was certainly not at all anxious to see her, but she had a right to see him when she chose, a right to make a scene if she chose, or many scenes. He moved toward the door when the telephone rang again.

"The lady says could she go up for a few moments?" said the clerk. "She says she's got papers for you to sign."

"All right," said Felix.

That, he thought, sounded like Ildina. He picked up the fuzzy green spread, neatly folded on a chair, and put it smoothly over the bed, moved by an almost unconscious instinct. It wouldn't be kind, it wouldn't be decent, to look too cozy and comfortable.

He heard the elevator door open and then opened his own door. It was Carrie, unfamiliar, very modish, in a black suit and a small black hat, and twinkling high-heeled pumps.

"Oh, it's you," he said.

"Well, I thought I'd better come," she said.

"Sit down," said Felix.

"Well, thank you," she said. "I can't stay long."

He could have laughed at her air of self-conscious propriety. I suppose Ildina's sent her with a message and that makes her feel important.

"Who told you to come here?" he said.

"Mr. Fuller has a man following you," said Carrie. "He got a phone call at dinner, and he came back and told Mrs. Tellier the man said you were here in the Washington."

"I see," said Felix.

"It's just dreadful in the house without you," said Carrie. "I just don't think I can stay."

She did not say this as if to flatter or to please him. It was an announcement of fact. She sat erect in the armchair, her ankles crossed, and for all her air of self-possession, she looked nervous and troubled.

"Honestly, Mr. Tellier," she said. "I think somebody ought to warn you that Mr. Fuller just *hates* you."

"Is that why you came?" Felix asked.

"Well, partly," she answered. "It is just dreadful to hear how he was talking about you. He said 'Give him enough rope and he'll hang himself,' and he said, 'If he don't, I'll help him.'"

"That doesn't matter, Carrie."

"Well, but Mr. Tellier, he's got it in for your friends. I mean about Mrs. Depew. I heard him say to Mrs. Tellier, pin that on West, and I'll see that the—' I *think* he said the Marlowe woman, or some name like that. Anyhow, he said she was after Mr. West's money."

"All right, Carrie. I don't want to hear this."

"Well, I brought you the two letters," Carrie said. "I thought maybe there was something in them."

"What letters?" His voice rose sharply.

"Well, they came for you but I just felt sure you'd never get them."

"Letters? In the mail?"

"No. A boy brought them. First time he came he handed it to me and *she* was right there. She said, 'Give it to me and I'll give it to Mr. Tellier.' The second time she opened the door herself and she took the note and she said to the boy she'd give it to you. But I just had a *feeling* you didn't get them. And today, when I was putting away her laundry, I saw them in the top drawer. And I thought—"

"Let's see them," requested Felix, and she opened her purse, thrusting a hand inside.

There were two big square envelopes of lemon-colored paper, both addressed to Mr. Felix Tellier. Both had been opened and sealed down again with Scotch tape. He tore the first one open.

Dear Felix:
You didn't answer my first note....

He put that down and opened the other one.
The paper trembled in his hand.

Dear Felix:
I couldn't write all this to anybody else on earth, but you're so understanding. And your own life isn't exactly heaven, either.

I'm really very fond of Roger. He's wonderfully generous and sweet, to me, and I do appreciate it. But, Felix, he's so frightfully *old!* Sometimes I want to scream, shut up in that house with all the old, old furniture and nothing I picked out.

Felix, I heard you saying today that you were planning to go to the Coast. Let me know just when you're going, and I'll come, too. Don't worry, Felix. I'm not thinking of a beautiful romance. I want to be silly and gay, and you're the perfect companion for that. We'll just have a little interlude, and then we'll come home and be good.

Let me hear, Felix.

Yours as ever,
Mimi.

He took up the second one again.

You didn't answer my first note, but what you said at the Yacht Club yesterday was meant for me, wasn't it? And you had a very *knowing leer*. I told Roger my sister wasn't well, and wants me to go out to San Francisco. He wasn't *too* sympathetic, but I think he'll come around. Anyhow, Piggy Debs is getting reservations on your plane! I shall come on board heavily veiled and run up to you when we reach Frisco. Then let's go to Chinatown, Felix. Let's go and sit in little bars with jukeboxes.

Don't be afraid of me, will you, Felix? I *never* make scenes. When we get home again, I won't expect you ever to *look* at me. But I'm so *bored*, Felix, and a little frantic, and a *little* bit afraid of myself.

See you Wednesday.

As ever,
Mimi.

CHAPTER XVII

He put the letters back into the big lemon-colored envelopes. He smoothed them out carefully.

"I thought maybe there'd be something in this," said Carrie anxiously. "I thought maybe if you could get something on her, she and Mr. Fuller couldn't be so mean to you."

"Thanks," he said.

She waited, looking at him with growing anxiety.

"Well, I acted for the best," she said uncertainly.

"Yes," he said and rose. "Thank you, Carrie."

She rose, too, looking up into his face with troubled eyes. Then he smiled at her and she was reassured. She smiled herself, and moved her shoulders.

"I certainly hope these letters'll help you out, Mr. Tellier," she said "I think it's *dreadful* to take other people's letters and not let them even see them."

He stood in the doorway until she got in the elevator, then he closed his door and stood near it. It was as if his lively blood had ceased to run. He was heavy, inert as a stone.

Now he knew. Now he knew what Ildina had done and why she had done it.

He went out and walked the three miles, and there was no sense of distance or of time. He turned into the road, and it was very dark there, under the trees, very quiet. He strode quickly and easily up the hill. He could have walked forever.

Turning the corner of the house he saw the lights in the long window of the library. He had not thought about the time. He did not know if it were late or still early. He mounted the steps of the terrace and opened the door with his latchkey. As he entered the hall, Leroy Fuller came out of the library.

"What do you want?" he said.

"I want to see Ildina," Felix answered.

"Nope," said Fuller. "You walked out and now you can stay out."

"I've got to see her," said Felix with a quick frown. "Where is she?"

"Did you hear what I said?"

"It doesn't matter what you say. Where's Ildina?"

"We're finished with you," said Leroy Fuller. "At last I've got Ildina to see what you are."

Over Fuller's shoulder, Felix caught sight of Ildina, standing motionless in the library, in that negligee trimmed with leopard skin. Her dark face was pale. She looked sullen and fierce and wretched.

"Ildina," he said. "I want to talk to you."

"No," she said. "You went to that hotel. You had that woman in your room."

"Never mind that. I've got to—"

"Never mind?" she cried. "You think I'll stand *everything!* Do you think you can leave me here and go to that woman!"

"Stop!" said Felix sharply. "This is serious!" He turned to Fuller. "Man, will you please go!" he said. "I've got to talk to my wife."

"Nope," said Fuller, standing squarely in the doorway.

They were both tall men, almost equal in height, both lean and hardy. Fuller was twenty-five years older, and he was Ildina's father. It was almost impossible for Felix to contemplate physical violence against him.

"Ildina," he said. "I want to talk to you about those two letters. The letters in the yellow envelopes."

All fierceness and defiance went out of her face. She looked at him in wild-eyed terror, like a child, very beautiful that moment.

"How did you get them?" she asked. "You *stole* them!"

"No."

"I know!" she cried. "It was that Carrie! I'll—"

She was moving toward the bell in the wall.

"Stop!" shouted Felix. "Don't be a fool!"

He caught Fuller by the shoulders and tried to swing him aside, but Fuller gave him a vigorous push and went to his daughter, took her arm.

"What's all this about?" he asked.

"He's found out," she said, still with her wide dark eyes on Felix's face. "Now he'll get rid of me."

"Found out what?" Fuller asked, evenly.

"This is between Ildina and me," said Felix. "Please leave."

"No!" Ildina said. "Don't go, Dad! He's just come to torment me."

"I've come back to help you," said Felix. "If I can."

"Suppose we sit down and talk this over," suggested Fuller.

There was a tense wariness about him. He pushed Ildina gently down into a chair and all the while he was watching Felix.

"Let's have it," he said.

No one spoke.

"Ildina," Fuller said. "Do you know anything about this shooting that you haven't told?" Still he got no answer. He looked away from Felix and down into his daughter's face.

"You mean you think she did it?" he asked Felix with emphasis. He waited a moment. "All right, my lad," he said. "You're wrong, as usual. But even if she had done it, I'd see her through it. I'd get her out of it."

Felix closed the door into the hall.

"You've been damn busy, getting her into it," he said. "If the police find out that it wasn't Ildina on the terrace with me, or if Carrie finds it out ..."

Fuller took a long, thin cigar out of his breast pocket and lighted it.

"Maybe I made a mistake about that," he said.

"You can take my word for it that you did," said Felix. "If you've managed to make the police doubt Carrie's story, if you've got them thinking it was somebody else on the terrace that night."

"You're thinking of her!" Ildina cried. "That's *all* you care about."

"I'm thinking of you," said Felix. "No one else."

His tone, curt and stern, surprised her. She looked into his face with a frown of wonder.

"Why?" she demanded.

I don't know why, Felix thought. It doesn't matter. I've got to help her, that's all.

"Let's see these letters you speak of," said Fuller.

"No," Felix said.

"They're from that woman," Ildina said. "Arranging to go away with Felix."

"Not quite like that," Felix said.

"Well, she meant it. She wrote—"

"It doesn't matter. I'll destroy them."

"No, you won't," said Fuller. "Give them to me. They might be useful."

I'll never do that, Felix thought. Mimi's dead. She's not going to be disgraced.

Standing in the big silent room with the massive furniture, the shelves of books that no one read, he thought of Mimi, who loved to laugh. Maybe she had married Roger Depew for his money. Many people said so. But maybe she had married him because he had asked her, had wanted her. Maybe she had thought she could be happy making him happy.

"Then we'll both come home, and be good," she had written. As if she had thought there was something alike about them, something they had in common, and had chosen him as the one who could understand her hour of rebellion.

Because she had turned to him, she was dead. Nobody must turn to him. He must never hold out his hand to anyone. Never.

"I didn't really mean to do it," Ildina said unsteadily. "Even after I'd read those—those shameless letters. When you said that you wouldn't go to her party without me, I was so happy, Felix. I thought she'd talked to you and you told her you wouldn't run away with her. But then, when you didn't come home …"

He turned his head to look down at her.

"When you leave me here alone, I think of—everything," she went on. "I know. I *know* you have all your grand times away from me. I know that when I'm here by myself, you're happy—with someone else."

CHAPTER XVIII

It was true. Here she sat, the woman to whom he'd promised a lifetime of happiness, and long, long go he had deserted her and left her to her own sullen misery.

"You told me so many lies," she said. "I thought maybe this was another one. I got dressed and went to the party, just to see if you really were there. It was horrible. Nobody wanted to talk to me. Everybody said 'Where's Felix? Isn't Felix coming?' It's *always* that way. I had champagne, a lot of it.

"I thought maybe I could get a little lively, myself. If I could forget you … Then Mimi got up. She said, 'People! What do you think Roger's giving me for a birthday present? A trip to the Coast! I'm leaving tomorrow!' Then when I saw how she looked—how triumphant …"

"What did you do with the gun?" said Leroy Fuller, after a moment.

"I threw it into a brook in the woods. I pushed it down in the mud." He rose.

"I think we could all have a little drink," he said, and went off to the dining room. He returned with a bottle of whisky and a decanter of water.

"We can swing this," he said. "Carrie's dead certain she saw Ildina on the terrace. She'll stick to her story. As long as this Marlowe girl keeps her mouth shut … Do you think she will?"

"If I ask her, yes."

"Felix!" Ildina said. "You can't—tell her!"

"No," he said. "I won't have to tell her anything. Just ask her."

They drank their tepid drinks, the two men standing.

"Ildina," said Fuller. "Get a good night's sleep. Take one of your pills. If you keep hold of yourself, keep cool and watch your step, we'll get you out of this."

He glanced at Felix and in his hard, strong-boned face there was a stricken look, almost an appeal. He was obliged now to count utterly upon the son-in-law whom he despised. He laid his hand on Ildina's head.

"Take it easy," he said.

In pain, in fear, she was the one creature in the world he loved. All her life he had given her what she wanted, or what she said she wanted. Faithfully and carefully he taught her that it was of paramount importance for her to get what she wanted. Faithfully and carefully he had trained her to guard what she had got. To put up signs, warning trespassers. To get and to keep.

She had wanted this man. And when a trespasser had menaced her possession …

"Good night," he said briefly, and went out of the room.

They were alone now. Felix stood beside her chair, very straight, his blunt-featured boyish face blank of any expression. She would speak and he was braced and ready for that.

"Felix," she said. "Why did you come back?"

"When I found out what trouble you were in, I wanted to help you if I could."

"Why?"

He was silent, seeking in vain for an answer.

"I don't know," he said at last.

"You *must* know."

"I don't. Simply it was the first thing that came into my head."

"You mean you thought it was your duty?" she said.

"No," he answered. "I'm afraid I don't do much thinking, Ildina. I'm not—deep. I just do things …" He paused. "When you're in such trouble," he said. "I guess this is where I belong."

"It's not as bad as all that," she said briefly. "Dad will see to it."

"I hope so."

"And even if it comes to the worst," she said. "Even if I was tried, do you think any jury would blame me for trying to defend my marriage?

That woman was trying to steal you. I'd only have to show her letters."

She did not think that what she had done was shocking and horrible. She did not even think it was very serious. But she could see by Felix's face that he did not agree with her.

"Nobody condemns a *man* if he shoots someone who's trying steal his wife," she said.

Let it go, he thought. She believes you can "steal" one human being from another, because she believes one human being can own another. Let it go. She's miserable enough, poor girl. And God know what's ahead of her.

"You don't love me," she said flatly. "You've never loved anyone, have you, all your life?"

It was only just, only decent that he should answer her. But it was almost impossible.

"Ildina," he said in a sort of desperation. "When I hear people talking about love, I think I don't know what they mean."

"You never loved anyone?"

"Plenty of people," he said. "My father, my mother."

"I don't mean that," she said impatiently. "I want to know. I've got to know if you've ever loved a woman."

"Yes," he answered.

"What woman?"

The sweat came out on his forehead, but he held his ground. It seemed to him that he owed it to Ildina to be honest. To find or try to find words for the things that he had never formulated in his own mind.

"More than one," he said.

"Tell me about them."

"I don't think I can," he said. "There was a girl in Boston, when I was in college … There was a girl in Trinidad … There was a dancer in B. A. …"

"Do you mean real love affairs? You mean you had a physical desire for them?" she demanded.

"Well, yes," he said apologetically. "That's part of being in love, don't you think?"

"Why did you love them?"

"Well … they were kind and pretty and sweet."

"Then why did you leave them?"

"It just happened that way," he said. "Something came up, and I had to leave."

"And what about the women? What happened to them—when you just walked away?"

"I guess they got on all right," said Felix. "I hope so. I don't see why not."

"And that's what you call love?" she said.

"All right," he said. "I do call it love when two people are kind and loyal and happy together. I've seen that other thing, in life, in the movies. Two people against the world. All right! I'm *not* against the world. I live in it. I like it. I like the people in it.

"I think it's damn ugly and evil, two people crouching behind a spite-fence they've built. There's no woman ever born who could be the whole world to me, and God knows I couldn't, and wouldn't, be the whole world to any woman."

She rose.

"All right, Felix," she said. "I guess that's the answer. That's not the way I love. I could have found plenty of rich men. But you set out to make me love you, and you did it. There's nobody else. Nobody, and nothing else. Whether you like it or not."

She was magnificent, pale, beautiful and doomed. She had committed a murder, for him. There was nothing she wouldn't do for him. And he wanted none of it. He had come here to help her. He was ready to go to desperate extremes to help her. But he could never take her in his arms again, never kiss her, or smooth back her rich black hair. It would be an ordeal to take her hand.

"Are you going back to the hotel?" she said.

"No," he said. "I'm staying here."

She moved toward the door.

"I'll tell Carrie to get the East Room ready for you," she said.

CHAPTER XIX

A squall blew up in the night and waked him. He opened his eyes and did not know where he was. He sat up in a strange alarm and then he remembered.

This was the East Room in the house where he had lived for nearly a year. He had passed it uncounted times. He had glanced in at the open door, but he had never set foot in it before tonight. There were other rooms here he had never entered. There were pieces of furniture he would not have recognized, things Ildina had bought. Things she cherished that he had never noticed.

As a rule he could fall asleep as quickly and easily as he woke. But not tonight. The utter strangeness of this room oppressed him. He got up to close the window and stood by it, looking at the trees that rocked in the wind. These are Ildina's trees, he thought. She owns them.

He thought of her lying alone in the room they had shared for so long.

He knew how she must look, pale and handsome, her black hair loose on the pillow. His gay and tender lovemaking had never brought a smile. Sometimes she wept, clinging desperately to him, and he would try to comfort her, without knowing what was wrong.

He could not comfort her now. He had come back here compelled by an impulse he could not understand. Her crime appalled him, and her callousness toward it; yet he had come back to stand by her, to help her if he could.

Love? he thought. No. Unless there's another sort of love … I don't know. Maybe she's right. Maybe I've never been in love. Never can be. I don't know.

Mimi? he thought. I suppose she was a little in love with me. Only a little. And that was something he could very well understand. It was far from admirable. If he had known about it, he would, tactfully and courteously have rejected the idea of a gay little holiday from Ildina, and Roger Depew. But he was not shocked, not disgusted; only sorry beyond measure that she was gone.

Taffy? he thought. His hear leaped with a queer eagerness. I was as if he saw her standing in a magic sunlight, everything clear around her, everything happy and innocent. But he was looking back at Taffy now. He knew it. All that magic was in the past. He could see, and his heart grew leaden, no future for himself.

The rain drove by. He opened the windows again and went back to bed. He fell asleep, and when he waked the strange room was filled with light and morning air. The curtains fluttered. Outside the windows, a leafy bough sprang up and down against a bright blue sky.

He took a shower in the strange bathroom and dressed, and smoked a cigarette, reluctant to open the door. Well, do I go to the factory today? he thought. Or is that finished? Is this just another day—or something new?

At eight o'clock he felt obliged to go downstairs. And it seemed to be just another day.

"Oh, good morning, Mr. Tellier!" said Carrie.

She didn't know, of course, what she had done in bringing him those letters. She didn't know how the three people in this house depended upon her story. But she did know that something had happened. And after having seen her Mr. Tellier away from here, she had a new air of intimacy that made him uneasy

"I'm terribly glad you're back," she said.

Better ignore this.

"Anybody else down?" he asked.

"Well, Mr. Fuller's out on the terrace," she answered.

He decided to ignore that, too.

"If you'll bring along my breakfast, please," he said, "and give me the papers!"

"Mr. Fuller took the paper," said the Carrie, giving him a sidelong glance. "I know you hate anyone to touch your paper, Mr. Tellier, but I just didn't dare say a word to *him*."

"Quite right," said Felix.

It seemed to him that Carrie would be pleased and interested to see trouble between him and his father-in-law, and with Ildina, too. He remembered, with a pang of regret, the things Ildina had said about Carrie. "Carrie's devoted to me … Carrie's absolutely loyal to me." But it was not so. No one was devoted to her. She had no loyal friends, no one at all but the two to men in this house, her father and her husband.

"The funeral's today," said Carrie.

"The— Oh! Mrs. Depew's?"

"Yes," she said, with satisfaction. "They say Mr. Depew's in such a state the doctors are giving him a drug so he can go. They say he looks like an *old, old* man."

Poor devil! Felix thought.

"It's eleven o'clock, at St. Mark's," Carrie went on. "And there'll be policemen hiding in the church."

"That's not likely," said Felix, displeased with her ghoulish content.

"Excuse me, Mr. Tellier, but it was somebody in the police that told me," said Carrie. "He said that the one that killed the person is sort of *drawn* to go to the funeral. Sometimes they faint dead away, he said, and sometimes they sort of glare."

"You talk too much," said Leroy Fuller from the doorway.

She looked straight into his eyes, her pretty face flushed scarlet and then grew very pale. She went out of the room straight as a dart.

"She'd better be handled with care," said Felix.

"No, I know her type," said Fuller. "But about this funeral. You and Ildina will have to go."

"Not Ildina," said Felix.

"She's damn well got to go," said Fuller.

"It's out of the question," Felix aid. "She can be ill—any excuse."

"No excuses. She's got to go, and she's got to look right and sit right."

"She's not going," said Felix carefully. "It's an inhuman thing to ask of her."

Even now, with their common purpose, they faced each other with all the old hostility.

"We'll—" Fuller began when the telephone in the library rang.

"I'll take it," said Felix.

But Fuller was ahead of him. He grabbed the instrument.

"Yes," he said. "Yes, he's here. For you," he said to Felix.

And he stayed where he was, standing near the desk.

"Felix?" said Augie's anxious voice. "Now, look, Felix. Take it easy!"

"What's up? Where are you?"

"I want you to take it easy. Felix. Everything will come out all right. They only let me have one phone call and I called you."

"Where are you?"

"Now, look, Felix. Keep cool. I'm not worrying. I'll just ask you to get in touch with my lawyer, Murray Blaustein. Wonderful man. He'll come right out."

"Where are you?" Felix asked again, keeping his voice level with an effort.

"Everything's going to be all right, Felix."

"Will you answer my question? Where are you?"

"Well, just at the moment, Felix, they've picked me up. They've got me down here at the County Jail. But it's a very nice place, Felix. Clean! You could eat off the floor."

Felix laughed.

"That's nice," he said. "Enjoy yourself, Augie. What's the charge?"

"Well, it's about that, y'know! That which happened at the Club. If you'll get hold of Murray Blaustein, Felix, I'll be grateful."

"What about bail?"

"Well … Not with this charge, Felix. But it's going to be all right. Absolutely! You take it easy."

CHAPTER XX

It occurred to Felix now that there was something extraordinary in this insistence upon his taking it easy, coming from a man in jail on a murder charge.

"Augie," he said, "is anyone else involved?"

"You mean T?" said Augie, lowering his voice. "Absolutely not serious with that party, Felix."

"Have they got—that party then, Augie?"

"Only for questioning."

"You mean in jail?"

"Only held for further questioning, Felix. No charge. She sent a telegram to her mother and it's going to be absolutely all right, Felix. She'd rather you didn't take any steps, Felix. She sent that message. Doesn't want you to take any, steps, Felix."

"Augie, what can I do for you?" Felix asked after a moment.

"Well, Felix, if you'd tell my butler to pack a little bag—pajamas, razor, and so on.... He'll know. He's a valet, too. And just get hold of Murray Blaustein."

"Can I see you?"

"Not at the moment. But I want you to know it's okay, and the other party, too. This place is absolutely up-to-date in every way. No vermin."

Felix laughed again. Augie ought to know, he thought. This is the second time for him. But it'll be a novelty for Taffy.

"Have to sign off, Felix. Only take it easy. They can't make this stick."

"All right. I'm in here pitching for you, Augie."

Felix hung up the instrument and sat on the top of the desk.

"Augie West's in jail," he said in a casual tone. "Charged with murder."

"He'll get out of it if he has a good lawyer," said Leroy Fuller.

"You dug up his past history," pointed out Felix. "It's a big help—for the police to know he's been suspected of murder before."

"If he hasn't got a good lawyer I'll get one for him," said Leroy Fuller.

"And Miss Marlowe," said Felix. "She's there, too. In a cell."

"They won't keep her long."

"You've done this," said Felix. "You set the police on her. And on Augie."

"Okay, I was wrong. I'll do everything I can to help them out."

"Everything?" said Felix.

He rose and again they stood facing each other.

"Just what do you mean?" asked Fuller.

"Here are two people," said Felix. "They're both remarkable people. Honorable, decent, splendid people. They're faced now with every sort of humiliation and disgrace."

"Tellier!" said Leroy Fuller. "This is the payoff."

"Well?" said Felix.

Fuller brought out one of his long, thin cigars, his brown, wooden face showed nothing at all.

"You've got those two letters," he said. "Take them to the police and you'll get your two pals out."

And get Ildina in.

"You're suggesting—?" Felix began.

"I'm not suggesting a damn thing," said Fuller. "I've got to depend on you and I never thought you were anyone to depend on. Only, you'll have to hurry up. If you're going to throw your wife overboard for that damn little squirt and your highfalutin girlfriend, I want to know. Quick."

Quick. This was what had come to the gay and friendly Felix, who lived without malice, without ambition.

"D'you love that girl?" asked Fuller.

"I don't *know* who I love!" Felix shouted. "And I don't know what I'm going to do!"

"I want to know now."

"You can wait," said Felix, and went out of the room.

He went out to the garage, where there was a telephone, and called Blaustein's office. Mr. Blaustein would not be in until ten, a girl's voice told him and he got the lawyer's home number from her and called him there.

"I'll be out at once," Blaustein said, in a resonant and very agreeable voice. "D'you know where I can get a room there?"

"I'll get you one at the Hotel Washington," Felix said. "And I'd like to see you, after you've seen Augie."

"I'll call you," said Blaustein and made a note of his name and address.

Felix hung up the receiver and went out of the garage. He lighted a cigarette and stood in the road looking about him, with a feeling almost of panic. He wanted to do something, to go somewhere. He wanted any sort of action.

But there was nothing open to him.

I can't make up my mind yet, he thought. I've got to know first how serious this is for Taffy and Augie. I've got to wait.

I'll go to the office, he thought. He had to get away from the house. He *could not* face Ildina until he knew what he had to do. He got into his car and started the engine with the same feeling of panic, tense with dread that someone could call him, stop him, drag him back into the house.

As he came in sight of the factory, he felt suddenly that he must look queer. He must look furtive, a man trying to escape. Heaven knew he felt queer enough. In his breast pocket were those two letters, and suppose something happened? Suppose he met with an accident, and someone else got hold of them?

He got into the elevator and it seemed to him that there was something wrong with it, very wrong.

"What's the matter?" he asked the operator. "What makes the car shake like this?"

"Same as usual, sir," the operator answered.

It's not, Felix thought. Suppose the car fell and he was knocked unconscious? They would take him to the hospital, they would empty his pockets. Someone would look at those opened envelopes.

There was no air in the car. It made him feel queer. He gave a long sigh when at last he got out.

"'Morning, Miss Larsen," he said, not looking at her. For she would see something in his face. "I'd like a big envelope. And get Perry, will you?"

He sat down at his desk, and put the two letters into a manila envelope, sealed it down and wrote on the outside.

Property of Felix Tellier. *Personal.*

Perry was the head bookkeeper, a very stout, youngish man in horn-rimmed spectacles, with a curiously sweet smile.

"Put this into your safe, will you, Perry?" Felix asked.

He had that fatal impulse to go on, to invent an explanation for wanting the envelope in Perry's safe, and not in his room. But he checked himself. What he was doing looked queer, but explanations would be still queerer. Let it go.

"I'll give you a receipt, Mr. Tellier," said Perry.

It would be too queer to refuse. But it was queer, at best, to have in his wallet that slip on which Perry had written, in his clear, beautiful hand:

Received from F. Tellier, one manila envelope marked "Personal."

CHAPTER XXI

If anyone found that in his pocket when he lay unconscious on the road. Or even here in the office … He remembered that fellow in Demerara. They stood talking in the little pub and the man had fallen to the floor like a felled ox.

Mistake to think of things like that. If you think of them, you make them happen. Or so they say. The fellow in Demerara had been middle-aged and heavy, the climate there was hellish. No use being morbid. If anyone does get hold of those letters, I'll simply say Ildina ever saw them, didn't know anything about them.

But if they asked *her* questions … she'd be sunk. She doesn't honestly realize what she's done. She can't. She lives in another world, where she thinks she can buy anything or do anything she wants. She doesn't know how much she makes people hate her. She doesn't know *anything*.

Except for her father, she was now utterly alone. And, for all her arrogance, her money and her father's faith in money, she was more helpless than anyone else. She did not know how to win anyone, how to persuade, even how to explain.

He thought of her in court, before a jury. Everything she said would be wrong, fatally wrong. No one would see her as a jealous woman, a wife driven to desperation by the fear of losing her man. She would seem, to everyone, like a barbarian queen, who thought nothing of destroying a possible rival.

And she was not a queen and she had no power.

Maybe Fuller can get her away, somewhere, he thought. Maybe I can. Out of the country?

"Have you looked at your memos, Mr. Tellier?" Miss Larsen asked mildly.

He looked at the pad on his desk, the list of appointments; he tried to put his mind on the work ahead. When I go home at lunch time, he thought, I'll have to talk to her. I'll have to make her see that if Bushey comes again, she must have a different manner. She must not antagonize. And he will come again.

Maybe he's there now, Felix thought. That won't do. She mustn't. He stretched out his hand for the telephone but drew it back. Telephoning would do no good. Perhaps talking direct to her wouldn't do any good, either. Bushey might have heard something. Mimi might have talked to someone. She could be pretty silly, he thought. Pretty wild. What if she told someone she was going away with me? Then Bushey …

The door opened and Ildina walked into the office. She was wearing a black skirt, a long-sleeved, sheer black blouse, a small black hat with a veil, black gloves. Her face was pale, as was natural to her, and best suited her. Only her full, scornful lips were heavily rouged. She looked extremely elegant and handsome.

He rose, startled, even frightened, to see her.

"Anything wrong?" he asked.

"No … It's time to start for the funeral."

Miss Larsen was not in the office. He moved to Ildina's side.

"Ildina," he said. "Go home. I'll say you were taken ill. You don't have to do this."

"Dad says I must."

"He's not God Almighty. He's wrong. You don't have to do this."

"I can do it," she said, "as long as you're with me."

"All right—*I* can't," he said. "I can't go to Mimi's funeral with you. Can't you see for yourself how it will be?"

"No," she said. "I'd like to go. I sent flowers."

"Why?" he demanded. "What do you mean by it?"

"I'm sorry," she said.

There she stood, tall, elegant, all in black, her black lashes lowered, saying "I'm sorry" for a wanton murder.

"Sorry for Mimi?" he said. "Sorry for poor old Roger?"

"No," she said. "I hardly knew them. They don't mean anything to me. No … I'm sorry I did something that's put us even farther apart."

"Ildina," he said. "You must have some sort of code."

"Yes, I have," she said. "And I stick to it. When I give my word, I keep it."

It seemed to Felix as if this were the last chance they would ever have to speak to each other.

"Ildina ... You can't think it's right to kill."

"You enlisted in the Navy," she said. "You thought it was all right. You thought it was a fine thing to kill anyone who wanted to destroy you. She wanted to destroy me by taking you away from me."

"Nobody could 'take' me away," he said. "I'm a free agent."

He could see that that made no impression on her.

"Felix, we ought to be starting," she said.

"I'm not going with you, Ildina."

"Dad said it would be very conspicuous if we didn't go together."

"Ildina, for God's sake, go home. I'll go by myself."

She looked at him, irresolute, darkly unhappy.

"Go home," he said again. "And Ildina, if Bushey comes, or anyone from the police, be civil. Be tactful. It's important."

"Felix," she said, "Will you *ever* get over this? Will things *ever* be the way they used to be?"

He had never known her to speak like this, or look like this with this dreadful humility. It was the impulse of his easy and compassionate spirit to reassure her, to give her some comfort, to push into the future the inevitable reckoning.

But something else was awake in him now. His own hour had come, when he had to face himself and his world.

"I'll try to help you through this," he said.

She turned away, and walked out of the office. He noted, irrelevantly, that she was wearing black nylon stockings. Complete mourning for the woman she had killed.

He did not tell himself now that this would be better, as time went on. He could not see one day ahead or one hour, only he knew that whatever came would be bitter and dark.

"Miss Larsen," he said. "Will you do me a favor? Will you just step out and buy me a black tie? I'm going to Mrs. Depew's funeral."

She loved to do things like that for him, and he knew it. He had no conceit about it. It seemed simply natural. Ever since he could remember, from the days when he had been a thin, nonchalant, cheerio little boy, there had been people like Miss Larsen. He liked them. He was grateful for them.

He got into his car and drove off toward the church. And he so dreaded the ordeal before him that he used his old, half-unconscious technique.

He stopped thinking about Ildina and about Mimi.

He thought of Augie. But that was too painful. After I've seen Blaustein, he thought, I'll know more about that. I'll be able to think....

Then, with a sigh, he turned his mind to Taffy. This was the road here they had driven together, only that little while ago. Nice, she had said, not to know where we're going. When she was headed toward a cell in the county jail and he toward his own disaster.

It's all my fault, he thought. I brought the whole thing on her. And if she were still in jail, she was there because, for his sake, she was still silent about being on the terrace with him. All his fault, yet he did not think of Taffy with guilt and remorse.

She can take it, he said to himself. He was a little surprised at the thought, but it stood firm under examination. It would be bad for her in jail. She would suffer discomforts, hardships. There might be people to bully and threaten her. But she could take it. She would get over it. She would come out of this unscathed.

Because she had in her something strong as steel. Because, beneath her gentleness and vagueness, she was sure and unshakeable. She's the one, he thought. She's the one I love and want. And need.

That came as no surprise. It was simply that he recognized something he had known for a long time, without understanding. He had come back to her, again and again, not, as he had imagined, to make her happy, to give her a good time, but because she was all he had to come back to, the one unchanging base of his careless life.

He saw now that he had always known this, and always feared it. There lay his destiny, the one companion to complete him and steady him, and he had escaped.

She's not for me, he thought, and he thought she was sorry about that. Sorry he had abandoned her, disappointed that he had made nothing of himself or his life. But still and forever, faithful to him, fond of him, in a way grown more and more aloof with every year.

CHAPTER XXII

The driveway before the church was lined with cars so he had to park around the corner. He walked back to the church and entered it. He sat down there among his fellow creatures. All of them facing together, in the same direction.

And it was worse than anything he had imagined. He saw Roger Depew with a blank stony face. He saw Mimi's sister, weeping. He sat among these people, and he felt himself an outcast. A criminal.

It was a frightful thing that Mimi should be killed and buried, hidden away, unavenged. My fault! he thought.

He did not go to the cemetery. He left the church with a nervous haste utterly new to him and he drove away, fast.

I'm going down to the shore, he thought. There was a place he had seen from the road, a spit of land covered with great boulders. It would be quiet there and lonely. He did not have enough gas to drive there and back, but he could walk. It would be good to walk.

But before he reached the parking lot near the station, he dismissed the idea. I've got to get home, he thought. He had to go back to Ildina. It was as if she were someone very ill, and there might be some dire change during his absence.

In his heart he did not, he could not, feel that there was any hope for her. He did not believe that she could evade the consequences of this thing she had done. He saw her as doomed, and he could do nothing but stand beside her until the inevitable hour came …

Later he stopped in at a drugstore and telephoned to the Washington. Mr. Blaustein had gone out. No, he hadn't said when he expected to be back. Yes, the operator would give him a message: "Please call Mr. Tellier as soon as possible."

I hope to heaven he's good, Felix thought. If he is, he ought to get Augie out at once, even today. There can't be any real case against him. And nothing at all against Taffy.

It was a shameful thing, a monstrous thing that they should be there in jail, even for an hour. I brought Taffy out here, he thought. I got her into this.

And he could not get her out of it. If he were to say that she had been with him, sitting on the terrace, it would mean immediate disaster to Ildina. He could not do that. I must seem contemptible to her, he thought, and he could not help that. Her mother would arrive, there would be lawyers, plenty of people with money and prestige, and they would get her out of there. He was not seriously worried about her, only sorry that their life together, all the golden happiness, had come to this.

As he opened the door with his key, Ildina came into the hall. She had taken off her mourning outfit and was wearing a white dress.

"I put lunch off," she said. "Come and have a cocktail first, Felix."

There was still that great anxiety in her dark eyes. She looked younger, with her arrogant assurance gone. She did not know what he thought, or what he felt. It was as if she were searching his face, to learn what she had done.

He followed her into the drawing room where Leroy Fuller sat with a glass in his hand. He glanced up and their eyes met in that implacable hostility there was between them. Only, something had changed. It no longer seemed to Felix that Leroy Fuller was master here.

"I've been talking to Ildina," said Fuller. "Or trying to. She ought to get away."

"She can't," said Felix. "Bushey wouldn't let her."

"He can't keep her. I want to take her out to Arizona with me for a few weeks. You can close the house and wind things up at the branch."

"Oh, that's finished?" said Felix.

"I'll put you in somewhere else. Chicago, maybe. I'll see. But I want Ildina out of the damn place."

"Do you want to go, Ildina?" Felix asked.

"Well, if you do," she said, with that new irresolution. "I think it would be nice to start somewhere else, all over again. Don't you?"

A car was coming up the drive. They were all silent, waiting. The doorbell rang and Carrie went along the hall.

"Mr. Blaustein is here to see you, Mr. Tellier," she said, pleased that the guest had asked for Felix and no one else.

"Who's he?" asked Fuller.

"Augie West's lawyer," Felix answered. "I'll see him in the library, Carrie."

"I'll be right there, too," said Fuller.

"No, thanks," said Felix. "I want see him alone."

"Nope," said Fuller. "This is my business as much as yours. Maybe, a lot more."

Felix looked at him thoughtfully. Is this worth fighting about? he was thinking. But in the end Fuller would have to know how things stood with Augie, so let it go. He could see Blaustein alone later on.

"I'd like to come," Ildina said. Felix went out of the room and left them to follow. Carrie had taken the visitor to the library, and he stood there, tall, strikingly handsome and distinguished, his hair gray at the temples, lines at the corners of his eyes.

"Mr. Tellier? I've just left Augie West."

"Ildina, Mr. Blaustein. My wife. My wife's father."

Blaustein bent his head politely. There was about him the indefinable aura of success. He took it for granted that he was known, and need not explain who he was and what he had done in the world.

"Sit down, won't you?" said Felix. "I'm very anxious to hear how it's going with Augie."

He had made up his mind to forget Ildina, and her father, and he was able to do so. They sat side by side on a sofa, and they were the outsiders now.

"Were you able to arrange bail?" he asked Blaustein.

"The hell with bail, Mr. Tellier."

"But they can't have that much of a case!"

"They've got a strong case, Mr. Tellier," said Blaustein.

He, too, was ignoring Ildina, and her father. He was studying Felix, with an interest he made no effort to hide.

"He was very insistent upon my seeing you, Mr. Tellier," he went on. "He wanted me to assure you this was nothing at all to worry about. That seems very much on his mind, Mr. Tellier. That you might be seriously worried about him."

And that looks queer to you, eh? thought Felix. You don't expect a man in jail to be so disturbed about a friend outside worrying.

"They can't have any evidence against him," he said.

"You don't expect much direct evidence in a case of murder," said Blaustein. "They've established opportunity. He could very well have been at the scene of the crime at the right moment. They've established that he had a gun, a small revolver of the type that was used in killing Mrs. Depew. This gun of his is now missing and he has no good story to account for that."

"But what motive could anyone invent for his doing such a thing?"

"The suggestion is that he went there with the intention of shooting a Mr. MacLoughlin who was standing directly beside Mrs. Depew."

"That's absolute nonsense," said Felix. "MacLoughlin had been causing Augie a certain amount of trouble, but nothing serious."

"MacLoughlin had told several people he intended to run Augie West out of Spruce Lake."

"I know that," said Felix. "But he couldn't have done it."

"The suggestion is that West believed he could do it."

"He didn't. But even if he had, he wouldn't commit a murder for the sake of living in this place."

CHAPTER XXIII

Blaustein smiled faintly.

"The non-legal mind is always concerned more with motive than anything else," he said. "But the more you learn of crime and criminals, the less important it becomes. It's almost indecent to say that anything, anything at all, can serve as the motive for a crime. Of course, beneath the ostensible motive lies the unconscious psychological motive, but that isn't suitable for a court of law."

"There's no motive here to bring into court."

"I put it to you this way, Mr. Tellier," said Blaustein. "Augie West and his brother were brought up in poverty. Not what would pass in Spruce Lake as poverty, not a household worried about mortgage payments, insurance premiums, taxes, but the grinding, constricting poverty of too little food, of crowded, sweltering rooms, of leaking shoes and patched, frayed clothing.

"The parents were immigrants speaking English with an accent that aroused ridicule. They did the best they could for their children. But this best was pitiably little.

"From his squalor and wretchedness, one child shot up like meteor, the first-born son. His great talent was manifest even in childhood. In his early twenties he was celebrated. He lavished every comfort and luxury upon the parents while they lived. He opened new worlds to his younger brother August.

"All the security, all the beauty, the wonder, the stir of life August had ever known came to him through this most talented brother. You have heard how this brother was lost to him. You will be able to imagine with what painful effort he began—alone—to build a new life for himself."

Blaustein sat smiling in his chair. He spoke without gestures. But the flexibility, the resonance of his voice was enough to cast a spell.

"We see August West coming to Spruce Lake, a prosperous little community priding itself upon its 'exclusiveness.' But, during the years of his brother's fabulous success August, too, had been accepted, nay, welcomed by the most brilliant and sophisticated circles in New York. He believes that he can repeat this. He buys a house, he furnishes it, he attempts to establish himself. And from every quarter he meets with rebuff.

"And now this man, frustrated, lonely, heartsick, meets a woman. A girl, young, charming, gently bred. It is like a dream to him that she accepts his attentions. He takes her out here and there, to a play, a restaurant. And every moment he speaks with her is poisoned by fear, fear that this cannot last, that he will lose her.

"He proposes that she come out here to the Inn. He intends to show her his home, his grounds, his style of living. He hopes passionately, desperately, that these will win her. And after she has agreed to come, and he is awaiting her, MacLoughin steps forward, with his threat to disgrace and ruin him."

"But it wasn't that way!" Felix protested, astonished and troubled.

"Possibly not," Blaustein said, smiling again. "I'm putting it to you as a hypothesis, Mr. Tellier. In the minds of a good many people, Augie's 'motive' will be entirely sufficient. He had the opportunity to hold a gun, now unaccountably missing. And he is not popular in this community. I think we might say that he has two strikes on him before he starts."

"But you can put up a case for him!"

"I'm not taking this case, Mr. Tellier."

"You're not going to desert him?" Felix cried.

"That's strong language, Mr. Tellier," said Blaustein mildly. He rose. "I have too much to do at present. I'm not able to take on another case. I'm sending Augie a young colleague—who'll look after him as well as possible."

"Do you mean you don't think Augie has any chance of getting off?"

"I'd never say that, Mr. Tellier. Juries are unpredictable."

"Couldn't you be persuaded? You're the one Augie wanted."

"I don't find Augie sufficiently cooperative," said Blaustein. "Well—before leaving, I'll repeat his urgent message to you, Mr. Tellier. That you're not to worry about him. Good day, Mrs. Tellier. Good day, sir. Good day, Mr. Tellier."

He went out of the room, erect and light-footed, and it was as if a great actor had made an exit, leaving the stage silent and empty.

Felix stood near the door, waiting. Leroy Fuller was lighting his pipe. Ildina leaned back on the sofa. Felix waited but neither of them spoke, and after a moment he turned away.

He went up to that guest room and locked the door. I've got to think, he told himself. But he did not think. He stood by the window, looking out at the drive.

Blaustein was making me see how it could be with Augie, he told himself. How he could be—lost. Would Ildina let that happen?

And would he himself stand by and let it happen?

"Oh, God!" he cried in his heart. "*What* am I going to do?"

Was he going to let Augie go through with this? Let him stay in jail for weeks, perhaps for months? Let him face the anguish of a trial for murder? Let him suffer the disgrace, the humiliation, the unforgettable dread and fear?

And if he were not acquitted?

Oh, God! he cried again with one of those gestures the stage has copied and stereotyped from nature. Both hands went to his temples. I can't let him die for Ildina.

He couldn't? Then was he going to Bushey and tell him the truth? Let Augie go. It was my wife who killed Mimi Depew. It's my wife you'll have to lock up in a cell. She's the one who must stand before the judge and jury, pale, handsome, haughty. Not really knowing or feeling or understanding the horrible thing she has done.

"I owned a man. He was *mine*. I kept him in *my* house. And this woman tried to steal him."

Their life together came into his mind in disconnected vivid pictures.

He remembered their first night in this house. She had led him from one room to another, pointing out a picture, a rug, a chair. Then standing by the staircase window, she had pointed out the view. And it's all *ours*, she had said. As far as you can see. We'll have a little privacy *here*, just by ourselves.

He had not understood, in those early days, all that she meant by that. He had been touched by her happiness in the house; he had taken her in his arms, and she had clung to him. He could almost feel her arms about his neck now, her heart against his, and now it was pitiable, and horrible. She wanted to cling to him and hold him fast, forever. She did not want even to turn her head and look at the rest of the world. And if he looked or laughed or waved a hand to anyone else, if was torment to her.

He was desperate to get away from her, to be free. Looking back he could see how ill he had done, how he had lied to her, at first reluctantly, and then casually and carelessly, for any reason at all.

He had never been frank and honest with her. He had never said, "I want and need other people. You alone are not enough for me."

Even now he was not honest with her. She would never see in his face the shrinking he felt. She would never hear in his voice an echo of the thought he had when he looked at her. Murderess.

She had sat there and listened to Blaustein. She knew, fully, what was ahead for Augie. And she had said nothing.

Am I going to let Augie go through *that?* he thought.

He wanted to think. He *had* to think. But he was not thinking. Only one thing, one sentence came back to him again and again. I can't denounce Ildina. I can't do it. Think it out. Think of it ethically. All right. Ethically you protect the innocent. Not the guilty. She's not a fine person, a valuable person. She's a jealous, wretched one. She's arrogant. And cruel. And Augie is generous and kind. And innocent.

I can't do it. Look back to that Bible class in prep school. "Forgive thy brother ... Love thy neighbor as thyself ..." Only I don't love myself so damn much, and who is my neighbor? Ildina or Augie? I don't know. I don't know what is right or what is wrong, but I can't denounce Ildina.

And why? It was not love. He did not love her. He would have been glad beyond measure if it had come about that they were never to see each other again. He cared far more for Augie than for her. Then what was there that so bound him?

CHAPTER XXIV

Standing there by the window, Felix remembered their wedding. Neither of them was a member of any church, but when Ildina wanted a church wedding he had found that quite natural and right. It was what people did. It was a convention. The vows you made were a convention. The people he and Ildina knew did not believe that nothing but death could part them, did not believe that lifelong love could be promised.

Yet in that pretty little Westchester church, something had happened to him. His mind, unused to making analyses, was beginning now to see what it was. He had, that day, taken on a responsibility. He had not realized that. He had thought of Ildina and himself as two young people who were going to live together because they believed they would enjoy it.

I don't want children yet, Ildina had said. Not until later, when we're more settled, more used to each other.

They had left the church a married couple. They had, in effect, announced to the world that they were partners, setting out to build a life, with the same goal, the same hopes. They had built nothing, they had had no goal, no hope except to keep the joy they felt in their lovemaking.

For family they had only Ildina's father and Felix's brother. They had no mutual friends. This marriage was of no importance to anyone else. And all that was left of it now, for him, was that inexorable sense of responsibility toward her.

He puffed at a cigarette and moved about the neat, impersonal room. I can't let her down, he thought. But I can't bear Augie like this. No, we'll have to get away. Fuller can arrange it. He can pull strings. We'll get on a plane and go somewhere. South America. We'll change our name. And then I'll write a letter to Bushey and tell him the truth.

He gave a long sigh, and sat down by the open window, curiously tired. That was how it had to be. Fuller may object to that, but this is one time when I have the upper hand. I'm going to tell Bushey or maybe Blaustein, and I'm not going to put it off too long, either. And Ildina's got to be out of the way when that happens. Fuller will understand the necessity of that.

He would have to go and talk to both of them together. And before long, he and Ildina would be gone. Swallowed up, lost, in an unimaginable future.

Life, which had always stretched before him like a sunny open road, was dark as a jungle now. But he accepted that. He had sat, smoking one cigarette after another, thinking of places where they might go, where he could earn a living. Where they would be unknown.

He spoke Spanish without effort and almost without accent. He had a fair knowledge of Portuguese. Brazil? he thought. Or the back country in Argentina, the oil-fields … Not a good life for a woman but she might have to endure it …

A taxi was coming up the drive and that worried him. Everything was menacing now. Bushey, the police, Blaustein. People he didn't even know about, coming to threaten that pale, arrogant, doomed girl.

He rose and looked down. The person in the taxi held out something to the driver and opened the door. It was Taffy, tall and slight, hatless, in a loose gray jacket and a dark skirt.

He ran down the stairs and opened the door.

"What's the *matter* with you?" he cried.

"Well, nothing, Felix," she said.

"Your face is dirty," he said. "Look at you! Your stockings. What did they do to you, Taffy?"

"I fell down when I came out of that courthouse, I saw a taxi, and I wanted to catch it and I slipped."

"What did you come *here* for?" he demanded.

"I came to see Mrs. Tellier," she answered.

He was astonished and alarmed.

"Well, you can't," he said flat "You'd better get going, Taffy!"

"I've really got to see Mrs. Tellier," Taffy said.

"Ildina's upset. Nervous. She doesn't want to see anybody."

"It's important, Felix," she said.

"Go back to the Inn."

"I'm not there anymore. They said they had to have my room for someone else."

"You mean they turned you out?"

"Well, you can't blame them," she said reasonably. "There were policemen and reporters and people coming all the time."

"Where are you going?"

"Well, I don't quite know at the moment, Felix. I've got to see Mrs. Tellier first."

"What do you want to see me about?" asked Ildina. "Who are you?"

She was standing at the head of the stairs and behind her was her father like her shadow.

"Marlowe," Fuller said. "She's the girl I saw in West's house."

Ildina came on down the stairs and at last they stood face to face. It was, to Felix, like a scene from a nightmare he had dreamed a hundred times, Taffy like an amiable schoolgirl with her long fair hair, her loose gray jacket. Ildina in that negligee trimmed with leopard skin.

"What do you want to say?" she asked.

"I'd like to see you alone, please," Taffy said.

"Nope," said Fuller. "Don't do it, Idina."

"Mrs. Tellier," said Taffy. "It's about Augie West."

Ildina glanced at her father, anxious and irresolute.

"Step in there," he said, nodding toward the library.

CHAPTER XXV

Felix went in with them. He felt like a ghost, invisible, ignorant. Taffy, *his* friend, belonging in *his* life, had not come here on his account. Her business was with Ildina only. Here they were, face to face, the two tall girls, and Taffy was so pitiably at a disadvantage. She was in Ildina's home. She was alone. She was so polite, so gentle....

"Mrs. Tellier, please let me see you alone," she said.

"No!" said Leroy Fuller.

"You can say anything you want in front of my father," said Ildina. As if Felix did not exist. He had, before this, felt himself a stranger in this house, but never as he did now.

"Mrs. Tellier," Taffy went on. "Augie's in prison, you know. Accused of something he did not do."

"That's for the police to decide," snapped Leroy Fuller.

"You see, Mrs. Tellier," said Taffy, "Augie knows who did it. He saw what happened. He was there."

"All right," said Fuller. "The police don't believe him or they wouldn't keep him locked up."

"He hasn't told the police," protested Taffy.

"All right!" said Fuller, again. "That's because he knows damn well the police wouldn't believe whatever cock-and-bull story he's fed you."

Taffy ignored him as she did Felix.

"He saw what happened, Mrs. Tellier," she said. "He got the gun from where it was hidden."

"Felix!" said Ildina. "Why did you let her come here?"

"He didn't let me," Taffy said. "He didn't know anything about this."

"Well, what do you want?" asked Leroy Fuller.

"It's for Mrs. Tellier to decide," said Taffy. "That's why I came."

There was a moment's silence, a dreadful silence.

"She's got nothing to do with it," said Leroy Fuller.

"It's a horrible thing for Augie to be shut up in prison," said Taffy. "It's horrible for him to know that so many people here are ready to believe he's guilty. It happened to him before, you know."

For the first time since they had come into the room, Ildina spoke.

"He'll tell—now," she said.

"No," Taffy said. "He won't tell the police. He made me promise not to."

"Well, *why?*" Ildina cried. "If he does—know anything?"

"He's Felix's friend," said Taffy.

"Damn nonsense!" said Fuller. "People don't do things like that."

"Augie's like that," said Taffy.

"And what have *you* got to do with it?" Fuller demanded.

"When he thought he was going to be arrested, he told me," Taffy said. "I guess he had to tell someone. He was so miserable about it."

"All right. My daughter's not interested in your Augie West. Let him tell his tale."

"Mrs. Tellier, he's not going to tell anyone," Taffy said. "He's there in prison. There's to be a trial, and however it comes out, it will be a horrible thing for him. They've already had things about him in the paper. About his brother, about his family."

"My daughter's not interested in this fellow," insisted Leroy Fuller.

"I talked to Mr. Blaustein," said Taffy. "He's very fond of Augie but he knew he wasn't telling him the truth and it provoked him. And worried him. He thinks the situation is serious, and he ought to know."

"We've had enough of this," said Fuller.

"It's for you to decide, Mrs. Tellier," said Taffy.

With her gentle face, her gentle voice, she was inexorable. Ildina looked at her for a moment and turned to Felix.

"Felix! Why don't you say something? Why don't you tell this woman you wouldn't *let* me say anything or do anything! Can't you speak?"

This was her chance, her last chance at honor and pride and courage. It was not for him, not for Leroy Fuller, to try to save her. This was Ildina's problem. And if she had it in her to face it honorably …

"Ildina," he said. "I'll stand by you."

"What!" she cried. "What! Do you think I'd sacrifice myself, *ruin* myself, for that common little nobody? Is that what you *want?*"

"It's for you to decide," he said beside Taffy.

"No, it's not," said Leroy Fuller. "My daughter's not interested in this fellow. She knows nothing about this business and she's got nothing to say."

"Augie gave me the gun he found, to keep," said Taffy. "I wrote everything down just the way he told it to me. If he's convicted I'll go to the police."

"Go to hell if you like," said Leroy Fuller.

"Felix," said Ildina, her dark eyes, brilliant with a sort of terror fixed upon his face. "Felix, is this what you *want?* You'd *let* me do that. Let me go to jail?"

"Ildina," he said. "It's not like that." He hesitated, caught in a familiar feeling of despair. She would not understand what he said or what he felt. "I don't want anything," he said, "except for you to do what you think is right."

Her eyes widened as if her terror grew.

"I thought you wanted to help me," she said.

"I do," he said, "but, Ildina, how *can* I?"

"I'll look after you," said her father. "Miss Busybody Marlowe can clear out now."

Then Ildina turned upon Taffy. And Felix's nightmare came true. All her violence, her confused pain and fury came down now upon Taffy alone.

"*You* did this!" she cried. "*You* made him want to get rid of me and get me locked up in prison, so that *you* could have him. He would have stood by me if you hadn't come. But no—you want to see me hanged, both of you. Well, you won't. I'll never tell. I don't care what happens to your Augie West. Let him talk."

CHAPTER XXVI

Ildina struck Taffy in the face, so hard that she staggered. She would've struck again if her father had not caught her arm.

"Take it easy, Ildina," Fuller said. "You shouldn't have done that. Now, listen, all of you. I'm going to get Bushey here and I'm going to tell him the whole story."

"Dad!"

"It's the only way out," he said. "You've got too much sense to believe the damn rigamarole these people have been feeding you. You don't believe that this fellow West would take the rap for something he hadn't done—out of chivalry, or whatever they choose to call it. Nope. He's holding out for something. I don't know what, but you can bet it would be plenty. And this girl here. You were right about her. She wants to get you out of the way. The whole thing's a racket, a holdup. We'll call it."

"If you could," said Ildina.

It was a strange thing to see the change in her. It was as if her father spoke a language she could understand, as if a great burden were lifted from her, as if she had come out of a dangerous and dreadful fog into clear daylight. She could believe the things he said. She could understand the motives he attributed to people.

"I can, all right," he said. "Felix, let's have those letters from the Depew woman."

"No!" Felix said. "She's dead. And her husband—"

"We're not interested in the dead Mrs. Depew or her husband. We're going to use those letters. We'll show that Felix was going to take a little jaunt with that woman. We'll show that at the same time, he was having an affair with this Marlowe girl."

"No!" Felix said.

"You'd been playing around with this girl for years," said Fuller. "You brought her out here to Spruce Lake. You brought her to this house, when you thought your wife was safely out of the way. We'll show that you drove Ildina desperate with your dirty love affairs."

"You'll leave Miss Marlowe out of this!" Felix warned.

"Don't kid yourself," said Leroy Fuller. "She's in it, up to the neck. I've had a report on her. Her mother had three husbands, two divorces. What do you think marriage means to her daughter? Not a damn thing. I dare say she was glad enough to see Felix marry a girl with money. Nice for both of them."

This was what Ildina could believe. She lived in a wilderness, a desert. She had taken a mate and she had wanted and tried to keep him alone, at bay against the world. Taffy, young and good-looking like herself, could be nothing but an enemy in her eyes.

Taffy was moving toward the door.

"Just a moment," said Fuller. "If my daughter goes through with this thing, gets your other boyfriend out of jail, will you admit to Bushey that you came here to carry on a love affair with Felix?"

"Yes," Taffy said with emphasis.

Felix did not look up as she passed him. He had dreaded a meeting between Ildina and Taffy, but he had never imagined it could be this bad, never had dreamed he could bring this humiliation and misery down upon Taffy. He could not defend her, not now nor during the hours that lay ahead. Ildina's safety was at stake.

Leroy Fuller lighted one of his thin cigars.

"You'd better be going, too," he said to Felix.

"No!" said Ildina.

"Use your common sense," said her father. "Your whole case is to show Bushey what provocation you had. You've got to make Felix out as bad as you can. He can't stay here."

"Then you'll come back later, Felix? When it's all over?"

"Ildina!" her father protested. "Let him go."

"I've got to know," she pleaded, "Are you coming back, Felix?"

He did not answer, he could not. She caught his sleeve.

"Answer me," she cried. "Do you mean you don't *care* anymore?"

"I'll do everything I can to see you through this," he said.

"I don't care about that!" she said. "If you're going to leave me—"

Their eyes met.

"I'm sorry," he said.

She gazed at him with doubt and growing terror in her brilliant eyes.

"But I did that—for you!" she said.

He forced himself to meet her look steadily. But he could not speak, even try to explain to her. She understood nothing. She believed that the monstrous thing she had done was a proof of her love for him. She had expected him to accept it in that fashion.

"I did *that* for you," she sat again. "And now you're deserting me! You couldn't!"

Her face pale and stricken, she turned suddenly away.

He heard the click of her high heels along the hall, up the stairs. He heard her door slam. She had done this so many times before. She would be up there now, her door locked, waiting for him to come, to cajole her into smiling.

"I'll pack a bag …" Felix said.

"Just a moment," said Leroy Fuller. "Let's have those letters of Mrs. Depew's."

"They're in Perry's safe. Here's his receipt."

"If you were the only one who knew what had happened, I wouldn't be using them," said Fuller. "I wouldn't be going to Bushey if it weren't for the other two."

"You can trust them," Felix told him.

"I don't," said Fuller. "Ildina couldn't go on living at their mercy. Either one of them might talk, any day."

"No," Felix said.

"You don't know much about human nature."

"I'll run up and pack a bag."

CHAPTER XXVII

Fuller seized Felix by the arms.

"Just a moment!" said Fuller. "As soon as you let me know your address, I'll send along the rest of your things. And a check for your pay, to date."

"Thanks," said Felix.

"Hold on! You've got plenty of trouble ahead of you, my lad. I can't keep you on, of course, and when his thing breaks in the papers, maybe it won't be so easy to get another decent job."

"I'll manage," said Felix.

"I never wanted my girl to marry you," said Fuller. "And I think she's well rid of you. She'll get a divorce without trouble. But you've behaved pretty well about this damn thing. I'll add something to that check of yours. Couple of thousand."

"No! I've got enough money. I don't want any more, thanks."

Leroy Fuller looked at him.

"You're one hell of a fool, Tellier," he said, almost with admiration.

Felix stopped in the doorway.

"After all," he said. "I won't bother with a bag."

Because all his things were in the room with Ildina.

"Well, good-by," he said to Leroy Fuller, and walked out of the house, empty-handed. Again he did not know where he was going, but there was no joy in that now, no feeling of freedom and hopefulness.

He felt that he had betrayed both Mimi and Taffy. He dreaded what was coming to them. Mimi's letters read in court, perhaps printed in the tabloids. Taffy so assailed …

It's unforgivable! he cried to himself. Yet he would have done it again. I don't know why, he thought. What Ildina did was utterly bad and horrible. She's not even sorry for it. I don't know why I care about saving her from the consequences. It's not justice. It's not love …

He stopped in at a little tavern and ordered a drink, sitting at a table in a dark corner. There was a row of men at the bar, but he felt unable to join them. He felt alone now, for the first time in his life.

I'll go in to New York, anyway for the night, he thought.

He took a long time over the drink. When he came out of the tavern the sun was low and the little village seemed to him infinitely sad. Never again would Mimi come driving down to the station, never would Roger Depew come, a little uneasy but secretly pleased by the gay friends she invited here. Ildina would leave here and probably Augie, too, would go now. Everything's finished, he thought.

He went into the waiting room to buy a ticket and Taffy was sitting there, all alone, her bag at her feet.

"Taffy," he said. "What are you doing here?"

"I thought you'd probably be along, Felix," she said.

He sat down beside her, his hands clasped between his knees.

"I don't know what to say to you," he told her. "I've done so badly, Taffy.

I haven't considered you. I've done you nothing but harm." He paused, desperately anxious to be honest with her. "A lot of the time I didn't think about you at all. I forgot you."

"Forget me again now, Felix," she said.

"You mean for good, Taffy?"

"No, no! Just for another while."

"I don't know how to *explain*," he said, frowning. "You must be pretty disappointed in me. I got you into all this trouble and I didn't consider you. I didn't put you first, ever."

"I didn't belong first," she said almost sternly. "I'd have been disappointed if you'd acted any other way."

He glanced at her clear profile.

"I suppose we shouldn't be seeing each other anymore," he said. "Until this is all over?"

"I guess not, Felix."

"Where are you going, Taffy?"

"Oh, I got a room in a hotel somewhere. Mother's coming back maybe tomorrow."

So here we are again, he thought. Not knowing where we're going.

"But I thought that we might have dinner together just this one evening," said Taffy apologetically "I thought maybe we could get out of the train at Yonkers, if it stops, and find a place where we wouldn't meet anyone."

"Yes," he said with a long sigh.

This is all I want, he thought. He leaned back, he put his hands in his pockets and stretched out his legs. There were bad times ahead, for both of them. There were things in the past that he would never forget, never remember without pain and regret.

But now, for this moment, he had all he wanted. All. Just Taffy beside him. She didn't care about coming first. She would never expect him to be her whole world, or demand from him her whole happiness. She was beside him.

Stay there, always, he thought. You never asked anything of me and I was too stupid. So damn stupid. I didn't see. Only, all the time you were the one, the only one. God knows I haven't much to offer you, but you won't see it that way. You'll say, Why Felix! You want to give me your whole life, you heart and your body, and your soul, if any?

Why, Felix! What a perfectly grand person!

I'd have been disappointed, she would say, if you'd done it any other way. I know how you felt about that miserable girl, living alone in a wilderness. You thought you could bring her out into the friendly, careless world where you lived. But when she dug in her heels, you stopped trying … You went your own way, and just came back, now and then, to her gruesome little cave. Maybe you could have …

The sands of the desert were heaving, the mouth of the cave shrunk and stones began to fall. Walling him in …

He sat up straight, with a start.

"Taffy!" he said. "Was that our train?"

"Oh, there'll be another," she said. "I thought you were sort of tired, Felix."

Farewell, Big Sister

The knob of my office door was turning, very quietly. I sat where I was, with my feet up on the desk. I just pressed a button that makes the right-hand top drawer slide open, where my .38 lay handy. If it was anybody okay, he would knock. If it was somebody out to get me, I was better off where I was. I could duck down behind the desk.

The door was opening, and it was a doll. All right. Still I stay put. A doll can be maybe worse than a man. But this one was enough to knock you out, just to look at her. She was around eight feet high, green eyes, blonde hair down to her waist, and she was well-stacked; she knocked the lamp off my desk when she came in the door.

"Sorry," she said.

"You got nothing to be sorry about," I said.

She sat down. I held out a pack of cigarettes and she pulled one out. I got up then and gave her a light.

"You Corney Bassard?" she asked.

"That's me," I say.

"I've heard about you," she said. "Only you never know what to believe."

"I do," I said. "If I didn't, I wouldn't get far."

"I hear you charge plenty," she said.

She crossed her knees then, and I came close to blacking out for a moment after a look at those gams, in purple nylon.

"I haven't got much," she said.

"I wouldn't know about that," I said. "What's your trouble?"

She took a long drag on the cigarette, and blew out the smoke in hard, quick, purple puffs.

"I want to find out who murdered my husband," she said.

"Hard to keep the cops out of a thing like that," I said.

"I had the cops in," she said. "They just said, why would it be a murder? They said he just walked out on me."

"Any chance it could be that way?"

She looked straight at me with those green eyes.

"Well, what do you think?" she asked. "It never happened to me yet."

"That's a thing I can believe," I said. "Give me the story, as straight as you can."

"It'll be straight," she said. "All through."

"Well," I said, "suppose we start off with your name."

"I'd rather wait for that," she said, "wait till I see if we're going to work together."

"All right, sister. Give."

"My husband disappeared about two months ago. We'd been married five years and—" She sort of choked up. "It was all right," she said. She waited a moment. "Then one night—he didn't come home. He'd said he was going bowling, like he often did. Said he'd be back around ten. That's the latest he ever was—ten, or maybe fifteen minutes later. Well, he didn't come. Didn't take anything with him, not a razor, or a toothbrush, not a thing. Just a couple of dollars."

"What was his job—where did he work?"

"He worked in a lending library," she said. "It's real small and his pay would make you sick, but he just wasn't ambitious."

"You work?"

"Well, sort of like a super. It pays the rent. Anyhow, Willie *was* steady. Never missed a day. He wouldn't walk out on the job—and on me. Why, he wouldn't even've walked out on the old pup we had, before it died. And that's another pretty queer thing. The old pup died the night Willie left. I guess it sounds silly, but—I sort of thought Walcher knew. I thought—maybe it was grief, the way he was so crazy about Willie and all."

"You hear of things like that," I said. "Go ahead."

"Around midnight I went to the bowling alley where he always went. Well, he hadn't showed. I stopped in a tavern where he used to go, oh, maybe once a week, for a glass of beer, but they hadn't seen him. I went to the police station and they just said take it easy and he'll probably show up by morning. I went to bed, but I couldn't sleep and early in the morning—before I was dressed, even—the cops came. They told me the library where he worked had been robbed that night. Well, you know the way cops think."

"Maybe you mean 'if,'" I said.

"They thought Willie had robbed the place and taken a powder."

"How much was gone?"

"Around sixty dollars."

"Did he happen to need any money very bad, very quick?"

"No. We've got a joint savings account."

"Well, what's your theory?"

"He might have gone down the street for a look at the library. He used to fix up the window, and he was real proud of it. And maybe a lookout there saw him while the safe was being robbed, and just conked him on the head."

"That happens," I said. "And then what d'you think they did with him?"

"They always have cars," she said.

"They do," I said.

"I've been twice to see the man that runs the bowling alley," she said. "He's a crook. He works a lot of small-time rackets, but he's got connections, all right. He's covered. I wanted the cops to get a list of who else was there that night, but they only asked Finny, and he gave them just the names he wanted. Ones that wouldn't talk."

"Meaning Fatso Finny?"

"Yes. I kept telling Willie not to go there, but he said everything was straight, and he met some nice guys. Once in a while he'd bring one of them home, and they *were* nice guys."

"You don't feel sure he didn't go to Finny's bowling alley then?"

"I don't feel sure about *any*thing," she said. "Only Willie's gone, and the cops think he cracked that safe."

"And you don't think so?"

"I *know* he didn't. I know what Willie's like. He wasn't close to anyone. He just liked to be with me. And Walcher. Find him for me—and I'll give you five hundred. It's all we saved together, in five years."

"Find him—alive?" I said.

She rose, and her blonde head cracked with the overhead light and smashed it.

"Sorry!" she said.

"Think nothing of it," I said. "But wa-ait a minute! Wait a minute! I want your husband's name and address, and some kind of picture of him."

She opened her purse and took out a snapshot. It showed a skinny, slope-shouldered chap with a handlebar mustache, shorts, striped blazer, standing beside a bicycle.

"Sure," I said. "But I'll need something less than ninety years old."

"That was just meant to be funny," she said. "We got it down at Coney Island. That's a false mustache."

"I want his name, address, age, names of friends and relatives, school—all you can tell me."

"His name was—*is*—Willard Van Stuyvesant. He lived with me on West Eleventh Street." She gave the number. "I don't know if he had any relatives, and he didn't have any close friends. I mean, he was friendly with most people, but not close."

"What's your name and present address?" I asked.

"Sylvia," she said. "I'm called the superintendent of this lousy apartment house. What used to be called a janitress."

I asked her a lot more questions, but she didn't give. It didn't make sense to me that a girl stacked like that would have to take a job like she had.

"If he's found dead …?" I said, and I didn't use any of my famous tact.

"*Anything's* better than not knowing," she said. "I get thinking that maybe he's lost his mind, and he's locked up somewhere, or …"

Her pocketbook was still open, and she brought out a wad of bills, with an elastic band around it.

"Keep it," I said, "Till I see if I get anywhere on this."

She came around the desk then, and kissed my cheek, and it was like a lighted match flicking my skin.

"Sugar!" she said, softly.

"Phooey," said I. "Well, you'll hear from me."

I started to work right away. I happened to be in the chips right then. I'd been paid off on a big job, so I could afford this. I went first to the lending library, and there was a dame there with gray hair and pince-nez, just what you'd expect.

"I thought the world of Willie," she said, beginning to cry. "And the customers did, too. He'd *never* do a thing like that. The policemen were here, and I *told* them that."

"Good-looking, was he?"

"Well …" said the pince-nez, "yes, *and* no. He was, well, I guess all of two feet shorter than his wife, and sort of spindly. But he had a fine head of hair, and he had beautiful eyes. Dark, y'know, and sort of sad, and he'd look up at you, like a collie does. Why, it was wonderful. Sylvia, his wife, she got offers to go in the movies, and television, and he didn't want her to, so she passed them all up, and she stayed there, doing that mis'able kind of super's work; she mops the halls, and all. Of course *he* did the real heavy work, before he left in the morning, and when he came home nights."

"Who does the hard work now?" I ask.

"Oh, she's found someone, but they say he's not much good."

A customer came in, and I start to leave pince-nez. But she's got a tag-line that just about knocked me silly.

"And I *told* the police over and over…. I said I *knew* Willie would never rob me—and anyhow, I asked them, why would he come back in the middle of the night and *break* the safe, when he had the combination?"

"He did?"

"Yes. He was the *only* one."

"Except you."

"No, I didn't want it. It made me nervous. I was afraid I'd tell it in my sleep, or doodle it on a pad when I was telephoning, you know."

"Sure. I know," I say, and take another look at that face. You're the one leaves her purse in the phone booth, you're the one drops her keys down a grating. You're the one gets locked in an icebox. "Thanks," I say. "Been nice seeing you."

Now, anyhow, I've got something to work on. If this fellow had the combination, he could have got out the money without her noticing. But even she might get suspicious if the safe wasn't broken open. He could've done it that way, to get the heat off him, but it's a hell of a risk for sixty bucks. He could have walked out on that blonde. Hard to believe, but it happens. Maybe he's murdered—and maybe he's shacked up real cozy with another dame. Accident? No. Accidents get found out. He went out to go bowling at Finny's, and Finny says he never showed. And what Finny says, you take. Finny don't look like much—cheap little apartment, wife does all the work, no swell clothes; but he's a big shot, all right. Owns hotels, chain stores, he's in the dope racket; that skinny little wife of his is just a front. He's probably got half a dozen long-stemmed beauties. I got to be careful.

You went up one flight of stairs to the Elite Bowling Alley; the stairs were steep and dirty and stinking, and the Bowling Alley was a punk show. But Finny was there, because this was his front; if kind of funny things happened somewhere else, plenty of people could tell you they saw Finny right here. Of course he couldn't be there all the time, with all the things he was running, so I took a chance maybe he'd be out, and I'd find a guy who might sing a little. But Finney was there.

"Well, if it isn't Bassard!" he said. "What gives?"

"Nothing," I say. "I'm just one of those Kinsey reporters."

"This is a bad place to ask questions," Finny says. "You better get traveling, sweetheart."

I did. I hadn't expected much, anyhow, and I go down those stairs as quick as I could, and step in next at the tavern she said he went to once a week for a beer, and the owner, who was doubling for barkeep, looked regular to me. Not scared, not jumpy. "The cops came around three or four times about Willie," he answered me, after he'd seen my card. "I can't tell you only what I told them. He came in here once a week, maybe once in two weeks. One beer, that was Willie. He never stood anyone a drink, but he got on good with everyone. Cheerful. I never believed that about his cracking a safe. Jeeze, he couldn't crack a flea."

I had six double ryes, and then I went back to my office. When I want to think something out, I put paper clips on my ears—fifteen, maybe twenty. It helps me, when I want to think.

I was beginning to see a lot of angles. I sat there a while, then I brought out a bottle of Bourbon. I gave myself a good shot of it, and then I went out to see that blonde, that Super, Sylvia. I got along to Eleventh Street, and I rang the bell that said "Superintendent." The buzzer clicked, and when I went in, a fellow came out of the back apartment—a sort of Swede he looked, with a lot of yellow hair like Harpo Marx, and yellow eyebrows. He was wearing a sort of football sweater with padded shoulders, and those pleated pants.

"I want to see Mrs. Van Stuyvesant," I say.

"No," says he. "She's resting."

"She'll see me," I said. "Tell her it's Corney Bassard."

"No," says he, but I gave him a shove out of the way and I went in. She's lying on a couch, in what I think they call a negligee, black, it was, and so thin you could see the pinkness of her right through it. She was smoking, in those short, quick, purple puffs.

"Why didn't you telephone, like you said?" she asked.

"Maybe I didn't have a dime," I said. "Or maybe I just wanted to see a super's wife at home. Finished all your chores yet?"

"I don't like you," she said. "I'm not going to hire you after all."

"Oh, I would, if I were you," I said. "I grow on people. You'd be surprised how they cling to me. Now, just one question. What was your husband's life insurance company?"

"I don't know," she said. "I don't know if he even had any. He tried once to talk about it, but I wouldn't let him. I said if he died, I didn't want any pay for it."

"I see!" I say. "What's money, anyhow? Who wants it? Not us, do we?"

"You're not working for me now," she said.

"Then you wouldn't be interested to hear about a clue?" I ask.

She puts out her cigarette and takes another out of the pack she's got beside her. Only the book of matches is empty; she tears it in two and looks at me, sidelong. I'm sitting on the edge of the table, and I give her one good, straight look, then I look all around the room.

"Nice place you got here," I said. That was true. It was a good floor plan, and kind of dark. I liked the way it was fixed up. Green carpet, pink walls, a lamp made like a sort of huge star with a red shade, some pictures on the walls; a big one of a house in Mexico, I guess, with some pale kind of people looking out of all the windows.

"All right," she said. "I'll buy it. Give me a light, and let's hear your clue."

I chucked her a pack of matches. "Wa-ait a minute!" I said. "Wait a minute. Did your husband ever have a plaid cap?"

"No," she said, very short.

"That's too bad," I said. "His initials in it, and all?"

"Where'd you find it?" she asked.

"Down on one of the docks," I said.

She goes on smoking for a while. I get up.

"Wait!" she says. "I've been thinking. He did have a cap like that, but he didn't wear it much."

"Here now?" I asked.

"I don't know," she says. "I just haven't had the heart to go over his things."

"Suppose I take a look?" I say.

"All right," she said, as if she was crying, with her head turned away. "In the bedroom closet."

He didn't have much of a wardrobe, but I went through the pockets of all his things hanging there.

"Cap's not there," I said.

"And you found it—on a dock?" she said. "What does that *mean?*"

"You tell me," I said.

"Are you going to the police?" she asked.

"I'll take another look first," said, and then I left her.

I went to a dock where I know the watchman, and he let me through. After a while I came back, with a lot of stuff in my hand, some of it dripping wet. You'll know later, I say, when he asks questions. But I got to see the cops first.

I stopped to pick up the cap from a little tailor where I'd left it, then I went to the station, and I showed them what I had. The wallet that had his name and address under a strip of cellophane had got sort of wedged in a girder and it was pretty dry; nothing in it but some snaps of his wife and a French franc. The checked cap was wet, but there was a handkerchief tied in a loop, with a lot of blood on it.

"Been used for a gag," I said.

"Nope. A sling," says Captain Canoodler.

You knock a man out, unconscious, maybe dead. You're going to dump him off a dock. But you put a sling on him, so he'll be comfortable. All right. All right. All right. Me, I don't mix it with the precinct captain.

I dictate a list to a cop, he types it, I sign it, Canoodler signs it. We talk a while; he says just what I expect him to say, and I get a few ideas into his head, which is not easy. Then I step in a bar and get a couple of double ryes, and then I get along to the blonde's. It is getting late now, after midnight. I ring the super's bell, and wait. I ring again, and do some more waiting. I didn't figure it would take the blonde long to put on as many clothes as she was apt to wear, but maybe she had curlers in her hair, or greaseless grease on her face, as I can't think of other reasons. Anyhow, I keep my finger on the bell, and after a while the latch clicks and I go in. The Harpo Marx character is standing there, all dressed, in a dark suit, even got a necktie on.

"What d'you want?" he asks.

"I'd like a couple of race horses," I answer. "I'd like a new car. I'd like a yacht, a lot of things. But right now I want to see Mrs. Van Stuyvesant."

"I'm not going to disturb her at this hour."

"Maybe she's up, reading a good book," I say.

"No," he says. "Her lights are all out."

"Where do you live?" I ask.

"I have a room—on the premises," says he.

"In the cellar, maybe," I said. "That's a good place to catch rats."

I saw that the door of her apartment was on the latch, so I give him a shove. One of his big shoulders went sliding down his back, and while he tried to push it back, I got by him, into the apartment. She was standing there, in some sort of long nightgown, pale blue; her feet were bare, and her toenails painted blue, her long blonde hair down to her waist.

"I got information for you," I say.

"Give," she said.

I had a copy of the list of what I'd brought to Canoodler, and I read it to her.

"God!" she said. "Then he was murdered, thrown off the dock."

I lit a cigarette and sat down on the edge of the table. She was crying, but plenty of dames can do that, any time they want. "Then—the case is closed?" she said. "Now they know—he's dead?"

"There's no case," I said.

"But all those things on the dock …!"

"They could have been planted," I said.

She gave me one of those sidelong looks, and took a cigarette out of a box. This time I gave her a light, her hand was shaking so.

"Anyhow," she said, "now they know—that Willie's dead."

"Nope," I said. "There's no case. No corpse. Nobody to accuse. Nothing to bring into court."

"But …!" she said.

"Yeah," I said. "But. The insurance people won't pay off till there's a body."

"But I don't want anything to happen to Willie!" she cried.

"Sure," I said. "But you'd have ten thousand bucks—"

"*Ten!*" she says. "I'd have fifty thousand."

"Well, no," I say. "You'd have ten, sister. You owe me a bill."

"You—rat!" she says. "You—"

"Change the record," I tell her. "I heard that one before. Ten is what you get—if I work for you. Otherwise, you go to jail."

She's puffing on her cigarette, little clouds of purple smoke.

"But …!" she says.

"But," I say. "If you want that ten thousand, you can have it. You don't even have to sign a note. You'll pay me when the insurance people pay you. Look how I trust you."

"But I'm *fond* of Willie!" she says.

"Ten thousand bucks worth?"

"I thought we could swing it together," she said, doing some more crying. "Willie knew I wanted—I needed a lot of things, and he thought—"

"Yeah, I know how Willie thought," I said. "But why the hell did you ever marry that poor little shrimp?"

She was really crying now, all right.

"He was—such a gentleman," she said.

I waited a minute, then I said: "Call in your handyman."

She waited a minute, two, then she opened a door to what was probably the bedroom.

"Come here, will you, please, Hans?" she said, and in comes the Harpo Marx character.

"I'm working for Mrs. Van Stuyvesant," I tell him, "and I'd like you to help me pick up some clues."

He looks at her, and she nods her head. So we go out, take him down to a friend's car I borrowed. We get in and drive away. "What's that, over your side of the road?" I ask, and when he turns to look, I give him a rabbit punch, and he's out. The Harpo Marx wig was easy enough to get off, but the eyebrows were pretty hard; they stuck. Well, anyhow, I did it. I had some bits of lead pipe and put them in his pockets, because I did not want him coming up too soon, and I drove down to the dock.

Of course, it is my profession to work for law and order, and if I was not ethical, I would lose my license. So that although the blonde knows it, I am thankful I was able to stop a big fraud from being put over on a life insurance company.

Glitter of Diamonds

It was raining, and blowing half a gale that autumn afternoon, and Lady Beryl was very restless. A tall, gaunt woman with wild red hair carelessly pinned up, wearing a gray wool skirt and a most incongruous green nylon blouse with crooked shoulder pads and many ruffles, she paced up and down the long living room of the house in Connecticut, lent her for the summer by one of her many American friends.

"Miss my exercise," she said. "If I could get out, even for a while...."

"But, Madame, this weather ...!" protested Mademoiselle Gervaise d'Arville.

"Call this weather?" said Lady Beryl. "Not me. No. What's keeping me in is that nephew of mine, Philip Phipps. He *said* he'd be here at 4."

"Madame has a nephew?" asked Gervaise, with polite interest.

"Shovels full of 'em," said Lady Beryl. "Nieces, too. You accumulate 'em, you know, when you've been married three times, like me."

"Ah. One sees that," Gervaise agreed. "Shall I then find on the radio something of interest, Madame, to pass the time?"

"No, thanks. No, *thanks!*" said Lady Beryl.

What the poor gal wants, she thought, is one of those news broadcasts. And then she'll want a little talk about Conditions, all over the place, and how damn-awful everything is. No, *thanks!*

"You are agitated, Madame. A cup of tea, perhaps—?"

Lady Beryl shook her head vigorously.

Some three months ago, she had had a letter from her brother, Sir Horace Lumms-Baggington, now in the British Embassy in Washington, in a post so confidential that even he himself had little, if any, idea what it was. There's this Mlle. Gervaise d'Arville, he had written. Very nice girl. Twenty-four. Very well-educated, nice figure, nice eyes, all that. They assigned her to me, to handle my French correspondence, and the trouble is, I haven't any, never did have. Girl's one of the conscientious kind, getting a neurosis, or one of those things, because there's nothing for her to do here. Fiddles around all day, trying to be useful, tidies my desk, and all that, and really it's getting on my nerves. Take her on as a companion for a while, will you, and I'll pay her salary.

Lady Beryl had answered at once. During her frequent visits to the States she had picked up many American expressions, which she used with relish and raciness. I want a companion, she had written to Sir Horace, just like I want a hole in the head.

But then, being by nature very generous, and unfailingly optimistic, she had torn up her letter and had sent Sir Horace a telegram. SHOOT GIRL ALONG. WILL PROVIDE.

She had definite ideas as to what was the best way to provide for any personable young woman, and as soon as she had seen Gervaise she had started a campaign. Sir Horace was right; she was a very good-looking girl, nice figure, fine dark eyes, eager, pretty face. Lady Beryl gave parties for her, she took her to parties, to the Country Club, to the Art Center, even to cocktail parties in New York.

In vain. The girl did not know how to dance, and did not wish to learn. She did not play bridge, or canasta. And, what was far more serious, she showed no interest whatever in any of the young men she met. She would, at any sort of gathering, unfailingly ferret out some elderly professor, or some gloomy middle-aged man with a wife and children, with whom she could engage in serious conversation about Conditions—always with a capital C—which they found equally alarming in Europe, Asia, Africa, and the United States.

"My dear girl," Lady Beryl had said to her, "take it easy. Relax. Enjoy yourself."

"Madame," Gervaise always answered, "in the world of today, how is that possible? Ah, no, Madame! For you, for Sir Horace, for the United States, which is now my country by adoption, I wish only to work my fingers to their bones."

This made things very difficult for Lady Beryl; she greatly disliked being obliged to thwart the poor girl. She had long ago learned that Americans believed all English people craved cups of tea at all hours, but Gervaise had superimposed upon this belief her own French theory of tea. It was, according to Gervaise, a medicine, a panacea. It was, she was sure, a tonic for the nerves, for the digestion, and a cure for insomnia. But, my dear, Lady Beryl assured her, I haven't any nerves, or digestion, or insomnia, and I don't *like* tea!

Still less did she like it when, if she was taking an afternoon nap, sitting in front of the fire, Gervaise would creep up behind her with a bottle of eau de cologne to rub the stuff on her forehead. Nor could she endure being read to. If you will give me your mending to do, Madame? poor Gervaise would ask. Well, I don't have any, Lady Beryl would answer, regretfully. I mean to say, she would explain, I don't seem to tear my clothes.

"Today," Gervaise would persist, "I make you an omelette *aux fines herbes*, Madame! That you will enjoy."

But the cook had objected so strongly to Gervaise's presence in her kitchen that there was no omelette. No, Lady Beryl had decided, this won't do. It's making a nervous wreck out of the poor girl and myself, too. Got to take steps.

And she had done so.

"Can't think what's delaying Philip," she said, scowling. "He's never late. He got a prize in school for punctuality."

"Your nephew, then, is a schoolboy, Madame?"

"Oh, Lord, no! He's—" Lady Beryl paused. "He's in business," she said, "and doing very well. Fine young chap. I've asked him out here for the weekend, a couple of times, but he refused." She looked at Gervaise obliquely. "Says he has no inclination for any social engagements. Not in times like these."

"Ah!" said Gervaise.

Ah it is, thought Lady Beryl. Well, we'll see. We'll just see. One has one's hopes, *n'est-ce-pas?*

The doorbell rang. "There he is!" cried Lady Beryl, and hastened out into the hall, before Millie, the housemaid, could reach there; she opened the door, and admitted a tall, lean, black-browed young man wearing a raincoat and a beret.

"Philip!" she said, with warmth. "This *is* nice. Long time no see, eh?"

"Yes," he said. "But I don't get out of town much these days."

Millie had arrived now; she took his raincoat and beret, and Lady Beryl led him by the arm into the sitting room.

"Gervaise," said Lady Beryl, "my nephew, Philip Phipps. Philip, Miss d'Arville, who is visiting me."

"I have the privilege of being employed as companion to Lady Beryl," said Gervaise. She said it courteously and pleasantly, but resolutely. No false pretenses for that girl, no talk of her being here as a guest.

All right, thought Lady Beryl, he'll like that. "Sit down," she said. "Sit down, both of you. What'll it be, Philip? Gin and tonic? Scotch on the rocks?"

"Nothing just now, thanks," said Philip. "I'd like to get the facts first."

"Sherry, perhaps?" said Lady Beryl.

"Not just now, thanks. Aunt Beryl, I stopped at the garage to see your chauffeur—"

"Lay off him!" cried Lady Beryl. "Johnson's a very fine fellow, and I don't want him bothered."

"Apparently," said Philip, "he knew nothing about this loss."

"No. Why should he? Nothing to do with him."

"Loss?" said Gervaise. "But, Madame...."

"Aunt Beryl," said young Phipps, "am I to understand that the members of your household have not been informed of this loss?"

"No reason why they should be. Now, do take it easy, Philip. Sit down.

Cigarettes? Cup of tea? Little chat?"

"It's important not to waste time in these cases," he said, not sitting down and not taking it easy. "The trail grows cold. No. Aunt Beryl, if you'll give me a brief résumé of the facts—"

"I did. Told you on the telephone this morning."

"I'd like a statement in writing. Signed by you."

"Well.... Later on, maybe. After tea."

"I'm sorry, but I can't agree to any further delay, Aunt Beryl. If you like, you can make an oral statement, and I'll take it down, for you to sign."

"Nonsense!" said Gervaise. "I can write shorthand, also I can type. For these, I have a diploma. If you permit, I will take down madame's statement."

Philip looked at her for a moment, and she returned his glance steadily.

"Very well," he said. "Thank you."

Gervaise hurried out of the room and returned with a notebook and a pencil; she sat down by the tea table, controlled but tense, all readiness.

"Now, Aunt Beryl," said Philip.

"Same like I told you on the telephone," said Lady Beryl. "Last Sunday, it was. Gervaise and I went to the Country Club, and Downy drove us. Cook had the afternoon off—we gave her a lift to her bus stop. Millie, the housemaid, had two friends here, all of 'em in the little sitting room they have. She had the radio on—and how! She always likes it loud enough to blast your ears off. Then, when Gervaise and I got back, the things were gone."

"Madame! But, if you please.... What things?" cried Gervaise.

"Oh, some—trinkets, you might say," Lady Beryl answered.

"You said over the telephone that there was a diamond ring missing, and a diamond clip," said Philip.

"Diamonds!" said Gervaise, almost in a whisper.

"In your insurance policy," Philip went on, "these two items are valued at nine thousand dollars."

"Nine thousand!" murmured Gervaise.

"You reported that these items are missing," continued Philip. "From where? That is, where do you usually keep articles of such value?"

"Oh.... Little boxes," said Lady Beryl.

"Where are those little boxes?"

"Oh, here and there. Bureau drawers, desk drawers, and so on."

"You understand, Aunt Beryl, that it is necessary to establish the fact that you took reasonable precautions against theft—"

"Certainly!" said Lady Beryl, in a tone of hearty agreement. "But the thing is, this tramp got in. This prowler."

"Have you any proof that an intruder entered the house?"

"Certainly," she said, again. "Saw his footprints, muddy tracks on the stairs, in my room."

"Muddy?"

"Muddy," Lady Beryl insisted.

"The weather on Sunday was cold and dry. How do you account for muddy footprints on that day?"

"Might have waded across a brook," said Lady Beryl.

"Who else saw those footprints, Aunt Beryl?"

"Dunno."

"You didn't call anyone's attention to them?"

"No."

"Why not?"

"Didn't want to make anyone nervous," Lady Beryl explained. "House full of women, y'know."

"Have the floors of your rooms and the stairs been swept since you saw these—" he paused —"these muddy footprints?"

"Lord, yes! They're swept every day."

"By whom?"

"Millie. Housemaid, y'know."

"Did she make any comment—?"

"No. They'd be dried up by this morning."

"You told me that you saw the ring and the clip just before you went out on Sunday. Where were they then?"

"In a box."

"Did you lock the box?"

"Well, no. I don't believe in locking things," said Lady Beryl. "You lose the key, and then where are you?"

"You were in the habit of leaving this box unlocked?"

"Of course! In fact, it *couldn't* be locked. Candy box, y'know. Holly wreaths on it, little angels, and so on. Very pretty. Your cousin Sam gave it to me last Christmas."

"This box, then, was accessible to anyone in your household?"

"I told you it was a *prowler*," said Lady Beryl. "Now let's have a spot of tea, or something."

"Aunt Beryl," said Philip, "I wonder if you realize the serious nature of the report you made—"

"Certainly I do. Thing to do is, to track down this prowler and get the stuff back. They'll be in a pawnshop somewhere, of course. I hear you're very good at this sort of thing, Philip. Irma tells me you're as good as a detective. A dick," she amended, with her great fondness for the

American localism. "A private eye. A shamus. But no, that's a cop, isn't it?"

"When a theft is reported to us," said Philip, "we make a prompt and thorough investigation. The first step—" He paused. "The first step is, to satisfy ourselves beyond any reasonable doubt, that a theft has actually been committed."

"What else could it be?"

"In a great many instances," said Philip, "articles are reported as stolen which have simply been mislaid. And ..."— another of his pauses—"the Griffin Mutual Insurance Company is very insistent upon obtaining evidence that *every reasonable* precaution had been taken against theft."

"All right, all right, all right!" exclaimed Lady Beryl. "That's just what you're here for, my boy. Stay two or three days, a week, investigate. Track down this prowler."

Philip turned to Gervaise.

"Miss d'Arville," he said, "have you, at any time, seen this box described by Lady Beryl?"

"I have, Mr. Phipps."

"Were you aware of the contents of this box?"

"In detail, no, Mr. Phipps. But I have seen it, and it glitters, as if diamonds...."

Millie now entered the room, carrying a large and heavy tray, on which were a tea service, plates of sandwiches, bowls of salted nuts and potato chips, a bowl of ice cubes, a decanter, and glasses.

"Ah," said Lady Beryl, "now we can relax. Be cheerful...."

"Just a moment, please!" said Philip, turning to Millie. "Your name, please. Your full name...."

"It's Mildred, sir. Mildred Bauer."

"Thank you. Miss Bauer, did you sweep the stairs and the floor of Lady Beryl's bedroom this morning?"

"Yes, I did!" the girl answered, alarmed and indignant. "I always do."

"Did you notice anything unusual on these floors?"

"No, sir, I didn't. And if it's anything that's lost, or was dropped, like a fancy pin, or anything, I'd of brought it straight to Lady Beryl, like I always do."

"Did you notice anything in the nature of footprints?"

"Footprints? You mean—like footprints?"

"Footprints."

"No, I didn't."

"Miss Bauer, were you here in this house yesterday afternoon, while Lady Beryl and Miss d'Arville were absent?"

"Yes, I was. And my girlfriend, Edna, she was here too, and her boyfriend, and they can tell you theirselves that I wasn't out of their sight a minute, and if there's anything funny, or missing, what I want to know is, why wasn't I told before the police was called in?"

"I'm not a policeman," said Philip, briefly. "I'm here to make inquiries with regard to the reported loss of a diamond pin and clip."

"Diamonds!" said Millie, in much the same tone Gervaise had used.

"Miss Bauer, in your opinion, would it have been possible for any outsider to have entered this house yesterday afternoon without your knowledge?"

"Well ..." she said, slowly, "I'd say no—with the front door latched, and we could see the back door through the kitchen, and the side door's always bolted on the inside. Only, you see in the movies how easy those crooks can get into houses, and we had the radio on, and maybe we wouldn't have heard footsteps, or—that thing they open locks with—electric grill."

"Miss Bauer," said Philip, "will you give me the names and addresses of the friends who were with you yesterday?"

"Yes, I *will*," she said, and began to cry.

"Philip, let her alone!" said Lady Beryl. "She's a nice girl and—"

"He can go and *see* my friends ..." said Millie. "If he's got suspicions, he can go and ask anybody that knows me. And he can go right upstairs now and ramsack my room."

"That's scarcely within my province," said Philip.

"Well, I don't know what's your providence, and what isn't," said Millie. "But if anyone's got suspicions of me, I got a right to have my room ramsacked."

"Nonsense!" said Lady Beryl. "Nobody suspects you, Millie."

"Lady Beryl," said Gervaise, "Mr. Phipps. Excuse me, please, if I offer a suggestion. But I have read much about such investigations, and I think it is in all cases customary to begin with a process of elimination of the members of the household. No?"

"Quite right," said Philip. "You are quite right."

"Then I ask you to search my room also, Mr. Phipps."

"No!" said Lady Beryl. "I won't have it!"

"Madame!" said Gervaise, with utmost earnestness. "Believe me, this search would be of advantage not only to yourself but to all of your household. It would help to establish the fact that these diamonds have not been mislaid, but that they have been removed from the premises."

"No!" repeated Lady Beryl, and then, almost at once: "All right!" she said. "I'll just rip upstairs myself and see."

"But, Madame! But no! To do that is to spoil all! This company of

Griffin might well say—ah! In advance of the search madame has flown up the stairs! She has concealed the diamonds!"

"*I* don't care what they say," said Lady Beryl, peevishly.

"But, Madame! There is your reputation to consider!"

"My reputation can look after itself," said Lady Beryl.

"Madame! I beg you, permit Mr. Phipps to search my room and the room of Millie."

"And there's another domestic, isn't there?" Philip asked.

"There's Mrs. McKenna, the cook," said Millie. "She's right out in the hall, taking it all in."

"If you'll ask her to step in …" said Philip.

A form appeared in the doorway, a short, stout woman, almost oval in shape, with high, round shoulders, like a belligerent Mrs. Humpty Dumpty.

"McKenna is the name," she said, "and the President himself could not set foot in my room. Let you lay a hand on me, and I'll go to law. For I've my rights as well as anyone, high or low."

"Mrs. McKenna!" said Gervaise. "Believe me, it is to your own advantage—"

"Is it so?" asked Mrs. McKenna, with irony. "I'll be up the stairs now, and I'll turn the key in the lock of my door and I will drop it in the pocket of my apron. And let anyone lay a hand on me—"

"Nobody's going to," said Lady Beryl. "Philip, just drop the whole thing."

"I'm afraid that wouldn't do," said Philip. "You've reported a loss and the company is obliged to investigate—"

"Well, I take it back," said Lady Beryl. "Cancel the report. The things will probably turn up, sooner or later, anyhow."

"Have you any reason for assuming that?" Philip asked.

"Because they do," said Lady Beryl. "There was this elderly clergyman, for example. Lost some very valuable book—thousand years old—something of the sort. And it turned up, buried at the foot of an oak tree in his garden. I mean, things like that. Now, just skip it. Drop it."

"Aunt Beryl," said Philip, "I'm obliged to put this bluntly. This attitude on your part will inevitably lead the officers of the Griffin to suspect that you were attempting to present a fraudulent claim."

"Or that madame was attempting to shield another," said Gervaise. "To one who knows the generosity, the kindness of Lady Beryl, that thought comes uppermost. Madame knows, or believes that she knows where these jewels are. And in her bounty of heart, she wishes to protect the thief. Mr. Phipps! Is it not obvious? When madame made her report, she did not know, did not suspect the one who is the thief. But now—all is otherwise. Is it not obvious, Mr. Phipps, that something has occurred—*between the time of the report and the present moment?*"

"Very well put!" said Philip. "Very well reasoned. Very good. Have you ever done any work of this sort, Miss d'Arville? Investigating?"

She smiled a little then, for the first time since his arrival.

"Only in fiction, Mr. Phipps," she said. "I read many stories of detection, and how much I enjoy those which are logical—"

Lady Beryl had quietly opened the door that led into the dining room and had reached the hall before there was a cry from Mrs. McKenna and an answering cry from Gervaise. She ignored them; she started to run up the steps. But they were after her. As she opened a door on the floor above, Philip laid his hand on her arm.

"Aunt Beryl," he said, "if you know anything, or suspect anything—" there was one of his pauses—*"now is the time to speak."*

"Says who?" demanded Lady Beryl.

"Mr. Phipps," said Gervaise, "this room which Lady Beryl had flown up to enter is *my* room. I believe that something has recently developed which has caused Lady Beryl to suspect me of this theft. And because of her bounty of heart, she has wished to discover the diamonds herself, to conceal them, in order to protect me."

"Criminy!" said Lady Beryl, in dismay. This is going to be hard to laugh off, she thought. They're both so doggone serious and logical and stupid. Dumb, that's what they are. They've just about spoiled the whole show. Just about—but not quite. I started this, and I'll finish it. So off we go, taking all the hurdles, and tantivity, and all that.

"Very good!" she said, and threw open the door, a little harder than she intended; it crashed against the wall. It was a large room, handsomely furnished, and scrupulously neat. Too neat, Lady Beryl thought, but then Philip's like that, too. She crossed the room to a secretary and let down the flap, disclosing a desk in beautiful order, letters arranged in the pigeonholes.

"But, Madame …!" said Gervaise.

"A secret drawer," Lady Beryl explained, and began scrabbling at the wooden panel between the rows of pigeonholes. "You turn something, pull something, push something."

"Permit me, Madame," said Gervaise, and reaching past Lady Beryl, she turned something and pushed something, and a little drawer shot out so violently that it left its groove and fell onto the desk, spilling its contents. In the light of the gray day the diamonds glittered blue and white.

Lady Beryl scooped them up. "Very good!" she said. "Now I've found 'em. Nothing's lost. Everything's fine. Your Mutual Griffin can be happy now."

"Aunt Beryl," said Philip, "I must ask for an explanation. I must ask why you made that claim, why you were insistent upon my coming all the way out here—"

"Nope," said Lady Beryl. "Nothing to say. I won't talk."

"Aunt Beryl, I am obliged to make some sort of report to my company. What—?"

"Tell 'em I mislaid the things. And then found 'em again."

"When there was a question of a search being made," said Philip, "you came directly to this desk, to this secret drawer. Am I to assume—?"

"Probably yes," said Lady Beryl. "Anyhow, drop it!"

"Aunt Beryl," he said, severe, but obviously very unhappy. "I've always had a great regard for you. Knowing your father and his reckless disposition, I could have understood your having some temporary financial difficulty. But *this* …?"

"Oh, do let me alone?" cried Lady Beryl, desperately. "You're persecuting me!"

"Madame," said Gervaise, "your nephew thinks only of your reputation. Mr. Phipps!" she turned to Philip, and never had she looked so handsome, so pale, so proud. "Mr. Phipps, it is I who took these jewels. *I* am the thief!"

"Hooey!" cried Lady Beryl, in a shout of anger and frustration. "That girl's as honest as daylight. She wouldn't steal a fly. No … that's not right. A crumb? No—what *is* it that people wouldn't steal? A pin, that's it! *She's* thinking of my 'repute.' I won't have it! *I* took those ding-blasted diamonds myself, and I put 'em there in the desk. And now I've got them back, there's no harm done, and it's nobody's *business* why."

Gervaise approached her, and laid a hand on her sleeve.

"Dear Lady Beryl," she said, "please believe that one understands how it is, in these times, for the members of the aristocracy."

"Who? *Me?*" asked Lady Beryl.

"It is so in all countries, dear Madame," said the earnest girl. "Taxes, confiscations, the loss of privileges, of power, of wealth. It is the beginning of a new order, Madame, a new democracy—the beginning, one hopes, of a better way of life. But the members of the aristocracy, however admirable, however guiltless they may be as individuals, must suffer, must become impoverished."

"But, my dear girl!" Lady Beryl began. Then she caught sight of her nephew's face and she became silent. He was looking at Gervaise—and with what a look! Respectful, admiring—almost human, thought Lady Beryl.

"Yes," Philip said. "Very well put, Miss d'Arville. But ethical values don't change."

"No," Gervaise agreed. "But in times like these, Mr. Phipps...."

"Well, yes ..." said Philip.

They actually believe they're talking, thought Lady Beryl. I suppose they could go on this way for hours.

"Now," she said, "you two nip downstairs and get your tea. I'm going to lie down."

She gave them what she hoped was a winning smile and moved toward the door, which Philip held open for her. As she started down the corridor, he closed the door, and, swiftly and silently, Lady Beryl returned, to stand outside the room.

"But I still don't understand why she did such a thing," Philip was saying.

"Ah, Mr. Phipps!" Gervaise said. "In these changing times ..."

"Well, yes," he admitted. "In any case—" one of his pauses— "I don't regret having come all the way out here, at the beginning of a very busy week. Because it's given me the opportunity of meeting you."

"You're very kind, Mr. Phipps. And now, if we go to our tea, perhaps you will tell me a little about your work of investigation. I shall be very much interested."

Lady Beryl hastened off to her own room, and closed the door. Ah! she said to herself, with a long sigh of relief. My "repute" may be a little dented, but it was worth it! Yes. *Ça marche*, okay, okay.

Very, Very Dark Mink

Pennington sat in the Company's office, smoking a pipe, because Captain Gregg might come in, and he despised cigarettes. "Just dropped in ...," he said, to Larkin, and hoped he sounded, and looked, very nonchalant.

Larkin was working ledger. "Yeah," he said.

"I was just wondering ..." said Pennington. "Surveyors still working on the old Dos Santos?"

"Finished," said Larkin. "She's in fine shape. She'll make her next run the fifteenth."

God! If old Gregg would just put in a word for me with the company—let me get back in Dos Santos ... I'm so damn sick of this Liverpool run.

"Lady for you on the telephone, Mr. Pennington," said the receptionist.

"*Couldn't* be," said Pennington, astounded. "There's nobody who'd know about getting me here."

"Well, one lady anyhow, Mr. Pennington," said the receptionist, archly. "She's called you up two or three times before."

"I'll see ..." he said, and rose, tall, slim, neat, boyish-looking for his thirty years. He sat down on the edge of the receptionist's desk and took up the telephone. He was sure it was a mistake, but it was rather gratifying that the receptionist and Larkin and another fellow working in a corner were obviously interested. "Pennington speaking," he said.

"Albert ...?"

He slipped off the desk and nearly fell; he hopped on one foot for a moment to get back.

"It's—you ..."

"I've been trying for days to get you. Albert, I *must* see you, at once."

"Why, certainly!"

"Where?"

"You say."

"At the Charleroy, on East 55th."

"Sure. Certainly. Right away."

He hung up, but he didn't get the instrument straight, and it fell off, dragging the base to the floor with a crash and the delicate tinkle of the bell. It frightened him, that little bell; it was like a ghostly signal.

"Oh ... I'm sorry ..." he said, and picked it up. "I'm *very* sorry. If you'll tell Captain Gregg I just stopped by. Same address—over in Staten Island."

"Yes, we have it," the receptionist assured him.

"Thank you," he said. "I'm *very* sorry."

He went out, into the narrow downtown street, where the autumn wind jumped at his throat; he set off for the subway station with his long, limber stride, and in his heart there was a sense of anger, and a great dread. It had taken him so long to get over Cynthia, and now, when he had at last stopped thinking of her, she had come back, like this. He could have endured it, he thought, if he had happened to see her somewhere, on a street, perhaps; he could, he thought, have felt only anger. But the sound of her voice, sweet, high, and clear, had so shaken him that he felt a sort of tremor; when he got his fare out of his pocket, his hand was unsteady.

"I'm terribly sorry, Albert," she had said, with tears raining down her face. "But I *can't* be treacherous to John. How could I, when he's always been so kind and good to me?"

"You don't love him," Albert had said. "And he's nothing but a damn stuffed shirt."

"I won't listen to that," she had said, sternly.

"And he doesn't love you. He couldn't love anybody. He married you because you were well-bred, and pretty, and one of the Vanderdorfs. Business asset for him."

"I *won't* listen!" she had cried.

And that had been the end. She had gone up to her room in the Royal Castle, that enchanting hotel on the top of a hill in the West Indies island of Conchita. His ship was sailing at ten, and he had been in the lobby by eight, thinking, feeling sure she would come, if only for a moment, to say good-bye. But she had not come.

There'll be a letter in Trinidad when I get there, he thought. And when there was not, all right, he thought, there'll be one in New York, sure to be. But there had never been a letter, or a telephone call; nothing, no word for over two years. Her husband, John Harrowby, was the President of the steamship company, and once in a while Pennington saw him, going into his office, or coming out of it, a big, handsome, heavy man with gray hair and a scornful curl to his nostrils, a man old enough to be Cynthia's father. A very much disliked man, because of his arrogance, his bad humor, his lack of any consideration, or even justice toward his employees. He would nod at Pennington, but without speaking; he scarcely knew him. One of our officers, that was all.

"I hate him," Miss Allen, his secretary had once said to Pennington. "Here it is, Friday afternoon, and he tells me he wants me *all day* tomorrow. When I had such a beautiful date, too. I don't know why I stand him—except that I'm saving up for my trousseau. And I don't see why his wife stands him. She's a sweet thing, and *very* pretty. Well, if she knew as much about him as *I* do ..."

The buzzer had rung for her then, and she had gone, and he hadn't had a chance to talk to her since then. I wouldn't have asked her any questions, anyhow. You don't do that, about a man you're working for. And anyhow, it wouldn't matter. I wouldn't go running to Cynthia with any tales I'd heard about her husband. It's all up to her. If she'd wanted to see me, I'd have come. Any time.

And what did I do, anyhow, that was so—unforgivable? misunderstood her—and when she told me, I told her how sorry I was. But, my God! Almost any man would have misunderstood.

They had met on board the *Dos Santos*, on the South American run. He was Second Officer, and she was a passenger of the utmost importance, the owner's wife; she had the best cabin, she sat at the Captain's table. The first night out, she had spoken to him on the promenade deck, asked him some questions; she had seemed to want to go on talking, and he was willing enough. He thought she was lovely.

It was she who had sought him out. She had asked him when he was off duty. Come and talk to me then, she had said, and she would be waiting for him, with a wide smile at the sight of him. Her husband had flown down to Rio but she didn't like flying; she was taking the ship to Conchita where he was coming in a day or two for some business reason, and then they would fly back to New York.

"But if you don't like flying—" Pennington had said.

"John's always thinking he can get me to like it," she had answered. "He's sure I will. He's going to buy a plane of his own, after we get home."

He found out that this was the first trip she had ever made. Except to Florida, for our honeymoon, she said. He had found out a good deal about her from their talks; she was the only child of a widowed mother, who had brought her up in what Pennington thought a preposterous and dangerous way. She had gone to a private school, and later to a Junior College; she had had plenty of girlfriends, but she had never gone out with a boy.

"Mother didn't want me to," she had told Pennington. "She said that any boy I liked was welcome to come and see me at home, and after two or three times she'd know if he was all right to go out with. But I hardly ever met a boy. If one of the girls asked me to a party, Mother said she'd have to meet the girl's mother, and—well, that was sort of embarrassing. I felt I'd rather stay home than tell that to any of my friends."

So she had stayed home; she had had no fun, no gaiety, no beaus. "But I loved school," she had told him. "I loved being in the plays we gave, and things like that. And Mother took me to lots of matinees and concerts.

She played the piano herself, wonderfully, and often she'd read out loud. She's a wonderful reader."

"I bet …!" Pennington said. It was plain that she hadn't been unhappy; she was not unhappy now. But she likes me, all right, he had thought. Once he had taken her hand, her dear little hand, and it was a few moments before she drew it away.

"How did you meet—Mr. Harrowby?" he had asked her.

"Oh, he's a friend of Uncle's, in Richmond," she had answered. "He'd been coming to our apartment for ages—over a year—before I ever dreamed how he felt. And then … He was so kind and nice to Mother and me … Mother's gone down to Richmond, but he sends her a check every month, and she comes to visit us, quite often."

She didn't love Harrowby; Pennington was sure of that. She admired him, and she had been taught to believe that wives love their husbands, automatically. She doesn't know what it means to be in love, Pennington thought. But she likes me, all right. And he liked her. It was more than liking; he was charmed by her, by her beauty, her gentleness, her courtesy, by her strange lack of worldly knowledge. I used to lie awake at night, and call her "the Sleeping Beauty." I hoped I'd be the one to wake her up.

Then the Captain had got a radio to stop overnight at Conchita, to wait for a belated cargo for inland.

"The old man's as sore as hell about it," Pennington had told her. "It's generally only a three-hour stop, and this throws out his whole schedule. Me, I like it fine. It's one of the prettiest islands, and there's a little hotel there I stopped at before. Run by a French couple. Wonderful food, wonderful view." He had gone on and on, talking about the Royal Castle Hotel, because it was growing harder and harder to talk to her, when this was the end.

"Where are you staying?" he had asked.

"Oh, some friends of John's have invited me there," she had answered. "The Governor's A.D.C. and his wife."

It was late afternoon when they came into the harbor at Conchita; the sea was deep blue and quiet; behind the pretty little town there were low hills, green, and almost treeless.

"The rainy season's just over," he had said. "In another month or so, you'd find everything parched and yellow."

"Couldn't you take me to your wonderful hotel?" she had asked.

He had been too much astounded to answer for a moment.

"But—the A.D.C.'s sure to come down to the dock and meet you," he had said. "It—I don't see—"

"I'll say I'm staying on board tonight to finish my packing," she had said. "Then, after he's gone, I'll come to your hotel. I'll certainly be there in time for dinner."

"Well ..." he had said. "Fine! Fine!"

But he hadn't known what to make of it. She doesn't know what a risk she's taking, he thought. In these little islands, everything gets around.

He had been on a hotel terrace waiting for her, and, after it had grown dark, a taxi had stopped, and out she had got. With a suitcase.

"I'll register as Miss Birch," she had said. "I've taken off my ring."

She had been excited, as he had never before seen her, or imagined her. She had been wonderful at dinner; she had not seemed naive but sparkling and joyous.

"I told the stewardess that I didn't feel very well and didn't want any dinner," she had said. "I told her I just wanted to rest, and not be disturbed until tomorrow morning. As soon as it was dark, I came ashore. I don't *think* anyone noticed me."

"Look here!" he had said. "Look here! I mean—why did you do this?"

"I wanted—only this one night ..." she had said.

All right; what would any man understand by that? He had been almost stunned by delight; as they strolled down the hill together, he could not speak for a time. Then he said, haltingly.

"You're so—very generous. You're—so wonderful—and beautiful—and darling."

"I'm not. I'm so glad you told me about this heavenly place. It's even better than you said."

He had put his arms around her, and she had permitted that, but when he had drawn her closer to him, she had pushed him away.

"Please, Albert, no!"

"Let's go back now," he said. "Your room's on the floor below mine. Shall I come—in an hour?"

"To my room?" she had said.

"I'll take care that nobody sees me. You can trust me, darling girl."

"To my room!" she had repeated, stopping on the driveway. "Did you think I meant—*that?*"

He had taken his arm from around her waist.

"Yes," he had said. "That's what I thought."

Then had come the tears, and all the rest of it. I'm terribly sorry, Albert ... I *won't* listen. And that was the end. Not a note, not a word from her. I don't want to see her now, he told himself. I don't know what the hell she wants, after all this time, but I don't want to go. She treated me as if I were a heel, a wolf, a cad. She ... He could not find quite the words for it, but it had been as if she had pushed him off a steep cliff, after leading him to the brink with her sweetest allurements. Then she had gone off, without a word, not caring what hurt he might be suffering. A hurt to his pride as a man, to the tenderness and honest devotion he had felt for her, a shock and a loss from which he had tried his best to recover, by not thinking of her, by forgetting her.

Only, he hadn't forgotten. Not any of it. When he came out of the subway, the wind leaped at him again, strong, very cold for October. Next month we'll be getting those damn North Atlantic gales, he thought. All right! I don't want to see her. A prude, that's what she is. A stupid, heartless little prude.

Has she changed, he thought. No; not in two years. She was—I thought she was lovely. Gentle, and kind. I thought she cared for me. A little anyhow. Well, she didn't care, and she wasn't what I imagined. The Sleeping Beauty. God, what a fool I was!

The Charleroy was a nice-looking place, with a striped awning over the porte-cochere; the room inside was somewhat dim, lit by rose-shaded lamps on all the tables; he did not see her until she raised a white-gloved hand. He crossed to her table in a corner.

"Well!" he said. "How are you?"

"Fine, thanks. And you?"

She was changed. She was thinner; there were faint hollows under her cheekbones; that dewy look had gone, that sweet freshness. Her dress was more sophisticated, a black dress with a high neck, a small black hat with a high loop of velvet on each side; over the back of her chair was draped a fur coat. She had a new poise, too; she seemed entirely at ease. He hated her for that, for being so unmoved at seeing him.

"I'm sorry to bother you," she said. "But there's something—"

"Suppose we have a cocktail first?" he suggested, and she agreed. "Cigarette?" he asked, and she accepted that, too. "You didn't use to smoke, or drink cocktails," he said.

"No ..." she said. "Albert, I want to tell you this *now*. I want to get it over with. It's—difficult."

Why come to me with your troubles? he thought. You've got a rich husband; you must have friends. Why me?

"Something gone wrong?" he asked, without even pretending too much interest.

"It's blackmail," she said. "And this time I can't pay."

"Too bad. It's always a mistake to start that."

"I asked you to meet me, because, you see, you're involved, too."

"*What!*"

"It was about a year ago. He said he had a note to deliver to me, personally, so I went to the door. He was very shabby, and I thought it was some scheme for begging. But he went away before I'd even opened it. Here it is."

From her black crocodile handbag she brought out an envelope, addressed in printing to Mrs. John Harrowby. The note he took out was printed, too.

I guess you would not like your husband to know you spent the night with Pennington at the Royal Castle Hotel. If you wanna keep this quiet, come to Staten Island ferry house at eleven tomorrow morning, and bring one hundred dollars in cash. A boy will come up and ask you have you got the ticket; and you give him the envelope. If you got anyone with you or watching you sure will be sorry.

"You paid this?" Pennington asked.

"Yes. There's been another one, every month, but I burned them up. This one's enough, isn't it?"

"It's plenty," said Pennington. "How much have you paid?"

"It's kept on getting more and more," she said. "I've paid twenty-six hundred dollars. He—or she—wants five hundred tomorrow. And I haven't got it. I can't ask John for it without making him suspicious, because he pays two hundred and fifty a month into my account, and he knows I haven't bought anything for a long time. And if I sold my rings, or my fur coat or anything, he'd notice that. But I can't pay it tomorrow."

"Certainly not. Don't ever pay another cent. What harm do you think your blackmailer could do you? He could tell your husband, but I'll take it for granted your husband will believe you when you tell him the truth. He might say you'd been a bit indiscreet, but—"

"But what about *you?*" she cried. "Don't you realize what it could do to *you?* You'd lose your berth, of course, and I don't think you'd ever get another with any other company, after they knew. And they would know, you can be sure of that."

Her poise was not so good, after all. Her hands gave her away; they were trembling! but her voice was steady, and she looked at him steadily.

"And what about next month, and the month after, and forever and forever."

"A great-aunt died a little while ago, and left me three thousand dollars. The lawyer says he can get at least half of it advanced to me, but not till next month. John won't have to know. Then I'll hire a private detective, and he'll end this. And I'll pay you back then."

"I see! You want me to pay this blackmailer five hundred dollars cash tomorrow."

"He's got to be kept quiet till next month."

The same thing, in a way. Make use of him, make a fool of him. Then good-bye. She knew what a Second Officer's pay was, and what five hundred dollars would mean to him. He was not extravagant, and that was simply because he didn't want extravagant things. He was a very moderate drinker, he had no use for gambling; he was bored by hectic parties; he didn't spend money on women, because he ardently disliked women who wanted to get money from him.

But, on the other hand, he was not thrifty. He got what he wanted, and it had to be good. His uniforms and his shore-going clothes were custom-made; his shoes, hats, shirts, everything he bought was of the best. He had a room on Staten Island with a retired tugboat captain and his wife, and he always brought home some present for the old lady at the end of every trip. He had a little niece, and he brought her presents; guava jelly, or a coral necklace, or something of the sort for his Mother's former colored maid, who did his laundry when he was ashore; he would lend money to a friend; he would help out someone in trouble. He bought and he spent what he wanted, and put the rest in the bank, without caring much about it. Why not? All he really wanted was some day to be master of a ship. There was no one dependent upon him, and he never gave thought to growing old or ill. But he resented this demand upon him, after what she had done to him, after these two black years.

"Damn convenient for the old lady to pop off just now," he said. "What would you have done, if she hadn't?"

"I don't know ..." she said. "I tried to think of ways, but I couldn't."

Her voice was not steady now, and her long, slim hands were tightly clasped.

"If you don't do it tomorrow," she said, "you'll be ruined."

"All right!" he said. "I'll pay it—to save my job."

The same thing, in a way. He had thought at first that she needed his help, but she wouldn't have it so. It's all for your sake, Albert.

She ordered shrimp salad and a cup of coffee, and he had the same. He didn't care.

"I suppose I'll have to give you the cash," he said. "I couldn't take it to the ferry myself."

"I'm afraid you will. I'll meet you wherever you say."

"You'd better choose the trysting place," he said, and saw the color rise in her thin, lovely face.

She understood that, anyhow, he thought. She suggested the lobby of a department store on Forty-second Street, at half-past ten. She rose, and he helped her on with her fur coat.

He went back to his room then. Mrs. Logan wanted him to eat with them, but he thanked her and said he had a date, because he didn't feel like talking. He went to a nearby diner, and on the way home, he bought a paper book and a couple of magazines. I'll go to bed, and read myself to sleep, he thought.

But he could not read. He opened one of the magazines, and then it came down upon him, like a stifling dark cloud, all the pain and the loss and the unbearable remorse. What would you have done, if the old lady hadn't popped off? he had asked her, and she had answered, I don't know. I tried to think of a way.

For a year she had endured this dread, this strain; the mark of it was plain. And she was thinking about me, he thought. Worrying about me, more than about herself. I love her. I love her, he thought. If I could only help her. The money's nothing. But maybe her legacy won't come in time. And if it does, she wouldn't know how to pick out a private detective. She might get hold of a crook, might get in a hell of a lot more trouble. If I could help her ... Find out who's doing the blackmailing. The stewardess? One of the crew? The taxi driver who took her to the Royal Castle? It could be any one of a dozen, a score of people. She didn't know; she hadn't any idea, of the risk she was taking. Or how I was going to see it. How I'd feel. It was my fault, the whole thing. I ought to have known she wasn't that sort.

He got up early and had breakfast in the kitchen with Mrs. Logan; then he went to his bank in New York. He got there too early, and he waited in the street for it to open. The wild, cold wind was still blowing. The sky was growing darker. Wind's shifting, he thought. In four clays, I'll be off—to Liverpool, and maybe this is the last time.

The bank opened, and he drew out a thousand dollars which was almost all he had, and asked for an envelope; then he took a taxi uptown to Forty-second Street. He was early for their appointment, but she was there before him, lovely and elegant in her fur coat and that winged black hat. But so pale, too fragile....

"Albert ...?" she said, as if it were a question.

"Look," he said, standing close to her and speaking in a low tone. "I brought a thousand, so that you wouldn't worry in case you didn't get your legacy in time."

He handed her the envelope, and she bent her head, to put it in her handbag; when she looked up, her dark lashes were wet, her dark eyes were shining with tears.

"I'll be back, the end of next month," he said. He waited, but she said nothing. "Can we have lunch together, then?" He waited again.

"Can I—ever see you again?" he asked, curtly.

"I—can't," she said. "I'm afraid."

"Of more blackmailing?"

"No!" she said, with a flash of her old spirit. "I can't—I mustn't see you again. That's why you never heard from me. I knew then, that night—I knew I mustn't see you again."

"You don't mean …? Look here, Cynthia …! You don't mean …"

"Yes, I do," she said. "I knew then. I knew—it *wasn't* a happy marriage. John's always been kind and generous to me, but … I haven't been a good wife to him. I wasn't … I couldn't pretend …"

"Yes …" said Pennington. "It was—you mean—it was me?"

"It can't be," she said. "John's my husband. I gave him—my promise—to be faithful—for better or for worse."

"Where do I come in?" Pennington asked.

"Nowhere," she said, with a smothered sob. "I can't betray John, when he's always been so good—never done anything … I can't ruin Mother's life for my own happiness."

"What about my happiness?" he asked.

"You're young, and you're very attractive. You'll find someone else."

"Cynthia! Look here! I—"

She laid her hand on his arm.

"Albert, I've *got* to go, or I'll be late. Albert, my dear, my dear, dear Albert …" She gave him a kiss on the cheek, so light, she moved away so quickly that she was in the street before he recovered himself. Again he helped her into a taxi, and again she was gone.

He walked all the way downtown to William Street, and strolled into his company's office.

"Miss Allen busy?" he asked the receptionist.

"The Boss-Man isn't here, but maybe she has a lot of work."

Miss Allen came out of the private office, cheerful and pretty.

"How's about lunch?" Pennington asked.

"Fine!" she said. "The tycoon won't be back till half-past two, so I've got a little time, for a change."

He had taken her out to lunch before; she liked him, and she was glad to go, but she had no illusions about the invitation. Probably he liked her company; most people did, but she was well aware that his chief reason was to hear about the office doings. Plenty of the other officers did that, and she knew exactly which ones she could talk to freely, and which ones were not to be trusted. They went to a restaurant where they had gone before, a nice little place.

"No, thanks," she said. "No cocktail, when I'm going back to work. But I can always eat."

"How's the trousseau coming along?" he asked.

"Too good to be true," she answered. "Mother and Dad are simply outdoing themselves, and a lot of old great-aunts, and uncles, and cousins that I hardly remember are creeping out from under rocks and giving me things. And we've got an apartment promised for the first of December. It is a horrid, dark little place and I know it has cockroaches. And it's in Jamaica—if you ever heard of that."

"Certainly. Know it intimately. It's the place where you change trains."

"We're glad enough to get it, though," she said. "I told you the *Dos Santos* is going out on the fifteenth of November, didn't I? I know you're interested; you were always so crazy about her."

"You get that way," said Pennington.

He realized that she was telling him what she thought he wanted to know, but this time the smart kid was wrong. He had remembered what she had said before. "If she"—Cynthia, she meant—"knew what *I* know about him," and he had come with the hope that he would find out something that would completely discredit Harrowby. If Cynthia found he had another woman, she'd change, she'd feel damn differently. Because she's like that. Prudish, maybe. Or maybe it's just honorable. Just good.

"They haven't decided yet about the personnel," she went on. "Except that Captain Decker's going to be in command, and he wants to choose his own officers. The board won't allow that, they say it leads to 'favoritism', and Harrowby wants to choose his own pets."

"That's the way things go," said Pennington.

"He has to watch his step now," she said. "Business hasn't been so good the last two years. But of course you know that. There's the new line competing with us, new ships, and better rates. And then there was that trouble with the union. The board didn't like the way he handled that. He *couldn't* negotiate. He just wants to rule everything and everybody. Now they're talking about a ten percent cut in salaries, and, boy! Will that hit him! He gets a big salary, but he's a terrific spender. A penthouse, and a French couple to look after them, and a new car that's out of this world. He plays the races, too."

"And his girlfriend …?"

"I didn't say he had a girlfriend."

"That's what I understood you to say, yesterday. But I thought …"

"Well, yes, he has," she said, "It's not much of a secret, anyhow. People have seen them around together. She's got a bit part in a Broadway show. I went to see it, out of curiosity, and she's certainly good-looking—if you like that type. One of those haughty blondes. *You* know. And what a name she's dreamed up for herself! Angela Verity, no less. She's got him roped and tied, all right, and he's plenty scared."

"Scared of her?"

"Yes. For one thing, he's got to keep respectable, or the board wouldn't stand for it, even if he is the President. They could vote him out, you know. And then she takes him for plenty, and he knows she wouldn't bother with an old stuffed shirt like him if he didn't give."

"How do *you* know what he gives her?"

"I guess I don't know the half of it," she admitted, and Pennington was pleased to see the color in her cheeks, the fiery look she had. Her anger and her scorn for Harrowby were, he thought, leading her to say more than she would like to remember later on. "But I can't help noticing things, can I? I have to get papers out of his desk, and twice I saw boxes from a jeweler. All right! I opened them. I know I shouldn't have but, after all, I'm human. One was a pin, a good one, too, and the other was a platinum cigarette case, with A. V. engraved on it."

Pennington didn't need to hear any more. This Angela Verity would be easy enough to find; he could ask questions, do a little bribing of elevator boys, maids, and he might be able to find a girl who hated her, and would talk. I could do that before I sail, he thought, and if Cynthia had the facts, if she knew for sure he'd been cheating on her … Only, of course, she wouldn't say that. She'd say "unfaithful," and I don't think she could take it. She'd never be unfaithful, to anyone. And she looks at marriage as an absolutely loyal partnership.

He wanted to get away now, and start his investigation, but Miss Allen had more to say.

"And that mink coat …!" she said. "You can see what a spot he's in, when a man in his position has to buy her a mink coat on the installment plan. I suppose she saw his wife wearing one, and told him she wanted one exactly like it. Well, she's got it, but how! When the first bill came from the furrier's, I thought it was just an ad, but I always open everything, just to be sure. When I saw it was a bill for a monthly installment on a mink coat, well! Three hundred dollars. *And* overdue! You could have knocked me down with a feather. The coat had a number, and one lunch time I went into the furrier's. Of course he'd have to pay something down on it, and carrying charges, but even I didn't know he's been getting these bills for almost a year. He told me not to open any others, so I haven't. But you can see what he'll do for his gorgeous blonde."

"Yes," said Pennington.

When at last he could get away from her, he started walking uptown, not going anywhere, just thinking. He went into a movie and sat through two shows, and he couldn't have told anyone much about them. He came out at seven o'clock, and he had made up his mind. He was going to take a chance, and he was staking everything in the world he valued on it. If he was wrong, if he failed, he would be disgraced, his career, that was his chosen life, would be broken and ruined, and Cynthia would be horrified, disgusted, lost for good and all. But I'm going to try it, he said to himself. I think I'm right.

He looked in the telephone book and called Harrowby's apartment. Harrowby himself answered, which is what uneasy men do.

"Pennington speaking, sir. Second Officer in the *Beresford*. I'd like to see you for a moment, sir."

"*What?*" said Harrowby. "See me in the office."

"It's a personal matter, sir."

"I don't see my employees here at home," said Harrowby. "Speak to me in the office, Pennington."

"Sorry, sir, but it's not a business matter. It's personal. It's—" He paused a moment. "It's about a mink coat, sir." There was a moment's silence.

"Very well!" said Harrowby. "Wait downstairs, and I'll see you in the lobby."

"I'd rather come up, sir."

"Well, you can't," said Harrowby, and hung up.

Pennington went directly to the apartment, got into an elevator at once, and when he rang the bell, Harrowby himself opened the door, the very image of dignity and prestige.

"Now, see here!" he said. "I'll have none of this. If you want to see me, go to the office."

"This isn't an office matter, sir," said Pennington. "Of course, if you'd rather I got the police—"

"The p—" said Harrowby. "Come in." He shut the door after Pennington. "What are you talking about?"

"I'd like Mrs. Harrowby to be here, sir," said Pennington, still with his polite Second Officer's manner.

"Well, she's not going to be," said Harrowby. But she was there already, in the long living room approached by a short flight of stairs. She looked like a school girl, in a black skirt and a plain white blouse; she was white as paper, and wide-eyed with fear.

"I have a friend who's a detective," Pennington said, not looking at her. "And he tells me he's seen Mrs. Harrowby—or his agents have seen—go down to South Ferry for several months, and give a sealed envelope to someone who approached her, and asked for 'the tickets'. This detective is sure it's blackmail."

She leaned back against the wall; none of them sat down.

"Blackmail," said Pennington, "is one of the dirtiest, lowest rackets there are. And anyone who's ever met Mrs. Harrowby would know that she's—beyond reproach. If she paid blackmail, it was only to spare someone else."

"She didn't," said Harrowby. "She— One moment."

He went out of the room, and came back with a bottle of Scotch and two glasses.

"Drink?" he asked Pennington.

"No, thank you, sir," said Pennington. "I also learned that a Miss Angela Verity has a fur coat—mink, dark mink, I believe, that's being paid for in installments. By the blackmailer."

Harrowby poured himself half a tumbler of Scotch, and gulped it down, neat.

"And—so what's your idea?" he asked.

"It's this, sir," said Pennington, still polite and quiet. "I think you've been blackmailing your wife, to pay for Miss Verity's mink coat."

Harrowby sat down, almost fell down, into a chair, and poured himself another big drink.

"You haven't any proof …" he said.

"I think I have, sir. Even for the police. You've given Miss Verity expensive presents. You've been seen around with her. You—"

Then he glanced at Cynthia, saw her still leaning against the wall. And his correct, polite manner vanished.

"You're a damn skunk," he said. "Getting money out of your wife, tormenting her, blackmailing her, to get money for your other woman."

Harrowby started on his other drink. He had faced angry union men; he had fought his own board. He knew when he could win, and he knew when he was licked.

"All right," he said. "What's the payoff? How much d'you want?"

"I want you to give your wife a divorce."

"All right," said Harrowby, without hesitation. "Is that what you want, Cynthia?"

He looked at her; her lips parted a little, but she did not speak. She could not. For a moment Pennington could see, and understand, what this meant to her, what he himself had done to her. She had given up her own happiness; she had resolved to spend all her life in a loveless and wretched marriage, because to her marriage was a promise, and she kept her promises. For a moment, he had the illusion that she was transfixed to the wall, the faithful, the innocent, the honorable, knowing herself most brutally exploited and betrayed. But I'll make it up to her, Pennington told himself. I'll make her happy.

"Well?" Harrowby asked. "Is that what you want?"

"Is it—what you want?" she asked. "Do you want—to marry—this other woman?"

"Well, to be frank, I do," he said. "I think she's going to be a famous actress, before long. She can entertain people. She—"

He stopped. But what he meant was obvious. She's everything that you're not.

"Then—you …" she said.

"All right!" said Harrowby, turning to Pennington. "Are you satisfied?"

"I want to be appointed Chief Officer on the *Dos Santos* when she sails."

"Chief …?"

"That's what I said. I've got my master's ticket. My record's absolutely clear."

"Well … And what else?"

"Nothing else."

"Then get out," said Harrowby.

Pennington looked at Cynthia.

"The Charleroy—at one, tomorrow?" he asked.

She raised her hand in a gesture he felt was assent.

"Now get out, you dirty blackmailer!" said Harrowby, and slammed the door after Pennington.

Blackmailer? Pennington said to himself, waiting for the elevator. Me? All right. I've got her out of this.

Shadow of Wings

It was late in the afternoon of a happy day that Stan Dickson first saw the shadow. He had just finished clipping the hedge, and he was sitting on the steps that led up to the veranda, looking out at the little tidal creek across the road. There was a small boatyard there, and an elderly man was using a hammer, with a clinking sound; down the street, someone was mowing a lawn. Celia was upstairs, putting the children to bed; he could hear her voice, and little Jenie's voice, loud and urgent; Jenie was four years old now, and filled with an almost desperate impatience. It no longer satisfied her to listen to a bedtime story; she wanted to compose her own, with someone to listen.

It made him smile to hear the jumbled story in that loud little voice, a bad wolf, a bad, *bad* witch, a naughty little rabbit, a good fairy, a beautiful princess. He took a pack of cigarettes out of his pocket and lit one; he smoked, well-pleased with his own life and with the tranquil Summer world. Maybe by the time little Pete grows up, there won't be any more wars.

The orange sun was swimming above the horizon, in a pale-green sky, throwing a fiery bar across the gray-green water of the creek. The old man's hammer clinked, but the lawn mower had stopped, and Jenie's voice had died away. There was another sound, somewhere in the offing; a plane, he thought, and watched for it. And then the shadow came across the face of the sun, a great flock of birds, some small, some with great wide wings beating. He heard a mewing cry, like that of a gull, he heard a fluty twitter, another unknown note; then they went sweeping past, and out of sight.

City-bred, he knew next to nothing about birds, and he frowned at the queer uneasiness that stirred in him. Damn nonsense! he told himself. Maybe this is the time of year they migrate; something of the sort, something perfectly natural.

He finished his cigarette, and went into the house. Celia was in the kitchen, beginning to dish up their early dinner. Libby was coming to sit with the babies, and they were going to the movies in the nearby town; they had made this a part of their sedate and cheerful routine. Stan did not mention the birds to Celia, but when she had gone upstairs to dress, he strolled into the kitchen where young Libby was washing the dishes. A nice girl she was, rosy and good-tempered.

"You know about these things," he said. "Do a lot of different kinds of birds often fly together in the same flock?"

"My *goodness!*" cried Libby. "Don't talk to *me* about *birds*, Mr. Dickson! My uncle Joe—he's got a truck farm, you know—why, he's creating and carrying on about the birds, from morning till night."

"Mean they're eating up the crops?" Stan asked, a little uncertainly. Because what did he know about birds? Only that farmers put up scarecrows, didn't they, to keep birds away?

"Oh, it's *lots* worse than that!" said Libby. "Why, it's even in the papers, Mr. Dickson, and the Government's sending people to find out about it. You see, the birds just aren't coming at all!"

"Coming where?"

"They aren't coming *anywhere*," Libby explained. "The crops are dying, and the trees are dying, because the birds aren't killing any of the insects. Why, you wouldn't believe how bad things are getting! The flowers, and even the grass …"

"I didn't know that birds were so useful," said Stan. "Maybe that's why our garden is so—let's call it unspectacular. Why have the birds quit on the job, Libby?"

"Nobody knows," she said. "Haven't you read about it in the papers, Mr. Dickson? Or heard people talking about it?"

"Well," said Stan, "the people in an advertising agency don't seem to talk much about birds."

"They'd ought to," said Libby, severely. "My father, and my Uncle Joe, and everybody, they all say there'll be a real famine in this country, in a few months, if the birds don't come back and kill the insects—worms, and beetles, and caterpillars, and goodness knows what—why, they're crawling all over the place."

"But I saw a big flock of birds, just a little while ago."

"I know," said Libby. "Everybody sees them—the biggest flocks of birds that ever came over here. Only, they don't *stop*. Not a one of them."

"But why not? They have to eat something somewhere, don't they?"

"Well …" Libby said. "Of course, I don't know if there's anything to it, but—well … some people say it's the Russians."

Stan bent his head, and flicked an ash off his sleeve, fighting back a grin.

"How would they manage that?" he asked, with polite earnestness.

"Well, I don't understand much about things like that," Libby answered. "But my father, he thinks they—" She paused, and putting her hands behind her, she leaned back against the sink. "What he calls it is '*deflecting*,'" she said. "Pop says that could be done, maybe. Something could be sort of sprinkled down from planes, something that would keep birds away."

Stan looked at her with a faint frown, a little impressed by her tone, and words. But only for a moment. Now, look here! he said to himself. These Russians "deflecting" the birds ... Come, come!

He went upstairs to wash, and when he came down, Celia was waiting for him. "Hello, Perfect!" he said to her, and he thought that she was just that, a tall girl, straight and proud, in a tailored white cotton dress that well set off her olive skin, her long dark eyes, her rich dark hair. She was handsome, she was intelligent, she was good-tempered, and she was superbly capable, as a mother, a housekeeper, an organizer. He was certain of a good dinner, and served on time.

"Celia," he said, "have you heard any talk in the village about birds?"

"Not in the village," she said. "But the old man from the boatyard stopped me in the street yesterday. He's a very nice old fellow, you know, and he often stops to speak to the children. But yesterday I couldn't get away from him. He went on and on about how the fish were gettin' 'out of control,' he called it. I couldn't quite follow him, but as far as I could make out, the gulls and the other seabirds had stopped catching fish, and the inlet, he said, is teeming with them. And some species, that the birds used to eat, are getting so numerous they're crowding out the others. He was very much worried. He said the balance of nature was being upset."

"I wouldn't know...." said Stan. "Maybe nature changes its balances now and then. Think so?"

"Stan, I'm just a child of the city streets. I don't know about nature. Only, I've read that when new species are introduced into a place, they can do a lot of harm. Rabbits in Australia, for instance."

"Yes," he said. "Yes, I've heard of things like that. You think, then, that maybe some new species of bird has come here, or been brought here, that's driving out all the other kinds?"

"Stan, I'm afraid I didn't take the old man's talk very seriously. Is it serious?"

"I don't know. We might take a look in the evening paper," he said. "Do you think it's important enough to be in the newspapers?"

"Probably not," he said.

He wanted it not to be that important; he wanted to laugh at the whole thing. But it was there, on an inside page, and he realized that the heading was one which, even this morning, he would have skipped without reading. SCIENTISTS STUDYING BIRD MYSTERY.

> Scientists from the Department of Agriculture have asked the assistance of ornithologists in making a survey of the changed habits recently observed in the bird life of the New England

States, and now reported to be spreading rapidly to other parts of the country.

The birds, which are an important factor in insect-control, have within recent weeks ceased to destroy various pests which formerly constituted their normal diet, and in consequence reports are pouring in to the Department of Agriculture of ruined crops, and, in some localities, of valuable timber forests succumbing to blights.

Unusually large flocks of birds, frequently composed of species hitherto regarded as inimical to one another, have been reported as flying over many areas, in a northwesterly direction. Observation planes report having occasionally seen these large flocks halting for brief periods of time in barren and inaccessible tracts, and then continuing their mysterious pilgrimages.

Scientists admit that at present they are at a loss to explain these unprecedented and increasingly serious phenomena.

BATS REPORTED JOINING BIRDS

Observers in Ohio report that vast numbers of bats have been seen flying in the wake of the great bird migrations. Mosquitoes in that region, formerly the prey of bats, are increasing to the dimensions of a plague....

There was more about grasshoppers, and worms, boll weevils, caterpillars, other insects with names unknown to Stan; he glanced through them, and handed the newspaper to Celia. She read it, frowning a little.

"Well ..." she said. "The scientists will find something—some new sort of spray to control the insects."

"They'd better," said Stan.

But lying awake that night, he remembered the flock of birds he had seen that afternoon, the cries he had heard, the sweep of wide wings, the flutter of small ones, the inexorable onward rush of this multitude, and he was filled with wonder and dismay.

The next day, people were talking about birds in the office. "Too damn bad the pigeons don't go away with the rest of them," Anderson said. "We could do without them, all right, but they're still around."

"But only in parks, and places where they're fed by human beings," said Miss Zeller, the receptionist. "It said so, on the radio."

"Very good; there's the solution," said Anderson. "If people want the birds back, then feed 'em. Strew bread crumbs all over the place, and whatever else they eat."

"No, but we need them to destroy *insects!*" said Miss Zeller, indignantly.

"Well, they've gone on strike," said Anderson. "They're tired of eating insects, and worms. I don't blame them."

There were other people who took his joking tone about the matter; there were others who showed a serious, but quite academic interest. But more and more people were growing worried.

When Stan went out to lunch, in a little restaurant near the office, the waitress brought him a menu with an anxious smile.

"There's an awful lot of things crossed out," she said. "But it just seems like things didn't come in to the market this morning."

Green peas. Crossed out. Corn on the cob. Out. Strawberry shortcake. Out. Purple lines through one item after another.

"They say it's the birds," said the waitress. "They're eating up everything—or something like that. Well, I guess the scientists will fix that up."

The evening newspaper Stan opened in the train had an article by a scientist, an ornithologist. It was, he said, erroneous to speak of the present phenomenon as a "migration."

> Our birds have not, in any area under observation, deserted their natural habitat, nor are they anywhere less numerous than usual. Nidification is normal. The remarkably large flocks of birds, comprising species never before observed in association, make from one to two flights daily, leaving their customary areas at fairly definite times, and returning after a fairly definite interval, ranging from three to eight or nine hours.
>
> The disturbing factor in these hitherto unexplained movements is that the birds are no longer feeding upon the insects and grubs which normally constitute their diet, and, in consequence, the Insecta are menacing crops, orchards, and all forms of plant life.
>
> It has been suggested that our birds are now being fed by what in marine life is known as "plankton." In the ocean, this consists of a continual rain of more or less invisible matter, drifting down from the surface through various strata of the sea, and providing nourishment for an amazing variety of marine life. It is suggested that some cosmic disturbance is causing a similar condition in the atmosphere, so that in certain regions the birds are now receiving sustenance from the air, ample and varied enough to satisfy their needs.

The man sitting beside Stan in the smoker had a different newspaper, and a different theory. "This fellow—" he said. "This scientist—he says here that experiments with the atom bomb have produced a radiation which makes insects poisonous to birds. And he says, 'Unless we can immediately find some effective method of insect extermination, this planet which we inhabit will become a desert.' The insects, he says, are going to take over."

Celia was on the veranda with the two children when he got home. "What's up?" he asked, surprised by this variation in routine; the children were always upstairs being put to bed at this hour.

"I wanted to see the birds," Celia said. "Stan, look! Here they come!"

They were visible now above the woodland across the inlet; they came sweeping on, across the face of the setting sun, casting a shadow on the calm green water; they flew over the road and past the house, mewing, twittering, honking, wide wings flapping, tiny wings spinning.

"Chickie ...?" said little Pete.

"Those aren't *chickens*," said his sister, scornfully. "They're big, big, *big* owls, and they eat little bunnies and—"

"Come on, children!" said Celia.

Libby was not here this evening, but Celia, as usual, had everything organized. She came downstairs, neat and fresh and pretty. But Stan, who knew her so well, saw something new in her face.

"Was it hot in the city, Stan?" she asked.

"Hot enough," he said. "What's on your mind, Perfect?"

"Oh ... Well ... The dairy sent around a notice that they'll have to cut down the milk supply, starting tomorrow. 'The destruction of large areas of pasture land by insects has seriously affected the production of milk in our herds.' But you don't catch me napping, no, sir! I had a bright idea. Right away, as soon as the notice came in the mail, I took the children in the car, and drove down to the village to buy up some cases of canned milk. Only, other mothers had had the same idea, all the mothers in a twenty-five-mile radius. It was—absolutely primitive, Stan! All of us fighting for cases of evaporated milk, telling how many children we had, and how extra-delicate they were, and then bidding against each other, offering two, three, five times the regular prices."

"But you got some," he said.

"Yes. Only, I don't like to remember how—how *fierce* I was. And the price ...! Stan, I'm sorry, but I haven't got a very nice dinner for you. I couldn't get any tomatoes, or lettuce, or green vegetables—"

"Take it easy, Cecily," he said, uneasy himself to see how disturbed she was under her air of good-humored amusement.

"And meat is getting scarce, too," she said. "And eggs. Stan, we'd better dig down into the old sock, and buy enormous stores—of everything."

"Yes …" he said.

But you can't beat the game, he thought. If it's going to be like that, we haven't that kind of money.

After dinner Cecily got a news broadcast on the radio. Experts in the nation's capital predict an early solution to the so-called 'bird-mystery' … In the meantime, citizens are urged to take immediate steps to control insects by thoroughly spraying all dwellings and outbuildings. Then foreign news, domestic politics, and then a little human-interest story, told in the commentator's celebrated whimsical style.

"From Vermont. A farmer, Leonard Bogardus, was arrested early today for firing a shotgun from the roof of his barn at Department of Agriculture planes. 'They came once before to spray that stuff all over my land,' Mr. Bogardus told representatives of the press, 'and after they had gone, I wrote to Washington, and I saw the mayor of Stoneham, that is our township, and I warned them that I would not let them come again. I tacked signs up on the trees, and one on the chimney. Planes Keep Out. Last time they came, their dratted spray killed my heifer and my cat and her kittens, and there isn't a *leaf* left on my fruit trees. No, sir! I'll fight these plaguy insects my own way. They don't do near as much harm as them scientists and their poisons.' Well, folks, the Spirit of Seventy-six seems to be still alive in Vermont."

And later. "Stop: Over three hundred deaths have been reported throughout the country from insecticides. The great majority of the victims are children, but some adults have succumbed after eating fruit or vegetables coated with certain sprays. The public is seriously warned to take every precaution—"

"Oh, switch it off!" said Celia. "Let's get some music, something silly. It's—the whole thing is probably exaggerated. And anyhow, the scientists will cope with it."

"The scientists," Anderson said the next morning in the office, "are a damn sight more of a menace than the bugs."

"They're the *only* hope we have!" said Miss Zeller. "They're just doing everything they can think of. They're sending planes to follow the flocks of birds to find out where they go, but the birds get scared and go into the woods. I—well, honestly, I'm *frightened*."

So was everyone else, whether frankly or secretly. The threat was developing with dreadful speed. There was something close to a panic in Wall Street as the stocks of the giant meat-packing and canning companies plummeted downward. And the lumber companies, the paper manufacturers, the publishing and textile companies were shaky.

The food situation had grown appallingly dangerous. The government issued stern warnings about hoarding; Congress was asked to rush through a bill imposing penalties for this, and authorizing a system of emergency rationing. In the meantime, prices rose and rose; Stan paid three dollars for his lunch of a ham sandwich, a cup of coffee, a piece of apple pie.

He read an evening newspaper over this lunch, read it with a cold and leaden fear. Red Cross Rushing Food Supplies to Cities. The first call had come from Pittsburgh, followed almost at once by New York, Chicago, San Francisco, Seattle. Speculators had hurried to buy up all available food supplies, dealers were charging fantastic prices, 'the low-income groups' were unable to pay for what few staples were left. There were babies without milk, sick people without nourishment; riots were reported here and there. A meeting of scientists, including ornithologists, meteorologists—

That's it, Stan said to himself. That's the matter with us, today. We all believe there are experts around, to fix up anything and everything. Soil erosion, rivers deflected, droughts, forests destroyed, natural resources wasted away. Never mind. Scientists will make food, control soil, or water. Plagues? Let 'em come; polio, flu, anything. Scientists will cope with them. They'll also deal with crime, insanity, sex, family rows.

But we're trained to look for an expert, in any sort of trouble. Don't try to do anything for yourself, ever. Don't monkey with the buzz saw. Don't you try to fix your own television set; you'll spoil it. Don't you try to figure out what sort of education and training your own children need. You'll ruin their lives. Call in a psychiatrist.

This is famine. Here and now. You've heard about it. You've read about it. But you thought it was something in Oriental countries, or something from the Dark Ages. Here it is. Here and now. Famine means death, and plagues, riots, insanity, and chaos. It's worse than earthquakes, volcanoes, hurricanes, tidal waves, because it's slower. But don't *you* try to do anything, little man. *You* can't do anything. Can't grow your own food, or go hunting for it, can't make your own clothes, build your own shelter. Can't even work for a living, unless someone else runs a train or a bus for you, and installs electric lights and telephones. Shut up! You're in the army now, little man. And there's no discharge in this war.

When he got to Grand Central at half past 5, it was like a dream in a fever. His train was going to be late in leaving; all the trains were late, either in leaving or arriving. Loudspeakers gave hoarse, furious announcements, as if to impertinent children who were trying to interrupt. Because of the serious food situation, it has been necessary to reroute freight and refrigeration trains in many sections.... The public is requested to accept minor transportation delays with patience.

Food First. They were making a slogan out of that. Food First.

There were fights, genuine hand-to-hand fights about the telephone booths. Stan gave up trying to call Celia, to tell her he would be late, and he was an hour late. The train was jammed; half or more of the commuters were carrying bags of food, anything they could get; one elderly woman had twelve cans of loganberries, a man had five pounds of cucumbers, and a gunny sack of brown sugar; a fellow Stan knew was sweating under the weight of a suitcase full of gin and rye bottles. All the liquor'll be gone in a day or two, he said.

Cigarettes were difficult to get, or cigars, or pipe mixtures. The tobacco crop was hard hit. The late editions of newspapers were strangely flimsy and small. Because of the pulp shortage, we can give our readers only the essential news at this time. And, of course, the baseball scores, the race track finals. The scientists … Hydroponics seen as possible solution…. Closed-seeding successful, say Kentucky farmers. Food supply ample for present, say experts, if hoarding is stopped. Share the food. Food First.

I hope Celia's not too much worried about my being late, he thought. But probably she's heard, on the radio, or from the neighbors, that the trains are late. It's damn hard for her, all of this. The women with children have the worst of it.

When he went up the steps of the veranda, she did not come to open the door for him. He entered, and stood listening, but he did not hear her upstairs with the children. He found her in the kitchen, where it was incredibly hot; she had a white scarf tied over her forehead, like a stoker; her hair was wet, and her dark lashes; she looked pale and strange.

"I've—been baking …" she said. "Making bread. Fourteen loaves…. I—never tried making bread before, but … Libby's aunt and one of her children died."

"Come out of here!" he said, sharply. "Come into the sitting room and I'll turn on the fan."

"I've got to—I've got to see …" she said, and opened the oven door. A blast of heat came out, and a sour smell.

"Two more loaves …" she said.

"I'll watch them. Come out of here!"

"Libby's aunt died, and her little boy …"

"That's too bad. Only I've never seen Libby's aunt, so I can't take it too hard."

"She bought ten pounds of rye flour. But there was something wrong with it. Something … It makes you go crazy. It kills you."

"All right. We'll cut out the rye flour."

"I bought ten pounds myself…. Ten pounds … I had to throw it all away. Ten pounds ... This ... This is all the other kinds of flour I could get. Buckwheat, potato flour, rice flour ... I—baked it quick—before it could spoil."

"Any dinner?"

"Oh, yes," she answered, with an attempt at cheerfulness. "Some nice homemade pea soup and—I've forgotten, but something else ... Oh, yes! Some nice—parsley ... And some delicious mint jelly I made...."

"Good!" said Stan.

I'm not a scientist, he thought. I'm not an expert, in anything. But, by God, I'm a man. I can try.

The plan came to him, then and there, before they sat down to that dinner. After they had gone to bed, he lay in the hot darkness and thought out the details. He did not feel in any way restless; he did not want to sleep.

At 4 o'clock he got up, very carefully and quietly. He dressed in the bathroom, and went down the stairs, carrying his shoes in his hand. In the hall closet which they kept locked he had a rifle and a box of ammunition. He had learned in the Army how to use a rifle; he was a pretty good shot, and when they moved out here, he had bought this rifle, with the idea of going hunting some time with some of the men he knew.

Only, I don't really want to go killing rabbits, squirrels, anything, he thought. I dare say I got an allergy in the Army toward shooting, or being shot.

He left the house by the back door. It was still dark, but he had a flashlight with him; he crossed the road, to the little ship yard, and a dog began to bark frantically. Shut up! he said to it, under his breath. You make me nervous. I don't want to have to shoot *you*. I know you, and you're a rather nice dog. Shut up!

He got into one of the rowboats tied up there; he unfastened the painter, and began to row across the inlet, and, in the hot, dark silence the noise of the oars seemed to him amazingly loud; squeak, dip, squeak, dip, a splash ... Shut up! he said to the oars. I want this kept quiet.

He stopped in midstream, and waited. A cigarette is a risk, he thought. But I'll take a chance that nobody sees it, or smells it.

He was intensely wide-awake, not tired, not impatient. Just ready. And little by little the sky was growing light, a gray and secret light. There's the east, he thought, but there's no sun yet. Maybe there won't be any today. But if it rains, then what? Will they come anyhow? Or what if it's too late, and they never come again?

Ten minutes to 5. No sun; only that gray light. And no hint of that sound he was waiting for; no sounds but the queer ones that come in the dark water, a little ripple, a little splash, something that seemed to jump up, and fall back; the whisper of leaves in the woodland. Five minutes to 5.

Here they come! he said to himself. And they came with a rush, like a great wind, twittering, mewing, cawing, wide wings flailing, tiny wings humming. He set the flashlight on end, and took aim, and the shots were deafening, horrifying, as if the sky cracked open. Six shots, and he brought two of them down, tumbling into the water. He rowed after one, and picked it up, and it flapped wildly on the boards by his feet. The other bird was swimming, slowly and clumsily, and he rowed after it.

It climbed out of the water by the boatyard, and he jumped out of the boat and followed it, carrying the other wounded bird in his arm.

"Hey! *Hey!* What are you doing?" shouted the old man.

"Let me alone!" said Stan.

The dog came rushing at him, barking.

"Call off your dog, or I'll have to shoot him," said Stan. "Let me alone."

"I'll get the police on you!" cried the old man. "Shootin' off a gun and—"

"Shut up!" said Stan, casually.

The bird that had been swimming was flapping across the road now; as he came near it, it took off, with an effort, flying low. It crossed his own garden, and he followed it; across a neighbor's garden, across another road, a field, and into a little wood. There he lost track of it, could not see it or hear it. He put the other wounded bird on the ground, and it struggled forward a little, and collapsed. He stirred it with a stick, and it moved again, and again lay flat. He gave it a merciful end with a bullet, and the sound of the shot made something stir in the bushes. It was the first bird, and once more it rose into the air and began to fly, slowly and clumsily.

I'm sorry, he told it. I'm damn sorry. But I've got to try. The sun was up, a blazing sun; the bird could make only short flights now, and then collapse. He followed it, through fields and woods, along roads and lanes, up hills, down hills. There were tears on his face when he stirred the wounded creature to go on again; he was glad when at last it died. He sat down beside it, exhausted, sick with pity, and contrition; he did not know where he was, or how far he had come, and for the moment he did not care.

Then he heard them. All through this monstrous journey, whether in the fierce sun, in the shade of trees, in gardens, in meadows, he had not once heard the sound of a bird; he had not been aware of this, but only of something strange and desolate in the summer world. And now he heard them, a multitude of them.

But we can't live without them! he cried aloud. They don't need us, but we've got to have them.

He did not know where he was; on a hilltop somewhere, overlooking a river. He listened, trying to decide the direction of the sound; then he left the dead bird lying in the sun and started down the hillside, over parched grass that was slippery underfoot. His rifle felt heavy, very heavy, but he must take it, wherever he was going. He must be ready to do whatever he might have to do.

That afternoon, a man walked into a garage in a little Connecticut township.

"I want to rent a car for twenty-four hours," he said. "Drive it myself."

He was dirty, his shirt was torn, his flannel trousers were muddy and wet up to the knees, his face was badly scratched, and he walked with a heavy limp.

"Got references?" the garage owner asked him.

"No. I don't know anyone here. But I'll give you a hundred-dollar deposit."

"Got your driver's license?"

"Yes. But—I don't want to show it just now. This is—private business. A hundred and fifty deposit."

"Sorry, man, but that's not good enough," said the owner. "My cars are all worth a lot more than that."

Some hours later, after it was dark, the man came back, and this time he had a rifle with him. He found the owner alone; he tied him up, and gagged him, and drove off in a small car, leaving two $50 bills on the desk.

The owner got himself free, and called the police, gave them a description of the car, and its license number. A little before 11 that night, a car with those license plates was intercepted, and the driver arrested.

But they let him go, in a hurry. He was a doctor, a well-known and respectable one. He had been sent for by a patient, and when he left the patient's house, he had got into his car and started home.

"Certainly I didn't look at my license plates!" he shouted. "Never thought of such a thing. If you policemen were worth your salt, things like this couldn't happen. Someone must have come along while I was with my patient, and stolen my plates and tacked on his own. It's an outrage!"

He was going to sue everyone, the police Captain, the Mayor of the town, the Governor of the state; he was going to write to all the newspapers, expose everyone; he was very tired, and he was furious.

With considerable difficulty, he was persuaded to accept apologies and go home, and the police were now alerted to find the car with the doctor's license plates. This they were not able to do at once, for it was then in a most unlikely spot. It was parked outside a police station in New Haven. "I want to see the chief of police here—and quick!" said the young man who had driven it.

"He's home. You can tell me the tale," said the sergeant at the desk.

"I want your chief," said the young man. "This is way out of your class." He was dirty, and muddy, with a torn shirt, a scratched face; it was obviously difficult and painful for him to walk. Nuts, that's it, thought the sergeant. And wouldn't the chief take me apart, if I called him up, this hour of the night, for some loony, or hophead, or whatever he is.

"Listen!" said the young man. "This is the biggest thing that's ever happened."

"Sure! Sure! And you're Napoleon, aren't you?"

"Listen!" said the young man, again. "Come out and see what I've got in my car."

The sergeant went with him out into the quiet tree-lined street. He turned on the light in the car, and he saw it.

"Jeeze!" he said.

Then he went back into the station, and called his chief. The chief was with them within half an hour, and he listened to the young man's story.

"My God …!" he said to the sergeant. "*I* don't know…. I don't know whether the man's insane, or not, but I'm not taking any chances. I'm calling Washington. Get McCorkle there for me."

He went back to the young man, and found him asleep, with his head on the desk. He shook him, until he opened his heavy eyes.

"Now, the best thing," he said, "is to get you right to the hospital—"

"No!" said the young man. "I'm going home."

"Be reasonable!" said the chief. "You've hurt your leg, and you've got some bad scratches on your face. You need treatment, and a good night's rest."

And a bath, he thought. You need a bath worse than anyone I ever came across before in my life.

"No. I'm going home," said the young man.

"Now, look!" said the chief. "You come driving up here, with—with that in your car, and a story which—well, which hasn't yet been substantiated in any way. If you refuse to go to the hospital voluntarily, there's nothing for it but to put you under arrest. But if you'll be reasonable … There are a couple of men flying here from Washington to see you tomorrow—"

"All right!" said the young man, after a moment. "Maybe these men from Washington will have enough sense to see the importance of this. I'll have to call my wife, though."

"We'll attend to that," said the chief.

"Don't tell her I'm in a hospital," said the other. "Say I'm detained in New York, on business."

So Stan went off, to a nice little private room in a hospital. There was a policeman sitting just outside his door all night, but he didn't know that. He was given a bath, his injuries were dressed, and he got an injection that sent him to sleep for over ten hours.

When he waked, a doctor came to look him over, and a nice young nurse brought him a pot of hot coffee, and orange juice, and fried eggs, and bacon, and toast, and he ate and drank all of it. Then the nurse lit a cigarette for him, and in a moment the men from Washington came into his room.

There were four of them. He was never to learn their names, or their functions, but they had, all of them, an air of authority. And a certain hostility. He felt that, at once, and it gave him a cold, queer feeling.

"This isn't an easy story to tell," he said. "In a way, I wish I—couldn't remember it."

"Take your time," said one of the older men.

"I went out early in the morning—yesterday, was it? Seems longer … I took my rifle, and I rowed out into the middle of the inlet, and waited for the birds to come over. Then I shot down a couple of them."

"Why?" asked another of the men.

"I thought that if I could manage just to injure one of them, I might be able to follow it. But I … They both died. I kept them going, as long as I could.… Drove them. Forced them on, until they both died. They were—I don't know what kind of birds, but they were pretty. One was gray. One had blue wings, and a white breast. I drove them on.…"

"Yes," said the second man.

"But the last one brought me to where I could hear the whole flock. And I found them. Down on the bank of the river. A very lonely place. There was a sort of pit dug there, in the mud. The birds were just leaving, after their morning feed, but there was still quite a lot of … It's pretty nearly impossible to—describe it. Insects, worms, a mass of crawling, creeping things moving at the bottom of the pit. Phosphorescent. Green, blue, yellow … And a stench like nothing you can imagine. I—feel as if I could never wash it off.…"

"Yes," said the second man.

"I was sitting down for a moment. Tired. I suppose I was pretty well hidden by the rocks, because the three men didn't see me. If they can be called men. They came down with parachutes. So small … But you saw the one in my car."

"Go on," said a third man. "You wish to assert that you saw three men descend by parachute? Descend from what? Did you see or hear a plane overhead at any time?"

"No."

"A balloon?"

"No. Nothing. They came down—very slowly. Their shoes—the things they had on their feet—were tremendously heavy.... They were not more than—say—three feet high, and wrinkled. Like raisins. They came down.... They had big containers full of these stinking insects—grubs—whatever they were, and they started emptying them into the pit. I got up then, and … This is the hardest part to tell.... Two of them were silent, all the time, but one of them … I can't tell you, because I'm damned if I know whether he talked to me in our language, or whether … I don't know if it's possible, is it? I mean, to get what's in someone else's mind without—any common language."

"What do you think this man was saying, or trying to convey to you?" asked the fourth man.

"He said—" Stan paused. "All right," he went on. "I'm going to put it that way. I'm going to tell you he said all this. Because whether or not he spoke, I—got it. He said that the place they came from—"

"Where was this place?"

"I don't know. Either he couldn't tell me, or he didn't want me to know. Anyhow, he said that their population had increased, and the place where they lived was too small and too poor to support them comfortably. They want to live here, on Earth. But they don't want us around. But they want everything else unchanged, the animals, the birds, the fish. The oceans, the mountains, the rivers. The trees, the flowers … He made it sound like Paradise. And he thought it could be like that. Without us."

"What was so objectionable in us?"

"He must have been here often, or heard a lot, or studied a lot. He said we ruined everything we touched. He said we've wiped out whole species of beautiful and valuable animals and birds. He said we use an incredible amount of our time, and energy, and ingenuity to finding new ways for destroying one another. He said we were too dangerous to keep around. So they've decided to get rid of us, and then take over."

"By warfare?"

"No. They don't go in for that. He said it seemed plain idiocy to them, to risk their healthiest young men in a war. No. They think we can be destroyed by getting the birds off the job. He said they had eleven pits like this one all over the country, and that what they put into them would lure all the birds away from any other food. He said it should be obvious why they started on this country, and after they had proved the method here, and they were proving it, they could go on to the rest of the planet. I asked him where the other pits were, and ... He didn't want to answer that one, but he did. I mean, it was all there, like a map—"

"All where?"

"Well, in his mind, I suppose," said Stan, with a growing reluctance. "I know how that must sound, but that's the way it was. He looked at me, stared at me. And somehow he knew he'd told me—let me know. And I could see—oh, hell! I can't help how it sounds. I'm giving it to you the way it was. I could see that he felt I knew entirely too much, and that this was one time when some killing had to be done. He didn't have any sort of weapon, and he was only half my size. But he was quick, and he was surprisingly strong. He jumped at me, and he brought both those metal boots, or whatever they were, down on one of my feet. Broke a couple of small bones, the doctor says. I knew what he meant to do."

"Yes? What did you think he meant to do, Mr. Dickson?"

"I didn't think! I knew. He wanted to throw me into that—that foul, stinking pit. He got hold of me around the knees, but I pulled away. And I shot him."

"And the other two who were with him?"

"They ... I don't know how they did it. I can just tell you what happened. They did something with their parachutes, and—they went up into the air again."

"And you allowed them to escape?"

"Yes," Stan said. "They—looked like birds. And—I didn't feel like doing any more shooting that day."

"Are you prepared to give us directions for reaching this pit, Mr. Dickson?"

"Well, I can tell you where it was. But I don't think you'll find anything much left of it. After the other two were gone, I—went—a bit berserk. I dug at the bank of the river with sticks, branches, my rifle, stones, anything, until I'd made holes to let the river run in and flood it. It—you see—the smell of it was—a bit too much."

"Then this pit which you claim to have discovered is not in existence, Mr. Dickson?"

"I don't think so. I hope it's completely flooded out."

"Then you have no evidence to offer, in corroboration of your story, Mr. Dickson?"

"No. What about the dead man in my car?"

"There's nothing in your car, Mr. Dickson."

"Look here!" cried Stan, sitting up straight in his bed. "Both the Chief and his sergeant saw that body."

"No detailed examination was made, Mr. Dickson. They are not prepared to testify that what they saw in your car was a body of any sort. It might have been a puppet, a toy of some sort."

"Where is it now?"

"There is no report of anything having been found in your car, Mr. Dickson," said the elderly man. "Moreover, we've received information that you had stolen the car you were driving."

"Look here! I left a hundred dollars deposit for that car."

"There is no record of that, Mr. Dickson. Furthermore, you were using license plates stolen from another car."

"Yes, I did that. I didn't want to be stopped by the police. I was in a hurry, to tell my story, and to show that body. To give someone in authority the location of the other pits. It seemed to me about as urgent as anything could be."

"Are you prepared to give us the locations of these alleged pits, Mr. Dickson?"

"Not offhand. But I wrote down all I could remember, while it was fresh in my mind. I made a plan, a sort of little map, on the back of an envelope."

"Where is this envelope, Mr. Dickson?"

"In my wallet."

"As a matter of routine procedure, Mr. Dickson, the contents of your wallet, and all your pockets were examined and listed. There is no record of such an envelope, with a map or plan drawn on it."

"Look here!"

The fourth man spoke now, for the first time, a stout, sandy-haired man with pale-gray eyes.

"Mr. Dickson," he said, "we're willing to accept this episode as a temporary aberration, caused probably by drinking."

"Provided," said the elderly man, "that we are assured it is 'temporary.' If any symptoms of a permanent obsession develop, we shall be obliged, of course, to take steps."

"What 'steps'?" Stan demanded. But he knew, by this time, what they meant.

"We can't have the public morale undermined by wild rumors," said the sandy-haired man. "The situation is bad enough, as it is. But it can be handled by the Government, and the scientists and experts employed by the Government, and it will be. Unauthenticated rumors might cause a panic to develop. And we can't allow such rumors to circulate."

"Meaning—?" said Stan. "That if I tell my story, to anyone, any time,

I'll be locked up in some mental institution?"

"If a permanent obsession develops—" said the elderly man.

There was a silence.

"Any objection to my going home now?" Stan asked.

"None whatever, Mr. Dickson," said the first man. "And you can rest assured that, unless you persist in some course detrimental to public morale, no charges will be brought against you."

"Damn white of you," said Stan.

He took a train home, and a taxi from the station.

I've got to have a story for Celia, he thought. But not the truth. I'll have to lie to her, and that won't be easy. It ought to be a good lie, only I don't seem very bright, just now. Could be I'm tired…. She'll probably know I'm lying, and that'll hurt her. But I can't tell her the truth. She couldn't believe it. Nobody ever will. I don't want to tell anybody, I don't want to think about it, or remember it. I don't want to talk at all.

But I'll have to talk. Stan, where have you *been?* Who, me? Oh, nowhere special. I was just having a temporary aberration. Much better now, thanks. The little house looked almost unbelievably pretty, this hot afternoon; the trees stirred in the light breeze; it was so good to get back.

Before he reached the top of the steps, Celia opened the door.

"Hello, Stan!" she said.

His heart sank, at the sight of her, so slender and straight and lovely, in her blue linen dress, smiling at him. But her nonchalance was not convincing, and she was pale; there was a look of strain about her dark eyes.

"Cecily …" he said. "I'm sorry."

And if only we could let it go at that, he thought. If I could sit down beside her, with my arm around her, or even just sit in the same room with her, and not talk, not answer questions, not make up lies …

"Stan, listen!" she cried.

He raised his head, frowning a little.

"I don't hear anything," he said.

"It's the birds, Stan! They're back again! They didn't go away this morning!"

"Good!" he said with an effort. "Fine!"

"Stan, come on in! You're just in time for the 4 o'clock news on the radio."

"Well, no, thanks, Cecily. I don't—"

"Come on!" she said, and held out her hand, and he took it and went into the house with her. A big tree outside shaded the windows here, giving a cool, greenish light to the living room that was neat almost to primness. That's how Celia wants things, he thought. Order, and decency, and peace … Only not that portentous voice on the radio.

"Turn it off, Perfect!" he said.

"But I want you to hear it, Stan," she said. "I heard the news at 3, and maybe they'll have more about it now."

"These pits filled with insects have been formed, scientists say, by unusual climatic conditions. Yesterday one of these pits was discovered in Connecticut, and two more have been found and destroyed this afternoon, one in Idaho, one in Virginia. These discoveries were made possible by a method devised by Dr. Wilbur Jonas, world-famous ornithologist employed by the Government in the preservation of wild life. Dr. Jonas has demonstrated that a bird's wing may be clipped in such a manner as to render its flight slow enough to be followed easily. This has led the experts—"

"Turn it off, Celia!"

"When I got up yesterday, Stan," she said, "you'd gone. And you'd taken your rifle, and all our cash. I wasn't very happy, Stan."

"Celia, I'm sorry. But—I couldn't leave a note for you. I didn't know—just where I was going, or when I'd get back."

"Birds in the vicinity of the three destroyed pits have already returned to their normal and invaluable function of controlling insect pests," said the portentous voice, "and scientists now predict that within a few days' time the food crisis will be ended—"

"The old man from the boatyard came over yesterday morning," she said. "He told me you'd been shooting birds from one of his rowboats. He said you were crazy, threatening to shoot his dog, and so on. But I thought I was beginning to understand. Only, I was worried…. When the night came, and I hadn't heard … I was frightened."

"Celia … I'm sorry."

"Then this morning the head of the police here came to see me. Early, before we'd finished breakfast. He asked me where you were, and I said I didn't know, and didn't care."

"Celia!"

"He was surprised, too. He asked if that meant that you and I didn't get on together. And I said it meant just the opposite. I said we didn't need to ask each other questions, ever. I said that wherever you'd gone, it was all right with me. Then he told me he'd heard from the police in New Haven, and that you were being 'detained' there. He said you'd told them some story about having saved the earth from an invasion from another planet. I told him you didn't know how to talk that way, and he left. But he came back, in less than an hour. He said there was nothing at all in the story he'd heard, and please not to mention it to anyone, and that you weren't being 'detained,' but would be home very soon."

"And so—" boomed the portentous voice, "due to the knowledge and skill and unremitting vigilance of our Government scientists and experts, the pits are being discovered and rendered harmless, our birds are returning, and disaster has been averted. Let us all be grateful to these modest and unassuming men, whose selfless labors have—"

She turned off the radio.

"You had something to do with this, Stan," she said. "I was sure of that, as soon as the old man from the boatyard came over here. Because, you see, I know you're not crazy. And I know you're not the sportsman type who goes out to shoot birds before sunrise."

He said nothing.

"If you don't want to tell me, Stan," she said, "it's all right."

"It isn't a question of not wanting to," he said. "I don't think I *can*."

"I guess there isn't anything you can't tell me, Stan. Want to try?"

"I don't know...." he said.

He lit a cigarette, and sat down on the arm of a chair, and she sat in a corner of the sofa, and he told her. He was slow about it, at first, cautious, groping, but after the beginning it was not hard. She had asked him a few questions, but when he had finished, she was silent.

"Celia …?" he said.

"You did it," she said. "You're exhausted, and half-sick, and you've hurt your foot. You'll never get any credit for it, or any thanks. Only—*I'll* always know, Stan."

"That's good enough," he said, quietly. "Celia, are you crying?"

"It's the—birds," she said. "Maybe all the rest of my life, I'll feel like crying—when I hear the birds getting ready for bed—or early in the morning—"

"Don't cry, Celia! Please!"

"In a moment," she said, "Libby'll bring the children home and I'll watch her feeding them—and I'll cook dinner—for you and me—and I'll be very gay and silly—so that you won't suspect—what I'm thinking. Their father, and my husband. Our man."

He crossed the room and sat down beside her; he took her hand and laid it against his cheek. "That's what I want to be," he said.

The Strange Children

Marjorie Smith sat up very straight in the car. When they swerved sharply round a corner, it sent her lurching against the side wall; when they made a sudden stop, it jerked her forward.

And it seemed to her that this was as it should be. Her blue corduroy raincoat was bulky, the collar rubbed her chin, and to her stern young conscience, this was right. Right and fitting to be uncomfortable, when you were doing something that you knew was wrong.

It *is* wrong, she told herself. I've always said I'd never do it. Never go to sit with children I hadn't met. It's not fair to them, or to yourself. If anything goes wrong, if they wake up, and call, it's a shock for them to see a complete stranger. And you can't do your best for them, if you don't know them at all.

But this Mrs. Jepson had been so insistent on the telephone, a few hours ago. Do *please* help us out, Miss Smith! We're more or less obliged to go to this thing at the country club; we engaged a table there, and invited these people to a late supper ages ago. And Katie, the maid who's been with us for years, was suddenly called away to a sick sister. Do, please, manage it somehow, Miss Smith! I've heard such wonderful things about you from Myra Williams. At half past eight?

I'd like to come earlier, to meet the children before they go to bed, Marjorie had said. But, my dear, the chauffeur's gone on an errand. I couldn't send the car for you until eight. I'll take a taxi, Marjorie had said. But, my dear, it's not *necessary!* Mrs. Jepson had cried. It's a perfect maelstrom here, without Katie. I'll have to get some sort of dinner for my husband and myself, and then we'll have to dress.... Really, it's not necessary. The children never wake up at night.

You never know when they may, though, Marjorie had said. And if there was a stranger there.... My dear! Mrs. Jepson had said, my children don't mind strangers the least bit! They're the friendliest children—almost *too* friendly, I sometimes think.

And then she had said, Miss Smith, my husband and I both realize how bothering this is for you. Being asked at the last moment, and such a bitter cold night, and not knowing us, and so on. We're going to make out a check for twenty-five dollars....

No, thank you! Marjorie had said. It will be my usual rate. If I come. Oh, well! We can argue about that later, Mrs. Jepson had said. There are stacks of new books here, my dear, and magazines, and Katie's left all sorts of things in the icebox—cold chicken, and chocolate cake, and salad....

Then she must have realized that she was off on the wrong track, and getting nowhere. The chauffeur says he can get this woman he knows, she had gone on. But I've seen her once, and I hate the idea of leaving the children with her. I'm quite sure she drinks, and suppose she set the place on fire, with a cigarette? That's always my great terror. Do, please, manage to come, Miss Smith, so that I won't have to get that woman.

I was a fool to say yes, Marjorie told herself. This woman who drinks might very well be just an invention of Mrs. Jepson's, to get me there. But if she wasn't an invention then I don't think much of this Mrs. Jepson. No matter how important her engagement was, to leave her little children with someone she didn't trust.

But people do things like that. You read about them in the newspapers. If I do decide to marry Johnny, and we have children of our own, I don't see how I could ever bear to leave them with anyone, unless it was Mother, or my own sister, or some old friend.... Because—I like children.

The car turned off the highway into a side road that seemed to plunge into a forest, black and frozen. The bare trees creaked in the wind; here and there stood a big old house, some with a light in a window, some in darkness. I suppose it's mostly a summer place, Marjorie thought. They always look rather forlorn in the winter.

Then, as they turned a corner, she saw ahead of them a bungalow, brightly lighted, trim and cheerful as a little launch in a harbor among grim old freighters. The car stopped; the chauffeur, who had not said one word, had not once turned his head, jumped out nimbly and opened the door of the car. Marjorie got out, went along the path and up the two shallow steps to the veranda. I'm glad the house is like this. It's cozy.

She rang the bell, and the door was opened almost at once by a big, heavy man in shirtsleeves and braces.

"Miss Smith?" he said. "I'm Jepson. Carl Jepson. This is very good of you. Very good."

His big shoulders sloped, his arms hung down in front of him, giving him a clumsy air. He was handsome, after a fashion, with butter-colored hair slick on his skull, good features, but marred by a curious expression of unhappy and almost stupid confusion. He looked at Marjorie, his light brows drawn together.

"You're very young ..." he said, in a loud tone.

"I'm twenty-two," she said, a little nettled at what she thought a criticism. "And I've had quite a lot of experience with children."

"Ralph, *darling!*" cried a gay, clear voice. "Let poor Miss Smith come in and get her coat off, do!"

It was the voice Marjorie had heard on the telephone that afternoon, a lovely and very persuasive voice. And Mrs. Jepson herself was like that: dark-eyed, slender, and tall, she persuaded you with a glance that she was your friend, your well-wisher, that you would be happy in her company. She wore a black dinner dress, a necklace of shining silver leaves and earrings to match, and she was charming.

"Ralph, darling, hurry up and finish dressing!" she said. "While I brief Miss Smith." She raised her arms in a gesture of shoving him away, and led Marjorie into the long, softly lit sitting room. "It's a weird little house," she said. "The children's rooms are down here, those two doors. And here's their bathroom. And here's the kitchen. You'll find lots of things in the icebox; just please take anything you like. And there's a radio, and a television, and a phonograph, and stacks of records. And don't worry about waking the children. *Nothing* bothers them. And here are books, and magazines, and cigarettes. And here's the telephone number where you can reach us, and the doctor's number. Will you be all right?"

"Yes, thank you," said Marjorie, a little stiffly. For, in her New England fashion, she found Mrs. Jepson a little too nice, too eager. "And the children's names?"

"There's Ronald; he's seven, and Jean, five. We won't be very late, Miss Smith. *Au revoir!*"

When she had gone, and the door closed after her, it was as if some fresh breeze had suddenly died, leaving the air stagnant; the little house was very still. The wind blew against the windows; an electric clock ticked, with a sort of purr; the refrigerator buzzed and whirred for a moment, and then was silent.

Ronald and Jean, Marjorie said to herself. Two little children here, in my care, and I've never seen them. If they don't wake up, I suppose I'll go home without having seen them, and they'll never know I've been here. I don't like it.

She took up a magazine, but she could not read. She was waiting. For the sound of a car going by outside, for the telephone to ring, for the icebox to start up again? For a board to creak, for a tap to drip, for a rustle, a sign? But there was only the wind, and the rain outside.

And then she heard it, a sound that should not frighten anyone: a low chuckle of laughter. It's one of the children, she thought. Still asleep, probably. And then a soft murmur, another soft laugh. She rose, and as she stood by the chair, she heard the patter of bare feet running. They're up, she thought. I'll have to see.

She went to the nearest door and turned the handle gently. But the door was locked. She tried the next one, and that, too, was locked. She knocked.

"I'm Marjorie Smith," she said. "I've come to see you. Open the door, will you?"

"No, thank you!" answered a little boy's voice, very resolute. "Go away, please."

"Go away!" echoed a little girl's voice.

"I just want to come in and say good evening—"

"No, thank you!" said the little boy. "We *never* let *anybody* come in at night, *never*."

"Just for a moment."

"Go away!" cried the little girl.

Marjorie stooped, and looked through the keyhole. The light was on in there; she could see a pink wall, a bed on which a little fair-haired girl in a blue dressing gown was sitting beside a dark-haired young man in a gray suit.

"Let me in!" she called, knocking more loudly.

"Go away!" said the little boy.

The young man in there said nothing, did not stir. I'm afraid! Marjorie thought. Who is he? What is he doing there? How did he get in? *I'm afraid*.

All right! Be afraid, then. It doesn't matter. Those children are in my care, and I'm going to get into that room. I'm going to find out who that man is. And I'm going to get rid of him.

She put on her raincoat; she fixed the front door on the latch and left it held ajar by a telephone book. Better to let the house grow chill than for her to take any chances of being shut out, away from the children.

The cold caught her by the throat, took her breath away. If only the house next door had one lighted window; if only there were some sound from the street, a car going by, a radio; if only there were someone....

The light from the children's room shone across the gravel path; she went close to it, and looked in. A dark little boy in a plaid dressing gown sat on the floor, hands clasped round his knees; the little girl still sat on the bed, and now the young man had his arm about her shoulders. Both the children were looking up into his face; they were listening to him.

With an effort, Marjorie pushed up the window from the bottom.

"Who are you?" she cried.

He turned his head and looked at her, with desperate, dark eyes. And then he was gone. He had not risen, or moved, but he was gone.

For a moment she held tight to the window sill, and it seemed to her that the wind went roaring through her head, so that she could see nothing, hear nothing. But the little girl's voice came to her, high and wild.

"Georgie! Georgie! Come back! Come back, Georgie!"

She climbed in over the sill; she stood in the room, dripping wet, her hair blown across her forehead.

"That's a fine way to treat me!" she said, laughing. "The very first time I come to see you, too. Making me go out in the pouring rain and climb in the window."

She had struck the right note.

"Well, you see," the little boy said. "Georgie won't stay if anybody else comes. Even Mommie. He doesn't want *any*body to see him but us."

"Katie sawed him, and she went away," said the little girl.

"Do you like him?" Marjorie asked.

They both looked at her, surprised, wondering.

"We like him the *best*," said Ronald. "He tells us stories, and he sings songs."

"And he stays here in the dark, too," said the little girl. "You go away now, and he'll come back."

"I can't go away," said Marjorie. "I promised your mommie I'd stay with you till she came home."

"We'd rather have Georgie, thank you," said Ronald.

"Some other time," said Marjorie. "I thought we'd all go out to the kitchen, and make some cocoa, have a little party."

It was nearly two hours before she could get them back to sleep. She made cocoa for them, and toast; she read to them, she played the phonograph records they wanted; she told them stories. They were, she thought, unusually attractive children, intelligent, reasonable, mannerly, and the little girl was beautiful, with great dark eyes and thick, fair hair, as fine as silk. But they were, both of them, curiously tense and excited; again and again they would turn their heads, they would look, they would listen.

"I thought it was Georgie," the little girl said.

Marjorie ignored that. She asked them no questions; she tried, in every way she could, to distract their attention from Georgie, to quiet them. When they had fallen asleep, she opened both their doors, and sat down in the living room. I got chilled when I went out, she told herself. That's why I'm so cold. The heat's not very good in this house. It's—there seems to be a draft somewhere. A very cold draft.

Almost all children invent imaginary playmates who seem absolutely real to them. When they're pretending they're one of these imaginary creatures, their voices change, and their expressions. If *they* feel absolutely sure they see one of those imaginary creatures, it might.... Thought-transference? People can be made to believe they've seen things, and heard things....

No, I did see him. I did hear him. And he—vanished. Is it my duty to tell Mrs. Jepson? Oh, how *can* I?

"Please don't be frightened," he said. "I'd very much like to come and talk to you for a few moments, but if you'd rather I didn't, I'll stay away."

The comfortable lamplit room was empty, but the voice was near.

"Where—are you?" she asked.

"I'll clear out, if you'd rather."

"*Where are you?*" she demanded, so loudly that she felt a sudden worry about waking the children.

"Well, I'm here," he said. "If you want to see me, I can fix it. But if you don't—"

She was silent for a moment, trying not to breathe so fast, so loudly.

"Yes. I do want to see you," she said.

Then he was there, standing at the other side of the table. He was young, and he was handsome, in a way, but his gray suit was shabby, and he looked tired to exhaustion, his dark eyes hollow.

"Who—are you?" she asked.

"My name is George Stewart," he said. "Or it was. But, you see…. It's hard to explain…. You see, I was murdered five years ago."

"No!" Marjorie said. "Things like that—aren't true."

"I didn't believe things like this, myself," he said, "until it happened to me. It's—you can't think how bad it is."

"Then why do you do them? Why do you—come back?"

"Well …" he said, in his gentle, tired voice, "we don't 'come back,' you know. We've never been able to get away. When you've been murdered, when you die—*at the wrong time*—you're caught here in this world."

"You mean—you're alive?"

"No," he said. "Not alive. And not dead."

"I don't understand," she said curtly.

"I don't think anyone does, quite," he said. "Some of the others like me have worked out theories—"

"You mean other ghosts?" she asked, and because of the dreadful confusion within her, she spoke in a scornful, sneering tone she had never used before in her life.

"That's what you call us," he said. "I've gone to see others I've heard about, in England, Ireland, Hungary. They'd all been murdered, even though sometimes it wasn't suspected. And one woman who'd been in a castle in Ireland for four hundred years told me it was because if you're murdered, it's not the *right time* for you to die. So that you *can't* die. You can't go on to the next world."

"And what's the 'right time' to die, may I ask?"

"This woman believed it was all predestined. You're born, she thought, with a natural lifespan, whether it's one day, or ninety years, depending upon the constitution you've inherited. Your inherited constitution will determine what diseases you'll avoid, and what ones will finish you."

"What about accidents?"

"She thought they were predestined, too. And it's true that if you go to a place where there's been some great disaster, a flood, a volcanic eruption, a train wreck, anything of that sort, no ghosts have ever been heard of there. No. It's only murder that makes us—as we are. Because murder, she said, doesn't *have* to happen. Nobody is born destined to be murdered, because nobody is born obliged to become a murderer."

"So if you've been murdered, you stay on earth, and try to hurt and terrify people?"

"I've never found a genuine case of anyone's being really hurt by a ghost," he said, with a faint sigh. "If people are terrified at the sight of us, that's not our fault. We go on and on, in a sort of despair, and nobody will listen to us, nobody will help."

"Why do they want people to listen to them? What sort of help do they want?"

"We want to be killed," he said.

"But you *have* been killed!"

"No," he said. "It wasn't the right time for us to die, so we couldn't."

"And when is this 'right time' supposed to come again?"

"Any time after we're murdered," he said. "We're ready then. Our life here is finished. We're longing, every minute, to get out of this world, and on to the next one."

"Well? Can't ghosts kill themselves?"

"I don't know," he said. "But they never do. They never even try. It's—I couldn't tell you how bad—how shocking the idea seems to us. No. We wait. We feel we *must* wait. Until we're taken."

"What do you mean by 'taken'?"

"We're killed," he explained, earnest and patient. "A building collapses, there's a stroke of lightning, a fire; in the war, some of us were killed by bombs. But often it's a long time. Such a long time.... That's why we're always looking for someone who'll be merciful enough to set us free. Even to listen to us, as you're listening to me."

"Why should the murdered people, the victims, be punished, and not the murderers?" she demanded.

"I don't know what happens to the murderers," he said. "But I'm certain that our waiting isn't meant as a punishment. I suppose—" He paused for a moment. "I suppose," he went on, "that if life is eternal, one hundred years, five hundred years, of waiting hasn't much significance. The way I see it, it's part of a plan, an order of things that we can't grasp.

But.... If you'll help me.... I give you the gun...."

"No! I couldn't! I couldn't! What happened to you, to turn you—into this?"

"Nella killed me," he said, casually.

"Nella?"

"Mrs. Jepson."

"*What!* What are you saying?"

"I was her lover," he said. "I suppose that's the word for it. Anyhow, that autumn, five years ago, she was sure Jepson suspected what was going on, and she wanted to get rid of me. She tried to bribe me—with Jepson's money—to go away somewhere. When I wouldn't do that, she got into a panic. She believed I was going to make a scandal, ruin her, make her lose Jepson's money, her social position, everything she valued."

"Were you going to do that?"

"No," he answered, simply. "I've never been like that. Never wanted to injure anyone. But she couldn't believe that; literally *couldn't*. She thought everybody was vindictive—and dangerous. She asked me to talk things over with her, and we drove in her car up to the lake. She was very quiet and serious; more reasonable, I thought. She'd brought along some drinks in a thermos, and she poured out one for each of us. I don't know how she managed it, but mine was poisoned. I wasn't watching her, particularly. I was smoking. I was looking out at the lake, at the autumn leaves floating on it. I was starting to tell her, once more, that she needn't worry, but that I wasn't going to give up my job here, my friends, everything, and go to Seattle, as she wanted, when the pain came.

"It was—like a thread spinning up and up, round the blade of the sharpest knife. Then it was cut into ribbons, and it was over.... She'd got me out of the car, onto the ground, when Jepson came. I don't know what made him come, or how he knew. But he was—overwhelmed, that's the word. Sick, with horror.

"Nella was stunned, for a moment. But only for a moment. Then she had her story for him. She said she'd never imagined the stuff she gave me would be fatal. She said she'd only wanted to knock me out for a few moments, so that she could get back some foolish letters she'd written to me. I'm sure Jepson didn't believe her. But he helped her. He tied a heavy stone on my ankles and another round my neck, and together they dragged me down to the lake and into the water, where it was deep.

"I stayed there, at the bottom of the lake, for a while, two or three days. But I knew, all the time, what had happened to me. I knew I could get out when I wanted."

"But how?" Marjorie cried.

"I don't know how to explain it," he said. "It doesn't seem strange to me. I can be anywhere I want, and it's no trouble, no effort. I can be here, or not here."

"You can disappear?" she said, unsteadily. "Vanish?"

"It doesn't seem like that, to me," he said. "To me, it's simply going away, somewhere else. It's hard for me to realize that I frighten anyone. I don't eat or drink, of course, because we don't need to. Nothing in us breaks down or wears out; nothing needs building up. But I'm just what I was, five years ago; the same blood, and bones, and muscles, the same mind. I can see, I can hear, I can speak. Why am I—terrible?"

"You're not!" she said, and it was true; all her cold horror and confusion had gone. "But why do you come back here? Is it to—make them remember what they did?"

"No," he said. "I don't care about Nella any more, and I'm only sorry for Jepson. He doesn't need any reminding. He's never got over it. He's—you can see it in his face, poor devil.... No, I've never let him see me here. No. It's Jean. You see, she's my child."

Marjorie began to cry, and that seemed to trouble him.

"I'm sorry," he said. "But I don't know where else to turn. It won't take a moment. If I give you the gun—"

"I couldn't! I couldn't! Please don't ask me! Can't you stay here—with Jean?"

"But don't you see?" he cried. "That's the worst of it. If anything should happen to her, if she should die, she'd go on, to the next world. And I couldn't. She'd be gone, and I couldn't find her. I beg of you—!"

The wind shook and rattled the front door; a freezing blast streamed in as it opened and Jepson stood there. Marjorie's lips parted, but before she could make a sound, there was a streak of yellow light, the crack of a shot, and George Stewart fell at her feet.

"I saw the whole thing from my window," said the woman who lived across the street. "And I called up the police at once. I saw Mr. Jepson go up on the veranda and look in at the window. I saw him open the door and when he was in the room, I saw him take out his gun and fire."

"I didn't mean to," said Jepson. That was what he had said to Marjorie, over and over, before the police came.

"Sure," said the police lieutenant. "You didn't know the gun was loaded. Only how did you get rid of the body so fast? Or was there a body? Did he—"

"No, he was dead, lieutenant. There wasn't any doubt," said Jepson. "This time," he added.

"Yes," said the woman from across the street. "I can identify the dead man. His name is George Stewart, and I used to see him here—" she paused. "A *lot*," she said, with malicious significance.

"Did you see Mrs. Jepson?"

"Yes. She got out of the car, and she went into the house right after he did."

"Mrs. Jepson, will you tell us …?"

"No," said Nella Jepson. "I have nothing to tell to tell you. I'm not obliged to give evidence against my husband."

She could not have said anything more fatal to him, and, thought Marjorie, she knew that, and intended it to be so.

"I didn't mean to," said Jepson. "I didn't think he was.... I didn't think there was anyone here."

"Do you wish to state that you did not see this man, when you fired a shot directly at him?"

Jepson wiped his forehead with a handkerchief. His heavy face was dazed and stricken.

"I didn't know I *could* see him.... I've thought about him, night and day.... I thought he was—gone."

"Come now, Mr. Jepson. Pull yourself together. Do you admit that you fired that shot?"

"Yes, I did. But I didn't think it would—do any harm."

"Why did you think that?" The police lieutenant waited. "Come now!" he said. "Why did you think it wouldn't 'do any harm' to fire a bullet in the man's back?"

Bear witness to the truth … Marjorie was saying to herself. Never mind about your pride. Never mind what people will think of you. Never mind how hard it is. Mr. Jepson *can't* say it. But I can. I must.

"The man was dead before Mr. Jepson came in," she said.

"Why, he was not!" cried the woman from across the street. "I saw him, with my own eyes, standing there, talking to you!"

"He was a ghost," said Marjorie, with an effort that made her voice husky and deep.

Jepson turned to her, his blurred eyes brightening with gratitude. "Yes!" he said. "Yes! You're—very kind...."

"McGraw," said the lieutenant, "take Miss Smith home in your car."

"I'd rather stay—"

"You're not doing any good here, Miss Smith," said the lieutenant. "We'll want to ask you some questions, later on. *Will* we want to ask you questions! Perfect eyewitness testimony to a murder, plus a virtual confession—and no body to tie it to. The corpus delicti without a corpus … You're the one who should be able to straighten it out; but just now you're—overwrought. Drive her home, McGraw."

"Overwrought," Marjorie said to herself. Hysterical, does he mean? Or crazy? Raving? She could imagine the spiteful woman from across the street telling this story with delight. A ghost, that Smith girl said. *Imagine!* The story would spread through the little suburban town; perhaps it would reach the ears of people who liked her and respected her, but wouldn't want to leave her in charge of their children anymore.

She could not save Jepson. His wife would not help him. He was doomed. He would go from here to a jail, if he was quiet, or a madhouse, if he insisted on the truth. She looked at him, and he smiled, and the blurred misery in his face had gone. It was as if his monstrous burden had at last been lifted, and he was at ease.

"Thank you!" he said, again.

The Legacy

Mrs. Lamb was working the crossword puzzle in her newspaper that afternoon when the doorbell rang. She rose, without interest; she expected nobody; she expected nothing at all. She opened the door, and there was her cousin, Laurie Jacobs.

"Oh ..." said Mrs. Lamb. "I didn't expect you. Come in, Laurie."

"God, it's cold in here," said Laurie.

"Yes, the heat's not very good," Mrs. Lamb agreed.

You got used to it, though; she scarcely noticed the chill anymore. She was wearing her purple felt slippers and a cinnamon-brown cardigan over an old black dress; she had just finished drinking her nice hot tea. The cup, without a saucer, stood crookedly on the radiator.

Laurie sat down and unbuttoned her mink coat. So *odd*-looking ... Mrs. Lamb thought. Like a buffalo, with her shoulders so high and heavy, and her thick blonde hair hanging loose about them. The rest of her figure was slim enough, and her face was young for her forty years, but her blue eyes were rather small, with a puzzled and suspicious look in them. I don't know why so many people call Laurie handsome, thought Mrs. Lamb. I never did, even when we were young.

"I'm going to Mexico," said Laurie. "Everyone seems to be going there. There seems to be a thing about it."

"That'll be nice," said Mrs. Lamb.

"Yes," said Laurie. "I need a change. Only, I'm bothered about Virginia. I don't want to let her go, but I certainly don't feel like paying her just to loaf while I'm away. I thought perhaps she could come and work for you, Edna, if I pay her wages. It would be nice for you."

"Thank you, Laurie," said Mrs. Lamb, "but there's not enough to be done in a little place like this."

"She can cook for you," said Laurie. "She can sew, too, and she can set your hair and do your nails. She's really wonderful, only she's got to be kept busy, or she gets queer."

"How d'you mean 'queer'?" asked Mrs. Lamb.

"Oh, I don't know ..." Laurie answered, in her flat way. "It's just that sometimes there's something about her ... Keep her busy, though, and she'll be all right."

"I really don't see how I can possibly let her come, Laurie."

"You can," said Laurie. "Let her sew. She can make bloomers for you, or whatever it is you wear."

That's the sort of thing ... thought Mrs. Lamb. Laurie *acts* like a buffalo, too, trampling all over people, and not even knowing it.

"Really, Laurie, I'm afraid I can't—" she said.

"Only for a little while," said Laurie, and rose. "I'm afraid I shan't have a chance to see you again before I leave, Edna. But remember, if anything happens to me, there's that thirty thousand for you in my will."

Mrs. Lamb made a little gesture with her hand, wincing at that familiar phrase. Laurie was always, always saying it, and always giving the exact sum. It's nothing so wonderful, either, she thought, considering all that Grandma left her, and the outrageous alimony she gets from poor Leonard.

"I don't see why anything should happen to you, Laurie," she said.

"Oh, planes and things ..." said Laurie. "You never know. I'll tell Virginia to come at nine on Monday morning, Edna. You'll be glad. You'll like her."

I won't be glad. I won't like her, thought Mrs. Lamb. She went to the door with her cousin and they kissed each other, as they had been doing since childhood; Mrs. Lamb stood in the doorway until Laurie got into the elevator, with her mink coat and her long blonde hair; then she closed the door and went back to sit by the tepid radiator. If Grandma had left me my fair share of her money, she thought, instead of absolutely disowning me, simply because I married poor Everett ...

Tears came into her eyes, perhaps because of Everett. But they had been married only eleven months before he died, and that had been nearly fifteen years ago; it was hard to remember him clearly, or her own feeling for him. The years had gone by with so little to mark them. I've been so poor, she thought; I haven't had anything at all. And there's Laurie, divorced from her second husband, and no doubt looking for a third. Laurie going off to Mexico, and forcing me to take that maid of hers.

I shouldn't have agreed, she thought. I shouldn't keep on doing things for Laurie, on account of that money. The money I'll never get. She's only a year younger than I am, and she's as strong as a horse. There's no reason why anything should happen to her—and I certainly hope nothing will. But if only she'd given me some of it, a quarter, a tenth of it, before this....

The more Mrs. Lamb contemplated the situation, the more disturbing, even appalling it looked to her. I cannot have that Virginia here! she told herself. She'll see my slips, and she'll see those awful blankets. She'll see everything, of course; she'll be snooping into everything. She'll see that I don't have any company and don't go out anywhere. And I know what servants are like. She'll be sneering at me all the time because I haven't any money or any social life.

She grew concerned with her own appearance which had not interested her for a long time. She was a tall woman, a little too thin, but with grace in her limbs; her features were delicate, her dark eyes were sad and vague in her pale face. If I made more of myself, she thought....

For a long time she had made nothing of herself. It was discouraging to have so little money for clothes; she could buy only the cheapest things and, though she had grown thinner through the years, she continued to buy the same size. I'll take that dress in, she would tell herself, but she never did it. She postponed everything possible in her life; she did not answer letters; she did not pay her bills until she was dunned for them; she put off buying any food for her dinner until the middle of the afternoon. I don't have to do it now, she would tell herself. Not yet. It was as if she were waiting for something, yet she expected nothing at all.

She had grown more than resigned to her solitary and dreamlike existence; she clung to it. And now this Virginia was coming into her retreat, an intruder, a spy. Mrs. Lamb used the four days left to her in a resentful effort to prepare for this, as best she could. She took the safety pins out of her slips and mended the shoulder straps; she sent one of her blankets to the cleaner's, although she was obliged to use her coat in its place. On Sunday she washed her hair and put it up in curlers.

She had seen Virginia several times in Laurie's apartment, but it was not her habit to observe people, or to think about them; she remembered only a quiet olive-skinned woman with a soft voice. She'll be insolent, though, Mrs. Lamb thought. She'll see that I'm poor, and servants despise that. I'll have to keep the upper hand, somehow.

At nine o'clock on Monday morning, Mrs. Lamb was ready for Virginia. She wore her dark-blue flannel dressing-gown; her dark hair was fluffy; a touch of lipstick brightened her pale face. It had long been her habit to spare herself in dishwashing; she would put a cup, a roll, a bit of butter in its wrapping paper out on a newspaper. This morning, though, she had spread a linen cloth on the table; she had set out a sugar bowl, a little cream jug, everything dainty. Virginia can clear this away, she thought.

At twenty minutes past nine Virginia had not yet come. She's being late deliberately, Mrs. Lamb thought, to be insolent. She thought that perhaps she would clear away the dainty breakfast and make her bed, so that when Virginia came she would say, oh, I thought you weren't coming, and I've done everything myself; there's really no need for you to stay today. Try to be on time tomorrow. Then she decided to wait until half past nine, and almost exactly at that moment, the doorbell rang.

"I'm sorry to be late, ma'am," Virginia said, "but Mrs. Jacobs gave me the wrong address and I had to go asking all around in the stores to find where you lived."

"I see!" said Mrs. Lamb.

Virginia had brought a little suitcase, and she stayed in the dark foyer to change her clothes; she came into the sitting room in a clean blue cotton dress, with white apron and cap, and Mrs. Lamb looked at her with a feeling of shock. I don't like her, she thought. She looks ...

The blue dress made her skin seem golden; her sleek black hair was parted in the middle and pinned in a thick knot at the nape of her neck; she was smiling gently, showing her white, even teeth; and the meek uniform, the smooth hair seemed a mockery of the woman's flaunting vitality. A—wanton, Mrs. Lamb thought.

The day was intolerable; even worse than Edna Lamb had foreseen, She set out pen, ink and paper on the desk, and sat down to write letters, but she could think of nothing to say to her very few correspondents, and in order to look busy, she did little games; she tried to see how many words she could make out of a book title. When Virginia had finished in the bedroom, Mrs. Lamb went in there; she put on her dress, her grey hat, and the sealskin coat which had been made over again and again, until from the voluminous long coat Aunt Bessie had left her it had now become an oddly jaunty jacket. She went out to market; it was a cold day, but she dawdled along, looking into the dull little shop windows until her feet were numb, her ears ached. I've got to go home, she thought, angry and miserable.

When she got home, she told Virginia she would have a light lunch, an omelette and a cup of tea.

"And make enough for yourself," she said.

"Thank you, ma'am," said Virginia, "but I don't ever eat any lunch."

This disturbed Mrs. Lamb beyond reason; she could not stop thinking about it. Why doesn't Virginia eat any lunch? she asked herself. Why does she work all day without eating? It's not natural. She glanced at Virginia, standing at the stove in the kitchen, strong, straight, voluptuously-rounded. It's not natural, she thought again, and something stirred in her mind. It's like—something I can't remember.

"I'm going to take a little nap now, Virginia," she said, when she had finished her lunch. "As soon as you've done the dishes you may go home."

"Yes, ma'am," said Virginia.

Mrs. Lamb was not in the habit of taking naps and she was not in the least sleepy; what she wanted was the relief of shutting a door between herself and Virginia. It can't take her long to do those few dishes, she thought. She'll be gone by two o'clock, or half-past, at the latest.

She lay on her bed and tried to read, but all the while she was listening for Virginia's light footsteps, for the sound of the front door closing. By three o'clock she could endure no more; she had to see if Virginia had gone without making herself heard; she had to know. She found Virginia in the kitchen, standing on a chair, taking everything down from the upper shelf.

"Oh, don't bother with that!" said Mrs. Lamb. "I'm not going to."

"I've got plenty of time, ma'am," said Virginia. "Unless you like your dinner very early …?"

"I'm going out to dinner," said Mrs. Lamb. "You needn't wait, Virginia."

At half-past five Virginia was still working at the kitchen shelves. Mrs. Lamb put on her hat and her sealskin coat, and stopped in the doorway.

"I'm going now," she said. "Good-night, Virginia."

"Good-night, ma'am," said Virginia.

Mrs. Lamb went to a nearby dairy lunch, and sitting at a table where she could not be seen from the street, she ordered toast and a pot of tea. She intended to stay a long time, but in a little while the dinner patrons began to come in; the waitress became openly hostile. Where can I go? thought Mrs. Lamb. What can I do?

She thought of the public library branch that was not far away, but when she came out into the street a thin, chill rain was falling. She nearly cried. I'm going home! she told herself. I don't care!

On the way back, she invented a story for Virginia. Her hostess, so she would say, had been called out of town by a sudden illness in the family. Such a *tragic* thing! *Poor* Rosemary! She realized then that she was talking half-aloud, in a strange, effusive tone such as she never used; she put a stop to that and went into the house; she opened the door with her key and went at once to the kitchen. Virginia was not there; she was not in the other rooms; she had gone, leaving the bed turned down, Mrs. Lamb's flowered nightdress laid out, everything in beautiful order.

Mrs. Lamb got a little supper for herself, and washed and put everything away, so that Virginia should not know she had eaten here. Then she sat down to work the crossword puzzle in the morning newspaper. Such heaven, to be alone, she thought. The puzzle was a little easy for her; she tried to do it slowly. "Mahomad's adopted son", one of the clues read. That's "Ali", she thought, and again something stirred in her mind. Ali, she thought … Ali Baba … The Arabian Nights …? That one—that woman who ate only one grain of rice …

Because she was a ghoul, and at night visited graves.

"Don't be silly!" Mrs. Lamb cried aloud.

The next day was still worse. When Mrs. Lamb came back from her marketing, Virginia had taken down all the curtains; the little apartment looked desolate, with a bleak light coming in through the grimy windows. She felt chilled.

"I'll do them up and get them all hung before I go," Virginia said.

It was much worse than yesterday. When Mrs. Lamb retired for the pretense of a nap, the people across the street could look into her bedroom; she pulled down the shade, and down came the roller; she tried to put it back, but something was wrong, and she could not. She did not want to lie down on the bed if people might be looking at her; she sat upright in a chair, once more trying to read. At three, she came out of her room, and Virginia was on the sill, outside one of the sitting room windows, cleaning it. Their eyes met through the glass, and Virginia smiled widely; her hand moved the cloth she held like the paw of a great cat.

I can't stand this! Mrs. Lamb thought. I'll have to get out. In haste, she put on her hat and coat; she took up her purse from the table in the dark foyer, and left the apartment. While she waited for the elevator, she opened the purse, as was her habit, to be sure she had her key. In a row along the bottom of the bag were four little bottles filled with capsules of a vivid yellow.

Virginia put them in there! she thought. It's poison. I know it! I know it! Poison is often yellow.

The elevator came and she got into it. It's poison, she thought. But as the old car descended, slowly and shakily, reason returned to her. There's no sense in that, she thought. Virginia would not put poison in my bag; she'd know I wouldn't take it. Unless it might be radium, or something that could come out through the bottles.

In the lobby downstairs she went into the telephone booth, and there she took out one of the bottles. It was a prescription for Mrs. Jones, one or two at bedtime; Dr. Bikley. All the little bottles were the same. Sleeping medicine, she thought. Then she noticed a blue comb, a blue cigarette case, and other things unfamiliar to her. No, she thought. I've taken Virginia's bag by mistake. These bottles aren't meant for me. No. Virginia's a drug addict. That's what makes her so queer.

Or she's a dope peddler. That's it! I shall go straight to the police, Mrs. Lamb told herself. I'll show them these bottles, and they'll put her in jail. I'll go to the police at once.

But her habit of indecision held her in the lobby. Where *are* the police? she thought. How do you find them? She could not recall ever having seen a police station in the neighborhood; certainly she had never entered one. They might be very rude, she thought. They'd ask me all sorts of questions. They'd find out that I wasn't paying Virginia, and they'd think … I don't know what. They might think I'd taken her bag on purpose for revenge. They might think I was mixed up in the dope ring myself.

Or suppose these bottles aren't anything at all illegal or wrong, but just something Virginia's got for some friend. Then what a fool I'd look like, and what a spiteful, malicious fool … No; I'd better not get myself involved in this at all. Very likely it's nothing at all important.

Or if it was serious, and they did send Virginia to jail, thought Mrs. Lamb, they couldn't keep her there forever. Someday they'd let her out, and then … Or there may be other people in it with her, and I don't know what they might do. It's not fair to expect a person like myself, a widow, living all alone, to get involved in a thing like this.

The elevator door opened with a rattle and she stepped into the car; she rode up to her floor and, being without her key, she was obliged to ring the bell and wait for Virginia to open the door. The overhead light was on in the foyer, making it glaringly bright.

"As soon as I got down into the lobby," Mrs. Lamb said, in a cool, pleasant voice, "I saw I'd taken the wrong purse. I didn't open it, but I suppose it's yours, isn't it?"

Virginia was looking at her with the lambent, steady eyes of a cat. She moved forward and held out her hand. And Mrs. Lamb saw that the thick gilt clasp had come undone, or perhaps she had not remembered to close it; the bag gaped wide open, and in the light the vivid yellow capsules twinkled. Virginia took the bag and closed it, and laid it on the table.

"I like working for Mrs. Jacobs the best of any of the ladies I ever worked for," she said. "When she comes home, she's going to take me back. You'll tell her how good I did for you. Won't you?"

They were looking at each other with the clearest comprehension. I have the upper hand, thought Mrs. Lamb, and I'm going to keep it. She doesn't want me to tell Laurie about these pills. She's afraid of me.

"You'll tell her, won't you?" Virginia asked again.

A chill ran across Mrs. Lamb's shoulders, making her arms tremble. Virginia's afraid of me, she thought. I must keep that in my mind and not be—nervous.

"It's my birthday tomorrow," said Mrs. Lamb, for no good reason, "and I'm going out to visit some friends in Greenwich. I may stay there two or three days. I'll let you know when I get back."

"Yes, ma'am," said Virginia.

She did not seem resentful, or at all surprised; she went away about her business and about half past five Mrs. Lamb heard the front door close. Now I'll have a little peace! she told herself. She was curiously exhausted, though; she lay on the couch in the sitting room until long after her usual dinner time before she could summon enough energy to go out and buy a little food.

But when she came back, when she opened the door with her key, she was able at last to realize her peace regained. She enjoyed her little dinner; she had a happy ending; when she lay in bed she felt triumphant. I've got rid of Virginia, she thought. I'll think of something to tell Laurie, when the time comes.

In the morning she laid out her breakfast on a newspaper, in the old style; she drank her coffee leisurely, and turned to the daily crossword puzzle. When the doorbell rang, she went to answer it, without interest. Virginia stood there, smiling, a little box in her hand.

"Happy birthday, ma'am!" she said. "I just baked this for you."

"Oh … Thank you," said Mrs. Lamb. "Thank you very much. I'm going away today, Virginia, so you needn't bother to stay."

"Yes, ma'am," said Virginia. "I'll just pack your bag and wash the dishes and tidy up."

"No, thank you," said Mrs. Lamb. "I can manage."

"I hope you'll like this," said Virginia, holding out the little box. She stood there, waiting.

Mrs. Lamb felt obliged to open it, and inside was a cake wrapped in oiled paper, a handsome cake with pink frosting.

"That's very nice of you, Virginia," she said. "Very nice indeed."

"I hope you like it, ma'am," said Virginia.

After Virginia had left, at five o'clock, Mrs. Lamb went into the kitchen to heat a can of soup for herself, and there, on the cabinet, was the pink cake, still wrapped in oiled paper. She knew I wasn't really going away, thought Mrs. Lamb, or she wouldn't have brought that. She felt obliged, however, to be civil about it, so she cut off a thick wedge and flushed it away in the bathroom. I couldn't possibly eat any of it, she thought. Not a crumb.

When she got into bed, an idea came into her mind, like a flash of light. Laurie will have to manage this, she thought. Laurie forced Virginia upon me, and Laurie will have to take her away. As soon as I hear from Laurie, I'll send her a wire. She has plenty of friends; she can make one of them take Virginia.

In the morning she dressed before breakfast and went down to look in her mailbox.

Facing the empty box, her hope all drained away. Laurie didn't write to me at all when she went to Canada, she thought; she didn't write to me from Sun Valley. When she used to go to Europe, sometimes it was months before I heard a word.

"Good morning, ma'am!" said Virginia's voice, startlingly close.

"Why are you here now?" Mrs. Lamb asked, sharply.

"I came early," Virginia answered, with a smile.

She wore a wide black hat, a black coat with a gardenia pinned on it; she looked opulent, happy, flaunting. I cannot stand her, thought Mrs. Lamb, and I won't, either. Only I don't want to say anything in front of the elevator man. She opened the door with her key and they entered the little dark foyer.

"Don't bother to change your clothes, Virginia," said Mrs. Lamb. "I shan't need you today."

"I'll just tidy up, ma'am."

"No," said Mrs. Lamb. "I don't want you to."

"Have to," said Virginia, taking off her hat.

It was open battle now.

"No!" said Mrs. Lamb.

"I never been fired off a job in my life," said Virginia, "and I'm not going to be now."

"I'm not—firing you," said Mrs. Lamb. "I never engaged you."

"Mrs. Jacobs told me to work here till she got back," said Virginia, "and I'm going to."

"You're not to come here anymore," said Mrs. Lamb.

"Well, I am here," said Virginia.

"If you come tomorrow," said Mrs. Lamb, "I shall send for the police."

She turned away and went into the bedroom, locking the door; she knew very well how unconvincing her threat had been; she felt helpless. I'm afraid of that horrible woman, she admitted to herself. I have been, from the very beginning. I shan't go near her. I'll stay in here all day, until she's gone.

At noon Virginia knocked at the door. "What would you like for lunch, ma'am?" she asked.

"Nothing," Mrs. Lamb answered.

At half past five Virginia knocked on the door, to say goodnight. "Good-bye!" Mrs. Lamb called, and Virginia went away; Mrs. Lamb heard the front door close. Now! she thought. Now I can go back to my own life and my own ways. It's over.

She went into the kitchen to make a cup of tea, and, just as the water was about to boil, the doorbell rang. She covered her mouth with her hand, looking about her in a panic. It's Virginia, she told herself. She's back. I won't let her in! I will not!

The doorbell rang again. She'll keep on ringing, Mrs. Lamb thought, and I can't stand that. I'll have to tell her to go away. Or send for the police. I mean it."

She opened the door, and there stood her cousin Laurie, in her mink coat, no hat on her blonde head, carrying a suitcase in her hand.

"Laurie! You've come home so soon?"

"I never went," Laurie said. "I've been up in Vermont." She sat down, in a suspicious, unhappy buffalo-attitude. "Have you anything to drink in the house, Edna?" she asked. "Whiskey, or gin, or even sherry?"

"I'm sorry, but I haven't," said Mrs. Lamb. "I was just making tea."

"Well, I'll take tea, then," said Laurie. "I'm so damn tired and cold ... I came here straight from the Grand Central. I wanted to see about getting Virginia back next week."

"Tomorrow," said Mrs. Lamb. "I don't want her here again, Laurie. I don't like her, at all."

"But she's a treasure," said Laurie.

"I don't like her at all," Mrs. Lamb repeated. "I wish you'd telephone to her, or send her a wire and tell her to go to you tomorrow. Not here."

"I can't," said Laurie. "I don't know where she lives."

"She's worked for you all this time, and you don't know where she lives?"

"No, and I don't care, either," said Laurie. "Have you any crackers, Edna? I couldn't eat a mouthful on the train and now I'm starving."

"I'll see," said Mrs. Lamb, rising. She could find nothing in her kitchen but that pink cake, wrapped in oiled paper; she cut a generous slice of it and brought it in to her cousin.

"It's good," said Laurie. "Only the frosting has a queer taste. What is it? What flavor?"

"I wish I had gone to Mexico," said Laurie. "I ought to get away. I wish I'd never gone to Vermont, never met that Colonel Mayne. He says he's getting a divorce, but they all say that. I don't know, anyhow ... There's something sort of sinister about him. Honestly, Edna, sometimes I'm afraid of him."

"Oh, are you?" asked Mrs. Lamb, not in the least interested. "Why, Laurie?"

"Honestly, Edna, if I turn him down again, I think he'd be capable of killing me," Laurie said.

She went on and on, and Mrs. Lamb sat with a polite look on her face, not listening anymore. Of course, part of it is simply conceit, she thought, but I dare say part of it true. I cannot understand it. Laurie's not young, and I don't consider her good-looking. Certainly she's not witty or interesting. It must be her money that attracts all these men.

"I'll be going along now, Edna," said Laurie. "If Virginia's coming to work for you tomorrow, I'll telephone her here, and she can open up my apartment. Dosia Woods has got me a room in the St. Pol for a day or so."

"That's nice," said Mrs. Lamb.

As soon as Laurie had gone, she turned on her little radio, a thing she very seldom did; sweet, delicate music came, and she sat listening, in peace. My life really isn't so bad, she thought. I'm poor, but I have a roof over my head. It's really quite cozy—without Virginia here.

It was a cold night, and she got into bed and read, until she was sleepy. Virginia will be gone tomorrow, she thought. That's all I want.

A bell was ringing and ringing, and she thought it was Virginia. I won't let her in, she thought, triumphantly. I will not. Then she realized that it was the telephone, and she got up, confused and alarmed, in the cold darkness.

"Edna …? This is Dosia … Oh, Edna! Poor Laurie!"

"What's wrong with Laurie?" asked Mrs. Lamb.

"Oh, Edna, she's gone!"

"Gone to Mexico?"

"No," Dosia said, a little impatiently. "She's passed on."

"Passed on?" Mrs. Lamb repeated. "To Vermont again?"

"She's dead!" cried Dosia Woods.

"That's not possible," said Mrs. Lamb.

"Don't say that!" said Dosia. "We took her to the hospital, Colonel Mayne and I, and she died. The doctors said poisoning. Food poisoning. Oh, poor Laurie! They didn't—"

Mrs. Lamb hung up the telephone while Dosia was talking; she sat beside it, with her mind blank. Simply impossible, she was saying to herself; simply impossible, all of it. She began to shiver, in her flowered nightdress, and she got back into bed, leaving the lamp alight.

That man killed her, she thought. Laurie said she was afraid he would, and he did. Laurie has—passed on. It would be dreadful of me to think about that thirty thousand dollars now, and I'm not thinking about it. Laurie was only a year younger than me. I never expected her to die.

Maybe I'll go to Mexico, myself, she thought. There would be a hot sun, a blue, blue lake, and in the center of it a boat or an island heaped with flowers, pink and white. People would be singing.

A bell was ringing again, but this time she knew that it was the doorbell; she knew it would be Virginia, and it was.

"I told you not to come," said Mrs. Lamb.

"Never been fired off a job in my life," said Virginia. "And I never will be."

"You can't come in," said Mrs. Lamb.

"Yes, I can," said Virginia.

With a shock, Mrs. Lamb remembered what had happened.

"Virginia," she said, sternly, "poor Mrs. Jacobs died last night. I'm very much upset, and I'm not going to be worried and annoyed by you. Go away at once."

Virginia began pushing at the door. Mrs. Lamb tried to close it, but she had not enough strength; as Virginia made her way in, Mrs. Lamb retreated, in haste, to her bedroom and locked the door. I'll go to see Mr. MacBride today, she I thought. I'm sure he'll get me some money, or advance me some, and I'll go away somewhere, anywhere. But suppose Virginia won't let me get out?

That's nonsense! she told herself. I'll get dressed, and I'll go when I'm ready. She had to wash, though, and she could not make up her mind to unlock the door and go out to the bathroom. You must! she told herself. You can't be so weak.

There was a knock at the door, a loud knock. She did not answer, and there was another knock; the knob rattled.

"Gentleman to see you!" called Virginia.

Mrs. Lamb did not believe that; it was, she thought, only a device to bring her out of her room. She kept silent, facing the door, and she thought it was bulging inward toward her; she thought it would fall flat in a moment, and Virginia would come walking over it, toweringly tall, great silver rings in her ears, her white teeth showing in a smile. I shall die, thought Mrs. Lamb.

"Colonel Mayne to see you!" cried Virginia.

He is the man, thought Mrs. Lamb; the murderer, the poisoner. He's here, in my house. What can I do? Call the police? But I can't get to the telephone, because he's in there. What can I do?

There was another knock at the door, and a man's voice spoke.

"Mrs. Lamb, I'm Colonel Mayne. May I see you for a few moments, please?"

I can't get away from them, she thought. They're both there. They'll get in. Help me!

Then her terror, risen to its crest, began to ebb; she drew a long breath and she began to think. There's no reason why he should want to do me any harm, she reasoned, and Virginia can't do anything to me while he's here. It's better with two of them.

"I'm coming," she called. "Just a moment." She went into the sitting room, standing so straight that her neck felt elongated.

"How do you do?" she said to the man who was standing there, a grey-eyed man in a grey suit, lean and tall, growing a little bald.

"I'm Colonel Mayne, Mrs. Lamb," he said. "Perhaps you've heard your cousin speak of me …? I'm sorry to disturb you—"

"I was asleep," Mrs. Lamb explained. Her voice sounded weak.

"I'm very sorry. But there's something I'm extremely anxious to find out. The police are investigating, of course—"

"The police?" said Mrs. Lamb.

"Dosia Woods told you, didn't she, that your cousin was poisoned? It's a poison that's frequently been administered in different foods."

"I see!" said Mrs. Lamb, earnestly.

"Dosia Woods thinks that Laurie came to her hotel direct from the station," he said, "but she didn't notice what time she arrived; no one seems to have noticed. And I want to be sure."

"I don't understand …"

"If she did come straight to the hotel," he said, "then she must have eaten the poisoned food on the train."

I didn't eat a mouthful on the train, Laurie had said.

"I want to know exactly what happened to Laurie," he was saying. "The police say there have been cases in which this sort of poison had been mixed in food by accident. I want to know whether this was an accident or—"

He paused. Or murder, Mrs. Lamb thought.

"I want to find out if Laurie stopped anywhere, anywhere at all, between the station and the hotel," he said.

"Why does it matter?" Mrs. Lamb asked, casually.

"It matters to me," he said. "I was—very fond of her … Dosia Woods told me that Laurie's maid was working here for you, and I thought that possibly Laurie might have telephoned, to speak to the girl, or to you. Or she might possibly have stopped in?"

Virginia must be in the kitchen, absolutely quiet, listening to every word. But she doesn't know, Mrs. Lamb thought.

"No," she said, "I didn't hear from poor Laurie yesterday. I didn't see her."

No sense in telling that man that Laurie came here, Mrs. Lamb thought, alone in her bedroom again. It would only cause trouble, and it has nothing to do with—what happened. Absolutely nothing. But if the police knew, they'd come bothering me with questions. They might think … I don't know what … They'd know about the thirty thousand dollars and they might think … Or suppose they feared I wouldn't pay?

That cake was meant for me. For me. Suppose I had—? No. It wasn't that cake. I won't think anymore about that cake. Nobody, not Virginia, not anyone knows that Laurie was here yesterday, and there's no reason why anyone ever should know. I'll go back to Mr. MacBride and get some money. I'll go to a hotel and never come back here. I'll simply walk out of here and leave everything. Virginia can't find me. Or if she does, I can cope with her, in a hotel. There'll be people to help me get rid of her.

She opened the closet door and stood there in her flimsy slip, looking at the row of dresses on hangers, all of them drab and dreary. I'm going to buy some new clothes, she thought, just a few really good things. I'm going to begin a new life, entirely different. I'll look up my old friends; I'll have a nice little circle. I'll travel; to Mexico, perhaps—

There was a knock at the door.

"No!" she called, and sprang forward to turn the key. But Virginia had entered.

"Why, how cold you are, ma'am!" said Virginia. "Get into your bed, and I'll bring you a nice hot cup of coffee."

"No," said Mrs. Lamb. "I won't."

"You're not fit to go out, ma'am," said Virginia. "You're all shaking. Get into your bed."

"No," said Mrs. Lamb. "I won't."

Virginia smiled.

"Look what I found!" she said, taking something out of the pocket of her apron.

"What is it?" asked Mrs. Lamb.

"It's Mrs. Jacobs's little compact, all shiny gold and her initials on it. I found it down beside the cushion in the blue chair."

I am cold, Mrs. Lamb thought. I am shaking.

"She must have left it here last week, when she came to say good-bye," she said.

"Oh, no!" said Virginia. "I turn that cushion every day. It wasn't there yesterday morning." She smiled again. "I found it just before you told the colonel you didn't see Mrs. Jacobs yesterday."

Mrs. Lamb reached for her dressing gown and put it around her shoulders.

"I'm going to the police," she said. "I'll tell them that Mrs. Jacobs did come here yesterday, and that she ate your cake."

"My pretty pink cake?" said Virginia, laughing. "Why, you ate it yourself. You told that old lady at lunch yesterday that it was delicious. No, I guess you won't go and tell the police that story. They'd think it was pretty funny you told the colonel Mrs. Jacobs wasn't here. But if you did, then I'd have to tell them how I found the compact, and that frightened you. I'd have to tell them I ate up the rest of that cake before I went home yesterday."

The dressing-gown fell to the floor, and Virginia picked it up.

"How much do you want?" asked Mrs. Lamb.

"Don't want anything," Virginia answered. "You could raise my pay, maybe, and you could give me a nice little present, now and then, when you get all that money."

"How much will you take to go away?"

"I'm not going away," said Virginia. "Never been fired off a job yet, and I'm not going to be now. I'm going to stay and look after you, night and day, the rest of your life."

I can't go to the police now, Mrs. Lamb thought. It's too late. I couldn't prove that Laurie ate that cake, or that there was anything wrong with it. I'd only look very—queer to them, very suspicious, telling that lie to Colonel Mayne. It's too late.

"Get into your bed, ma'am," said Virginia, "and I'll make some coffee. I'll look after you."

I'll never know about that cake, Mrs. Lamb thought. She kicked off her shoes and lay down on the bed. I'll never get rid of Virginia, and I'll *never know*.

Friday, the Nineteenth

When Boyce came downstairs, the table in the breakfast nook was set, and Lilian was moving about, quickly and crossly, in the kitchen. He had once thought her pretty, a neat, small, dark-haired woman, but he no longer liked to look at her, or to think about her. Her quickness had no grace in it; she bustles, he thought, that's the word for it, slamming things around, always cross, always with a grievance.

If she knew about Molly …! he thought. It was almost funny that, with all her accusations, her suspicions, she never suspected the one thing that mattered. She had accused him of 'flirting' with the dreary blonde next door, of 'carrying on' with his secretary. Yet she could see him and Molly together, here, in her own house, and feel no uneasiness. I asked Molly and Ted over this evening, she would say, or, why don't you call up Ted and see if they'd like us to come over?

He sat down on the bench beside the table, and he hated it; everything red and white—red and white checked curtains at the kitchen windows, the cabinet drawers full of little knives, spoons, all with red handles, even the can opener, the eggbeater. Her life was made up of things like that. There had to be a blue shower curtain in the bathroom, and a blue bath mat; she was always looking for blue soap. And worst of all was her closet; her dresses all in green cellophane bags, her jaunty hats in green cellophane, her high-heeled shoes in the pockets of a green ruffled bag.

He was sick of this little house, of the smug suburban street and the people who lived on it; he hated his job. He was sick of everything but Molly.

And what did that amount to, after all? He and Molly had never had more than a few minutes alone together; while Ted was in the kitchen mixing drinks; while Lilian was at the telephone in the hall. Then, in their little moment, their hands would meet, in a desperate clasp; they would kiss, without a word. They had never had time for words; Lilian would come back, with a full report of her conversation with a neighbor; Ted would come in with drinks on a tray, always whistling.

All through the war, Ted had been the most important figure in his life. Time and absence had made Lilian grow fainter in his mind; all his past life had become a little shadowy; only Ted was the friend dearer than a brother, the indispensable comrade. Now he was an enemy, like Lilian, to be outwitted; the sight of his ruddy face, the sound of his fluty whistle were odious.

"You've got to trim the hedge when you get home tonight, Donald," said Lilian, taking away his empty cereal bowl and setting down a plate of eggs and bacon before him.

"Not compulsory," he said.

"It is!" she said. "It's the only ragged, nasty-looking hedge on the street."

"Terrible," said Boyce.

"Well, it is," she said. "And if you haven't any self-respect, Donald Boyce, I have. If you won't trim that hedge, I'll *pay* someone to do it."

"I'm not interested in the hedge," said Boyce. "Or the street."

"I know that," said Lilian. "You're just too superior. Every other man on this street has a better job than you have, and *they* can trim their hedges, and do lots of little things—"

"For God's sake," said Boyce, "let's not start this again. I pay the rent—and everything else. But it's *your* house. You run it to suit yourself. You love it."

"What else have I got left?" she asked.

Sitting in the smoker, Boyce held up a newspaper so that nobody should talk to him, ask him to play gin rummy, bother him. The quarrel had made him feel sick; one of the worst quarrels they had had; he wanted to forget it, and to think about Molly. God! he said to himself. When you think what life could be like—and what it actually is.... If Molly and I could go away together....

He had never thought anything like that before. He had never seen her, never heard of her until six months ago when Ted had come to tell him about his marriage. And, because Ted was not an enemy then, but his friend, he had moved heaven and earth to get Ted a house on the same street. I want you and Molly to meet, Ted had said.

At Grand Central, Boyce took a taxi downtown to the office. If Lilian knew it, he thought, she'd never stop talking about my 'extravagance.' All right! What she doesn't know won't hurt her. And she's never going to know about my last two raises. Damned if I'm going to spend all the best years of my life in that office, just for Lilian's benefit.

He was thirty-eight now, the same age as Lilian, but anyone would think she was older, she with her sulky mouth, her quick, graceless bustling. He was tall, limber, fair-haired and grey-eyed, with a look of boyish good humor. Even now, shaken by that quarrel, he was good-humored and friendly to the others in the office.

He was popular here; he got along well with everyone; he had been like that in the army. Lilian likes to quarrel, he thought. Every one of these wretched women she gets in to do a day's work now and then does something that makes her angry. The last one washed the bath mat in something that faded it, so that it doesn't match the shower curtain, and that's a tragedy. That's her life.

What else have I got left?

Let her find something else. Let her be something else. He turned to his work, routine work which he could handle without effort; it was dull enough, but it soothed him.

"Someone on the telephone for you, Mr. Boyce," said the secretary he shared with three other men.

He picked up the telephone without interest, and for a moment he did not believe what he heard.

"Not—you?" he said.

"Yes," she said. "It's Molly. I just wondered if you could get off a little early, and we could have a cup of tea?"

"Yes," he said. "Where?" He had to be careful; there were a dozen people who could hear every word.

"I'll meet you in the lobby of your building, shall I? At four?"

"Yes," he said, again.

He could not believe this; he could not understand it. They had never tried to meet alone; never mentioned it, and, in all his wretched longing for her, Boyce had never seriously made any sort of plan for meeting her. They had never even had a talk together; there had been nothing but those handclasps, those kisses, hurried and dangerous and silent.

He went at once to the head of his department.

"Will it be all right if I leave a bit early, Mr. Robinson?" he asked. "There's something my wife wants me to look after." *Why did I say that?* he thought. *But it didn't matter.*

He was down in the lobby at ten minutes to four in a curious anger. *If she's going to say we mustn't see each other anymore,* he thought, *I won't listen. If she's going to start talking about Lilian, about Ted being my friend, I won't listen, that's all. Nobody's obliged to live a life like mine. It's hell. Everybody has a right to try to get out of hell if he can.*

There was, he thought, something hellish and insane about the activity in the lobby, the clacking of heels on the tiled floor, the people, all hurrying, silent, preoccupied, getting in and out of elevators, going up, going down, all in a hurry. A boy in a hurry with six bottles of a popular soft drink; a girl in a hurry with a sheaf of papers; a stout man with his straw hat pushed to the back of his head, in a hurry to go up, a thin woman in pince-nez coming down in a hurry.

He stood where he could watch the entrance, and people came in and out, one after another. Why didn't anyone know anyone else? Why didn't anyone say hello, or smile? And why didn't Molly come?

It was five minutes past four. She's not coming, he thought. He knew that. He was so sure of it that he was not going to wait. She's changed her mind, he thought. It's too much of a risk. She can't take it. He was so sure that he went to the newsstand and bought an evening newspaper; he went out of the building, and she was there, her black-gloved hand on the revolving door.

"You're late," he said.

"Only a minute," she said. "Where can we go?"

"There's a rather nice little place near here where we can get a drink," he said. "Unless you insist on tea...."

"I don't care," she said.

They set off along the narrow downtown street, crowded with these hurrying people, jaded in the fierce midsummer heat. He glanced at her sidelong, and his anger increased. She was a tall girl, broad-shouldered and lean, in a dark-green dress and a wide hat that looked countrified here. She walked so easily; she alone was cool and easy.

She's not pretty, he thought. Her face with high cheekbones had a gaunt look, a hungry look; her mouth was too big. Not pretty; not a girl, either. She's as old as Lilian, and she's divorced and remarried. She's no girl.

"Here we are," he said, and took her arm, to steer her into a tavern. It was dim in here, with a sour smell; two big electric fans spun with a hollow roar, like wind in a tunnel. They went to the back of the room and sat down in a booth, facing each other.

"Oh, beer, thanks," she said.

He ordered a rye for himself and lit cigarettes for both of them: "I've got a job!" she said.

"That's nice," said Boyce.

"It's such a *funny* little job," she went on. "It's with a woman radio writer. She wants me to come in three days a week and stay in her apartment in the Seventies, to take telephone calls and open the mail and do a little typing. So that she can stay out at her country place."

The bar was blankly and strangely silent; even the bartender was gone; only the fans were spinning, sending against his face a thin stream of musty air. He sat looking down at the table; then he glanced up at Molly, and her dark eyes were brilliant in her thin face.

"You're going to be alone in this apartment?" he asked.

"Yes," she said. "From nine to five. Starting tomorrow."

Their eyes met steadily.

"Shall I come tomorrow?" he asked.

"Yes," she said....

She had to leave at five.

"I told Ted I'd meet him on the five-forty train," she said.

"I don't want you to go," Boyce said.

"I don't want to go, either. It's been so wonderful," she said, "this little time alone together. I love this funny little bar; I've loved every moment here. I wish today would never end."

She rose and stood, pulling on her gloves; he rose too, and suddenly she came to his side; she put her black-gloved hands on his temples and kissed him, hungrily and desperately; he held her close to him, so that he could feel her heart beating.

"I *must* go, Donald!" she said. "Till tomorrow!"

"Till tomorrow," he said.

"*Will* you trim the hedge, Donald?" Lilian asked, as she opened the door.

"All right," he said.

The morning's quarrel would never be mentioned; that was how it was with them now. In the early days of their marriage, he had always been able to end her quick-tempered little outbursts with a kiss, a smile, a joke. But he was tired of that; tired of her instant remorse. Let her nag; let her sulk. He put on an old jacket, and taking up the pruning shears, he went out of the house into the last of the afternoon sun.

"Hello, Boyce!" said the man next door, trundling his lawn mower. "No rest for the weary, eh?"

After tomorrow I can stand all this, Boyce thought. Because then he would have his secret life, his own life with Molly. The shears made a sharp biting sound; the lawn mower rattled; two radios were playing nearby, music on one of them; on the other a woman's voice, monstrously sweet and false, was talking on and on. I'll be so damn glad when this day is over, Boyce thought.

Lilian talked, while they ate dinner. She was angry and hurt and sulky, but she could not help talking. She had to tell him what she had said to the gas company; what the milkman had told her about those people who don't pay their bills. Boyce was polite, in a bleak aloofness. Oh, did you? Oh, really?

"I've got to go in to the office tomorrow," he said.

"On *Saturday?*"

"On Saturday. But there's no need for you to get up. I'll stop in Grand Central and get a bite."

But he knew she would get up; her alarm clock waked him in the morning. He had bought an alarm clock for himself, to keep in his own room, so that she should not come in to wake him, grasping him by the shoulder, speaking sharply. Donald! *Donald!* Now, *don't* go to sleep again!

He lay in bed until he heard Lilian go down the stairs, and he tried to think about Molly. But he could not, and he could not feel anything except a desperate impatience to get away, out of this house.

Lilian had his breakfast on the table when he came downstairs.

"Another hot day," she said. "And the paper says hot tomorrow."

He hated her to look at the newspaper before he had read it. I'll order another one for you, he had said. No, she had said. It would just be a waste of money. *I* don't have time to sit down and read newspapers. Only once in a while I like to glance at it.

She had opened the newspaper and turned over a page. He folded it back, and frowned a little. Senate Committee Calls McGivney. They printed that yesterday, he thought, and this one too. Hotel Cashier Foils Hold-up. He glanced at the weather report. Continued warm and sunny. Highest temperature in upper 80's. Tomorrow and Sunday—

"This is Friday's paper!" he said, angrily.

"But it *is* Friday, Donald," said Lilian.

He looked at her for a moment and then turned away.

"It is Friday," she said again.

He did not want Lilian to drive him to the station. "I'll walk," he told her. "It'll do me good."

"But you'll miss your train, Donald."

"All right. I'll get the next one," he said.

It made no difference what train he got this morning; he was not going to see Molly until noon. He was leaving early only because he wanted to get away from that house. He set off down the street, walking fast, too fast for this hot weather, to get away from Lilian. Fool …! he thought. She doesn't even know what day of the week it is.

"Hi-ya!" called a cheerful voice, and Matthews, his next-door neighbor, slowed down his car. "Hop in, and we'll give you a lift to the station, Boyce."

"You're going in to town today?" Boyce asked, as he got into the sedan with Matthews and his wife.

"What?" said Matthews. "Well, why not?"

"You don't often go in on Saturdays, do you?" asked Boyce.

"But this isn't Saturday, man!" said Matthews. "It's Friday."

Boyce felt his throat contract; his mouth was dry. Take it easy! he told himself. You and Molly made a mistake, that's all. A mistake about what day of the week it was. That happens, now and then. Nothing unusual. Nothing to be upset about. I'm glad I found out in time, though; otherwise I shouldn't have shown up at the office today.

Only this was not the day he was going to see Molly. There was all this day to go through, with his wearisome job; dinner with Lilian, another evening, another night, like a desert to be crossed. Molly will have realized our mistake by this time, he thought. She'll take it for granted that I'll come tomorrow instead of today.

He sat down at his desk, and his routine work seemed to him like yesterday's; he went out to lunch with the same fellow-worker.

"Well, Friday's fish day," Haley said. "I think I'll have a try at this codfish."

"You said that yesterday," said Boyce.

"I certainly didn't say that yesterday was Friday," said Haley, a little offended.

"No, no," Boyce said, quickly.

It seemed to him that he had never felt such hot weather; he felt sick from it, and stupid. He went back to his desk, back to those papers that were like yesterday's papers, and his hands were unsteady.

"There's someone on the telephone for you, Mr. Boyce," said his secretary.

"It's—you?" he said.

"Yes," Molly said. "Donald, could you get off a little early—?"

"Yes," he said.

"I'll meet you in the lobby of your building at four," she said.

He went at once to Robinson.

"Will it be all right if I leave a little early, Mr. Robinson?" he asked. And then, because he thought Robinson was looking at him in an odd way: "There's something my wife wants me to look after," he said.

He was in the lobby at ten minutes to four, but this time he was not restless or troubled. He knew she would come.

"Wasn't that a queer mistake?" she said, as soon as she came. "For both of us to be so sure that yesterday—"

"Let's go and get a drink," said Boyce. "I could do with one."

It was dim in the tavern, and very quiet; only the big fans spinning, sending a stream of musty air against his face.

"It's such a *funny* little job," she said. "It's with a woman radio writer—"

"Yes," he said. "You told me yesterday."

They were silent for a moment.

"How was your day, Donald?" she asked.

Like yesterday, he thought. But, with a great effort, he answered in his usual debonair way.

"This new office boy we have …" he said. "I sent him up to the eleventh floor with a claim—"

He stopped short, because of the look on her face.

"But I told you that yesterday," he said.

"Yes," she said. "You did."

She rose and stood before him, pulling on her black gloves.

"Until tomorrow, Donald!"

"Until tomorrow!" he said.

I'm not going to say anything to Lilian about going in to the office tomorrow, he thought. I'll simply set my alarm, and get out of the house without waking her.

But her alarm clock waked him; when he went downstairs, she had his breakfast ready.

"Another hot day," she said. "And the paper says hot—"

"Shut up!" he said.

"Donald!" she cried.

"Sorry," he said. "Hot weather nerves. I'm sorry." He waited for a moment. "Hand me the newspaper, will you please, Lilian?"

When he saw it, he grew blind for a moment; he could not draw a breath for a moment. The date line was Friday the nineteenth.

He was waiting for her in the lobby at ten minutes to four, and he did not even notice the passing of time until she came.

"Donald," she said, "what's *happened?*"

"I don't know," he said.

"It's hard to see how we could both have made such a mistake about the days of the week," she said. "I mean—"

"Let's go and get a drink," he said. "I could do with one."

It seemed to him that the tavern was darker than before; the air stirred by the fans was sickeningly tepid; he and Molly were alone; even the bartender was gone.

"It's such an *idiotic* mistake!" she said, and laughed.

"Don't do that!" he said.

"What d'you mean, Donald?" she asked.

He did not tell her how he hated her laugh, harsh, loud, ringing in his ears.

"But tomorrow we'll forget all this," she said, laying her hand over his. "Won't we, darling?"

The touch of her hand in its black glove made him wince.

"I've got to go now," she said. "I promised to meet Ted on the five-forty."

"Yes," Boyce said. "Yes. You'd better go."

And, he thought, if only she would never come back.

She looked haggard and ill when she came into the lobby the next day a little after four.

"I don't understand this," she said. "It can't *still* be Friday."

"Let's go and get a drink," said Boyce. "I could—"

"For God's sake, don't say that again!" she said. "I'm sick of it."

"We'll go somewhere else this time," he said, and he took her to another bar nearby. But there was a sign on the door. Closed For Repairs.

"I know another place," he said.

"I haven't time," Molly said. "I promised to meet Ted on the five-forty."

"So I've heard," said Boyce.

They went back to the tavern.

"Let's sit at another table," said Molly.

They sat down at a table nearer the door, but the heat there was intolerable; the air from the fans did not reach them.

"Let's try the next table," Molly said.

"It's no use," said Boyce, and led the way to the table where they had first sat.

"*Why* is it no use?" she demanded. "Do you mean you think it's got to go on like this?"

"What do you think, yourself?" he asked.

Their eyes met, in a long look of wonder and fear.

"For God's sake, haven't you any ideas?" she asked. "Aren't you going to do anything? This is—simply hell."

"Yes," he said. "I think you're right."

They met the next day, because he had something to say to her.

"I don't pretend to understand this," he said. "I don't know what's happened to us. Nobody else seems to notice anything wrong. It keeps on being Friday the nineteenth.... But I thought of this. Perhaps if we don't see each other again, we can get out of this."

"Let's try it!" she said eagerly. "Let's shake hands on it."

He took her black-gloved hand with a shiver of aversion.

"We promise never to see each other again," she said, and he repeated it. She took a sip of her beer, and she gave her harsh little laugh. "Our wonderful love didn't last very long, did it?" she said.

"It never began," said Boyce.

"None of that!" she said, angrily. "You were crazy for me. You'd have done anything to get me."

"Oh, no," he said. "I never even thought of doing anything for you.

Except a little lying, to Lilian and Ted."

"Keep quiet!" she said.

"Or you for me," he said. "We weren't going to give up anything for each other. We were just going to take, all we could get."

She rose. "I'm going," she said. "I've got to meet Ted on—"

She stopped abruptly, and turned away, leaving him at the table.

If only it works ... he thought. Oh, God, if only this is the end! And he thought that it might be; hope was rising in him. If we don't see each other again, he thought, it *has* to stop. Maybe even making up our minds never to see each other again will stop it. Maybe tomorrow.... Oh, God, if only tomorrow will be Saturday....

He went home, more tired than he had ever been in his life, yet he slept poorly, restless in the hot dark. If this thing is over now, he thought, I'm going to make some plans. I'm going to start saving my money, so that I can get away. I'm—tired. If tomorrow is Saturday, I'll take it easy, all Saturday and Sunday.

But if it isn't Saturday.... I've got to be prepared for that. It may take a little time to stop this thing. Only I'm so damn tired....

The sound of Lilian's alarm clock waked him, and he got up at once; he went downstairs, barefoot, in his pajamas, to bring in the newspaper. His hands were trembling as he held it up, his eyes did not focus. But he thought he saw an S, bold and black.

"Donald!" called Lilian from the head of the stairs. "Why ever did you go rushing down—?"

"Come here," he said. "Come here and tell me...."

The newspaper rattled in his shaking hands.

"What's—the date?" he asked her.

"But, Donald—" she said, looking up into his face.

"What's the date, I say?" he shouted.

"But it's Friday, the nineteenth, of course," she said. "Donald, aren't you well?"

"No," he said. "It's just the heat. Let me alone."

I've got to have patience, he thought. As long as we've stopped seeing each other, this thing will have to end. If not today, then tomorrow. As long as I don't see her.

Lilian drove him to the station.

"Bye-bye, Donald," she said, as he got out of the car.

"Bye-bye," he said, with a twitch of a smile, and started along the platform.

"Hello, Sarge!" called Ted's voice.

There was no escape from this. Boyce had to go all the way in to New York with Ted; he had to listen to Ted talking about Molly.

"This job she wants to take …" Ted said. "I wish she wouldn't do it. She went through hell, in her first marriage, you know. I want her to take it easy now, poor girl."

"I see!" Boyce said.

"Maybe Lilian could talk to her," said Ted. "Lilian's a regular little homebody; maybe she could persuade Molly it's better to stay home."

"Maybe she could," said Boyce.

"Lucky break for us, that the two girls get on so well together," said Ted. "Sometimes a marriage will pretty well break up a friendship between two men, if the wives don't hit it off."

Shut up, you fool! Boyce was crying in his heart. Shut up, and let me alone.

"Well, be seeing you!" said Ted, when they reached Grand Central.

"So long!" said Boyce.

His work was the work he had done yesterday; he made the same minor mistake he had made yesterday. He had lunch with the same man.

"There's someone on the telephone for you, Mr. Boyce," said his secretary.

It can't be Molly, he thought. She wouldn't do that.

"Donald," she said, "I've got to see you."

"Well, you won't see me."

"I've got to! Donald, I've found a way out for us."

"I don't give a damn. I won't see you."

"Donald, it's our only chance."

"All right," he said, after a moment, and hung up the telephone.

He realized that he had been speaking loudly and violently, yet no one had noticed. If Robinson will only notice, he thought. If Robinson would say, What? You want to get off early again? This won't do, Boyce.

"Certainly, Boyce," said Robinson.

He was surprised to see how ugly she was, pale, gaunt, moistening her lips with the tip of her tongue. As they walked to the tavern, he thought of names for her. Hyena, he thought, and that pleased him best.

They sat down at the table together.

"All right," he said. "Let's hear your idea."

She did not answer.

"Come on!" he said. "Let's hear it."

"Donald," she said, "I—can't remember."

"What d'you mean?"

"There was something ... something I had to tell you. But I can't remember."

"Damn you!" he said. "You mean you got me here for nothing?"

"There was something," she said, in tears. "I know there was. But I can't remember."

"You've spoilt everything," he said.

"*I?*" she said. "You're trying to blame *me* for this? It's *your* fault. That first time we met, in your house, the way you looked at me...."

"I hope to God I never have to look at you again," he said.

She rose, and began pulling on her black gloves.

"Now I've made up my mind," she said. "Now I know what I'm going to do. I'm going to tell Ted what you've done to me. I'll tell him how you've been making love to me, how you planned to come to that apartment. He'll forgive me, but he'll *kill* you."

Their eyes met again, in a complete understanding. She wanted Ted to kill him. And Boyce would have been utterly happy to see her dead here, on the floor, this instant.

He stayed on in the booth after she had gone, because he was so tired. But after a while the noise of the electric fans began to worry him, and he rose. Again, as this morning, his eyes did not focus; the bar seemed filled with smoke. When he went out into the street, the sunshine was smoky; the crowded street seemed completely empty. No people, no traffic, not a sound. I hate her, he thought. I hate her so much that I can't see, can't hear.

He saw the truck, though, towering above him; he heard a monstrous confusion of sound, roaring, thundering, little squeaks and yelps. He went spinning high up into the air and then he came down with a thud so hard, he thought, that he broke through the street into a black, wet stairway, and he fell down it, thudding on every step, heavy, yet soft as a rag.

He could hear Lilian's voice, almost in his ear.

"Donald! Donald, darling!"

Her voice, he thought, was too insistent. But she was trying to call him back from the place where he was lying, and it was a very lonely place; he thought that he would be glad to go back with her. It would be good, he thought, to sit in the kitchen with the red and white checked cloth. Lying here was very lonely and Lilian, at the very least, had long been his companion. She was holding his hand now, and he was willing that she should keep on doing that.

In a way, he felt very comfortable. He was lying, he thought, on a cloud, and if he chose, he could move his hand a little and send the cloud floating off, away from Lilian. But he had also the choice of remaining here; it was clear to him that he lay in the most delicate balance.

Let Lilian hold my hand, he thought. I'll go back with her. I won't mind trimming the hedge. No, he thought, I'll like it. He could recall the sharp sound of the shears in the late summer afternoon; he could remember the feel of the grass under his feet; he could remember some sweet fragrance, a flower, perhaps, or the blossoms of a fruit tree.

Now he heard a loudspeaker calling Dr. Dawson Dr. Dawson Dr. Dawson; he could hear Lilian sobbing; he heard some sort of jingling table go by along the corridor. He liked to hear these sounds; he wanted to come back; he wanted to put on his shoes and walk out of here. Poor Lilian ... he thought. He had been gone away from her for a very long time; he had left her alone, but he thought he could get back, find her young and pretty as she had once been, always a little cross because she felt herself not pretty enough.

There was another sound, though; a sweet and delicate little bell. It was growing clearer and louder. A fire alarm? he thought. The other sounds were very dim now; Dr. Dawson Dr. Dawson, oh, Donald, darling, come now, Mrs. Boyce, nurse.... But the bell grew louder and louder, ringing in his ears.

"There's someone on the telephone for you, Mr. Boyce," said his secretary.

That's Friday the nineteenth, he thought. I wish this day would never end, Molly had said. And it never had. If he went back there would be nothing else.

He sighed, and let his hand drop from Lilian's careful clasp. He moved his fingers a little, to push off the cloud on which he was stretched; he lay stiff and quiet under the sheet and floated away.

Dr. Dawson Dr. Dawson. The telephone bell was ringing, and Molly was waiting. But he was not coming back.

Mollie: The Ideal Nurse

"But, Rob," said Mrs. Keating, "you can't deny that it was—well—at least *suspicious*."

"Pshaw!" replied her husband, with vigor. "Nothing but surmise, anyway. And in *any* case, she was justified."

"But a murderess!" protested Mrs. Keating. Her husband scowled at the word.

"You women!" he exclaimed. "You are never satisfied. Here you are with an ideal nurse, and you cavil at—at a mere suspicion. You've forgotten, I suppose, how it was before she came."

Forgotten that time, that awful time before Mollie came? Never in life would Mrs. Keating forget it. Her mind reverted with amazing vividness to the day that was the climax of the awfulness and the end of it. She remembered it and said no more of her suspicions.

She remembered how she had been sitting at the window, where she could watch her three terrifying children playing on the lawn; remembered how dowdy and dreadful she had looked, with her red eyes and her frowzy hair, how worse than dreadful she had felt, how hopeless, how helpless.

The front door had banged, and out came a lean, wooden man, who strode down the garden path, jerked open the gate, slammed it after him, and disappeared in the direction of the railway station. Her husband, in a frightful temper. There had been a scene at the breakfast table; his tea had been weak and cold, the eggs hard as bullets, the toast revoltingly pale and soft. And the baby, somewhere out of sight, had wailed miserably all the time.

"What's the matter with this breakfast?" Keating had demanded.

"Cook has her hands full," she had explained. "She's taking care of baby, and she doesn't know how very well."

"Why the devil don't you get another nurse?"

"But, Rob, I don't know how. I don't know where to look for a really good, trustworthy woman. I'm not used to American ways yet."

Keating had become quite violent.

"You'll have to find out. It's your *business*. Your business either to find a nurse or to learn how to keep that child quiet yourself. I will not be bothered with this sort of thing."

She had begun to cry, which helped nothing.

"Oh, Lord!" he shouted. "Can't you do anything but sit there and snivel? Look at this breakfast. Not fit to eat, the house all upset. What's the matter with you, anyway? Simply because a poor old ayah dies, everything goes to pieces."

And so on, until Mrs. Keating had got up and left the table, sobbing. Her husband watched her go, and if it hadn't been for her dressing gown, he would have gone after her. But that outrageous thing of dingy flowered flannel trimmed with purple ribbon, with a long, trailing fold at the back—this garment, combined with her tears and her untidy hair, quite hardened his heart. Of course he realized that it was hard for her after that languid existence in India and the years of utter reliance upon the ayah, but still it didn't do to overlook the fact that he was being made very uncomfortable and that it wasn't wifely, wasn't decent, of her to allow any such condition.

So, deserted and rebuked, sat Mrs. Keating in her room. She was expected, she well knew, to dust and to make beds, as cook couldn't do that and likewise walk unceasingly up and down the nursery with a baby suddenly grown sleepless. But she felt too ill and miserable and too hopeless. The little she could do wouldn't make any impression upon the dreadful confusion, daily growing worse.

She was thinking something about wishing she had never been born or had never married Rob or had never come to America, when, glancing dutifully at her quite unmanageable children, she observed a stranger in the garden, a sturdy, gray-haired woman, respectably dressed in black, with a voluminous skirt that flounced about her square-toed boots as she walked. She was talking to the children with that manner and that smile recognized at once by Mrs. Keating as being absolutely the proper sort, at once adult and full of authority, without being irritating.

She patted young Robert's head, and went on her way, disappeared round the corner of the house, headed evidently for the back door. No doubt cook admitted her, for presently Mrs. Keating, with some surprise, heard soft-soled boots come squeaking up the stairs, and there stood the stranger in the doorway of her room.

"Good morning, ma'am," she said in a pleasant voice. "Please to excuse me for coming up, but the cook tells me you're not very well, so I didn't want to trouble you. I heard you wanted a nurse, so I stopped in. I'm a nurse, ma'am, and looking for a proper situation."

Now, Mrs. Keating was almost irresistibly inclined to accept this placid and kindly woman as a gift from Heaven without further questioning. She knew that there would be no faults or flaws in her. But the wraith of her husband forbade any such course. She was obliged to be what he would call sensible. So, apologetically, with an absurd feeling that it was an impertinence to interrogate this wise woman old enough to be her mother, she murmured something about references.

"Have you had much experience?" she inquired.

"I have, ma'am. Eighteen years with Mrs. Lyons down the street a bit. *She'll* tell you anything you'd like to know. Only mention Mollie to her. Six children she had, and I've brought them all up from the day they were born."

She waited for another question, but Mrs. Keating could think of none to ask. So Mollie herself inquired:

"What food do you give your baby, ma'am?"

"I don't know. You see, I had an ayah—an Indian woman—who took entire charge of—of everything. Of course I wouldn't expect anyone else to do what she did—"

"There's nothing could be done by any heathen woman that I couldn't do," said Mollie, respectful, but stern. "You can safely leave everything to me, ma'am, as Mrs. Lyons will tell you."

"I'm sure of it," Mrs. Keating began, and again recollected her husband and her own role of competent mistress. "Would you tell me why you left Mrs. Lyons?"

"The children grew up," said Mollie, soberly. "It's hard, when you've been with them day and night for all them years, but it's what's to be expected. It's nature."

"Well," said Mrs. Keating, "I don't see why—if you like it, you might try the place for a while, and see how we get on together."

"Yes, ma'am," said Mollie, and stood for a moment looking quietly at her new mistress. Then, as she looked, her sunburned and impassive face broke slowly into an indulgent smile.

"Everything will be all right now," she remarked kindly. "Lie down, ma'am, and rest."

Mrs. Keating not moving, she took matters into her own hands, made the bed deftly, and, patting the pillows, said soothingly:

"Come now, ma'am, lie down! There, I'll take them hairpins out of your hair and make a braid that'll give your head more comfort. Now! Wait and I'll cover up your feet and close the shutters. After a bit I'll maybe bring you up a cup of tea."

She was gone, stepping softly, shoes squeaking comfortably, vast skirt rustling.

Mrs. Keating fell asleep, closed her eyes upon a complex and troubled world, opened them upon peace. Mollie, coming up with a tray, had tactfully waked her, propped her up with pillows, brushed and coiled her hair, opened the shutters to let in the gay spring sunshine, and left her to drink her tea in heavenly comfort and quiet. She stopped long enough to give her detailed information about her young family, and went serenely about her business again.

When Keating got home that evening, he encountered a delightful peace and orderliness in his household. He was prepared to be amiable, anyway, to atone for his morning ferocity, and this evidence of reform on the part of his wife still further softened him. He started up the stairs with a whistle absolutely cheerful, when a stout, gray-haired stranger appeared before him, finger to lips, and whispered:

"Hush, sir! The baby's asleep! The children are in the nursery, sir."

So he went into the nursery and found them there at tea, clean and contented, and with a new air of restraint that profoundly pleased him. They were evidently being "managed." He watched them for a time in solemn satisfaction, and then went into his wife's room to compliment her—indirectly, of course—upon her judgment and discrimination.

"You seem," he said, "to have found a very good, useful sort of woman."

Mrs. Keating, refreshed, rested, at ease regarding the future, had not the least intention of telling her husband that she hadn't found Mollie, that Mollie had, in fact, simply materialized. Neither did she intend to let him know that she hadn't investigated the apparition's references, and never meant to, either.

"Rob," she said firmly, "she is absolutely the *ideal* nurse!"

And she was. Undoubtedly. She went out that evening, and returned later with a large valise, and installed herself in the nursery, whence day after day she ruled the household with wise tyranny. She was infallible, supreme, beyond appeal, yet so discreet that no one resented her authority; not even the irritable master chafed under it. Within a month she had become the indispensable, inevitable thing, the sun, one might poetically say, of their universe. They relied upon her for everything good, yet took her as a matter of course.

Keating was, I think, the only one who really appreciated her. To see her in the evening, sitting in the dimly lighted corridor outside the nursery door, hands folded, rocking placidly, prepared apparently to wait there eternally; or to watch her on the lawn with the children, watchful as some mother animal, and as little interfering; to observe her limitless discretion, to hear her calm voice, satisfied his very soul. They never spoke to each other except for a "Good morning, Mollie," and a "Good morning, sir," decorously exchanged. But he, with his profound British propriety, and she, with her inborn Irish decorum, were always in accord, always understood each other. Not for them to inquire, to experiment; they were of the elect who knew by instinct and tradition what was the right and proper course at all times.

So you may imagine how amazing and disgusting it was for him to hear that Mollie had a "follower." Mrs. Keating had long ago heard rumors, which she preferred to keep to herself. The cook had told her of a mysterious man whom Mollie supplied with table scraps. She had rebuked the cook for tale-bearing, and told her she was quite sure Mollie was incapable of anything improper.

"I don't care," she said to herself, "how many followers she has. I *know* she's a perfectly respectable woman, and I'm not going to interfere with her."

It was on a Sunday that Mr. Keating discovered the thing. He was weeding a beloved flower bed when he heard voices at the back of the house and went quietly to see. He saw Mollie handing an immense sandwich to a man.

"Here," she said somewhat ungraciously, "take this. It'll last you till dinner time. And don't you be hanging about here, Steve. It won't do."

As the man went off with his sandwich, Keating made a point of getting a good look at him, and was shocked. A man of perhaps fifty, with an alarmingly red face, drooping black mustache, a heavy, beefy, slovenly fellow without a collar. Keating at once decided—or insisted—in his own mind that this was Mollie's reprobate brother. It could not be otherwise; it should not be. He kept as silent in regard to this follower as his wife did.

For months the follower haunted the premises, resolutely ignored by everyone. He really wasn't any trouble even to the cook. He appeared once or twice a week and got a package of food, scrupulously selected by Mollie from what would otherwise have been wasted. It represented on her part a struggle between honesty and propriety and a nice balance achieved. She wouldn't rob her employers of the very meanest scrap, but neither would she give to any human being food that wasn't clean and decent. She used to stand out on the back steps in the dusk, talking to the man, and after a bit he would go away with his honest package, while she returned to the kitchen, affable, but not to be questioned.

Apart from the follower, this remarkable woman had but a single weakness and a most amazing one. This was a passion for tobacco coupons. She even ventured to break her silence with Mr. Keating and to address him on the subject, to his great surprise. It was a Sunday evening, cook's night off, and Mollie was obligingly waiting on the supper table. They had finished; she was taking out the cold pudding when Mr. Keating lighted a cigar, and she suddenly spoke to him.

"Excuse me, sir," she said, "but isn't that one of them Victor cigars?"

He stared at her.

"Yes," he said.

"I take the liberty of asking, sir, because—I don't know whether or not you've any use for the coupons they give with them. Two with every Victor. Because, sir, if you haven't any use for them—"

"Never keep them," said Keating.

"Are you collecting them, Mollie?" his wife inquired.

"Yes, ma'am," she replied, with modest triumph. "I've near a thousand. Mr. Lyons used to give me all he had, and—other people. When I've two thousand," she added, "there's an elegant tea set, a hundred pieces, I have me eye on."

After that Keating was punctilious in preserving the coupons given with the Victor and bringing them home to Mollie. He showed an unaffected interest in her tea set, too; she showed him the picture of it in the catalogue of premiums, and assured him that she had gone to see it in person and that it was still more imposing in reality than in the picture. It is not impossible that he consumed more Victors than he really wanted or were good for him. He would have done more than that for the excellent woman. What is more, he thoroughly understood her ambition. Mrs. Keating had kind-heartedly suggested buying a similar tea set and presenting it to Mollie as a Christmas gift, but he refused. He knew that the thing would lose all its virtue that way. It must be pointed out and displayed as having been secured with Victor coupons; otherwise it would be like any ordinary tea set.

In view of his strong sympathy with Mollie, then, one may imagine his feelings on that miserable evening when they came across the follower in so disgraceful a way. They were returning from the theater; they had come decorously up the garden path in the moonlight, arm in arm, and there he was, lying on their front steps, drunk and asleep and snoring.

Keating shook him.

"Get up!" he cried roughly. "Be off with you!"

"A—a tramp," Mrs. Keating suggested, although she had perfectly recognized that red face and that black mustache.

"Of course," her husband answered impatiently, and shook the man again, with more violence. "Here! Wake up! Be off with you!"

But he was not to be roused, and he couldn't be moved. They went in and left him there, snoring under the moon, a shameful blot upon Mollie's fair name. With solemn duplicity Mrs. Keating suggested sending for the police to remove the creature, and was immeasurably relieved when her husband refused, as she had expected he would. Her heart almost stopped beating at the very idea of losing Mollie, of losing dignity, comfort, security.

Mr. Keating suffered from the same anxiety, because he, too, had immediately recognized the follower. He got up early the next morning, a Sunday, and looked quietly and cautiously out of the front window. The man was still there and still asleep, a yet more disgusting object in the morning sunshine, his mouth open, his dank black hair plastered over his red forehead. He was dressed in a flannel undershirt, a pair of outrageous old trousers, and carpet slippers. Where could he have come from in such a costume? And what possible quality in him could appeal to that soul of propriety that was Mollie?

Unfortunately, steps must be taken; the follower couldn't any longer be ignored. Keating put on a dressing gown and went quietly along the hall to the nursery, whence came a cheerful babel properly hushed for Sunday.

He knocked on the door.

"Mollie," he called, "will you come out and speak to me for a minute?"

She appeared without an instant's delay.

"Yes, sir?"

"There's a man outside. I believe he's known to you. He's been there all night, drunk. If you think you can get him away quietly—"

"Yes, sir," she answered, without the slightest change of voice or expression; "I think I can. Perhaps you'd be so good, sir, as to sit in the nursery for half a minute. They'll look at their picture books like lambs. And the baby's asleep."

For no one else under the sun would Keating have taken sole charge of his children for any fraction of a minute; now, however, he consented at once, and was sitting meekly enough in Mollie's big rocking chair when she re-entered.

"He's gone, sir," she said.

Keating got up.

"We—there's no need to mention the occurrence to anyone," he said. "Only don't let him hang about, will you?"

Mollie shook her head sadly.

"I'm afraid I can't help it, sir," she answered. "I've done my best. But when once this sort of thing begins there's no hope. He's my husband."

Try as she would to remain respectfully calm, the tears stood in her eyes, and her lips quivered.

"It's a great cross to me, sir," she said. "He's hounded me from place to place. All the time growing worse and worse, the way his kind always does. Since I've left Mrs. Lyons, I've had no peace at all. I've tried my best. We lost our little home two years ago because of his—ways, and—and every time I've set about saving up again, he—"

She couldn't go on for a minute.

"I'm sorry, sir, and ashamed that *you* should be troubled by him when you've been so kind. And I did love the children, indeed I did. But now that he's got in the way of coming here, there'd be no end to it. I've got to go."

"Nonsense!" said Keating; "we shan't hold you responsible for that—for him. And perhaps you could get rid of him once and for all. I'll speak to my lawyer—"

"In my church, sir, we don't look on it that way. He's my husband, that I chose of my own free will, and I've got to put up with him the best I can till one of us is dead."

She dried her eyes.

"I'll see that Mrs. Keating's not too much put about by my leaving," she said. "I'll take it on myself to find a new nurse."

Mrs. Keating was overwhelmed with dismay when Mollie told her.

"Oh, no!" she entreated, "don't go! We'll find work for your husband. He can take care of the garden or the furnace if you'd like."

"He wouldn't stick to it, ma'am. He says the only thing to keep him straight and sober would be a home of his own again. So I think I'll try it once more, ma'am. 'Tis no use trying to keep a situation, the way things is now."

They helped her in every possible way. Keating was generous beyond his wife's expectation; gave lavish assistance toward furnishing the little home, and took great trouble to find a job for Steve. He even "talked to" Steve, tried to impress upon him how fine a wife he had, and how he ought to honor and cherish her. Steve quite agreed, was even fulsome in his praise of Mollie, but said it was almost impossible to cherish anyone who was so much away from home.

"Whin we're settled, boss," he said, "you'll see! I'm a fine fellow, I am, and a great hand for work, give me only something to work for. You'll see, boss."

No one, however, was able to have any faith in Steve. He was so obviously just what he was and nothing more, and he so shamelessly traded upon the indulgence extended to Mollie's husband. He had an exasperating, cunning air about him. "You'll do it for Mollie's sake," his expression seemed to say triumphantly, while he humbly asked the most outrageous favors.

The last day came; the new nurse, hopelessly inferior and wholesomely impressed with that fact, was installed after a course of training personally conducted by Mollie. Mollie, bag in hand, her eyes still red from taking leave of the children, came in to bid good-by to Mr. and Mrs. Keating. And Mr. Keating gave her a final gift of a package of Victor coupons sufficient to complete her hoard. This gift moved her inordinately; she found it almost impossible to maintain her composed, respectful manner. She would, one felt, have liked to kiss his hand or fall at his feet or do something equally extravagant. Mrs. Keating's handsome and thoughtful farewell gift was as nothing at all in comparison.

"O Mr. Keating, sir!" she cried, "all *these!* Oh, I'm sure, sir, you've no need of so many Victors!"

"I bought a few boxes in advance," he told her. "They'll be all the better for aging. Don't worry; they won't be wasted."

He had, in fact, by this time acquired an incorrigible appetite for Victors; he never afterward smoked any other brand. They had become more or less hallowed by the worthy creature who had so well cared for his children.

She had a final request, in absolutely the proper tone of deference and pride mingled. If, when she did get that tea set, Mr. and Mrs. Keating would do her the favor to come and see it in her own home? They agreed readily, and at last she left, the door closed after her; she was gone. Once again there descended upon them that old fear well known to all parents, that fear of their children. They dreaded lest they should hear the baby cry or Robert's voice in his nightly demands for drinks of water, handkerchiefs, or assuagements for his spiritual alarms. Once again had the whole alarming load settled upon their shoulders, for now there was no Mollie. The new nurse, good enough in her way, found it necessary to come to them for instruction on every possible point, from safety pins to prayers. She was earnest, kind, trustworthy; but she was not authority.

In the course of time came a letter from Mollie.

> Mrs. Keating, dear madam, I have it all planned to get the Tea Set on Saturday morning and if you and Mr. Keating and master Robert and Miss Lucy would call by in the afternoon there would be home made ice cream and cake which would not hurt them and they would I know like to see the plates with birds on as I often showed them in the premiums book Mollies Tea Set they called it. Respectfully yours
>
>   MOLLIE DILLON.

The Keatings arrived at what Mrs. Keating imagined would be the expected hour, at three o'clock, or thereabouts. To do honor to Mollie the children were dressed up as she loved to see them, decorous and well-starched and wearing gloves. She met them at the door of her flat, not dressed up herself, because Steve's income never stretched to include clothing. Food, shelter, and his whisky consumed it all. But she was, of course, neat and clean, and beyond measure correct in an old white linen dress given her years ago by Mrs. Lyons. She led them into the tiny parlor and invited them to sit down, but was pleased and flattered when they asked to be shown about the place. Stiff, orderly, hideous, every inch of it, everything brand-new and shining, a "parlor set," a "dining room set," a "bedroom set," all designed and executed for the world's Mollies and, accordingly, giving them absolute satisfaction. And all so clean and beautifully cared for as to be a little pitiful, as were, above all, the many tokens of the gratitude the good woman had inspired in her life. There were photographs of all the Lyons family at various ages, and pictures relating to older services, records, indeed, of a long life of service, faithfully and competently performed; little presents from the children she had loved. And beside these were all sorts of trifles carelessly thrown away as of no value by those for whom she had worked, which were somehow decorative in her eyes, paper fans, dinner favors, painted candy boxes. Mollie liked her home "cozy," and there were few bare spaces on the walls or on the floors.

They reviewed every part of her domain, and then went back into the parlor for the ceremonious chat required. It was then for the first time that Keating and his wife noticed something very wrong in Mollie's look, an expression altogether new to that composed and pleasant face—the look unmistakable of one suffering from an intolerable outrage. She sat down and talked to them, the first time she had ever sat in their presence with idle hands, but she not at all embarrassed, because the situation was altogether correct. She was in her own home and mistress of it and entitled to her due meed of consideration. No; it was not embarrassment or constraint that disturbed her; it was some emotion profound and novel. Her pleasant, ruddy color had faded, her lips were compressed; there was a sort of classic and repressed fury about her.

Presently, after a decent interval, she rose, excused herself, and vanished into the kitchen, whence came sounds of dishes gently handled, the clinking of knives and forks, and her firm footsteps passing to and fro.

"The ice-cream!" murmured young Robert.

"And we'll see the tea set!" his sister added. Then Mollie drew aside the curtains that shut off the dining room, showing a table lavishly set with cakes, jellies, a tall cylinder of ice-cream, and smoking cups of cocoa. They all walked in soberly and sat down in their appointed places.

"But, Mollie!" cried little Lucy.

"Yes, my pet?" asked Mollie.

"The *tea set!*"

Something very wrong here! There they were eating from earthenware plates, cups and saucers that didn't match.

"Isn't—wasn't—" ventured Mrs. Keating.

"Steve hasn't come home with it yet," said Mollie.

Two spots of bright color came out over her high cheekbones; she could not maintain her lifelong reserve.

"When I saw he wasn't going to work this morning," she went on, "I said to myself I'd send him to fetch the tea set. He'd not been drinking at all. I thought I'd be safe trusting him. Coupons is not like money, either. I sent him at nine o'clock. I thought it would give me a grand chance to get plenty of water heated, the way I could wash it as soon as he'd bring it."

She had an air of trying to force back a torrent of words, almost a physical struggle. A few more escaped her.

"I'd the shelves all scrubbed the night before," she said, "and clean scalloped paper with a fancy green edge laid along them, all ready."

"And you've heard nothing of him since nine o'clock this morning?" Mrs. Keating asked.

"No, ma'am; I have not."

Mr. Keating suggested that perhaps he had met with an accident.

"Yes, sir, I dare say," she answered grimly.

They resumed eating. But her delicacies had lost their flavor, had turned pathetically bitter on their cracked plates. Even the children were impressed and very grave; they knew as well as any one that this feast without the tea set was a wedding without a bride, a travesty, a mockery.

Dusk came, and Mollie lighted a wonderful lamp made of two round halls of blue china, one on top of the other, with a design of pink roses painted over it. They had gone back into the parlor again, and it was evident to all of them that the occasion was over, that it was time to go home. Yet they lingered; Mrs. Keating couldn't make a move. Suddenly and loudly the front doorbell rang; Mollie went to answer it, and returned, followed by Steve.

Perhaps some obscure instinct of self-justification made them remember him forever afterward as almost superhumanly repulsive; or it may be that he really was so. Mrs. Keating described him later as looking "drowned in whisky." He had, she said, such a disgustingly *wet* look, his long black mustache, his hair, his red face. And he had his usual offensive manner; he was collarless, unshaven, he reeked of whisky, and he had the gross politeness of a beggar.

Mr. Keating looked at him severely. "Well, Steve," he said, "let's see the tea set."

"I ain't got the tea set, Mr. Keating, sir. I used them valu'ble coupons for something more useful-like, as'd benefit the two of us."

"O Steve!" murmured Mrs. Keating, reproachfully. But Mollie, standing by, said nothing at all.

Steve laid a paper bundle on the table in the bright light of the blue china lamp and began to unwrap it—a jumble of cords, blocks, staples, and hooks.

"What is it?" Mr. Keating asked, with a frown.

"Well, boss, I went, like the old woman told me, and got the tea set."

There was a faint sound from Mollie, but no one turned toward her.

"Just like in the book it was. Mighty fine and pretty. *Too* fine and pretty for us, I thought, and I said so to a young fella I seen outside. 'Take this instead,' says he, 'I'll give it ye for yer chiny.' He was standing outside." Outside what, Steve did not say. "'Step in,' he says, 'and I'll show ye my little invention,' says he; 'T will save yer life,' says he, 'and isn't that worth more than cups and dishes and plates and jugs and the like?' So I steps in, and he shows me how does it work. So after I'd sat with him a bit, to be sociable-like, I came home."

There was a long silence.

"Come on!" Keating said suddenly to his family. "Time to go."

But Steve wouldn't hear of that; he insisted, with a pompous, half-defiant insistence, that they should wait and watch him demonstrate the little invention. And for Mollie's sake, rather than that she should see Steve knocked out of the way, Mr. Keating complied.

Steve led the way into the kitchen and lighted the gas jet there, revealing those empty shelves covered with clean scalloped paper, prepared for the tea set. They all stood about awkwardly, Mrs. Keating holding her little girl by the hand, Mr. Keating in the doorway, the inquisitive young Robert near the window where Steve was securing his contrivance. It took a preposterous length of time. His hands moved busily, and he whistled under his breath, while close beside him, handing him this, that, and the other tool, tying knots, straightening tangles, stood his silent wife.

"Ah!" he cried at last, triumphantly, and opened the window. A raw, wet wind came blowing in, making the gaslight flicker and lifting his sodden hair from his forehead. He leaned far out and threw out one end of his device. The metal weight at the end of it clanked dismally on the stones four stories below.

"She's down," he announced, and sat down on the window sill, with his legs hanging out.

Mr. Keating seized him by the coat collar.

"Come in here!" he cried. "Do you want to kill yourself?"

"No, I don't, boss. But I'm going to show you how this little invention works. In case of fire—"

"Don't play the fool. Come in!"

"Mr. Keating, sir, I'm going down on my fire escape," said Steve, solemnly and loudly. "No one at all can stop me. I know all about it. I understand it. I tried it this morning with the young fella that invented it."

"Rob, don't let him!" cried Mrs. Keating.

Keating tried to haul him in, but Steve was a much larger and heavier man than himself, and he couldn't move him.

"Come in!" he cried again. "You are drunk. You don't know what you are doing."

The sound of their voices had attracted the attention of the neighbors; windows across the narrow court were opened and heads thrust out.

"What the hell are you doing there at all, Steve?" called out a friendly voice opposite. "Get the legs of you inside."

"I'm going down on me new-invented fire escape," Steve answered him. "The more of you watches me, the better. 'T will be a lesson. Ye'll all want thim whin you've seen me."

Without an instant's warning he disappeared. Mrs. Keating shrieked, but his voice reassured her, and the sight of his face reappearing just above the sill, looking more drowned than ever.

"Don't be uneasy, ma'am," he said. "I've only to let meself down now. Whin the iron weight comes up here again, you'll know that I've touched the ground. Now, then, Mollie, take another look that all thim ropes is tight."

Mollie turned to Mr. Keating as if she were about to speak; but she turned away again abruptly and leaned out of the window; she was busy there for what seemed to be a long time.

"Hi!" shouted her husband. "Whatever are you doing, Mollie? You've only to see that thim ropes is all tight."

Mr. Keating came forward, exasperated and alarmed by her fumbling.

"Let me see—" he began, but Mollie sprang back suddenly, almost upsetting him.

"All right!" she cried. "Go ahead!"

And suddenly, like a shot, the iron weight came whizzing up and crashed through the top of the window.

They didn't comprehend for an instant. Then came a babel of shrieks and shouts.

"Take the children home at once," Keating ordered. "Get a taxi somewhere. Hurry up and get out."

Mrs. Keating obeyed blindly, hurried down the long flights of stairs holding Lucy by one hand and Robert by the other, flew down the dark, narrow street in a panic.

"Don't talk!" she commanded the children, sharply. "Wait till your father comes home; he'll tell you all about it."

They were forced to go to bed unsatisfied, and their mother had a solitary and anxious dinner, for Mr. Keating didn't come home until ten o'clock. She jumped up when she heard a cab stop before the house, and hurried to the door.

"O Rob!" she began, but saw behind him the portly form of Mollie, with that very same black bag—composed, placid Mollie.

"I'll go into the kitchen, ma'am, if I may, and ask cook for a cup of tea," she said, and disappeared before having been quite realized by Mrs. Keating.

"I suggested her coming back to us," said Keating, "and she seemed pleased. I thought you'd be glad to have her."

Mrs. Keating didn't trouble to reply to so obvious a statement.

"Then is Steve—" she asked.

"Dead. One of the ropes slipped. The police came, of course, and an ambulance, and so on. But it was too late. And, upon my word," he added vehemently, "it's a good thing, too. Worthless brute!"

Mrs. Keating remained silent for some time, frowning thoughtfully. "Rob," she said at last.

He started in a guilty way.

"Well?"

"Are you sure—do you think—the rope really *slipped?*"

He scowled at her, but she persisted.

"Because, Rob, I'm quite *sure*. I saw her pulling one of the little hooks or screws or—"

"For the love of heaven!" cried Keating, jumping up, "if that's not just like a woman! Can't let well enough alone. Weren't you *longing* to have her back? Didn't you tell me morning, noon, and night that she was *the* ideal nurse?"

"She is, of course," his wife replied, but couldn't resist adding, "She *is* the ideal nurse—even if she *did*."

I'm the Man You Killed

When Agnes had finished the dishes, she ran up the three flights of stairs to her room. It made her out of breath to run; there was a blazing color in her thin cheeks, but she didn't care. Matt would be waiting for her, and she was in a hurry.

She put on her white raincoat and an old black hat, and ran down the stairs again. Mrs. Dorf was in the hall. "Where are you going, in this weather, Agnes?"

"Out," said Agnes, looking straight at her.

It was queer how different she was since she had known Matt. Before that she had been almost afraid of Mrs. Dorf and the other people in the house. And she had been so tired all the time; she had never wanted to go out; if she had had any spare time, she went to sleep. She had liked to sleep better than anything.

She wasn't a bit tired now, though. She went down the steps and along the street toward the boardwalk. The wind and the chilly rain blew in her face, but she didn't mind that for herself. Only for Matt.

"It's a shame!" she thought. "Raining like this, and it's Saturday night."

Last Saturday had been the first warm day of the season, and he had done such a grand business. The season was so short … In just these few months he would have to make enough to pay for all that setup.

The lights along the waterfront were misty in the rain; the boardwalk felt spongy underfoot; the sea was invisible, except when a curling white crest rose on an inky wave, but she could hear it all the time, that thud against the sand, and the little hiss as the waters spread and were dragged back again. She was afraid of the sea, but she didn't want Matt to know that, when he loved it so. "Loves it more than me," she thought.

But that was all right. Matt was like that, and she didn't want him any different. Even if sometimes it made her cry, that didn't matter.

His place was all lighted up, and the ducks were going along, clicking and jerking, in an endless parade. They always made her smile, with an immense affection. Even when a rifle shot hit one of them, it just dived nose down for a moment, and then came up again, and went on with the others. Matt could shoot them, one after the other, never missing; he had wanted to teach her, but she had told him she didn't like the crack of the rifle.

"You're a sissy," he had said, smiling at her.

He didn't really mind that. In the beginning, she had been afraid that he would stop liking her if she couldn't be lively and laughing; she had tried to be, but she couldn't. And now she knew it was all right. Sometimes in the evenings when there was no crowd, he would close up his place early, and they would go down and sit on the beach. He would put his arm around her, and she would rest her head on his shoulder.

"Go to sleep, you lazy little devil." he would say.

"It's not much fun for you to be out with a girl that don't talk."

"I don't want to hear you talk."

She went to the door in the wall beside the ducks, and opened it. The back room, where Matt lived, was empty; the cot was neatly made up with an old grey blanket over it, the enamel coffee pot stood on the gas ring; it was all bare and clean and fresh with the salt air. She took off her raincoat and sat down in the rocking chair he had bought specially for her; she leaned back and rocked, listened to the rain and the clicking of the ducks.

"Matt's gone for cigarettes, maybe," she thought.

He knew she was coming, and he would be back in a few moments; she didn't mind waiting. She liked to sit here in Matt's clean bare room, and think about him. An unshaded electric bulb hung from the ceiling; it was so bright that she closed her eyes ... Saturday was a bad day at the boarding house; lots of extra people came for the weekend, and Mrs. Dorf always got mean and cranky.

"I'm not scared of her now, like I used to be," thought Agnes.

It had used to make her feel sick, when Mrs. Dorf got yelling at her. But now she didn't care. Didn't care much, anyhow.

"The worst thing is, I get so tired," she thought. "She hired me for a waitress. Never said anything about me helping do the rooms and all those stairs. I'm a fool to put up with it. I'd ought to look for another job. Only I get so little time off—and I'm so tired ..."

It was queer, she thought, that when you were so tired, you'd rather stay in a hard job that you hated than look for something else.

But when the summer was over, and Matt went away ...?

"He said maybe he'd go on a ship again. That's what he wants to do—be a sailor. And what'll I do, with Matt gone?"

She would not think of that. He was here now, and he was so nice to her, nicer than anyone else had ever been.

"Maybe that's just his way," she thought. "Maybe he don't love me. He never said he did."

She opened her eyes and sat up straight, at the sound of something knocking somewhere.

She listened, and then she got up and opened the door. There was a man standing at the counter, knocking on it; he turned toward her.

"I'm looking for a man by the name of Flynn," he said.

A great fear came over her. Like a scarecrow, the man was, slight and small, in a coat so big for him that the sleeves came halfway over his hands; his face was white as chalk, too, and his blue eyes were so bright; just blazing, they were.

"He's out," she said.

"Well, he'll be in," said the other. "I'll wait."

"If you give me your name, I'll tell him you came."

"Name's Wilkin, but that won't mean anything to him."

"Well, why do you want to see him?"

"That's for him and me to talk about. You his wife?"

"No."

Wilkin took off his sodden hat, and as he moved his head, she saw his profile, and was startled.

"He's real good-looking …" she thought, only half aware of the classic beauty of those pale and clean features, the fine set of that head. Somehow it was dreadful for this scarecrow to have so noble a head.

"I'll wait," he said.

"If I knew where Matt had went …" she thought. "If I could just tell him this fellow is here."

For, without reason, she felt this scarecrow to be a menace. He was turning up the long sleeves of his overcoat now, showing delicate wrists and thin hands; he took up one of the rifles.

"You got to pay first," she said.

He laughed.

"Me?" he said. "Not much!"

He began to shoot, and he never missed. At each crack, a duck dipped forward, tail in the air, went on a little like that, and then came up again. He was reloading the rifle.

"You stop that!" she cried, but he laughed again. Crack, went the rifle, and another duck dived down. She was crying now; she caught his sleeve, and the big overcoat slipped off one shoulder.

"Crying, are you?" he said. "Crying over Matt Flynn? You must love him, all right."

"That's none of your business."

"You're pretty," he said. "Those big blue eyes … I wish I had a girl like you."

His eyes were blue, too, very clear, a little hollow; he was staring at her and smiling, and she hated him.

"Maybe you'll leave Matt and take up with me," he said.

"I wouldn't look at you!" she said. "If Matt was to hear you, he'd kill you."

He gave a loud, hooting laugh.

"He'd kill me, would he?"

"You better get out of here before Matt comes!" she said. "Because I'm going to tell him how fresh you been."

They both heard the sound of footsteps then, coming quick and light along the boardwalk.

"All right. That's him," said Wilkin. "Tell him. Just go ahead and tell him!"

Matt came into the light then; he was wearing an old pair of pants and a grey sweater and his black curly hair was damp. His lashes were wet, too, and that made his grey eyes look gentle.

"Hello, kid," he said. "Been waiting long? I had to go and see a fellow … Got a customer here?"

He looked down with a smile at Wilkin, that careless smile of his.

"No, mister," said Wilkin. "I wouldn't be a customer, because I haven't got a cent. You and me was in a ship together once, and I thought maybe you'd give me a meal."

"What ship was that?" asked Matt.

"The *Balamine*, on Puerto Rico run. Maybe you forgot her."

"I don't forget a ship," said Matt. "Only I don't remember you."

"I was in the galley. I haven't got a berth now. I haven't got a cent. I thought an old shipmate would maybe help me out."

"Sure I'll help you out," said Matt. "I haven't got so much myself, but I guess I'm better off than you."

He smiled again; he didn't worry about Wilkin, thought Agnes, and he ought to worry. Something about Wilkin …

"Come in the back room," said Matt. "I'll give you some coffee and something to eat."

"No!" said Agnes.

"What's wrong with you?" asked Matt. "You can come along."

"I want to talk to you," she said.

"Sure." said Matt, laughing. "Wait till I get this bird fixed up."

It was dreadful, to let Wilkin into the room where he lived. He just stood there, and watched Matt moving around in that quick, sure way.

"I'll make the coffee, Matt," she said.

"You can't make it as good as me," he said, and that was true. But it was mean of him to say it in front of Wilkin; it made her feel stupid and useless and ashamed. She sat down in the rocking chair, her rocking chair that Matt had bought for her, and she too watched Matt.

He had everything so neat. He had built a box onto the window, and he had butter in it, and bacon and eggs; a lot of things. He had made two shelves inside an upended box, and he had a little frying pan in there, a little saucepan, and some knives and spoons. He set the coffee pot on the gas ring, and made good, thick ham sandwiches.

"Why don't you sit down?" he said to Wilkin.

"My clothes are soaked," said Wilkin. "Gee, but it's cold! Haven't got a drop of whisky, have you, mate?"

"Coffee'll do for you," said Matt. "Take off that coat."

Wilkin took off the big overcoat, and he had no shirt or jacket underneath, only a cotton singlet.

"Have a cigarette?" said Matt.

Wilkin took a cigarette and lit it and inhaled. And that made him cough. Agnes had never seen anyone cough like that; you could see that it hurt.

"What's the matter with you?" asked Matt. "You sick, or something?"

"It's me throat," said Wilkin. "I had an accident."

He sat down on a box, and went on smoking, with that cough shaking him every few moments. He began to talk to Matt about ships and ports, and Matt got interested. He didn't pay any attention to Agnes; he didn't seem to notice how Wilkin kept looking at her.

"I'd go home," she thought, "only I don't want to leave Matt alone with him."

It was just miserable, to sit there, with Matt not even looking at her.

"He don't love me," she thought. "He never really said he did. He never made love to me. Just kissed me once in a while. He's been nice to me, but he's nice to everybody. I guess he's just sorry for me …"

The wind had risen, and the rain came dashing against the window.

"What a night!" said Wilkin. "Can you maybe lend me a dollar, so's I can get a room, shipmate?"

"No," said Matt. "But you can sleep here. I got another cot and a blanket."

"That's all I want," said Wilkin. "A roof over me head and something to eat. That's all there is to life."

"The devil it is!" said Matt, staring at him. "That's not living."

"You're different," said Wilkin. "Strong as an ox, you are. And you got a nice girl, and everything. But I lost me health. I never got over that accident."

"What kind of accident was it?"

"I don't like to talk about it," said Wilkin.

Agnes got up, and put on her hat and coat.

"I'm going home, Matt."

"I'll walk along with you," he said.

"That's right!" said Wilkin, with that loud, hooting laugh. "You want to look out, when you get a nice, pretty girl like her. Somebody might steal her."

"Shut up," said Matt. And she loved the way he said it; she loved the way he took hold of her arm when they got outside in the wind and the rain.

"Matt ... That's a funny kind of a fellow ... I wish you'd put him out."

"Couldn't put a dog out in this weather."

"Make him get out tomorrow morning, will you, Matt?"

"Leave it to me."

"You're too easy, Matt. Matt ... I don't like that fellow ..."

"Why?" he asked, and his voice changed. "Did he try to get fresh with you?"

His fingers tightened on her arm.

"No," she said.

"I'd wring his neck if he did," said Matt.

She was laughing to herself in the dark, and crying, too. "You wouldn't care," she said.

"Wouldn't I? You're my girl," said Matt. "And don't you forget it."

"It's a wonder you wouldn't look at me, then, all the evening."

"Come around tomorrow morning, before there's any crowd."

"Mrs. Dorf'd never let me off in the mornings!" she cried.

"If I clean up, this summer," said Matt, "you can walk out on Mrs. Dorf."

She was afraid to ask him what he meant, afraid he didn't mean anything. He was just being nice to her, maybe.

"I got my eye on a place down here," he said. "It's over a store. Steam heat, and everything. We'll move your rocking chair in there, and you can just sit there and rock and get rested."

"You mean— for us to get married?" she asked, unsteadily.

"What else would I mean?" he said, and squeezed her arm.

"Well, you might ask me do I want to marry you?" she said, haughtily.

He laughed, and put his arm around her shoulders.

"You got to," he said. "It's your fate."

She was so happy that a sob came in her throat. But still she was afraid.

"Do you think it's like that, Matt?" she asked. "I mean—fate?"

"Sure!" he said. "When I was only sixteen, an old black woman down in Trinidad told me I'd never get drowned. I believe it. There were times when anyone but me would've been drowned. But it couldn't happen to me."

"You won't go to sea anymore, will you, Matt? I mean—if we were ever to get married, you wouldn't go?"

"I got to go," he said. "You wouldn't understand how it is. I've tried, two or three times … But after I been ashore a few months, I get sick of it. Only, I'll come back to you, every time."

Mrs. Dorf wouldn't give her a key; she had to ring the bell and wait.

"Go on, Matt." she said. "Or she'll see you."

"Let her see me!" he said, and stood beside her on the steps until Mrs. Dorf let her in.

"That's a good-looking fellow," Mrs. Dorf said, when she had closed the door. "You want to look out and not let him make a fool of you."

"We're going to get married," said Agnes.

"That's what they all say," said Mrs. Dorf.

She couldn't spoil things, though. Agnes went up to her room on the top floor, and undressed. The rain was drumming on the roof above her, and she remembered how it looked, falling on the black ocean.

"I'll miss him something terrible while he's away," she thought. "But he'll come back, like he said. I love him so … I didn't know there'd ever be anything like this.…

When the alarm clock waked her in the morning, it was still raining. "He won't make any money this weather," she thought. "It's a shame." Her heart felt like lead. She tried to be happy, remembering how Matt had talked about them getting married, but it didn't seem real.

"I feel so mis'able this morning," she thought. "Could it be a sign? A sign something's going to happen? That fellow that was there … I wish Matt hadn't of let him stay. I hope he's gone. I just hope I'll never set eyes on him again." She wanted to hurry with her work today, but the boarders never would get up Sunday mornings. When she had finished waiting on the tables at lunch, she wanted to go, but Mrs. Dorf got angry.

"Seven rooms to do, and a big dinner to cook!" she cried. "And all you think of is running out after that fellow of yours." Agnes helped her with the rooms, but then she would go.

"You got to be back by six!" Mrs. Dorf said.

"Well, I never was late yet, was I?" said Agnes.

"You going out, all dressed up like that, in this rain?"

"Well, they're my clothes!" said Agnes, angry herself. "I paid for them. I guess I can wear what I like."

She put on her raincoat over her long pink and black dress, and she took an umbrella to protect her big black hat. There wasn't much wind today; the rain fell straight and steady, but the sea was running high, one long grey roller after the other breaking on the wet sand. There were two men in swimming; they came out of the water and ran along the beach, fast, as if they had just escaped some danger in the heavy grey ocean. A woman passed her, pushing a baby in a go-cart, almost running.

"I'll be mad if Wilkin's still there, so's I can't talk to Matt," she thought.

She went straight into the back room, and Wilkin was there, asleep, she thought. He lay on a cot, covered with a blanket, and his overcoat on top of that. But then she saw that his eyes were staring at her.

"Hello, beautiful!" he said.

"Where's Matt?"

Wilkin sat up, still in his singlet and trousers.

"He took a boat and went somewheres to get us some fish," said Wilkin. "Matt and me are going to have a nice bit of fried fish for our dinner."

"How long d'you think you're going to stay here?" she asked, one hand on her hip, the big hat making a shadow across her eyes. She threw off the raincoat and sat down in the rocking chair; she smiled insolently. But she was afraid she would cry in a minute. The very room was changed, spoiled; that cool, neat look was gone. The cot where Wilkin had slept gave it a curious air of disorder and poverty.

"Me?" said Wilkin. "Don't you like me?"

"No."

"Well, you better like me. 'Cause I'm not going, see?"

"You think Matt'll let you live here for ever and ever?" she demanded.

"Yes, I do! 'Cause he can't help himself. I got a right to live here and eat here. I got a right to take his girl."

He stood up, barefoot, then, with that finely set head of his, that face that was strangely and horribly beautiful; his hollow eyes were fixed on her.

"And I'll tell you why," he said. "Matt don't know. He don't remember me. But I'm the man he killed."

The room was dim this grey afternoon; the rain pattered on the roof and ran down the windowpanes. She could hear the music of the merry-go-round down at the end of the boardwalk; it was far away; everything was far away.

"You're crazy," she said. "If—if anyone'd killed you, you'd—be dead."

"I came back," he said.

She could not look away from his face that was so pale, his hollow, brilliant blue eyes.

"Matt killed me," he said. "But I came back."

"No … You couldn't … No!"

"And he can't never hurt me again. You can't kill a man twice."

"You're crazy!" she cried.

"Crazy? Not me! But it's a wonder I ain't. What I been through! I dream about it … Down in Martinique, it was. There was a kind of casino, on the hill, all lighted up, people sitting there drinking, some of them singing … Me. I was down by the water, talking to this yaller girl. Just the lowest of the low, she was. Couldn't even speak English good. She wanted my money. Well, she didn't have no right to it. I'd give her some, and it was plenty. Then she starts screaming at me. I wasn't going to hurt her. On'y the way she was screaming got on my nerves. It sounded—it got on my nerves. All I did was put my hand over her mouth. And then he comes along, running down the steps from the casino. The yaller girl gets at him … He didn't know what she was saying, no more than what I did, the lingo she talked … But he didn't care. Wouldn't listen to me. He hauled off and gave me a sock in the jaw, knocked me back into the sea. Cripes! There's sharks there, and barracuda that's worse than sharks, and I can't swim a stroke. I yelled to him. 'Mate!' I said. 'I can't swim!' 'All right, sink then,' he says, and I drowned."

"You couldn't of drowned. Because you're alive right now."

"I drowned, I tell you!" he said, savagely. "Went down in that black water, and drowned. Died. A man knows it, if he dies, don't he? Well, I died. It was …" His eyes dilated; he was looking at her, but she knew he did not see her.

"So that's what it's like," he said. "That's the way it is when you die. At the end, when you've quit fighting and choking, it's … There's no use to try to tell you what it's like. On'y, at the end, it's all right. But they wouldn't let me stay dead. Had to drag me out and get me back, and that was—Cripes!"

His eyes were as clear as blue water. "Brought me back," he said. "Just when I'd got over all the bad part of it … I was terribly sick. Got my throat sort of choked … I was in the hospital then, and I couldn't figure why this had to happen to me … Why I had to die twice … Then it came to me why it happened that way. I was meant to come back and find the man who did that to me."

"Matt didn't mean …" she said, faintly.

"I said, 'Mate, I can't swim!' And he said, 'Sink, then.' He meant it all right. So I made up my mind I'd find him. My ship sailed without me, 'count of me being so sick. But soon as I got well, I went around asking questions, like I was looking for a friend. I found out what ships'd been there. I found out his name."

"You could easy make a mistake."

"I didn't make no mistake. Last night, talking to him, I asked him was he down in Martinique at that time, on that ship. And he was. I've found him. It's took me nearly a year, but I met a fellow who knew him and where he'd went. So here I am."

She believed him. Looking at his white face and his clear blue eyes, she believed that he had come back.

"Now I got a right to everything he has," he went on. "I can live off him, long as I like. And I can take his girl."

"D'you think he'd let you?"

"He can't help himself!" cried Wilkin. "He don't remember me or anything, but he sort of knows he's got to do what I want. In the end, I'll tell him. The very last thing, I'll tell him. I'll say, 'I'm the man you killed down in Martinique.'"

"You mean you're going to try to kill Matt?" she said. "Why, if you was to even say a word he didn't like, he'd—kill you."

"No," said Wilkin. "He couldn't kill me twice. The next time it's my turn."

"I'm going to tell him—"

"No, you won't. 'Cause as soon as he knows, it's finished. Soon as you tell him, he'll try to get rid of me, and then it'll be my turn. I won't have to do nothing much. Anything I do'll kill him. Because it's got to be that way."

"Listen!" she said. "You know Matt didn't mean to—to do that. He's so strong, and all ... He thought you'd be all right. Matt's terrible kind. Real softhearted."

"He stood there on the beach, and he said, 'Sink, then.'"

"He didn't know. He swims so good himself, he just couldn't believe anyone else couldn't swim. You just tell him—how it was, and he'll be sorry. He'll help you out. Look at how good he is to you anyways, without his knowing."

"Can't help himself. Something makes him do that. It's justice. I got a right to everything he's got. And I got a right to his life."

She wanted to pray, but she could not. Maybe God would forgive Matt for what he had done, but He wouldn't save him from Wilkin in this world. That was justice. And Matt couldn't save himself, no matter how strong he was. She looked away from Wilkin; her glance fell upon the box with the shelves, where the pots and pans were neatly stowed away, and her fear was engulfed in a wild surge of tenderness. She could hear the ducks clicking along ...

All this belonged to Matt. He was so strong and so smart; he loved being alive. No one else was so much alive as he was.

"No!" she cried to herself. "Oh, no! He can't die now, when he's young. He wants to go back on a ship. He hasn't had his life yet. He's so full of fun ..."

It was as if she could hear Matt laughing, see him smiling down at her. It was as if he were still holding her arm, the way he had last night when they went along together in the rain.

"I couldn't live without Matt," she thought. "But he could get on without me. He's real fond of me, but it's different, with men. He'd go on a ship, and when he got to those far-off places, he'd forget." Matt's life was the most important thing in all the world. It was almost as if there wouldn't be any world without Matt.

"I'll stay here as long as I like," said Wilkin. "And you'll be nice to me, too."

"Suppose I was to tell Matt—all this?" she said.

"Go on and tell him! He'll get mad, and if he tries to do me any harm, I'll kill him. Take a good look at me! Matt'd make two of me. But that don't matter. He killed me once, and he can't do it again. It's my turn now, and you know it!"

He rose and came over to her.

"I got a right to everything he's got," he said. "You, too. You got to stop being so mean to me."

"I'm not mean to you," she said. "It's only because I love Matt such a lot."

"Well, you better stop loving him," he said. "'Cause you'll never have him. You better love me."

She looked up at him, and smiled, a soft, provocative smile.

"Maybe," she said. "I don't know ..." His hand fell on her shoulder, and she let it lie there.

"I got to go now," she said. "D'you want to walk along with me a ways?"

"You think you can fool me," said Wilkin. "You're just being nice to me, so's I'll let Matt alone."

She shrugged her shoulders.

"All right!" she said. "I don't care if you come or not. You're not the only man in the world, and Matt isn't, neither. There's some fellows in the house where I work would be glad of a chance to take a walk with me."

With that smile, her eyes narrowed; she looked insolent, she looked beautiful, and she knew it. She had never before been sure of her beauty, had never dared make use of it.

"I'm going," she said. "You can come or not—I don't care."

"I'll come," he said. "Wait till I get me coat and hat."

"I'll wait outside," she said. "I won't wait long, neither."

The rain was falling steadily, and she had left her umbrella behind. But she wasn't going back for it; she wasn't ever going back into that room.

"Hello, missy," said the Jap who had the place next to Matt's. You rolled balls along a board, and if you got the ball into one of the right holes, there was a prize. A tea set, a funny little doll, things like that. "You get wet," he said, laughing. He was always laughing.

Matt liked him, so she liked him, too; she laughed, too, with the rain blowing in her face. He had a light inside his place, and she could see those teacups hanging up, and a blue and white table cover, just as she had seen them so many times. An anguish of loneliness swept over her; it was dreadful to think that she wouldn't see them again. It made her cry, but the Jap kept on laughing.

"You get wet," he said.

"Sure, I'll get wet," she said, laughing. Then Wilkin came out, like a scarecrow in that big overcoat; when he saw the little Jap, he laughed. It was so lonely, thought Agnes, for other people to laugh when she was crying.

She stopped crying almost at once, though.

"I'm supposed to be back and get that table ready," she said. "But maybe I'll take some time off. You're a sailor, the same as Matt, aren't you? Have you been all those places he's been?"

"Yes, and one more place!" said Wilkin, with a hoot of laughter. "I been dead, and he hasn't."

"Well, I don't want to hear about that anymore," she said. "If you're going to talk about that, I'm not going to walk with you."

"What do you want to talk about? All the pretty girls I seen?"

She let him boast; she pretended to believe him, so that he would go on. They came to the street where she should have turned off the boardwalk, but she did not stop. Her big black hat was limp now; the long skirt of her pink and black dress was wet and cold about her ankles. They were down at the end of the boardwalk now, the part where the fire had been a month ago. The little shops were black ruins; the rain brought out that smell of charred wood. Nobody ever came here anymore.

"Let's go out on the pier." she said.

"You're crazy!" said Wilkin. "Got a chain across to keep people off, 'cause it ain't safe."

"It's safe enough for me," she said, scornfully. "I been on it hundreds of times. That's where I'm going, but you don't have to come."

"There's a sign says, 'Danger. Keep Off.'"

"All right, keep off!" said Agnes. "If you're scared."

She had only been here once before, taking a walk with Matt. It had been a bright day then, with the sun glittering on the water.

"First time there's a heavy sea, that pier'll go," Matt had said. "The shorings are just about burnt through."

She had thought it desolate then, that sunny day, with Matt beside her. But now, in the rain, with Wilkin … The sea would be grey underneath, and cold. But she wasn't going to think of the sea. She had not looked toward it once since they started. She could hear it, though, and as she climbed over the chain, she could feel it, thudding against the rotten pier and making it tremble.

"It's not safe, I tell you!" cried Wilkin.

"Matt says it's safe, and he knows. Matt and me often came out here, to look at the water."

She had to go forward, to make him come. The boards felt soft under foot, the whole structure shook. He was climbing over the chain now.

"Come back," he said, angrily.

"All right! I'll just walk out to the end and see if Matt's boat is anywhere around."

"I'm not coming." he said. He was afraid; she heard fear in his voice. She looked back over her shoulder, and smiled at him.

"Aren't you coming with me?" she asked. "When I get it in my head I want to do something. I just got to do it."

"That's the way women are," he said. "Curse them all!"

"We'll just walk out to the end, and look for Matt's boat," she said. "And then—maybe you'd like to come back to the house with me."

He was coming after her. He was afraid, but he had to come.

"I'll take a hold of your arm," she said. "Case my heels catch between the boards." He took her arm and drew her dose to him; he was speaking, but she did not hear him. Any minute now … The next board might be the one to go … And that would be the end of him. He couldn't swim. The end of her, too.

"I wish I could've told Matt," she thought.

The wind blew harder out here; a gull went screaming by overhead; the waves came crashing against the pier.

"There's Matt!" cried Wilkin. "Wait till he sees me here with his girl!"

She had to look then. She saw the awful grey waste of water that moved upward to the horizon and down again, in a sickening swing. And she saw Matt rowing toward them, his boat sliding up the side of a great wave, and then lost, swallowed up, coming up again.

"Matt!" she called, with all her strength.

"Hey, Matt!" cried Wilkin. "Ahoy, shipmate!"

A shift in the wind brought their cries to him; he turned. But he was too far away for her to see his face, or her eyes were blurred. She wanted to see his face once more … She pulled Wilkin forward, but he shook himself free.

"You're crazy!" he shouted. "The pier—"

The boards crumbled beneath his feet; he clutched at the railing, and it was an empty shell. He went over backward, with a scream …

She stood alone on the end of the pier, with the gaping hole at her feet.

The boards on which she stood shivered and swayed, the wind rushed at her.

"Don't—move!" shouted Matt.

How had he come so near? When she looked down, she saw his boat almost beneath her. He was taking off his shoes. "Mate! Help! Help!"

That was Wilkin.

"Matt!" she cried. "Don't! Don't! Matt … He'll kill you!"

Matt didn't even look at her. He shifted the oars, and dived overboard. She saw him swimming; she saw Wilkin's thin arm catch him round the neck, and they were both gone.

She had been lying there so long in the rain, not stirring, just like a wet heap of clothes. They thought at first that she was dead. It was hard to reach her, harder still to carry her back. But when they brought her into the coffee shop, she opened her eyes. She didn't say a word, just lay there. The music from the merry-go-round was very loud; "O Sole Mio" it was playing. She turned her head a little, and looked up into Wilkin's clear blue eyes.

It had to be like that.

"Matt …" she said, trying to tell Matt. "I tried …"

"Give her some whisky," said a voice. "I think she's going!"

"Listen!" cried Wilkin, frantically. "Don't go! Don't die! Matt's going to be all right! Listen! He saved my life, see? There was a high sea on, but he jumped right in after me. I made a grab at him, 'cause I was so crazy-wild. But he saved my life! D'you see? He took that chance. Risked his life. And he saved my life. D'you see? It's square now."

"Matt's dead," she said, so faintly that only Wilkin heard her.

"He's not dead—and I'm not dead!" His blue eyes were blazing. "D'you see how it's worked out? There was another chance given him, and he saved my life! I pretty near killed him, the crazy way I was fighting. But I didn't! I couldn't! I couldn't even hurt him now. D'you see now how it is? All square!"

Someone raised her head, and held a flask to her lips; she swallowed a little of the liquor, and it went in a fiery course along her nerves. Life, coming back …

Game for Four Players

When Desiree got out of the elevator, she was in a bad temper, her handsome face was sullen. But as she walked through the dismal and almost empty lobby of the third-rate little hotel, she changed all that. She transformed herself; her impatient walk became a languorous glide, one foot almost directly in front of the other, her dark lashes were lowered, her full red lips were set in a pouting and enigmatic half-smile. She was dressed in a black suit well fitted to her ripe young body; her long hair, now a glittering auburn, brushed her shoulders.

She paused at the top of the wide stone steps leading to the Paris Grill; it was a dramatic pause, and she hoped it was being noticed by someone who might be even a little useful. But, my God! What d'you expect, in a joint like this? she thought. I wouldn't even try here, if it wasn't for Ramon. But he … God, he makes me mad!

The Paris Grill was a big dark room, filled with small tables on which dim little lamps burned; on one side was a long bar with eerie blue lights. The television was turned off; the windows were closed, this cold and rainy night, and the Paris Grill was very, very quiet, in its own queer way. The few people sitting at tables were eating in silence; the row of people on the bar stools were silent. It's—just spooky, Desiree thought. I'll never do this again. It's too risky.

She went down the steps, slowly and gracefully, and moved through the shadowy room, to what seemed the most promising table. Nick, the waiter, came up to her, and she glanced at him through her downcast lashes.

"I guess a Scotch and soda, Nick," she said, clearly. "I'm real tired, rehearsing that show all day."

That worked, the way it almost always did. The stout man, alone at the next table, had turned his head to look at her. It always kind of soothed them to hear you had a job. Not just a floozie, on the make.

"I'm just so tired," she said to Nick, when he brought her drink. "I don't even feel like eating any dinner. I guess I'll just go upstairs and curl up with a good book. Life of Marie Antoinette, I'm reading, and it's wonderful."

I bet it is wonderful, too, she thought. It was nice of that fellow on the train to give it to me, a five-dollar book, and brand-new. You'll enjoy it, he said. *He* didn't think I was so dumb I wouldn't like a good book.

God! I wish I *could* go upstairs now, and anyhow just start that book.

I don't want to go on with this thing. It makes me nervous. The last time, I told Ramon I wouldn't do it again. I told him it made me so nervous, it gave me a headache. I must say he was nice about it, that time. Tears in his eyes.

But not this time. He made me real mad today. All right! he said. This room is thirty a week, and we owe two weeks now. The manager said either we pay up tomorrow, or we get out. I wouldn't mind getting out of here. This place gives me the creeps, and there was a cockroach in the bathroom. Only they certainly wouldn't let me walk out with a suitcase. No, I'd have to leave all my things here, the nice things I got when I was married to Steve, and the things I got since then. Only there's not many of them.

And how about you getting a job, may I ask? I said to Ramon, and then, of course, he blew his top. He practically says he's too good to get a job, and nobody wants anybody that plays the piano as well as he does. Well, in the beginning, I had faith in him, and he had a job then, in the Night-Owlery, and pretty good pay. I don't know if he walked out on it, or if he got fired. But anyhow, the way things are now is getting me down.

Steve had absolutely different ideas about a girl. He just wanted to lavish things on me, and me not to worry. If he hadn't got so mean and sarcastic, and trying to make me live in that little town where all the women were jealous of me.... If Steve had been nice about things, I'd have stayed with him. I'd be there in Texas with him right now. And even if it was hard for me there, I wouldn't have to be doing *this*. This makes me nervous. Suppose somebody was a detective, and you didn't know it …?

Well, I guess I could tell a detective, if I met one. I'm a pretty good judge of character. That man *looks* all right …

Only, he looks like such a lot of other men. Middle-aged, sort of fat. Got a wife back home, in the sticks. I mean, you know just how he's going to talk …

She let her dark lashes brush her cheeks, and then glanced up at him, a sad, vague look. A tired, lonely look.

"Nick," she said, as the waiter moved near her, "could I please have some ice water? My throat's sort of tired, from all that rehearsing."

"Sure! Sure! You ought to take it easy," Nick said, always willing to play it her way.

"If you'll excuse me, miss … But I thought I heard you say something about rehearsing …"

The stout man had risen; he stood beside her, smiling, but a little scared.

"Yes, I did," she said, quietly.

"I take a lot of interest in the stage," he said. "There's a niece of mine, she was playing in a Broadway show last year. Sue Carlyle was her stage name. Maybe you've heard of her …?"

"I don't know," said Desiree, in the same quiet tone. Not prissy, acting shocked, but just quiet, dignified, ladylike. "Oh, *thank* you, Nick!"

"Well, look here …!" said the stout man, "I'd certainly think it was an honor if you'd have—" He paused. "A glass of wine with me, maybe?"

"Oh, thanks, but I've had a drink," she said. She raised her eyes, and smiled a little. "Afraid it was a whiskey …" she said.

"Well, what's the matter with whiskey?" he demanded, heartily, much encouraged. "Personally, wine doesn't agree with me. Makes me feel sort of logy. But whiskey, now … If you'd allow me to order you another, miss …?"

"I really *shouldn't*," she said. "But when I'm tired …"

He pulled back a chair and sat down across the table from her. Still a little scared, she thought. Well, let him be. That's all right, up to a certain point. Only you've got to be careful not to overdo it. Hard to get, that's all right, but if you give the impression that there just isn't any hope at all, most of them just fold up and quit.

"What about a little something to eat?" he said. "I don't know how the food is, in this place—"

"Oh, it's quite good," said Desiree. Not being too grand, and looking down on things. Just sort of natural and unaffected. You've got to study *every* move, she thought. You can't ever relax. It makes me nervous. I hate doing this. I won't do it again. I don't care what happens. I hate it, and it's a risk. You could get arrested, if anybody squawked. Only, of course, mostly they don't. For their own sakes.

"I'm from Topeka," the man said, "but I know little old New York pretty well. Pret-ty well. Been here I don't know how many times. There are a lot of people say they don't like New York, say the people aren't friendly, and all that. Well, I never found it like that. I've met some of the finest people here … Oh, maybe you'd better order, miss. Er … you know what's good here."

Another headache, Desiree thought, wearily. You've got to pick out things that are sophisticated, things he maybe never ate before, so he'll get the right impression. But you don't want to run him up a big bill. Like a gold-digger.

Well, she had found a good way to handle that, if there was a waiter like Nick, who would play it your way.

"Any frogs' legs tonight, Nick?"

"Frogs' legs!" the man said. "That's something *I* never tried."

"Sorry," Nick said. "Haven't got 'em tonight."

No Lobster Thermidor tonight. Or any other night, in a joint like this.

No Vol au Vent. That was about as far as she could go.

"The lamb's real good tonight," Nick suggested. "Mint sauce, peas, French fries. Okay?"

Okay. And how's about another little drink while it's coming up? This was the biggest problem, every time. How much should he drink? It's so darn hard to tell, with a stranger. I mean, what would be all right for one man will hit another like a ton of bricks, all of a sudden. It's funny, how *quick* that happens, sometimes. And when they drink too much, they're just no good. They're a nuisance, and they can make trouble. Serious trouble. Even the police ...

God, but I'm tired! I wish I didn't have to do this. It *worries* me. It's a strain. It's so dark in here I can't see the other tables—and maybe there's someone better than this hick. Well, I'm stuck with him now, though.

"Porter, my name is," he said.

Oh, yeah? Pullman Porter maybe? "My name's Desiree Devon," she said.

"Well, look now!" he said, frowning. "Haven't I heard that name somewhere?"

You've got good hearing, if you did. Because I never heard it myself till six months ago.

"Radio, was it?" he asked. "Or TV?"

"Oh, well!" she said, smiling a little. "I'm no star, you know."

"You will be!" he said. "You will be, all right! A girl like you ... You've got everything. Looks, personality, class, everything. Say, I like that little blouse you've got on. That little bit of ruffles."

"Do you? I'm glad," she said, leaning back in her chair as he leaned across the table.

Another little drink? No. He's sure to have one, maybe two, after I've gone upstairs. No. This is where I've got to get busy.

"'Fraid you'll have to excuse me," she said, with an anxious little smile. "But I'm just so tired ... It was a lovely dinner, and I certainly enjoyed meeting you, Mr. Porter."

"You can call me Tom, can't you? Wish you would."

"Maybe I'll see you again, some time, Tom."

"Hey! Where are you going now, Desiree?"

"I've just got to go upstairs and lie down, Tom, I'm so tired, and my head sort of aches. A couple of aspirins, maybe."

"You—you're staying here, in this hotel?"

"Oh, yes!"

"Well, look, Desiree ... Suppose I just come up with you ...?"

"Why, I couldn't do *that!*" she said. "What would the hotel people think?"

I wonder do you know the answer to that one, Mr. Porter from Topeka? Most of them do, and maybe you're not as dumb as you seem.

"Well, look, Desiree," he said. "Suppose you go on up now, and a little later I go up. Get out of the elevator at another floor, see?"

So you do know the answer, wise guy.

"Well, honestly, I don't know, Tommy. I don't know if I ought to let you do that."

"Look! You trust me, don't you, Desiree?"

Sure! You'd be surprised.

"Just a little chat. I'd like to hear about your work—that TV and all. Maybe—"

He looked at her, and it was a different kind of look. He'd been thinking things over, and he wasn't scared anymore.

"Lot of ups and downs in theatrical work," he said. "Maybe I could help you out, some way …"

"Nobody can help me, Tommy," she said, somberly. "I've just got to sink or swim, all alone."

She rose, and so did he.

"Look …!" he said.

"No, Tommy," she said, "I don't want to bother you with my troubles. I'm just tired, and kind of disheartened, that's all."

"Look, Desiree! Tell me the number of your room, and I'll be along. I—I want to hear your troubles. I might be able to—help some way …"

"Honestly, Tommy, you make me feel like crying …"

Well, then … Room four-o-eight. In about fifteen—no, make it ten minutes. I don't want you to have too much time for drinking. Or thinking, either. God! Suppose some time you got this far, and then the guy never showed? Suppose you sat up there, waiting and waiting, and he never came? Honestly, I think I'd want to kill myself, I'd feel so humiliated. And Ramon—think how *he'd* talk?

I'm pretty sick of Ramon, and that's the truth. I thought it was the real thing, real love. I wouldn't have come with him, if I hadn't thought that. I'm not that kind of a girl, man-crazy. No. Lots of times I *hate* men. I really do.

Ramon opened the door when she knocked. All right, he was handsome—in that gigolo way. Dark, sort of graceful, that smile that showed his white, even teeth,

"What have you got your eyebrows raised up that way for?" she demanded.

"Nothing," he said, putting his arm around her shoulders. "My little beauty. Little wild tiger-cat."

He stooped, and laid his cheek against hers, and if she could only close her eyes, and rest her head on his shoulder ... Don't be such a fool! She pulled away from him.

"Better get going, Ramon," she said. "I'm expecting company."

"If you knew what this does to me ...!" he cried. "When I'm waiting— not knowing what's going on in here ... When you're so beautiful ..."

"Be brave!" she said. "Better hurry. I told him ten minutes. Then add— let's say another twenty minutes, or maybe half an hour would be better."

"I'd like to kill him!"

"Why don't you?" she asked, looking straight at him. "He'll be along any minute."

She took off her coat and her dress, and put on a pale-blue nylon negligee, Chinese slippers, and all the while she watched Ramon, moving quickly about the little room and the bathroom, putting away his razor, his dressing gown, all his belongings. Then he took up his overcoat and his hat, and went out, without a word.

Love! Desiree said to herself. When you think of all I've given up for Ramon, and all the sacrifices I've made, and look where I am now! I *hate* this room. Nasty, cheap, dirty little room, and a nasty, cheap hotel, and here I sit, waiting for that fat hick. Maybe he can "help me out!" Sure! Just coming up here out of pure kindness. Sure. Men make me sick. Love ...

All right! It won't do any harm to be crying when he comes. And it's not crocodile tears, either. I honestly do feel miserable, and all nervous. Suppose Porter's drunk too much, and then, when Ramon comes ... Well, suppose this is the time it doesn't work? Suppose Porter makes a row, instead of coming across ...? Suppose he gets the *police?* Gosh! This thing is such a strain ...

There he is now. I *hate* him. Coming sneaking up here, pretending to be so sympathetic and all ... And what do I know about him? He seemed to be well-heeled. Expensive clothes, and plenty of bills in his wallet, and he has that sort of prosperous way about him ... I don't know. I guess it's intuition, but I've never been wrong yet about that.

She went to the door and opened it.

"No ..." she said, almost in a whisper. "No ..."

"Oh, come now, sweetheart!" said the man standing there. "Aren't you glad to see your own loving hubby?"

"Steve ..."

"Been a long time, hasn't it, sweetheart?" he said, and putting his hand on her shoulder, he moved her aside and entered the room. He was so big, toweringly tall, he looked, and with that smile on his tanned, lean face. A terrible smile...

"Steve ... Please ... Please go away. I'm sick. It's—the flu. Please ..."

"What?" he said, closing the door. "After all this long time? I've been trying to find you, honey-chile, even got detectives—"

"Steve! But—Steve! *Detectives?* But why?"

"I'll tell you, sweetheart. That's what I'm here for."

She moved, backward, almost staggering, and sat down on the edge of the bed. He lit a cigarette and stood before her, looking down at her and still smiling.

"Not quite as pretty as you were a while ago, sweetheart," he said. "Skin's kind of sallow, hair's kind of lifeless. Maybe you haven't been eating right, and that's a pretty cheap kind of little wrapper you've got on, isn't it? You used to be mighty fussy about your clothes—"

"Oh, let me alone! Tell me why you came—"

"I will," he said. "Don't worry. I will. When you walked out on me, year and a half ago, you left a little note. Remember that little note, sweetheart? 'All my dreams are broken,' you wrote. 'I thought at last I had found true happiness, but all your family and friends high-hat me and just ignore me, and you never say a word—'"

"Oh, let it go!"

"I didn't like that note, sweetheart. I didn't like a woman walking out on me. I've got to go on living in my hometown, and I'm not going to be 'poor old Steve.' I'm going to get free from you—"

"I told you, in that note, you could get a divorce ..."

"I sure will, sweetheart. But not your kind of divorce. Not for desertion. This is going to make headlines. Your picture in the tabloids. No alimony."

"I never asked you for any."

"Well ..." he said, glancing around the mean little room. "Don't you think I can figure you'd be asking me for something, pretty soon. Anyhow the detective I hired found you here a couple of days ago, and he called me up, and I got a plane this morning. And there you were, honey-chile! There you were, in that lousy little restaurant, batting your eyes, playing a poor middle-aged sucker for a square meal and a couple of drinks. Kind of hard way to make a living, isn't it? I got your name from the barkeep, and here I am. I hear your name is Mrs. Devon. Well, I'd sure like to meet Mr. Devon. I've got to meet him."

She leaned forward, clasping her hands tight.

"Listen, Steve! Steve, please—please go away now! I'll call you up later. I'll meet you later, anything—"

"Anything?"

"Yes! If you'll just please go away now."

"But I want to meet Mr. Devon, sweetheart."

"Steve! You're so *cruel* …"

There was a knock at the door.

"Steve!" she whispered. "For God's sake—go in the bathroom and shut the door. Just for a *minute*—just till I speak to—"

"No, sweetheart," he said, and stepped across the room and opened the door. Mr. Porter was standing there.

"Listen, Mr. Porter …" she said. "I'm terribly sorry—but—but this is my brother, just flew up from Texas—"

"The little lady gets sort of absent-minded, sometimes," said Steve, still smiling, always smiling. "I'm not her brother, mister. I'm her husband."

Porter came in, closing the door after him.

"Honest to God, Mr. Porter," Desiree cried. "I didn't know he was coming! He'll tell you that himself, if he's got *any* decency."

"Haven't any," said Steve. "This was a date, then? I thought she'd finished with you, after you paid the dinner tab."

"No," said Porter. He took a clean handkerchief out of his pocket, wiped his forehead. "I could see that the young lady was all upset and unhappy, and she was good enough to say I could step up here for a little chat."

"Sure!" said Steve. "She's a very obliging little lady. Very obliging!"

"Now, look here, son," said Porter. "There's no use to take that tone with the poor girl. She's miserable; been crying. Maybe you are her husband—"

"There's no 'maybe' about anything I tell you," said Steve. "Get that clear."

"And maybe you're not," said Porter, undisturbed. "But if you are, you ought to be ashamed of yourself."

"*What! Me?*"

"Yes, you," said Porter. "Talking like that to a lady. Acting as if her telling me to step up here for a little chat was something suspicious."

Desiree looked at him in blank wonder. He's standing up for me! she thought. Steve could take him apart, with one hand, but he's facing right up to Steve, taking my part. Why, he's—

She heard the elevator door open and close. *Ramon!* she thought. Oh, God! I'd forgotten … Oh, I wish—I was dead! Oh, what can I do?

There was the sound of a key in the lock, and, quick as a cat, Steve stepped into the bathroom, and pulled the door half-closed.

"Mr. Porter," said Desiree. "Oh, please …! I honestly didn't … I don't know … I didn't—mean it to be like this …"

"There, now!" said Porter, and pushed her gently back on the bed. "You mustn't get so upset, Desiree. Why, you're shaking like a leaf—"

"Here, you!" cried Ramon. "What are you doing here with my wife?"

"Ramon!" she said. "Don't! It's all right."

Oh, if only I can keep Mr. Porter from knowing! Oh, God, please help me to keep him from knowing! Because he was nice to me. He was standing up for me. And I'm so—miserable. I'm so ashamed.

"Ramon!" she said, again. "It's *perfectly* all right. Mr. Porter—"

"All right? For this man to be in your room, and—and—All right, is it? We'll see about that! I'll get the hotel manager up here—"

"Ramon, shut up!" she cried. "This isn't—"

"The old badger game," said Porter, softly.

Desiree was appalled. You wouldn't think he was the kind that would have ever heard about *that*, she thought. He does know.

"You'll find your name in every newspaper—" Ramon was saying.

"Oh, shut up!" she cried. "You try that on Mr. Porter; and I'll show you up."

"You dirty little—"

"None of that," said Porter. "You've come to collect, of course. That's the game. All right! I'll give—"

"Don't!" Desiree implored. "Don't give him anything! He's not—"

"Ten dollars," said Porter, taking out his wallet.

"Ten dollars!" said Ramon. "Maybe that's money where you come from, but not here, mister. Not in this town. A hundred—"

"Twenty," said Porter. "That's the limit."

"Twenty—and a hundred," said Ramon.

A shout of laughter came from the bathroom, and Steve pushed the door open.

"I never …!" he said, raising his hands. "This is the richest …! This is the best story …!" He choked with laughter. "Wait till I tell them—back home …!"

He looked at Ramon, and Porter, and Desiree, huddled back against the wall.

"What d'yuh know! A four-handed—badger game …!"

He laughed and laughed, his loud, joyous laugh.

"Sweetheart," he said to Desiree, "you're sure out of luck. You lose this game, all right. Mister, put your wallet away. This glamor boy doesn't get any cut. Because *I'm* her husband, see? Right, sweetheart?"

"Yes," she said.

It doesn't matter, she thought. I'm finished. I never felt so miserable and ashamed before in my whole life. I just wish I were dead.

"The old badger game—with *two* husbands," said Steve, wiping away the tears of his laughter. "That's cheating, honey-chile. You're barred from this club, from now on in. Come on, you two! I'll stand you both to a drink down at the bar."

Let them go. Tomorrow, they'll put me out of the hotel, and I've only got three dollars. And they'll keep all my clothes. I don't know what I'll do. But I won't go back with Ramon. Never! I hate him! I hate men! I hate—I don't know. Myself, maybe.

"Come on! Come *on!*" said Steve.

"I'm staying, to talk to Miss Devon for a while," said Porter.

"Oh, I see!" said Steve, cheerfully. "It's all right, with the two husbands gone? Well, she's a nice girl, mister. Only, her dreams are broken …"

"She's a dirty little double-crosser," said Ramon. "She put me on to this. She begged me to do it."

"I didn't! I didn't! That's a *lie!* I—"

"Now, now!" said Porter. "Don't get so upset, Miss Devon. Thing is, I've got my sister here. She runs a little sort of a mission for the Indians, and she's been looking all over for a young lady to help her. I think you'd be just the right one."

"Wh-*what!*" cried Steve. "What! Desiree in a *mission?*"

"God help the Indians," said Ramon, and he, too, laughed a little.

"Let's go get that drink," said Steve to Ramon. "This sure calls for a drink."

"Miss Devon's just the type," said Porter, as the men were leaving the room, almost shouting it, daring them to deny it.

Then there was the murmur of laughter and speech in the hall; that faded away, leaving a complete silence in the room.

Porter looked at Desiree and smiled; he chuckled, forcing the sound out, as though he were obliged to make it. "The old badger game," he said, scoffing at it, a racket that was beneath him. He moved the two steps that separated them. He took Desiree's hand.

The clasp and his expression said, "This makes it official. Now we're partners."

Desiree looked at him, puzzled—but only for a moment. What a fool I've been, she thought. Men! Oh, how I hate men. They all have their approach. And now that I come to think of it, there's something mighty familiar about that missionary line. Still he does have a way about him. Maybe he's not so young—or as handsome as Ramon—but I mustn't forget he's got a wallet of money. Of course I know money isn't quite everything. Just the same I must try to pull myself together. Only, it's been a kind of nerve-wracking evening. I do hope Tommy Porter's game is a little easier on the nerves …

People Do Fall Downstairs

Captain Martin Consadine, Commissioner of Police in the island of Puerto Azul, lay back in his swivel chair, his neat dark head resting against the back, his feet up on the desk. The Venetian blinds were down, the electric fan was spinning gently, and he was perfectly quiet in the dimness. He was not asleep, though, or even drowsy in the heat of the tropic afternoon; he was simply taking it easy while he could.

He had been in Puerto Azul only a month, and he had not yet quite got the hang of the place. But that did not trouble him. He had been a policeman in Ceylon, in Demerara, in Trinidad, and elsewhere; he had almost forgotten Ireland, where he was born, London, where he had been trained. Wherever he was sent he would settle down, and would get on courteously and fairly with whatever people happened to be there; nothing was exotic to him any longer, nothing was strange.

There was a knock at the door, and Constable Merribell entered.

"Sah!"

"Yes, Constable?"

Merribell was invaluable to him, a portly colored man of calm and decorous demeanor, with a colossal knowledge of the island and its inhabitants.

"Lady on the telephone, sah. Will not tell me what she want. Say she got to speak to 'the captain'."

"I'll take it," said Consadine, rising, tall, straight, a little gaunt; a handsome man in his own disciplined fashion.

He went into the anteroom and took the telephone.

"Commissioner Consadine speaking," he said.

"Commissioner, is it?" said a fervent voice. "God be praised I've a man like yourself to talk to, and not a monkey out of the zoo."

That voice, that accent, made him smile a little.

"What is it you want, madam?" he asked.

"There is bad trouble here," she said.

"Trouble where, madam?"

"It is Captain Jarvis's house, and there is trouble."

"What sort of trouble?"

"Once you're here," she said, "it'll be plain as daylight to a smart man like yourself, Commissioner. Will you come now, as soon as you can?"

"I'll have to have more information, madam," he said.

She was silent for a moment.

"If it was in New York, now," she said, coldly, "the police'd see for themselves what was wrong, and not be wasting time on the tillyphone."

"This is not New York, madam."

"And well do I know it!" she cried. "If it's information you're wanting, the Captain's brother is hurt, how bad I don't know. But there is *more to come.*"

"What is your name, madam?"

"The name," she said, "is Mrs. Gogarty, and I am the cook. Will you not come, Commissioner dear, and see for yourself?"

"I'll need more information—" said Consadine, but Mrs. Gogarty had hung up.

The sensible thing would be to send Merribell to look into this matter. Certainly Mrs. Gogarty had given no reason why the Commissioner should go in person. And yet he thought that he would go. Something in the woman's voice, and her words, stirred an old and long-forgotten emotion in him. He felt that Mrs. Gogarty was a fine woman, sensible too, and not easily flustered. He turned to Merribell.

"Do you know where a Captain Jarvis lives, Sergeant?"

"Oh, undoubtedly, sah! Captain Jarvis very well known in the island, sah, and highly esteemed. Live out on the South Shore now."

"What sort of captain? Army?"

"Oh, no, sah. Marchant Marine. Been coming down here for years on he ship. Third Mate, Second Mate, Chief; Captain. Then he ship torpedoed, and the faculty of hearing damage."

"Is he married?"

"Oh, no, sah. Single gentleman. But he brother and he brother wife here now from New York."

"What about them?"

"Brother wife a very quiet lady, sah. Stay home all the time. Never see she."

"And the brother?"

"He drink, sah," said Merribell, gravely.

"Well, we'll drive out there," said Consadine.

Merribell squeezed in behind the wheel of the small car, and they drove through the town, past the cane fields and up a hill, to the shore road that ran along the cliffs. Nothing grew here but short, rank grass and here and there a tamarisk tree; in the old days of great estates no one had lived here, but now there was a settlement of five or six new houses, high above the road, without walls or fences, and looking very lonely in this empty world. Merribell stopped the car before the last of them, a white wooden house, narrow and ugly, already bleached and weather-beaten, and Consadine got out and started up the long flight of steps cut in the rock.

Everything was completely quiet in the blazing afternoon sun; the road behind him was empty; as he reached the top of the steps he could see the Caribbean stretching out to the horizon, blue and empty. And this disturbed him. *I shouldn't have come without more information,* he told himself.

He rang the bell, and the door was opened promptly by a nonchalant young fellow in dungarees.

"I'd like to speak to Mrs. Gogarty," said Consadine.

The young man turned his head.

"Gogarty," he called. "You're wanted."

Then he came out, passed Consadine down the steps of the veranda, and disappeared round the corner of the house. Consadine waited a moment and then, because he did not like Merribell to see his Commissioner standing ignored outside the house, he entered the hall.

It was a cramped, ungracious house. From the narrow hall rose a narrow and very steep stairway, and against the wall facing it stood a colossal hat rack that was almost like a crazy little house in itself, with a seat and tiers of shelves and wooden antlers and a round mirror.

A door opened upstairs, and a girl began to descend the stairs; a very pretty little blonde, slim and full-bosomed, in a sleeveless black-and-white striped dress with a halter tied in a saucy bow at the nape of her neck.

"Yes?" she asked, polite but unsmiling.

"I'd like to see Mrs. Gogarty, please," said Consadine.

She looked surprised, and why shouldn't she?

"It's—there's nothing wrong, is there?" she asked.

He was a man of authority, and he must not allow himself to feel abashed.

"I'm the Commissioner of Police, madam," he said. "We've been informed that there's been—some trouble here."

"Oh!" she said. "Well, yes. My husband fell down the stairs. But Doctor Buller has seen him …"

And there's no reason for *you* to be here.

"If you'll give me an account of the accident, madam …?" said Consadine, stiff and aloof to cover his secret chagrin.

"I was in my room when I heard the fall," she said. "I came down, and Francis—that's Captain Jarvis, my brother-in-law—was already here. He called out the window to Hazen—"

"Who is Hazen, madam?"

"He's the handyman. He came in, and he and Francis—Captain Jarvis—carried my husband upstairs. He was unconscious."

She began to cry, very quietly, and that disturbed Consadine.

"Doctor Buller saw your husband?"

"Yes. He said to keep him very quiet, and he'd look in tomorrow morning."

So there it was. A drunk had fallen downstairs, and here was the Police Commissioner making a marvelous fool of himself.

"I'm sorry to trouble you," he said, "but I'd like a word with Mrs. Gogarty."

"I'll get her," said Mrs. Jarvis.

"Don't bother. If you'll tell me where I'm likely to find her …?"

"I suppose she's in the kitchen," said the girl. "That's just down the hall."

"Thank you," he said, with formality, and went down the hall, opened a door, went through a pantry and into the kitchen, where he found the young fellow in dungarees washing his face at the sink.

"Where's Mrs. Gogarty?" asked Consadine.

"I wouldn't know," answered the other, drying his face and his sturdy neck on a roller towel.

Consadine did not like his tone. Above all, he did not like his own position, wandering around here, looking for this outrageous Mrs. Gogarty.

"I'm the Commissioner of Police here," he said. "I want your name, address, and occupation."

"The name," said the other, "is Hazen. Louis. Address is Toronto Villa. Occupation is licensed hack driver."

"What are you doing here?"

"Working on the electric pump, and the car. I was in the Merchant Marine in the war, and I sailed with Captain Jarvis once. Now whenever he wants anything done, he sends for me."

"Were you in the house when the Captain's brother fell?"

"Nope. In the garage. The Captain yelled out the window to me, and I came. I helped him carry Bill upstairs."

"Was—William Jarvis conscious at that time?"

"Out like a light," said Hazen, cheerfully. "I thought he was dead."

"You're well acquainted with the family?"

"Me?" said Hazen, with a grin. "Why, I'm just a deck hand that shipped with the Captain. I couldn't be 'acquainted' with his family, any more than a dog could."

He spoke with an easy good humor, very sure of himself; he looked squarely back at Consadine.

"I come here to do odd jobs," he said. "And five, six times I was sent out to find Bill Jarvis when he was missing. He blacks out when he's drinking."

"I see," said Consadine. "Now I'd like you to get Mrs. Gogarty for me."

"*I* wouldn't know where she is," said Hazen.

"Find her," said Consadine.

"They wouldn't let me go running around the house."

"She lives here, I suppose?"

"And how!" said Hazen. "Her husband was the Captain's pet steward, and when he died, the Old Man sent for her. She thinks she owns him *and* the house."

"I see," said Consadine again.

He was very much at a loss now, but he was absolutely determined to see this Mrs. Gogarty, and to get an explanation from her. *I'll send Merribell in to look for her*, he thought, and went out through the pantry.

As he came into the narrow hall again, someone was coming down the stairs—a big man, heavily built, strikingly handsome, with black hair, bold black brows, bold, steady grey eyes that looked pale in his deeply tanned face. He came on leisurely and stopping a few feet from Consadine, he took a small hearing aid out of his pocket and adjusted it.

"Well, mister?" he asked.

This was almost too much for Consadine, but he stood his ground.

"I'm the Police Commissioner, sir. I'd like to speak to Mrs. Gogarty," he said.

"Now, what's *she* been up to?" asked the other, with a broad smile. "My name is Jarvis, mister, and I'm responsible for Mary Gogarty. What's she done? Been pulling somebody's hair?"

"Oh, no. Nothing. Routine," said Consadine. "If I can see her for a few moments, please …"

"She's upstairs, sitting with my brother. Doctor said he might be comin' to his senses any minute, and we're standing by. It's Mary Gogarty's trick now. I'll get her for you."

"Suppose I go up?" Consadine suggested.

"If you like. This way, mister."

Jarvis led the way up the stairs, and opened the door of a bedroom, dim, with the Venetian blinds down; the big double bed, covered with a mosquito net, was pulled out from the walls, for a better circulation of air. A woman sitting by the window rose at once, a sturdy little woman with thick black hair in a tight knot on the top of her head, a fine color in her cheeks, fiery blue eyes.

"Well, here she is," said Jarvis. "Mary Gogarty, here's the police after you."

He spoke loudly, probably more loudly than he knew, and Mrs. Gogarty put a finger to her lips.

"You're right," said Jarvis, in a whisper. "Step out into the hall, Mrs. Gogarty, and find out what's going to happen to you. I'll stay here till you come back."

"I'll just take a look at the patient," said Consadine.

"No," said Jarvis. "Doctor said not to disturb him."

"I shan't disturb him, sir," said Consadine. "I'm used to these cases."

He went over to the bed and drew aside the mosquito net. A man was lying there, tall and straight, in white shirt and trousers, a neat white bandage round his head. He had once been a handsome man, but he had grown haggard and sick. And he had a look Consadine had seen often enough before. He raised the man's wrist.

"Here, mister!" said Jarvis behind him. "Better not do that."

Consadine bent and laid his head against the man's chest. Jarvis pulled him by the shoulder and he straightened up and faced him.

"I'm sorry, sir," he said. "I'm very sorry—but this man is dead."

Jarvis fell back into a chair so heavily that it creaked; he looked up at Consadine with blank eyes.

"I killed him, mister," he said.

"You did not!" said Mrs. Gogarty. "Don't be listening to him, Mr. Commissioner. He—"

"I knocked him down the stairs," said Jarvis. "I killed him. You can take me along with you, mister."

Consadine took the key out of the door.

"Both of you step out of the room, please," he said.

Jarvis did not move. He had put the hearing aid back into his pocket and sat slumped in his chair, looking at the man on the bed. Consadine touched him on the shoulder.

"I did it," said Jarvis. "I killed him."

"Step out of the room, please," said Consadine, but still Jarvis did not move.

Mrs. Gogarty went to his side.

"Captain, dear, come along now!" she said, coaxingly, and he rose.

"Like Cain …" he said.

Mrs. Gogarty took his hand and led him out of the room, to a room along the hall. He went in there, stumbling a little, and closed the door after him. Consadine locked the door of the room where the dead man lay.

"Commissioner, dear, I'll tell you the whole truth," said Mrs. Gogarty, "the way it happened."

"Later," said Consadine. "Show me where the telephone is."

She led him downstairs to a sitting room, heavily furnished, where a telephone stood on a marble-topped table. She gave him Doctor Buller's number, and stood beside him while he called it. Fortunately, the doctor was at home.

"Commissioner Consadine?" he said. "Yes? Yes? What can I do for *you*, sir?"

"I'm speaking from Captain Jarvis's house, doctor. You saw William Jarvis after his accident?"

"Yes, yes. Bandaged him up, and left him to sleep it off."

"Your patient is dead," said Consadine.

There was a moment's silence.

"That's—most unfortunate," said Buller. "*Most* unfortunate. It—" He rallied; his voice became louder, and with a note of resentment. "It's very difficult to diagnose those cases, particularly when they're complicated by alcoholism. All the symptoms were characteristic of a simple concussion."

"You didn't think there was any possibility of his dying?"

"That's absurd, sir!" shouted Buller. "No doctor would answer a question like that. There's always the possibility of unforeseen complications in a head injury."

"But you didn't expect him to die?"

"Certainly I did!" cried the doctor. "I mean to say, I was fully aware that complications might develop—"

"I'd like you to come over here as soon as you can," said Consadine, and went out to the car, where Merribell sat waiting in calm patience. He sent him to fetch Nicholson, the Police Surgeon, and turning back to the house, he found Mrs. Gogarty standing in the doorway.

"Now will you listen to me, Mr. Commissioner?" she asked sternly.

"Yes," said Consadine, and went after her, down the hall and into the kitchen.

"Why did you ask me to come here, madam?" he asked.

"You were needed," said she.

"I'd like something more definite than that," he said. "At the time you telephoned to me there was no occasion for alarm."

"I knew there was worse to come," said Mrs. Gogarty. "And wasn't I right, Commissioner?"

"You mean you thought William Jarvis's injury was more serious than the doctor suspected?"

She was silent for a moment, and he studied her face, with the high cheekbones, the long upper lip, the dark blue eyes. A passionate, stubborn face, he thought.

"Commissioner dear," she said, "to tell you the truth of it, I wasn't clear in my mind when I tillyphoned. Only when I saw Mr. Bill lying there, white as death itself, I knew there was worse to come. And wasn't I right? Isn't he lying there dead this moment, murdered by the two of them?"

"What two?"

"Mrs. Bill and that Louis."

"What grounds have you for saying this?"

"I know it," said Mrs. Gogarty.

"How do you know it?"

"Commissioner dear," she said, earnestly, "Mr. Bill could never have been killed by that fall."

"Why not?"

"Because," she said, "he wouldn't have been *let* be killed. The Captain's the finest man ever drew breath, and God Himself wouldn't let him kill his own brother."

"Accidents can happen to anyone," said Consadine.

"Commissioner, sir, it was the two of them did it, plotting and planning together."

"Have you any evidence that Mrs. Jarvis and Hazen were engaged in any sort of conspiracy?"

"I have."

"Do you wish to make a statement, madam?"

"And what else am I doing?"

"Do you wish to make a statement, to be taken down in writing and later to be signed by you?"

"I will sign anything at all," said Mrs. Gogarty. "All I want in the world is to see the poor innocent Captain easy in his heart, and that murdering pair—"

"You must be careful in making accusations of that nature, Mrs. Gogarty. Have you any evidence—?"

"I've seen the looks they give each other."

"That's not evidence," said Consadine.

"It is good enough for me," said Mrs. Gogarty.

"Have you anything definite to tell me? Any *facts?*"

"Holy Mother of God!" cried Mrs. Gogarty. "Isn't it fact enough for you that Mr. Bill's lying there murdered?"

"Madam," said Consadine, "there's no evidence whatever of murder. Captain Jarvis has stated that he pushed his brother downstairs in the course of a quarrel. He and Hazen carried William Jarvis upstairs—"

"Herself wint up, too," said Mrs. Gogarty.

"Mrs. Gogarty, when I arrived here you were in the room with William Jarvis. Who was there before you?"

"It was the Captain himself."

"Have you any reason to believe that he left that room for any length of time?"

"I have."

"Did you *see* Captain Jarvis leave the room?"

"I did not."

"Then how do you know that he left it?" Consadine asked, marveling at his own patience.

"Because the two of them couldn't have murdered Mr. Bill unless the Captain was out of it," said she. "I tell you it wouldn't be *let* happen. The Captain wouldn't be *let* kill his own brother."

"Mrs. Gogarty," said Consadine, "do you realize how your accusation would sound in a court of law?"

"I do!" said she. "Put me before a jury of Christian beings, and they'd believe me."

"It's not a question of 'believing' you, Mrs. Gogarty. You haven't given me any evidence, not one single fact pointing to collaboration between Mrs. Jarvis and Hazen."

"'Collaboration', is it?" said she, with irony. "That's a word is new to me. But if you mean were they carrying on, they were that."

"Did you ever see them alone together? Ever hear them arrange a meeting? See them exchange notes, anything of that sort?"

"Never," she said. "And I didn't need to. The two of them were carrying on, and they wanted to get Mr. Bill out of the way, God rest him. He was not good at all to a woman, the way he was drunk all the time, and roaring up and down the island. But that didn't give the two of them the right to murder him and let the poor innocent Captain take the sin on himself, and him so generous and good to her—"

"Captain Jarvis is—fond of his sister-in-law?" Consadine asked, very cautiously.

"I know what's in your mind," said Mrs. Gogarty, "as well as if you'd spoke the words. You are wrong. Mrs. Bill's got a way with her, a tweedly way would please many a man." She looked at Consadine. "The Captain, God help him, thinks she's a saint on earth, and that's the whole of it. It would never come into his head at all that his brother's wife would be carrying on with that Louis. But Mr. Bill thought of it, many a time."

"How do you know that, Mrs. Gogarty?"

"By the way he'd be looking at the two of them."

"Mrs. Gogarty," said Consadine, "you haven't given me one single fact to support your theory—"

"'Theory!'" she cried. "It's the truth I've told you, and you've a right to take the two of them off to jail, before there's more harm done."

"There's no case against them, Mrs. Gogarty."

"And you'll take himself off to the jail?"

"I'm obliged to charge him with manslaughter, Mrs. Gogarty," said Consadine, rising. "But he'll be admitted to bail."

She rose too.

"I've told you the truth of it," she said, "and if you will not believe it, so much the worse for all of us."

He went out of the kitchen, annoyed with himself for the stir of uneasiness her words and her tone had caused in him. *She's an utterly unreasonable woman*, he thought.

He felt it his duty to break the news to young Mrs. Jarvis, but he was much relieved when Doctor Buller arrived, before he had found her. The doctor was in a belligerent mood; a dapper little grey-haired man with a self-important air. He was still more affronted by the arrival of young Nicholson, the Police Surgeon; he went upstairs with him, in cold silence.

Consadine waited in the lower hall, and presently they came down again.

"At the time that I examined the patient," said Buller, "the symptoms were those of simple concussion. Complicated, of course, by his condition of alcoholic intoxication."

"I see," said Consadine. "Are you both agreed about the cause of death?"

"Depressed fracture of the skull," said Nicholson.

"Caused by what?"

"By what?" cried Buller. "Why, the man fell all the way down a steep flight of stairs, and hit his head against that—that thing there."

"Then you're ready to state that the fall could have been the cause of the fracture?"

"'Could have been?'" said Buller, more and more outraged. "It *was*. There's no question at all about it."

"There's no possibility that he could have got his head injury before or after his fall?"

"Certainly not!" said Buller.

"Well …" said the serious young Nicholson, in his amiable manner, "I think we'll have to admit that the injury *might* have been done by some instrument."

"My good sir!" cried Buller. "You have the evidence of everyone in this household that William Jarvis fell down these stairs. You can see for yourself how narrow this hall is. It would be almost impossible for anyone—especially a tall man—not to strike his head on that—thing. That's quite good enough for me. I don't need any fantastic 'instruments' to satisfy me as to the cause of death in this case."

And it's good enough for me, too, Consadine thought. *Mrs. Gogarty told me nothing of any value whatever. Utterly unreasonable woman. Her whole story's an invention.*

Doctor Buller offered to break the news to Mrs. Jarvis.

"I'll take the poor girl home with me," he said. "My wife will be glad to look after her."

This seemed to Consadine a very good idea, and he went himself to the Captain's room. He knocked, waited, knocked again, and getting no answer, he turned the knob and entered. The big man was standing by the window; he did not turn until Consadine touched him on the shoulder.

"All right," he said. "I'm ready, mister."

"I'd like an account of the accident, Captain," said Consadine, but Jarvis did not answer.

"He cannot hear you at all," said Mrs. Gogarty, from the hall behind him, "when he's not using the contraption."

"Ask him to use it," said Consadine. "I want a statement from him."

"Captain," said Mrs. Gogarty, speaking close to his ear, and very clearly. "Captain, dear, the Commissioner wants to speak to you. Will you put on the contraption, he asks?"

"No," said Jarvis. "I quarreled with my brother and I killed him. I'm not going to discuss the quarrel now, or any other time. It's nobody's damn business. I killed my brother. For God's sake, isn't that enough?"

He has the look of a bull at the end of a fight, Consadine thought, *so big, so strong, so tormented.*

"Cain ..." the Captain said. "Like Cain."

Consadine had a solitary and formal dinner in his bungalow; then he went out, to walk up and down the garden path while he smoked a cigar. And here he was a trespasser, in a strange and secret world. There was no breeze tonight, only a smothering blackness, perfumed with unknown flowers; things chirped and rattled in the grass, things moved with a rustle in the branches of the trees, things scuttled across the path; some night bird made a gurgling sound.

He had thought he was used to all this, used to anything. But tonight, a man without a home, he was homesick, and it was Mrs. Gogarty who had done this. He felt very angry at that stubborn, utterly unreasonable woman.

He thought of the pretty little blonde, but only for a moment. She was better off without her sodden husband. Captain Jarvis was the tragic, the epic figure. There had been a score of people ready to go bail for him; he had had any number of invitations, of offers to accompany him, but he had gone home alone. There would be no legal punishment for him, Consadine was sure of that, but for the rest of his days he would be remembering what he had done. It happened so often, it happened so easily. One moment of anger, one blow of a fist could crash through the whole structure of a life.

Like Cain, he had said. But Cain had killed his brother deliberately, because of his bitter envy. And Jarvis? Had Jarvis envied his brother, perhaps? Envied him his wife? Envied him, hated him, because he was not deaf? Those things could be in a man's heart, and the man not know it. They could be behind a blow, giving it a dreadful force.

Well, I don't know, Consadine thought with a sigh. *Maybe a breeze would spring up with the moon. A fresh, sweet breeze coming over the sea …*

He went to bed, under his mosquito net, and after a while he fell asleep.

The telephone waked him, and he got up in haste to answer it.

"Commissioner, sir, will you come quick?" said Mrs. Gogarty's voice, with a curious ring in it. "For there has been another accident."

"Who is it?" he asked.

"Let you see for yourself," said she. "There'll be nothing disturbed at all till you come."

"Somebody hurt? I want full information—"

"Let you come and get it," she said, and hung up.

He was very angry at Mrs. Gogarty. For a moment he thought of calling her back and demanding a complete explanation. Only he knew he would not get it. *You can't do a damn thing with that woman,* he thought. *I won't go.*

I won't go, he thought, while he dressed. He called Merribell and told him to bring along the Police Surgeon; he went out on the screened veranda to wait for them.

"What's happened?" the young doctor asked.

"Accident," Consadine said, with unusual curtness.

"What sort of accident?"

"I don't know," said Consadine.

"Who's hurt?"

"I don't know."

The doctor was silent then, and Consadine made up things for him to be thinking. *Consadine's not fit for this job. Hopeless! Getting me out of bed at one o'clock in the morning to go to an accident, and he hasn't* had the wit to get the most elementary information. Must have lost his head completely.

They passed the Botanical Garden. It was like a dense black jungle, and there was a bird in it that sounded like an owl choking to death while the whistling frogs piped away, jeering. There was a light in Jarvis's house, and as the car drove up, Mrs. Gogarty opened the door.

She was wearing a white cotton dress with short sleeves that stood out like wings. There was a fine color in her cheeks; her black hair was very neat, her blue eyes were alight. She looked handsome, and somehow dangerous.

"Come in, the lot of you," she said politely, and stood aside.

Louis Hazen was lying on the floor at the foot of the stairs, with blood running down from one temple and soaking into the shoulder of his white shirt. His eyes were half open; his face was grey with a mortal weariness; his breath came in a faint moan.

"The man's bleeding to death!" said the young doctor, on his knees beside him. "Send for the ambulance!"

Constable Merribell stepped forward, and Consadine turned to Mrs. Gogarty.

"How did this happen?" he asked sternly.

"He fell down the stairs," said Mrs. Gogarty, in a ringing voice. "And *now* will you believe me? Isn't it the judgment of God?"

He looked at her with a narrow, hostile glance.

"I want to talk to you," he said. "In here."

He gestured towards the sitting room, but she ignored that.

"This way, sir," she said, and started along the hall. He restrained himself from catching her by the sleeve and pulling her back; he followed her into the kitchen.

"Now I want a complete and sensible account of what's happened," he said.

"Yes, sir," she said, with a docility that did not at all reassure him. "I'll tell you the whole truth of it. I was feeling that low in my mind, I went down the street to ask the colored woman that works for the Porters would she come and keep me company a while. She is a good woman, only she is superstitious, the way they are here. Ah, well, they're not to be blamed, for they haven't had the education we have. She came back with me, but she wouldn't go into the house at all, for some notion she had about Mr. Bill. So I brought two chairs out on the little back porch, and there we sat, with thim insects. I can't stand them!" she cried. "Heathenish things, flapping in your face, and some of them like a puff of dust in your nose—"

"Get on with your story, please," said Consadine. He didn't need to be told about those insects.

"I will, sir. We were sitting out there, the two of us, with thim insects, when we heard him come falling down the stairs, bumping and banging, like a sack of coal. In I went to see what was wrong, and Rose, she came along too, forgetting her notions. He was lying there, and he was unconscious. Rose ran off, scared out of her wits entirely. I tillyphoned to yourself and I waited, and after a bit he came to. 'Give me some whisky,' he said, and then, 'give me some water,' he said. But I wouldn't disturb anything at all."

"You wouldn't give him water when he asked?"

"I would not," said Mrs. Gogarty, with a virtuous air. "How would I know it wasn't the worst thing in the world for him? No, sir. I leave him lay. And now you'll be taking him off to the jail, will you not?"

"To jail? Why?"

"God help us, Commissioner dear!" she cried. "Don't you see it now? I told you the two of them killed Mr. Bill, and you would not believe me. It was God Himself sent him falling down the stairs, so you'd *have* to believe it."

"Why should his falling down the stairs make me believe you?"

"And why did he ever go *up* the stairs?" she demanded. "What was he doing here in this house in the dead of night, if it wasn't carrying on with her? Indeed, he could never have got into the house at all if she hadn't let him in, for I'd locked and bolted the front door, and Rose and myself were sitting there by the back door."

"You have a point there," said Consadine slowly.

For if young Mrs. Jarvis had been "carrying on" with Hazen, her husband's death took on a different look.

"Where is Mrs. Jarvis?" he asked.

"She's shut up in her room," said Mrs. Gogarty. "And never a sound out of her, with all the noise he made, falling down the stairs. She is shut up in there, shaking and trembling, because she knows her sin is found out."

"I'll speak to her," said Consadine.

When he knocked at her door, she opened it after a moment. She wore a white dressing-gown, and she tried to look startled; she tried to look drowsy, rubbing her eyes.

"What's happened?" she asked.

Consadine told her.

Oh, no, she said. She had been sound asleep, and had heard nothing. Not a sound. Hazen? she asked with a look of amazement. What was he doing here? He must have come to talk to the Captain about something.

"I'll ask the Captain," said Consadine.

"No!" she said. "It would be cruel to disturb him now."

"I'm afraid I'll have to," said Consadine. "He must have let Hazen into the house."

A familiar excitement was rising in him, although his composed and quiet manner gave no hint of it. The little blonde did not look pretty to him now. She moistened her lips, and glanced at him, and glanced away.

"The front door must have been left open," she said. "It often is."

"Not this time," said Consadine. "So the Captain must have let him in." He paused. "Mustn't he?" He waited a moment. "I'll go and ask him."

"No! Please!" she said. "He's been so good to me.... I haven't any money, or any place to go.... And he's so—straitlaced. He'd never understand. He'd turn me out. I—I did let Louis in. But it wasn't anything wrong. I just wanted to speak to him about"—her glance flickered over Consadine's face—"about the garden," she said. "*Please* don't tell Francis."

"No way out of it," said Consadine. "He's got to know about this other accident, and he'll have to know how Hazen got into the house."

"He won't have to. We can tell him that the door was left unlocked. Louis'll agree to that."

"Mrs. Gogarty won't."

"She's a devil!" cried the girl.

"Think so?" said Consadine. "I can't waste any more time, Mrs. Jarvis. I'll have to see the Captain now."

Then it happened. He had seen it happen before, and always to his advantage, as a policeman. Yet it was, he thought, the ugliest and sorriest thing there was to see. Lover against lover, friend against friend, brother against brother, the cornered and the frightened turned as she turned now.

"You can't think what my life has been like.... My husband was drunk all the time. Francis was wonderful, but he didn't *understand* ... I know I shouldn't have listened to Louis—but there wasn't anyone else. I was so lonely."

Consadine was not touched by any pity for her.

"You helped Hazen to kill your husband," he said. And he knew what her answer would be.

"I didn't! I didn't! I didn't even know he was thinking of such a thing—until it happened."

Lover against lover. She was desperately anxious now to tell it all. Doctor Buller had said that Bill Jarvis would recover—and Bill was going to talk.

"That's what they quarreled about, Bill and Francis. Bill was trying to tell Francis—horrible things about me—and Louis. And Francis wouldn't listen. He hit Bill. I didn't know that Louis was going to do—that."

Until she had seen Hazen take a spanner out of his pocket and shift the bandage, just a little, and strike a carefully planned blow.

"I haven't any money or any place to go.... Louis can't look after me—yet. But later Francis was going to help him start a garage for himself—"

"Get dressed, please, Mrs. Jarvis," said Consadine.

She began to cry, catching his sleeve. But that did not trouble him.

"Get dressed, please," he said. "We'll have to see the Attorney General."

He went out into the hall, closing her door behind him; he was going towards the Captain's room when he saw something that stopped him; he bent over, turning his flashlight on the floor.

The Captain did not answer his knock; he turned the knob and entered the room; he had to shake the sleeping man to rouse him. He had to fetch Mrs. Gogarty to persuade the Captain to use his hearing aid.

Mrs. Gogarty began to cry.

"Captain darlin'!" she said. "You're as innocent as a babe unborn—and didn't I know it? I knew you wouldn't be *let* do a thing like that, the grand man you are."

He stood silent, sick and dazed by what he had heard.

"Captain darlin'!" said Mrs. Gogarty, tears running down her face. "Couldn't you take heart now, when that's not weighing on you anymore? When it's not—like Cain?"

He patted her shoulder, and after a moment he managed a smile for her.

"You're a fine woman, Mary Gogarty," he said. "You're a good friend."

"Just a moment," said Consadine, as Mrs. Gogarty was moving away. He went out into the hall with her.

"Just a moment," he said again, and pushed aside a queer little rug that lay at the head of the stairs. He turned on his flashlight, to show her a jagged hole in the carpet.

"Yes," she said. "That's why I put down the bit of a rug."

"That rug wasn't here when I first came upstairs," said Consadine.

"I put it down afterwards, so you wouldn't see how poor looking the carpet was."

"That hole wasn't in the carpet yesterday," said Consadine.

"Was it not?" she asked, with an air of interest. "It must be the mice got into it."

"That hole was *cut*, Mrs. Gogarty."

She looked back at him steadily.

"Terrible sharp teeth thim mice have," she said.

"Mrs. Gogarty," said Consadine, "that hole is extremely dangerous. Suppose the *Captain* had wanted to go downstairs tonight? He might very well have caught his foot in it, and pitched all the way down."

Mrs. Gogarty's blue eyes were still fixed steadily upon him.

"No," she said. "He wouldn't have been *let*."

Most Audacious Crime

Captain Consadine, Commissioner of Police in the Island of Puerto Azul, sat at his desk writing out a report for the Governor. He liked this paperwork, this putting of complex and troublesome human affairs into neat tabulation; so many charges, so many convictions, so many acquittals. This record of his first six months on the island was good, very good, and he was proud of it.

"You're busy …" said an apologetic voice, and he looked up to see Doctor Atkins standing in the doorway, a tall, lean, sandy-haired man in a rumpled white linen suit.

"Come in, doctor!" said Consadine. "Come in! What can I do for you?"

The doctor entered the office and sat down heavily in a chair.

"I don't know, Consadine …" he said. "I don't know whether there's anything in this or not."

Consadine pushed aside his beautiful report and sat waiting, neat and alert. He had a great admiration for the tired doctor and a growing affection for him; he was willing to wait as long as necessary to hear whatever he had to say.

"D'you know a man called Joblyn?" asked the doctor.

"I've seen him," said Consadine "Fellow with a black beard; wears shorts. An American."

"That's the one. He's a geologist down here on some sort of survey. Well, about two weeks ago he came into my office, in a bad state. I diagnosed some form of poisoning and I took what measures I thought indicated, and when he was in a condition to talk, I asked him what he'd been taking. He told me he'd been down at North End, looking for rocks or whatever it is those fellows look for, and he said he'd eaten the seeds of a plant growing there. He said he often did that.

"I told him, in my best professional manner, that it was a damn fool habit and he agreed. I wanted to take him to the hospital then, for a thorough check, but he wouldn't go; said he felt fine, but that he'd be much obliged if I'd drive him home. I had no patients waiting, so I took him along, and on the way he was very insistent upon my not letting the ladies know what had happened to him. He said it would worry them, and I couldn't see any good reason for not agreeing to that. I drove him home and I had tea with his wife and her aunt."

From his breast pocket the doctor brought out an object incongruous with his rumpled and careless appearance, but familiar to everyone who knew him; a fine gold cigarette case, engraved inside from a grateful patient. He took out a cigarette and held it between two fingers, looking absently at it.

"Well, Consadine …" he said. "Day before yesterday I was called out to the Naval Hospital for a consultation with a young doctor there. We saw his patient, and then he took me to his quarters for a drink and a talk. In the course of the conversation, he mentioned a queer thing that had happened the day before. A man had come into his office, suffering from symptoms of what this chap diagnosed as digitalis poisoning. The doctor treated him, and when he was sufficiently recovered to be questioned, the patient said he'd been eating the seeds of a plant."

"Joblyn?"

"Yes," said the doctor.

"He must be the biggest fool that ever walked on earth," said Consadine.

"He's not. He's an intelligent man."

"Then how do you account for his doing a thing like that *twice?*" asked Consadine, with a certain indignation.

The doctor struck a match and lit the cigarette he had been holding.

"I couldn't get the thing out of my mind," he said. "And this morning I called up Doctor Blumstein at the Botanical Gardens. Asked him what sort of plant could cause digitalis poisoning. He said foxglove."

"And this Joblyn goes straight for foxglove, every time they let him loose?" asked Consadine.

"There's no foxglove growing on the island, Consadine," said the doctor. "Blumstein was very definite that it couldn't grow here."

"Ha …" said Consadine, annoyed by this fantasy. "What's your Joblyn up to, then?"

"What do *you* think, Consadine?"

"Suicide?" suggested Consadine "Fellow takes poison, and then panics and runs to a doctor?"

"From what I've seen of Joblyn," said Doctor Atkins, "I don't think he'd lost his nerve. Certainly he wasn't in any panic when he came to my office."

"Very well," said Consadine. "He didn't eat foxglove seeds by mistake as he told you, and you don't believe he tried to commit suicide. Very well—what do you think?"

"I don't know, Consadine," said the doctor. "I don't know. The thing's been troubling me a great deal, ever since I heard from Blumstein, and I made up my mind to come and tell you the story. Leave it to you to decide what steps to take."

"What steps d'you think I'd be taking?" asked Consadine.

"Tell you what I'd like, Consadine," said the doctor, presently. "I'd like you to come to the Joblyns to tea with me."

"Now, why?" asked Consadine.

"I'd like to get your impressions, Consadine."

"I'll come," said Consadine. "But I warn you, doctor, I'll get no 'impressions.' I can't read people's faces. I can't tell by looking at people whether they're lying or not."

The doctor rose, and took up his battered hat.

"Thank you, Consadine," he said. "I'm glad you're coming."

The doctor returned at four o'clock, and he had made an attempt at spruceness; he wore a fresh linen suit, and a bow tie, checked green and brown. But he was not designed by nature to look neat; his sandy hair grew in rough little spouts; there was something awkward in his walk and in his gestures. Beside him, Consadine looked formidably straight and foursquare in his white uniform; his dark face under the white helmet looked severe.

"Better tell me something about these people," he said, when he was settled in the doctor's shabby little car.

"Well, there's Joblyn, of course," said the doctor, "and Mrs. Joblyn and her aunt, Miss Fanning. Americans, from somewhere near Boston."

"You think one of these women's been trying to poison Joblyn."

"Consadine! I've never said, never implied anything of the sort."

"Couldn't be plainer," said Consadine. "You said you didn't believe it was attempted suicide, and if you'd really thought it was accidental, you wouldn't want to bring me into it. Very well. That means you think someone's given Joblyn poison, twice, and both times he's tried to shield this person. His wife, I suppose."

"Consadine," said the doctor, with energy. "Mrs. Joblyn is one of the most charming women I've ever met. She—" He paused. "She's charming," he said.

Ha …! Consadine said to himself, surprised by the doctor's choice of a word. He had heard Atkins speak of so-and-so as a fine woman, someone else as a brave woman, a good woman. But charming …? He felt a considerable curiosity now; he wanted to see this woman the doctor found charming. But, all the same, he thought, if there's been any poisoning going on, she's the likely one. The wife.

"Is Joblyn a well-to-do man?" he asked.

"No," said the doctor. "Nothing but his salary. Miss Fanning's the one with the money."

"Never heard of a man being poisoned by his wife's aunt," said Consadine.

"Consadine," said the doctor, "there are probably a great many things in this world you've never heard of."

I doubt it, thought Consadine. I doubt it. If you've been a policeman in Dublin and London, *and* the Malay states, and Trinidad, I doubt it.

The doctor drove through the town and uphill, to the road that ran along the cliff overlooking the sea. Now there was visible before them, on the summit of the hill, a big white house, with a double gallery, a cupola, all the filigree of a bygone era, standing in a forlorn jungle of a garden.

The door was opened by a buxom grey-haired woman in a snug-fitting grey linen dress.

"Oh, doctor?" she said, with no great show of cordiality. "Come in."

"Miss Fanning, Captain Consadine."

"How d'you do," said Miss Fanning.

She led them into a big room with a bare polished floor, in which was gathered a nondescript collection of furniture, a fine old mahogany sofa, covered with rotting brocade, basket chairs, a marble-topped table and a surprisingly modern coffee table.

"Sit down!" ordered Miss Fanning. "My niece will be down in a moment."

She herself sat down on the edge of a big wing basket chair, erect and unsmiling, looking down her pointed nose.

"How do you like Puerto Azul, Miss Fanning?" asked Consadine, politely.

"I despise it," said she.

"The—climate?" asked Consadine.

"The climate," said she, "and the people. I never saw such a lot of lazy, good-for-nothing, absolutely unreliable people. When we first came here, I was warned that I'd have to have two servants to do the work one would do at home." She laughed, angrily. "Three of 'em couldn't do it."

She's like my Aunt Kate in Dublin, thought Consadine—the same fresh complexion, the straight back, the bulldog jaw. A holy terror is the same anywhere in the world, he thought.

Miss Fanning now went on: "This house—" she began, and stopped, turning her head, at the sound of a step on the stairs.

"My niece," she announced. "Natalie, here's the policeman, Captain Consadine."

Consadine looked up with interest, and considerable disappointment, at the woman Doctor Atkins found charming, a pale little woman in a bunchy blue cotton dress, her soft dark hair somewhat untidy. She gave him a vague little smile, a soft little hand, and sat down in a corner. She made no effort to start a conversation, she leaned back, her ankles modestly crossed, and the big and dreary room became silent.

"Would you like to see my garden, Captain Consadine?" asked Miss Fanning, suddenly.

"Very pleased," said Consadine, rising as she did, and following her down the hall and out of the front door. Brisk and straight and somehow modish, she led him along a gravel path to the back of the house, to four green wooden boxes set end to end on the ground. In them grew a few delicate little flowers, ghostly little flowers, stirring in the hot wind, blanched beneath the fierce sun.

"They're not worth looking at," she said, frowning. "Nothing will grow in this Godforsaken place."

She turned away from her flowers and stood looking out at the blue sea. "So you're a policeman," she said. "What made you come here?"

"Doctor Atkins was good enough—"

"It was the cat, wasn't it?" she asked.

"What cat?" asked Consadine.

"I suppose you heard about it in some roundabout way," she said. "Everything gets out, in this place where they have nothing to do but gossip and backbite from morning to night."

She fell silent, and Consadine let her alone. She didn't answer questions, she didn't let you finish a sentence; she went ahead, he thought, like a juggernaut.

"I'll tell you exactly how it happened," she said. "When we first came here, the house was overrun with mice, and I got a cat from the grocer, a young cat. I can't say I'm very fond of cats, but I like 'em better than vermin. I fed Nellie well, and she was earning her keep, catching mice. Well!"

She looked at Consadine, her thin lips compressed.

"I happened to get up extra early that morning," she said. "I daresay it was Howard Joblyn going downstairs that waked me, without my knowing it, because I'm a very light sleeper. Anyhow, the sun was just coming up when I looked out the window. And there was Howard Joblyn, streaking across the grass, in his dressing gown. He was carrying something, but I couldn't see what it was. He put whatever he was carrying down in one of my flower boxes, and he came hurrying back into the house. I got myself dressed, and I went out to see what he'd put in my flower box. And it was Nellie, the cat. I could see she was dying, and I telephoned for Doctor Willis, the veterinary, and he got here just before the cat died."

She was looking straight at Consadine.

"He didn't need to tell me Nellie'd been poisoned," she said. "I knew that already. We were standing there talking, when along came Howard Joblyn, and he told his story. He said he'd got up very early and gone down to the kitchen for a glass of milk. And he said he'd looked out the window and he'd seen Nellie, nibbling at one of my flowers. He said she must have eaten the foxglove."

Entirely too much foxglove, thought Consadine.

"Did Doctor Willis agree with that?" he asked.

"Yes."

"But you don't agree with him?"

"What do *you* think?" asked Miss Fanning.

"I suppose it's possible," said Consadine.

"Do you?"

"What explanation did Mr. Joblyn give you?" he asked.

"None," said she. "Because I never asked him for any."

"What's your object in that, Miss Fanning?"

"I don't want him to know that I'm on my guard," she said. "I want him to go right on with his schemes, and never suspect that I'm watching him. I'm not worrying. I can take care of myself very well indeed. But—" She paused. "If anything should happen to me," she said, "now you'll know where to look."

"No, I won't," said Consadine, finding a certain relish in speaking as bluntly as she.

"Howard Joblyn wants to get rid of me. For my money."

"You're leaving money to him?"

"No. To my niece. But she's a lackadaisical little thing. Once I was out of the way, Howard Joblyn would be able to get anything he wanted out of her. He hates me, too," she said, with a complacent smile.

"Have you anything definite—?" asked Consadine.

"Here he comes!" said Miss Fanning, "I'll tell you more later."

Joblyn was coming along the unshaded road, a thin, tall man with a black spade beard. He was wearing shorts and a white helmet, and he walked with an exaggerated action in his bony knees.

"Ah! Captain Consadine!" he cried. "We met once at the Yacht Club, I believe. This is a pleasure!"

"Thank you, sir," said Consadine.

"Anything official?" Joblyn asked. "Am I going to be deported as an undesirable alien, because I wear a beard?"

"No, sir," said Consadine. "Doctor Atkins brought me here to tea."

"Suppose we all go into the house, then," he said. "I think perhaps I can offer you something more interesting than tea."

Doctor Atkins had moved nearer to Mrs. Joblyn in her corner; they were talking quietly together when Joblyn and Consadine entered the room.

"Glad to see you, doctor!" said Joblyn, heartily. "And Natalie, how are you, my dear? Beginning to stand the heat better?"

"Yes, thank you, Howard," she answered, in her gentle little voice.

"What'll it be, people?" he asked. "I'd like to recommend my famous whisky sours. That suit everyone?"

"Very nice …" said the doctor.

"Very!" said Consadine.

"That suit you, Aunt Josephine?" asked Joblyn.

"I'll mix my own drink," said Miss Fanning.

Nice life for little Mrs. Joblyn with those two, thought Consadine. She sat in her corner, pale and quiet, with no air of being mistress in her own home. No … thought Consadine. A thin time, as the Americans say.

A thin time. A thin little woman, as if crushed out flat between two relentless opponents. Miss Fanning was talking to the doctor, and Consadine sat covertly watching the hostess as she leaned back, her hands clasped in her lap, her grey eyes fixed upon the wall before her. Fine eyes, she had, and pretty hands.

He saw her start; he saw her hands fly apart, her eyes grow wider; her lips opened as if she were about to speak, or to give a cry. She was looking into a mirror that hung on the wall, and the mirror faced the open door of the pantry where Joblyn was moving about. What had he done, to startle her so?

She recovered herself almost at once; she lowered her thick black lashes; her breast rose and fell in a long, quiet sigh. But Consadine was not satisfied; he wanted to know what she had seen in the mirror.

Joblyn came in now, carrying a tray of glasses, and directly he entered, Miss Fanning went into the pantry. Joblyn set the tray on a little pedestal table beside his wife, and the doctor and Consadine came forward, each to pick up a glass.

"Excellent!" said the doctor, politely, at his first sip.

"Excellent!" Consadine echoed, although he did not relish the acid lemon flavor.

Miss Fanning returned, carrying a glass with an air of triumph, and sat down on the end of the sofa. Almost at once there came a loud knocking at the back door, and she set her glass down on the pedestal table and rose.

"Pshaw!" she said. "That's old Crowell after his money."

She opened her purse and looked into it.

"Howard," she said, "will you be good enough to lend me five shillings?"

Joblyn rose and began to feel in his pockets, and the knocking at the door started again.

"Impudence!" cried Miss Fanning. "Thank you, Howard."

As she left the room, Joblyn began to talk, telling them of some experience of his in Canada; he laughed often, he imitated dialects, but he was not amusing.

Miss Fanning came back and flounced down on the sofa.

"That old Crowell ...!" she said. "Five shillings is far too much for the little work *he* did."

On and on she went, sipping her drink. And Consadine sipped his, and the sour lemon flavor set his teeth on edge.

"I'm sorry, Mrs. Joblyn," he said, suddenly, "but I'm afraid I'll have to be going."

"I'll drive you home," said the doctor.

"No!" cried Joblyn. "You've got to have another drink, you two."

They both declined, but he kept on, with embarrassing insistence.

"Just one more! Just a short one!"

It was as if he could not bear to let them go. He came to the car with them, taking Consadine's arm, while Doctor Atkins and Mrs. Joblyn stood on the veranda talking.

"Let me tell you a joke I heard the other day," said Joblyn, still holding Consadine's arm.

It was a long story, and in no way entertaining. The doctor had come up to them, and waited, his foot on the running board, while Joblyn went on and on.

"Ha ... Very good ..." said Consadine, at the first pause.

"Excellent!" said the doctor, and got into his car. They set off, leaving Joblyn standing in the treeless road before his cheerless house.

"Consadine," said the doctor, "there's something I think I ought to tell you."

"Go ahead," said Consadine.

"When Joblyn was in the pantry, mixing the drinks," said the doctor, "I happened to be standing by a mirror that gave me a plain view of him through the open door. I was watching him, for no particular reason, and I saw him take a small box out of his pocket and drop some tablets or pills into his drink."

"How d'you know it was his drink?" Consadine asked, sharply.

"Because he left it in the pantry when he brought the other drinks in on a tray," said Atkins. "Naturally, I kept an eye on him after that. I saw him go back and fetch his drink. After all the rest of us had ours."

"What did you think he was doing? Trying to commit suicide?"

"If I'd thought that," said the doctor, "naturally, I'd have intervened. But as I told you before, Consadine, I don't consider Joblyn at all a suicidal type."

"Then what do you think?"
"I don't know."

Consadine was dining at the Yacht Club that evening. He was sitting in the lounge and sipping a gin tonic, thinking about Joblyn and Miss Fanning. And about little Mrs. Joblyn. In a poisoning case, he thought, eight times out of ten it's— He smiled faintly to himself. *Cherchez spouse*, he thought, rather pleased with the phrase.

A waiter moved quietly to his side "Excuse me, sah, Doctor Atkins on the telephone."

Consadine went out into the hall where the booth was.

"Consadine?" said the doctor's voice, subdued and toneless. "I'm here, at Joblyn's. You'd better come at once."

"What's wrong?"

"Miss Fanning died a few moments ago. There are definite indications of—poisoning."

"I'll be there," said Consadine.

When he reached the ornate old house, it was blazing with lights; the neglected garden had a greenish glow like a stage jungle. As Consadine mounted the steps of the veranda, the doctor opened the door.

"I want to send for the ambulance," he said. "You'll order a post mortem, of course, and the sooner the better."

Consadine followed him up the stairs to a bedroom. The doctor turned down the sheet that covered Miss Fanning, and Consadine looked down at her for a moment.

"It was too late when I got here," the doctor said. "Mrs. Joblyn told me that as soon as we'd left. Miss Fanning complained of feeling ill, and came up here to rest. Mrs. Joblyn looked in on her several times, and she became very much worried. She wanted to send for me, but Miss Fanning wouldn't allow it. When she couldn't rouse Miss Fanning, she called me, but it was too late."

"You think it was digitalis?"

"The symptoms indicate that. But I'll need a chemical analysis."

"What time would you say she'd taken the stuff?"

"Judging from what Mr. and Mrs. Joblyn have told me about the onset of the symptoms, I should be inclined to say that the digitalis was taken probably—not certainly, but probably between four and five this afternoon."

"Well, we'll know more, later on," said Consadine. "You can send for the ambulance. Now, where are Joblyn and his wife?"

"I left them in the drawing-room. You'll bear in mind, Consadine, that this is a great shock to Mrs. Joblyn …?"

She did not look shocked. She was sitting in the same corner, in the same bunchy blue dress; she raised her pretty grey eyes to Consadine's face with a look of clear trust. Joblyn had been pacing up and down the room; he stopped now and stood with his head up, his chin outthrust, so that the black beard jutted out; he was pale, and sweating profusely, but he looked confident, even jaunty.

"This is a horrible thing, Captain," he said. "Horrible. Personally, I can't pretend to any great grief, but on my poor wife's account...."

He wants to talk, thought Consadine. Then by all means let him talk.

"It's what you might call a tragedy of errors," said Joblyn. "What you might call a strange, a striking example of poetic justice. You see, Captain, the poisoned drink was meant—for me!"

"Why d'you think that, Mr. Joblyn?"

"I *know* it," said Joblyn.

"Mr. Joblyn," said Consadine, "do you wish to make a statement?"

"I do," said Joblyn.

"I have to warn you, sir—"

"Oh, yes! I know!" said Joblyn, almost gaily. "It might be used against me. That doesn't worry me, Captain."

"Doctor Atkins can tell you about my visit to him," Joblyn went on. "That was the first time I was poisoned—"

"Just a moment, please," said Consadine. "You wish to state that you were poisoned, sir?"

"Yes!" said Joblyn. "Twice! Naturally, I knew who'd done it, but for my wife's sake, I tried to keep it quiet. I told both the doctors I'd been eating foxglove seeds, and—"

"Just a moment, please. What is the name of the person you believed had given you poison?"

"I'm sorry, on my wife's account," said Joblyn, "but the thing can't be kept quiet any longer. It was Josephine Fanning. She hated me. She tried in every way she knew to set my wife against me, and when that didn't work, she tried to kill me. You noticed how Miss Fanning insisted upon mixing her own drink this afternoon? How she went into the pantry alone? She used plenty of digitalis this time, and it was meant for me. Only, by some chance, the glasses were switched."

"Mr. Joblyn," Consadine said, looking up, "what were those pills you put into a drink this afternoon?"

"Pills …?" said Joblyn. "I? Pills?"

"I have a trustworthy witness, sir, who saw you—"

"Oh!" said Joblyn and laughed. "I'd forgotten that." He wiped his forehead with his handkerchief. "Here they are!" he said, and from the pocket of his shorts he brought out a little tin box labeled aspirin.

"Sodium bicarbonate," he explained. "I'm not much of a drinker; no head for it. So that when I do take a drink or so, to be sociable, I add a couple of these five-grain tablets. I've been told that sodium bicarb lessens the toxicity of alcohol."

He has a good story, thought Consadine. A damn good story.

"Take them, Captain!" said Joblyn, holding out the little box. And when Consadine made no move, he pushed the little box against his chest. "Take them! Get them analyzed! You won't find any digitalis here."

"Why do you think digitalis has been used, sir?" asked Consadine.

"Because Miss Fanning had digitalis in her possession," said Joblyn. "She had a prescription for it, from some doctor in New York—"

"But, Howard," said little Mrs. Joblyn, "Aunt Josephine never had that prescription filled."

There was a silence. Joblyn glanced at his wife, and again he wiped his forehead with his handkerchief.

"You're mistaken, my dear," he said. "I've seen your aunt taking those pills."

"But, Howard, I know I'm right!" said Mrs. Joblyn. "I went with Aunt Josephine to that doctor in New York, and she didn't like him. She told me she didn't believe there was anything the matter with her heart. She said she wouldn't touch his pills, and she wanted to tear up the prescription. But I begged her to give it to me, and I put in into my purse, in case she ever did want it, in a queer place like this."

"I'd like to see this prescription, Mrs. Joblyn," said Consadine.

"I'm so sorry," said Mrs. Joblyn, "but it disappeared out of my purse."

"When?"

"Well, let me see ..." she said frowning a little. "Oh, yes! The time I missed it was the day my husband had to go to Barbados for a week. I remember, because I had to clean out my purse, to look for a paper my husband wanted, before he left." She laughed, a little sadly. "I never did find it," she said.

Joblyn's story was no longer damn good, and Joblyn was no longer jaunty.

"Mr. Joblyn," said Consadine, "you understand that if you had a prescription filled in Barbados, we can easily trace it?"

Joblyn was looking at his wife as if he had never really seen her before.

"Yes ..." he said. "That's what I did. Yes. I'll tell you the whole thing. The truth."

He sat leaning forward with his hands on his knees, his dark eyes desperately earnest; with his beard and his bony bare legs and arms he looked, Consadine thought, like one of those ancient prophets you see in paintings.

"I swear before God," he said, "that what I'm telling you now is the truth."

"You wish to retract the statement you've already made?"

"Yes. I swear before God that this is the truth. I didn't want to tell it—because—I didn't want to. It—the whole thing—was an attempt to discredit Miss Fanning. That's *all* it was. I swear I never intended—never thought of doing her any actual harm. She made trouble between us, between my wife and me. My wife has a little money of her own—very little—two or three thousand dollars. I—I—wanted to borrow it. For a project. For—research. But Miss Fanning's influence ... When I went to Doctor Atkins and the other doctor, I'd taken digitalis myself. I wanted it to be traced back to Miss Fanning. To—discredit her."

"What about the cat?" asked Consadine.

"I didn't mean to kill it. I—I simply wanted to observe the symptoms, so that I could—act more convincingly."

"And this afternoon?" asked Consadine.

"I put some digitalis pills into my drink. *My own drink*. If anyone saw me, then they saw it was my own glass. I used a lot of the stuff. I meant to drink a little, just a little. Just enough to produce symptoms—while you were here, Captain. I thought you'd investigate. I thought—I intended you to find the box of digitalis pills upstairs, with Miss Fanning's name on it. Miss Fanning's prescription ... I put the pills into *my own drink*. It was never meant for *her*. But somehow the glasses must have been shifted."

He was silent for a moment; then he turned quickly to his wife.

"Come to think of it ..." he said. "You were sitting here by the table all the time, Natalie. You were the only one who didn't move about the room at all. You—perhaps *you* moved the glasses on the table, Natalie? I mean—pushed them around?"

She was looking at him with her clear gaze.

"Is that what you *want* me to say, Howard?" she asked, earnestly.

"Mrs. Joblyn!" cried the doctor.

"I want to say whatever will *help* Howard," said Mrs. Joblyn.

Mr. Parry, for the defense, did his best, and it was a brilliant best. His client, he told the jury, would not deny that he had plotted to discredit Miss Fanning. But before judging his actions too severely, consider, gentlemen, the provocation.

He presented a picture of Joblyn, the devoted husband of a lovely young wife, driven to desperation by Miss Fanning's efforts to ruin his marriage, to destroy his whole life's happiness. He described Natalie Joblyn as a faithful and affectionate wife, but unduly influenced by the aunt who had brought her up, and perhaps without any great strength of character.

Howard Joblyn's story might be called fantastic. He did not deny that it was fantastic; a plot such as would occur only to a scientist, immersed in his work, and pitiably lacking in worldly wisdom. It was fantastic, if you like, but every statement made by Joblyn was supported by evidence. He called Captain Consadine and Doctor Atkin to attest that Miss Fanning had gone into the pantry alone to mix her own drink, *after* Joblyn had distributed the other drinks. His client did not deny that he had put digitalis tablets into his own glass, for the purpose of inducing symptoms, which he believed would be attributed to Miss Fanning's machinations, thus discrediting her and forcing her to leave his household. But an unforeseen, a monstrous accident occurred.

The Commissioner of Police himself, as well as Doctor Atkins, has given evidence, gentlemen, that all the glasses used on that afternoon were identical in size and shape; the drinks in them were identical; there was no way to distinguish one from the other. And, for a moment, on the occasion of a trifling disturbance, Howard Joblyn and Miss Fanning both set their glasses down on the same table, among the other three glasses. The same two unimpeachable witnesses have attested to that.

"I now call Mrs. Joblyn," said Parry.

She was in mourning, and she looked very pretty, very young. Mr. Parry led up to his question gently, almost tenderly. Yes, Mrs. Joblyn had sat all afternoon beside the table where the glasses stood.

"Mrs. Joblyn," said Parry, "did you at any time move any of those glasses?"

"Yes," she answered, resolutely, "I put my husband's glass where my aunt's had been, and her glass where he'd left his."

She remained resolute under cross examination.

"I don't know why I did it," she said. "I just did."

Had she moved, or touched any of the other glasses on the table? No, just those two. No, she had had no purpose in doing so. I just did it, she said.

Sir Hector Lomax, the Attorney General, said that he was amazed, and he looked so, a tall, thin man with a monocle and haughtily-arched brows. He was amazed, he said, by the defense—if defense it could be called—that had been offered to them. The accused admitted that he purchased—in Barbados—with a stolen prescription—the poison which later caused the death of the unfortunate Miss Fanning. The accused was seen, by no less a witness than the Commissioner of Police, putting pellets, tablets, pills, whatever you wish, into a glass of whisky. Miss Fanning drank from that glass. And died. You have heard something of the hostility that existed between the accused and the unfortunate lady. You have been informed that the wife of the accused is the sole heir of the late Miss Fanning's considerable estate.

The defense, the entire defense, rests upon the assumption that, by accident, the deceased somehow obtained possession of the wrong glass. The defense has called only one witness to the fact that *any* glasses were changed, or moved, by anyone. Gentlemen, you have heard that witness. If you are convinced that this witness—the wife of the accused—shifted *just those two* glasses, among the five on the table, and for no reason whatever....

I suggest, said Sir Hector, that this witness should never have been brought into court. Legally, she could not be required to testify against her husband. But I suggest that, in her innocence, and acting under instructions not properly understood, she *has* testified against her husband by a statement unacceptable to a reasoning mind.

Gentlemen of the jury, Sir Hector said, I consider this the most audacious crime that has ever come within my experience. A murder committed in the very presence of the Commissioner of Police....

On the evening of the day the trial ended, the glass began to fall.

"Hurricane weather ..." Atkins said, sitting beside Consadine in the Yacht Club lounge. "Very oppressive."

"And they found Joblyn guilty," said Consadine, slouched in his chair in an attitude of gloomy dejection very uncharacteristic of him.

"I was talking to Sir Hector," said the doctor. "He doesn't think Joblyn will hang."

"I don't, either," said Consadine. "There'll be an appeal—a commutation, something of the sort. No ... It's the damned injustice of the thing. *She* killed Miss Fanning, of course."

He had never said this before to the doctor, but Atkins showed no shock, or even surprise.

"You can't be sure, Consadine," he said. "You don't know that she saw Joblyn put the pills into his glass."

"I do know," said Consadine, "I told Parry about it. But, as he said, you can't go into court and say you saw a woman give a start and begin to stare into a mirror. That's not evidence."

He stretched out his legs and lit another cigarette.

"I don't think she meant to kill her aunt," he went on. "I happen to believe Joblyn's story. But Mrs. Joblyn didn't know anything about that, and when she saw her husband doping a drink, she'd naturally think it was meant for Miss Fanning. It's my opinion that she switched the glasses, hoping to get rid of Joblyn, meaning to give him what she thought he'd fixed for Miss Fanning."

"You have no evidence …" said the doctor.

"No. None," said Consadine. "Well, anyhow, she's succeeded. Poor Parry was nearly out of his mind, when he heard her statement on the stand. He told me he'd coached her so carefully. She was to have said simply that she remembered shoving the glasses about on the table, in an aimless sort of way. That would have been easy to believe. And it might have saved Joblyn. But to this moment, Parry believes that the outrageous statement she made on the stand was a touching attempt to help her husband."

"Perhaps it was …" said the doctor.

"No," said Consadine, curtly. "She didn't say much, either in court, or while Joblyn was making his statement to me. But every word she did say tightened the noose around Joblyn's neck. She knew it. She's got rid of her husband and her aunt now, both the people who were bullying her, and she's inherited a nice little fortune."

He sat up straight.

"Sir Hector and his talk about Joblyn's 'most audacious crime' …!" he cried, angrily. "And how about little Mrs. Joblyn? She tried to murder her husband right under Sir Hector's nose …!"

"You did everything humanly possible to help Joblyn, Consadine."

"It wasn't good enough," said Consadine. "I've failed."

The doctor rose and crossed the room to the barometer that hung on the wall. He began tapping it with one knuckle, as if knocking at a door that was not going to open.

I've failed, Consadine said to himself.

Then another thought came into his mind. But, by God, I was right! he cried to himself. Before there was any crime committed at all, I knew who was going to do it.

The Daring Doctor

Lieutenant Dennis Consadine, newly-appointed Deputy Commissioner of Police in the Caribbean island of St. Jerome, was a very fortunate young man. His new job was almost entirely routine work, paperwork, patient dealing with idiot complaints; the pay was nothing wonderful, the lovely little island was subject to droughts, hurricanes, and occasional earthquakes. But he had been blessed at birth with one of the greatest gifts a man can have, a steadfast and cheerful confidence in himself.

Oh, *you* think you can do *anything!* his older sister had used to cry, in exasperation. And so he did. If he set out to climb a tree, up to a squirrel's nest, and he fell and hurt himself, that did not seem a failure to him. He simply lay in bed, and planned how he would do it next time, when his leg was mended.

He had a bull-neck, broad shoulders, and a deep chest. His curly black hair grew low on his forehead, and he had quick, deep-set dark eyes, and a long, humorous upper lip. But his looks had never been a handicap to him; he was liked wherever he went, and that included the ladies. And why not? He expected people to like him just as he expected to succeed in what he undertook.

He was sitting in his office this morning, studying a new form that had just been sent to him from London. What arrangements have been instituted in your district, he was asked, for the psychiatric examination of a: accused prisoners, b: convicted prisoners, c: juvenile offenders, and so on and on. Through the open door he could see the anteroom, where his invaluable Sergeant Mayblossom sat at his desk typing, a stout colored man, looking soft as a teddy bear in his very snug white uniform, but in reality hard and muscular and alert, knowing everything about the island.

He rose now, and quickly and quietly closed the door of Consadine's office. That meant that some unofficial visitor had come in. And, when he could, he disposed of nuisances without troubling Consadine.

But this time he could not. For a time, Consadine heard a woman's voice behind the door; the words were inaudible, but the tone was unpleasant as the buzzing of a fly, flat, insistent, running over the deep, grave sound of Mayblossom's voice. After a time, the Sergeant knocked at the door and entered.

"Lady here, sah ..." he said, grimly. "American lady. And she say she sit here till she see the Captain. Tell she no Captain here. Ask she to write down complaint. But she will not, sah! She say it a Personation Case, very serious."

"Know who she is, Sergeant? A tourist?"

"No, sah. Name is Cobby, and husband a learned man. They rent one of Mr. Olsen's houses for one year, sah."

Olsen's houses were small, cheap, and unfashionable, not attractive to tourists.

"Husband a professor, sah," the Sergeant went on. "Come down here to write a great book. Everybody speak well of he."

"And how do they speak about Mrs. Cobby?"

"Mrs. Cobby don't partake of social life, sah. But—" He paused. "Nobody like to work for she."

"Know why?"

"Only hear gossip, sah. Say she very mean. But she say this a Personation Case, and very serious, and she sit here, sah …"

"Well, bring her in," said Consadine.

Another crank, another nuisance. But it was part of his job to deal with them, and he had been remarkably successful, so far. He rose as Mrs. Cobby entered, and he smiled. But not she. She was a stout and shapeless woman, horribly dressed; a round Panama hat with a long blue-and-white dotted scarf hanging down her back was perched upon her lank grey hair; she wore a dark purple silk blouse buttoned up to the chin, a long skirt of black denim, black oxfords. She had a wide, tight mouth, turned-up nose, small, chilly blue eyes, and, incongruously, a soft pink-and-white complexion.

"Sit down, Mrs. Cobby!" he said, and she did sit down, in *his* swivel-chair, behind the desk.

This was a complication. He did not like asking her to move, but he would, he felt, be altogether too much at a disadvantage if he left her there, and sat in the straight chair on the wrong side of the desk.

"It's a bit cooler over here—" he began.

"I never thought it was a good idea to come to this tropic isle," said Mrs. Cobby. "I didn't, indeed. I said all I could, but the Professor had this notion that here and here only could he finish writing this wonderful book of his. It's his Sabbatical year, you know, and why we couldn't spend it in our own home, in peace and quiet, I do not know. But come here he would."

"I'm sorry …" said Consadine, with an air of polite sympathy. "If you'll sit over here, Mrs. Cobby, you'll find it cooler—"

"I don't care *where* I sit, I'm sure," she said. "I'm so upset about this case. And I cannot get the Professor to take it seriously. No. He'll wait till we're all murdered in our beds before he'll take any steps about this impersonation."

"If you'll just sit over here, Mrs. Cobby, and give me a resume …?"

Her little cold blue eyes regarded him fixedly. "Sit over there?" she repeated. Apparently she grasped what he wanted. "It doesn't matter where I sit," she said, and did not move. "I haven't any time to waste," she went on. "This woman I've got now … She calls herself a cook, but I say—" She gave a dry, short laugh. "*I* say she does a lot more *eating* than *cooking*. I'll have to get back to the house, or she'll be feeding half the island."

"Now, if you'll give me the facts, Mrs. Cobby …" said Consadine. He had given up about his chair; he remained standing, and trying to look alert and amiable. But she's the most damn' irritating woman I ever came across, he thought. That voice …

"No," said Mrs. Cobby. "Come to this tropic isle we must, because this wonderful book couldn't be written in the United States. And we must bring this Danish girl, if you please. Here she is, with a nice room all to herself, and servants to wait on her, and that typewriter clattering and rattling so that you don't know where to go, for a little peace and quiet. Well!" She laughed again. "I suppose that when there's a great masterpiece being written, the rest of us have to make sacrifices."

"This case …?" said Consadine. "Has someone been annoying you, Mrs. Cobby?"

"Annoying me?" she repeated. "That's not what I'd call it. No! This man is impersonating my husband, all over the island."

"What man?" Consadine asked.

"Doctor Pauli, he calls himself, but what his true name is nobody knows. The very first time he came, I knew there was something queer. But that girl Karen, she was completely carried away. I've told her she's not to let anybody set foot in the house on Wednesday nights—"

"Why Wednesday, Mrs. Cobby?"

"That's the night the Professor and I go to the movies," said Mrs. Cobby. "Well, three weeks ago, as soon as we're out of the house, this Doctor Pauli comes ringing and jingling the doorbell, and up jumps this Karen, and opens the door! 'Oh,' she says, 'at first I thought it was the Professor. And when I saw that it wasn't, I didn't want to ask him to leave. He was so *pleased*,' says she. I dare say he was. All these swindlers and impostors are 'pleased.' It's part of their stock in trade. So there he was, if you please, sitting on *my* veranda, and telling that girl his wonderful tale. He's a professor, too, he says, from some foreign country, Vienna, or some such place. Then, off he goes before we get home."

"Well …?" said Consadine.

"*I* don't think it's 'well'," said Mrs. Cobby. "I think it's very queer, and dangerous. Because, if you please, back he comes—the next Wednesday night! The one night we're always out."

"Did he know you'd be out?"

"Oh, no!" she said, with that ugly little laugh. "Oh, no! He's as innocent as an unborn lamb. He says he's come again, to see Professor Cobby. Out Karen goes, and sits on the veranda, talking to him. Such fun to talk to, she says. Fun, indeed! And the rest of his gang prowling around the back of the house, most likely."

"Was this Karen alone in the house, Mrs. Cobby? No servants there?"

"No, *thank* you!" said Mrs. Cobby. "I cannot and I will not have any of those native people sleeping in my house. The woman comes in time to get breakfast—always late, too, and she goes home after she's washed the dinner dishes. And what she takes with her would feed a regiment. Scraps, she says."

"Has the man come again?"

"No," she said. "But he wrote a note, out there on the veranda, and left it for us. Here it is."

She stood a great, shiny black bag on the desk and opened it, and brought out a folded piece of lined paper, torn from a notebook.

"Dear Colleague!

"It would seem that Bad Luck is pursuing! Two times I come in the hope to see you, and two times am I disappointed!

"So, now I propose a new stratagem! Will not you and your lady-wife be my guests at dinner, what evening you shall appoint, at the Hotel Royal Duke? I am changing my lodgings, but a reply to this little shop will reach me. Hackey's Cosy Corner, Burnt Rocks.

"Your work in the glorious history of United States is well-known to me, and esteemed most highly. It is perhaps too much to hope that you have heard of my little works on the great Thomas Jefferson and Benjamin Franklin. But, I hope for the honor to entertain you soon!

"With sincere respect to your lady-wife, and to yourself, my esteemed colleague, please believe me

"Your most humble servant,
"Thomas Pauli.

"President Vienna Institute
of Comparative History."

"Well?" said Mrs. Cobby, as Consadine returned the note.

"Afraid I don't quite see …" said Consadine. "Do you mean that this man is impersonating a Doctor Pauli?"

"Indeed I don't!" said she. "*He's* impersonating the Professor!"

"But—"

"Three times it's happened," she said. "This woman I sometimes talk to, at the market, she said to me that she'd seen the Professor at Moon Beach the day before."

"And she hadn't?"

"Indeed no! He was in his own house working, that afternoon. Then this young man from the Cable Company who keeps dropping in … Karen encourages him. He said he'd seen the Professor in the bar at the Royal Duke. The Professor's never been in a bar in his life, and he's not going to start now, at his age."

"Do you know where your husband was, at the time he was reported—?"

"I do, indeed! He was fishing."

"And the third time?"

"The third time was yesterday," she said. "And *I* was the one who saw him. Here, in the town, it was. I'd been buying some new teacups—I believe that cook breaks them on purpose—and when I came out of the shop, there he was, just ahead of me, walking up that hill to the Post Office. I called 'Henry! Henry!' But he didn't answer. So I hurried after him, and I tapped him on the shoulder, and he turned around. And it wasn't Henry!"

"You mean there's a strong resemblance between your husband and this Doctor Pauli?"

"It's a lot more than that!" said she. "He had a white suit, and a straw hat, exactly like Henry's. And he walked like Henry. He was trying to be like Henry. If I hadn't had a good look at him, in the bright sunlight, I'd have been sure it was Henry."

"Did his face resemble your husband's?"

"Indeed it didn't!" she said. "It was a nasty face, sneering and jeering. And what's more—" Her little eyes glittered with triumph. "He was wearing a red *necktie*. You know what *that* means!"

He knew what she thought it meant. "That's not necessarily—"

"He's a Communist!" she said. "Who else would go prancing around the streets in a red necktie? The whole thing's a Communist plot, and that girl Karen is in it. I dare say she's only a cat's-paw, but those Europeans can't be trusted. Why else would this Pauli man know when we'd be out?"

"Then why should Miss—Karen have told you about his coming to the house?"

"She was ordered to. That's how they work. Blind obedience. No questions asked."

"Yes … but, Mrs. Cabby, to be frank with you, I can't see that you have any cause for complaint against this Doctor Pauli. He hasn't committed any injury, hasn't made any threats. Why don't you accept this invitation of his, and have a talk with him?"

She rose, pushing herself up by her hands on the arms of the chair.

"*I see!*" she said. "*I* see! This man is impersonating my husband, making people think they've seen him in bars, and goodness knows where else, ruining his reputation. He's come sneaking and skulking to our house twice when he knew we'd be out, and who's to know if he didn't get at the Professor's papers?"

"Has your husband any notes or papers of a secret or confidential nature, Mrs. Cobby?"

"Certainly! Everything about this wonderful book of his is a secret. I'm not allowed to see one word of it, not me. Not his wife. Oh, no! Only this girl, and heaven knows who *she* is."

"Is your husband a scientist, Mrs. Cobby?"

"Ask him," she said, "or that girl. Not me. *I'm* only his wife. But it doesn't matter. I see very well how things are. You're on that Pauli man's side. I needn't expect any help from you and your policemen. Very well! I'll write to Washington. I'll tell them that an American citizen is being impersonated by a Communist in your British colony."

"I'll look into the matter, Mrs. Cobby," said Consadine, invincibly good-humored. "And in the meantime, don't worry, will you? You can telephone us, you know, at any time, day or night."

And you will, he thought, with resignation. *You will!* He opened the door for her, and she went out, past Sergeant Mayblossom, and into the corridor.

"Cranks," he said, "take up a lot of our time, Sergeant."

"That is right, sah," said Mayblossom, gravely. "But we know they got to be heeded. In the war days, we had to take on extra men to handle the reports kept coming in, telephones, unanymous letters, people coming in person. Saw a strange light, saw someone flashing signals, heard someone speaking in the German tongue. Baseless rumors, the most of them, but now and then …"

"Now and then one was right," said Consadine. "Yes … That's a primary rule in police work, eh, Mayblossom? Never ignore a crank. Because he may put you on the track of something important."

"You are right, sah!" said Mayblossom. "And also he can be up to something queer hisself. They are cunning, sah, sly as a mongoose."

"Yes. Now get me the Immigration people, will you?"

He went back to his desk, and his own chair now, and presently a call came through. "Department of Immigration," said a girl's voice, fatigued and annoyed.

"Lieutenant Consadine speaking. Will you see what you've got on a Doctor Pauli." He spelt the name. "Tomas Pauli, from Vienna."

"Very well, Lieutenant," she said, implying by her tone that she would do her duty, no matter what brutal and unreasonable demands were made upon her. "I'll call you back."

Consadine lit a cigarette, and looked at Constable Green's report upon the arrest of a 'prowler'. The telephone rang.

"Henderson speaking, Lieutenant. We haven't turned up anything about a Doctor Pauli. Mind spelling the name? Thanks. When did he come here?"

"I don't know," said Consadine. "I don't know anything about him, and I'd like to. He couldn't be here without having gone through your hands, could he?"

"Not possibly. Of course, he may be using another name from the one on his passport. That happens, you know, and we don't like it much. We'd better check. Where does your Doctor Pauli live?"

"Changing his lodgings, he said, and picking up his mail at Hacky's Cosy Corner, at Burnt Rocks."

"But, look here, Lieutenant! Aliens are required to notify you people of any changes of address."

"We haven't had any such notification for weeks."

"Well …" said Henderson. "I'll grub around in the files a bit more. But I'm damn sure we haven't any Pauli."

"Just a minute! What about a Professor Cobby, an American, and his wife, and a Danish girl with them?"

"Very fine girl," said Henderson. "Very! Intelligent, and all that."

Doesn't sound too fascinating, Consadine thought. Henderson was continuing. "The Professor's absolutely sound. Came here to write a book. Professor at Columbia. What? No. I don't know what he teaches. He's a nice fellow. But the missis! Oh, lor'!"

"Yes," said Consadine. "She's just been here. Well, let me know if you turn up anything that might apply to this Pauli, will you?"

He then left the office in charge of Sergeant Mayblossom, and got into his little car, to drive out to Burnt Rocks. I'll look into this myself, he thought. It's too damn vague and nebulous to put anyone else on it. This Pauli hasn't done anything objectionable, as far as I can see. As for his impersonating the Professor, there's no reason to believe that. What motive would he have for that? No. There's often a chance resemblance between strangers that's very striking. And if they're both professors … For all I know, all professors may look more or less alike.

He drove steadily along the East Shore Road that ran over the top of the low cliffs where grass and bush grew, parched and yellow now in the dry season. It's not a case at all, he thought. Only, it's a bit queer about this Pauli. No record of him, no address. Even if he isn't up to anything wrong, it's queer, in a place like this.

Hacky's Cosy Corner belied its name. It was a small wooden shed with a corrugated iron roof, standing forlorn under the burning sun on the empty road. Inside there was a counter, three or four stools, a glass case so low that any customer would need to bend double to see the sad little collection of bead necklaces, paper fans, playing cards, pink and blue cellophane boxes. On three sides were shelves, stocked with tinned foods, hammers, nails, toys, patent medicines, paper novels, paint brushes, an assortment so varied, so confused, that Hacky himself had long ago given up. He would serve you with ginger ale, pink, yellow and white sodas, at the counter, but anything else you wanted, find it for yourself.

He was a clean but somewhat ragged old colored man, wizened and bald and melancholy.

"Perfesser Pauli? Yes, sah, I know he. He come in here, and he pay me a pound, if'n I keep he mail. I say I will do so, sah, only ain't no mail ever come. What he look like?" This question seemed to dismay Hacky momentarily; he stared at Consadine. Then:

"He a pleasant-spoken gentleman, sah. Grey hair. Tall or short? He betwixt and between, sah. No, sah; not fat. He spry. No, sah, I do not know where he live. I do not know where he come from or where he going to, when he leave here. No, sah; he don't come in no car. Come on foot. Might be he get out of the bus down the road." His toothless mouth stretched in a grin. "Might be he flew down out of the sky, sah. Or climb out of the sea."

"Might be," said Consadine. "Next time he comes in, Hacky, try him with a few questions. Notice all you can about him, clothes, so on. Ask your neighbors about him. And if you get any information, let us have it."

"I will do so, sah!" said Hacky.

Now then, thought Consadine, getting back into his car, we'll have to take this to headquarters. I'll have a word with Professor Cobby himself.

The Cobbys lived on the outskirts of the town, in a district of depressing and impoverished gentility. Their old wooden house stood on a corner, with overgrown empty lots on either side; cramped and narrow, it had the look of a disdainful spinster drawing up her shoulders. The small garden in front was neglected, with purple morning glories running riot over everything. He went up onto the veranda and rang the bell. The door was opened by Mrs. Cobby.

"Oh!" she said, with that little laugh. "So here you are, Captain!"

"Lieutenant," he said. "Yes, I'm looking into this matter, Mrs. Cobby.

Now, if I could see the Professor for a few moments—"

"No," she said, flatly.

"I'm afraid it's necessary—"

"Well, it isn't," she said. "He's busy. I'll come to your office tomorrow morning and tell you anything you want to know."

She tried to push the door shut, but Consadine kept it open with his shoulder.

"What's this? What's this?" asked an amiable voice, and over Mrs. Cabby's shoulder Consadine saw a slim, straight, grey-haired man in pince-nez.

"Professor Cobby?" he asked. "Lieutenant Consadine, Deputy Police Commissioner. If you could spare me a few moments, sir—"

"By all means!" said the Professor. "Anna, my dear …" He smiled at Consadine. "Mrs. Cobby is very jealous in protecting my working hours," he said. "But when it's a case of the police …! Come in, Lieutenant."

It was an ugly little house, hot, dim, overcrowded with cheap and tasteless furniture and with no trace of a tropic atmosphere, not so much as a flower to be seen. The Professor led the way to the dining room. The center table was covered with books and papers, the sideboard too, and in a corner a girl was sitting before a typewriter on another table.

She rose as they entered, and looked up at Consadine with a half-anxious smile; she was a little thing, fair-haired and grey-eyed, slim and very neat in a brown and white checked gingham dress. The word for her, Consadine thought, was 'appealing.'

"Karen," said the Professor, with a sort of academic archness, "the police … In the person of Lieutenant Consadine. Lieutenant, my invaluable secretary, Miss Jensen. Sit down, Karen. Sit down, Lieutenant!"

In came Mrs. Cobby, closing the door after her. "I *don't* see," she said, "I don't, indeed, see why the professor has to be disturbed in the middle of this great book. He's never seen this Doctor Pauli, and what you imagine he can tell you I do not know."

"Oh, it's—apropos of Pauli?" said the Professor. "My wife is convinced that he's a sinister character—impersonating me, and so on. But I think her anxiety is—" He smiled again. "Unnecessary," he said. "I hope to see the doctor before long, and then perhaps I can reassure my wife. I know something of his work. Along the same lines as mine."

"Is it scientific work, sir?" Consadine asked.

"Well …" said the Professor, again somewhat arch. "Not unless you will concede that history is a science. American history—"

"Why they should be called Americans I cannot understand," Mrs. Cobby interposed. "These Ponce de Leons and Pere Marquettes,

Frenchmen and Spaniards and Englishmen ... And now this Doctor Pauli, another foreigner—"

"I see!" said Consadine, politely enough. "Now, sir, if you can give me any information—"

But the Professor had none to give; he had never seen Pauli; he had no idea where he might be living, or when he had come to the island.

"Miss Jensen," said Consadine. "You've seen Doctor Pauli twice, I understand? Can you give me a description of him?"

"Not a very good one," she answered. "Because, you see, both times it was in a dim light—"

"*I'm* the only one who's seen this man in the bright daylight," said Mrs. Cobby. "He's a nasty, sly-looking creature."

"I thought he was—very agreeable," said Karen. "Very gay, very courteous. He had little jokes, you know. And highly educated!"

She was enthusiastic about Doctor Pauli, and that, Consadine thought, might be a mark against the doctor. Plausible swindlers were only too often admired by pretty young females. No, she answered Consadine, Doctor Pauli had not told her where he lived, had not said anything that could provide a clue.

"You mistook him for Professor Cobby, Miss Jensen?"

"Only for a moment. There was not much light."

And she had nothing else to tell. "Only, he's *nice*," she said.

Mrs. Cobby gave her short ugly little laugh.

"Oh, yes!" she said. "Very nice, I dare say! Worming his way to this house, and ruining the professor's reputation—a typical Communist. Maybe *you* dote on Communists, but *I* don't."

The girl rose and went quietly out of the room, and Consadine rose, too. He had found out nothing at all, and he wanted to get away. It was not easy, though, to escape from Mrs. Cobby. She blocked his way, her flat voice going on and on, her bitter spite and suspicion toward Pauli, a more veiled malice against the girl Karen, resentment and contempt toward her husband. He intervened, from time to time. Come now, Anna, my dear ... No reason to be upset, my dear ...

In the old days, Consadine thought, when at last he got out of the house, they used to take women like that, dunk them in a pond. A shrew. A common scold. A sound idea, too. They're dangerous troublemakers.

He drove down the quiet street, past the quiet, dreary little houses, and he was about to turn into the highway when a small figure in a neat checked dress waved at him from the roadside.

"Could I speak to you, please?" she asked.

"Hop in," he said, "and we can drive a bit."

"I'm sorry, but if I'm not back in ten minutes, she'll carry on so—"

"She's pretty difficult to get along with I imagine," he said.

"Yes," Karen said, and was silent, standing in the full blaze of the sun, a green silk handkerchief tied over her bright hair. "It's horrible."

"I'm sorry for the Professor."

"I'm not," said Karen.

"You're not?" Consadine asked, surprised. "It seems to me pretty hard for him, with a wife like that."

"He shouldn't have a wife like that," said Karen. "He should have stopped her, in the beginning. He shouldn't have let her bully and humiliate him. It's his fault, all his fault."

"Easy enough to say. But, after all, a man can't be bickering all the time. A man wants a little peace and quiet—"

"Peace—at any price?" said Karen. "I think it's shameful, to let yourself be trampled on, instead of showing pride and courage. And it's cruel, too. To her."

"To *her*, eh?"

"Certainly! When he lets her act like that, he hates her for it. It's all *his* fault. If you knew ..." There were tears in her eyes, and she tried to blink them away. "My father sent me here, to finish my education—and I took two of Professor Cobby's courses at Columbia, in American history. He was—not only a fine scholar, but so witty, and original ... Everybody in his classes admired him, and respected him so ... When he offered me this job, I wrote home—how happy I was, and how proud. I— didn't know. And I wish, I wish I'd never found out—what he's really like."

"Look here!" said Consadine. "Get into the car, and we'll drive a bit. You're crying, you know."

"No, thank you. I just wanted to tell you this. I—well, I don't want to sound conceited, but I'm pretty sure that Doctor Pauli likes me, rather a lot."

"That's not hard to believe," said Consadine.

"The last time he came, I think he knew that the Professor and Mrs. Cobby wouldn't be home. It would be easy enough to find out. The cook knows, and she could tell other people. And I—well, I have an idea he'll come tonight."

"You think so?"

"And if he does," she said, "I'm going to tell him the whole thing. About Mrs. Cobby going to the police, and saying he's impersonating the professor, and that he's a Communist. I'm going to warn him, so that he can defend himself. Because he's a *nice* man. Please don't think I'm silly about him. He's old enough to be my father. I just *like* him. He's intelligent, and gay, and polite. And nice."

"I see …!" said Consadine.

"Now I'll have to hurry home," she said. "And next week, I'm going back to New York."

"I see!" said Consadine, again.

I like that girl, he thought. And I'm damn sorry for her. Sorry she's been so disillusioned about her precious Cobby, and now I'm afraid she's going to get another shock about her 'nice' Pauli.

Because there's something wrong about him, something very wrong, very queer. I don't know whether he's actually impersonating Cobby and I have no idea if he's a Communist, or not. But I think he's a crook. He's an alien, and not registered, and nobody knows where he lives, or when he came here, or what he's doing. No. I'll have to have a little talk with Pauli. As soon as it was dark, he drove back. He left the car on the next street, and he waited on the corner, behind a tree, until he saw the Professor and Mrs. Cobby come out of the garden and start down the street. They walked slowly; for a long time her flat, persistent voice floated back to him.

Then, when they were out of sight, he opened the gate, and entered the unkempt little garden, to the hiding place he had already chosen, behind a clump of bushes. He sat down on the ground, hands clasped around his knees, and he waited, with the patience that was essential to his profession. He wanted a cigarette; he wanted to stand up; he felt a sudden and almost irresistible impulse to cough. But he stayed quiet; he waited.

The shabby street was very quiet. Now and then a car went by, or footsteps sounded; a night bird made a gurgling sound; in the distance someone whistled a mournful calypso song. And all the time, from inside the house, came the muffled clicking of a typewriter. I'll bet she's a good worker, he thought. A good kid. A pretty kid. I'm sorry.

There were footsteps in the street again, hurrying, and in a moment the gate creaked. He looked out through the bushes, and he saw a quick, light figure going up the path. But Cobby? How did he get here without the missus?

The man went up the steps, and Consadine heard the bell jingle inside the house. In a moment, Karen opened the door, and light flowed out. And it was not Cobby; it was a man with thick dark hair, and he wore a jaunty yellow and black striped bow tie.

"Tonight I have good fortune?" he asked, a marked accent in his cheerful voice. "I find my colleague at home?"

"Well, no, Doctor Pauli," Karen answered, and her voice sounded very young and earnest. Consadine could see her fair hair glitter. "Doctor Pauli, I wish you'd tell me … You knew the Professor wouldn't be here, didn't you?"

"Yes," he said, after a moment. "I confess. It is you I wish to see, Miss Karen. Before I come here for the first time, I see you, in the garden, in the street, many times."

"But you don't have to come in this—this secret sort of way. I don't like—"

The gate creaked again, and it was Mrs. Cobby who entered, a shapeless form moving slowly and heavily.

"Don't let her see me!" cried Pauli. "Let me in!"

"I'm sorry, but I can't let you into the house—"

"Let me in!" he cried. "She mustn't see me! I'll get out by the back door."

"No!" Karen said. "You can't!"

But he pushed her aside and entered the house, slamming the door behind him. Mrs. Cobby came up the steps.

"Aha!" she said. "So *that's* how it is! Aha!"

"I'm sorry—"

"Oh, yes! You're sorry. So the Professor's in it *with* you, I see! We never sit together in the movies, you know. I have to sit up front, because I'm nearsighted, and he has to sit as far back as he can. Well, tonight the picture was a nasty, immoral one, and I wouldn't stay. I got up, and I walked back to where I'd left him. And he'd gone. So along I came, and just in time to see you letting that Pauli man into my house."

"I'm sorry he got in, Mrs. Cobby," said Karen. "But he was going right out by the back door."

"Oh, no, he won't!" said Mrs. Cobby. "No, indeed, he won't. The back door's locked, and I have the key in my purse. And the screens are all nailed to the windows. Oh, no! Your fine Doctor Pauli won't get out. He's in my house this very moment, and I'm going to see him. He's in there, plotting and planning with my husband."

"The Professor hasn't come home, Mrs. Cobby."

"Oh, indeed? You expect me to believe that, do you? Do you think I don't know that the three of you, my husband, your fine Doctor Pauli, and you, sit here in my house, hatching up some way to get my money away from me, and goodness knows what other wickednesses? No! In I march!"

As she entered the house and closed the door, Consadine mounted the steps.

"Oh! You're here?" Karen said. "I'm afraid you'd better not stay, just now. It's—you see, Doctor Pauli's in the house, and Mrs. Cobby's gone in after him, and the Professor's not home. It's—"

"Look here!" said Consadine. "You won't like to hear this, and I don't like telling you. But—the Professor *is* Doctor Pauli."

"But—no!"

"Sorry, he is. It's the best sort of disguise there is, when it's almost nothing. A bit of a wig, a fancy necktie. The whole art of it is a different way of smiling, of talking, taking on what you might call a different personality. Clever."

"But Mrs. Cobby ...!"

"Yes," said Consadine. "I'm afraid he's in for a bad time, poor devil."

They both heard that sound, not a scream, but a sort of hooting shout; they heard the thud. Consadine threw open the door, and before them, Mrs. Cobby came rolling and bumping down the narrow staircase, like a great bundle.

Karen started to run toward her, but Consadine stopped her. "Wait!" he said, and knelt down beside Mrs. Cobby. He moved her a little, pushed back her hair, felt her pulse, laid his head against her chest. Then he rose.

"Don't touch her," he said. "Call the Police Station, please. Tell them to send the ambulance and a couple of men here at once."

"Then she—?"

"She's dead. Hurry up with the call, please."

They waited for the police, standing in the little hall, with Mrs. Cobby lying on the floor.

"I did it," the Professor said, again and again and again. "I did it. I killed her. I hit her on the temple with a brass book end, and I pushed her down the stairs. I did it. When she found out, I had to kill her. Pauli was my only way to get away from her, and when she found out I was Pauli, I had to kill her."

Twice Consadine gave him the official warning, but he paid no attention to it.

"I did it. I had to do it, I had to get away from her. I wanted to talk to Karen. I wanted to laugh. I wanted a glass of beer. I had to get away from her. I invented Pauli so that I could get away from her. But she caught me, before I'd changed my necktie. Then, you see, I couldn't ever be Pauli again. I couldn't ever get away from her again. So I had to kill her."

"Here's the ambulance now," said Consadine, tuning to Karen. "I'll drive you to the hotel. You can't stay here alone."

The Professor, too, turned to Karen.

"*You* understand, don't you?" he asked, with great anxiety. "I didn't mean any harm to anyone. If I could just have kept up the Pauli thing—had a talk with you sometimes, had a good laugh, a glass of beer ... But when she found out, then suddenly ... Suddenly I—could see— it was the end."

"No," Karen said, later, when Consadine was driving her to the hotel. "It wasn't sudden. It had been building up, for years and years. He let her treat him—in that shameful way—and it made him hate her."

"Now you're crying again," said Consadine.

"Because—now I'm sorry for him."

"I don't imagine he'll hang," said Consadine, "What with this Pauli disguise, and so on, I think he's pretty certain to get off on an insanity plea."

"And be shut up somewhere," Karen said. "Be a prisoner again …"

"Yes," said Consadine. "Maybe what you said is right. Maybe it's always like that. Always life imprisonment—for cowardice."

The Chain of Death

PART ONE—A HOUSE IN SUSPENSE

The telephone rang, and Clement reached for the instrument, took down the receiver, and said "hello" in a muffled voice, without glancing up from the book that lay open on his knee.

"A lady to see you, sir."

"A lady?" he repeated, startled. "No!"

There was no lady now alive in the world whom he wished to see, and none who had any right to come disturbing him in his own flat at this hour of the evening.

"Ask her what's her name."

There was another pause.

"Says it's a relative, sir."

Clement frowned and sighed.

"Well ... All right! Let her come up!" he said.

For, like most people, he had female relatives and they were, he thought, capable of anything. He hung up the receiver and rose, a big man, with a stoop to his heavy shoulders, and cold blue eyes, and a grizzled mustache that did not conceal a mouth like a steel trap. His friends—and his enemies—had a nickname for him; his name suggested "cement," and so did his disposition, and they called him "Old Portland."

He looked about the room to see if everything were in order. It was a big, high-ceilinged room, filled with massive old furniture, a heavy and somber room, lit only by a green-shaded lamp on his desk. It was a wet, chilly night, but one of the long windows was open at the top and the rain blew in a little. He didn't care; rain would not hurt the ancient solidity of his furniture, and he never left anything about that the wind could flutter.

The bell of his flat rang and he went out into the hall and opened the door. Standing there in the brightly lit corridor was a girl: a thin, dark, vivid young creature, bareheaded, with a fur-trimmed wrap over a black evening frock.

"Sorry to bother you, Uncle Barty," she said casually.

"Ha! Lois ..." he said. "It's you.... Come in!"

Neither of them made any pretense of smiling; he stepped aside, and she went past him into the gloomy sitting room. For a moment she stood there, looking about her, then she slipped off her wrap and sank into a huge leather armchair, while Clement stood looking down at her.

She was the only child of his only sister; but that fact failed to touch him. Also, she was now an orphan; and that did not touch him, either. Her father's death had been tragic; but when he had last seen the girl, at the funeral three weeks ago, she had not appeared grief-stricken.

Since childhood she had been remarkably self-sufficing, and to Clement entirely unappealing—a careless, arrogant, self-centered young nuisance. He had never troubled himself about her, and she had never before seemed aware of his existence.

From her rhinestone bag she took out a silver case and a lighter and lit a cigarette. And now he observed that beneath her nonchalant manner she was much agitated; her hand was not steady, her breathing was rapid.

"Do you know why I've come?" she asked brusquely.

He sat down on the edge of a table.

"I suppose you're in some sort of difficulty," he said.

"I don't get in 'difficulties,'" she retorted scornfully. "And if I did I wouldn't ask anyone else to get me out of them."

"Well, then ...?" asked Old Portland in his muffled voice.

"It's about father," she said, and was silent for a moment. "Of course you read all about it in the newspapers."

Old Portland now lit a cigarette for himself.

"I can't say I read all about it," he answered. "Simply the main facts."

"What facts?"

He glanced at her sidelong before he spoke.

"I read," he said, "that some three weeks ago your father was shot dead by a burglar he'd surprised in the act of stealing the silver."

He made no attempt to soften the statement, and she did not flinch.

"That's the tale," she said, and was silent for a moment. "The police are satisfied with it. Everyone else is—except me."

"And what's your idea?"

Again she was silent for a moment. She was sitting within the circle of light from the shaded lamp, and he saw that her young face had grown pale and grim.

"I never believed in that burglar," she said. "And now—I'm sure."

"Is that feminine intuition?" asked Old Portland. "Or have you any evidence?"

"It's evidence enough for me," she answered slowly, "but I've got to have another opinion. I want the opinion of someone who doesn't give a hoot for us—someone who'll try to find out the truth, and not care who gets hurt by it."

He looked at her with a new interest now; she had suddenly become a human being and not a type.

"Let's hear all about it," he said.

She opened her bag again, and took out a folded paper.

"I've written it down," she said. "Just the facts. I haven't said anything about the people, because you can judge for yourself when you see them—"

"See them?" he interrupted.

Her dark eyes looked steadily into his blue ones.

"I thought you'd come out," she said.

"Well, why? I've got work—a life of my own."

"I thought you'd come, though," she said.

"But why? I don't mean to be hard, or anything of that sort—but I don't see … I wasn't a friend of your father's. I'm not particularly interested in abstract justice. It's not my job to punish the guilty. Why me?"

He waited with considerable interest for her answer. And he made up his mind that if she reminded him that he was her mother's only brother, if she said she needed his help, he would acknowledge her claim and would go.

"I ask you," she said, "because you're—impersonal."

That answer a little disappointed him.

"If I'm so impersonal," he said, "why should you expect me to be interested enough to give up my time to this—wild-goose chase? You haven't told me anything yet."

"It's all in that paper," she said. "If you don't agree with me after you've read it, then—all right."

"Then you'll find someone else?"

"No," she said in her scornful way. "There isn't anyone else. I'll just try by myself."

"You're bound to avenge your father?"

She rose and took up her wrap.

"It's not that," she said curtly. "Only I'm satisfied, myself, that the person who killed him is still in the house. And I'd feel responsible if anything else happened."

He had risen too.

"Expecting another—crime?" he asked.

"Yes," she said. "Maybe *that's* nothing but 'feminine intuition'—but I do."

"Hold on!" he said, as she moved toward the door. "This isn't settled yet, young lady!"

"There's a boy waiting for me outside in a taxi," she said. "We're going to a play. It's late already."

"Step in on your way home."

"I can't. I'll have to hurry for the last train out to Moorewood. I'll ring you up tomorrow morning."

"This boy who's waiting … like him?"

"No," she said. "Not much. But I was glad to get away from that house for an evening."

"Why do you stay there if you're uncomfortable? Can't you visit—"

"I don't care about being comfortable," she said disdainfully. "And I told you I thought something was going to happen there."

He did not point out to her that this was illogical; indeed, he did not find it so. One didn't run away from a place where things were going to happen. She was struggling impatiently with her wrap, and as he stepped forward to help her he caught a glimpse of her profile, her clear, clean features, her fine, dark brow. An old memory stirred in him.

"Do you remember your mother?" he asked.

"No," she answered curtly.

She faced him again, with her eyes narrowed; then, under his steadfast glance, she frowned and her eyes widened, grew serious and thoughtful,

"Did you ever read anything of Dr. Watson's?" she asked.

"Never heard of him."

"He's the behaviorist, you know. He thinks that your environment—your early training—is the only thing that counts."

"Nonsense!" said Old Portland, "Character—that's the thing. Napoleon said it: 'Character is destiny.'"

"I guess you don't know," she said. "I guess you were brought up in that nice, old-fashioned way. By nice, old-fashioned, *sure* parents."

A queer little vision came to him, of the breakfast room of his old home; his mother, gracious and gay, sitting behind the coffee urn; his father, absent-minded, a little stiff, but so courteous, punctilious even to his children … For an instant he recaptured the very feel of those summer mornings of his childhood—the perfume of the stocks in the garden, the aroma of coffee, the glitter of the sun on silver and glass, all the sense of clean, cheerful well-being.... It had been a long time since he had thought of any of those things.

"Yes …" he said, half to himself.

"Well," she said, "things like that count. People *told* you what to do—and you did what you were told until you got into nice habits. But when nobody tells you anything—"

"Your stepmother's taken a great deal of trouble—"

"You needn't think I'm complaining," said she. "I was just thinking out loud. Well … read that paper, won't you? And I'll ring you up in the morning."

He went out into the corridor with her, stood at the head of the stairs, watching her as she descended.

Then he went back into his austere room, sat down in one of the tremendous chairs, with his long legs stretched out. He was thinking of what she had said.

"Environment ... no!" he said to himself. "No; it's character that counts.... She's got character—that girl...."

He thought of his sister. Certainly Lois did not resemble that gentle, pretty mother of hers.

"And she doesn't take after her father!" he thought.

He had always regarded the late Gilbert Emery as the most unnecessary and objectionable man alive, and the fact of his being dead gave him no halo. No wonder his daughter was running out to theaters three weeks after his death.

"But that notion of hers," he reflected. "Nothing in that, of course."

He took down the receiver and spoke through the telephone.

"See if you can get me the newspapers for the twenty-seventh of last month," he said.

He didn't ask whom he was speaking to; he didn't know; he didn't care. What he wanted done would be done. And within fifteen minutes the hall boy came up with those newspapers, crumpled and by no means clean, but smoothed out and neatly folded now.

"The janitor happened to—"

"All right!" said Old Portland, and gave him a tip. Then he sat down and began to read, with care, the accounts of his brother-in-law's tragic accident. They all agreed; things were perfectly plain and straightforward. At a quarter past twelve on the morning of the 27th a shot had been heard by several members of the household. The first person to reach the dining room from which the sound came had been Mr. Barrow, Emery's secretary. He testified that he had found Emery, in pajamas and dressing gown, lying on the floor by the sideboard, shot through the heart—and that he had seen a man running across the lawn. Captain Marcus Snow, a relative of Mrs. Emery's, had also seen this man from an upper window. Several valuable pieces of silver had been taken from the sideboard. The police were in possession of important clues.

There had been an inquest, with the obvious verdict of murder by some person or persons unknown. There was no suggestion of anything more than a burglarious assault.

"No," he thought. "The girl's upset—overwrought. I'll have a look at her precious paper, though."

As he unfolded it, he was surprised to find, not a schoolgirl scrawl, but

very neatly typed pages, headed "Confidential."
The first page bore the title:

PERSONS WHO I BELIEVE WERE IN THE HOUSE
AT 12:15 AT NIGHT ON THE 27TH
1. Myself.
2. My stepmother, Lydia Emery.
3. Marcus Snow.
4. Jack Barrow.
5. Elsie Evans.
6. Duncan Sommerfield.
7. Selma Petersen, the cook.
8. Agnes Croly, the housemaid.

ALIBIS
1. I claim that I was reading in bed.
2. My stepmother says she was asleep.
3. Marcus Snow says he was sitting smoking by the open window in his room.
4. Jack says he was reading in the library.
5. Elsie says she was studying in her own room.
6. Duncan says he was out.
7. Selma says she was in bed and asleep.
8. Agnes says the same.

Nobody can corroborate anyone else's statement. Nobody admits seeing anyone until Marcus Snow ran downstairs when he heard the shot, and met Jack. I have figured out that any of the persons in the house could have fired that shot, and run up the back stairs, which are very near the dining room.

Excepting the servants, whom I don't know much about, everyone in the house had a pretty good reason for wanting to kill my father.

The second page was headed:

REASONS FOR DOUBTING THE BURGLAR THEORY
1. I heard father go past my door and downstairs at least half an hour before the shot was fired. It is pretty certain that he went to the sideboard in the dining room, because he always did. So there must have been a light in the dining room half an hour before the shot was fired. That would mean that the burglar came in *after* father, and shot him.
2. When I got down there, I am sure I saw the silver filigree bowl on

the sideboard. I went upstairs when they carried father up, and after that it disappeared.

3. Everyone in the house is suspicious and miserable. I am sure that not one of us believes in that burglar.

Old Portland read this document through twice. Then he took down the receiver again.

II

Down the great flight of steps in the Grand Central came Lois, like a haughty princess, her little dark head held high, her fur-trimmed wrap held about her with one hand. Old Portland watched her with a sort of severe admiration.

Then she caught sight of him, stopped short, and came on, unsmiling as usual.

"Where's the boy?" he asked.

"Just left him," she said. "I've had enough of *his* company. I've got to step to get that last train—"

"No," he said. "Wait!"

He was pleased to observe that she did wait, without question, standing before him and looking at him. He realized then that he was rather proud of her. People turned to look at her. He detested her powder and lipstick and short hair, her wisp of a dress, her high-heeled silver slippers, her general air of insolent assurance. But he liked the way she stood, so straight and proud, and he liked the look in her black eyes.

It did not occur to him that people likewise turned to look at him; that he was a conspicuous figure, not only for his size, but for the force, the relentless intelligence, in his handsome face.

"Anyone could tell you were somebody," she observed.

"Who?" he demanded.

"You look darn distinguished," she proceeded.

"Bah!" said he. "Now! I read your paper. I don't admit that there's anything in it. And if there is it's not my business. But I'm going with you—"

"We'll have to get along—"

"I'll drive you out," he said. "Now! I suppose somebody was going to meet you at the Moorewood station—"

"No," she said. "I'd have got a taxi. You see, Lydia's idea is to trust me."

"Well, it's a good idea, too."

"No, it isn't. Because it's not real. She's always awfully worried and miserable about me. But she thinks that if she pretends to trust me it'll keep me straight."

"Come along!" said Old Portland abruptly. "My car's outside."

As she followed him, he had vague memories of Young Ladies he had known in his youth. They had had—at least, some of them had had—a gracious charm he saw no more in the world. But at this moment Lois surpassed them. Not one of them could have set off anywhere without putting things on, arranging and composing herself, consulting people. And Lois, bareheaded and in silver slippers, was ready to go anywhere.

He felt, too, that she would appreciate his car and his masterly driving. He turned his head to ask her if she herself drove, and he saw that a man was running after them across the rotunda.

"Is that a friend of yours, Lois?" he asked.

She looked back, and a singular change came over her face, a look of bitter and insolent recklessness. She stood still and waited, and the man came up and caught her by the arm. Neither of them heeded Old Portland. They were absorbed in some drama of their own, looking only at each other, in anger and pain and a sort of fear.

The man was young and extraordinarily handsome, but in a fashion especially repugnant to Old Portland. He was too heavy, obviously badly out of condition; his dark face was haggard and drawn; there was a theatric air of dissipation about him, like a stage villain. He even had the little black mustache proper to a villain, and an overlarge seal ring on one finger and diamond studs in his shirt.

But he was not being theatric now. He gripped the girl's arm fiercely and his eyes blazed.

"I've been looking for you all evening!" he said. "I've rung up all your friends—all the ones *I* know—"

"I went to a show," she said coldly. "Any objection?"

"Did you forget you'd asked me out for the weekend?"

"No. I thought you'd be able to get that far by yourself."

"Where are you going now?"

"My uncle is driving me home." That reminded her of her uncle's presence. "Uncle Barty," she said, "this is Duncan Sommerfield."

"I've heard of you, sir," said the young man, holding out his hand. Clement took it, said "Ha!" and nothing else.

"You'll have to hurry if you want to get that train," said Lois.

"Look here, Lois—" he began.

She turned to her uncle.

"Can we pick him up at the Moorewood station, Uncle Barty?" she asked.

"We can," said Old Portland curtly.

"Then I'll see you there, Duncan," she said. "If you get there first, wait for us."

And without another word or glance she turned her back on him and walked on with her uncle.

Neither of them spoke until they had entered Central Park.

"Who's *he?*" asked Old Portland.

"He's what the tabloids would call my 'millionaire sweetheart,'" said Lois.

"What do you mean by 'sweetheart'?"

"We're engaged, in a way."

"What do you mean, 'in a way'?"

She was silent for a time. Through the bare branches of the trees he could see the lights in towering apartment houses and hotels, blurred in the rain that pattered on the top of the car and rattled against the windows.

"I mean," she said, "that sometimes I think I'll marry him, and sometimes I think I—can't."

He drove out of the park at 110th Street and turned up Seventh Avenue.

"Making a problem out of it, eh?" he said. "That's what women always like to do."

"I don't think you know much about women," said his niece.

That made him angry for a moment, but he got over it.

"Maybe not," he said. "Suppose you try to explain."

She did not answer for a time.

"We couldn't be engaged before," she began in her scornful tone, "considering that Duncan's just got his divorce."

He was glad it was dark. He had heard and read enough about the changed viewpoint of the present day, but hitherto he had been perfectly indifferent. Only—this was different…. He thought of things he would like to do to Duncan Sommerfield.

"Father wanted me to marry him," she said.

"Oh, did he?" said Old Portland frigidly.

There was another silence.

"Do you care for the fellow?" he asked.

"I'm trying to," said she.

"What do you mean—trying to?" he burst out. "Why should you try to?"

"Well, I've got to care for someone, haven't I?" she cried, as hotly as he. "I can't go on like this! I—I'm not—*human!*"

He was startled and profoundly touched.

"I don't quite see …" he said.

"Duncan's wild about me," she said. "And he's just going to pieces. I could—do a lot with him, I guess.... But I don't want to talk about it anymore. I've had some—perfectly rotten scenes with that boy. It's—I'm sick and tired of—everything!"

"Well … suppose we discuss your—mystery," he suggested.

He felt her start. And he remembered what she had written: "Everyone in the house had a pretty good reason for wanting to kill my father." Sommerfield too? He would have liked to ask about that, but he could not endure to mention the fellow's name.

"Tell me something about these other people," he went on. "Elsie Evans—Snow—the secretary—what's his name?"

"I'd rather you saw them first," said she. "I want to hear your impression first, and then I'll tell you what I think."

"I imagine it was the secretary fellow who answered the telephone—"

"Telephone? When did you telephone?"

"As soon as I decided to come. I'm not in the habit of arriving uninvited at people's houses at one o'clock in the morning. I asked your stepmother if it would be convenient for her."

They were out of the city now, on a wide boulevard that stretched endlessly before them like a black river, bordered by lampposts whose globes seemed melting in the downpour. They were driving in the teeth of the wind now; the rain was like hail.

"Lydia doesn't like Duncan," said Lois abruptly.

"Doesn't, eh? Why?"

The girl did not answer for a time. "If I don't tell you someone else will," she said. "Lord knows, his wife has enough to say about her troubles. She says he threatened to kill her. I don't know if it's true. I don't care. I admit he's got a pretty awful temper, but she'd provoke anyone." She paused. "You might as well hear all the bad things about him. Everybody knows them. He drinks, and he gambles. The other things about him, the decent things, nobody wants to hear."

Nor did Clement want to hear them. He had taken a profound dislike to Sommerfield, and the thought of this girl, this child, and her "engagement" filled him with a passionate anger.

"But I've got to go slow," he thought. "Got to be careful here …" And aloud he said: "Now, about these motives—?"

"Duncan didn't have any 'motive,'" she said. "He was about the only one who didn't have one."

He smiled faintly to himself at her quickness.

"Ever talked to him about it?" he asked.

"No," she said. "I—didn't want to. I haven't talked about it to anyone but you."

"I'd like to know why you chose me."

"Well …" she said. "Because you're like me."

"Like you?" he repeated, startled.

"Yep," said she. "I feel pretty sure you'd see things the way I do. I mean, you wouldn't care so much about punishing anyone. You'd just help to keep anything else from happening."

He thought that over for a time.

"What do you imagine is going to happen?" he asked.

"I don't know," she said. "Only—when you get there, you'll know. You'll—feel it. It's like living on top of a volcano. There's a sort of horrible atmosphere—of suspicion and—and dread."

"But what do you think I can do, my dear child?"

"Oh, I can't tell you!" she cried impatiently. "When you get there, I guess you'll see...."

"You don't want me to find the guilty person—if the guilty person's not that burglar. You simply want me to come and observe this 'atmosphere,'" he went on remorselessly. "I'm not very sensitive to 'atmosphere.' I don't—"

"Look here!" she interrupted with vehemence. "I've asked you because I can't handle this alone. I'm worried. And you've *got* to help me!"

"All right!" he answered meekly.

They drove on in silence, through the wind and the rain, and Old Portland was smiling to himself.

"Turn to the left for the station," said Lois.

He did turn, and drew up presently beside the platform. It was empty, and the rain drove across it.

"He'll be in the waiting room," said Lois. "The train got in twenty minutes ago."

She jumped out and ran across the platform; he saw her silver slippers twinkling, splashing in the wet. She was back almost at once.

"Waiting room's locked," she said, getting into the car again. "Let's see if he's in the drug store."

He drove across the street to Hague's All-Night Drug Store. There was no one there but a sleek young man in a white jacket, sitting at a small table and reading a magazine.

"Hello, Harry," said Lois.

"Hello, Miss Emery," he answered, rising.

"Is the last train from New York in yet?"

"Came right on time," said Harry. "Mr. Barrow came up by it, and he sure was mad!"

"Why?"

"Well, there was only one taxi come to meet the train, and he let it go. Said your car was coming to meet him. And he waited in here about ten minutes, and then he telephoned up to the house, and they told him the car started long ago. Must of had trouble on the way. He stayed a while cursing out your shover, then he tried to get the taxi on the phone, only the garage was closed up, and he's walking. Been gone about twenty minutes."

"Didn't anyone else come by that train, Harry?"

"Nary a soul," said Harry cheerfully.

Old Portland had been listening to this dialogue with a curious satisfaction.

He liked the girl's way of talking to that Harry. She had the careless frankness of a well-bred boy; not any kind of ladylike condescension.

"By Jove!" he thought. "If she was a boy she'd be all right. It's only when you judge her by feminine standards—"

"That's—queer, isn't it?" she asked.

"Not so very. He's changed his mind about coming, that's all. He impressed me as the sort of fellow who changes his mind pretty easily."

He saw that she was very much distressed, and his heart sank. Did she really care so much for that cad?

"I'll telephone," she said, and went into a booth.

Old Portland bought a cigar from Harry, and lit it, and they conversed about the weather until Lois came out again.

"Come on, Uncle Barty," she said. "Night, Harry."

And, once they got into the car: "I telephoned to his flat in New York," she said. "He's not there."

"There are one or two other places in New York where a man might be."

"No," she said. "Something's happened to him."

"That's a little too psychic," said Old Portland. "You've absolutely no grounds for saying that."

"I know it," she said, unexpectedly apologetic. "I don't mean to be hysterical and silly. I really have got a feeling that something's happened, but I know that lots of times these feelings don't amount to anything."

Old Portland had been at sea for half his life, and he had in him superstitions older than his cynical common sense. Old memories stirred in him of "feelings" that had been amply justified.

"What does your feeling tell you has happened to him?" he asked, scornfully because his uneasiness made him angry.

"That he's dead," she said.

He started the car and, swinging round the corner, left the lights of the station and Hague's All-Night Drug Store behind. The rain rattled like hail against the windows, the wind came in a rush. And he had a "feeling" himself, a feeling that death and disaster were in the air tonight.

"We'd better keep an eye out for Jack," said Lois.

"Who's Jack?"

"Jack Barrow. If he's walking, we might pick him up in a moment." Her voice was a little unsteady for a moment, but she conquered that and went on: "I'd better tell you a little about Jack before you see him. Because you wouldn't get a very good first impression of him, like this."

"Do you want me to get a good impression?"

"Yes, I do."

"Like him?"

"No; I hate him. That's why I want to be fair. Drive slowly, won't you? ... You see, he's in love with Lydia."

He was glad of the darkness, so that this brutally outspoken young creature could not see that she had shocked him. To speak that way of her father's wife, and her father dead only three weeks!

"I see!" he said.

Then once more he was startled by her quickness. She seemed to read his mind from the tone of his voice.

"There's nothing in it," she explained. "I mean, Lydia never encouraged him or anything. And father knew about it. You couldn't help knowing. He simply adores Lydia in an abject way.... I hate that sort of thing! And Lydia ... But I suppose that's the way she was brought up. To be gracious, you know. Like a queen. She couldn't imagine being friendly with a man. And men never feel friendly to her. They just cringe."

"She seemed to me a very charming woman."

"She is. Too darned charming. I don't see any sense in that."

"Don't think it's possible for a woman to have a good influence?"

"Not charming women," said Lois. "They just make men miserable. She makes Jack miserable. And she makes him worse. He's begun drinking."

"Like Sommerfield?" he said, and was sorry he had said it. But her appraisal of the older woman's charm had somehow nettled him.

"I know," she said. "I don't seem to be much good in the influencing line myself."

He would have liked to shake hands with her then, he so admired her honesty.

"I'm not running down Lydia," she went on. "She's wonderful, in lots of ways. I'm fond of her. And she's terribly unhappy. I only— I think I see him!"

Ahead of them a man was striding along the road. He passed under a street lamp, and Clement had a clear glimpse of him, tall, slight, his coat collar turned up, soft hat pulled clown. Lois had opened the door of the car.

"Hi!" she called. "Jack! Jack Barrow!"

He turned and stopped, waited until the car reached him, and got in without a word. Clement expected some sort of introduction, but none came, and he snapped on the light for a good look at the newcomer. And he was startled, almost alarmed, by the wild and desperate look of the fellow. He was brown as a gypsy, with a narrow face and long dark eyes and a bitter mouth; and now, in his limp hat and sodden collar, he looked as if he had been wading through mud and rain for hours.

"Why didn't you wait for the car?" asked Lois.

"I don't mind the rain," he answered briefly.

"You didn't happen to see Duncan anywhere, did you?"

He jumped as if the question were a gun.

"No!" he cried with a sort of violence. "Why should I see him?"

Finding himself completely ignored, Old Portland started the car again, and that recalled Lois to her social duty.

"Uncle Barty," she said, "this is Jack Barrow. Jack—my uncle, Mr. Clement."

"I believe I saw you at the funeral, sir," said Barrow, and getting no answer the conversation dropped.

Clement wanted to think. Sommerfield had made a poor impression upon him; young Barrow made no better. Indeed, there was something of the same air about him, a suggestion of intolerable tension and dread.

"Damned queer lot ..." thought Clement uneasily.

He was a remarkably good driver, but that night he nearly had an accident. In turning a corner he came full into the blinding glare of the headlights of another car speeding along in the middle of the road. He swerved aside, and they would have passed without further trouble, but the other driver lost his head, jammed on the brake, skidded in a half circle, and stopped across the road not six inches from Clement's car. Barrow began to swear almost hysterically.

"Shut up!" said Lois sternly. "There's no harm done. Wait! Why, it's Stevens!" She opened the door of the car and called:

"Stevens!"

"Yes, miss," answered a soft, drawling voice. "It's all right."

"Then get out of the road," said Old Portland.

"Yes, sir. I'm stalled. Half a moment."

The man jumped out, to crank his engine. Clement saw him plainly—a tall, loose-limbed young fellow with a pleasant face.

"Where on earth were you going?" asked Lois.

"To the station, miss, to meet Mr. Barrow."

"But you're so late!"

"I had tire trouble, miss."

"But why—" she began, and stopped. "We've got Mr. Barrow here," she said.

He started his engine, backed aside, and let them pass. A long trip, this seemed to Clement, but at last they turned into the drive of the late Gilbert Emery's house.

"We'll let Jack out here," said Lois, "and I'll go round to the garage with you, Uncle Barty."

They stopped under the portico. Barrow got out, and Clement turned the car.

"Don't you see—how queer …" she said. "Jack had had at least twenty minutes' start of us, and he'd only gone half a mile."

"I thought of that myself," said Clement.

For a moment they stood looking at each other. And he realized that, within a few hours, this child had become of supreme importance to him. The realization did not at all surprise him; it seemed inevitable.

"Do you think that perhaps he met Duncan?" she asked, "and said something to make him go away again?"

"Is there anything he *could* say?"

"Yes," she said slowly. "I guess there is."

"What?"

"It's—about a girl," she said. "Nobody thinks I know about it … The housemaid…. The night father was shot, I saw Duncan with her, holding her hand…. It was after father'd been brought upstairs. I'd left my little bag down there in the library, and I was going to run down the back stairs. I saw them, halfway down…. I went away quietly: they didn't hear me. But just as I was going to shut the door of my own room, I saw Jack go along the hall and open that door. If he saw them too, he'd have something to hold over Duncan's head."

"Lois!" cried Old Portland. "Child! Good God! That man—that man with a wife … a drunkard, a gambler—carrying on some low intrigue with a servant girl…. Lois! You can't—you can't seriously think of a man like that!"

"I don't know how to explain," she said. "Only—Duncan's the only person who ever *needed* me. The worse he is, the more he needs me. He's—sort of lost his bearings, like I have. He doesn't know what to do with life. He's—lost. And he—needs someone—so awfully badly …"

Her voice was unsteady, but not her glance. And looking into her face, with its proud honesty, its incurable courage, he felt a thrill of pride in her.

"You're a young fool!" he said. "Same idea women had in your grandmother's day. Marry a rake to reform him."

"It's not that—" she began, with her invariable willingness to explain, when Stevens came into the garage.

"Hello!" she said. "Did you have any more trouble?"

"No, miss," he answered in his soft drawl. He was standing bareheaded before her now, and it occurred to Clement that the fellow looked curiously out of place here, clad in uniform.

"Looks like a cowboy," he thought.

And as he looked at him he saw something odd.... Lois had spoken again, and Stevens had smiled a little, and from the corner of his mouth there came a tiny trickle of blood. He wiped it off quickly with the back of his hand, and continued to grin with his lips closed.

But the impression had been made. He had, in that instant, looked horrible; his pleasant sunburned face had been altered; he had put Clement in mind of a once faithful sheep dog that had suddenly turned killer.

He tried to dismiss this fancy; he was angry with himself for having it. But while he and Lois ran through the rain to the house, there it was, that image of the soft-voiced, good-looking young man with blood running out of his mouth....

Under the portico Lois stopped to draw breath.

"Perhaps Agnes will open the door," she said.

"Agnes?"

"That's the housemaid—the one I told you about," she said.

There was a bright light here, and by it he saw how his niece looked, with her dark hair wet and ruffled, the fur collar of her wrap matted.

"You look like a drowned rat," he remarked.

"I wish you could see yourself!" she retorted. "You look like a—pirate."

"No wonder! The way you've dragged me around in the rain and mud at my time of life."

Then, for the first time that evening, she smiled. It was a funny little smile, half grudging.

"Thank you—lots!" she said.

"Come on, you little drowned rat!" he said brusquely. "Ring the bell!"

The door was opened very promptly, but not by any housemaid. It was Lydia Emery herself who stood there.

"Oh, I'm so glad!" she cried. "It's so late! I was—worried.... Lois! My dear! You're drenched!"

She held out her hand to Clement and he took it, a little uncomfortable. After all, he was the brother of Emery's first wife; perhaps Lydia didn't like seeing him.

"I have a splendid fire for her," she went on, "and hot coffee and—"

"I guess I'll go right to bed, thanks," Lois interrupted. "'Night, Lydia;

'night, Uncle Barty!"

She ran off up the stairs, and the two persons left in the hall, alone together for the first time in their lives, were aware of a considerable constraint.

But Mrs. Emery was well disciplined in social matters.

"You'll have a cup of coffee and a sandwich, won't you, Barty?" she asked, with only the faintest hesitation before his name.

"Thanks, yes," said he, and followed her down the hall.

He had seen her only two or three times before. She had seemed to him then a charming woman, and she seemed even more so now. She was much younger than Emery had been, not more than thirty, he guessed, very slender, with clear, fine features and remarkably beautiful bronze hair. But, though young, there was nothing girlish about her. She had a mature poise and dignity.

"I like her," he thought.

The room to which she led him was very attractive this wet, chilly night. A fire of wood blazed in the hearth, an electric coffee percolator bubbled. But Clement was not too pleased to see a stranger there.

"This is Captain Snow," she said. "Mr. Clement."

The two men greeted each other without shaking hands. Then they sat down, and, as he lit a cigarette, Clement covertly inspected the other.

He liked the look of this fellow. There was something cool and solid about him which Clement could at this moment appreciate profoundly. He had this evening met two men whom he did not like; he had been so often reminded of Gilbert Emery, whom he had always found particularly objectionable; he had been dragged into an atmosphere of feverish distress, of very ugly complications. And here at last was someone of his own sort.

Lydia talked because she felt it her duty to talk, and the two men answered her politely enough, but with a sort of detachment. The clock struck one, and Lydia stirred as if she were going to rise. But she did not rise, and a long silence fell.

"Lois seemed to expect this Sommerfield down tonight," Old Portland observed. "I don't—"

He stopped, astounded by the look he got from Snow—a blank, icy glare that entirely changed his inexpressive face. It was an outrageous look. Old Portland's brows drew together in an ominous frown. Then he remembered Lydia, and turned his head. And found her staring at him, white as a ghost.

"*Is* he—coming?" she asked.

"He didn't get the last train, anyhow," said Clement.

"I hope—" she began in her pleasant, polite way; she tried to smile, but her upper lip twitched, and abruptly a loud sob burst from her.

"G-good night!" she cried, rising. "Sleep—well …" And hurried out of the room.

The two men stood facing each other. Snow no longer wore that outrageous look; his face was blank again.

"Like a spot of Emery's prewar whisky?" he asked.

Clement forgot to answer until Snow repeated the question.

"All right, thanks," he said, and sat down again.

He had come here in a skeptical mood. He had realized that there might be something in his niece's contention that her father had not been shot by a burglar, chiefly because it was very easy to believe in people wanting to put Emery out of the way. But he had not believed at all in her notion that something else was going to happen. Now he did believe that. Now he saw that there were here a score of invisible threads making a dark and evil pattern.

He thought of the haggard and reckless young Sommerfield; he remembered the strange appearance of Jack Barrow, and his unaccountable delay on the road in such weather; he remembered what Lois had told him—that Barrow loved Lydia. He remembered with great disquiet how the chauffeur had looked, with that trickle of blood from the corner of his mouth. He thought of Lydia's recent agitation; and, still more, he thought of Snow's frigid, baleful look.

"No …" he said to himself. "There's something going on here—something I don't like...."

Snow set a glass down beside him.

"I hope we'll get good news of Sommerfield," he remarked amiably.

"Good news, eh?"

"Yes. That he's broken his neck—or that someone's broken it for him!"

PART TWO—DEATH STRIKES AGAIN

There was a brief silence.

"You don't like Sommerfield, eh?" said Old Portland.

"No," said Snow, in the same amiable tone; "I don't."

Old Portland had had a wide and varied experience in dealing with men. He had quarreled with his father at an early age and had gone to sea. He had been captain of a cargo steamer when his father had died, leaving him a considerable fortune, and he had given up the sea then, and had walked into his late father's office one morning and taken charge of the business. And though he had known nothing of that business then, he had done remarkably well because of the other things he knew. He was cautious and not disposed to be overtrustful of his fellow creatures; but he could, when he liked, give an excellent impression of bluff outspokenness.

"I met him for a few moments in New York, you know," he said. "And I didn't like him myself."

That seemed to encourage Snow.

"It's a damned shame to see a girl like Lois interested in a swine like that," he said. "I'm glad you've come down here. Perhaps you can get rid of him."

"Oh, well!" said Old Portland. "The thing will probably blow itself out. She's young. In the course of time she'll lose interest in him, I dare say."

"But in the meantime," said Snow, "he'll make trouble."

"What trouble could he make?"

Snow, thought for a while before he answered.

"I mean …" he said, "that he'll cause a lot of—idle gossip.…"

"Oh, well!" said Old Portland again. "That doesn't amount to much."

But, though he spoke with an air of good-humored carelessness, he was very much on the alert. He had been aware for some time that Snow had some purpose in mind; he was also aware that Snow was no more outspoken than he was. He needed handling, this fellow.

"The trouble is," said Snow, "that Sommerfield might make a great deal of unpleasantness. Perhaps I'd better tell you the whole story."

"Good!" said Old Portland.

"Of course we had the police in here, asking questions and rooting around. Not very pleasant for anyone—and worst of all for Lydia. And when they'd gone Sommerfield put on his little show. Began talking about what fools the police were: 'That's one burglar they'll never catch!' I tried to shut him up; he'd been drinking. 'Well,' he said, 'as long as they don't try to pin it on some poor devil of a crook they've got a down on, I'll hold *my* tongue. I'm not losing any sleep over Emery's timely departure!'"

"And what did he mean by that, d'you suppose?" asked Old Portland.

Snow glanced at him sidelong; then, with an effort:

"I'd better tell you, in case you hear of it from someone else. Otherwise it wouldn't be worth repeating. But—evidently the swine had some idea in his muddled head that it—wasn't a burglar."

"Ha!" said Old Portland.

"Naturally, you can see that if he spreads that idea all over the place …"

There was another silence.

"Then he didn't care much for Emery, either?" said Old Portland musingly. "I gathered that they were pretty friendly."

"Nobody on God's earth 'cared much' for Emery," said Snow. "He—" He stopped and lit another cigarette, and once more Clement saw on his face the shadow of that frigid, baleful look. "If you'd been here," he went on, "the last evening Emery was alive … It was—" Again he stopped. "Like a cat in a bird cage," he continued. "He was at the top of his form that night. He had something to say to everyone—something that hurt…. And no one was able to hit back.

"There was his wife, badly handicapped by her antiquated idea of loyalty and decency and good breeding. He reminded her of how he supported her father, and helped him out of a pretty nasty jam. Then he touched up young Barrow—who'd drawn his salary six months in advance. Then he had a few little remarks for Elsie Evans."

"Who is she, anyhow?"

Snow drew on his cigarette for a moment.

"She's a girl," he said, "a kid, a poor young devil, full of crazy ideas—or ideals. I saw her once, ten years ago, when she was a kid of nine or ten—funny little kid with long yellow hair, dressed like a charity child. Her mother was a cousin of Emery's—one of those thick-skinned social climbers. When she died, Emery volunteered to pay for the girl's education. That sounds kind, but it's—otherwise. He was simply buying another victim.

"The girl's mad to study medicine. She has this idea of 'serving humanity,' and she thought she had to put up with anything and everything so that she could go on studying. She cried that night, though. And Sommerfield got flicked on the raw, and slammed out of the house. And Barrow took refuge in the whisky. And Lydia just sat there…. Sort of evening you don't forget in a hurry."

"And you were there, too?" said Clement. "Were you enjoying yourself, too?"

"I?" said Snow pleasantly. "I was just sitting there, thinking."

Old Portland, too, sat thinking for a time.

"And you believe that Sommerfield's likely to make trouble …" he said, as if musing.

"You can see for yourself that an idea like that … And it seems to me … Emery's gone. Nothing can bring him back. Best thing is to—let matters alone."

"Hardly ethical—" murmured Old Portland.

"I'm not concerned with ethics," said Snow briefly.

"But—" said Old Portland, glancing up suddenly, "if you and Barrow both saw the burglar escaping? I don't see what grounds Sommerfield has for his tale."

"We only saw a man. It was too dark to recognize him."

"And Sommerfield was out at the time of the shooting?"

"Yes."

"I wonder where."

"God knows," said Snow.

"Didn't the police ask him any questions?"

"They got a good account from Stevens—the chauffeur, you know. He swore that Sommerfield was in the garage, talking to him, from eleven o'clock until they heard the shot and ran over to the house. And that satisfied the police and the coroner's jury. Sommerfield's a rich man—well known, good social position. He was apparently on good terms with Emery. No reason for suspecting him of any sort of complicity."

"But you do?" said Old Portland, so suddenly that Snow started nervously.

"No," he answered curtly. "I don't suspect anyone. I don't give a damn who did it, anyhow. The only thing that interests me is to see that—the people who are left aren't dragged into a shameful scandal." He rose. "Perhaps, after you've thought it over, you'll see my point of view—and do what you can to keep Sommerfield quiet. Now, if you'll excuse me, I'll be getting to bed.... By the way, can't I show you your room?"

"I know the way, thanks. I stayed here the night of the funeral. Good night!"

"Good night!" said Snow.

As he looked after him, Clement noticed that he walked with a limp. "A mettlesome lad!" he observed to himself. "And capable of making a good deal of trouble on his own account, I should think. Well, we'll see...."

It was nearly two o'clock now, but he felt no desire to go to bed just yet. The silence of the house pleased him. He roamed about the room, glanced at the books, and then went over to the window to take a look at the weather.

The trees were tossing and creaking in the high wind; the rain dashed against the panes. But he saw, shining steadily through the turmoil, a bright light from a window.

He looked at it; then he spun round on his heel, crossed the room noiselessly, glanced up at the dark stairs, and went along the hall to the hat rack. He put on his overcoat and hat, and silently unlocked and unchained the front door, and slipped off the catch, so that he could get in again.

It was black as the pit outside, and the rain blew in his face. Nevertheless he set off without hesitation. He was sure he had the location of the garage well fixed in his mind, and self-distrust was not one of his weaknesses. It was his way to make up his mind suddenly and vigorously, and he had been right so often that he had now the utmost confidence in his own decisions. He went on head down against the wind. He stopped only once, to hit the flashlight he carried against a tree, hard enough to break the bulb.

He was right this time, too, for in a few moments he saw again the light that shone from an upper window of the garage.

He knew what he meant to do here. He was not concerned with the problem of Emery's death, but he was very much interested in Sommerfield. He had listened to Snow with alert attention, and two points had particularly interested him. One was that Sommerfield's only alibi was furnished by this chauffeur; the other was that Sommerfield had boasted that the "burglar" would never be discovered.

Evidently Snow believed that Sommerfield knew who had committed the crime and was in great dread of his telling what he knew. But Old Portland was not so sure; he had heard too much boasting with nothing behind it.

"Now, if Sommerfield actually was in the garage with the chauffeur when it happened, he can't *know* who did it. He's only guessing. In that case, I'll call his bluff and make it hot for him. But if he wasn't there—if the chauffeur was lying—then I'll make it still hotter for him."

For what he wanted was to discredit Sommerfield in the eyes of Lois. The other aspects of this case were, he thought, better let alone. Emery was small loss to the world; he was gone, the deed was irreparable; better let it alone and think only of getting rid of Sommerfield.

He knocked briskly on the door of the garage; for it was no part of his policy to seem at all furtive. But he was surprised by the result. Instantly the light upstairs went out. He knocked again. No answer; no sound but the rush of the wind and the drumming of the rain. He waited; then he banged on the door with his torch.

"Who's there?" asked a voice, so close that he started.

"I'm from the house. Miss Emery's uncle."

The door slid back at once, and revealed the garage, flooded with light now, and the chauffeur standing before him in pajamas.

"I saw a light here," said Clement. "I've smashed my torch and I couldn't find my way back to the house. Have you got a spare light?"

"Yes, sir," said Stevens. "If you'll step in—"

Old Portland did step in, and Stevens ran up the stairs at the back of the garage. He was barefooted, and still barefooted when he ran down again with a flashlight. He was pale, too, and his mouth was swollen on one side and his sandy hair all on end.

"My idea was," said Clement, in a confidential tone, "to take a look at the grounds and so on while everyone else was asleep and out of the way. I'd like to get a notion of how this burglar came and went and so on. It's a queer case...."

"Yes, sir," said Stevens. His teeth had begun to chatter—and no wonder, standing barefoot on the cement floor.

"It interests me," Old Portland went on. "The police say the burglar got in through the dining room window, and in that case ... But see here! I'd like to have a few moments' chat with you. Can't we go upstairs to your quarters, Stevens? It's pretty cold down here."

Then he discovered something new.

"I'm afraid not, sir," said Stevens, in his soft drawl. "I'm sorry, but— I've got a friend of mine up there, and—I reckon he wouldn't like to be disturbed."

"Well, you know," said Old Portland, with a laugh, "that looks bad, Stevens! Might think you were sheltering this burglar, eh?"

Stevens' swollen lip twitched in a faint smile.

"Never thought of it that way, sir," he said. "I hope you won't feel you have to mention this up at the house, sir. My friend's been drinking, and I brought him here to sleep it off. He'd get in trouble—and so would I—"

"I don't think I'll find it necessary to say anything," said Old Portland kindly. "Good night, Stevens. Thanks for the light." He moved toward the door; then, as if by an afterthought, he stopped and looked back. "By the way, you and Sommerfield did not see or hear anything that night?"

"No, sir; not until we heard the shot."

"You were upstairs?"

"No, down here."

"Now, that's a queer thing," mused Old Portland aloud. "Sommerfield seems to know ..."

"Know *what?*"

Clement glanced at him, and the chauffeur seemed aware that his manner had been unseemly, for he smiled—a strained and apologetic smile.

"I mean, sir," he said, "that if he claims he heard or saw anything while he was here, it makes me look like a fool—or a liar."

"Well, of course—anything he says has to be looked into."

"I'd—I'd like to hear what he said."

Old Portland appeared surprised and a little shocked; but in his heart he felt an unholy thrill of excitement at how well he was drawing the other.

"The proper authorities—" he said. "Well, you'd better go to bed now, Stevens. Toothache?"

"Yes, sir," said Stevens. "I—yes.... I—I'd be very much obliged to you, sir, if you'd tell me what—Mr. Sommerfield's been saying."

"It can't affect you, Stevens," said Old Portland, looking still more surprised and shocked. "You gave evidence that Sommerfield was here with you from eleven o'clock until you heard the shot. If he's expressed any—suspicions, they'll be thoroughly investigated by the proper authorities."

"If he's expressed any suspicions," said Stevens gently, "he was a hound, and a damned liar."

Old Portland looked steadily at him. Stevens looked back at him, with his swollen lip twitching and his blue eyes very brilliant.

"If Sommerfield's tried to pin this on someone else—" he said.

"If he suspects anyone, it's manifestly his duty—"

"All right. Then it might be *my* duty to do a little talking, too."

"Stevens!" said Old Portland severely. "You're implying that you've withheld—"

"You're Miss Lois' uncle," Stevens interrupted. "You'd better try to get this investigation stopped—on her account."

"Not at all. It's her wish, naturally, to learn the truth."

"She's engaged to Sommerfield," said Stevens. And he was not speaking like a chauffeur now; he was not respectful.

"Sommerfield happens to be the one person—except yourself—who has an alibi—"

"If it comes to a showdown—"

"I can assure you," said Old Portland, "that it will. That's what I'm here for. I'm going, personally, to see that Sommerfield's statement is thoroughly investigated."

"Well, then," said the other, "I reckon I'll land in jail."

"The police will give you all the attention you want," said Old Portland briefly. But he knew he was to learn more, and an odd excitement filled him.

"The police had better be kept out," said Stevens. "They're satisfied. They're busy looking for the burglar—"

"*I'm* not satisfied, though. After what Sommerfield said—"

"He's just a doggone hound and liar!" said Stevens. "And I reckon I'll do a little talking myself now. That alibi of his isn't so good."

"You mean he wasn't here?"

"I mean *I* wasn't," said Stevens.

There was a moment's silence.

"First I saw of him that night," said Stevens, "was after the shot. I was standing out in the road, talking to a fellow I know. I started running up to the house, to see what was up, and I met Sommerfield coming away from the house. He stopped me, and told me to say he'd been in the garage with me."

"Why did you consent?"

"He paid me," said Stevens. "And I fixed it up with the friend I'd been talking to."

"Well," said Old Portland, in an easy, amiable tone, "you'd better get to bed, Stevens. Worst thing in the world for a toothache—standing around barefooted. Good night!"

He was well aware that he left the chauffeur bewildered and desperately uneasy by this sudden retreat, but that caused him no remorse.

"So he's trying to saddle Sommerfield with it," he said to himself. "We'll see...."

Although Old Portland was so late getting to bed, he waked early the next morning. And he had no impulse to turn over and go to sleep again. An odd restlessness possessed him—an uneasy sense of haste and urgency.

"All nonsense!" he said to himself. "I've done what I wanted to do. I've found out that this fellow Sommerfield was lying. Now I can talk to him. I'll tell him that if he doesn't disappear I'll make it hot for him. As for the rest of this little mystery, it doesn't concern me. I don't know, and I don't care, who killed Emery. It's Lois I'm interested in."

He was a little surprised at this interest. Now, in the light of a bright spring morning, the whole thing seemed far more fantastic than it had on a rainy night. He had never before felt this unreasonable anxiety about any human creature. He had been fond of his sister, genuinely sorry for her in her wretched marriage; he had been a faithful friend to her, but always a little aloof. She had never confided in him, and never appealed to him for help or advice, as this young niece had. And he had never worried over his sister, that gentle, old-fashioned woman, as he did now over the cool, cocksure Lois.

He got up, bathed and dressed, thinking with the same uneasiness of this thoroughly unpleasant situation in which he found himself.

Now, he had one weakness, and he knew it—he chose to call it not crossing bridges until he came to them; but it was something more than that: it was a refusal to admit the existence of any bridges. He would not consider the possibility of danger and difficulty until they leaped out at him.

He tried this morning not to see the fatal flaw in his plan; he would have continued to deny it if it had not been for this new affection that had come to him. For Lois' sake, he sat down and looked at a very ugly possibility.

Suppose that, when he had the interview he intended to have with Sommerfield, he should hear—what he did not want to hear? Suppose that when he threatened Sommerfield to expose his perjury, his false alibi, Sommerfield should confess—or, more than confess, should boast—that he had killed Emery? Then what?

"Damn it all!" he thought. "If he does that—then I'll be—what do they call it?—an accessory after the fact. I'd be simply saving the neck of a scoundrel...."

Well, then, suppose he delivered the scoundrel up to justice?

If Sommerfield were tried, the fact of his engagement to Lois must be made public; all sorts of things would come to light.

"And what's more," he thought, "if the fellow was arrested Lois would stand by him. She's a young idiot. She'd call that playing the game. She'd refuse to believe he was guilty.... Well, perhaps he isn't. I hope to heaven he isn't!"

Nothing could have pleased him better now than to believe Sommerfield innocent of anything worse than perjury.

"And I'll have to find out first," he thought, with a sigh. "I can't threaten the fellow, or try to get rid of him, until I know more about this. It may be that he only witnessed the crime—"

Then why did he keep quiet about it? Whom had he seen?

"Snow was right," he thought. "This thing's better let alone."

And why was Snow so anxious for Sommerfield to be discredited, not listened to, his story not believed? What did Snow know?

Lois had said she felt sure something was going to happen....

"What's the matter with me?" thought Old Portland angrily. "Getting to be a regular old woman!"

He opened his door and went out into the corridor. Very quiet there; all the other doors closed.

So he too was very quiet—went down the stairs without a sound. It occurred to him that he would like to take a look at the dining room undisturbed, and he went in there.

It had that dismalness peculiar to dining rooms, which are somehow almost always the least cheerful rooms. It faced west, and there was no sun; there was a huge polished walnut table, austere carved walnut chairs, a monstrous sideboard....

"Are you from the police?" asked a voice behind him.

He turned, considerably startled, and saw in the doorway a tall, broad-shouldered girl, straight as a ramrod, with flaxen hair, and wearing horn-rimmed spectacles; a handsome girl, but with a sternness about her thin, fine face and a curtness in her voice that did not please him.

"I am not," he said. "Why should I be?"

"I've never seen you here before," said she.

"My loss," said Old Portland dryly.

She kept on looking steadily at him.

"Do you mind telling me who you are?" she asked.

"My name's Clement. I'm Lois' uncle. And you're Miss Elsie Evans."

"How do you know that?" she demanded, surprised.

"Because you couldn't be anyone else," he thought, "and you fit Snow's description. What did he say?— 'full of crazy ideas—or ideals.'"

But he preferred to remain mysterious, and merely smiled faintly.

"Are you expecting a visit from the police?" he asked.

"They'll have to come back," she said frigidly. "They can't just drop a thing like this."

"Suppose they catch the burglar? May have caught him already."

He saw the color rise in her thin cheeks.

"They probably will," she said. "They'll find some poor, wretched, hunted creature who's never had a chance in his life, and they'll use him as a scapegoat for their own inefficiency."

"Have they been inefficient?"

"Does it seem to you that the police and the judges and the lawmakers have ever been anything else?" she demanded. "For thousands of years the privileged classes have had exactly the same problem of so-called crime to deal with, and have they ever made one single step of progress? They don't want to. There's nothing they want less than justice. What they want—all they want—is to hunt and torment and crush the unprivileged."

Suddenly Old Portland felt very sorry for this girl. He remembered what Snow had said about her mother—"one of those thick-skinned social climbers"—remembered that Snow had seen her "dressed like a charity child," remembered that she longed for education, so that she could "serve humanity," and that Emery had made her cry. He thought to himself that a good deal of suffering had been required to make her what she was now.

"I think we're getting on a bit," he said, almost gently. "The underdogs are coming up—"

"They're not!" she cried. "You simply don't know. Your life has been protected from knowing and seeing the real conditions."

He thought of his life twenty years on cargo steamers, but did not mention this.

"It's just the same now," she went on. "It'll be the same in this case. The police will arrest *someone*. And it will be someone poor. That's the great crime. Cousin Gilbert was a rich man. Someone poor will have to suffer for his death."

"But it's not likely that anyone who wasn't poor would steal the silver."

"If it ever was stolen."

He concealed his alert interest.

"Must have been," he said. "The police came. No doubt they searched the house—"

"They searched the servants' rooms," said she. "Naturally. And they asked *them* plenty of questions, and investigated their records. If they'd known how poor *I* was, they'd have asked me more questions."

"Oh, well," he said soothingly. "Anyhow, of course you told 'em all you knew."

"I don't know anything."

He took out his cigarette case and held it out to her.

"No, thanks!" she said curtly.

He lit a cigarette for himself.

"Lois was talking to me—" he began carefully.

"Lois!" she said, and her fine face was transfigured with a bitter contempt. "Do you know Lois' idea of justice? She thinks it's an injustice if she can't have everything she wants. You can't even talk to her about ideas. The moment anyone shows the least sympathy for misery and poverty, she simply says, 'Bolshevik.' That's her notion of argument. She's an arrant snob."

He recalled Lois' effortless friendliness toward the young man in the drug store, and toward Stevens—the queer, half-cynical tolerance of her judgments upon her fellow creatures.

He thought that anyone in trouble would receive more mercy and generosity from the worldly-wise Lois than from this young servant of humanity.

But he could also imagine that Lois, without ever knowing it, might a thousand times have hurt and humiliated the oversensitive Elsie.

"Don't you get on very well with Lois?" he asked mildly.

"I don't ever try to 'get on' with anyone in this house," said Elsie. "They all look down on me and I have nothing but contempt for all of them. I have to stay. Cousin Lydia said she'd 'be obliged' if I'd stay a week. And as I depend on her now for every penny, I've got to do it. I tried working my way through college—and I ended in the hospital. If I want my education, I've got to suffer for it. I've got to cringe."

"Lydia didn't impress me as domineering."

"She's not. She hasn't any spirit, any pride, really."

"She seems—"

"Oh, I know how she 'seems'! The perfect ideal of the lady."

The girl was well started now; nothing could stem the tide of her bitterness.

"I've sometimes wondered," she went on, with a short laugh, "if blackmailing would really be much more dishonorable than this—cringing for every penny."

"It's certainly more risky," said Old Portland.

"I'm not afraid of risks. I ... Think what it is, to stay here, and see Lydia treated like a heroine, when *I know* ..."

"The only things one really knows," said he curtly, "are what one has actually seen or heard. The other—"

"I have seen," she said. "I have heard."

"What have you seen and heard?"

"Why should I tell *you?*"

"There's no reason," he said. "Unless you'd like to."

"You'd only take *her* side."

"Are you sure of that?"

She looked at him, with a faint frown.

"Well, wouldn't you?" she demanded. "You'd stand by Lydia, wouldn't you, no matter what she'd done?"

"Very likely," said he.

"Even if you knew she'd deceived her husband?"

A great disgust overwhelmed him; he had wanted to learn everything he could about Emery's death, but he did not want to hear *this*. He remembered that Lois had told him Jack Barrow was in love with Lydia, but, as Lois had put it, there had been nothing sordid or base in it.

"I don't know it," he said curtly.

"And you don't want to, either," said Elsie. "Well, do you think I like to know it, either?"

Something in her voice arrested him; he glanced at her, and was surprised to see tears in her eyes.

"For years—" she said, "I thought it was—a beautiful thing.... I was only fourteen when I first found out.... I was here, visiting with mother.... I wasn't an attractive child, and she liked me to keep out of the way.... I was wandering around in the garden, and when I came by the library window I heard them. It didn't seem to be a bit wrong to look and listen. It was—like a beautiful play.... She was sending him away; they were saying good-by. He kept saying, 'I'm so sorry, Lydia; I'm so sorry ...' And she was crying. 'God bless you, darling,' she said."

The girl was crying herself; she took off her blurred spectacles, and Old Portland was startled by the change that made in her; her face looked worn and pitifully young.

"I remembered it—all these years," she went on. "I thought—it was so beautiful. I thought—they were—so honorable. And then, when I came back two weeks ago, *he* was here again. They hadn't—really parted. I suppose they've been seeing each other all this time."

He looked at her with compassion but also with a sort of curiosity. Were these tears, this pain, only for a lost illusion, a lost faith in human nature? Or was there something else, of which perhaps even she herself was unconscious?

He thought of Barrow, a good-looking young fellow, no doubt romantic in the eyes of the girl.

Then he thought of Lydia.

He had seen her only half a dozen times. After his sister's death he had expected to see no more of Emery; but now and then an invitation had come, and it had seemed to him decent to accept. And Lydia had always been just what she was now, a gentle, courteous, obviously unhappy lady.

Considering what her husband was, it was by no means impossible that she might have found young Barrow's devotion balm to her hurt pride. But as for carrying on a love affair with him—

"No," he thought. "She's not that sort. And Lois said so, too."

He then addressed the unhappy girl before him.

"Look here!" he said. "I dare say you'll call me a plutocrat, or an aristocrat, or a grinder of the faces of the poor—whatever it is you call the people who are able to make a good living—but I believe you're altogether wrong about this. There may be some—sentimental attachment—"

"If you could see the way they look at each other!" she cried. "In that—way—"

"Good Lord! Didn't you ever look at a man 'that way'?"

"No," she said. "Never."

There was something stern and somber in her answer. She was, he thought, the sort of girl who would love in a desperate, tragic, never-smiling fashion, and he felt even more sorry for her.

"You're making a mountain out of a molehill, my dear girl," he said.

To his surprise, she caught his hand, held it in a convulsive grip. And there flashed through his head a great wonder at the confidence these two young creatures, Lois and Elsie, showed in him.

He was not sympathetic; he belonged steadfastly to another generation. Yet that did not in the least discourage them.

"I wish I were!" she cried. "He was so kind to me when I was a little girl.... He was kind to me—when nobody else was. He's so changed now...."

But, thought Old Portland, puzzled, Barrow couldn't be much older than she herself. When she had been a little girl he must have been no more than a boy, and boys are not usually kind to small girls.

"Now, see here!" he said. "I think you're altogether wrong. And, in any case, it's not your business. Lydia's being very kind to you. It's not for you to judge her, or to pry into her private affairs. Forget all about it. You're going to be a doctor, aren't you? That's enough to keep anyone interested. I always wished I'd known more about it. Once, on the Valparaiso run, I had to cut off a poor devil's finger. Never forgot it."

Her grasp on his hand tightened.

"But don't you see ..." she said, very low, "that when he was so kind to me—long ago—and now to see him—ruined—dragged into this horrible thing—by *her* ..."

"What horrible thing?"

She looked at him, and did not answer for a moment.

"It's not his fault," she said. "If you could have seen him that evening.... Cousin Gilbert was—dreadful to Lydia. And he—couldn't stand it."

"Yes," he thought. "Poor young devil! She's certainly in love with Barrow."

"He couldn't stand it," she repeated. "And when he got up to go out of the room, I heard her say in that helpless, hateful way of hers, 'Please don't mind, Marcus—'"

"*Marcus!*"

"That's Captain Snow's first name."

"Captain Snow?"

"Why, yes," she answered, with a frown. "Of course. There's the housemaid ... I don't want her to see my eyes."

She hastened out of the room, and Old Portland stood where he was with something new to think about now.

He went out into the garden, to smoke a pipe over the new idea. So Elsie Evans believed that Snow was in love with Lydia....

"If that's true," he thought, "it's a bad job."

For Barrow was no more than a reckless, hot-headed boy, but Snow was something very different. He recalled that cold and baleful look of Snow's. No, Snow was a man, and a level-headed, purposeful man. Whatever he did would be properly planned and executed.

The fatally weak point in any case against Sommerfield had been the lack of a known motive. If Elsie Evans was to be believed, Snow had a motive. He had sat there that evening listening to Emery tormenting his wife with his brutal talk. Probably he had heard that sort of thing before. And if he loved her ...

There was also another, still more unpleasant aspect of the case. By her husband's death Lydia inherited a nice little fortune. Suppose she cared for Snow, and he was simply an adventurer who would take advantage of her love and marry her for her money?

An adventurer of that type might well want Emery out of the way.

"I'll have to find out more about Snow," he thought.

He discovered that he did not want to find out anything more about anyone here. He saw, in every direction, nothing but distressing complications. If Snow had done this thing, and it should be proved, and Lydia did care for him, it would mean more agony for a woman who had already suffered cruelly.

But could he stand by and see the fellow marry Lydia? "No," he thought; "I've got to know more about him. Now, whom can I ask?"

As if in answer to his question, a shout reached his ears: "Hello, Uncle Barty!"

And, turning, he saw Lois coming out of the house. She wore a dark dress, sleeveless and very short, which seemed to him singularly like a bathing suit.

She was the perfect embodiment of that new sort of girl he had often thought deplorable. But this morning it occurred to him that these girls were considerably easier to deal with than their more gracious and dignified predecessors.

He could at once begin to ask Lois questions without even trying to be tactful.

"Hello!" he called back, and waited while she ran toward him across the wet grass.

"You'll take cold, coming out like that," he said.

"Never do," said she.

"See here!" he said. "What do you know about this Captain Snow?"

"Well …" she answered. "It's rather pathetic … But why? Are you sleuthing?"

"I want to know."

"Well, you see, he gets sort of attacks—of being loony," she said seriously.

"Loony?"

"I mean, something happened to him in the war, and every once in a while he goes off his nut."

"In what way?"

"Oh, awful rages. He went for father once—started to choke him; only luckily Stevens heard the row and dashed in. Father was very decent about it. He said nobody ought to hold it against Marcus. I like him. But lots of people won't have anything to do with him."

"Any other instances?"

"I've heard plenty, but I don't pay much attention. You're sleuthing on the wrong track, Uncle Barty, if you think he did—that. It's not a bit like him. I mean, I suppose he might do a thing like that, but he'd never cover up his tracks and lie out of it."

"Ha!" said Old Portland, musing. "And he's one of the people who say they saw the burglar escaping.... Ha! ..."

"Let's eat," said Lois. "I'm hungry. I've been trying to get Duncan on the telephone, and they say in his hotel that he's not in. That means he never came in last night. He'd *never* be up and out at eight o'clock." She paused a moment. "It worries me," she went on. "He's capable of doing—pretty silly things."

Old Portland silently hoped that Sommerfield had done the most rash and foolish deed possible. But aloud he said:

"When you first spoke of this affair, you said that practically everyone had a motive. Yet, whenever I mention a name, you always say not that one—*he* couldn't *possibly* have done it."

"Well, that's how I feel," she admitted. "It doesn't seem possible—and still it happened."

"And you want to find out what's happened—no matter who's hurt?"

"It's not that. I told you. It's simply that I don't want—anything else to happen. You see, no one's gone away. Everyone who was here that night is here now. So—whoever did that is here now. I—get thinking of that at night sometimes ..."

There was a moment's silence.

"Lois," said Old Portland curtly, "I'm due for a holiday. Want to come with me? We'll go to France for May. Ever seen Paris in May? Then we'll go up through the Black Forest. Norway in July."

He was, in his heart, a little nervous. He could not imagine how she would receive his proposal.

"I'd—love it," she said a little unsteadily, and laid her hand on his shoulder. "Only we've got to settle all this first. Now, come on! Let's eat."

As they turned toward the house, a sound arrested them.

"Was that a cat?" asked Lois. "Or a fellow creature?"

"Don't know," said Old Portland, frowning, while in his ears there echoed still that thin, wailing cry. "Wait! Is that someone running?"

"From the garage," said Lois.

She ran across the lawn, and he followed her to the hedge that lined a gravel path. He caught sight of a girl in a black uniform flying along. She turned her head; he saw her eyes dilate with terror, and she collapsed suddenly, lay in a heap on the path.

It was a sturdy hedge; no getting through it. They had to follow it down to the garage before they could reach the path.

"It's Agnes," said Lois in a matter-of-fact tone. "She's fainted. Don't look so worried, Uncle Barty. Fainting isn't serious. I'll get some water from the garage."

She was off, and Clement was left alone with the unconscious girl.

Perhaps fainting was not serious—but it looked serious. The girl at his feet was horribly white, a very pretty young creature with an innocent softness in her face. Agnes. This was the girl who interested the unspeakable Sommerfield.

Well, it didn't follow that he interested her. In her straight black dress this girl had the look of a little strayed nun affrighted in the outside world. Such a neat, young little thing. He felt very sorry for her, and very uneasy.

"Never understood this fainting business," he thought. "I suppose it startled her to see us looking over the hedge."

Then he heard Lois' step on the gravel, and with profound relief saw her coming along the path carrying a tin dipper with great care.

He had begun to smile at her, when he noticed the look on her face.

"Lois!" he cried. "What's the matter?"

Without answering she came on steadily and set the dipper down on the path beside the unconscious figure of the girl.

Then she looked at him, straight in the face. She spoke without a tremor, but her mouth had an odd tenseness.

"Duncan's there, in the car," she said. "I'll look after Agnes if you'll go and see …"

Her quietness was more effective than a scream. He knew at once that something was terribly amiss. Without a word, he went toward the garage.

The door was open, and in the cool gloom he saw the big car. He crossed to it, and he saw, propped up stiffly on the seat, a figure wrapped in a rug, a chalk-white face with closed eyes.

He got up on the running board and, opening the door, leaned forward and touched the man's forehead. It was cold as stone.

He stepped down on the floor again, and, still with his eyes upon that still figure, felt in his pocket for his cigarette case. For that was his profound instinct—to collect himself, to realize a situation, never for an instant to let go.

His first clear thought was of Lois. He went to the door. But the path was empty; both girls were gone. For an instant he stood there, remembering how she had come from the garage after seeing—that; had come steadily, not so much as spilling a drop of water.

"By heaven!" he said to himself. "She's a thoroughbred!"

Now he must act. He had turned back to the car, when a panting voice spoke behind him:

"Mr.—Clement!"

It was Stevens, haggard and breathless.

"I've been up to the house, sir—looking for you.… I wanted to see you first.…"

Old Portland lit a cigarette. "Well?" he asked.

"I found him this morning—beside the boulevard—"

"Begin at the beginning," said Clement briefly.

"All right," said Stevens, growing cooler and cooler himself. "The cook telephoned over from the house about half an hour ago, asked me to run down to the village and get another bottle of cream. So I took the car.... It was early. The boulevard was pretty empty. I wasn't hurrying.... Then I saw a man's hat near the roadside. I slowed up a little. I thought I saw an arm. I got out. And I found him. He'd been run over. So I brought him back, and I tried to find you.... I didn't want to frighten any of the women...."

"You shouldn't have touched him. Didn't you know that?"

"My God! I couldn't have left him there like a dawg."

"You shouldn't have touched him until the police had seen him."

"He was soaked through. Must have been lying there in the rain all night.... I couldn't leave him there that way."

"Telephone to the police at once," said Clement. "I'm going up to the house."

"Hold on a minute!" said Stevens, who had once again lost his respectful manner. "Help me to carry him upstairs and put him on the bed."

"You let him alone. Notify the police first."

"No!" said Stevens. "I wouldn't treat a dawg like that."

"You're a blamed fool," said Old Portland. "The man's dead. It doesn't matter to him anymore—"

"Down in Texas where I come from," said Stevens, in his soft drawl, "we wouldn't treat a dawg like that. I'm going to lay him out decent. I reckon they won't hang me for *that*."

Old Portland frowned, surprised by this superb sentimentality in a young man he had not imagined so constituted.

"I'll notify the police myself," he said. "Where's your telephone?"

Stevens pointed it out, and Clement took down the receiver.

"Police station!" he said. And as he said it a great weight seemed to descend upon him—a great dread and dismay.

PART THREE—A KILLER AT LARGE

"The chauffeur here found a man dead by the boulevard this morning," Clement told the police. "He picked him up and brought him back here. His name is Duncan Sommerfield—an—an acquaintance of Mr. Emery's.... All right!"

He turned back to Stevens.

"They're sending someone up at once," said he.

"Yes, sir," said Stevens, unexpectedly deferential again. "Will you tell Miss Lois, sir?"

Clement looked at him; saw the young man standing, cap in hand, looking at the car, for all the world like a movie hero.

"You'll be asked questions, Stevens," he observed.

"Yes, sir," said Stevens. "I reckon everyone will be."

"They may reopen the question of that alibi of Sommerfield's."

"I don't see why, sir."

"Don't you?" said Old Portland, and walked off, with a heart like lead.

It did not seem to him very probable that Sommerfield, a young man of almost unlimited resources, had come out here alone, had gone walking in a downpour of rain along the lonely boulevard at night, and had been accidentally run over. Not very probable.

He thought of Stevens as he had seen him last night, with the little trickle of blood running from the corner of his mouth. Stevens, who had brought the dead man back. And he remembered a saying of his old nurse, from the remote days of his childhood:

"Them as hides can find."

Then suddenly he remembered Barrow striding along that empty road—Barrow, with that desperate look on his face.... And no good reason for being where he was.

Wherever he looked there was confusion, darkness. But in his mind there was one definite thought: He believed now that Emery had been murdered, not shot down by an escaping burglar. And he believed that Sommerfield had been murdered.

"There's a killer loose here," he thought.

Clement had an opportunity, that morning, of observing some of the practical difficulties which the police encounter. He had thought the police either pretty indifferent or pretty stupid for having accepted Emery's death so readily at its face value. But this morning he saw matters in a new light. He found the men who were sent to investigate efficient, civil, and painstaking, and he saw what an almost impossible task they had.

For no one told them anything that could help. He did not, himself. They knew nothing of the relations among these people. By dint of patient questioning they got the bare facts, and it was surprising what a straightforward case those facts presented.

Lois told them, and Clement corroborated, that they had met Sommerfield in the Grand Central, apparently on his way to catch the last train out to Moorewood. After that, no one had seen him again, alive.

No one had noticed him getting off the train. Barrow said that he himself had swung off the last car and ducked under the gate.

He had looked toward the station, but, not seeing the car that should have come to meet him, had gone to Hague's drug store and tried to get a taxi by telephone.

Then he had set off on foot, being presently picked up by Clement and Lois.

The fact that he had gone only half a mile in twenty minutes on a night when no one would be disposed to loiter never came to light at all. No one was particularly interested in his movements, anyhow; for he obviously had not run over Sommerfield.

The driver of the only cab that had met that train said he thought he had seen a man alight, but had not been interested; an old customer, an alderman, had come by the train and had at once driven off in his cab.

Stevens was questioned more closely. He said he had left the house in time to meet Mr. Barrow by that train, but he had punctured a tire, and, the weather being so bad, had stopped at a garage to put on his spare. Two mechanics at the garage corroborated this. They had not particularly noted the time, but they said it had been after twelve. Then Stevens had gone on, and had presently met Clement's car. And Sommerfield's body had been found some distance nearer to the station than the place of that meeting, on a part of the road which Stevens had not reached.

The police examined the spot where Stevens declared he had found Sommerfield, and the evidence was unmistakable in the sodden ground. Stevens repeated the account he had given to Clement. The cook had sent him for a bottle of cream; he had noticed a hat; he had stopped, got out, found the body, and recognizing it had brought it back. He was sharply reprimanded for having done this, but he was not at all contrite.

The body was examined by the police doctor and later by Lydia's own doctor. They both said the same thing. The unfortunate man had been knocked down and run over, the wheels of a heavy car crushing in his chest. There were no other injuries, except a severe bruise on the back of the head, for which his fall could well account. In his pockets were a considerable sum of money, a gold cigarette case, and he was wearing a valuable wrist watch.

It was by no means an unheard-of thing for a motorist to run down someone and escape without ever stopping to see what damage had been done. In this case, it seemed that the driver, with some paltry remnant of decency, had at least dragged his victim's body aside from the road. There was absolutely no clue to the perpetrator of this; there was no reason whatever for suspecting a deliberate murder.

In a surprisingly short time the reporters began to arrive. What interested them was the rumored engagement between Sommerfield and Lois. Old Portland would have sent them away, none too tactfully; but Lois did not agree with him.

"That's a mistake," she said. "They'll print something anyhow, and I'd rather it was my tale than theirs. I've got a pretty good line. You can listen."

He did listen, and marveled. She was graver than he had yet seen her, but perfectly cool. She said they had not been engaged, only old friends, and that Sommerfield had been a friend of her father's too.

"Both of them dead inside of three weeks," she said somberly. "It sort of shows you, doesn't it, how lawless the country's getting. Gunmen, and reckless drivers ..."

The reporters took that all down, along with the simple account of Sommerfield's fatal accident. The car sent to meet the train having been delayed, and the only taxi engaged, he had set off on foot, and on the boulevard had been run down and killed by an unknown motorist. Then she added a few more remarks about the "growing lawlessness in the country."

Old Portland saw what she meant to do. Inevitably Sommerfield's death would recall her father's shooting, and she had decided to point out the connection herself, and herself supply an explanation. She then told them that Mrs. Emery was prostrated, and that she herself was "just about all in." She shook hands with all of them, and they departed.

"You handled that well," said Old Portland.

But as she turned to him there was no look of triumph on her face, only a great weariness and grief. "We could have prevented it," she said, "if we'd let Duncan come in the car with us. I knew something was going to happen. I could have saved him!"

"My dear girl, if he'd simply waited at the station for us the accident would never—"

"You needn't bother to call it an accident to me," she said.

"What's this? More feminine intuition?" he asked. For he wanted her to think it was an accident.

He had noticed before that she never took offense, but was inevitably ready to explain her own point of view and to listen to his. Even now, after this atrocious shock, in all her sorrow and fatigue, she answered him with valiant patience.

"You see," she said, "I knew Duncan better than anyone else did. He'd never dream of starting to walk to the house on a night like that. If he wanted a taxi he'd get one, if he had to buy out a garage. And there's another thing. You saw the things they took out of his pockets. There was his cigarette case. I know he always carried that in his breast pocket—and it wasn't even dented."

"What do you make out of that, Lois?"

"I haven't had time to do much thinking—yet," she said soberly. "But I've got to. It's up to me to see that nothing more happens."

"Good God, girl! You're not expecting—"

"Everyone's still here," she said. "Whoever killed father and Duncan is *still here*."

Old Portland's scalp prickled; a shiver ran along his spine.

"If you believe that," he said, "you ought to tell the police."

"That's about the last thing I'd do."

"Why?"

She stood for a moment, staring at the ground.

"I'm going up to Lydia now," she said. "She's badly upset."

"One moment! What are Barrow and Snow staying on here for?"

"Jack's got work to finish, winding up father's estate. He was his secretary, you know. And Marcus—Lydia asked Marcus to stay. Anyhow, it's better for them to stay, now, until after the inquest."

He stood looking after her as she walked off, that girl who within three weeks had lost her father and her fiancé, or whatever she called Sommerfield. She had had no illusions about either of them; yet, thought Clement, she mourned them honestly. She was involved now in tragedy and crime as well as grief, and how sane she was, how strong, how steadfast!

"By heaven, she's got to get out of this," he thought. "I suppose she'll have to attend the inquest, poor child. But after that she'll have to get away. Then the rest of 'em can stay here and go on with their killings, if they like."

He had had no breakfast but a cup of coffee gulped down in haste, and he had been smoking incessantly all the morning; he felt altogether out of sorts.

"I'll take a walk," he decided. "Have to find out first what time lunch will be."

He rang, and very promptly the housemaid, Agnes, answered his ring.

"Feeling all right again?" he asked her.

"Yes, sir," she answered, with a pretty blush.

And she looked all right again. An extraordinarily attractive young person, with her dark hair and her blue eyes and that soft innocence about her.

"Life must be pretty hard for a girl like that," he thought; but compassion did not deter him from asking certain questions that he had in mind.

"Must have given you a nasty shock," he said sympathetically, "going into the garage like that. I suppose you were looking for Stevens...."

"It was the cook sent me to call him in to breakfast, sir."

"And when you went past the car you happened to look into it," he proceeded. "I think I heard you cry out."

"Yes, sir."

"No wonder!" said he. "Enough to upset anyone. And then, I suppose, the police bothered you with a lot of questions?"

"No, sir," she answered in her subdued, respectful little voice.

"The newspaper men?"

"No, sir. They didn't talk to me at all."

"I'm afraid we haven't finished with them yet," said Old Portland, sighing. "Sommerfield was a fairly prominent figure—in certain circles.... Visited here a good deal, didn't he?"

"Yes, sir."

He was not getting much out of *her*. He could not even read anything in her shy, pretty face.

"Well!" he said, with another sigh. "I suppose there are some people who won't be much upset by this. A fellow like Sommerfield must have had plenty of enemies."

She raised her eyes to his face, and he saw in them the same look of terror he had seen across the hedge; then her lids closed and a deathly pallor came over her. He sprang forward and caught her arm. She swayed for a moment; then she opened her eyes again.

"Sit down!" said he. "I'll get you some water."

"No, thank you, sir," she said, almost inaudibly. "I've me work to do."

Old Portland put a bill into her hand. She thanked him and went off, leaving him confused.

"Now, what does this mean?" he thought: "Did she care so much for Sommerfield? Well, hang it all! I'm not going to ask women any more questions. Makes me feel like a brute.... I'll take a walk. I need to think. Haven't had any time for thinking since I came out here."

He went into the hall, took his hat and stick, and, opening the front door, stepped out on the terrace. Immediately the door opened again and Elsie Evans came out.

"Mr. Clement!" she said. "I want to speak to you!"

Perhaps it was a lingering remorse for the effect of his questions upon the housemaid; whatever the reason, he felt sorry for Elsie. Her dark dress looked so shabby in the bright spring sun, her young face so worn.

"Certainly," he answered. "Come and sit down here!"

She followed him to a stone bench at the end of the terrace, and they sat down side by side.

"You won't like what I have to say," she began.

At her peremptory tone his sympathy commenced to dwindle.

"Won't I?" he said.

"No. You'll try to deny it. You'll think up all sorts of excuses."

"See here!" said Old Portland. "Let's take it for granted that I'm a bigoted, thick-skulled imbecile to start with. It'll save time. We'll assume that I'm incapable of understanding anything you say and that I have a constitutional prejudice against the truth. Now we can go on."

"Oh …" she faltered, very much taken aback. "I didn't mean it that way…. I only meant … I only thought that—your sympathies would probably be on the side of—"

"Of Mammon," said he. "They probably will be. Now, what's the latest crime committed by the plutocrats?"

"I only meant," she said, "that I could see things that other people, who hadn't had my experience, wouldn't think of looking for."

He felt sorry for her again; her with her experience.

"Everyone else," she went on, "was perfectly satisfied with that burglar theory. Well, I wasn't. I worked on a newspaper all summer, and I came in contact with criminals. I thought, from the very beginning, that it was something different. I nearly gave myself away to you this morning when I said 'if the silver ever was stolen.' Do you remember?"

"Yes."

"And now I know!" she cried triumphantly.

"Go ahead!"

"Well, this morning, after this other thing—after they'd taken Duncan away—I made up my mind…. I wanted to look at Cousin Gilbert's will. Of course he didn't leave a penny to me—but I wanted to see all the people who benefited. I knew there was a carbon copy in the safe in Jack Barrow's room, and I knew the combination—"

"How?"

"Cousin Gilbert told it to me, the night he was killed. He sent me to get something for him. Jack wasn't fit to do anything then. So this morning, when I knew Jack was busy in the library, I went into his room and opened the safe. And I found in it—a silver filigree dish that was supposed to have been stolen from the sideboard!"

Her blue eyes were bright behind her spectacles; her triumph shocked him.

"Nevertheless," he said, "finding that dish doesn't by any means connote that Barrow—"

"But it does!" she cried. "When you realize that Jack was terribly in debt, worried sick about money troubles. When you realize that he owed money to Cousin Gilbert and that he hated him."

"And you'd be glad if you could prove it was Barrow?"

"Certainly I'd be glad to find out—"

"You'd like to help to send the fellow to the electric chair?"

"Oh, I don't—mean that!" she cried, paling. "It's only that I—I want to see—innocent people cleared from suspicion …"

"Nobody's been accused."

"But someone will be! Duncan's death will bring it all up again."

"Elsie," said Old Portland, using her name for the first time, "why did you come to me with this story?"

"Why …" she faltered, "because—you seem—you seem to be—the right one—"

"I'm not the right one," he said, rising. "I wouldn't lift a finger to help hound that fellow to ruin—to death."

She had risen too, looking at him in dismay.

"I didn't think of it—that way," she stammered. "I only wanted to spare other people …"

"What other people?"

Her face grew scarlet, then pale again.

"But—don't *you* want to see justice done?" she asked.

"I'm not sure if I know what justice is," he answered.

There was not a vestige of that triumph on her face now.

"But—do you think I ought to—just do *nothing*—when I've found out …?"

"What have you found out? That Barrow has a silver dish that doesn't belong to him. Ask him about it."

"But if I ask him … Don't you see? … He'd—"

"Then if he were guilty he might have a chance to escape from justice? And that wouldn't do, would it?"

Her eyes still questioned him in wonder and dismay.

"But—what do *you* think I ought to do?" she asked.

"It's impossible for me—"

"Don't say that!" she interrupted, seizing his sleeve. "Just tell me! I'll do whatever you say!"

He was surprised and considerably touched by that.

"Suppose—" he began, when the door opened and Agnes came out and crossed the terrace.

"Lunch is served, sir," she said, paying no attention to Elsie.

He nodded briefly and looked after her thoughtfully as she returned to the house. Then he turned back to Elsie.

"Suppose we have a talk with Barrow," he said. "You and I?"

"All right," she answered. Then, as they moved toward the house:

"Perhaps I'm not—quite so horrible as you think," she said unsteadily.

"You're remarkably poor at reading my thoughts," said he.

That lunch was, to Old Portland, a very nightmare of a meal. Lydia had seated him at the end of the table. On one side of him sat Lois, cool and self-possessed as usual, but very silent and with reddened eyes. On his other side sat Elsie Evans, who never once spoke a word. Beside her was Captain Snow, stiff and impassive. Next to him, at the other end of the table, sat Lydia, pale, obviously half ill, but making her valiant effort to talk, to be the good hostess. And the only one who played up to her was Barrow, at her left hand. He talked, thought Old Portland, a little too much, and ate too little.

A more careful study revealed that Barrow was not so young as he looked—about thirty-five probably, not a boy.

There was about him an indefinable air of uneasiness and misery which disturbed Clement profoundly. In debt, Elsie had said, "worried sick about money troubles." ... And he did not look like a man who could endure any sort of trouble with much fortitude. He was the type that hits back at ill fortune. But a murderer? A man who could shoot his employer and rob him, and go on as if nothing had happened? ...

It occurred to Clement that most murderers had to go on as if nothing had happened. And also in his mind every moment during that interminable meal was this perfectly plain fact. Of all the persons here, Jack Barrow was the only one who had demonstrably been able to kill both Emery and Sommerfield. He had been in the house the night Emery was shot—and he had in his room a silver dish stolen from the sideboard. He had certainly passed the spot last night where Sommerfield met his death. And Sommerfield had died after having hinted that he knew more than he had told about the first tragedy.

Clement entirely lost track of the conversation. He drifted off into a sort of daydream in which he saw Barrow, neat and slender in his blue shirt and dark trousers, walking down a corridor at the end of which stood that Chair....

He roused himself with a start as Lydia pushed back her chair and rose.

"If anyone—" she began, and stopped. "Lois, you'll look after everyone, won't you?" she asked.

"Yep," said Lois briefly. "You'd better go and lie down."

With a polite smile that included everyone, Lydia withdrew. Lois leaned back in her chair and lit a cigarette.

"Does anyone need any looking after?" she asked.

"You do, yourself," thought Old Portland. "This is harder for you than for anyone else."

But he knew better than to say that. She would not like it. Just then she turned her head, and their eyes met. She laid her hand on his for an instant, and then rose and left the room, leaving with him the memory of her tear-stained young face, her steady eyes.

"My God!" he thought. "She's got to get away from this thing—from this whole atmosphere. The child's suffering—and no one seems to bother about her. Of course Lydia's cut up—but she's an older woman. She ought to be able to help the child."

He rose, with a frown, and would have walked out of the room if Elsie had not touched his arm. Then he remembered.

"If you're not too busy, Barrow," he said, "can you spare me a few moments?"

Barrow did not seem at all suspicious or alarmed by this request.

"Certainly," he said. "What about the library? I've got all my papers and so on in there, so that if you want any information—"

It was obvious that he thought Clement's talk would be concerned with Emery's estate. Not remarkable, considering that he had been the brother of the first Mrs. Emery, and that a part of the estate consisted of property left by her.

This unsuspiciousness should have pleased Old Portland in his role of investigator, but it did not. He followed Barrow along the hall to the library in an uneasy and unhappy humor.

"Sit down!" said Barrow. "Have a cigarette? It's—"

He stopped, and for the first time looked startled; for Elsie had come into the room and seated herself near the window.

"Is Elsie in on this?" he asked.

"Look here!" said Old Portland. "I don't care to—take you by surprise. I give you fair warning that this is—a pretty unpleasant business."

He closed the door into the hall, and stood near it.

"It's a matter of a—a silver dish," he said curtly. "Found in your room."

A blank silence followed. Reluctantly he glanced at Barrow, and saw how the words had stricken him.

"Now's your chance to explain, Barrow," he said.

"I have nothing to say," said Barrow.

"Yes, you have," said Old Portland. "You're not speaking to—an enemy. Naturally, the thing has to be cleared up, in justice to other people; but, beyond finding out the truth, I've no concern with it."

Again Barrow was silent for a time.

"Then—in that case," he said—"if you take the dish back, and I clear out …"

"Not quite good enough, Barrow," said Old Portland. And he thought he was not likely ever in his life to go through a more difficult scene than this. He felt that he would remember all his life how Barrow looked, that neat, slender young fellow in his blue shirt and dark suit, trapped here, and well aware of it. His eyes were desperate, but he spoke quietly.

"I'll—make a bargain with you," he said. "I'll—enable you to—get the rest of the missing silver—if you'll give me twelve hours' start of the police."

"Barrow," said Old Portland, almost gently, "do you realize that what you're saying doesn't accord with the theory that Emery was shot by a burglar—"

"It doesn't affect that in the least," said Barrow. "The burglar was frightened before he'd collected anything. He got away. I saw him."

"How did you see him from the library window and yet get into the dining room in time to take—"

"I simply shoved the stuff into a drawer in the sideboard," said Barrow. "Then I came down later and got it. No one thought of searching just then."

He spoke with a sort of careless ease, but his face was pitiable to see, so strained, so white.

"You've got all the silver, Barrow?"

"Yes. I'll tell you where it is, if you'll give me a chance to get away."

"Why was that one dish in your room?"

"I meant to pawn that," he answered, "in case I had to get away. I'd have left the ticket behind."

He brought out his cigarette case, but his hand shook so that he dropped it, spilling the cigarettes on the carpet.

"Have one of mine?" said Old Portland, producing his own case.

Barrow looked at him sidelong—an odd look.

"You don't seem—very—very prejudiced," he said.

"Well, you impress me as pretty amateurish at this game," said Old Portland. "I don't think you've had much experience in—stealing, Barrow."

"No," said Barrow. "You're right. I—haven't."

Old Portland struck a match for him, and he inhaled deeply.

"I'll—tell you where the silver is," he said. "I'll write a—confession that I—took it. If you'll let me go."

"You wouldn't be likely to get far, Barrow."

"All right. If I'm caught, I'll have to pay."

"There'd be a pretty heavy payment demanded, Barrow. You'd better face the facts."

"I—have," said Barrow.

He was in torment, and gallant in his ordeal.

"You said you ran in after the shot, and found Emery dead. You were there, with him, when Snow and the others arrived. If you admit that you took the silver, Barrow—"

Barrow said nothing.

"Do you understand?" asked Old Portland.

"Yes," said Barrow; "I understand."

"You understand that you'll inevitably be accused of murder, Barrow?"

That word was like a blow to Barrow. He sank down into a chair, and stared at the floor, in a stony silence. Then, in a moment, he pulled himself together.

"It's—not inevitable," he said. "If you get the stuff back—and I get away—you can—let it drop."

"It would be out of my hands, Barrow. The police would have to know that the silver had been returned."

"Well," said Barrow, "suppose I confess—everything—and then shoot myself. That makes a nice, neat ending."

"No!" cried Elsie, and the two men started violently. They had forgotten Elsie. "No!" she cried again. "Oh, let him go, Mr. Clement! It's—*horrible!* I never thought … Let him *go!*"

"You started this," said Clement.

"I didn't realize … It's so—horrible! …" She had risen, and stood gripping the high back of the chair. "Do you know who's really responsible for Cousin Gilbert's death? It's he—himself!"

They both stared at her, and she looked back at them, her thin cheeks flushed, her blue eyes brilliant behind the spectacles.

"*He's* responsible!" she cried. "No matter who actually fired the shot! He was cruel—bad—hateful. He hurt everyone who came near him. Long ago he used to encourage my mother to do—foolish things—to—to toady to people. He's been a bad influence in my life ever since I can remember. *He* started that vile lie about Captain Snow—"

"What lie?" asked Clement.

"That he has fits of insanity. There's not one word of truth in it! One night Cousin Gilbert said things to Lydia—dreadful things—and Marcus knocked him down. Then Cousin Gilbert called for Stevens. He told Stevens that Captain Snow mustn't be blamed—that he had these attacks…. He got the story going—in a sort of sympathetic way—'poor old Snow.' And Marcus couldn't deny it without bringing in Lydia's name. It's spoiled his life. Whatever he does, people see signs of his 'insanity.' When he's been impatient—or careless—like anyone else—people have thought it just another sign…. Nobody will trust him…." She stopped, and bit her lip; her eyes brimmed with tears.

"He's done harm to everyone! No one could be in this house—without growing worse for it. He made Duncan Sommerfield worse—he made Marcus so bitter and different. Jack—you know all he's done to you—"

"No," Barrow interrupted. "Emery—nobody's responsible for anything I've done—except myself."

It gave Old Portland singular pleasure to hear that. It probably wasn't true; he thought it more than likely that Emery had exerted a strong influence for the worse on Barrow. He thought Barrow reckless, careless, easily moved to anger and resentment.

"But he's a *man*," thought Clement. "He's taking this well."

"*I* know what he's done to you," Elsie went on. "I've seen him—encouraging you to drink—encouraging you to borrow money from him and then sneering at you. It was Cousin Gilbert's own fault! He started all this hatred and bitterness. I didn't realize what I was doing! I'm sorry! Jack, I don't—blame you for what you did!"

With tears running down her cheeks, she held out her hand to Barrow, and he took it, looking at her with a sort of incredulity.

"You think—I shot him?" he asked.

"I don't care!"

"You think I shot him?" he repeated.

Her eyes widened; she stared at him with an expression Clement could not reach. "*What* ...!" she cried.

Barrow turned to Clement.

"D'you think I did it?" he asked.

"I'll believe anything you give me your word is true," said Clement.

"Then—" began Barrow, "I'd like to tell you something that"—when he was interrupted by the entrance of Snow, who came in through one of the open French windows.

"Sorry!" he said. "Is this a private conference? Or may I stay?"

Nobody answered him, but he seemed quite undisturbed by that. There was a new cheerfulness about him, an air almost gay.

"I've got an evening paper," he observed. "The first account of our little show down here. Extraordinary, isn't it, that the thing's in print already?"

With something like a shock, Clement realized that during this talk with Barrow he had forgotten Sommerfield, forgotten that there was a second death to be taken into account.

"A second death—" said Snow, exactly as if he had read his thoughts. "Of course the newspaper's playing that up. Now, if we were in a detective story or a play, there'd have to be a third one—"

"We're not, however," Old Portland interrupted curtly, for he did not like the look of Elsie Evans.

"Don't want any more faints," he thought. "Why can't that fellow hold his tongue?"

But Snow kept on.

"It's all here," he said, indicating the newspaper he carried. "Even photographs—of Sommerfield, and of the boulevard, with the usual cross to mark the fatal spot. They've called Sommerfield the 'millionaire clubman,' and they speak of the 'death car.' Nothing's been forgotten. And there's a little editorial about 'the growing lawlessness in the country,' introducing Emery—"

"Very amusing, no doubt," said Old Portland, more and more annoyed.

Then he remembered how Snow had spoken last night: "I hope we'll get good news of Sommerfield—that he's broken his neck—or that someone's broken it for him!" …

"I've been talking to our chief of police in Moorewood," Snow continued. "The inquest will be tomorrow. He's going to subpoena Stevens, and you, Barrow, and you, Clement. And Lois …"

"Lois?"

"Matter of form. Simply to say what she saw in the garage. And young Agnes, of course."

"Let me see the paper!" said Elsie abruptly, and when Snow handed it to her she went out of the room.

After a moment Old Portland followed her. But he did not go upstairs; he opened the front door and went out on the terrace. And as he was strolling along there in the sun he heard something he was not meant to hear. The library windows were at the end of the terrace; as he passed them he heard Snow's voice:

"It's a damned lucky thing—for some people—that Sommerfield's out of the way."

There was no answer to this remark.

"He would have talked," Snow went on. "And now he can't. That ought to be—an object lesson—for other talkative people."

Still there was no answer.

"And *you'll* hold your tongue," said Snow evenly.

This time Barrow's voice answered him, sounding shaken and very young in comparison with the other's cool insolence.

"I'm not taking orders from you—you swine!"

Clement stood motionless, expecting to hear the sound of a blow. But not a sound came, and he walked on, profoundly disturbed.

As he turned the corner of the terrace he came upon Elsie Evans, standing close to the back window of the library. She did not see him or hear him; she was staring into the room, one hand pressed against her heart.

He turned back quietly, and hurried into the house. He looked into the library, but Snow sat in there alone, smoking his pipe and reading a magazine.

"If we were in a detective story or a play," Snow had said, "there'd have to be a third death...."

Certainly Snow had seen his wishes in regard to Sommerfield most strangely fulfilled. Did he have a prevision …? 'A third death ' …

Once again old Portland felt a chill run along his spine, a prickling of the scalp.

"I've got to think this thing out!" he said to himself. "I've been no more use since I came here than a figurehead. I've got to *think*."

He wished to begin at the beginning, to marshal his facts in orderly array; but he could not dismiss the feeling of haste that was upon him, an almost panic sense of haste. For suppose *something else* were to happen? Suppose something else were already prepared?

Whoever had killed Emery and Sommerfield was still at large. Only by learning who the murderer was could he protect this household.

"I'll have to begin with Emery's death," he said to himself. "And I'm not going to worry about motives. Almost anyone, some time in his life, has cause to want to kill someone else. I have, myself. But I haven't done it. No; it's not a question of cause, but of character, temperament—whatever you like to call it. The thing is, who's capable of a murder here?"

He was strolling up and down the lawn, now, hands clasped behind him, big shoulders stooped.

"Sommerfield's out of it. He may have been killed because he knew who did it, but he didn't do it himself, or why was he killed? Then there's that fellow Stevens.... He says he was talking to a friend when they heard the shot. If that can be proved, it lets him out. I'll find out about that.... Then there's Barrow.... I don't think it was Barrow. I don't think it was Stevens.... Then there's Snow.

"Snow had a long score against Emery, because of that tale of his 'insanity.' According to what Elsie says, Snow's in love with Emery's widow. Snow was certainly threatening Barrow just now. Told him to hold his tongue. Held up Sommerfield as an example of what happens to people who talk too much.... It's physically possible for Snow to have fired that shot and gone up the back stairs and come down later.

"But Sommerfield … Snow was in the house when we got here last night.... But, after all, I don't know what time Sommerfield was killed. He may have been lying there dead when we drove past. Snow may have been out of the house earlier in the evening. That's another thing I've got to find out."

He felt that his reflections were tending a little too clearly toward

Snow's guilt, and he distrusted that. There were too many things that did not fit in: Barrow and the silver, Stevens with his cut mouth, other less tangible things—glances he had seen, inflections in this voice or that, something in the very air to make him aware that there was so much he did not know.

"First thing to do," he reflected, "is to investigate Stevens' alibi. If it holds, then he's eliminated, and that's something."

As he walked toward the garage his thoughts turned again to Lois, and with a heavy anxiety. He hated the prospect of her appearing at the inquest; he hated to see her here in this atmosphere of sordid tragedy, with heaven knew what more horrible disclosures ahead of them. He remembered her as he had seen her at lunch, with the marks of tears on her face, so plucky, so honest, so very much alone.

Her father had no doubt been fond of her in his own egotistic way, and she was loyal to him; but he had been no comfort or help to her. Sommerfield had been even less; she had thought only of what she could do for him, never of what he could do for her. Elsie detested her; Snow and Barrow seemed perfectly indifferent; and Lydia, though she was kind and conscientious, had, he thought, very little understanding of the girl.

"She's got to be taken away from here," he thought. "Got to meet a different sort of people. Now, there's that young Martin in the office. Good-looking boy; plenty of character; got brains, too. He'll get on. Just the sort ..."

He stopped.

"My God!" he exclaimed. "Am *I*—matchmaking?"

He was shocked; he went on toward the garage with a quick stride and an ominous expression, intent upon nothing but the investigation of Stevens' alibi.

When he entered the garage, he noticed that the big car was gone. Only the two-seater was there, and his own car. He called Stevens, but there was no answer. He stood for a moment meditating.

"Last night," he said to himself, "Stevens wouldn't let me go upstairs; said he had someone there—a friend.... I might do a little investigating now."

The idea was repulsive to him. "Snooping," he called it to himself.

"Well, if I don't snoop," he thought, "if I'm so damn' squeamish, I'll never learn anything. And I've got to find out. I've got to see that nothing else happens."

That spurred him on. Going to the door, he glanced all about. No one in sight. Then, crossing the garage, he mounted the stairs down which Stevens had come the night before. There was a door at the head of the stairs, and it was closed. Once again he turned away—when he heard a sound inside the room, a rustle.

He knocked, and there was no answer. And he was extremely reluctant to open that door and walk into Stevens' quarters.

"What do I expect to find, anyhow?" he asked himself. "And suppose the fellow comes back and catches me snooping?"

Another department of his brain informed him that clues must be sought for everywhere, and that he could certainly hear the car coming in plenty of time to get down the stairs. So he turned the handle and entered.

PART FOUR—WHAT LOIS TOLD

Clement found himself in a neat and somewhat austere bedroom, with nothing in the least remarkable except a row of squirrel skins pegged out on the wall, like a line of headless little victims with arms raised to cry "Kamerad." Half smiling, he stepped forward to examine them—and saw, on the chest of drawers beneath them, a green purse.

It was undoubtedly a woman's purse, and, he thought, a cheap and tawdry article.

"None of my business," said that part of him which disapproved of detective work.

"Everything's your business," said the other department. "If you find that Stevens is involved with some woman, it may give you just the clue you need."

He stood looking down at the purse for a few moments. Then he took it up and opened it. He found in it a perfumed handkerchief without any initials, and six hundred dollars in bills of large denominations. There was nothing whatever to identify the owner.

He knew this was a clue, all right. But a clue to what? He had no idea.

Perhaps it was Stevens' own money, his savings. Then why put it in a woman's green purse? Well, why not, if he wanted to?

Perhaps it belonged to some friend of Stevens. But why should she leave so large a sum of ready money in this careless way?

What was more, he did not see how he could decently ask Stevens any questions about it. He had no evidence of anything against Stevens, nor had he any authority for his snooping. He put down the purse, and after a more careful examination of the room he descended the stairs and went out of the garage.

On his way to the house he suddenly remembered the squirrel skins. It was something more than probable that the skins were trophies of

Stevens' own prowess. And if Stevens could shoot squirrels …

"I'll have a talk with him," thought Old Portland. "I'll get something out of him—if I use my wits. In the meantime I might find out something more about him from the other servants."

It occurred to him then that the staff was very small for a house of that size—only a cook and a housemaid. He was sure that in his sister's day there had been another servant—a parlor maid.

"I hope there's one now," he thought. "I'm not going to tackle that Agnes again."

Nor could he possibly go into the kitchen and ask questions of the cook. He thought it over for a moment, then he went up to his own room.

"I'll ring my bell," he thought. "If Agnes comes, I'll tell her I want to speak to the other girl. And if there isn't any other girl I'll have to think of something else."

He rang, and stood waiting. He heard a light step in the hall outside, and a knock on his door. Stepping forward, he opened the door, and found Lydia there.

"I heard you ring," she said, smiling. "The parlor maid left last week, you know, so I came myself. Please don't mind telling me what you wanted!"

He was silent for a moment, very much taken aback.

"The agency is sending out two girls this afternoon," she went on. "Sisters. They have wonderful references."

"But—that girl Agnes?" he asked.

"Oh, she's gone!" said Lydia casually.

"Gone?"

"Yes. She wasn't very strong, you know, and all these—horrible things upset her badly. So I let her go."

"But she's wanted at the inquest tomorrow, Lydia!"

"No one told me that," said Lydia. "And, anyhow, it can't make much difference, can it? She only saw poor Duncan there in the garage, and you and Lois both saw him too."

"Lydia, you shouldn't have let her go! It's—it may lead to trouble. Where has she gone?"

"I'm awfully sorry," said Lydia. "I don't know. But it can't make such a difference—"

"Where did she go?"

"I really don't know. She took an early train, after lunch," said Lydia. She was polite, as usual, but evidently not at all impressed with the wrongness of what she had done. "I believe she told me where she was going—to her sister; but I really don't remember."

He decided to say no more until he had done more thinking, and he wanted to get rid of Lydia for a moment.

"What was it you wanted, Barty?" she asked in her gentle way. "Please tell me."

"I only wanted to know what time you have dinner," he said.

"I'm afraid it may be rather late tonight—with two new girls. But you'll have tea, won't you, Barty? They'll be here by five."

"Thanks," he said. "Sorry to have troubled you, Lydia."

"You don't trouble me, Barty," she answered. "I'm so very glad you're here."

For a moment her dark eyes regarded him steadily; then, with a smile, she withdrew and he closed the door.

"That girl had some reason for going," he thought. "Her behavior was—queer—altogether. Apparently Sommerfield was interested in her. She fainted when she found him dead—or did she faint because she saw us? She shouldn't have been allowed to get away! Lydia shouldn't—"

But he could not find it in his heart to blame Lydia.

"She doesn't suspect that there's anything wrong," he thought. "She's not the sort of woman to suspect things like that.... The thing is, how will the police take this?"

He walked up and down the room in a sort of rage, trying to piece together the things he knew into some logical entity. He could not. Barrow, Snow, Stevens, Agnes, Sommerfield—they all flitted through his mind now overshadowed by suspicion; the very house seemed filled with a brooding shadow.

"This isn't getting me anywhere," he thought angrily, "I've got to act. There are still these two things to do—test Stevens' alibi, and find if Snow was out of the house last night. I'll try the garage again; the fellow's back now, perhaps."

A new idea occurred to him: Very likely he took Agnes to the station. She may have told him where she was going.

He went out of his room, closing the door behind him and descended the stairs. And in the lower hall he met Lydia coming from the door that led to the kitchen.

"They've come," she announced. "Stevens has just brought them from the station—and they seem like very satisfactory, capable girls. It's such a relief!"

He looked down at her with a smile, and she, raising her soft eyes, smiled back at him, so gentle and fragile a creature, so pitiably ill adapted for any role in this ugly tragedy. She was thinking of nothing but her little domestic problems, innocently unaware of what was going on about her.

"I'm very glad," he said. "Now you'll—"

He stopped short, almost with a gasp. For he noticed that in her hand she carried that green purse.

"I mustn't startle her," he thought, and pulled himself together. "What's that?" he asked, touching the thing with his finger.

"That's my purse, Barty."

"Pretty gaudy, isn't it?" he pursued, smiling again.

"Oh, I wouldn't take it out anywhere, now that I'm in mourning!" she cried, shocked, "But I thought that just in the house—"

"Of course! I was only joking," he said.

But never in his life had he been farther from joking; never had he felt so bleakly dismayed. It was not possible for him to believe that Lydia, in her quiet fastidiousness, had ever owned or used that cheap, tawdry purse of imitation leather with its big brass clasp. He had seen it last in Stevens' room, with six hundred dollars inside it; he saw it now in her hand. He was certain that she was lying—and lying so easily and adroitly, with no trace of confusion in her pretty manner.

He managed to smile again as she passed him, but he was utterly sick at heart. A great desire seized him to stop here at this point—to find out nothing more.

"If I can persuade Lois to come back to the city with me tonight!" he thought. "I could get hold of young Martin—or someone else—take them out—to a theater—to dance—"

He remembered Lois' face at lunch; not much disposed for dancing just now. And he knew, too, that she would not come away now. She wanted to know the truth. She was not afraid of anything that might happen.

"I've got to go on with it," he thought. "Even if *I* don't—it'll go on by itself now."

So once again he set off for the garage. And all the way he could think of nothing but Lydia with that green purse in her hand.

He did not want to know anything more about that purse; he did not wish ever to think of it. But he had to think of it.

"She may have left it in the car," he thought. "And Stevens found it and kept it until he had a chance to return it."

Only, Lydia had not been out in the car that day; and if she had, she would surely have missed a considerable sum of money like that at once, and moreover he could not believe it was her purse at all.

There was in him a terrible smoldering rage against Stevens which he knew he must control. He found him in the garage, cleaning the car, and whistling over his work.

"Stevens!" he said.

"Sir?" said Stevens cheerfully.

"I'm still worrying about that burglary," said Old Portland. "I want to know more about it. You said Sommerfield wasn't with you when you heard the shot. You were here, upstairs—"

But he did not catch Stevens so easily.

"No, sir," said Stevens. "I was out by the road, talking to two fellows."

"Did they hear the shot?"

"I reckon they did," said Stevens.

There was a moment's silence.

"I suppose they were the same men—the same friends who saw you in the garage last night—when you had that tire trouble," observed Old Portland.

"No, sir," said Stevens. "They weren't."

"Oh! You've got four friends ready with alibis!" said Old Portland. For the sight of Stevens, so cool and easy, was fanning his smoldering rage into a blaze. He wanted above everything to find Stevens guilty; he hated Stevens—because of that purse.

"Maybe you'd like to talk to the four fellows, sir," said Stevens, with a faint, unpleasant smile.

"I think I should," said Old Portland.

"I'll take you in the car, if you like. I won't get out. You can talk to them alone."

"Very good! I'm ready," said Old Portland, and got into the car.

But as soon as they started he saw things in a new light. Suppose he found these alibis questionable? Suppose he found Stevens guilty of shooting Emery? Then what would follow? What would be made public?

He forced himself to face a supposition that sickened him. He knew Lydia's marriage had been a wretched one for her. What if she had, in her unhappiness, been led to think too much of Stevens? Things like that did happen. That purse was the sort of thing Stevens might have given her.... She might have put the money into it for him....

"She's not like that!" he cried to himself.

But she had lied to him. And she had let Agnes go away. Because Agnes knew too much to be allowed to appear at the inquest?

Again he thought—better to stop here, to learn no more. And again he realized that, even if he stopped, the course of events must inexorably continue. One death had already led to a second—it was like a chain; and the next link was even now forging.

The beginning of it all was Emery. He had sown evil, and evil was being reaped.

Stevens stopped the car before a little stationer's shop near the station.

"Just ask for Joe Borelli," he said. "He was one of the friends I was talking to when I heard the shot."

"I've got to go on," thought Old Portland, and entered the shop.

Joe Borelli was a serious young Italian with a wooden leg, more than willing to talk. He described, with gestures, the events of that night.

"We was driving home from a wedding, me and Tony Scori. We see the light in Steve's winder, and we holler. Steve comes out. We wanner tell him about the wedding. He stands there, talkin'. All of a sudden—crack! 'Sounds like a shot!' is what I say, and Steve he begins to run. I got one game leg. I can't run so good. And Tony he don't like any shooting. So we wait. By and by the police come along ..."

For a long time Clement stood in the little shop listening to Joe, but with only half his mind. The man's words and manner had convinced him from the beginning; he believed now that Stevens had been, as he said, out by the road when the shot had been fired. But that did not mean that Stevens knew nothing about the shooting. He might know too much. That money might have been a bribe....

As a matter of routine, he had a talk with Tony Scori, who had been Joe's companion. Then he went to the garage and talked to the mechanics there who had seen Stevens the night before. It was as if fate arranged for all these persons to be available, so that he need have no further suspicion of Stevens.

As they drove homeward he was aware for the first time of a great fatigue. It was less than twenty-four hours ago that Lois had come to his flat, and from that moment he had had no peace.

He straightened his big shoulders and sighed, and once again set his mind at the miserable problem.

Stevens had not killed Emery; he had an alibi. And Sommerfield had not shot him, for he himself had been killed because he knew too much. Unless, thought Old Portland, he had had an accomplice, who had grown frightened. That idea offered new possibilities. Who was a likely accomplice for Sommerfield? Barrow?

He began to think more deliberately, now, of Barrow's story. He admitted that he had stolen the silver; but when Elsie had accused him of the killing he had seemed genuinely startled and shocked. He had, on the whole, made a favorable impression upon Clement, in spite of that theft. Yet it must be remembered that if he were the murderer his own life was at stake, enough to make the most straightforward man develop a certain cunning. He had certainly been extremely anxious to get away....

"My God! Perhaps he's gone!" thought Clement.

He was about to tell Stevens to hurry, but he checked himself. If Barrow were not the killer, let him go. And if he were—let him go. With him would go the vague menace of another tragedy.

But the facts did not fit in with Snow's threat. Snow had warned the other to hold his tongue. Was that because Snow himself was the murderer and Barrow knew it? And Sommerfield had been killed because he too knew it?

They had reached the house now, and Clement got out. And when he entered the house he found a man waiting in the hall, to subpoena him to appear at the inquest the next afternoon. He put the paper into his pocket and went into the drawing room, where Lydia was sitting behind the tea table. Barrow had not gone away; he was there; and so was Elsie Evans, and so was Snow.

"Oh, Barty?" said Lydia. "But isn't Lois with you?"

"No!" he answered, instantly alarmed. "Why—?"

"The man wanted to give her one of those papers, you know; but I couldn't find her anywhere, and I thought she'd gone out in the car with you."

"No," he said again. "When did you see her last?"

"I suppose she's gone for a walk, then," said Lydia. "She often—"

"When did you see her last?" he repeated, in so strange a tone that Lydia glanced up, startled.

"Why—after lunch," she answered. "She came up to my room with me and massaged my head until my headache was gone. Then she went—I don't know where she went. I didn't think of asking her. She doesn't like to be bothered—"

"Hasn't anyone seen her?"

He looked from one face to another, but no one answered him. A cold fear rose and rose in him.

"She's got to be found at once," he said.

"But, Barty!" protested Lydia. "She doesn't care for tea. She often goes out by herself and doesn't come back until dinner time—"

"She's got to be found!" he repeated. "And if I can't find her—at once—I'll get the police in."

"Barty! But—why? Barty! You don't think anything's happened to Lois?"

Lydia had risen and faced him with terror in her eyes. He could feel sorry for her, even in the midst of his own overwhelming alarm.

"I think—she ought to be found," he said more gently.

"But *why?* You must have some reason. You must know—of some danger to her—"

He did not know how to answer, and was silent. It was Barrow who spoke.

"Is there any particular reason for upsetting Mrs. Emery this way?" he demanded.

"Damned inconsiderate," said Snow. "She's had enough anxiety as it is."

Not for the first time, it occurred to Clement that Lois, who must seem to the world a spoilt child, a pampered and indulged young creature, was actually, and had been all her life, neglected and disregarded. Snow and Barrow thought only of Lydia. And Lydia, though she was no doubt alarmed by his tone, would not otherwise have been alarmed. The girl had sat with her, massaging her head …

He turned away abruptly.

"I'll just see—if I can find her," he said curtly. When he reached the hall, he glanced back into the drawing room. He saw Snow pouring a cup of tea for Lydia, saw Barrow bending over her, saw Elsie Evans looking on at this with a singular expression on her face. He paused for a moment, with some dim idea that this scene had some significance, was somehow important. Then he dismissed it from his mind and went up to his room for his hat and stick.

The sun was going down; the last rays were shining into the tranquil and pretty room. He stood by the open window, looking at the sky swimming in soft colors, and he thought that if anything had happened to Lois his life would be worthless to him. No matter that until yesterday she had meant nothing to him; ever since she had turned to him in her trouble, she had meant everything, all the kindly and tender things he had missed in his life, the child he had never had. He had come here for her sake, and now she was gone!

What if she had met with an "accident" like Sommerfield's? If she were lying at this moment by some roadside …?

He strode across the room, got a light overcoat and hat from the wardrobe, picked up his stick, and was about to go out to look for her—heaven knew where—when it occurred to him to fill his cigar case. He always traveled well supplied with his favorite cigars and enough cigarettes for emergencies. He had put them into a drawer. As he was in the act of pulling out the drawer, he noticed an envelope lying on the chest. It was addressed to "Uncle Barty."

He tore it open. It began without any salutation:

I find I haven't got a bean. I don't want to borrow from anybody. As soon as you can get away without anyone noticing it, will you come to Oak Vista and bring me some money? It's about a mile, north, straight along the boulevard.

Please don't tell anyone where I am, just yet. They won't begin to worry for hours.

Lois.

He gave an immense sigh that seemed to lift his heart and leave it exquisitely light. Then he went down the back stairs and out through the kitchen, with a brief nod to the astonished servants. He felt no compulsion to relieve Lydia's anxiety by disregarding Lois' wish. Lydia was being well looked after.

He stopped thinking entirely as he strode briskly along, enjoying the air. He felt quiet, content, almost gay, because nothing had happened to the child, after all. On the boulevard it was not quite so pleasant. There was a stream of cars going along, and no footpath.

He kept an eye out for "Oak Vista," whatever it was, and presently he was rewarded by the sight of a signpost: "Turn here for Oak Vista." He did turn, and in a minute had reached a large and respectable-looking house standing on a small hill in the midst of wide lawns. He thought at first it must be the home of some friends of Lois. Then, as he drew nearer and saw the long row of rocking chairs on the veranda, he thought it must be a boarding house of a superior sort.

He went up the drive, mounted the steps to the veranda, and looked for a bell. Through the screen door he could see into a lounge which had not the look of any superior boarding house, and then he saw Lois, lying back in a big wicker chair, smoking a cigarette. He pushed open the door and entered, and she sprang to her feet.

"Thanks!" she said briefly.

Immediately a waiter appeared and stood at his elbow. Old Portland looked at the waiter's face, glanced again about the lounge, and ordered a whisky; then he drew up a chair beside his niece and sat down.

"Father used to come here," she explained. "I knew they wouldn't mind my staying until you got here. And it's quiet enough until later in the evening."

"What are you doing, waiting here in a roadhouse?"

"I haven't any money."

"What do you want money for?"

The waiter returned with the drink, and assiduously turned on three or four little gold-shaded lamps. Old Portland could see the girl's face more clearly now, its pallor, its fatigue.

"I don't know whether I'd better tell you or not," she said. "I don't want to be treacherous. I guess you'd better just give me some money."

He took a wallet from his breast pocket, took out one bill which he kept for himself, and handed her the wallet.

"Forty dollars there," he said. "I don't carry much cash. I have a check book here. How much more do you want?"

"No more ..." she said. "I just want enough to get into the city...."

"I'll drive you in, Lois. No point in my staying after you go."

She shook her head.

"You've got a summons, or whatever they call it, for the inquest. I saw the man, and I dodged mine."

He had forgotten his cigars, after all; he took one of her cigarettes and lit it. "Now you'd better tell me the whole story."

"I don't know …" she said reluctantly. "I've been thinking about that for a good long while. I don't know if it's fair to you. I mean, you might think it was your duty to—to—take steps—if you knew. And if I made you promise beforehand not to take steps, then you'd think you were being dishonorable, and you'd be miserable. I knew you'd help me anyway, whether I told you or not. I knew you'd let me have some money. And I'd like to go and crouch in your flat until this inquest's over. I don't think the police would bother much about me. I'm not an awfully important witness. If Lydia just tells them that I couldn't stand being in the house and went away for a rest, I guess they wouldn't do anything."

"She's used that tale once already," said he, "About Agnes."

Her steady eyes rested on his face for a moment; then she glanced down at her clasped hands.

"Did she tell you?"

"Yes. Told me she'd let Agnes go because the girl was upset. If the tale is repeated—if another witness is too 'upset' to give evidence—" He paused, and again she looked at him.

"It's not the inquest I mind so much," she said. "I guess I could hold my own there. It's going back—to that house. I'd rather do—about anything else in the world—than ever go back there."

He wished that she would cry, wished that she would in some way relax the fierce hold she kept upon herself.

"You needn't worry about making me miserable," he said. "The only reason I came was to help you, and that's all I care about now."

"It wouldn't worry you—not to take steps?"

"It would not."

Her lips quivered, but in a moment she had recovered herself.

"Well, you see …" she said … "I've just found out—who shot father."

He got up, paced across the lounge, and sat down again.

"I think I know," he said.

For in his mind was a vision of that little scene—Lydia behind the tea table, and Barrow and Snow waiting upon her.

There was only one person whom both those men would shield at any cost.

"I don't want to hate her," said Lois. "I don't want to punish her. But I—" Her voice broke. "I don't think I could bear to see Lydia again."

The waiter reappeared. Old Portland had not touched the drink on the table beside him, and never intended to do so; but he ordered another, so that they should be left in peace.

"Then—you think …?"

"I'm afraid—I'm pretty sure," she said.

"Let's get out of here!" said Old Portland abruptly.

She rose without a word. He put down a handful of change for the untouched drinks, and a substantial tip, and they went out. It was twilight now, and it seemed to him that the wind had grown colder.

Instead of going down the boulevard she turned off into the woods, and he followed her. The quiet there among the dark trees suited him well. Their feet made no sound on the path strewn with pine needles.

"Lydia …!" he said to himself, with a sort of dull horror. "*Lydia* …"

It did not occur to him to protest against Lois' statement. In the first place, the girl was neither rash nor stupid; she did not talk at random. If she said this thing, she had reason for it. And in the second place, appalling as the idea was, it did not seem impossible. He found himself able to believe that that fragile and gentle creature, driven to desperation, could have done such a thing—could, with that dreadful weight upon her mind, have continued to behave courteously, graciously. Naturally, inevitably, Snow and Barrow would try to protect her. Any man would. He himself.

"See here!" he said. "Does anyone else know?"

"Agnes," she answered, "and Marcus Snow, and Jack Barrow, and possibly Stevens."

"My God!" he said, half to himself. "If all those people know—there's not much chance … I don't see … just what's to be done."

"No jury'd ever convict *her*," said Lois.

Her tone and her words shocked him. He thought of Lydia in the dock—Lydia stared at, photographed, examined, cross-examined, reexamined, in the pillory; all the details of her wretched marriage made public. And Lois could speak of it like that!

"It's—unthinkable that she should stand trial," he said shortly.

"That's what generally happens, though, after a murder," said Lois.

"Good Lord, Lois!" he cried. "Haven't you any—natural feeling? Lydia's been so kind to you—"

"Well, you see," said Lois, "the man who was killed happened to be my father. He wasn't—a general favorite, but—I loved him."

Now Old Portland felt ashamed of himself. Lydia was not the only one who was suffering, who had suffering before her.

"Yes …" he said. "I know. I …"

The girl stumbled a little over a root. He caught her arm, and kept his hold of it.

"Yes ..." he said. "I suppose it's natural for you to feel—that you want justice—"

"I don't," she said. "I don't want her punished, or hurt in any way. I'll do all I can to help her. Only—I don't want to see her again ever."

"How did you find out?"

"By accident. After lunch I sat with her for a while. Then I went back to my room. And I got thinking about Duncan.... They've kept his body at the undertaker's in Morewood until after the inquest. And I thought ... Duncan was awfully sentimental. I thought he'd like it if I—went to see him there, and brought some flowers. Only, I hadn't any money. So I thought I'd borrow some from Lydia.

"I was just going to knock at her door, when I heard Agnes in there, crying: 'Oh, I can't face that inquest, ma'am! I cannot!' I may not have got the words exactly right, but I guess it's pretty near. I heard Lydia answer: 'You needn't, my dear. Take this money and get away, at once.' Then Agnes said: 'It's *you* I'm thinking of, ma'am. I can't bear to think of you in such trouble.' And Lydia said: 'There won't be any trouble, Agnes, if you keep quiet.'

"Then Agnes began to cry about 'maybe Captain Snow or Mr. Barrow would let on,' and Lydia said: 'They won't, Agnes, ever.' Then she began giving her directions where to go, so that she wouldn't be found, and I went away.

"I felt then that I had to be sure, so I sort of jumped on Jack. It was rather mean—but I had to.... He was in the library, working, and I went in very quietly, and I said: 'Jack, what's the best way to protect her?' I thought he'd faint, or have a fit, or something."

She paused a moment.

"I'm sorry for him," she went on somberly. "He had such a crazy plan. He told me he'd stolen the silver to make it look like a burglary, and that if Lydia was accused he was going to say he'd done it."

"He was sure—?"

"He saw her," said Lois. "He'd told her that he saw her and that he'd never say a word."

"And Snow?"

"I think he only guessed. Anyhow, when Jack said he'd seen the burglar running across the lawn, Marcus said he'd seen him too. And of course Jack hadn't seen anyone out there."

They went on in silence for some time.

"What do you mean to do, Lois?" asked Old Portland at last.

"Nothing," said Lois. "Just shut up and go away."

"I'm afraid that won't do," he said. "Agnes' going may not make much difference, especially as the police seem to take the case as an unquestionable accident. But if you go too—if you leave the house now—"

She did not answer.

"About Sommerfield …" he said. "What is your opinion of that, Lois?"

"I think Jack did it," she said. "I think Jack met him, and knocked him down, and left him for dead on the boulevard. Perhaps he was dead. Or perhaps the next car that came by—finished him, and when the driver saw he was dead, he just dragged him to the side of the road and went on."

"Any grounds for thinking that?"

"Yes," she said. "When Jack told me what he'd done—about the silver—and how he meant to confess that he'd fired the shot, I told him that he was a fool. I told him that if he wanted to do a crazy thing like that, he'd better leave a written 'confession' and clear out. And he said there were other things. He said: 'I'm as guilty as hell, anyhow; I don't care what they do to me now.' So I—figured out the rest of it for myself."

Again they went on in silence. And now Old Portland was thinking only of his niece.

"If she could get away—before this thing breaks," he thought. "It can't be kept quiet. Too many people know. It's bound to come out, sooner or later...."

It occurred to him suddenly that both he and Lois were guilty in the eyes of the law.

"Accessories after the fact," he thought.

The wind was bitter now, the little wood dark as an old forest. There was death and shame and heartbreak all about them. His fingers had unconsciously tightened on her arm. *She* was his responsibility, his own flesh and blood, like his own child to him. How could he protect her, save her from the atrocious ordeal that must inevitably come? Murder will out.... Lois would be a witness—against her stepmother for the murder of her father.

Unexpectedly they emerged from the wood and were facing the road which led to the Emery house.

"I'll go home—if you say it's best, Uncle Barty," she said.

"Lois!" he said. "My dear …"

She buried her head on his shoulder, both hands clutching his collar, and she cried, dreadfully and silently.

There was nothing he knew to say. He could only hold her in one arm, and pat her shoulder, murmuring: "There, my dear.... There! I'm sorry! …"

In a few moments she recovered herself.

"Go slowly!" she said, with all her old imperiousness. "I don't want to get to the house looking like this."

They crossed the boulevard and went on slowly.

"What shall I do?" she asked. "Let them give me the summons to the inquest?"

"I'm afraid so."

"And what else?"

"Nothing," he said. "There's nothing to be done now but to wait. And to hope it will blow over. After the inquest we'll get away—travel, eh?"

"You bet!" said Lois.

His heart was like lead when the lighted windows of the house came into view. His very soul shrank from the thought of crossing that threshold, of seeing Lydia.

But Lois set him an example. As far as he could see, she was just as usual. The new parlor maid opened the door, and Lois stopped to talk to her.

Then he saw Lydia coming out of the drawing room, and a sort of terror seized him. He turned away, that he might not witness the meeting between these two.

"My dear!" he heard Lydia's gentle voice. "We were wondering where you'd gone."

"I went up to Oak Vista," said Lois carelessly.

"Oh, but, Lois! Do you think you ought—?"

"I just went for the walk," said Lois. "There wasn't anybody there—and I didn't try any of Louis' chained lightning." They were speaking quite as usual.

"There's a man waiting in the kitchen with a paper," said Lydia. "For that inquest. I'm so sorry."

"Oh, well!" said Lois, with a sigh. "Bring him along."

Old Portland went upstairs then, and wished he might stay there. But that was impossible; there was dinner to be got through, and the evening.

It was all easier than he would have imagined possible. And that was due to Lydia and Lois. Lydia was exactly the same gracious hostess she had always been, and Lois was, if anything, a little more polite than was her habit.

After dinner, Lydia, Clement, Barrow, and Snow made up a table for bridge.

Just after the clock struck eleven they finished a rubber, and Lydia suggested that it was time for bed. No one disputed that. It had been, Clement thought, the longest day of his life.

He did not much look forward to bed, though. Locked in his own room, he lit another cigar and began to think. He dreaded the inquest beyond measure. It seemed impossible that nothing would be revealed.

And into his weary brain there came a new and terrible idea. What if the police suspected already? They might have some sinister surprise to spring tomorrow. Even now they might be watching the house, where their prospective victims were neatly trapped and sleeping in their cruelly false security....

But was anyone sleeping in this house? As he strained his ears, he thought he heard a board creak in the hall; he thought he heard a door close softly.

"I'm likely to keep on hearing things," he thought.

His imagination seemed out of hand. He did keep on hearing things. He even fancied he heard a groan.

He called himself a fool. But then he heard it again, and close to him. Then a door opened and closed, and he heard a hurried step outside. He got up and opened his own door quietly. And that groan was not imagination. It came from the next room to his—Barrow's room.

He thought instantly of suicide. He did not wait to knock. He tried the handle, and, finding the door unlocked, opened it and entered. The room was black.

He saw a dark shape move.

"Who's that?" he cried.

The dark form was silhouetted against the pale square of the window. He sprang forward, but he was just too late. The man had disappeared—had jumped out of the window. He leaned out. Below him, on the grass, he saw a figure lying very still.

He stumbled and groped for the light, and turned it on. He saw Barrow lying on the bed with his eyes closed and a towel tied over his mouth.

He ran out into the hall, and then he met Lois, in her dressing gown.

"Whose door banged?" she began. "I—"

"Call Snow," he said. "And then go to Barrow. Something—wrong there. Let me have your torch."

She handed him the torch she carried. In the dim light of the hall, he saw her dark little face alert and cool. Then he ran down the stairs, unchained and unbolted the front door, and went round to the side of the house, beneath Barrow's window. There was no one lying there now.

The house was built on a hillside and the distance to the upper window was no more than eight feet. It was possible for a man to make that jump unharmed; but he had seen the figure motionless there, as if stunned or hurt. He flashed the torch about him. Nothing to be seen but the lawn, the dark trees.

He tried the back door, and found it locked. As he stood, thinking, he heard a car come out of the garage and down the drive.

He raced across the lawn. The door of the garage was open, and all the lights on. The big car stood there, and his own, but the two-seater was gone. He called Stevens, but there was no answer. He went upstairs. The room there was in disorder; the squirrel skins were gone from the wall. For a moment he stood there, dazed, not knowing what to do or what to think. Should he telephone to the police? No. Not until he learned what had happened to Barrow.

He turned toward the house again, with something like despair in his heart. He could not understand this—could not know if this were the last act of the tragedy, or part of some chain he had not yet suspected.

PART FIVE—THE CHAIN OF DEATH

A faint rain had begun to fall and Old Portland stood still for a few moments, glad to feel it cold on his face. Before him he could see lights in the upper windows of the house, and he thought it must have been the same the night Emery was shot: lights, hurry, tears, and a great dread.

He felt certain that Barrow was already dead, or dying. He was sorry for that, in a dim way; or rather he knew he was going to be sorry, when he had time. But just now there were other things that must be thought of and done.

The police would have to be notified, and Stevens arrested.

"But I'm going to tell Lydia first," he thought. "I'll give her time to make any arrangements she wants."

For, with Stevens captured or even under suspicion, the whole story must be revealed. The police would want to know why Stevens should have attacked a guest in the house; they would ask questions....

He set off across the lawn again. Downstairs the house was as he had left it—tranquil; only one soft light in the hall; and he heard none of the sounds from overhead which he had expected, no footsteps, no doors opening and closing, no voices.

It worried him unreasonably. It seemed to him as if this tragedy, too, were to be hastily buried, somehow made plausible to the world—as if this chain of death were still being forged, link after link, by invisible hands.

He mounted the stairs. The hall upstairs was quiet, too, and all the doors closed. But, at the sound of his step, Elsie Evans came out of Barrow's room. She was fully dressed, and on her face was a look harder, more bitter, than he had seen before.

"Oh! It's you!" she said.

"Is—Barrow—?" he asked.

"He's getting on," she said briefly.

"Getting on? You mean—"

"I mean that I've been left alone to look after him!" she interrupted vehemently. "Everyone else is 'tired.' But I'm too poor to be tired. I'm to stay up all night—"

"Then he's not dead!" said Old Portland, with a long sigh of relief. "I suppose the doctor'll be here any moment."

"There's not going to be any doctor," said Elsie. "It's not necessary."

Without ceremony, he took her by the arm and moved her aside, and went into the room. Barrow still lay there. He certainly was breathing, and groaning faintly, but there was a sickly, dreadful pallor on his face; he looked to Clement like a man half dead already.

"You'll have to get a doctor," he said sharply. "Don't you realize—"

"Tell Lydia, then," said Elsie. "It's her business, not mine."

He shrank from that task.

"I'll take the responsibility myself," he said. "Who was that fellow they had before?"

Even as he spoke, he realized that calling in the doctor was equivalent to calling the police.

"Does—Lydia know—the condition he's in?" he asked.

"She's been in here," Elsie answered. "She cried, and got faint, and did all the other proper things. Then she asked me if I'd stay and look after him, and she's gone back to bed."

"Any idea what's the matter with him?"

"I've been studying medicine for two years," she said. "I dare say I know that much. He's been chloroformed—and he doesn't react very well."

He was silent for a moment.

"I've got to speak to Lydia," he was thinking.

Then, without a word, he went out into the hall, to Lydia's room, and knocked at the door. It was opened by Lois, still in her dressing gown.

"Lois," he said, "I'll have to speak to her."

Their eyes met.

"All right!" she said. "Come in!"

Lydia, in a black fur-trimmed negligee, was lying on the bed with her eyes closed; but as he drew nearer she opened them and sat up straight.

"He's not worse?" she cried.

"I don't think so. I don't know. But … Lydia … don't you *see?* It's—absolutely necessary to send for a doctor."

"But Elsie says he'll be quite all right in the morning."

"We'll hope so. But, Lydia! Don't you want the poor devil to have proper attention?"

"Yes ..." she said. "Only—Elsie says she can look after him. And if the doctor comes ... We've had so much—talk—already ... Oh, Barty! If he is quite all right in the morning, what is the use of making more trouble and misery?"

"D'you think he'll be satisfied to let matters drop?"

"Oh, I'm sure he will!"

"Lydia, do you know who did this?"

"Why, no," she said. "How could I know, Barty?"

"Then why do you feel so sure Barrow will let it drop? If it is a thief, for instance, why should he simply let him go?"

"Oh, Barty!" she cried despairingly. "Why can't you—let well enough alone?"

He could have smiled at her choice of words.

"It doesn't seem to be very 'well,'" he said. "Please face this thing. Barrow's subpoenaed to appear at the inquest tomorrow—"

"He'll be able to go. Elsie said so!"

"It's possible that Elsie's mistaken. He looks—pretty bad to me. Suppose he dies?"

Her hand flew to her heart; her dark eyes widened.

"You've got to face it," he went on. "Barrow has been attacked under your roof. He's getting no medical care—and his assailant is having all the time he wants for making his escape."

"If you'll just wait—until Jack's better ... Perhaps he won't want to—prosecute ..."

"You know who the man is?"

This time she did not answer. The room was quiet. He heard a little clock ticking briskly. Lois stood by the window, looking out.

"Barty," said Lydia at last, "I'll—leave it to you. You must do as you think best."

With all his soul he protested against that. It was intolerable, to make him responsible for her ruin. But he said nothing. She was lying back again, her eyes closed, her face drawn with fatigue, helpless and without hope. And he was to take the steps to set in motion the inexorable machinery that would send her—heaven knew where....

He turned away, went out of the room and back to Barrow. As soon as he entered, he was aware of a strong smell of chloroform.

"Funny I didn't notice it before," he thought.

He went over to the bedside.

Elsie was not in the room. Barrow lay there as before, still with that deadly pallor, on his face. But surely there had not been this reek of chloroform before! …

He thought he understood now. He crossed the hall and knocked on Snow's door; waited, knocked again; and presently it was opened. The room was dark, and Clement perceived here a new and unmistakable smell—the smell of whisky.

"See here, Snow," he said. "I'd like you to come and sit with Barrow for a while. He's—"

"Can't," said Snow unsteadily. "I had a filthy toothache, and I—took a drop too much. No good—to anyone—just present…. S-sorry, old man…."

His door closed, and Clement stood in the hall, thinking fast. He was not sure where Elsie's room was, but he believed it was round the corner of the corridor, and he went there. From under a door he saw a ribbon of light; he knocked and she answered.

"It's Clement," he said.

"What do you want?"

"I want you," he said.

He heard a chair pushed back, and he turned the handle and opened the door. He found her just risen from a table where she had been writing, and before she realized what he was doing he had caught up the sheet of paper lying there.

"Give it to me!" she cried.

"Sit down and keep quiet!" he threatened, and to his relief she obeyed. Then he looked at the paper:

You must get away at once, before Jack has a chance to tell. You *must*. I know he means—

That was all, but it was a good deal.

"So you've been adding a little more chloroform, eh?" he said. "Just to help things along?"

She did not answer, but her eyes met his steadily. "Who's the note for?" he asked.

She smiled a little, and remained silent.

"Do you realize, what you've let yourself in for?" he went on. "Now I'll certainly call in a doctor, and he'll have to know. If Barrow dies—"

"He won't die," she said scornfully. "I can bring him round in half an hour if I want."

"Then you'd better want."

"I will," she said, "if you'll agree not to send for a doctor."

"I'll agree to wait half an hour."

"Give me my note!"

He shook his head and put the note into his pocket. He had not even begun to think of this new development; he was for the moment almost incapable of thinking.

"Come along!" he said. "I'll go with you—and stay with you for half an hour. Then, if I'm satisfied …"

They returned to Barrow's room, and Elsie fetched a jug of cold water.

"Is she in love with Stevens?" he thought. "She must know who did this.... But she probably doesn't know yet that he's got away. She wanted to warn him...."

He had taken out his pipe to light it, but in his overpowering weariness he forgot it, sat with it in his hand. He couldn't think just now. Elsie was moving quietly about the room.

"Got to keep an eye on her," he thought. "She's capable of trying that trick again, under my nose. She's—"

Something thick descended over his head. He struggled to rise, but the sickly sweet scent of chloroform was in his nostrils, stealing into his brain. He kicked over the chair; he raised his hands to tear off the suffocating thing over his head. But he was finished....

He was aroused by a sharp slap on the cheek, and, opening his eyes with a great effort, he saw Lois kneeling beside him.

"Say something!" she commanded; and, when he could not comply, the wet towel she held descended again and struck his face.

"Damn it! Stop that!" he cried angrily.

He imagined then that he saw her begin to cry, but he felt too sick to care. He closed his eyes and silently endured the waves of nausea that swept over him.

"Uncle Barty!" he heard her urgent voice in his ear. "Just tell me what's the right thing to do for you.... *Please* open your eyes!"

He managed to do so, and he saw that she was undoubtedly crying—tears raining down her cheeks.

"Do you want brandy, angel?" she sobbed, staring anxiously at him. "Or hot coffee—or ice—or something?"

What he really wanted was to be let alone, but he did not care to tell her that. He patted her hand, and lay still for a moment, remembering....

"Barrow?" he said, so suddenly that the girl jumped.

"I don't know …" she answered dubiously. "I don't know much about sickness and things like that."

He struggled up on one elbow. He was still there in Barrow's room. The lights were on; it was still night.

"What time is it?"

"Nearly two."

"Where's Elsie?"

"She's gone."

"You mean—left the house?"

"Yep. Her hat and coat and bag are all gone."

He succeeded in getting to his feet with her assistance, but he very hastily sat down again. She opened the window wide, and he drew deep breaths.

"Let's have a look at Barrow," he said, rising.

"Lean on me, angel," said Lois.

With a faint smile, he ruffled her hair, and crossed the room, unsupported. Barrow lay there, still groaning.

"A little while ago he got awful," said Lois. "He flounced and yelled and tried to hit me when I held him. I—he looks—pretty bad, doesn't he?"

It seemed to Old Portland that he looked very bad indeed.

"We'll have to get a doctor at once, Lois," he said.

"I know. I tried. But someone's cut the telephone wire."

His head was clearing now, the nausea and giddiness leaving him. Neither he nor Lois wasted any words upon the *fait accompli*. If the wire was cut, it was cut.

"My car's still there," he said. "I'll drive to the doctor's."

"No, I'll go—"

"No!" said he, in the arbitrary voice which had carried instant conviction on his ship and in his office. But his niece was unimpressed.

"Listen first to the reasons," she said severely. "In the first place, I don't think I can manage Barrow—if he gets that way again. He's delirious. I had a bad time—and he may get worse."

"Get Lydia to help you."

"Lydia!" she said with a sort of sorrowful gravity.

"Snow."

"I've tried him. He won't even open his door. Just yells that he's 'no good.'"

"Well, there are three servants."

"And they're going to stay where they are," said Lois. "There's no knowing what Jack will say."

"I'll tie him—"

"I wish you weren't so obstinate," said she. "Even apart from Jack, you don't know the way to the doctor's. I'll get there in half the time."

He could not deny that she was right; yet the thought of her going off alone at this hour was unbearable to him.

"We're wasting time," said she. "I'm going."

"I'll go out to the garage with you."

"You can't leave Jack."

"I can," he said; and without further hesitation he tied the unconscious man's ankles together with a towel, tied another towel to that one and knotted it firmly to the foot of the bed; then he poured water on the knots.

"It'll take a bit of doing to undo *that*," he remarked. "And I'll hurry back. Come along!"

She went into her room, and came out wearing a leather coat and a small hat, with her bare feet thrust into shoes. With extreme disapproval he observed that she wore silk pajamas.

"You'll take cold," he said.

She did not even bother to answer that. They went downstairs quietly, and out of the front door.

"How did you happen to find me?" he asked, as they were crossing the lawn.

"Well, after I'd got poor Lydia asleep, I wanted to see how Jack was getting on. The room was all dark. I called to Elsie, but there wasn't any answer. And I heard Jack groaning…. So I turned on the light, and I saw you lying on the floor. That was just about the final straw. I thought that if anything had happened to *you* …" She paused. "I'm going to take one of those first-aid courses," she went on. "It is—horrible not knowing what to do. I ran to telephone to the doctor, and I found the wire cut. So I tried to remember what people did in books and plays. I put water on your face, and I tried flicking you with a wet towel…. Did Elsie do it?"

"Couldn't have been anyone else."

"But why?"

"I don't quite know. But now—"

"Now it'll have to come out," she said, with immeasurable regret in her voice. "I suppose there's no way that we can stop it?"

"No way, Lois," he said.

There was a silence.

"And Elsie did that to Jack, too?"

"That's a little obscure. I caught sight of a man in the room. He jumped from the window, and I saw him lying on the ground. But when I got there he was gone, and a moment afterward the car drove out of the garage."

"But why should Stevens do that? To—help—her?"

"I don't know," he said. "Well, here we are!"

The garage door was still open and the lights on. He made for his own car, and was looking to see how much gasoline the tank held, when he heard a sound.

"Just a moment!" he said, and ran up the stairs. He glanced into the upper room, closed the door, and ran down again.

"Hop in!" he said. "And drive carefully. Don't, on any account, stop or speak to anyone, and bring the doctor back with you. Don't—"

"I was driving cars before you were born," said his niece, in a good imitation of his own manner, and drove out of the garage.

He went upstairs again and opened the door.

"Come!" he said briefly.

Elsie Evans stood facing him.

"I won't!" she said.

But he had already discovered that her defiance was a flimsy thing.

"See here!" he said. "I have no time to waste. If you won't come willingly, I'll have to make you."

She shrugged her shoulders, and picked up her bag. He took it from her, and they set off together.

"Elsie," he said, "I'll help you—if I can, if you'll explain."

She made no answer.

"Lois has gone for the doctor. You can see what that means. For God's sake, you poor little devil, tell me the whole story, and we'll see what's to be done."

But she would not speak a word. They entered the house and went upstairs. He glanced in and saw Barrow lying as he had left him, apparently asleep.

"We'll talk out here," he said, "in the hall, so that we won't disturb Barrow."

Then she spoke for the first time.

"You'd better just feel his head," she said. "Tell me if it's hot."

"Do it yourself."

"I won't."

Clement was afraid to disregard her words. He entered the room and went to the bedside. The door slammed. As he turned he heard a key turn in the lock outside. And then he heard her knocking on the door opposite, heard her voice, desperate with entreaty:

"Marcus! Marcus! You *must* go—this instant! It's your *only* chance! I've locked him in—but Lois has gone to get the doctor. And Jack will tell.... Oh, Marcus! For God's sake, Marcus!"

He heard that other door open, and a dreadful cry from the girl. Then the key turned in the lock of his door, and Snow stood before him.

Clement could not repress an exclamation himself. For Snow's face was contorted with pain; there was a cut on his cheek bone; he had one arm in a clumsy sling made of two neckties.

"Clement," he said, "look after the girl, will you?"

Over his shoulder Clement saw Elsie leaning against the wall, with her eyes shut.

"You need a bit of looking after yourself," he said curtly.

"I'll do," said Snow. "I'll sit down a minute."

He advanced, crossed the room, dragging one foot to the chair by the window; and it was plain that every step was agony to him.

"Look after—the girl—" he said, lowering himself into the chair.

But Elsie came in herself then, and knelt beside him.

"Marcus! ... Let me see ... your arm!"

"Don't be a nuisance!" he said. "I'll do."

"Then it was *you*, Marcus—who jumped out of the window? You—not Stevens?"

"Me," he said.

"Why?" asked Old Portland.

"It was a mistake," said Snow easily. "I heard Barrow groaning, and I came in—and found him unconscious—but talking.... I didn't like what he was saying, so I tied something over his mouth. Then I heard someone coming, and I turned out the light. And *you* came in. I didn't want to explain my—rather questionable behavior, so I jumped. I knew the ground was soft there. I thought I could manage.... It knocked the wind out of me, but only for a moment. I got up, and luckily found the back door unlocked, and got up here. I'm sorry I haven't been—very useful this evening...."

"But now, Marcus!" cried the girl. "Even now you can get away! The little car's still in the garage."

"But, my dear kid, I don't want to get away."

"Oh, Marcus!" she cried. "After all I've done for you!"

"Why, what have you done?"

"I gave Jack the chloroform—to keep him quiet—so that you'd have a chance to escape. I heard him say he was going to 'explain.' ... Oh, come! I'll help you! You know how to drive. I can't do that—but I'll go with you. Don't—*don't* waste any time! Lois will be back. It's your only chance to escape!"

"Escape?" he repeated.

"I know Mr. Clement won't tell. And I'd rather die than tell. No one else knows but Jack, and he can't speak yet."

"Knows what?"

"He does know! At first I thought *he'd* done it, but when I found it was you—"

"You mean—shooting Emery?" said Old Portland.

She turned to him.

"You *said* you'd help me. Then help me now! Help me to get him safely away! He's suffering horribly—he's ill ... He's the only person in the world who's been truly kind to me. My one friend ..."

Over her head, the two men looked at each other.

"Don't you see that it's no use?" she cried. "Lois is bringing a doctor. He'll insist on knowing.... Stevens is gone. When he doesn't turn up at the inquest tomorrow, the police will come again ... It can't be hidden any longer."

"No," said Snow. "I don't suppose it can."

"Then, quick!"

"It was kind of you to try to help me," said Snow. "It was ... you're a good little Bolshevik, Elsie. But I'm afraid I'll have to stay."

His hand rested on her hair; she looked up into his face, pulled off her spectacles.

"I'd have given my life for you, Marcus!" she said, with a sob.

"I don't deserve it, dear kid."

"At first I thought you were just trying to shield Lydia."

"Elsie!" said Lydia's voice.

She was standing in the doorway, in her black wrap, with a look of shocked distress on her face.

"What are you saying, my dear? I— Oh, Marcus! What's happened to you?"

"Nothing," he said. "I—had a fall."

Old Portland drew up a chair for her.

"But, Elsie, my dear!" she said. "I really don't understand.... You said—Marcus was trying to shield me?"

"I thought that, at first."

"I don't wish anyone to shield me," said Lydia, with quiet dignity. "I'm quite ready to take the consequences of all that I've done. I hoped it would never come into court; but if it does, I'm ready. I'm not ashamed—and I'm not sorry."

"See here!" said Snow. "Let's not talk any more ... Lydia, Elsie's found out!" His eyes were fixed on her face with terrible intensity. "Please listen to me! Elsie's found out—and I admit it: I killed Emery."

"Marcus!" she cried. "But that's—carrying chivalry *too* far! It's splendid of you, but it's—really too much. I can't let you say that."

"I do say it."

"No, Marcus!" said she.

Her voice was as soft as ever. She looked distressed, but nothing more. And, thought Old Portland, she never would show any more emotion. In her polite gentleness there lay hidden an invincible strength, and an invincible pride.

"No, Marcus!" she repeated. "And it's quite unnecessary now. They have a good start."

"A good start?"

"They?" said Snow and Clement together.

"I don't think they'll be caught," she went on. "Stevens is really very clever and resourceful. I wouldn't let them tell me where they were going, so that I can honestly tell the police I don't know." She looked at Snow. "It was very splendid of you, Marcus, to think of such a thing," she said. "I felt quite sure that you knew, and Jack, too. I hoped—" For the first time her voice grew a little unsteady. "I hoped that, for Gilbert's sake, we could manage to keep this quiet."

"But what—" Elsie began, when Old Portland bent over her.

"Keep quiet!" he murmured fiercely.

"When Stevens told me about Duncan," Lydia went on, "I was afraid it wouldn't be possible to keep it all a secret. It was wrong and wicked of Stevens—but one can't help being sorry for him ... And his love seemed to me—a beautiful thing."

Again she paused.

"Go on! Go on!" Old Portland urged her, but silently.

"I don't think he had actually intended to kill Duncan," she resumed. "But there was surely murder in his heart. You see, Duncan had *seen* what happened—had actually seen the shot fired. And he was—horrible about it ... So that night—only last night, was it? It doesn't seem possible, does it?"

"No ... it doesn't ..." said Snow politely.

"He got to the station just as the train came in, and Duncan got into the car at once. He sat beside Stevens, and he began to talk ... in a horrible way—about her ... and what trouble he could make, if he liked. And Stevens stopped the car and threw him out. He drove on a moment, and then, he told me, he realized how wrong that was, and he went back. And before he could get there, another car ran over Duncan. It's so terrible to think of! But Stevens is sure that poor Duncan was unconscious from the fall.

"The driver of the other car didn't even stop. Stevens caught a glimpse of his face, looking quite wild.... Then Jack Barrow came up and they carried Duncan out of the road. He said that all night he lay awake thinking of Duncan out there in the rain, and first thing in the morning he brought him here. He really was sorry. You can see he had—some feeling of decency."

"But—" said Old Portland, "—I don't understand—"

"It was all very simple," Lydia explained, with a sort of courteous patience. "He felt quite certain no one had seen Duncan get into the car. He took a short cut and came to that garage from the other direction, as if he were just coming from the house. He did something to the tire on the way, to make it all seem quite right."

In the silence that followed, Barrow muttered and tossed. She rose and went over to the bedside, laid her hand on his brow.

"Exactly—how much did Sommerfield say he saw?" asked Old Portland, very carefully.

"Everything. He was on the terrace. He saw Agnes snatch up the revolver that poor Gilbert always had on his desk at night, and fire."

"Shot him down in cold blood?" said Old Portland.

Then he saw a faint color rise in Lydia's cheeks, and he was sorry he had said that. Knowing the late Gilbert Emery as he did, he could well imagine that Agnes had shot him, not in cold blood, but in the hot blood of anger, perhaps in fear. She was a pretty and unprotected young girl, and Emery had been—Emery.

"I think," said Lydia steadily, "that Agnes must not be too much blamed. Her love for her husband—"

"Husband?"

"She and Stevens were married last week. I was happy to help them a little. I was willing to do anything I could to help her get away. I gave her money, but Stevens returned it to me."

And that, thought Old Portland, explained the purse. Everything was pretty well explained now by Lydia's words. And her silence in regard to Agnes' motive for the shooting was still more eloquent.

There she stood, straight and slender, fatigue in her face, and a look very grave, but at heart untouched by the tragedy that had blackened her world. She had done what she believed to be right. She had cared nothing at all for policemen and judges and other such masculine devices. She had tried to protect her dead husband's quite unprotectable reputation, but she had thought first and foremost of the luckless little housemaid. It never had occurred to her that she herself had been suspected.

And it never must! Clement had been willing to obstruct the course of justice, thinking her guilty. Barrow had removed the silver to establish a burglary theory. Snow had gone so far as to make his preposterous "confession." And she was never going to know any of that.

Elsie rose to her feet.

"Of course you'll have to tell the doctor that I gave the chloroform to Jack," she said shortly.

Lydia looked at her kindly enough, yet, thought Clement, with considerable aloofness. For Lydia would understand her housemaid far better than she would Elsie.

"I don't think it will be necessary," she said. "I'm quite sure that Jack will be perfectly willing to say it was an accident. And Dr. Porter is so nice. We'll send for him—"

"Lois has gone to get him now," said Elsie. "Anyhow, I don't care what happens."

"My dear!" protested Lydia.

"I don't! I've—just made a—fool of myself—"

"I suppose your idea was to help Stevens get away," said Lydia, a little doubtfully. "Though I'm sure you were mistaken. Jack would *never* have told." She sighed a little. "If it really becomes necessary," she said, "I have their confessions. Stevens insisted upon leaving them, in case anyone else should be accused. But I shan't produce them for a week at least— until they are both safely away. And never at all if it can be avoided."

She stopped and listened.

"There's a car!" she said, and turned to the two men with her gracious air of deferring to their superior judgment. "If it's Dr. Porter, don't you think that perhaps I'd better see him first?"

"Certainly!" said Clement. "By all means!"

She went out of the room, and after a moment Elsie turned to follow her.

"Too bad, Elsie!" said Snow.

"I don't care!" said she.

"But your theory, my dear kid! About the poor always having to pay— no one willing to help them—"

"Oh, let me alone!" she cried.

"Sorry!" he said. "But this'll probably go on for years. Now you've got to marry a man who not only has a bit of money, but who's going to keep on trying to make more—"

"I haven't got to!"

"You have!" Snow assured her. "You've compromised yourself irrevocably. Clement heard you. He heard you say that—"

"Stop!" she cried. "Oh, how can you! When I've known for years and years how you feel about Lydia."

There was a moment's silence.

"As a matter of fact," said Snow, "you don't know anything about anything. Got a cigarette, Clement? Thanks!" He struck a match with a shaking hand, but his voice was level and cool. "And I'm not going to explain. Only that in my younger days I made a fool of myself, and Lydia was very kind to me.... Just lately, after I'd met you at that studio tea, I wrote to her. I said I thought that if you ever grew up you'd be someone worth knowing. And she was delighted. She asked you here, *and* me. I hadn't seen her for years, but she was just the same. She's a prejudiced woman. She's an unreasonably loyal friend. She thought you had only to see me for a week or so to adore me. So you came, and I came, and now you've got to marry me and stop being a female doctor."

"Never!" cried Elsie.

"But, my dear girl!" protested Snow. "Look at me, utterly neglected here, with any number of broken bones! Look at Barrow! My dear girl, *look* at your two patients! Don't you see what an utterly rotten little doctor you'd be?"

She drew herself up proudly; but, to save his life, Clement could not help bursting into a laugh. She looked at him furiously; then, with something like a sob, she began to laugh herself. Clement had not heard her laugh before, and it seemed to him very touching, as if she did not know much about laughter.

"I thought," said Snow, "that Lydia'd do you good. She belongs to the strait-laced, law-abiding past generation…. Look here! You'd better clear out before the real doctor comes. He might not approve of your— treatments."

She ran out of the room, and Snow glanced at Clement.

"And otherwise," he said … "we might as well leave the explanations to Lydia?"

"I agree with you," said Old Portland.

Two days later Old Portland sat at dinner in the hideous and forbidding dining room of his own flat.

The inquest was over, not postponed, as he had feared, because of Stevens' flight. The police were certainly looking for Stevens, but so far they had found no trace of him except the car, discovered in a garage in a neighboring town. They understood, now, why he had disregarded his subpoena. Lydia had explained to them. It appeared that Stevens and Agnes had been married the week before, and that they had helped themselves to certain petty cash, no doubt to start housekeeping. Of course, this was reprehensible, but Lydia said she would never prosecute.

Barrow had attended the inquest, and given the evidence required of him. Dr. Porter had been called, too, as he had been summoned when Stevens had brought the body of Sommerfield to the house. He deposed that Sommerfield had been dead when he saw him, and his opinion of the injuries was the same as the police doctor's.

Captain Snow had not been required to attend, which was a good thing, as he had slipped on the stairs and broken his arm and sprained his ankle. Nor did Elsie have to appear. She was still visiting Mrs. Emery, and had decided not to return to medical college.

All over. All explained. And now in the hideous and forbidding dining room sat Old Portland, facing his niece, and between them sat young Martin.

Seen away from the office, Martin was notably younger, and his conversation, to his employer, was not very interesting. But it seemed to entertain Lois.

"As soon as he's out of the hospital," young Martin was saying, "he's going to hop off again. And he's promised to take me on his trial flight."

"Well, I'll send a wreath," said Lois.

They both smiled. That was their idea of a joke. Their eyes met; they were appraising each other, in the merciless fashion of their years; and they smiled again.

"Ha! …" said Old Portland to himself, with boundless satisfaction.

THE END

Elisabeth Sanxay Holding Bibliography
(1889-1955)

NOVELS

Invincible Minnie (1920)
Rosaleen Among the Artists (1921)
Angelica (1921)
The Unlit Lamp (1922)
The Shoals of Honour (1926)
The Silk Purse (1928)
Miasma (1929)
Dark Power (1930)
The Death Wish (1934)
The Unfinished Crime (1935)
The Strange Crime in Bermuda (1937)
The Obstinate Murderer (1938; reprinted as *No Harm Intended*, 1939)
Who's Afraid? (1940; reprinted as *Trial by Murder*, 1940)
The Girl Who Had to Die (1940)
Speak of the Devil (1941; magazine version as "The Fearful Night," reprinted as *Hostess to Murder*, 1943)
Kill Joy (1942; reprinted as *Murder is a Kill-Joy*, 1946)
Lady Killer (1942)
The Old Battle-Ax (1943)
Net of Cobwebs (1945)
The Innocent Mrs. Duff (1946)
The Blank Wall (1947)
Miss Kelly (1947)
Too Many Bottles (1951; reprinted as *The Party Was the Pay-Off*, 1951)
The Virgin Huntress (1951)
Widow's Mite (1953)

STORIES/NOVELETTES

Patrick on the Mountain (*The Smart Set*, July 1920)
The Problem that Perplexed Nicholson (*The Smart Set*, Aug 1920)
Marie's View of It (*The Century Magazine*, Dec 1920)
Mollie: The Ideal Nurse (*The Century Magazine*, Jan 1921)
Angelica (*Munsey's*, May-Oct 1921)
The Married Man (*Munsey's*, Dec 1921)
The Foreign Woman (*Munsey's*, July 1922)
Hanging's Too Good for Him (*Munsey's*, Sept 1922)
Like a Leopard (*Munsey's*, Nov 1922)
Lost Luck (*The Bookman*, Dec 1922)
"Hanging's Too Good for You!" (*The Novel Magazine*, Jan 1923)
The Girl He Picked Up at Coney (*Metropolitan Magazine*, Feb/Mar 1923)
The Aforementioned Infant (*Munsey's*, Mar 1923)
It Seemed Reasonable (*Munsey's*, Apr 1923)

BIBLIOGRAPHY

Unless Experience Be a Jewel (*The Sovereign Magazine*, Apr 1923)
The Business Girl (*Woman's Home Companion*, May 1923)
Horseshoe Over the Door: Stories (*Woman's Home Companion,* May, June, July, Aug 1923)
Old Dog Tray (*Munsey's*, May 1923)
The Matador (*Munsey's*, June 1923)
The Hick (*Woman's Home Companion*, June 1923)
The Down-and-Outer (*Woman's Home Companion*, July 1923)
A Hesitating Cinderella (*Munsey's*, July 1923)
The Postponed Wedding (*Munsey's*, Aug 1923)
The Disgruntled Boarder (*Woman's Home Companion*, Aug 1923)
With Unbowed Head (*The Century Magazine*, Aug 1923)
This is Life (*The Nation*, Aug 15 1923)
The Marquis of Carabas (*Munsey's,* Sept 1923)
Out of the Woods (*Munsey's*, Oct 1923)
Miss Flotsam and Mr. Jetsann (*The Dial*, Nov 1923)
Benedicta (*Munsey's*, Dec 1923)
Keeping the Boy at Home (*Woman's Home Companion*, Dec 1923)
Nickie and Pem (*Munsey's*, Feb 1924)
His Remarkable Future (*Munsey's,* Apr 1924)
His Own People (*Munsey's*, July 1924)
Who Is This Impossible Person? (*Munsey's,* Aug 1924)
Ye Gods and Little Fishes (*The American Magazine*, Aug 1924)
Mr. Martin Swallows the Anchor (*Munsey's*, Sept 1924)
Too French (*Munsey's*, Jan 1925)
A New Story (*The Grand Magazine*, April 1925)
The Good Little Pal (*Munsey's*, Apr 1925)
Flowers for Miss Riordan (*Munsey's*, May 1925)
Mrs. Prunes (*Woman's Home Companion*, May 1925)
Something Human (*The Grand Magazine*, May 1925)
Marionette (*The Century Magazine*, June 1925)
Sometimes Things Do Happen (*Munsey's*, June 1925)
Miss What's-Her-Name (*Munsey's*, July 1925)
The Long Night (*Ladies Home Journal*, Sept 1925)
The Wonderful Little Woman (*Munsey's,* Sept 1925)
As Patrick Henry Said (*Munsey's*, Oct 1925)
The Worst Joke in the World (*Munsey's*, Nov 1925)
As Is (*Munsey's*, Dec 1925)
That's Not Love (*Munsey's*, Jan 1926)
Rosalie Gets Out of the Cage (*The American Magazine*, Feb 1926)
The Thing Beyond Reason (*Munsey's*, Feb 1926)
Dogs Always Know (*Munsey's*, Mar 1926)
Highfalutin' (*Munsey's*, Apr 1926)
Bonnie Wee Thing (*Munsey's*, May 1926)
Memory of a May Night (*Pictorial Review*, May 1926)
Vanity (*Munsey's*, Jun 1926)
The Compromising Letter (*Munsey's*, July 1926)
Miss Cigale (*Munsey's*, Aug 1926)
Blotted Out (*Munsey's,* Sept 1926)
Pale Pink Crime (*Woman's Home Companion*, Sept 1926)
Human Nature Unmasked (*Munsey's*, Oct 1926)
Chris Had Gone (*Ladies' Home Journal*, Nov 1926)

Home Fires (*Munsey's*, Dec 1926)
Totally Broken Reed (*Woman's Home Companion*, Mar 1927)
The Grateful Lunella (*The American Magazine*, May 1927)
The Old Ways (*Munsey's*, July 1927)
By the Light of Day (*Munsey's*, Aug 1927)
Out for a Good Time (*Woman's Home Companion*, Oct 1927)
For Granted (*Munsey's*, Nov 1927)
The Warning Leer (*Detective Story Magazine,* Nov 26, Dec 3, Dec 10 1927)
Incompatibility (*Munsey's*, Dec 1927)
In Chains (*McCall's*, Dec 1927)
One Misty Night, (*The American Magazine*, Feb 1928)
Derelict (*Munsey's*, Mar 1928)
Half an Hour Late (*Woman's Home Companion*, Mar 1928)
This Road Is Closed (*The American Magazine*, Apr 1928)
Inches and Ells (*Munsey's*, June 1928)
It Is a Two-Edged Sword (*McCall's*, June 1928)
Too Late (*Liberty*, July 21 1928)
Proud and Pig-Headed (*Pictorial Review*, July 1928)
Outside the Door (*The Elks Magazine*, Oct 1928)
Hard as Nails (*Liberty*, Oct 20 1928)
Important Things (*Liberty*, Nov 17 1928)
A Dinner Date (*The American Magazine*, Jan 1929)
Vera's Superior Smile (*Pictorial Review*, Jan 1929)
Saving Up (*Liberty*, Jan 5 1929)
Flow and Ebb (*Liberty*, Jan 26 1929)
Without Benefit of Police (*Complete Stories*, Feb 1929)
The Sin of Angels (*The American Magazine*, Apr 1929; *The Grand Magazine*, Jan 1939)
Dare-Devil (*The American Magazine*, June 1929)
Little Deeds of Kindness (*Liberty*, July 6 1929)
Broken Faith (*The American Magazine*, Oct 1929; *Cassell's Magazine of Fiction*, July 1930)
Prelude (*The Delineator*, Sept 1929)
Far-Off Hills Are Blue (*Woman's Home Companion*, Oct 1929)
Carline (*Liberty*, Oct 12, 1929)
Rose-Leaves (*Liberty*, Jan 18 1930)
The Chain of Death (*Liberty*, May 24, May 31, Jun 7, Jun 14, Jun 21 1930)
On Condition (*The Elks Magazine*, Sept 1930)
Miss Pettijohn (*The London Magazine*, Sept 1930)
Mrs. Herbert's Notion (*The Delineator*, Nov 1930)
Absolutely Different (*Maclean's*, May 1, 1931)
The Girl in Armor (*Street & Smith's Detective Story Magazine*, Aug 8, Aug 15, Aug 22, Aug 29 1931)
Porthos (*Maclean's*, Sept 15 1931)
It's All Right for Men (*Liberty*, Oct 10 1931)
Humility (*Maclean's,* Nov 15 1931)
Brides of Crime (*Street & Smith's Detective Story Magazine*, Nov 7, Nov 14, Nov 21, Nov 28, Dec 5 1931)
The Preposterous Mrs. Manders (*Woman's Home Companion*, Mar 1932)
Hound's Bay (*Street & Smith's Detective Story Magazine*, Mar 5, Mar 12, Mar 19, Mar 26, Apr 2 1932)
Wonderful Day (*Good Housekeeping*, Jan 1933)

BIBLIOGRAPHY

If It Hadn't Been for Laurel (*Liberty*, Jan 28 1933)
Some Unknown Woman (May 1933)
"Bring a Man, Dear" (*The Delineator*, June 1933)
No Personal Calls (*Maclean's*, July 15 1933)
That Woman (*The Delineator*, Oct 1933)
October Night (*The New York Daily News*, Oct 29 1933)
Like Father, Like Son (*The Novel Magazine*, Jan 1934)
Unknown Land (*Collier's*, Jan 13 1934)
Mrs. Cochrane Mayne and Mrs. Haggerty (*The Novel Magazine*, March 1934)
A Man Can Take It (*Collier's Weekly*, May 12 1934)
The Green Bathtub (*Collier's Weekly*, June 16 1934)
Vital Interlude (*Redbook Magazine*, July 1934)
The Last Night (*The Passing Show*, July 14 1934)
Porthos (*Maclean's*, Sept 15, 1934)
All She Could Get (*Collier's Weekly*, Sept 15 1934)
The Unfinished Crime (*Street & Smith's Detective Story Magazine*, Nov 10 1934)
Guest of Honor (*Maclean's*, Dec 1, 1934)
Don't Care! (*Cosmopolitan*, Dec 1934)
"I Could Brighten Your Life!" (*The American Magazine*, Jan 1935)
The Bride Comes Home (*Cosmopolitan*, Feb 1935)
Dawn Smile (*The Strand Magazine*, Apr 1935)
The Root of Evil (*Collier's Weekly*, Apr 27 1935)
Nobody Would Listen (*Mystery*, Aug 1935)
Somebody's Cynthia (*Collier's Weekly*, Aug 3 1935; *The Passing Show*, Nov 2 1935)
It's Time Life Began! (*Redbook Magazine*, Dec 1935)
Touch of the Spur (*Maclean's*, Dec 1, 1935)
You Never Can Tell (*Collier's Weekly*, Dec 14 1935; *Grit*, June 1936)
Unscathed (*Ladies Home Journal*, Jan 1936)
Lost (*Redbook*, Feb 1936)
Cross Purposes (*Collier's Weekly*, May 30, 1936)
Can Do! (*Pictorial Review*, July 1936)
Bermuda Murder (*Street & Smith's Detective Story Magazine*, July 1936)
Scandal (*Woman's Home Companion*, July 1936)
Background (*Redbook Magazine*, Aug 1936)
The Pink-Soap Princess (*Maclean's*, Aug 1, 1936)
Intent to Kill (*Street & Smith's Detective Story Magazine*, Sept 1936)
Night Life (*Redbook*, Sept 1936)
Murder Solicited (*Street & Smith's Detective Story Magazine*, Nov 1936)
I'm the Man You Killed (*Mclean's*, March 1, 1937)
Third Act (*Pictorial Review*, Apr 1937)
Drifting (*McCall's*, May 1937)
Wedding Day (*Cosmopolitan*, Sept 1937)
The Nicest Little Lunch (*Cosmopolitan*, Nov 1937)
Echo of a Careless Voice (*McCall's*, Jan 1938)
Proud Girl (*This Week*, July 17 1938)
Illusion (*Good Housekeeping*, Aug 1938)
They Take It So Lightly! (*Cosmopolitan*, Oct 1938)
Two Passes for the Show (*Liberty*, Nov 5 1938)
So Sort of Proud (*Good Housekeeping*, Mar 1939)
Cad? (*This Week*, May 21, 1939)
Money Can't Buy It (*Liberty*, Aug 5 1939)

Open That Door (*Liberty*, Aug 26 1939)
Blonde on a Boat (*The American Magazine*, Dec 1939)
Late Date (*Cosmopolitan*, May 1940)
Proposal (*McCall's,* May 1940)
On Yonder Lea (*Good Housekeeping*, Aug 1940)
Lesson for Pete (*This Week*, Oct 6 1940)
Tropical Secretary (*The American Magazine*, Feb 1941)
Tomorrow's Not Soon Enough (*McCall's*, Mar 1941)
What It Takes (*Grit*, Mar 9 1941)
Loved I Not Honor More (*Liberty*, Apr 12 1941)
The Fearful Night (*The American Magazine*, June 1941; expanded to *Speak of the Devil*)
Another Baby (*Woman's Home Companion*, Nov 1941)
I'll Never Forgive You (*The American Magazine*, May 1942)
Not Goodbye But Au Revoir (*McCall's,* Oct 1942)
The Kiskadee Bird (*Cosmopolitan*, July 1944)
The Old Battle-Ax (1943; abridged, *Liberty,* Mar 18 1944)
Mrs. Henry Gibson (*Cosmopolitan,* Aug 1944)
Bait for a Killer (*Collier's Weekly*, Sep 30 1944, as "The Blue Envelope"; *The Saint Mystery Magazine*, Mar 1959)
The Unbelievable Baroness (*The American Magazine*, May 1945)
The Net of Cobwebs (*Collier's Weekly*, Jan 6, 13 & 20, 1945)
Ten-Cent Wedding Ring (Cosmopolitan, Feb 1945)
Funny Kind of Love (as by Elizabeth Saxanay Holding, *Boston Sunday Globe Magazine*, Nov 11 1945)
Invictus (*The New Yorker*, March 23 1946)
Farewell to a Corpse (*Mystery Book Magazine*, Oct 1946)
The Other Mrs. Minor (*Cosmopolitan*, Sept, Oct, Nov 1946)
"Be Careful, Mrs. Williams" (*Cosmopolitan*, July 1947)
Second Marriage (*Cosmopolitan*, Apr 1948)
The Bird of Time (*Cosmopolitan*, May 1948)
The Stranger in the Car (*American Magazine*, July 1949)
People Do Fall Downstairs (*Ellery Queen's Mystery Magazine*, Aug 1947)
Friday, the Nineteenth (*The Magazine of Fantasy and Science Fiction*, Summer 1950)
The Legacy (*Liberty*, Dec 1950)
La Signora from Brooklyn (*Cosmopolitan*, Dec 1951)
Farewell, Big Sister (*Ellery Queen's Mystery Magazine*, July 1952; hardboiled satire)
I'll Never Leave You (*Woman's Home Companion*, Oct 1952)
The Death Wish (*Cosmopolitan*, Feb 1953)
Most Audacious Crime (*Nero Wolfe Mystery Magazine*, Jan 1954)
Shadow of Wings (*The Magazine of Fantasy and Science Fiction*, July 1954)
Glitter of Diamonds (*Ellery Queen's Mystery Magazine*, Mar 1955)
Mrs. Daugherty & Mrs. Depew (*Canadian Home Journal*, July 1955)
The Strange Children (*The Magazine of Fantasy and Science Fiction*, Aug 1955)
Very, Very Dark Mink (*The Saint Detective Magazine*, Dec 1956)
The Daring Doctor (*Alfred Hitchcock's Mystery Magazine*, Mar 1957)
Game for Four Players (*Alfred Hitchcock's Mystery Magazine*, June 1958)
The Blank Wall (*Alfred Hitchcock Presents: My Favorites in Suspense*, 1959)
Seeing Nellie Home (*Woman's Home Companion*; *A Diamond of Years—The Best of Woman's Home Companion*, Doubleday, 1961)

www.ingramcontent.com/pod-product-compliance
Lightning Source LLC
LaVergne TN
LVHW010146070526
838199LV00062B/4271